EARDLEY HALL.

A TALE BY ELLEN T——, AUTHORESS OF ROSE SOMMERVILLE, &c.

CHAPTER I.

I'll pull you sweet flowers, to wear if you choose them,
Or, after you've kissed them, they'll lie on my bosom;
I'll fetch from the mountain its breeze to inspire you,
I'll fetch from my fancy a tale that won't tire you;
Oh, your steps 's like the rain to the summer vex'd farmer,
Or sabre and shield to a knight without armour;
I'll sing you sweet songs till the stars rise above me,
Then, wandering, I'll wish you in silence to love me.

How frequently it occurs, in families where all are loved and cherished, that **one** for some reason, known perchance only to themselves, nestle closer to the parental bosom, and claims a double share of tenderness, to whom all without a thought **of** discontent yield their palm of love; and are willing cheerfully to sacrifice their hopes and yet such a one more often than another is doomed, in after years, to pain and sorrow, to bear a burden of anguish, and none to share it with them; to suffer in silence and alone pangs rendered doubly acute by recollections of their early happy years, when not even the winds of heaven were permitted to visit their cheeks too roughly; and more than this, the child who has been loved and treasured above all others will sometimes be the only one whom the parent is destined (as it were in punishment of his idolatry) to see resolutely choose the path of vice and sorrow—two little words, but what an amount of suffering do they convey, especially to the mind of a parent, who is conscious that the cup of their best beloved is filled night and morn with that bitter portion; the knowledge that this only too often occurs, ought surely to guard families against the fatal error of petting and consequently spoiling one of its members, fitting them by silly indulgence to stand alone, and, as men or women, act well their part in society; but, no, in spite of all, there is scarcely a family in which some wild, wayward girl, or noble, high-spirited boy is not made a pet of by the others.

Thus it was in the family of Mr. Clarence, lately a rich merchant; he had amassed sufficient property to enable him to retire on a handsome competence some few years previous to the opening of our tale, and with his family, consisting of his lady, two sons, and two daughters, occupied a very pretty villa in one of the numerous villages that skirt the suburbs of London.

Lucy Clarence, the merchant's youngest child, had from her earliest infancy been the chief favourite of her doating parents. Naturally of a wild, impetuous, and wayward disposition, there was yet much about her so soft, yielding, and loveable, that her brothers and sister were never actuated by the slightest feeling of envy, as regarded their more favoured sister; on the contrary, they appeared to feel that she merited preference, and were thankful she had obtained it.

Besides, too, Lucy was their junior by six years, and for a long while she bore the endearing epithet of "Little Lucy," and then she was so lovely, so artless and bewitching, that she won the love of all with whom she came in contact, without the slightest effort.

At the time we desire to introduce her to the reader, Lucy had nearly attained her eighteenth year. In stature, she was somewhat below the middle height, and of rather slight make, yet her figure was of the most faultless and exact proportions. We have said she was lovely, and her beauty was of that soft and touching kind that appeals, irresistibly, to the feelings of the beholder; fair, even to an appearance of extreme delicacy, there was yet a radiant bloom upon her cheek, which a word would sometimes suffice to deepen into the richest brilliancy,

> "And when angry, for e'en in the tranquillest climes,
>   Light breezes will ruffle the blossoms sometimes,"

the short passing storm but seemed to awaken new beauty, for it gave a richer lustre to her eye, and a sweeter animation to her countenance, which, when in perfect repose, might, by a fastidious person, perhaps, be considered rather wanting in that sweet grace. Her hair, which was of the lightest shade of brown, was allowed to flow free and unconfined in natural grace over her neck and shoulders, whose lily whiteness might be detected peeping out here and there between its rich and sweeping folds; and her eyes, oh! how can we attempt to describe her eyes!—large, languishing, and soft, they were indeed the eyes of love, and matched the heavens in their pure unsullied brightness.

We are, as Byron says, "a great admirer of fine eyes," for, when full of expression, they are capable of making a plain face sweet and interesting; and none could boast of more lovely enchanting eyes than Lucy Clarence, and their soft bewitching glances had kindled the flame of love in the breast of Harry Wilmot, a true, warm-hearted young friend, who, with his sister, resided in close vicinity to the Clarences, and to whom Lucy, with the hearty consent of her parents, was betrothed.

To be sure, they had at one time hoped their fond, darling child might form a more prudent alliance; but when the honest, open young man had, with perfect hu-

EARDLEY HALL.

A TALE BY ELLEN T—,

AUTHORESS OF "ROSE SOMMERVILLE," "RAVENSDALE," ETC. ETC. ETC.

LONDON:

PUBLISHED BY E. LLOYD, SALISBURY-SQUARE, FLEET-STREET,
AND SOLD BY ALL BOOKSELLERS.

mility, preferred his suit, at the same time making a full and candid statement of his circumstances, from which it appeared he possessed ample means to maintain their beloved Lucy, in the station of life she now occupied, and, moreover, on being consulted, she blushingly confessed feeling a decided preference for the young man, the family unanimously declared in favour of his suit, and in a few short weeks Harry Wilmot was about to lead the fair Lucy to the altar.

"What a happy girl you are, dear Lucy," said her sister Jane, as she hung fondly over her, entwining a wreath of the sweet scented jasmine in her luxuriant hair.

"You have always been a spoilt child," she continued, "and I should grieve if you were about to leave us to link your fate with any one but Harry Wilmot."

"Why should you make so great an exception in his favour, Jane," replied the young girl, turning her full blue orbs upon her sister's face.

"Because, dear Lucy, he loves you. Ah! I should scarcely call it love; it is rather a deep, thoughtful, devotedness, concentrated wholly and solely in yourself!"

"If that is all," replied her sister, with a slight degree of confusion, which she strove in vain to conceal, and averting her face from the other's gaze, "if that is all, it is not saying much, for another might regard me with an equal amount of tenderness."

"Can you think so, Lucy," returned the other, in a tone of slight reproach.

"Most certainly," said her sister. "One man is as capable of loving as another."

"Oh! dear, dear sister, I cannot bear to hear you say so," said Jane. "Few men, I truly believe, love with that utter abandonment of selfish feelings that so particularly characterises the addresses of Harry Wilmot."

"Well," replied the lively girl, laughing, "I will endeavour to look upon Harry as the very *acme* of perfection; a woman of course naturally desires to think highly of the man to whom she is shortly to be united for life, and it will therefore be an easy task to dwell only upon the best traits in his character."

There was something in the tone in which her sister spoke these words that left an unpleasant impression on the mind of Jane, it seemed as though they were intended purposely to reassure her, and that in sober truth Lucy did not love Henry with that truthful affection he so well merited.

Alas! and was it possible, thought Jane, that her sister had accepted her first suitor merely because he was such; the light opinion with which she appeared to regard his numerous good qualities, and more especially his love for herself, made her more than half suspect that such was the case. There had ever been a total want of affectionate warmth in her conduct towards her lover, but this her sister had put down to the natural timidity and delicacy of her sex; but of late, Jane had remarked that, so far from such feelings wearing off, they seemed to grow upon her, and an almost entire indifference to the young man appeared to invade her heart, there were times too when Jane had retired to weep, at the cold, not to say unkind behaviour of her sister towards herself; but then she remembered that Lucy had been unfortunate enough to be a spoiled child, and dried her tears, resolving for the future to be less ready to take offence at what probably was never intended to vex her.

Still, though she continued to practise towards her sister the most exemplary patience and self denial, Lucy, once so sweet-tempered, when all were anxious to oblige and please her, become gradually fretful and irritable in the extreme; it seemed, indeed, with difficulty that she restrained her temper in the presence of her lover, and apparently forced herself to receive him with kindness and consideration. None observed this change so sensibly as Jane, her heart throbbed with anxious and painful forebodings, as she looked forward to the expected marriage of her sister, and she resolved even at the risk of incurring her displeasure, to speak to her seriously concerning her affection for her lover.

"Dearest Lucy," she began, one afternoon, as she accompanied her sister in her usual walk in the grounds, which surrounded the villa, "will you be offended with me for speaking plainly and seriously to you?"

"What is it you wish to say?" replied her sister petulantly.

"Do not be angry with me, love," said Jane, kindly; "remember I am your elder sister, and what I wish to say is intended affectionately towards yourself."

"You always appear to think, Jane," replied Lucy, pouting her pretty lips, "that possessing the advantage of a few years in point of age, gives you the right to lecture and scold me on any occasion you deem fit."

"No, love," returned Jane, "I do not wish to scold you, but to tell you in plain, sober truth, that I do not think you love Henry Wilmot as — he deserves to be loved," she added after a slight hesitation.

"Indeed! and when, may I ask, did you make that interesting discovery?" said Lucy, in a tone of satire.

"Sister," replied Jane, without heeding the unkindness of her speech, "you are not yet the wife of Henry, and though you have certainly allowed matters to proceed very far, yet, thank God, it is not too late to break off the match. Harry, I feel assured will release you from an engagement that I fear you hurried into without due consideration; be open, be candid with him, and tell him you cannot return his affection; and you will find he is too honourable to keep you bound by an engagement which the heart does not sanction."

"How is it possible, Jane," replied her sister, angrily, "that you can know I do not love Harry Wilmot. You, at least, appear thoroughly sensible of his merits, and if I am not mistaken, would have no objection to stand in the position I now occupy."

The face of Jane glowed with indignation as her sister gave utterance to those words, and she answered with more show of resentment than she had ever manifested before.

"You sadly mistake me, Lucy, if you suppose, even for a passing moment, that were Harry free as air, had he, indeed, never been your suitor, but in the first instance have offered his hand to myself, that I should have accepted him. No; I do not, and never could love the young man with that fond devotedness I conceive I ought to regard the man I made my husband, neither do I believe you so regard him."

"As you discredit my assertion," replied her sister, "I feel myself at liberty also to discredit your's. If you did not love Harry yourself, you would not be so quick-sighted, or so easily perceive the want of affection in another."

Jane felt too deeply hurt to reply to her sister's speech, and she walked by her side in silence, pondering, as she did so, on the motive that could induce her sister to persist in wedding a man she did not love. For Jane was assured of this; she might like—she might respect Harry Wilmot, but love him, she was convinced beyond the possibility of a doubt, she did not; she grieved for the wilfulness of her sister, she would have advised her kindly and tenderly, but the wayward girl scorned all control, and seemed resolved to act as she thought proper; and Jane saw, with a feeling of acute sorrow, that all attempt to argue with her sister was useless, for the future she must abstain from any allusion to the subject.

CHAPTER II.

"Oft must my soul the question undergo,
Of—dost thou love? and burn to answer, no!
Oh! hard it is, that fondness to sustain,
And struggle not, to feel averse in vain;
But harder still the heart's recoil to bear,
And hide from one—perhaps another there;
He takes the hand—I give not, nor withhold;
Its pulse—nor checked—nor quickened—calmly cold;
And when he quits, it drops a lifeless weight
From one I never loved enough to hate."

It is evening—the evening of the day on which the conversation recorded in our last chapter took place between the sisters—Harry Wilmot has just pressed his farewell kiss on the unresisting lips of his betrothed bride, Lucy Clarence—the night is fair and beautiful, and as the pair stood on the threshold of the door, looking up into the calm blue sky, and then down upon the sleeping flowers at their feet, where the light breeze rustled their tender leaves, and scattered their soft perfume upon the balmy air.

"Lucy," whispered the young man, as he passed his arm round her slender waist, and drew her closer to his side, "one more word before we part, tell me, my girl, what has rendered you of late so cold and reserved in your manners towards me, even now," he continued, in a tone of slight reproach, "you shrink from me, as if——"

"You are somewhat bold, Harry," interrupted Lucy, as she endeavoured to free herself from his embrace.

"Have we not confessed a mutual attachment? And are you not in the course of a few short weeks to become my wife?" replied her lover.

"It is true; but still, methinks, that is not a fair excuse for your freedom."

"Lucy," exclaimed the young man, in a tone of deep sorrow, "you were not always thus cold and reserved. It is better for us both, that I should speak freely now. Lucy, it is with bitter anguish that I have remarked a change gradually stealing over you, since the younger son of Sir Richard Eardley came over to the hall, yonder."

A deep crimson, plainly visible by the soft light of the moon, flitted across the cheeks of Lucy, and she seemed for the moment painfully distressed, which her lover perceiving, he instantly began to blame himself for his rash speech.

"Forgive me, dearest," he said, pressing her hand tenderly in his own, "I meant not to pain you, but——"

"It matters not," interrupted the young girl, endeavouring to speak calmly. "Walter Eardley (and she seemed to breathe the name with difficulty,) has left for London, some time since, and it is very improbable he will ever return," this was followed with a sigh.

"Dear Lucy," replied the young man, "I will not suppose you capable of giving me your hand, while your heart is estranged. Dearly as I love you; aye, dearer than my own life, I will not perfect my own happiness at the expense of your's; if you love that young Eardley, in preference to myself, you are free, dear Lucy, to give him your hand. I can make any sacrifice for you, ah! even my life, could it secure you bliss."

"How strange you talk, dear Harry," replied the girl with a slight embarrasment in her manner; you almost make me doubt your love, you appear so ready to resign me."

"Then you love me, Lucy, as dearly as ever?" said the young man eagerly. She replied by pressing his hand to her lips, and then with a little hesitation said:—

"You must make some allowance for the natural reserve of my character, dear Henry. "I may not be the less capable of loving fondly and affectionately because I am to outward appearance cold."

"God bless you, Lucy, for those words, to me, the sweetest that have ever been breathed from those lips, pardon, love, all that my impetuous feelings have led me to say that sounded like reproach, you will not refuse this dearest?"

"I scarcely know," replied Lucy, "for to speak the truth, I am greatly inclined to chide you."

"No, no, returned her lover, you will forgive me, I am sure you will."

The young girl slightly returned her lover's warm embrace, and then breaking from his arms, hurriedly bade him good night, and hastening to the privacy of her own room, covered her face with her hands, and wept long and bitterly.

"It is useless," she exclaimed, clasping her small white hands impetuously. "My fate is sealed, I must wed Harry, I must, indeed; I have struggled hard to love him, but it is in vain; love dwells but with the free, it is impossible to command affection; but Harry will be content with the semblance of it, he knows not the state of my feelings, and never shall."

Intent upon her own sorrowful reflections, she had sate by her window for hours, little heeding the flight of time, and the evening was now far advanced; all the inmates of the villa had retired to rest, saving Lucy, who was too disturbed in her mind to permit herself to think of slumber, or perhaps she was actuated by other motives in thus remaining up and alone; for occasionally she ceased to weep and listened intently, as though in the expectation of hearing some sound. And when after the lapse of some considerable time a loud musical whistle struck upon her ear, she trembled violently from head to foot, and twice she essayed to move in vain, and not till it had been once or twice repeated did she gain courage to show herself at the window, in answer apparently, to the signal.

In a minute more, she stole stealthily from the room, and down the stairs. And crossing the hall, she opened a side door, and stepped out upon the lawn.

She was instantly joined by a tall, handsome man, who clasped her rapturously in his arms, as he rained down kisses on her blushing cheek.

"Dearest Lucy," he exclaimed, "I almost despaired of seeing you—indeed I was on the point of leaving, fearing that our interviews had been discovered, and——"

"Dear Walter," she exclaimed, affectionately, as she clung to his embrace, "I know what you were about to say, but believe me, nothing on earth would have prevented me seeing you this evening, this once more," she continued, sobbing "to tell you that it must be for the last time."

"The last time! how so, my love?" he replied in an accent of surprise. "You are not grown weary of me?"

"Weary of you!" exclaimed the young girl, sobbing convulsively. "Oh! Walter, Walter! You know not, you never will know how dear, how very dear, you are to my heart." And she leaned her head upon his shoulder and wept, as though her heart would break.

The young man strained her to his bosom, and kissed off the fast falling tears, but for a time remained perfectly silent.

Of which silence we desire to take advantage, in order to introduce him to the reader, which is the more necessary, as he is destined to play a prominent character in our little history.

The younger son of a rich baronet, Walter Eardley contrived to live in a style of almost princely extravagance, though in what manner he obtained the means of doing so was only known to himself.

Descended from a long line of noble ancestry (we use the word noble, as appertaining to exalted character and worthy deeds), he possessed in common with many others, a high reverence for rank and station, and a proportionate dislike to employing his time or talents in any useful occupation, and though apparently receiving but a small allowance from his father, who lavished the chief part of his estates on his eldest son, who was destined to succeed him; yet 'ter refused with disdain, several offers he received from men of standing in society (with whom his father's position brought him into contact), of augmenting his income by employing his spare time in mercantile affairs. None that ever bore the name of Eardley had ever been known to contaminate their fingers by engaging in trade, and with trade Walter was resolutely determined to have nought to do. No, he would contrive to live as he best might. It was whispered, that for this noble resolution, he received a handsome reward from his brother, who could not brook the idea of Walter entering on any undertaking derogatory to their boasted family.

In the neighbourhood of Eardly Hall, little was known of the baronet or his family; he had married in early life the youngest daughter of Earl Grey, whom, report said, had been forced into the match greatly against her inclination, by her haughty and unfeeling parent; she was a fair, delicate girl of nineteen, and looked anything but a happy bride when she accompanied Sir Richard to spend the honeymoon at Eardley Hall. Indeed, there was such an appearance of resigned anguish imprinted on the pallid brow that it called forth the deepest sympathy from every beholder.

The peasants, all of whom were assembled to greet the owner of the estates upon which they lived, when they gazed for a few brief moments upon the lovely, yet saddened face of the young bride, suppressed the joyful exclamations that had risen to their lips, and the bridal party were received in respectful silence.

Their stay at the Hall was brief. But the domestics whispered to the villagers that even that short period sufficed to prove the marriage was an unhappy one. They left to spend the season in London, intending, as it appeared, shortly to return, but such intention was frustrated; through what means was never ascertained; but the baronet suddenly broke up his London establishment, and with his lady withdrew to the continent. Rumour with its hundred tongues was busy in finding out manifold reasons for the sudden determination of the baronet, but all of them, after much canvassing, were rejected as wholly destitute of truth, and when year after year passed by, and Sir Richard Eardley still remained an alien to his country, the interest which had been kept alive by the expectation of his return, began by degrees to abate, till his name was rarely mentioned in the village.

When, after the protracted absence of two-and-twenty years, great excitement was manifested in the village by the unlooked-for and undoubted return of the baronet to England, accompanied by two young men, said to be his sons. Of his lady no mention was made, but it was concluded, from her not being of the party, that she must have died abroad.

Sir Richard was greatly altered; from being of an exceeding frank and open disposition, he had evidently become suspicious, morose, and sullen.

With his two sons he had paid a short visit to the Hall, immediately after his return to England, but in such strict seclusion did they live, that though the young men were naturally objects of intense interest in the village, they avoided being seen as much as it was possible by any but their own domestics.

All, therefore, that was known of them was, that they were exceedingly handsome, and strongly resembled each other; the elder, Richard, being thought most to favour his father, and Walter, the younger, was spoken of as the very picture of his mother.

Their stay at the Hall we have said was short, but it was sufficient to bring Walter Eardley on intimate and affectionate terms with Lucy Clarence.

They first met accidentally, and Walter, struck with her extreme loveliness, early sought another interview; he at first found Lucy shy and backward in receiving his advances, but his handsome person and gentlemanly manners soon won upon her heart, and ere many weeks had fled, they mutually confessed a fond and ardent passion for each other. Lucy loved him, as woman can but once, with the tender self-sacrificing affection of her sex; indeed her love for Walter Eardley approached almost to a species of idolatry. And he was well calculated to awaken such a feeling in the bosom of a warm hearted and inexperienced girl like Lucy.

Tall, and remarkably well-made, he had just entered his twentieth year, amazingly fair, with the exception of a peach-like blossom that sat on either cheek; his chestnut hair waved in luxuriant curls over a beautifully formed forehead of the purest white, his eyes (bright, expressive orbs) were, in colour, of a dark hazel, and shaded by long, black-fringed lids; a handsome, well-shaped nose, and a mouth round which, when he smiled, a thousand dimples played, shewing teeth of the finest ivory.

To these natural charms young Walter added many acquired graces, his manners were particularly pleasing, and the soft, low tones of his voice sounded sweet and musical upon the ear.

Educated entirely abroad, born even in a foreign clime, he possessed all the polished grace of an Italian; warm, ardent, and aspiring, good-tempered, apparently amiable and lively; such was the young man who had won the trusting love of the fair and lovely Lucy.

From her own lips, soon after their first meeting, he learnt that she was the affianced bride of another; skilled in the sophistry of the world, he won her affection almost without an effort; he loved her dearer than aught else on earth, (always excepting himself), but then he loved her for her personal charms alone, for that beauty which the lightest accident or illness might totally eclipse; he never gave thought as to her mental attractions, neither had it ever entered into his imagination that he was doing her an injustice, a cruel wrong, in seeking her love without the intention of making her his wife, and yet, strange to say, he considered himself strictly an honourable man; had any even hinted a word against his honour, his arm would have been instantly raised to avenge the calumny.

To Lucy he had never breathed aught concerning his father or brother, otherwise than to assure her he was wholly dependent on them for support, and that he was well aware they would never sanction a union between himself and her; he would take her to London, and provide an elegant house for her, every luxury, even to profusion, would he scatter round her path, bearing his name, none but themselves should ever know that she was not in truth his wife.

Lucy, we have said, fondly and ardently loved him, but she had been educated in strict virtuous principles, and her heart recoiled with horror from his proposal; in vain did he strive to induce her to comply, all his persuasive eloquence availed nothing, and the young man found himself compelled to leave the hall with his father and brother, without gaining the consent of Lucy; but he felt that she was too fair and bright a conquest to be thus easily abandoned, and after the lapse of a few weeks he returned privately to the hall alone; none in the village knew of his arrival, even Lucy was ignorant of it, till his well-known signal sounded on her ears; to hasten down, to sink half-fainting into her lover's arms, while a joyful exclamation burst from her lips, was the work of an instant; they met again and again, but always in the darkness of the night, so that none knew of the stolen interviews. Lucy felt that she was doing wrong, and at last resolved to break the chains that held her soul in bondage, she would see him once more, to bid him farewell, to tell him they must meet no more. She did so; as the reader is aware, the result he will learn in the next chapter.

CHAPTER III.

No, Hinda, no, the fatal flame,
Is nurs'd in silence, sorrow, shame,
A passion without hope or pleasure,
In thy soul's darkness buried deep.

If Lucy could have called to her aid the courage she so much lacked to defend her virtues, what an amount of degradation and suffering would she have spared herself and those who were near and dear to her; but she could not fortel what the future would bring forth. A little reasoning, had her mind been sufficiently calm to have done so, would have told her how widely she was straying from the paths of rectitude, and from the morals that her preceptors had laboured hard to instil into her mind. Her sister, Jane, as we have seen in the preceding chapter was not unaware of her uncourteousness to her lover of late, but little did she think on what a fearful precipice her younger sister, the idol of her parents, stood. From the manner in which she parted with Harry Wilmot, we might be led to think that Lucy had really been sincere in her words and actions. When Harry left her he was quite elated with the happy termination of their interview, which at first bore so gloomy an aspect; he resolved to banish the unworthy thoughts he had entertained, and only to think of her as the pure idol his imagination had ever pictured her, and as he continued walking towards home, he soliloquised—

"Oh, how happy shall I be when the day arrives that is to unite me to my beloved Lucy. But one thing now remains, and that is to prevail upon her, at an early opportunity, to name the day that is to make us one. I have the hearty consent of her parents, and the good wishes of the whole of the family, therefore I ought to make myself happy till the time arrives for the consummation of my bliss. I will endeavour to do so."

He ceased to speak, and walked on in a meditative mood, with his eyes fixed upon the earth. As he proceeded, gloomy thoughts seemed to be passing in his mind, and he started at the slightest ruffle among the dry leaves that covered his path, and ever and anon he would look around him to see from whence the sound proceeded. If his mind had been in its usual and tranquil state, he would have traced the noise to its right cause, he would have known that it emanated from the leaping of frogs, which noise he had been accustomed to from his infancy; but his mind was now so purturbed that he could not recognise those familiar sounds. He put his hand on his forehead as he said—

"My brain is surely disordered; such strange things seem to be enacted in my mental vision which quite bewilders me; they are so opposite to the bliss that was mine but an hour ago. No, no," he said, "such can never be the case! What is young Eardley to her? it is only a foolish fit of jealousy that has seized my imagination! I will eradicate the idea from my memory!" He had now arrived at the gate of his own house, when the voice of his sister aroused him from his abstraction.

We will now return to Lucy and Walter Eardley, who we left in each other's embrace in Mr. Clarence's garden.

"Dear Lucy!" said the young man, after the two had remained locked in each other's arms for some minutes in silence; the young girl raised her head, and smiling through her tears, looked affectionately upon her lover's face; "You say you love me," he continued in the clear musical tones that were natural to him, "and yet how can I believe you when you refuse to give me the only proof of it I ever asked; my love for you, Lucy, is such that I would resign my nearest and dearest friends for your sake, and for me you are unwilling to make the slightest sacrifice. Is this consistent with the fond passion you profess for me?"

"Would we had never met," sobbed the unhappy girl, as she rested her head once more on the shoulder of her lover.

"This is unkind towards me, love," whispered the young man, "the hours we have spent together though few and far between, have been the sweetest and brightest of my life. I can never regret having known you; no, the memory of our meetings will ever be fondly treasured in my bosom, and when in after years, I can look with calmer feelings on the past, I will endeavour to picture you happy, and blest with him you have chosen in preference to myself."

The young girl sobbed aloud.

"I will not, my love," resumed her lover, "inflict my presence longer upon you. I see, I feel, that it has no other effect than to render you miserable. Yes, I," he continued, "whose only thought and desire was to make you happy, have caused your gentle bosom to throb with anguish; kiss me, love, once more, and I will go to wander forth alone. Life will be to me a blank; the world a wilderness; but, if you are happy, I will strive to be content."

"Walter, Walter," exclaimed Lucy, gazing on him with reproachful tenderness, "you will break my heart. Heaven only knows how dear you are to me, and yet you can coldly question my love. I would not, could not act so unkindly by you."

"If you love me," replied the other, and he laid great stress upon the words, "why refuse to consummate our mutual bliss? it rests entirely with yourself to render us both happy or miserable for life. I will not, my love, wrong you, by supposing it possible that you can be happy as the bride of a man whom you do not love. Then why hesitate to confirm your own bliss with one who adores you, and whom you have so frequently declared you love?"

"Were it in your power to marry me, Walter," replied the girl, earnestly, "I should not for a moment hesitate."

"Alas!" returned the young man, in accents of sorrow, "that you should allow such foolish scruples to stand between yourself and happiness. Marriage," he continued, warmly, "is a useless ceremony to such as love like us; you do not, Lucy, doubt my faith or constancy?"

"Oh! no, no, I do not, I cannot doubt your truth."

"Nor I thine, my love, we need no bonds of man's creation to enchain our hearts as one. We are already fast bound by the sweet and rosy fetters of love; what need of more? Will repeating a few words in the presence of a priest (human, and mutable as ourselves) render our love more sacred, or our hearts less inclined to change? No, Lucy, give me the satisfaction of knowing that you rest satisfied with my love, my fond, warm, ardent love, that you rise superior to the silly prejudice of vulgar minds, whom nothing but a church and priest can satisfy; as if these could shackle and enslave the affections. If love is insufficient to keep hearts constant, rest assured, Lucy, nothing on earth will."

With such subtle reasoning as this, did Walter Eardley seek ruthlessly to break down the barriers which parental precept and inherent virtue had reared in the breast of Lucy Clarence, to protect her from the temptations and sins to which the young are ever, more or less, exposed.

Never before had vice assumed so much the semblance of virtue, or presented itself to her unthinking mind in such alluring colours; she listened to the soft, musical tones of her lover's voice, and listening, she was lost. Alas! why did she not cast the tempter from her; poor girl, she loved, and the wily arguments brought forward by the young man, sunk deep into her heart, and she began to regard his preposition with much less horror.

"If," she said, tremblingly, "I could persuade myself that I was acting right, I would resign all, everything for your love, but if you should grow weary of me——"

"I forgive you, dear Lucy," replied the young man, with an air of deep mortification, "the implied doubt, though I feel more hurt than I can tell you. I love you with no light or passing affection, but a passion, that I can fearlessly say, is lasting as time itself. I have the greatest confidence in your love for me, and can look forward to years made sweetly blessed, by spending them together. And yet so anxious I feel, that you should never repent of the step I now urge you to take, that I will no longer press you on this subject. You shall decide wholly for yourself; to-morrow I leave for London, if you determine to go with me, then indeed, I shall be blest."

"And," said Lucy, enquiringly, "If I still refuse?"

"Then," replied her lover, "I must go alone; must bid an eternal adieu to love and happiness, must shun this spot above all others, as ruinous to my peace; I shall probably return to the Continent to spend the remainder of my life in vain regrets."

"And we shall meet no more," said Lucy, tears almost choking her utterance.

"It were better so," replied her lover, mournfully; "to meet again would arouse thoughts and feelings we must learn to suppress; dearest Lucy, sometimes think of me with kindness and pity," and pressing a fond, warm, lingering kiss upon her lips, he endeavoured gently to disengage himself from her circling arms.

"Stay, stay," said the young girl, clinging convulsively to him, "I love, I madly love you, and for this love, I am willing to lose state, station, heaven, mankind's, my own esteem; remember this, Walter, if ever you should be tempted to forsake me, if another should endeavour to usurp that place in your heart I now hold, remember, I beseech of you, that I am fallen, terribly fallen, even in my own estimation, to convince you of the truthfulness of my love. Alas! we cannot look into the dark future, or I would gladly learn in what manner our affection is destined to close." And then, withdrawing herself from her lover's warm embrace, she stood in the full, soft light of the moon, her dark blue eyes raised to the orbs above, her face beaming with wild excitement, and one arm slightly extended, she looked like one inspired, as she said, in a tone that almost awakened awe in the mind of her hearer,

"Walter, I trust neither of us may have cause in after years to repent the decision I have come to this evening, but be that as it may my fate is determined, my destiny is closed, linked with your own, be it good, or evil, blessed with joy and happiness, or cursed with sin and sorrow, blighting the heart's best feelings, I must share it with you; I have no power to do otherwise, my fate is sealed, my doom is cast, in the same mould as your own."

"My own dear girl," replied the young man, "you must not talk so sadly. You will fill my heart with sad and evil forebodings; you consent to be mine let that rapturous thought banish all other feelings.

"It does, it does," replied Lucy, sinking once more covered with blushes into her lover's arms. "Alas! how little they know of me, who regard me as cold and unimpassioned. I knew not what the true meaning of the expressive word, love was, till I knew and loved yourself."

"Nor I, dear Lucy," replied Walter, pressing warm kisses on her glowing cheek. "Let me be to you, father, brother, husband, friend, all, all in one; this time to-morrow, love, we meet to part no more; till then, dear girl, adieu!"

"Farewell, for the last time," repeated Lucy, "henceforth I am your's alone."

Once more seated in the calm seclusion of her own chamber, Lucy had leisure to think over the events of the last half-hour. She wept bitterly at the thought of the cruel ingratitude and deception she was about to practice towards her tender parents, and the thought of the bitter sorrow that would be their portion, on discovering her flight, rent her heart with anguish; several times she was tempted to alter her determination; but then her lover rose before her mind's eye, and she felt that she could resign all but him. Long and severe was the struggle between duty and inclination, and she tried hard to persuade herself that she had gone too far to retract.

The night was far spent before she rested her aching head on the pillow; even there, her

> " Dreams were those of troubled sleep,
> From which 'twas joy to wake and weep;
> Visions that will not be forgot,
>   But sadden every waking scene,
> Like warning ghosts, then leave the spot
>   All withered where they once have been.'

Lucy had a difficult part to act; to conceal from the eyes of her tender relatives the sad and bitter feelings that filled her breast. The plea of bodily illness, which she might well have urged, would, she well knew, awaken such extreme anxiety concerning her, that she forbore to use it. How drearily the day passed on, it seemed as though it would never close; she endeavoured to buoy up her spirits by the thought of the bliss she should experience in her lover's society; but it was useless, as a deep and settled gloom appeared to involve all with whom she came in contact. And very early in the evening she retired to her chamber, in order to avoid seeing Harry Wilmot, whom she felt certain would call, and employed herself in preparing her wardrobe for her departure.

This done, she wrote a few lines to her sister, and concealed it in one of the drawers, and then seated herself at the window, and calmly awaited the hour of departure. Yes, there she sat, almost as immovable as a statue, silently watching the stars of night as they came out one by one, and anon casting her eyes towards Eardley Hall, a fine, romantic building, with "bastion worn, and turret grey," and which now stood boldly out in the midst of the deepening gloom of evening; and as she did so, she wondered if it would ever be her lot to look upon it again. It had ever been an object of interest in her eyes, before she had become known to Walter; but, now that she was connecting herself, in a manner, with the fortunes of its owners, she naturally felt a redoubled interest in the mansion. She regarded it with a half superstitious feeling of reverence; it had witnessed her midnight meetings with him she so ardently loved; she had sat by her window when he was absent, gazing upon the dwelling that had become irresistibly dear to her, as appertaining to him, for hours, till at length she looked upon it almost in the light of a friend, and, strange to say, she felt sad and thoughtful at the prospect of seeing it no more. And as she gazed, and gazed again, to her distempered imagination, it seemed to frown darkly upon her.

"It is too late to retract," she inwardly exclaimed, as a boding thrill shot through her heart, "my doom is fixed, be it for good or ill."

The hours crept gradually on, and still she remained gazing from the window, without the slightest appearance of impatience, as though she heeded not the flight of time, till the well-known signal of her lover aroused her to action.

Surely there was something in the very tones of his voice that fascinated her every sense, for a glow of intense delight illuminated her countenance, and she rose hastily from her seat, trembling with eagerness, the instant she caught the well-known sounds.

"Be quick, dearest love," he whispered, in a loud but beautiful and distinct tone. "All is in readiness, and I am impatient to be gone."

Slow and stealthily she crept down the stairs, and opening the door, stept out upon the threshold for the last time.

The young man received her rapturously, clasped her for a moment fondly to his heart, and then directing a servant, who accompanied him, to take charge of her box, he encircled her slender waist with his arm, and urged her at a rapid pace towards the open road; here there was a travelling-carriage waiting their arrival, they stepped in, the door slammed, and in a few minutes they were whirling away at a rapid pace towards London.

Her head resting on the shoulder of her lover, while she felt the warm kisses on her lips, and listened to the peculiarly soft, honied tones of his voice, Lucy forgot faith, home, father, all—all but the object of her heart's idolatry, for whom she had sacrificed the best and purest feelings of her young heart.

———

CHAPTER IV.

" Then, when thou speakest of me, never say
' He could forgive not.' Here I cast away
All human passions, all revenge, all pride ;
I think, speak, act no ill—I do but hide
Under these words, like embers, every spark
Of that which has consumed me, quick and dark,
So let oblivion hide this grief—the air
Closes upon my accents ; as despair
Upon my heart—let death upon my care."

HARRY WILMOT had been left an orphan when quite a youth, without a relative in the world, save an only and much beloved sister.

They mutually inherited from their father a small patrimony, with which they purchased a farm ; and, by unremitting care and industry, in a short time reaped the reward of their efforts. No farm was in a more flourishing condition than Harry Wilmot's—no dairy so clean and so well stocked as his sister Clara's ; and no two persons were so deservedly beloved, both by rich and poor, as the brother and sister. Contented, light-hearted, and happy, most devotedly attached to each other, they knew not what care or sorrow meant.

Henry was the elder by three years, of a kind and gentle disposition, but capable of strong and ardent attachment. Clara, who in age was scarce three-and-twenty, possessed, naturally, a firmer mind than her brother, never being known to yield, in the slightest degree, when convinced that her opinion was correct ; yet good-tempered, amiable, and open to conviction if in error, she rose superior in character to the weakness and foibles that frequently appertain to her sex ; indeed, she possessed an almost masculine understanding and decision of character, was clever, high-minded, and affectionate in disposition, most devotedly attached to her brother, for whose sake she had refused many excellent offers of marriage, that she might superintend his little household.

Rather above the middle height, Clara Wilmot was pronounced by competent judges to possess a form of the most faultless symmetry.

Though by no means what would be called handsome, or even pretty, her complexion was yet so clear and heathful, and her dark eyes shone as brightly, and she moreover possessed that index to the mind, an expressive countenance, that never failed to please and interest the beholder.

Three years had the brother and sister passed on their little farm, contented and happy, when Clara gradually noted a change stealing over her brother ; he became thoughtful and at times even sad ; grieved to observe this change, she watched him narrowly ; and quickly came to the conclusion that he was in love. Though in many respects disappointed at the discovery she had made, as if she rightly judged it was likely to lead to their separation. Clara wavered not for a moment in the praiseworthy determination of seeking an explanation with her brother, and learnt with surprise that the object of his attachment was the pretty, volatile, and light-hearted Lucy Clarence.

Astonishment chained her tongue, and Harry, interpreting her silence into a disapproval of his choice, ventured to express a hope that on becoming better acquainted with Lucy she might be willing to receive, and love her as a sister.

"My dear brother," replied Clara, affectionately resting her hand upon his shoulder. "I admire, I love Lucy, as a pretty simple child, but will her parents think you, be willing for her to share our humble fortunes? they so love and doat upon her that I fear they contemplate a more brilliant match for the sweet girl; but," seeing a shade of disappointment pass over her brother's countenance, "I may be mistaken; faint heart, you know, dear Harry, never won fair lady, you must lose no time in seeking her hand; go at once to her parents and lay before them a plain statement of our circumstances; and I hope you will prove successful."

"And you, dear Clara, will be willing to extend your love, and affectionate interest to Lucy."

"The woman who will hold towards you the tender and holy relationship of wife, will be treasured in my heart, as a dear and precieus sister."

"You must still remain beneath this roof, dear Clara," said her brother turning to kiss her cheek.

"That Lucy shall decide; as you love her, Harry, lose no time in seeking her hand."

Thus urged, the young man gained courage to solicit from her parents the fair hand of Lucy, his suit was accepted, the wedding day named, and everything appeared to proceed prosperously.

It very frequently happens, that women most love and admire in each other the qualities they are conscious of being deficient in themselves, hence Clara speedily found herself regarding the spoiled and self-willed Lucy with the most affectionate interest, still she felt that in the most essential respects, she was not the sort of woman calculated to make her brother happy; but as Lucy had fully decided that Clara should continue to reside with them, she hoped to counteract the few failings that were perceptible in her friend, who would not be called upon to manage any part of the farm business, that would still remain under her own care. Lucy, too, appeared to return the affection she inspired in the breast of Clara, there was such true nobility in her character, joined to such good temper and amiability, that the young girl both loved and respected her friend.

Harry, poor fellow, was so overjoyed at his sister's approval of his choice, and so tenderly and devotedly attached to Lucy, that he indulged in the most delightful anticipations for the future, nor so much as dreamed they might never be realised, till the sudden arrival of Sir Richard Eardley at the hall, accompanied by his two sons, worked, in a short time, a great and painful change in the manners of his betrothed bride.

Accident, too, made him acquainted with the fact, that Walter Eardley had seen and spoken with Lucy, and though he could not learn that aught beyond common civility had passed between them, yet, the saddened appearance of the once volatile Lucy, when the young man quitted the village, made him fear that his good looks (of which report spoke highly) had made an impression on her young heart. Grieved and hurt at this suspicion, which was confined entirely to his own bosom, he yet loved Lucy too well and fondly to hurt her feelings, by hinting a word even of his fears, till her extreme coldness led him to suspect he was no longer beloved; he then generously resolved to give her an opportunity of releasing herself from the engagement that subsisted between them, which resolution led to the conversation recorded in our second chapter, and which, unfortunately ended in fully restoring the young man to the belief that all his fears were utterly groundless, and that the coldness and reserve in Lucy's manners were to be wholly attributable to the natural timidity of her character.

The next day Harry Wilmot felt more blythe and happy than he had done for weeks before; Lucy still loved him, yes, he was convinced that he was as dear to her heart as formerly; in the evening, according to his daily custom, he walked over to the villa, to see and converse with Lucy, and great was his disappointment, on learning from her sister, that indisposition compelled her to retire to her chamber.

Filled with vague and uneasy forebodings, the young man returned home, but his sister's lively converse soon succeeded in banishing them from his mind, they sat together till a late hour discoursing on the future, which Clara endeavoured to paint in bright but not too glowing colours.

"As long as I remain single, and you and Lucy desire it, I shall still continue to reside with you," said Clara in answer to some remarks of her brother.

"Why Clara, you have surely no thoughts of marrying," replied her brother laughing.

"Well, I see no reason," returned Clara, endeavouring to conceal a slight degree of confusion, "that you should put me down for an old maid. to be sure I have refused several eligible offers as the gossips call them, but then you must remember, Harry, that I acted under the idea that you intended to be a bachelor.

"True Clara," replied the young man, "and I am sure it would please me to see you united to a worthy person, but really there is no one about here that I think good enough for you."

"I am infinitely obliged to you, I am sure," said Clara laughing, "for entertaining so favourable an opinion of my merits; but joking apart, dear Harry, depend I will never even promise my hand to any one, till I have obtained your cordial approval."

And it being now late, the brother and sister separated for the night. The nature of their avocation required them necessarily to be early risers, and when they met at breakfast Harry stated his intention of calling at the villa to inquire if Lucy had recovered from her last night's indisposition.

An unwonted sadness, for which he could not satisfactorily account, pressed heavily upon his spirit, but he trusted the sight of Lucy perfectly restored to health would banish the unwelcome gloom.

On arriving at the villa, it was yet so early that the family had not all assembled. Jane alone was stirring, and welcomed the young farmer who was so soon to become her brother, with her usual cordiality.

"You have come thus early to inquire after Lucy's health?" said Jane, when the first warm greetings had been exchanged.

"Yes," replied the young man, "I confess feeling extremely anxious concerning her; more, perhaps, than the occasion warrants. And so she has not yet risen? I will wait while you go to her room, and enquire after her health."

"I will go at once," replied Jane, "and I have no doubt I shall find her perfectly recovered, as she complained of nothing beyond a slight head-ache."

And Jane instantly departed on her errand; but a few minutes elapsed before the young man was startled by an half-suppressed exclamation of surprise, and scarcely knowing what to think, he hastened from the room to seek the cause. He was met by Jane on the staircase. Her face was of ashy whiteness, and her whole appearance betokening some terrible calamity.

"Good God!" exclaimed the young man, "what has happened; keep me not in suspense, I beseech of you. Lucy is——"

"Gone," replied her sister, in accents of the deepest sorrow, "gone, alas! I know not where." And without the power of saying more, she leant her head against the young man's shoulder, and wept aloud.

Harry Wilmot was thunderstruck at this unlooked for announcement, he could scarce credit the evidence of his senses; surely he could not hear aright. Suddenly a gleam of hope shot across his mind, brief as delightful.

"Cheer up, my girl," he said, addressing Jane, "you have alarmed yourself unnecessarily; this fine morning has tempted Lucy to walk in the fields before breakfast, by way of removing all trace of her late indisposition, and I have been silly enough to allow you absolutely to frighten me."

"No, no," sobbed Jane, "she has gone for ever, her bed shows no signs of having been used last night, and could any doubt remain, the removal of her wardrobe must surely dissipate it."

"Alas!" exclaimed the young man, "is it, can it be possible that she has voluntarly left us? Cruel, unfeeling girl; some deep and powerful motive must surely have actuated her to a line of conduct, so utterly at variance with her disposition, which by nature is kind, open, and generous; and yet, I am at a loss to find one."

"My poor mother," said Jane, endeavouring to calm the violence of her grief, "this unlooked for occurrence will break her heart."

"Jane," replied the young man, "are you well assured that your sister has left no letter to apprise us of her purpose, and explain, perhaps, what now appears so inexplicable—the motive that has induced her thus to act."

"I never thought to look," replied Jane, "but it is most probable she may have done so; indeed, I can hardly think it possible she would be cruel enough to leave us in suspense as to her motive in thus quitting friends, who have only loved her too well." Saying which, she once more returned to her sister's room, and opening a drawer, discovered a letter addressed to herself, with which she speedily rejoined the young man. Opening the welcome epistle, they mutually read as follows:—

"DEAR JANE,—While writing these lines, I picture to my mind the surprise and anguish of yourself and my dear parents, at discovering my flight. I know you will regard me as cruel and selfish, when I inform you that I voluntarily quit all who are dear to me on earth, for the sake of one with whom I could not part. When I accepted the offered hand of Henry Wilmot, my heart was free, and I persuaded myself that I loved him, as well as it was possible for me to love, but I was soon deceived. Accident brought me in contact with Walter Eardley soon after his arrival at the Hall, and I soon learnt to love him, as I had never loved before. Having said so much, you will have guessed that he is the companion of my flight; we confessed a mutual passion, and I required but little persuasion to induce me to consent to an elopement. Be it your task, dear sister, to comfort and console our parents, and Henry Wilmot. That they may pardon the seeming ingratitude of my conduct, is the earnest prayer of your affectionate sister,

"LUCY."

"Cruel, misguided girl," exclaimed the young man, in a voice hoarse and broken with emotion, as he dropped the letter from his hands; "God knows, that although she has wrung my heart with the acutest anguish, I pity and forgive her. It being her own voluntary act, I cast aside all feelings, that would tempt me to seek revenge. May she never know," he added solemnly, "what bitter anguish is now my portion, and will be till I die."

"Harry," replied Jane, tears almost choking her utterance, "she is unworthy of your love; the knowledge of that should induce you to cast her image from your heart."

"The task is more difficult than you imagine, Jane," replied the young man; "pride will doubtless assist me, but I have loved, I do love her, too well, thus suddenly to tear her from my bosom. I must delegate entirely to you," he continued, "the painful duty of beaking this sad and unlooked for misfortune to your parents; when I have calmed the violence of my own grief, I shall be happy, if possible, to endeavour to mitigate theirs."

CHAPTER V.

"We part!—Oh Leon, I must dare, nor tremble
To meet those looks no more!—Oh heavy stroke!
Sweet brother of my soul: can I dissemble
The agony of this thought? As thus she spoke,
The gathered sobs, her quivering accents broke."

HARRY WILMOT, poor fellow, had indeed, received a heavy blow by the elopement of his betrothed bride with another: so sad a change had passed over his countenance that when he presented himself once more before his sister, she was absolutely alarmed at his appearance.

"Dear Harry!" she exclaimed, in accents of the deepest sound, "you are ill, or some dreadful calamity has befallen you. Speak! tell me at once which it is."

It was some relief to the young man to pour his sorrow into the bosom of his sister. A sister who had ever made his lightest grief her own; who had shared

THE STOLEN INTERVIEW OF LUCY CLARENCE WITH WALTER EARDLEY.

his every joy, and soothed his hours of care; to whose counsels he had ever listened, convinced they were calculated to make him a wiser and a better man. Harry was naturally possessed of but a small share of firmness, and this, perhaps, had occasioned him to lean (more than others) on his sister for succour and advice. And he now more than ever felt that he required sympathy. And yet Clara listened to him in silence; she started as he mentioned Walter Eardly, as being the successful lover of Lucy; and a deep burning blush of indignation sat upon her cheek, but she was silent, not one word even of consolation or sympathy did she offer. Her bosom heaved evidently in painful throbs, and she appeared as though she were mentally engaged in endeavouring to conquer some violent emotion; still she spoke not.

"Clara," said the young man, hurt at her supposed want of sympathy; she started at the sound of his voice, and regarded him steadfastly. "Clara," he continued, "you do not appear to feel for my sorrows. Deep, bitter, humiliating as they are, they do not awake that ready sympathy. I never before sought of you in vain."

"Neither do you now," she replied quickly, "out—" she hesitated, and then throwing herself on her knees before him, "Oh! brother, brother," she exclaimed, "pardon me this first deception I have ever practised towards you."

"Deception—you practised towards me?" repeated the young man with unfeigned surprise.

"Yes, yes; I, whom you looked upon as all openness and candour, but you will forgive me. Oh! say that you will forgive me; there are but two of us, we have not a single relative in the world, save each other."

"Clara," returned her brother, "speak plainly; tell me what I have to forgive, for I confess I am utterly at a loss to understand you."

"Listen then," said Clara, hiding her burning face upon his knees; "I know this Walter Eardley, and with shame must confess that I have secretly encouraged his addresses; say, my brother, that you pardon this first act of deception, and from this moment I dedicate myself to revenge the wrongs he has heaped upon us both. He knew from my lips that Lucy Clarence was your betrothed bride, and —and—"

"Say on," said her brother, in a voice husky with emotion; "wretched girl, tell me all; you have dishonoured our name, and my arm it must be that shall revenge the wrong."

"No, no, my brother, not so; neither must your arm be raised against the life of another. You, who never so much as trampled on a worm—no, it must not, shall not be, anything else but that—never—never."

As she spoke she rose from her knees, and threw her arms energetically round her brother's neck.

"Alas, Clara," he exclaimed, affected by her earnest manners, "I never should have believed that you would deceive me."

"Brother," replied Clara, "I beseech of you, let this conversation remain a secret between ourselves. Walter, I am convinced, loves me. That love shall now be turned to gall and bitterness, and made the means of revenging the injury he has done us both."

The young man shook his head.

"This conversation will be buried for ever in my bosom," he returned, "none shall know how deeply we are dishonoured; but for this scheme of revenge, it is wild and impracticable."

"No, brother, it is not," said Clara emphatically, "but you mistake, we are not dishonoured; we are crushed, broken spirited, cast down, if you will—but dishonoured, never."

"You confess, Clara," replied her brother, "having secretly encouraged the addresses of this Walter Eardley. They were not honourable overtures, or what need of deception, especially towards me, your only brother, to whom your welfare and happiness has ever been most dear."

"And yet I can fearlessly affirm, that Walter never breathed a word into my ear that I need blush to repeat. He spoke of marriage, and strenuously urged me to consent to a secret union."

"The villain!" muttered Henry, between his closed teeth. "He not only sought to rob me of my bride, but likewise of my only sister; the thought is maddening. And yet," he added, after a short pause, "I can scarcely perceive it possible that so young a man could be capable of such deceit and treachery."

"Nevertheless such is the case," replied Clara, "see and read for yourself;" and she drew a letter from her bosom, and placed it in her brother's hand.

He opened it, and glanced momentarily over the contents.

"It is strange," he said, as he returned it to her; "when, Clara, did you receive this?"

"Last night," she replied.

"It is almost imcomprehensible," returned the young man. "He surely must have entertained feelings of affection for Lucy, or he would not have burdened himself with such a companion."

"It would seem so," replied Clara, "but it is no part of my intention to upbraid him with the duplicity of his conduct. No, my delight will be to keep him in ignorance of the knowledge I have obtained, encourage his advances, lead him to suppose that I still return his passion, and hurry him to the confession of open and honourable proposals. Then, when he feels assured of securing my hand, at the very moment when he arrives to lead me to the altar, at once throw up the duplicity I have practised, and triumph in his sufferings. This is the revenge, the only revenge I seek, and I am resolved to obtain it, cost what it may; my efforts will be untiring. I shall heed no difficulty, and in the end I feel convinced I shall triumph. Cheer up, brother!" she continued with increased animation, "and all may yet be well."

"Clara," he replied, "your wild and improbable scheme will only result in disappointment; abandon it, therefore, I beseech of you. You acknowledged having nourished an affection for this young man in your bosom, that alone will prevent you."

"Stay, brother," interrupted Clara, "it is possible for love to turn to hate, nay, such has often been the case. I feel, now, surprised even at my own folly in having listened to Walter's addresses; all love has vanished totally from my breast. I cannot love again, for the freshness of my heart is gone."

The young man wound his arms around his sister's form, and pressed the tenderest kisses of paternal love upon her cheek, as he said—

"My own sweet sister, our happiness is mutually shipwrecked; the same storm has been fatal to us both—one hand has ruthlessly severed our souls from bliss; let us then forsake the love of all others, and cling alone to each other for love and tenderness; let us again, as in days gone by, be all the world to each other. Oh, how oft in childhood's hours have we shared every joy, and divided many a little sorrow; there are but two of us, dear sister, give up, then, all thoughts of revenge, and the remainder of our lives, be they short or long, may yet be passed in peaceful serenity."

"Dear brother," replied Clara, melting at once into softness, "I will be guided entirely by your wishes."

"But what, then, will be your intention regarding that letter?"

"I will return it, with all others I have received from him, without accompanying them even with a single line, depend upon it; Harry, he will guess the cause, and feel mortified by my contempt."

The young man signified his approval; and once more reinstated in his good opinion, Clara was content. It were sad indeed, that the sin of one should cause misery to so many, but Clara felt that it was no uncommon case, and exerted herself to banish the gloom from her brother's countenance, but, from that sad hour, he became an altered man, the smile was banished for ever from his lip, and sorrow had set her seal upon his once open, happy brow. Clara marked this change with bitter anguish; but even this was not all, for severe as it was, it might have been borne, but she shortly became aware that his health was fast giving way, that ere long her beloved and sole remaining relative would sink to "that bourn from whence no traveller returns," long she sought in vain to disguise this painful truth from her own mind, but it at length became so apparent that it forced itself upon her, in spite of all her efforts. Many and bitter were the tears she shed when alone, but Clara was possessed of fortitude and strength of mind seldom found in one of her sex, and she was therefore enabled to look forward to the end with calmness and resignation.   Mr. and Mrs. Clarence mourned deeply for the loss of their daughter; their two sons were travelling on the continent, and to Jane entirely devolved the task of cheering and soothing their afflicted minds; the poor girl did her utmost, but they were discontented and unhappy, for awhile they indulged the hope of again hearing from their Lucy, but as time wore on, and no tidings of her reached them, they gave up all in despair.

"She is unworthy of our anxiety, unhappy, deluded girl," said her father, when conversing of his absent daughter.   And yet while he spoke, the tears fell thick from his eyes; her mother, too, for months wept almost incessantly; their hearts had received a wound which only time could heal.   Jane exerted herself to the utmost, to supply the place of her sister to her unhappy parents; deeply, too, did she sympathize with the affliction of Clara, and often would she walk over to the farm, to mingle her tears with those of her friend.   Long and weary were the winter months that followed the elopement of Lucy, and when spring, soft and warm, once more began to smile upon the earth, it was evident to all that Harry Wilmot would soon pass away; poor fellow! he made no complaint, nor no murmur of discontent escaped his lips, but consumption, that fell tyrant, had marked him for its own.   Clara strove in vain to dissemble her anguish, even in the presence of her beloved brother.   To part with him, her sole relative, to be left in the wide world alone, was terrible to contemplate.   And when she thought upon the cause that had thus brought him low, her heart throbbed with anger and resentment. "And is it possible I could once love the man who has wantonly wrought such an awful amount of misery?" was a question she repeatedly asked herself, and she shrunk with horror from the thought.   But she consoled herself with the hope that he might one day be made to feel the very pangs he had inflicted on her brother.   So much, and so deeply, did she dwell on this, that it at last became as it were a part of her being.   Yes, fondly did she cherish in her heart the hope of revenging the injury inflicted on her brother; this was her darling object, for this she wished to to live, aye, were it necessary, even a life of toil and sorrow.

CHAPTER VI.

"Ah ! thine be the gladness, and mine the guilt !
Forgive me, adored one, forsake if thou wilt,
But the heart which is thine, shall expire undebased,
And man shall not break it, whatever thou may'st.
And stern to the haughty, yet humble to thee,
This soul in its bitterest blackness shall be,
And the days seem as swift, and the moments more sweet,
With thee by my side, than with worlds at my feet."

TWELVE months have elapsed since Lucy quitted her peaceful home, and the kind and affectionate relatives who surrounded her.   And Harry Wilmot, her betrothed husband, has passed from earth away; he died praying for her happiness, and with his latest breath pronounced her forgiveness.   Clara knelt beside him.

"Her hands were clasped, her eyes upturned, dropping their tears like moonlight rain."

Yet there was light around her brow, a holiness in those dark eyes, and a sweet and holy calm settled on her spirit.   Pressing her lips fervently to the icy ones of her departed brother, she whispered gently—

"Farewell, dear Harry, I would not wish you back again to this dull cold earth. You are now safe landed on a happier shore, where we shall ultimately meet again."

From this moment she stedfastly avoided looking again upon her brother's face.

"Do not urge me," she said, to those who would have persuaded her to look upon him once more. "I am now resigned and tranquil, I can remember him as he was in life and health, and thus do I ever wish to recollect him."

After seeing her brother laid in the quiet grave, in a sweet, green, sunny spot, in the village churchyard, where the children frequently assembled at morn or dewy eve, to gather the beautiful wild flowers that grew in rich profusion there, a spot where the young man had often loved to linger when blest with health and strength, and where, his sister was assured, many who knew and prized his worth, would mark well the spot where, "after life's fitful fever, he slept well."

"Nor lose it from their memory, beneath the deepest snow."

Clara resolved to bid adieu to the little village, and take her part in the great world; she was alone and friendless, and the scenes by which she was surrounded reminded her too strongly of her lost happiness, for her to dare to expect to regain her peace while residing there. The sale of the farm, which Clara was happy to dispose of to a young man, who, by dint of great industry, had saved sufficient to enable him to start in life, realised so small a sum, that even with the strictest economy it would barely suffice to procure the necessaries of life, and Clara, therefore, determined to seek some employment which might enable her to make up the deficiency. And while turning over in her mind the most desirable manner in which to employ her time and talents, she learnt from one of the domestics at the hall, that Sir Richard Eardley was desirous of meeting with a young person who might be willing to become companion to his, the baronet's sister, who was spoken of as being a widow lady in delicate health, and Clara instantly resolved to proffer her services, which were thankfully accepted, and an early day named for her departure to London. Clara considered herself exceedingly fortunate in so easily procuring this situation, and yet it was with a swelling heart that she bade adieu to her native village. She had, to be sure, few friends to leave; yet she was beloved by many, and their kind warm parting affected her almost to tears; with Jane Clarence too, for whom she felt a tender interest, she was grieved to part, but the promise of an epistolary correspondence cheered her heart. The journey to London was performed by stage, and it being the first time Clara had ever visited that great city, she was completely dazzled on her arrival by the number and brilliancy of the shops, and the immense traffic from all quarters. Clara was preparing to alight, and had already desired the guard to procure a coach, in which she might proceed to her destination, when a tall and elegant young man, possessed of great personal beauty, presented himself at the coach door, to enquire for a young lady who was about to proceed to Mrs. Mortimer's. Bewildered by the novelty of her position, Clara, without for the moment glancing at the stranger, announced herself as the person he was inquiring for, when the young man starting with unfeigned surprise, uttered an exclamation of astonishment, which induced Clara to regard him more steadfastly, and the name of "Walter" escaped her lips as she sank back almost motionless.

"Yes, call me so, dear Clara, always call me so," replied the young man in the low musical tones that were so peculiarly his own.

The sound of his voice served to recall her scattered senses, and she commanded herself sufficiently to enquire his errand.

"I came here, dear Clara," he replied, "in obedience to the desire of my father, in order to convey a young lady to the residence of my aunt, little dreaming I should meet with you; but come, love, allow me to assist you to alight, the carriage is waiting to convey you to your future home."

It was with extreme difficulty Clara could conceal the horror she felt at the young man's presence, but she commanded her feelings sufficiently to give him her hand, though she inwardly shrank with loathing from his touch. He pressed her hand tenderly within his own as he led her to the carriage, and then having placed her in it, seated himself by her side. As soon as the vehicle was in motion he turned to his companion, who compelled herself to appear pleased with his attentions, and carrying her hand respectfully to his lips, said—

"I will not now, dear Clara, seek to convince you of the injustice you did me in so abruptly breaking off our correspondence, nor attempt to describe the anguish I have endured through your coldness; we shall now meet again often I hope, dear Clara, and I shall thus have opportunities of reinstating myself in your good opinion; your brother——"

"Is now no more," replied Clara, in a voice broken with emotion, "his happiness as well as my own were shipwrecked, and this it is that has driven me a wanderer from my home."

The young man was silent, and Clara felt pleased to observe that he seemed to feel deeply the communication she had made of her brother's death. There was a painful pause. The brow of Walter darkened, and the expression of his countenance, usually grey, changed to one of a deep sadness; he still retained the hand of Clara in his own, and when he again spoke, his voice trembled perceptibly as he gave utterance to what he wished to say.

"Dearest Clara," he began, "time may perhaps explain much in my conduct that now appears cruel and unjustifiable; till then, will you promise to suspend your judgment of me?"

Clara murmured a faint affirmative.

"I love you," continued the young man, "as God in heaven knows, with sincerity and truth. I desire to obtain my father's consent to our union. Since we last met, much has occurred to induce me to condemn a secret marriage. I will wed you, dearest, in the presence, and with the consent of all whom I am bound to consult; or, cost me what it may, I will resign all pretensions to this dear hand."

"This looks well," thought Clara, and she mentally exclaimed—"My brother. I will avenge you yet, if he really loves me as he would have me believe. I will lead him on to gaining his father's consent to our union, and then, at the last moment, when all is in readiness for the ceremony, I will dash his fondly cherished hopes to the ground; he shall feel the very pangs recoiling on his head, that he so cruelly inflicted on my beloved brother; for this end will I endure his hateful presence, will smile and bless him now, that I may wither him with my contempt hereafter."

"Being but a younger brother," resumed her companion after a short pause, "I cannot, dear Clara, ever anticipate placing you in the station of life you so well deserve to move in; but, though before I became acquainted with you, I steadfastly refused all offers of augmenting my income by accepting a mercantile appointment for your dear sake, I will gladly bow my pride, and eagerly, thankfully, accept what I have heretofore refused."

Clara felt, even in spite of herself, affected at the earnestness and apparent openness of his speech.

"There can be no deception here," she mentally exclaimed, "I am convinced he loves me, and yet, in all probability, he spoke in the same strain to the unfortunate Lucy."

And at the recollection of her friend, she longed to enquire of her companion, what had become of the unhappy girl, but—she forbore, she had a part to act that required her to be exceedingly wary, or she would probably defeat her own ends. When Walter Eardly spoke again, it was on a subject of deep interest to Clara, as it concerned the lady with whom she was about to take up her abode.

"My aunt," said the young man, "with whom I hope you will be happy, is an authoress of some celebrity, and your services will be chiefly required as an amanuensis; you will find her kind and amiable, though possessed of some eccentricity, and you must not allow her to impose too much labour upon you."

Clara expressed her surprise at this announcement, as it was the first intimation she had received as to the manner in which her time would be employed, but the knowledge was far from unpleasing, as copying was an occupation she might pursue without arousing herself to feigned cheerfulness she could not feel, and she gratefully expressed herself to this effect.

"I must caution you," said Walter, "not to intimate to my aunt, on any account, the friendship that exists between ourselves, and if, by any chance you should see me in her presence, receive me as an entire stranger."

" Is not this request," replied Clara, " at variance with your expressed determination to seek me openly as your bride ?"

" I ask it but for a short time, dearest, I hope a very short time ; in the meanwhile, Clara, you will not, I hope, feel offended if I entreat of you to avoid seeing or speaking to my brother ; Richard is frequently a visitor at my aunt's residence, and did he see you, I should tremble for the result ; a professed admirer of beauty, and a libertine to boot. It is not, love, that I doubt your faith," he added, seeing Clara was about to make an indignant reply, " but should Richard unfortunately conceive a passion for you, it might prove fatal to my hopes. At present, it is indispensably necessary that our affection should remain a secret ; under these circumstances you will not, I feel assured, refuse to grant my request."

Clara instantly assented, and the carriage which had been proceeding at a rapid pace through the western part of the city turned into a pretty quiet, shady grove, and finally stopped before the entrance of a small but elegant cottage, which stood in the centre of a beautiful garden ; the soft perfume of the violet, mingled with the fragrance of the rose and honeysuckle ; the trellised walls of the cottage were completely hidden by the climbing jasmine and clematis ; the porch was thickly shad d with the bright green leaves of the ivy. Clara was delighted, she possesed a passionate fondness for flowers, and the elegant arrangement of the garden spoke to the good taste and sensibility of the owner. No employment is at once so sweet and graceful as the cultivation of flowers. A love for their soft perfume and varied tints is confined to no station or condition, it pervades all ranks from the peer to the peasant. How often in our walks have we stopped to admire the neatly and prettily cultivated garden of the labouring man, who, rather than forego the pleasing avocation of attending to his plants, will willingly snatch an hour or two from his nightly rest, to devote it to so pleasing a purpose. And the rose will bloom as sweetly in the small patch of ground that adjoins the cottage of the poor, as in the large and flourishing parterre of those who are rich in this world's goods, the same dews of Heaven will water them, and the same bright sun shine alike on them. On alighting from the carriage, a servant in neat livery approached to conduct Clara to the house, and Walter Eardly, with a fond, lingering pressure of her hand, bade her farewell, and at the same time whispered a promise of a speedy meeting. The short time they had been together during the ride had sufficed to captivate the heart of Clara with the fascinating manners and appearance of the young man.

" Alas," she thought, as she mechanically followed her conductor into the interior of the abode, " that such wickedness and duplicity should dwell in the breast of one possessed of such an enchanting form and face, how sad that vice should lie concealed beneath so winning an exterior."

In the hall, Clara was met by a genteel looking young girl, who informed her that Mrs. Mortimer was at present engaged in her study, but that she had given her orders to conduct Clara to the apartments prepared for her reception. Clara bowed in compliance, and followed the girl up two separate flights of stairs, on reaching the top of which, she opened a door, and on entering the apartment, Clara was pleased to discover that it was tastily arranged as a sitting room ; this and the one adjoining, which was fitted up as a sleeping apartment, Clara was given to understand were intended for her own exclusive use.

" My mistress," said the girl, " desired me to say that she hoped you would at once consider yourself at home, and order whatever refreshment you may require after your journey, and she will be happy to meet you at dinner, an hour hence."

" That being the case," replied Clara, " I will decline taking any refreshment at present," and dismissing her attendant, Clara proceeded to change her dress, and having satisfied herself by a hasty glance at the mirror that her toilet was *comme il faut*, she sat down by one of the windows, which commanded a view of the garden, and indulged in a fit of meditation.

Her thoughts naturally recurred to the young man with whom she had so lately parted, and spite of her most strenuous efforts, she could not command her feelings sufficiently to regard him with that detestation and abhorrence she conceived his conduct so well merited. There was something so extremely fascinating about the person and manners of Walter Eardley that at once conquered the young and susceptible of the opposite sex; his smile alone was victory. And although Clara was of a firmer mind and prouder disposition than the generality of young women of her own age, yet in her extenuation, it must be remembered that to this youth her first vows of love had been paid; he had been the worshipped shrine at which she had offered her heart's warm idolatry, and though he had fallen immeasurably in her estimation, yet love lingered o'er its idol still, not that she for an instant wavered in her expressed determination to revenge her brother's death, by making the destroyer of his happiness suffer the very pangs he had inflicted upon him, yet, as we said before, she could not entertain towards him those feelings of hatred she so much wished. In the midst of these reflections, Clara was aroused by a summons to dinner.

CHAPTER VII.

" Proud has been my fatal passion !
    Proud my injured heart shall be !
While each thought, each inclination,
    Still shall prove me worthy thee !
Not one sigh shall tell my story,
    Not one tear my cheek shall stain ;
Silent grief shall be my glory—
    Grief, that stoops not to complain !"

WHILE Walter's affections were thus apparently once more bestowed upon Clara, and he was whispering in her ear the tender words of love, the unfortunate Lucy, in the hour of woman's greatest peril, was left alone and unattended, save by the hirelings of service. Poor Lucy ! she is much altered since we last presented her to the reader, sorrow and anxiety have done much towards eclipsing her personal charms, soul-withering care has already set his seal upon her young brow, the rose has faded from her cheek, the lustre from her eye. Yet for all this, there was more beauty in her matured charms than in the pretty girlish attractions that had pleased, for a time, the wandering eye of Walter Eard'ey. On their first arrival in town the young man was pleased and proud of his fair companion, her comfort and happiness engrossed his every thought ; established as mistress of an elegant house, where profusion scattered her lavish gifts around, evidently idolised by the only being on earth whose love she ever wished to win, we need scarcely say, that Lucy deemed herself happy. And yet, in the midst of gay and animated scenes, whither she was constantly accompanied by Walter, sad and regretful feelings would flit across her breast, and fill her heart with anguish. Yea, even when most gay,

" Sad thoughts, she knew not whence or why,
Would suddenly o'er her spirits fly ;
Sometimes so strange, so undefined
Were these strange dreamings of her mind,
That not of life, or earth they seemed,
But shadows from some world unknown."

More oft, however, it was the thought of friends who had so loved and cherished her, and whom she had so cruelly and ungratefully deserted. Yet sedulously did she conceal all sombre and regretful thoughts from her lover ; he never approached, but the same soft winning smile that at first enchanted his roving heart, played round her mouth, and fondly gave him welcome, words of tenderness ever fell from her lips, and to all appearance Lucy had totally forgotten all, but him. Ye inexperienced in the world as she was, Lucy frequently wondered how the young man contrived to support the utter extravagance in which he indulged, both as to the style in which they lived, and the expensive dress and ornaments with which he constantly presented her. Once she ventured gently to hint as to the probable means he possessed of supporting so extensive an establishment; but a frown,

SIR RICHARD EARDLEY VISITS LUCY SHORTLY AFTER HER ACCOUCHMENT.

the first she had ever seen upon his brow, completely silenced her, and she never again alluded to the subject. The first eight months they spent together were passed in a constant succession of gaieties; balls, masquerades, theatres, and the like were visited, till Lucy was absolutely indifferent, not to say weary of them, and was by no means sorry at this period to perceive that Walter began to hint that it would for a time be advisable for them to live in a state of more domestic retirement. And yet, though Lucy eagerly embraced the idea, the young man seemed loath to tear himself from his accustomed pleasures, and another month passed without any change, when one morning Walter, who had been absent for a few hours, hurriedly returned, and told Lucy that they must instantly prepare to quit their present abode; he had become deeply involved in debt; his father, to whom he had applied, refused to assist him, and his brother was absent from town, but on his return he hoped to be able to manage his affairs, but in the interval he stood in momentary danger of a prison; indeed his only chance of escape was instant flight. Lucy was shocked beyond measure at this intelligence, and though now within a few months of becoming a mother, she instantly exerted herself to hasten their departure; in a few hours all was in readiness, and Walter conducted her to the outskirts of London. Having seen her settled in her new abode, he left her with only two attendants, under pretence of having to meet some persons concerning the management of his affairs. Lucy was nervous and low spirited, which Walter's return with a gloomy countenance did not tend to banish; she now, for the first time since their acquaintance, began to tremble for the result of their connection, and to fear, perhaps, not without good reason, that his love was beginning to decay; this was greatly increased, when, as week after week passed by, he invariably framed excuses for repeated and almost continual absence. Still, though she wept his absence, and mourned for his return, she carefully refrained from whispering even a word of reproach; she knew too well, that if love and unvarying gentleness could not win him back to her side, nought else on earth could. As he ever urged the unsettled state of his affairs in extenuation of his absence, Lucy's fears would undoubtedly have been lulled to sleep, had not his manners towards her assumed a painful change; he was no longer the tender, amiable friend and lover; on the contrary, Walter's brow was the seat of constant gloom and sternness, his temper became irritable in the extreme, and his whole conduct towards her neglectful, even to unkindness. Left for hours and days entirely alone, poor Lucy had time and food for reflection; much and often she wept the apparent loss of affection in one whom she only loved too well, for whom she had sacrificed her all. Bitterly too did she repent the false step she had taken, and much would she have given, could she have purchased back her innocence and guiltlessness of heart; yet she loved him still, and fondly did she look forward to the birth of her child, which she hoped might become the means of restoring to her once more the affection of its father. Proud had been her fatal passion, and now, deeply injured as she was, her heart was full of pride, silent grief was all her glory, grief that stoops not to complain. Such command did she possess over her feelings, that not once even did Walter surprise her in tears. When she wept, which was far from unfrequent, she turned away to shed her tears alone. The anguish of her mind undoubtedly made sad ravages in her fair face, yet the look of silent sorrow, that was so indelibly imprinted on her countenance, was accompanied with a gently interesting expression, most pleasing to behold. Yet Walter seemed utterly indifferent to both, the unsettled state of his affairs appeared to engross all his thoughts. Lucy voluntarily renounced all the luxuries and pleasures to which she had been accustomed, contracting even her necessary expenses. Yet still Walter declared his circumstances were too narrowed to meet her demands; not the slightest preparation had been made for the expected infant, and rather than involve him in farther expense, Lucy cut up the chief of her own wardrobe to make frocks and robes for the as yet unborn child. She robbed her dresses of the rich lace, with which in happier hours Walter loved to see them trimmed, in order to make caps and frills for her babe. How much she tasked her invention to contrive the scanty materials, so as to make the greatest number of articles, and when all was done, how scantily was the little basket stocked, and yet how neatly was it arranged; the fond, tender solicitude of a mother was visible even in the fold of each small article. And now her hour of anguish rapidly drew nigh, and with a mixture of hope and fear, she tremblingly awaited its approach. Poor girl, how much she needed the tender sympathy of a dear relative, who, with words of hope and comfort, might sustain her fainting spirit in that dread hour; but, alas! woman's heart grows fonder when her dream of bliss is o'er—she loved Walter, if possible, more ardently now, than when she quitted her home, and all who were dear for his sake. And this love made her content to struggle on; yet, when the first symptoms of indisposition assailed her, and he whom she so treasured was far away, and none to whom she could breathe her anxiety was nigh, her courage for a time failed her, but she soon recovered from the despair which had threatened to overwhelm her spirit with anguish, and the presence of an elderly lady, a near neighbour, who hearing of her situation, kindly offered her services, greatly helped to sustain her fortitude, which was at length rewarded by the birth of a fine and healthy boy. Oh! what sweet extatic sensations filled the heart of Lucy, as she pressed this first dear pledge of love to her maternal bosom,

> "And kissed its hands, and kissed its face,
> Delighted with its infant grace."

Every wish of her heart seemed now obtained, every pain assuaged; and she shed tears of grateful joy as she felt her little treasure nestling close to her bosom. Oh! how she trembled for fear it might be torn from her arms, how her heart palpitated with joy as she watched her darling, with its downy cheek fondly pressed against her own, sink into its first soft slumber. Three days passed gently on, and the newness of her bliss began to give place to anxiety for the continued absence of Walter, who had not once all that time paid her even a passing visit. Towards noon on the fourth day from the birth of the child, Lucy had sunk into an uneasy slumber, from which she was aroused by the startling announcement that a gentleman particularly desired to see her on matters of business; Lucy never doubting but that he must be commissioned to call upon her by the absent Walter, desired the servant to apprise him of the delicate state of her health, and at the same time to enquire the stranger's name. Lucy, it must be confessed, watched with a degree of feverish impatience the return of her messenger, but great was her astonishment to hear the name of her visitor announced as Sir Richard Eardley, coupled with a request that he might be admitted to her chamber, if only for a few moments; she had none to consult as to the propriety of doing so, and she felt as though she dared not refuse, and yet it was with faltering accents that she granted permission for his introduction to her room; the pallor of death overspread her countenance as she listened for his approach, and when he entered she was so overcome that she was on the point of fainting; scarcely could she gain courage to look upon the man, who probably held her destiny in his hands, but when she did so, the result was in a measure favourable. Sir Richard Eardley was apparently little more than fifty years of age, of a tall, commanding figure, and a benevolent expression of countenance, which, however, was rather clouded by an unusual degree of sternness that sat upon his brow; he had evidently in his younger days been remarkably handsome, indeed he was now what is termed a fine looking man. Approaching the bed on which poor Lucy lay, for the time deprived (by the agonised emotions of her mind) of the faculty of speech, the baronet apologized for his intrusion, and begged her to compose herself.

"I have, madam," he concluded, "but to request your frank answer to one or two questions, and I will instantly withdraw."

Lucy gained courage to murmur a faint reply, to the purport that she would be happy to oblige him so far as it was in her power.

"To be brief then, madam, rumours having reached my ears to the effect that my youngest son had formed an imprudent alliance, which had unfortunately deeply involved him in debt, I deemed it right to enquire fully into the circumstances that led to it. And having from good authority ascertained that you were the lady who had assumed his name, I wish to hear from your own lips whether or not you possess a legal right to it."

Lucy trembled excessively, she had a soul above the meanness of attempting deception, and yet, how deeply humiliating to be compelled to avow her own dishonour, and to whom? the father of him who had wrought it; the presence too, of her nurse, nearly an entire stranger, offered a severe restraint, and thus it was with the utmost difficulty she gave utterance to the monosyllable, "No."

"I am answered," replied the baronet, "and must beg, madam, that henceforth you will abstain from assuming a name to which you acknowledge having no proper title. I am tenacious," he continued "of a name that has never yet been in the remotest manner linked with dishonour; neither shall it be, if I have power to prevent."

Lucy trembled yet more, she had no power to express her thoughts, or she might have intimated to the haughty baronet that his own son had already dishonoured a name of which he expressed himself so tenacious. As Sir Richard turned to leave the room, he for the first time appeared to observe the infant, which was lying on the nurse's knees before the fire; it was one of the prettiest little mortals on which the sun had ever shone; and Lucy, justly proud of her new-born treasure, followed the eyes of the baronet as they rested on the child.

"Sweet innocent," she thought, "you at least will surely interest your proud relative in your favour."

It lay with its pretty little dimpled hands crossed over its heart, the very picture of infantile grace.

"Poor little wretch," said the baronet, bending for an instant over it. "It would indeed be a blessing, if it pleased God to take you."

Lucy scarce stifled a groan of anguish; she was oppressed with suffocation, to the very verge of fainting; fortunately a flood of tears afforded her seasonable relief at the moment Sir Richard closed the door behind him, and, stretching out her arms, she clasped her infant to her breast.

CHAPTER VIII.

"It is the spirit's bitterest pain,
To love, and to be loved again;
And yet, between a gulf which ever
The hearts which burn to meet, must sever."

"THEN you positively refuse, Jane, to listen to my proposal," said a pale, but peculiarly intellectual-looking young man, to Jane Clarence, as he walked by her side, in a sweet shady lane, one warm summer's afternoon.

"I do, I do," replied the young girl, energetically; "consider for a moment, Henry, what it is you propose, and then, I am sure, you will not be angry with me for refusing to entertain it."

"I am not angry with you, Jane, neither do I blame you for exercising what I may perhaps be tempted to regard an over-due caution; in respect to the future, I am poor and friendless, there is nothing whatever in my lot to induce you to leave a comfortable and a happy home, nothing but my own deep love; if that could have made amends for the loss of worldly enjoyments, it would have been ever and only yours."

"I believe it, Henry," replied Jane, "I believe it all, and, oh, you might do me the justice of attributing my refusal to share your lot (dear to me above all others) to anything but selfishness; could aught tempt me to quit my parents, it would be, dear Henry, the blissful hope that I might share and cheer your humble fortune."

"If," said the young man, without heeding the remarks of his companion, "you refuse to accept my offered hand, to-morrow I shall start for London alone; there," he continued, proudly, "my talent, I hope, will be appreciated, and I shall have an opportunity afforded me of competing for those laurels I am so anxious to gain. Oh, Jane," he continued, warmly, "blest with thy dear presence, I should have felt certain of success; thy smile, thy dear approving smile, would have moved my soul to repeated and untiring efforts, thy tender gentle words would have soothed my wayward spirit, and rocked all troubled thoughts to sleep. Blest with a loved and loving wife, no temptation would have possessed the power to move me, for thou would'st have made me strong in virtue, and in wisdom's might."

"And so I will, dear Henry, though at a distance from you; in every temptation think that I am nigh. I have the strongest confidence in you, place the same in yourself, and you will never have cause to regret my present determination," replied Jane, who was affected even to tears.

"Then your determination is fixed and unalterable?" said the young man, in a tone of disappointment.

"Listen to me one moment, dear Henry," returned Jane. "Your own ardent imagination will not permit you to view the future in its most probable, though at the same time, its most sombre colours. You urge me to quit my parents, whose hearts are already crushed and wounded, and who depend upon me for love and tenderness, and dear father (here her voice became nearly inarticulate) sensibly declines in health, and I sadly fear he will not much longer require my care; nothing then on earth will ever induce me to leave my parents, not even with their own consent, while they stand in need of my services, but were it otherwise, dear Henry, and I was free to give you my hand, I could not for your own sake become your wife under existing circumstances. Go to London unburdened by the expense attending such a companion as myself. You have yet all your fortune, all your friends to find."

"Then you refuse to share my poverty?" said the young man in a tone of bitterness.

"I love you too well to consent to becoming a useless and expensive burden to you. It is most probable that you will find many noble and generous patrons of your delightful art, but should it prove otherwise, and you should be doomed to see your little purse daily grow lighter, it will be some satisfaction to know that you have none save your own wants to provide for."

"Oh, Jane," sighed her companion, "I little thought you could argue so coldly; it evinces a want of affection I scarcely thought to find in you whom I have so long and so fondly loved."

"I shrink with horror," replied Jane, "from the bare thought that it is possible you might ever regret having induced me to become your wife, and that it is, joined to my fixed determination not to quit my beloved parents, which induces me to negative all your proposals, and my heart assures me that you will one day approve of my resolutions."

"It is useless to say more," returned the young man; "I am henceforth a solitary being, ambition alone will urge me to the path of fame, none will smile upon my efforts, or weep for my anxieties."

"Say not so, dear Henry; while I live, there will at least be one being to whom your success and triumph will be dear above all else on earth, who will daily mourn your absence, yet glory in the cause that occasions it."

"It may be so," said the young man, doubtfully, "but remember, Jane, you have refused to give me the lightest proof that my welfare is dear to you."

"You have asked the only proof that I cannot give, but be not angry with me, dear Henry, let us at least part friends, if nothing more."

"I will not detain you longer, Jane," replied the young man; to lament what seems inevitable, is the action of fools. God bless you!—I will endeavour to forget the dream of bliss that I have so long encouraged in my heart. And for the future I will devote myself more ardently than ever to the acquirement of fame."

Saying which, he released her hand, and Jane, who had now closely approached her parents' habitation, without a word more hurried to her own apartment, there to shed her tears of heartfelt anguish, alone and unheeded. Henry Fergusson had been her accepted lover for years, he was the first being for whom her heart had beat responsive to that first warm passion life only once may know. Of origin by no means inferior to her own, he was yet poor in purse, but proud and sensitive in spirit. He loved Jane Clarence for her gentle feminine attractions, and before the ill-timed flight of her sister, Jane had half promised that she would seek her parents' consent to their union; but that unfortunate affair unsettled all their plans. With true filial affection, Jane refused to augment the anguish of her bereaved parents by proposing herself to quit their roof. In the meantime, adverse circumstances deprived Henry of his little all. From his earliest youth painting had been his passion; he was now desirous, if possible, of turning his knowledge in that art to account. His talent was not likely to become matured or appreciated in a small village; therefore, he would visit London, and there, he fondly hoped, acquire fortune and celebrity. With a light heart, and a still lighter purse, he prepared for his departure; filled with the most sanguine hopes for the result of his undertaking, he resolved to persuade Jane to consent to accompany him: he could not bear the thought of parting with her, whose gentle, yet wise counsel had for years animated his heart. He thought but little of the sacrifice he required of Jane, and never doubted but her love for him would induce her to yield a ready assent to his wishes; deep then was his mortification, when he found himself deceived in his anticipations: Jane could not love him, he thought, if she were so unwilling to make a small sacrifice for his sake. Henry Fergusson was naturally of a proud, high-spirited, warm, sanguine temperament, but impetuous in the extreme. No person, surely, could be more suited to curb and rein in the faults of such a character than Jane Clarence, mild, gentle, and open to conviction; yet firm in purpose, conscious of falling into error, never suffering herself to be persuaded to do aught that interfered with the dictates of her conscience. She loved Henry, as woman can only love, but this did not blind her to his failings, and often had she occasion to exert over him the control which she possessed, and ever made him wince by her counsel, nor did she shrink from administering reproof, if she saw that he needed it. Still she had the strongest confidence in his love; admired and reverenced the many noble traits in his character, and, moreover, was ready to sacrifice her fondest hopes, could it in any way tend to his exaltation or preferment. Thus she was enabled to look forward to his departure to London without any weak, silly fears that she might be forgotten in the ardour of his pursuits. She met him by appointment on this afternoon, to receive his parting adieus, and was prepared to endeavour to moderate his somewhat too sanguine expectations, when, alas! she was grieved at receiving from his lips a proposal that was utterly incompatible at once with honour and duty. She could not, whatever inclination might have urged, quit her parents, who now more than ever depended on her care; her father's health daily failed, and, when he was gone, who but she could comfort and support her mother? and then, too, as she so emphatically declared to her lover, her acceptance of his proposal, could she with honour do so, would most probably burden him with an expense he might for some years find it difficult to meet. Grieved and hurt, Jane most certainly felt, at finding her motives wilfully misunderstood; yet, that did not render her less firm, and though she could not repel the starting tear, she carefully removed all traces of sorrow or anxiety from her countenance before she again met her beloved parents. And none, to witness the playful gaiety of her manners, the lively converse with which she sought to beguile the time, and make it pass pleasantly away, would for a moment even have thought it possible that her bosom was the seat of sorrowful anxiety. Henry, we have said, was mortified at the supposed coldness and want of affection in one to whom he had been so long and so ardently attached, but he was more than mortified, for he was vexed and angry, his self-pride had received a wound, by Jane, as he considered, thinking infinitely more of the comfort and happiness of her parents than she did of him, forgetful that the claims of those dear relatives were far prior to his own. In this mood the young man parted with the object of his affection, and in this mood he arose the following morning, and started on his journey; he conceived that he was ill-used, and consequently was right in resenting the supposed injury. But we defy any but the very sullen and morose to remain angry with one they love, when they find themselves journeying rapidly from their side. The morning was warm and beautiful, and the fresh breeze fanned the young man's feverish brow, and animated and invigorated his spirits; the last object that caught his eye as he looked, from the top of the stage, a farewell to his native village, was the time-worn turrets of Eardley Hall, which standing on an eminence, and being moreover of loftier height than any other building, looked down, as it were, proudly and grimly upon the passer-by, standing alone in its glory, a true picture of solitary grandeur. It was truly a noble edifice; much of its original beauty had undoubtedly fled, still there was a venerable appearance clinging round its time-worn walls that excited an interest in the beholder, and if those old walls had possessed the power of language, no doubt they could have recounted many a wondrous tale and strange exciting incident. As the young artist beheld the venerable building gradually fading from his sight, and he felt himself hurried from his dear native home, and the gentle girl whom he had so early learnt to love, a remorseful feeling began to take possession of his breast, and conscience whispered that he had been unkind and unjust in his conduct towards her; her long enduring affection merited a better return than the selfish anger he had manifested at her rejection of his proposals, a rejection which he shrewdly began to suspect was founded on praiseworthy motives. He was strongly inclined to vacate his seat, and hasten back to seek her pardon, and acknowledge his own injustice, but his natural good sense prevailed, and he determined to continue his journey, and immediately on his arrival write to her entreating her forgiveness. This was by far the wisest plan, nor was he slow to put it in practice; the journey was safely and pleasantly performed, and with unbounded joy the youthful traveller found himself in the heart of the great city of London. In such a large and wealthy spot he felt certain of speedily realising wealth and fame; then with what joy should he be enabled to return to his village, and fetch his beloved Jane to share his name and splendour; he no longer regretted her refusal to accept his premature proposals, he was now well content to earn his laurels before he won his bride. Such thoughts as these warmed and animated his bosom as he sat down to write to his betrothed, and all the sanguine hopes of his heart found vent in in that letter, which breathed nought but love and tenderness. In due time this letter was received by Jane, and her eyes filled with tears of gratitude as she perused the contents. " I knew," was her inward exclamation, " that Henry would do me justice—he is impetuous, but never intentionally unjust ;" and with renewed cheerfulness she applied herself to the pleasing task of attending upon an invalid father, and sustaining the fortitude of her mother.

CHAPTER IX.

" Let fate do her worst, there are moments of joy,
  Bright dreams of the past which she cannot destroy,
  Which come in the night time of sorrow and care,
  And bring back the features which joy used to wear.
  Long, long, be our hearts with such memories filled,
  Like the vase in which roses have once been distilled,
  You may break, you may ruin the vase if you will,
  But the scent of the roses will hang round it still."

CLARA eagerly obeyed the summons to dinner, anxious for the introduction which was about to take place between herself and Mrs. Mortimer ; and half fearing the lady might not be impressed in her favour from her utter want of knowledge of fashionable life, Clara was naturally possessed of an innate refinement and love of good breeding, and she was therefore unawed by the rich and costly appearance of the house and its appointments, and so far acquitted herself to perfection, for nothing in her manner gave token that she was unaccustomed to move in the sphere of life in which she was now placed. On entering the dining room, Clara was met by a lady of middle age, of prepossessing, nay almost fascinating exterior, who stretched out her hand most cordially, and kindly gave her welcome.

"I trust," said the lady in a low musical voice, "that you will find everything managed to your satisfaction, and frankly state whatever you may wish altered."

Clara was charmed beyond expression, both with the manners and person of this accomplished lady, and could scarcely find words sufficient to express her deep sense of her kindness. Seated at dinner, Clara had leisure to observe Mrs. Mortimer more accurately. Rather above the middle height, her figure was elegant and lady-like. Of fair complexion, chestnut hair, and hazel eyes, her chief charm was in the constant and varying expression of her countenance, with which was blended a pleasing and subdued melancholy; her voice was habitually low, but musical and clear, and Clara thought she detected in the aunt a strong resemblance to her nephew, differing of course as regards age and sex. She seemed but little disposed for conversation, and the dinner passed without any remarks beyond what courtesy demanded.

"I shall be engaged in my study for the remainder of the evening," said Mrs. Mortimer, as she rose to quit the room, "which will prevent me having the pleasure of meeting you again. You can employ the evening in endeavouring to familiarise yourself to your new abode; to-morrow I may, perhaps, require your services."

Clara bowed in acknowledgment of her kindness, and once more seated in her own room her thoughts were free to float and flow. So far as she was now able to judge, she was by no means displeased with the situation in which she was placed; it appeared at once replete with comfort and independence; there was nothing to remind her that she was an hireling, or offend the dignity and purity of her mind. And in spite of the many bitters which were infused into her cup of happiness, she was still blessed with moments of joy, which came in the night time of sorrow and care. The evening was spent in calm reflection; the form of Walter Eardley, it is true, would occasionally flit across her mind, leaving a dark cloud, as it were, hanging over her spirit, and giving her thoughts a tinge of sadness; but melancholy thoughts are not always the most unpleasing, particularly to a sensitive mind. The next morning Clara had breakfast served up to her in her own room, immediately after having partaken of which, the servant brought her a quantity of manuscript, of which she was desired to make a fair copy. All alacrity, Clara set about her task, but she found it one involving more labour than she had anticipated; the writing was very illegible, and so many lines were crossed off and others substituted, that it was a work of considerable time to decipher it, and moreover it was destitute of punctuation of any kind, so that she was compelled to make sense of it as she best could, neither was the subject of sufficient interest to enliven the hours of labour. A treatise on matters of which she was profoundly ignorant, could not by any possibility awaken her sympathy. The work went slowly on, notwithstanding Clara's efforts were unceasing, and before she had completed many sheets, the entire was demanded as being concluded. With shame Clara confessed her inaptitude for the task, and expressed a hope that when the novelty of the occupation was worn off, she might be enabled to succeed better. Mrs. Mortimer smiled as she replied—

"I have no doubt, my dear Miss Wilmot, you find a difficulty in deciphering my characters, but when you once get thoroughly used to my hand, you will do wonders. You must understand," she continued, "that when I am composing, my ideas are so quick that I am obliged to note them down with the greatest rapidity, or they are entirely lost, this will account for the illegibility of my writing."

Clara thanked her for her consideration, and dinner being now ended (for it was during that meal the above conversation took place), offered to retire once more to resume her labour.

"I should be sorry to tax you too much," replied her employer, with an air of extreme consideration, "at the same time I am very desirous to have the work complete; indeed I promised the publisher he should have it to-morrow, so if you can contrive, without fatiguing yourself, to finish it this evening, I shall feel myself greatly indebted to you."

Clara constantly complied, but not till the evening was far advanced did she have the satisfaction of her work complete, and then she retired to rest weary in body and mind. Thus doomed to perpetual employment, two months passed slowly on, and Clara notwithstanding every effort to bear cheerfully the fatiguing labour, began to find that her health and spirits daily declined. So constantly was she

confined to her desk, that no time was allowed her for even necessary recreation, and, accustomed as she had been from infancy to active employment, the greater part of which consisted in out-door-exercise in the pure air of the country, rendered her present situation more distressing than it would otherwise have been. She saw but little of Mrs. Mortimer, the greater portion of whose time was spent in her study, and Clara frequently wondered how that lady contrived to keep in such good health, while devoting herself to an employment which two months' trial had served to convince Clara was a destroying labour. But Clara never took into account that by far the most fatiguing part of the employment devolved upon herself. Mrs. Mortimer was undoubtedly possessed of great talent, her works were received with unbounded applause by the literary world, and scribbling a few pages when the humour pleased her, was by no means a very arduous task. And for which not only did she greatly augment her income, but likewise gained honour and renown; while to the poor amanuensis was delegated all the laborious part of the profession, and for which she received a pittance barely sufficient to procure necessaries. This is no uncommon occurrence: frequently do authors of high literary attainments, and whose abilities procure them an almost princely revenue, employ an amanuensis or secretary, to whom they delegate all the trouble, and consequent anxiety, of preparing their works for publication, at a salary they would in all probability blush so name. We cannot receive the excuse which is frequently urged, that plenty of persons are to be found not only willing, but eager to embrace their terms, small though they be. To such argument we reply, "their poverty, but not their will, consents;" how many unfortunates are doomed to choose between the veriest pittance and positive want; it is the knowledge of this induces us to express ourselves warmly on this subject; we cannot bear the thought, that in England, proudly and arrogantly vaunted a free country, that so many of her sons and daughters should be enslaved and oppressed by their fellows; the love of country pervades, we fully believe, all bosoms; surely

> There lives not a man with soul so dead,
> Who never to himself hath said,
> "This is my own, my native land."

And we can say of England, in the language of one of our best poets,

> "With all thy faults, I love thee still."

But at the same time we should like to see those faults corrected, and cannot refrain (out of very love for our country) from using our humble efforts to expose, and, if possible, aid in eradicating them. As the first step towards this, we consider that a far more equitable remuneration should be paid for labour of all kinds, but more especially we feel ourselves called upon to urge the claims of our countrywomen, many of whom, aye, far more than our readers would perhaps readily believe, are compelled to exist upon a trifle, wholly inadequate to their wants, because, forsooth, of the low price paid for services, which in many cases are in themselves invaluable. Mrs. Mortimer engaged Clara at what might be termed a liberal salary. And to mere thoughtlessness was to be attributed the severe amount of labour she imposed upon her. She met Clara every day at dinner, when she usually wore an air of cheerfulness, and most certainly never even hinted that she found the amount of labour too much for her health. But Clara was of an uncomplaining nature; there were none to feel an interest in her welfare, none to whom her health and happiness was dear, and there was not enough of selfishness in her disposition to induce her to utter complaint. No, she struggled on unmurmuringly, though the bloom of health gradually faded from her cheek, and a sickly pallor usurped its place. Seated one morning at her desk, engaged in copying a manuscript, which was more difficult even than usual to decipher, and endeavouring almost in vain to conquer the lassitude that oppressed her, she was interrupted in her task by the entrance of a servant who placed a letter on her desk, and instantly withdrew. Clara glanced at the handwriting, and her heart throbbed with a sensation she could scarcely define, for she recognised the well remembered characters of Walter Eardley. In her present state of mind, aught that gave rise to new ideas afforded a sweet and seasonable relief to her tire-worn mind, and gladly did Clara welcome this unlooked-for epistle.

"I thought that he had entirely forgotten me," she murmured, as she broke the seal. "And that I should be thus deprived of putting into practice my scheme of revenge."

In this frame of mind, and desirous of embracing the opportunity it appeared to offer of once more renewing their intimacy, Clara proceeded to read the contents. It was short, but warm, tender, and expressive; indeed, so eloquently was it written, that she felt charmed in spite of herself; pure, respectful, yet passionate love, was breathed in every word, which was singularly well chosen. A thousand times did she read this short but expressive letter, and each time with renewed satisfaction; she felt it so truly flattering to her vanity, to know that the man who possessed such personal and mental graces, as to make him an object almost of adoration to her own sex, should be thus tenderly devoted to herself. So wrapt was she in these thoughts, which cheered and soothed her spirit, and made toil itself seem easy, and devoid of ill, that for the time her scheme of revenge was forgotten, but it speedily returned to rob her of her bliss. And she resolved, cost what it might, to pursue the line of conduct she had marked out for herself. In compliance with the expressed wish of her lover, she returned a short, and in some respects a doubtful answer to his warm and expressive letter, which was speedily followed by another, equally as tender, eloquent, and pleasing. Thus glided away two months more; the correspondence between Clara and Walter Eardley was constant and frequent, the breathing eloquence of the young man's epistles had exerted a species of fascination over the mind of Clara, there was such a beautiful ingenuousness, such a warm enthusiastic adoration expressed in every letter, that at once interested her, and charmed her. After they had thus corresponded two months without once speaking to each other (for Clara declined most positively his pressing entreaties to be admitted to an interview, for she dreaded if it were discovered it might not only injure him with his relative, but most likely deprive her of the means of subsistence), Clara at length consented to meet him in the grounds which surrounded the house, in the dusk of the evening. And yet, as the day approached, how many agitating conflicts pervaded the breast of Clara. She now began to repent having consented to a personal interview. If his letters had so charmed and entranced her mind, would not the soft bewitching tones of his musical voice, the irresistible sweetness of his smile, and the graces of his person, in all probability exert a baneful influence over her? If the exquisite sensibility which breathed through every line of his epistles, his ardent professions of adoration, had combined to shake her feeble resolution, would not a personal interview be productive of far worse consequences as regarded her own happiness? Still her promise was pledged to grant him this one interview, and she therefore felt herself bound to redeem it.

CHAPTER X.

"Power and splendour could not charm me
I, no joy in wealth could see !
Nor could threats or fears alarm me,
Save the fear of losing thee.
Let the bosom prone to ranging,
Still by ranging seek a cure,
Mine disdains the thought of changing,
Proudly destined to endure."

THE unexpected and truly unwelcome visit of Sir Richard Eardley was productive of the worst effects to Lucy; so painful indeed was the tumult of feelings that swelled her breast, that for a time they actually endangered her life. Utterly neglected (at a time, too, when she surely possessed the strongest claims upon his tenderness) by him for whom she had sacrificed her all, and whom, in spite of his many faults, she still ardently loved, poor Lucy's case was indeed a pitiable one; true, all her sorrows were the consequence of her own sin, yet does she not the less possess an undoubted claim upon our sympathy. With returning health there came to her no return of the fond hopes that she had once so proudly nourished, and but for the treasure she possessed in her darling babe, life would no longer have had a single charm for her. Walter appeared to have wholly deserted her, and her jealous heart foreboded, too truly, a rival as the cause. Her illness had involved her in expenses to which she could oppose no reasonable mode of payment, her tradesmen were clamorous to have their claims settled, and their insulting illiberality preyed deeply on her spirit, and was only to be equalled by their unbounded impositions. The state of her mind, which was in constant agitation, prostrated her strength, and rendered her incapable of action; she perceived a growing coldness in the looks and manners of her attendants; and guessed but too easily the cause; their wages had been allowed to accumulate, and seeing no probable means of payment, they grew careless and discontented. For some months Lucy tacitly endured this accumulation of misery, in the hope, though oft deferred, that Walter would voluntarily return to her side; she loved him still, and shrank from exposing him to the humiliation of making his cruel conduct known to his father, but at length she found that it was impossible to hold out any longer; sorrow had made sad and fearful inroads on her constitution; her child, who was now all the world to her, grew delicate, and required comforts which she was powerless to procure. The dread of losing this sweet treasure without whom she would have been thankful to meet death, unaccompanied by the crime of suicide, roused her to exertion. By dint of careful enquiry she learnt the town residence of Sir Richard Eardley, and addressed a letter there to his youngest son, complaining of the wrongs to which his cruelty had subjected her, and entreating, for the sake of her infant, that he would use his utmost exertion to relieve her from her embarrassment. To this letter she received no reply, and after waiting a considerable time she wrote again, expressing herself still more warmly, and representing in glowing terms the destitute state of her unfortunate infant. A week of anxious sorrow elapsed before she received an answer, but when it did arrive, it poured balm and consolation into her wounded heart; it was written kindly, and even eloquently expressed the deep regret he felt at being compelled in a measure to absent himself from her side, contained a small remittance for present necessities, and promised to see her on the day but one following. The heart of Lucy appeared lightened of half its burden; when he beheld their child, she doubted not but that the sight of its pretty innocent features would impress him strongly in its favour. All would yet be well; it was surely possible he might be able to offer a reasonable excuse for his protracted absence. Thus she permitted herself to indulge in the hope that Walter still loved her, and with a thankful heart she prepared for the anticipated visit. Her child she dressed with unusual care, and her own now slender form she arrayed in a robe of white muslin; at length the appointed hour arrived, and Lucy began to tremble with apprehension.

"Oh! surely she will not doom me to disappointment," she exclaimed, half aloud; but scarcely had the words escaped her, when a thundering knock at the door startled her. The next instant she heard his well known footsteps ascending the stairs; she became giddy with the intensity of her own feelings; the door opened, she was conscious that the form of him she had loved too well once again blessed her longing sight, but her head swam, her breath came thick and short, she made an effort to rise from her seat, but was prevented by Walter, who, with one stride across the room, was again by her side, and heaving a deep convulsive sigh, she sank half fainting on his bosom. With kind and tender words, breathed in his own peculiar, low, musical tones, he sought to cheer and sustain her drooping spirit; his arm encircled her waist; her head rested on his shoulder, while she gazed with eyes that filled with tears of rapture, on his open, manly brow. Oh! how fondly she loved him. How true, how tender, how constant is woman's love, when not even unkindness or neglect can estrange her affection. Yet Walter had no love to answer love like this, his affections were estranged from the early object of his boyish love; and she was no longer the object of his heart's warm adoration; he had learnt to love again, and no more, oh! never more, could she be to him his universe; that dream of bliss was o'er, and sad to the trusting girl at his side was the awakening. Still the young man sedulously concealed from his companion the state of his feelings, whispered words of love again fell pleasantly on her ear, and she yielded herself to the pure, heart felt bliss, that she was still beloved. Walter pleaded in excuse for his protracted absence that his liabilities were so extensive, and his means of meeting them so narrow, that he had been forced to remain in concealment, the horrors of a prison staring him in the face; and this alone had prevented him hazarding a letter, fearing it might by some unfortunate mischance lead to his discovery.

"But I have now, my dear Lucy," he continued in conclusion, "entered into an arrangement with the chief of my creditors, and therefore you may henceforth expect to find me a constant visitor."

Lucy was content; she implicitly believed every word he gave utterance to, and not the slightest reproach escaped her lips. And when she presented to him their child, rich in infantile grace, and Walter taking it in his arms pressed a father's first kiss upon its downy cheek, and declared he had never seen so beautiful an infant, her heart swelled with pride and joy.

"And he is like thee, dear love; his eyes are thine, his brow, his lips, and so he ever keeps, one arm in sleep pillowing his head just as did'st thou," broke in murmurs half inarticulate with emotion, from the lips of the fond mother, as she hung over the couch of her first-born child. True and holy, beautiful in its endearing simplicity, is the love of a mother; and never had Lucy known such bliss as now; her heart was full of rapture, and throbbed with the noblest and purest emotions. The evening sped quickly on. Ah! all too quickly for the tender bosom of Lucy, for the period now quickly approached that was destined to destroy all the fairy visions which had filled her mind with dreams of happiness. Walter left her, with a voluntary promise of a speedy return, though grieved that they were so soon to part. Yet, as he declared that at present it was absolutely necessary for the proper adjustment of his affairs, Lucy uttered not one word of discontent or even sorrow. Cheered with this hope, she smilingly bade him adieu and retired to rest, her bosom throbbing with joy and gratitude; the next day passed in peaceful serenity, and the next, the third, she received a letter, a cold unkind letter, from him whom but two days before had met her with apparently unbounded affection, briefly informing her that they must see each other no more. The anguish of her feelings on reception of this epistle, it is beyond the power of language to describe; she could scarcely believe it possible that he could thus so suddenly and cruelly desire to desert her, and to leave them, without friends or provision, to the tender mercies of a cold and unfeeling world. It could not be possible, and yet there was his own writing to vouch for the accuracy of the statement; he did not even condescend to inform her of his reason for this sudden determination, and but for the sake of the child, she would never have enquired.

> "Oh, within her bosom beating,
> Mingling passions wildly reign;
> Love with proud resentment meeting,
> Throbs by turns of grief and pain."

Actuated by a deep and burning sense of her injuries, she replied to this unfeeling epistle, in a letter in which she poured out the anguish of her sorrow, and expressed in glowing terms her indignation and proud resentment of the cruelty of his conduct towards herself and their unhappy child, and entreated him, for the sake of her helpless child, to think well, before he resolutely doomed it to sorrow and privation. For her infant alone, did Lucy make this effort to move its unfeeling father in its favour; as far as she was herself concerned, she felt that she had lost his love for ever. For many long months of anxious sorrow, hour by hour she counted o'er, looking forward to the morrow—every day she loved him more. Aye she had loved him, dearly loved him through an age of worldly woe, how ungrateful she had proved him let her mournful exile show. Lucy felt that now she had nothing to hope or fear beyond procuring a provision for her child; sweet innocent, all unconscious of his mother's pangs, he nestled closely to her bosom, and slept in peaceful slumbers there. And as the unfortunate Lucy folded her arms about him, and gazed with rapture on his budding charms, her tears fell fast and thick upon his sunny brow, and her heart once more turned towards the dear friends she had deserted, and falling upon her knees, with streaming eyes she exclaimed—

"Oh, God! thou hast meted it unto me, even as I deserved."

Happiness cannot, never does, go hand in hand with sin; joy may riot for a moment, but sorrow will inevitably follow close in the footsteps of the guilty, while peace, if not happiness, will as surely bless and cheer a virtuous mind. Lucy was now deprived of all for which she had sacrificed her peace, but how bitter was the reflection that the very arm which once embraced her, had been destined to inflict in her bosom a cureless wound. She would willingly have resigned all but his love; even the resemblance of it was indescribably dear to her agonised heart, but to be thus crushed, trampled to the dust, by the man for whom she had made such a terrible sacrifice, was almost more than she could bear. She had secretly nourished the hope, that on the birth of her infant Walter might possibly be induced to make her his wife, to reward her trusting love by giving her a right to his name and protection. Then she would gladly have communicated once more with her dear relatives, whose loss she had never ceased to mourn, but even in her moments of mirth and gladness she had felt their loss hang heavy on her heart, and would have endured much to be enabled again to embrace them, and to receive that loved caress. Alas! she was now well assured that she had resigned true substantial happiness in order to pursue the phantom disappointment. Yet even in this moment of complete despair, when oppression bowed her to the earth, she did not blame Walter, for her heart retained too vivid a recollection of the visit she received from his father, Sir Richard Eardley, and she doubted not for an instant that he was the moving cause of all. Alas! when once a woman stoops to error, where can she look for a friend to shield her from the blasts of adversity; none deem it worth while to stoop to pity and save the unfortunate. The mind of Walter she had ever conceived to be nobly and honourably organised, and she could not bring herself to believe that a heart which she fondly thought to be the seat of every virtue, could possibly become thus suddenly cruel and unjust. Lucy was well aware that the young man was entirely dependent upon his father, and he had ever manifested a decided aversion to his becoming acquainted with the intimacy that existed between them. He was now likewise deeply in debt, and Sir Richard, no doubt, stipulated that the connection should be entirely broken up if he interfered to relieve him from his embarrassment.

CHAPTER XI.

"All things are sold: the very light of Heaven
Is venal: earth's unsparing gifts of love,
The smallest and most despicable things
That lurk in the abysses of the deep,
All objects of our life, even life itself,
And the poor pittance which the laws allow
Of liberty, the fellowship of man,
Those duties which the heart of human love
Should urge him to perform instinctively,
Are bought and sold, as in a public mart
Of undisguising selfishness, that sets
On each its price, the stamp mark of her reign."

ARRIVED in London, Henry Fergusson's first step was to secure suitable apartments; he was naturally desirous to embark without any unnecessary delay in the purpose for which he had left his dear peaceful village, namely, the acquirement of wealth and fame. The most populous part of the city he conceived to be the best for a young artist, who had none to aid him either with advice or recommendation. On the morning, therefore, after his arrival ne sallied forth in quest of rooms that might serve his purpose, without demanding too much from his small finances. He found, as the reader will readily imagine, plenty of apartments, any of which would have suited him to admiration, but the amount of rent demanded was such as absolutely to startle him. He had been in the habit of seeing really genteel and elegant houses let in the country for a mere trifle, and now the demand of forty or fifty pounds for two rooms of no very large dimensions, he actually regarded as an unjust extortion. And greatly annoyed he felt to observe that whenever he ventured to hint at the extravagance of the charge, a smile of pity evidently at his want of knowledge played round the lips of those to whom he thus expressed himself. Three days were spent in vain attempts to procure cheaper lodgings; at length, trembling at his own temerity, and yet in despair of doing better, he engaged two rooms in one of the large thoroughfares in the city, at the yearly rental of forty pounds, the first quarter of which was paid in advance in default of being able to procure respectable reference; a few necessary articles of furniture were purchased at an equally dear rate, for, being an entire stranger in London, and possessing no knowledge of the intrinsic value of the articles he required, the extortion he experienced was unbounded. A large brass plate bearing the name of Henry Fergusson, artist, was placed in the inner door; the outer one stood constantly open, and on the posts of which were displayed a few miniature portraits, with the inscription under them, "Likenesses taken in this style two guineas." There was moreover a bell handle close by, and written under it the words, "Ring and proceed to the first floor." Thus, having ordered all that was deemed requisite, the young artist settled himself in his new abode and waited patiently for his first engagement. When we say he waited, we do not wish it to be understood that he was idle, for he immediately engaged himself on a painting, and the darling wish of his heart was to see it in one of the public exhibitions; he had commenced it while in the country, and it was now far advanced towards completion; the subject he had chosen was the death of Nelson, thinking that a national subject would please the popular taste. This was a work of deep interest; it occupied his time by day and his thoughts by night; he never wearied in his efforts, it was a labour of pleasure; he fondly lingered over its minutest detail, and saw a thousand beauties in it, which would probably be never seen by any eye save his own. Indeed, as he proceeded, this feeling grew into an affection for the offspring of his genius; he could not bear the thought of giving it the finishing touch; day by day he continued his engrossing employment, scarcely allowing himself time for requisite exercise. Hope indeed whispered to him a flattering tale, a tale too bright to be realised in this cold sordid world. Alas! what a vast number of persons daily, nay, hourly, passed the door of his residence, and how many little groups were almost constantly gathered round the door, to gaze upon the miniatures, but none ever appeared to think it possible that the artist might be poor, and that it would be a charity, a good and generous deed, to employ him to execute some little trifle, even if such were not exactly needed by them. Great inroads had been already made upon the little hoard of Henry, and he became sorrowfully aware that it was fast dwindling away. But his picture was now progressing rapidly; indeed to any but the eye of an artist, it would even now have appeared complete. Yet there were many little touches wanting—a little more colouring here, a little more shade there, and a few lines required bringing out more bold, and others softening down, and then it would be done. Still it repeatedly happened, that as soon as one part was pronounced perfect, another required some trifling touch. So greatly had he become attached to his painting, that it was with a regretful feeling he at last declared it complete—the thought of parting with it was painful in the extreme. He had become so tenderly attached to this offspring of his genius, that the bare idea of separation was fraught with sadness, still he felt that it was inevitable, and cheered by the fond hope that others would doubtless admire it equally as himself, he affixed to it a price he by no means considered as equivalent to its merits, and despatched it to one of the public exhibitions. Great was his mortification, a few days subsequently, when he paid a visit to the exhibition in order to view his cherished picture, to find it hung in an obscure corner, in the worst possible light, where many persons passed it without even remarking that a painting was there. Grieved and vexed beyond the power of expression, Henry could not refrain from loudly complaining of the injustice, but to all his remonstrances was opposed the simple fact that the place it occupied was the only spot vacant, and a promise of removal on the first opportunity that offered. Henry felt that he could do nothing but submit, at the same time his spirit was ruffled and his mind depressed. Indeed, this little incident, simple as it may seem to the reader, sufficed to over-power him with despondency; he now appeared for the first time, to recollect that he had been in London several months, during the whole of which time constant and repeated calls had been made upon his little purse, and so far from having it bene-fited during his stay, he had not so much as earned a single sixpence. His pic-ture appeared now to be his sole resource, and he trembled with apprehension, that, unless it were speedily moved to a more favourable site, the exhibition might close without its sale being effected. This was almost the first desponding feeling his sanguine heart had ever known, and as he neared his temporary abode (for he never called London home) he strove hard to rid his bosom of so troublesome a guest. A group of idlers now gathered round the door, examining the portraits, and occa-sionally venturing upon a little criticism by no means flattering to the artist. Among the loiterers were two ladies, one of them young and handsome, the other some years her senior. The eldest of the two ladies spoke in the very highest terms of one of the miniatures, to which she directed her companion's attention. She ran on with a series of flimsy remarks and affected phrases, which at once convinced Henry that she laid claim to the title of a connoisseur, although her observations proved that her real acquaintance with art was exceedingly small. But she sought in vain to secure the attention of the younger lady, who candidly declared that her want of taste, or of that knowledge of the subject which would enable her to form a proper judgment, prevented her from participating in her companion's amusement.

"I am surprised, my dear," exclaimed the elder lady, "that you can contem-plate such a perfect specimen of art in silence. I feel it quite impossible to refrain from expressing my admiration."

"But," urged the young lady, "if we have no genius for such things, it is impossible to take so deep an interest in them."

"We shall see," replied the other, "the exhibitions are now all open, and I intend to visit every one of them, and I hope before the close of the season to convince you that your present opinion is an erroneous one, and that, in truth, you are pos-sessed of a perfect genius for painting."

The young lady smiled good humouredly as they resumed their walk, but the artist thought that her features wore a look of incredulousness, as though she were determined not to be convinced. He felt assured that the elder lady had no right or true appreciation of the art to which he had so sedulously devoted himself. She evidently possessed an ardent admiration for a science of which, to judge from the few remarks that fell from her lips, she literally understood nothing. And the artist could well understand the utter weariness the unfortunate girl must experience if doomed to listen to her constant criticism. Henry certainly might have felt flattered by the high encomiums the lady had lavished upon the work of his hands, but unhappily for her discernment the most faulty miniature had been selected as the object of her warmest admiration. This beguiled the young man of a smile, and he shrewdly suspected that her companion who refused to give an opinion, was, in all probability, the best judge of his art. When Henry Fergusson once more entered his room, and seated himself at his easel (for he had already commenced a fresh subject) he could not entirely cast from his mind the conversation he had overheard between the two ladies; the elder one he conceived to be wealthy beyond the shadow of a doubt, and he pondered deeply in his mind, whether, if she knew he were poor, she would deem it worth while to patronise his unassuming merit. It mattered but little as in all probability he would never see her again, still it would have pleased him, if he could have known that among the busy moving crowds in which he lived, all were not actuated by the sordid selfish motives that chiefly characterised the few with whom he had become acquainted. Poor Henry had been dearly made to feel, since his short residence in London, that all things were bought and sold, aye, even the pure

[THE STOLEN INTERVIEW OF LUCY AND WALTER.

light of heaven, so that the poor were forced to live in habitations possessed of an insufficiency of light and air, those sweet pure blessings which are God's own free gift, but man to his fellow man denies the boon. He had peeped into some of the narrow thoroughfares with which London abounds, but shrank with horror from the spectacles they presented, narrow crowded alleys, houses ill-ventilated, and, if possible, worse drained, where men and women, and children, were huddled together, filled his heart with the keenest anguish. The hardships to which the poor we exposed were doubtless greatly exaggerated, to his mind, by his having so late left the pure fresh air of the country. And as he would sometimes rem standing at his window for half an hour, watching the passers by, he would turn asi to check the starting tear at the sad recollection that he was alone among a crow that not one of the many who daily passed his door cared whether he were livi or dead, when but a short time before, so many kind voices gave him good morro and so many bright smiles welcomed the coming day. He felt his lot to be s and lonely; there was not even one being to whom he could breathe his anxietic or whisper his hopes and fears. His heart yearned, oh, how earnestly, for symp thy to pour all his sorrows into some friendly bosom. He thought of Jane; h letters were his only solace, and yet he could not commit to paper the many tria that daily, nay, hourly, beset him; he must be content to struggle on, hoping ev against hope for better days. In the meantime, in proportion as his purse gre light his heart grew heavy; he had fallen into arrears with his rent, and for tl first time in his life (and which cost him a severe pang), was obliged to get in debt for a few trifling articles. He now depended solely upon the sale of h picture to release himself from his present difficulties. And yet, in spite of r peated remonstances, it continued to occupy the obscure corner in which it h first been placed, and finally the exhibition closed, and his picture, apparently h last resource, was returned to him unsold.

"Well it might be," was his bitter reflection, "when it had hung in a corne where no one could see it, or if they chanced to do so would scarcely remark augh beyond its defects."

"After all," soliloquised Henry, "merit is not so certain of meeting wit success as I fondly hoped to find it."

Still he did not regard his picture as rejected, or his abilities depreciated, for a yet it had scarce been seen. And had his circumstances permitted him to retai it in his possession till the term of the next exhibition, he doubted not that h should be more successful, but necessity compelled him to seek a purchase without delay.

CHAPTER XII.

"Oh! yes, I could love thee, yes love, though rejected,
Like Adam, when sadly from Paradise driven,
To look on his home, he turned sad, and neglected,
So I could gaze on thee, my Eden, my Heaven."

At length the evening arrived that was to witness the much dreaded interview between Walter Eardley and Clara Wilmot; many days and weeks had elapsed since they last met, during which time they had constantly corresponded; and the warmest adoration had been expressed by the young man, coupled with unbounded assurances of lasting affection in many sources of the most eloquent epistles. Still Clara's heart beat high, and her bosom throbbed with anxiety as the hour drew nigh; indeed, it were almost impossible to describe the variety of conflicts that agitated her breast at the important moment when, the labours of the day completed, she sat by her window awaiting the signal of her lover. She admired Walter, and felt grateful for his affection; to her he was the most engaging of created beings. The correspondence that had been carried on between them had filled her mind with the most exalted notions of his mental attractions, and which needed but little more to deepen into a warm passionate love, and yet there was a gulf between them that she shuddered as she contemplated, and which she was well aware nothing could remove, or do away. At length a handkerchief waved at a little distance beneath her window, yet the signal was rendered almost imperceptible by the dusk of the evening. With trembling limbs, Clara cautiously stole down the staircase and entered the garden. Walter instantly advanced to meet her, and taking her hand, uttered a few words scarcely articulate. Emotion deprived Clara of the power to reply, and she suffered him to draw her arm through his own and carry her hand rapturously to his lips. The moon was rising fair and bright, and Clara dreaded being seen out at so unusual an hour by any of the domestics, and yet, the graces of person that so marked her lover, the irresistible sweetness of his smile, the tenderness of his melodious voice enchanted her soul, and chained her to his side. Yet Walter hesitated to prolong an interview which might prove dangerous to the comfort and happiness of Clara should they be discovered, and after a few more words of the most affectionate nature, uttered in his own musical tones, they parted. Alas! if her mind had previously been influenced by admiration, it was now awakened into a warmer and more enthusiastic feeling. Alas! alas! how was it that he, whom she most wished to hate and contemn, was gradually winding himself round her very heart-strings. They met again and again, each time with renewed transport; their walks sometimes continued till past midnight; nothing could at once be more delightful or rational than these interviews. The polished and fascinating manners of Walter contributed greatly to enliven their meetings, and won insensibly upon the heart of Clara. He sung with exquisite taste, and sometimes at Clara's request the tones of his voice would break upon the stillness of the night, when she would listen as one entranced, and to her ear it sounded like more than mortal melody. Alas! how bitterly she began to lament the distance that destiny had placed between them, how fondly would she have idolised such a husband. How often, in the ardent enthusiasm of her heart, had she formed the wish that they might be united; but no, thoughts she would fain have forgotten came back to rob her of her bliss, to poison her happiness, and she felt that she was destined to revenge her brother's sorrows, but at the same time to sacrifice herself. Still she could not as yet break the magic spell that bound her senses. The present was fraught with bliss, though the future looked dark and full of sorrows. Many and frequent were the interviews, not a day passed without seeing or hearing from each other. Walter's attachment seemed to increase daily, and Clara loved him with all the ardour of which she was susceptible. How little now did she heed the fatiguing employment in which her days were spent, it precluded thought, and that was something gained. The unhappy girl wilfully blinded herself to the sins of which she knew him to be guilty, and though she longed to enquire the fate of her young friend, the betrothed bride of her beloved brother, yet she felt incapable of doing so; she doubted not that he had separated himself from the object of his guilty love. Yet she could listen to vows of affection that by right were not her own, nor ever dreamed that he who had once changed might change again. No, she yielded to the sweet delusion of loving and being loved. During this time, she saw but little of Mrs. Mortimer; they usually met at dinner, but their conversation generally turned on general subjects; she had once or twice expressed her entire approval of Clara's arduous duties, and urged her to unceasing application; this she was by no means backward in performing, for employment, constant and unceasing employment, now became necessary to drown reflection, which at every interval of leisure was fraught with the most painful stings. Her days were spent in irksome toil, and her evenings in anxious happiness. And as might well be anticipated, her health suffered materially, the lily usurped the place of the once warm blushing rose upon her cheek, and her form which had been symmetrically round, lost its fine proportions. A lassitude, totally unfitting her for employment, frequently oppressed her spirit, and she would remain seated at her desk, without the power or energy to proceed. Nothing but the desire she felt to drown thought, would have compelled her thus to sacrifice her health and spirits. Mrs. Mortimer at length, apparently no great observer, remarked that she did not look well, and enquired if she felt the confinement too fatiguing. Thus encouraged, Clara ventured to reply, that having been accustomed to constant out-door exercise, her health was certainly not so good since she had been engaged in so sedentary an occupation.

"This is bad news," replied the lady, "I am excessively grieved that your health should suffer—perhaps you would like to see a physician?"

Clara answered with a faint negative.

"Let me see," returned the lady. "I have just commenced a new work, and for which I am greatly hurried, or I should have been happy to have spared you for a few weeks; but if you are quick, it will soon be accomplished, and then I shall be pleased to afford you an opportunity of spending a short time in the country, which I hope will suffice to fully re-establish your health."

Clara thanked her, for she felt really grateful for this concession, though scarcely knowing how to avail herself of it, without entirely breaking the truth to Walter. Sometimes she felt half resolved to inform him of all, and quit for ever the temptations to which she was exposed; but the delight of daily seeing and conversing with him was too dear to be easily abandoned. In their frequent meetings Walter would sometimes allude to the subject of their marriage, the only impediment to which appeared his total want of the means by which to support them in comfort.

"With you, dearest," he whispered, one evening as they wandered by moonlight, arm-in-arm, their whole thoughts and hopes concentrated in each other. "With you I could be happy, upon the veriest pittance; but I love you too dearly, too devotedly, to plunge you into the vortex of misery, which poverty, and its consequent ills, must necessarily entail."

"Secure in the possession of your heart," replied Clara, "I desire nothing more—in that I count all my future treasure—

> When with thee, what ill can harm me?
> Thou canst every pang assuage,
> But when absent, what can charm me?
> Every moment seems an age.
> If the storms of fortune press thee,
> I shall weep to see thee weep,
> And if relentless cares oppress thee
> I will lull those cares to sleep."

"Sweet Clara," returned the young man, gazing passionately on her upturned face. "Thou art indeed my bosom's friend, it wakes to joy my morning song, checks every pain, soothes every woe.

> Yes, fondly loved, as fondly too admired,
> Still feeling cherishes what worth inspired.

Superior worth, that triumphs over all. Yes, Clara, believe me, that it is thy noble mind, far more than the graces of thy person, that has won my heart, that binds me to thee through good and ill. And now to tell thee what I fear thou'lt gravely smile at. Sometimes, thoughts vague, strange, and undesired hover o'er my spirit, and appear to whisper of coming ill.

> Oh, is it that there lurks indeed,
> Some truth in man's prevailing creed?
> And that our guardians from on high,
> Come in the pause 'twixt toil and sin,
> To put our senses' curtain by,
> And on our wakeful souls look in,

and warn us of coming ills, which in this manner so frequently cast their shadows before them."

He ceased, but the tones of his voice still thrilled upon the ear of Clara. She became pensive in the extreme, and for some time they wandered on in silence; her lips were mute, she could not as yet impart to him the bitter vow to which she had given utterance, and which now was past all recall; she felt as though she were compelled to keep silence till the last moment, when, all doubts and troubles cleared away, he should openly seek her hand; she shuddered as she pictured to her mind the bitter anguish of her lover when all should be known. Oh, surely then, he would not urge her to break a vow that was characterised as sacred. The hour of parting arrived, an hour always sad and sorrowful. Yes, though they parted at eve to meet again on the morrow, they could scarce tear themselves asunder.

"Clara," said the young man, as they stood under the friendly shadow of an elm, through the leafy branches of which the young moon shed a subdued and mellow light. "I hope ere long to renounce a secrecy ;which is hateful to my heart, and foreign to my nature; bear up, my girl, a short time, and I hope that happiness will reward your love."

"And you?" replied Clara, in a voice half articulate with contending emotion. "And you have a secret, Walter, that should be a trouble to your conscience, and yet deny me the poor gratification of participating in it with you? I thought you had learned ere this to trust me with your joys and sorrows."

"Dearest," replied the young man, looking in the eyes of Clara, which were fixed upon him. "I have a secret, but it is not of much importance, therefore you must excuse me entering into the particulars just at present, but I trust the time will come, and that soon, when I shall be delighted to do so, and to reward your love, and take you to a home fitted for such a being. I am convinced, despite all dark forebodings, that we shall, we must, be blest; now one kiss—another; and adieu."

Clara tore herself from his encircling arms, and with kisses yet lingering fond and warm upon her lips, retired to give vent to the anguish of her bosom in tears —bitter agonising tears.

————

CHAPTER XIII.

"Love, by fickle fancy banished,
    Spurned by hope, indignant flies;
Yet, when love and hope are vanished,
    Restless memory never dies.

Yet ere far from all I treasured,
    Ere I bid a last adieu,
Ere my days of pain are measured,
    Take the song that's still thy due

Yet, believe, no servile passions
    Seek to charm thy vagrant mind;
Well I know thy meditations,
    Waving as the passing wind.

WE last left Lucy anxiously awaiting a reply to the letter she had despatched to Walter; in which, we have already informed the reader, she poured out the sorrows of her mind, and besought him, for the sake of her child, to redress the wrongs he had heaped upon her unhappy head. Alas! long she waited in agonised suspense, but received no reply. In the anguish of her soul she again addressed him, she complained, perhaps too vehemently, of the injustice he had done her, and most solemnly conjured him at least to assign a just cause for thus suddenly withdrawing himself from her society, when lately he had only seemed happy while endeavouring to evince his affection towards her, and earnestly entreated him to consider her situation, now every hour rendered more irksome. She was deeply involved in debt, which she despaired of ever being able to discharge. For his sake she had quitted her home, and all that was dear to her. The retrospect was dreadful, still more so the future, that loomed through the darkness. Without any honourable resource of any kind for herself and a darling child, that depended wholly on her for support, she knew not where to turn for succour or advice; assailed on every side by the malice of enemies, and could she have bowed her pride to seek their protection, would no doubt have been reproached by her friends. So circumstanced, the sorrows and struggles of her mind became intolerable, and nearly deprived her of reason. Rumours reached her to the effect that Sir Richard Eardley was exerting himself to settle the affairs of his son; several creditors declared their claims had been honourably met. To him then, for whom she had made every sacrifice, and to whom she owed her present embarrassments, she ultimately conceived herself entitled to look for redress; her letter still remained unanswered, and she determined in person to represent to his father her destitute condition. Painful in the extreme was the humiliation to which she felt she should be exposed in representing to Sir Richard Eardley the cruelty and injustice she had sustained from his son; yet no alternative presented itself to her bewildered mind, and she therefore resolved to lose no time in seeking redress at his hands; she had frequently heard him spoken of as a man of the most unspotted integrity and uprightness, and though the little she had seen of him was not calculated to impress her in his favour, she wavered not in her determination. And yet her heart beat almost to suffocation as she approached the lordly mansion of Sir Richard. She had purposely dressed herself with studious neatness, and pressed to her bosom, now the seat of violent and contending emotions, her darling boy, sleeping all unconscious of his mother's sufferings. It was some minutes before she could gain courage to give the gentle knock that at length announced her. The door was immediately opened by a servant in rich livery, who regarded her with a somewhat supercilious air, as she made known her desire to speak to his master. There was a lady-like appearance about Lucy, palpable, even in her humble attire, that commanded respect; and the servant, desiring her to be seated, said he would enquire if Sir Richard were at liberty to receive her. A tedious quarter of an hour elapsed before the return of the servant, who at length appeared, and desired her to follow him to the library, where Sir Richard would be happy to receive her. Poor Lucy trembled so much that her limbs almost refused to do their office, and it was with great difficulty she supported her infant, who still slept sweetly in her arms. Alas! to what bitter mortification—to what deep humiliation had not one false step exposed the unfortunate Lucy! If all that she had borne of anguish and self-denial had arrayed themselves in a bodily shape, and presented all their deformity to her bewildered gaze at the moment she was revolving in her mind the contemplated desertion of home and friends, she would have started back with horror, and steadfastly shunned their near approach, even at the expense of the gratification of the present moment, and yet a little, but a very little, foresight was needed on her part to enable her to regard the future in its probable light. She could scarcely expect aught but sorrow and humiliation from an attachment which had for its basis no solid foundation. What is begun in guilt will assuredly end in grief and disappointment. Lucy was on this occasion spared some embarrassment, for on entering the library the baronet instantly recognised her, and quickly guessed the purport of her visit. Sir Richard bowed stiffly, and pointing to a seat, remarked that he scarcely need enquire to what he was indebted for the honour of this unexpected visit, as he presumed it arose more on his son's account than his own. The manner in which these words were spoken, far more than the words themselves, cost Lucy a severe pang; had she been the most abject being, the baronet could scarcely have treated her with more freezing hauteur. She had no power to reply—her spirit was crushed and wounded, yet pride came to her aid, and repelled the tears that would fain have forced themselves to her eyes.

"It is utterly useless, madam," resumed Sir Richard, "to endeavour to draw my son again into a connection humiliating to himself and disgraceful to his family, and from which I have happily succeeded (though not without difficulty) in extricating him."

He paused, but Lucy made no reply; observing which, he again went on in the same blunt strain—

"The fact is, madam, my son is on the point of forming a most advantageous alliance. Your good sense will therefore, I hope, convince you of the utter fallacy of again attempting to force yourself upon him."

This, then, was the reward of her trusting love; she who had forsaken all for him, now that he was weary of her fleeting charms, he cast her from him without a thought even of her sufferings.

> "What was she then ?—a toy for dotard's play,
> To wear but till the gilding frets away."

So maddening was the thought, her whole soul seemed changed. Wronged, spurned, reviled!—oh! sweet would be revenge,—yet softer thoughts speedily chased the bitter ones away. Grief almost choked her utterance, yet she strove hard to calm the turbulence of her emotions, and at length contrived to inform Sir Richard she came not there that morning with any other intention than to inform him of her destitute condition.

"Well, madam," replied the baronet, "what do you intend to do with your child?"

Lucy was silent.

"I will tell you what to do," he continued; "work for it."

Even the worm will turn if you trample upon it, and Lucy, naturally gentle, felt her spirit roused to anger by the unfeeling conduct of Sir Richard, and with more energy than she had ever before shown, indignantly informed him that his son was the acknowledged father of her child, and to him she should look for the means wherewith to support it.

"If he contemplates marrying another," she continued, "though so incredible does it appear, that I can scarcely believe it, he will find it more to his advantage quickly to meet the claim I undoubtedly have upon him, or I will take steps to make the lady acquainted with the cruelty and almost unheard-of oppression he has practised towards me."

Saying which she rose to quit the room.

"Wait a moment," said Sir Richard, anticipating her movement. "Rather than anything unpleasant should occur to prevent my son from forming an alliance which is so very desirable, I am willing to provide for his offspring, if you are agreeable to confide the child to my care."

"You wish me to part with my child!" replied Lucy, her eyes flashing with anger and resentment.

"I merely said," returned the baronet, "that I was willing amply to provide for it, if you chose to entrust it entirely to my care."

"Cruel, unfeeling, insulting offer!" said Lucy, in a tone of angry excitement. "Good God, to what misery and contumely have I not subjected myself, and all for the sake of one who pays me back with scorn and contempt, but I despise and renounce them all!"

"As you think proper to refuse my offer of providing for the child," replied Sir Richard, "I can do nothing more; it is useless further to trespass on my time. But let me warn you against attempting in any manner to interfere with my son, and——"

But Lucy was gone! She heeded not the parting admonition of the baronet. She held her infant more closely to her bosom, as though she dreaded it being snatched from her, and pressing her lips to its cheek, she murmured—

"Sweet innocent!—did they want to rob me of a treasure all their wealth would not suffice to purchase. Walter," she continued, "thou hast spurned, crushed, and trampled on me; now beware, for I am thy evil genius. Strange that love should turn to hate! Yet the change to hatred is at least to feel I will not tamely endure thy cruelty—thy chosen bride shall learn the extent of thy baseness. From this moment I turn my thoughts and energies towards discovering what I know thou would'st fain hide from me."

Filled with such thoughts as these, that followed each other in rapid succession through her mind, Lucy arrived once more at her own habitation. Truly unfortunate, the sufferings of her mind threatened to overpower her, and cause reason to desert its throne, but, for the sake of her child, she bore bravely up. And yet she was possessed of no means wherewith to meet her current expenses; one thing was parted with after another, till near all was gone. The house in which she resided was, of course, a useless expense upon her hands, and she therefore determined to part with it without delay. A tenant was speedily found, and, collecting the few things that remained, she removed to a lodging in close vicinity to the town residence of Sir Richard Eardley, determined narrowly to watch the movements of Walter, and discover to whom he was engaged. With great difficulty she procured a little needlework, and by dint of close application contrived to procure common necessaries for herself and infant, more she could not do. Some trifling articles of jewellery, all that now remained to her, she carefully hoarded to meet any exigency that might occur; and, though peace had passed for ever from her breast, she strove to bend her spirit to the humble circumstances in which she was now placed. In the meantime, her sister Jane was smoothing the passage of a beloved father to the tomb; to which he was now rapidly hastening, bowed down with sorrow for the loss of a beloved child. Oh, would that I could see her once more, to tell her that she is forgiven—to entreat of her to forsake the path of guilt, and to return to that of virtue, was language that frequently found vent from his over-charged heart. Were it possible he could have known that the child for whom he thus daily mourned, was day and night shedding the tears of bitterness, or suffering from sorrow and constant privation—her who had been so delicately nurtured, exposed to hardship, scorn, and humiliation—oh! how gladly would he have opened his arms to receive back his erring, but repentant child; with what sweet tears of rapture would he have welcomed her once more to his arms and heart; but it was otherwise ordained, and he must die without looking upon her face again.

CHAPTER XIV.

The iron rod of penury still compels
Her wretched slave to bow the knee to wealth.
How many a rustic Milton has passed by,
Stifling the speechless longings of his heart,
In unremitting drudgery and care?
How many a vulgar Cato has compelled
His energies, no longer tameless then,
To mould a pin or fabricate a nail?
How many a Newton! to whose passive ken
Those mighty spheres that gem infinity
Were only specks of tinsel fixed in heaven,
To light the midnights of his native town.

POVERTY doth indeed compel the noblest geniuses to bow before the shrine of wealth. Their proudest efforts sink into nothingness before the iron rod of penury. Alas! that wealth should exert so baneful an influence; but so it is. Gold is a god whom all worship, and to whom all other things give place. None ever was made to feel this more acutely than Henry Fergusson. His money was now nearly all gone, his landlord was pressing for the rent, and his few other creditors equally clamorous. The night dreams of hope, which had so long sustained and cheered him, began to fade before the stern realities of life. There was none with whom he came in contact sufficiently refined to enter into his feelings. He had promised his landlord to discharge the arrears of rent the instant that he succeeded in disposing of his painting—that painting he so fondly cherished, and so dreaded to part with. He gazed upon it again and again with a regretful fondness, before he could determine to bid it adieu. Round it were entwined so many feelings that assumed an almost sacred character; but necessity knows no law, and he felt regrets were useless. So, endeavouring to assume a cheerfulness he could not feel, he set out to seek a purchaser. He bent his steps towards the west-end, and, with a sort of desperation, forced himself to enter the first fashionable printsellers. Several ladies were engaged in looking over a variety of paintings, and making therefrom a selection; and he waited an instant till a shopman approached, and inquired his errand. With a manifestation of embarassing timidity, Henry made known the purport of his call, at the same time offering to display his picture.

"I am sorry," replied the person to whom he thus addressed himself, "that I

FANNY MOWBRAY.

cannot hold out any hopes of effecting a purchase; we are totally overburdened with such things, and trade is now at a perfect stand-still."

"You will allow me, at least, to offer it you for inspection," replied Henry, displaying his picture.

The young man shook his head as he answered—

"At present, we have more of such things on our hands, than we can at all dispose of."

At the instant that Henry was about to turn away in disappointment, a young lady, simply but elegantly dressed, and who was accompanied by an elder lady, whose stylish appearance caused him instantly to recognise her as the person who passed such high encomiums on one of his portraits a short time previously, entered the shop. The younger lady attracted the gaze of her companion towards the painting Henry held in his hands, and at the same time inquired the price. Henry modestly named the sum.

"You know I am no judge," she said, addressing her companion, "but I have actually taken a fancy to this picture, for the subject itself interests me."

"Why, Fanny," replied the elder lady, in astonishment, "you do indeed surprise me by the display of a taste, indeed I may say judgment, for which I have always given you credit, though you never would allow that you possessed it."

"Neither do I now," returned the first spoken; "as I said before, it is the subject that pleases me."

"The subject, of course, is highly interesting, and cannot fail to please, but the painting itself is a perfect masterpiece of art; the features and the expression of the countenance of the dying Nelson are perfectly exquisite."

The young artist blushed at the high encomiums of the lady, for the expression and features of Nelson had pleased him less than any other portion of his work, and he could scarcely suppress a smile at the want of correct taste in one who evidently considered herself a perfect judge of the art. At this moment his eye met that of the young lady's, and great was his surprise to observe, from the smile that played round her lips, that feelings similar to his own evidently pervaded her breast."

"I was right in my conjecture," was his inward thought; "this young lady, I am convinced, has more knowledge of painting than she cares to have known."

Henry was interrupted in his reflections by the elder lady, who demanded the price of his picture, and he roused himself from his reverie to reply.

"You are too modest in your demands, sir," she replied, as soon as he had stated the sum, "and, therefore, I shall not hesitate to make a slight addition."

"Perhaps this gentleman will have the goodness to bring us the painting this evening, when I shall be happy to arrange with him for the purchase of it," interposed the young lady.

Henry, of course, was all alacrity, and having received a card from the ladies, took his leave. Seven o'clock was the hour appointed for the introduction of Henry to the house of the first acquaintance he had found during nine months' stay in London, and he looked forward with some little anxiety as regarded the result. The ladies were apparently rich, liberal, and easy to please, and he hoped that he might be fortunate enough to gain their future favour and recommendation. Now, indeed, there appeared to dawn a prospect of brighter days, when his untiring patience and indefatigable industry might meet with a slow but sure reward. He thought of Jane, his first and only love, the recollection of whose mild and unobtrusive virtues, and gentle trusting love, had never failed to warm his heart and animate his spirit, when borne down and crushed with the bitter blasts of adversity. And now that his hopes were brighter, and his prospects evidently on the eve of improvement, he delighted himself with the hope that he might ere long return and seek her for his bride. Henry Fergusson was as free from all personal vanity as a young good-looking man well could be; it was, therefore, perfectly pardonable that he should this evening have taken unusual care in the arrangement of his dress, and several anxious glances did he cast in the mirror to convince himself that his appearance was satisfactory. And yet when he stopped before a large and fashionable house, at the western part of London, he glanced with sorrowful regret at his plain black clothes, which it must be confessed were all the worse for nine months' wear, though brushed and adjusted with scrupulous neatness. His gentle tap was directly answered by a servant in genteel though plain livery, and on giving his errand, Henry was conducted into an elegant and spacious apartment, where the two ladies were seated, who instantly rose to welcome him. The picture, the object of his visit, was placed in the best possible light. High encomiums were showered on his genius and ability by the elder lady with such valuable rapidity, that it completely overpowered the young man with embarrassment, but a few discriminating remarks made by the young lady, and which showed that she possessed a correct judgment, sufficed to restore him to his wonted easy and unaffected manners.

"You must know," said the elder lady (whom Henry discovered to be a rich widow of the name of Belmont), "that I have a perfect passion for painting; indeed, I am never happy unless I have got a brush in my hand. This must be my apology for asking your opinion of a few sketches at present incomplete, but which I hope to finish in the course of the ensuing winter."

Henry unhesitatingly expressed the pleasure it would afford him to inspect the collection, and in another minute he found himself following his conductress to what she styled her studio. Never had Henry found it more difficult to praise the paintings of another; and yet he conceived it necessary to say something in favour of the most execrable sketches it had ever been his painful lot to inspect. At length one was exhibited of rather a more pleasing character than the others, and Henry availed himself of the opportunity of lavishing some praise. A few cows and sheep, which occupied the back ground, especially attracted his attention as being really very well executed, and he warmly expressed his approbation. A smile of peculiar acuteness played round the dimpled mouth of the young lady, whom her companion addressed as Fanny, while Mrs. Belmont looked confused as she confessed they had been put in by her young friend.

"Then I am convinced," replied the young man, smiling in his turn, "that she has more knowledge of the art than she would have us believe."

"That is exactly what I am always telling her," replied Mrs. Belmont, "and yet, strange to say, she constantly denies it, and indeed tries to persuade me that she knows nothing whatever about drawing. I have taken her to all the exhibitions, and pointed out the merits and defects of every picture individually; still, for all that, she is so perverse that I never can get her to even give an opinion."

"Well," returned the young lady, slightly blushing, "you must give me credit for beginning to approximate to your views, as likewise having benefitted by your dissertations, for I have not only given an opinion, but actually become a purchaser."

This was said with a playful gaiety that appeared natural to the young lady, and Henry began to feel interested in her character, and remarked for the first time since he had been in her company that she was, if not decidedly handsome, at least very good looking. Fanny Mowbray—such he learnt was her name—was tall, and exceedingly well, though rather slightly made. A clear olive complexion was set off by a pair of sparkling black eyes, and teeth of the fairest ivory; rather pale, save when excitement tinged her cheek, and lent an additional lustre to her eye. She looked about twenty; was of pleasant agreeable manners, and naturally of a lively turn of mind, which rendered her a pleasant companion; and her conversational powers at once charmed and prepossessed the young man in her favour. The time flew unheeded by, and when Henry at length bade them adieu, he received a warm and pressing invitation speedily to renew his visit. It was indeed with a light and happy heart that Henry wended his way home. His purse was well stocked, and he had every prospect of preferment. His first care was with scrupulous exactness to pay every debt that he had been forced to contract. This reduced his money to comparatively a very small sum; yet as his second attempt at painting for the exhibition was now rapidly advancing, it cost him no uneasiness. A week elapsed, and Henry, though most desirous of again paying a visit to Mrs. Belmont, had at present refrained from doing so, when one morning he was surprised by a call from that lady, accompanied, as usual, by Miss Mowbray. For a moment the young man was more vexed than pleased, as his toilet was far from having received those finishing touches the company of ladies required. But the good-humoured apologies of his guests for having thus unexpectedly inflicted their company upon him, sufficed to restore him to his usual placid mood. They expressed themselves delighted with the numerous small sketches that lay scattered about the room, and in his new work, on which they found him busily employed, they manifested a deep interest.   The subject was an Italian sketch, a copy from one of the first masters, and the artist expatiated on its beauty with all the ardour such a subject was calculated to inspire.

"You have never had an opportunity of studying in Italy?" said the young lady in a tone of inquiry.

"No," replied Henry, "great as my desire has been to visit that land of beauty and romance, I have never yet been enabled to gratify it."

"It is a pity," replied Mrs. Belmont; "such undoubted talent as you possess, would do justice to the fairy, lovely scenery of sunny Italy."

Henry felt flattered.

"You do me more justice than I deserve, madam," he replied. modestly, "yet I often think, that if Heaven has a blessing in store for me, it is, that I shall one day stand beneath its blue unclouded sky."

"You speak with the ardour of a poet as well as a painter," said the young lady, smiling.

"Well, Fanny," said Mrs. Belmont, in a tone of reproof, "the two are very closely connected—a painter has the same appreciation of the beauties of nature as a poet, and the same glowing imagery fills the mind of both."

Before they left, Mrs. Belmont engaged the young artist to dine with her on the following day.   Nothing loth, he accepted the invitation. Both ladies were anxious to please and interest their guest; the time spent in their society passed rapidly and pleasantly away; the void that once dwelt in his breast was now filled—he felt grateful for the kind attentions so lavishly bestowed upon him, and the intimacy that was thus begun, speedily ripened into a warm and sincere friendship.

CHAPTER XV.

"Deep in my soul that tender secret dwells,
    Lonely and lost to light for evermore,
Save when to thine, my heart responsive swells,
    Then trembles into silence as before.
There in its centre, a sepulchral lamp,
    Burns the slow flame—eternal—but unseen;
Which not the darkness of despair can damp,
    Though vain its ray, as it had never been."

CLARA was seated at her desk, employed at her usual wearying occupation, but there was a langour, heavy and oppressive, hanging over her once buoyant spirit. In vain she strove to command her attention to her task, thoughts free and unshackled roamed from her present occupation, and fixed themselves on scenes and objects more dear.   She loved,—yes, though she hardly dared to confess it, even to herself, she loved Walter Eardley with that passionate self-denying love which is so often the peculiar feature of a woman's affection.   Yet how many bitter, saddening reflections did the knowledge of this love bring to her heart!   Sad, indeed, was her destiny.   Long had she endeavoured to deceive herself as to the real state of her feelings regarding Walter; but she felt that it was no longer possible to disguise the truth.   She loved him with that true devotedness that would have induced her gladly to sacrifice all things else—to part with even life, rather than with him— to nourish in her young heart the secret of his love, as the first dearest blessing Heaven could give.   She felt that the only pang her bosom dare not brave, would be to find forgetfulness in his. How bitter then, how soul-harrowing, to know that ere long she must crush that budding bliss, must bid him think of her no more, though not even the darkness of despair could damp the love that she knew would survive all other feelings in her breast. Without his love life would no longer be endurable, and he loved her in return; yes, she was assured that he regarded her with the same fond ardour that she entertained towards him. She was not relying on plighted vows—she knew too well that man's faith to woman is a trifle dying upon the very breath that gave it birth. But these were moments that would be enshrined in her heart for ever, when, if there be truth on earth, he spoke it then, when their whole souls seemed blended,—when thoughts would sometimes take a tone of sadness, and then unconsciously grow glad again. Her pen dropped from her hand, and, thrown back in her chair, Clara had abandoned herself to the thoughts that so sorrowfully oppressed her. She was aroused from this fit of gloomy meditation by the entrance of a stranger, who advanced timidly towards her, her eyes bent on the carpet. At a loss to account for this unexpected interruption, Clara rose from her seat and politely enquired the nature of her business. The stranger was young and interesting, though clad in the humblest habiliments, and carried in her arms a pale and delicate looking child. At the sound of Clara's voice she started, and raising her eyes to her face, fixed on her an earnest and searching look, and had not Clara supported her to a seat, and gently removed the child from her arms, she trembled so violently, that she must have fallen to the ground. Her countenance was overspread with the deadliest pallor, and she appeared to be suffering from the most painful excitement. With innate delicacy Clara carried the child to the further end of the room, and affected to be engaged in endeavouring to attract its attention; thus giving its mother an opportunity of recovering her composure. She had been thus employed a few minutes, when she was startled by the voice of the stranger, who, not without difficulty, managed to breathe her name. There is something in the tone of a voice to which we have been once accustomed, which, though unheard for years, never entirely fades from the memory. We may have ceased to remember it—it may be to us as though it had never been, but let it be breathed again in after years, and it instantly touches a chord which perchance has been long silent, but which never fails to vibrate back the sound once so welcome and so dear. Those we loved in early years may be separated from us till their features are entirely forgotten. Time and sorrow may so alter the face and form that we once so much loved to look upon, that we may meet again in after years and fail to recognise them; but the voice is ever the same. The tones that charmed us once never fail to charm—its music sounds as sweetly on our ear in the well remembered strains, after absence has effaced all other recollections from our memory. Clara experienced this at the moment the stranger uttered her name—it sounded familiar to her ears. She had heard that voice before, she was convinced, though where, she was puzzled to remember. She hastened towards her; one glance was now sufficient. Yes—altered, changed entirely in every feature, yet she felt assured she beheld before her no other than her early friend, Lucy Clarence.

"Alas!" she exclaimed, taking her wasted hand and carrying it to her lips, "is it indeed you, Lucy, that I behold after so long and painful an absence?"

The young girl hid her face on the bosom of Clara, and wept aloud.

Great as had been her sin, oh, had she driven her from that resting place,

"Her's had been more or less than mortal heart,
But good or ill, it bade her not depart."

She folded her arms affectionately round her, and suffered her to weep out her sorrow, uninterrupted by questions or reproof. Poor Lucy!—this was the first time since her departure from home, that she had experienced the sweet relief of knowing that a sister's heart commiserated and sympathised with her sorrows. Tears were an inexpressible relief to her aching breast. Oh! how often had she courted their softening aid in vain, but now they gushed forth warm and bright, moistening the parched feelings of her bosom, and invigorating her with renewed fortitude. She was soon sufficiently recovered to impart to her friend the object of her visit.

"How strange and unexpected, dear Clara, is this meeting," said Lucy, raising her head from the bosom of her friend.

"Then you came not here purposely to see me?" replied Clara. "I thought——"

"No, no," interrupted Lucy. "I hope, dear Clara, oh! how earnestly, that my surmises are incorrect. Tell me you do not know—you do not love, Walter Eardley."

The burning blood rushed tumultuously to the very temples of Clara, as Lucy hurriedly put the foregoing questions, but she spoke not.

"Alas!" resumed Lucy, as she viewed the confusion of her friend. "Then I am not mistaken. You love him, and—and,"—here she spoke with difficulty—"it is to you he is about to be united. You deserve happiness," she continued with more animation,—"but, oh, do not deceive yourself with him; you cannot—will not find it. The man that is capable of deserting one—the only crime which she e'er could own was loving him, and him alone—and dooming her and his child to poverty and sorrow, when but a little, a very little sacrifice might have saved them both from its bitter stings—oh! such a one, dear Clara, can never make you happy. He must be lost to every feeling of honour and tenderness, and I entreat of you not to trust your happiness to nis keeping. Believe me, I am actuated now by no unworthy motive—no jealousy mingles with my anxiety to prevent you forming an alliance, which I am assured you would live to repent."

Lucy spoke these words with unwonted energy, and Clara gazed sorrowfully on her pallid face—so pale, that not even the excitement of her feelings lent it even a transient bloom. It was white as parian marble, and her eyes were sunk and hollowed; and then the expression, the dead despondency of those sunk eyes—

> ——"The withering blight,
> That sin and sorrow leave where'er they light."

Clara felt her whole soul moved to compassion; still it cost her a bitter struggle to renounce him whom she so ardently loved, that not even his sin could extinguish the flame of love that beamed so brightly in her breast—with his faults, and they were many, she loved him still. After vainly endeavouring to calm the tumult of the feelings which agitated and oppressed her mind, she spoke in a subdued and trembling voice—

"I confess, dear Lucy, that I have loved, and still do love Walter, how dearly you may conceive when I tell you that not even the knowledge of his unkindness towards yourself can efface his image from my heart. No, there it is enshrined in fadeless truth and beauty."

Lucy groaned as she scarce articulated—

"Another victim! Oh! Walter, how much will you have to answer for!"

"No, no, dear Lucy," replied Clara, eagerly; "as regards myself, he has nothing to answer for. He sought my love honourably, and I gave it freely."

"If I thought," said Lucy, in a reflecting tone, "that you could be happy with him, God knows I would not seek to prevent you becoming his bride, but——"

"Stay, Lucy," replied Clara, "and hear me solemnly declare that the wife of Walter Eardley I will never be. You have nothing to do with this determination," she continued, "there is a vow registered in Heaven that will effectually prevent him ever being to me more than he is at this present moment; less, he cannot be. I encouraged his attentions in the vain belief that I might thus win his love, and revenge the injuries he had heaped upon my unfortunate brother—while my own heart remained free and unshackled; but I found it impossible. His many attractive qualities have made an impression upon it, too deep to be effaced. But enough, dear Lucy; satisfied with my assurance, let us now converse on some less painful topic." And in the hope of diverting the attention of Lucy, who was evidently weak and ill, she began to praise the beauty of her child. Poor Lucy burst into a flood of tears as Clara pressed the boy to her bosom and fondly kissed his cheek.

"And can you, Clara, thus fondly caress a child of sin and shame?" found vent upon her overcharged heart.

With tender words and affectionate solicitude, Clara at length succeeded in tranquillizing the mind of Lucy. It was with undisguised feelings of anger and resentment that she learnt the cruelty that Walter had practised towards Lucy and her unoffending child; indeed she could scarcely conceive it possible that he could thus act. There must surely be some mistake—some misunderstanding. Sir Richard had probably deceived him into the belief that he was himself providing for her wants, and had likewise intercepted her letters; such a construction of the seeming mystery was far from impossible. And the representation of Sir Richard that his son was about to form an advantageous marriage, she regarded as an invention on his part to prevent, if possible, Lucy troubling him again. So ably did she argue this point, that Lucy at length became a convert to the opinion. With gentle force Clara insisted that Lucy should remain with her the entire day, and in the tenderest manner made her acquainted with her brother's anguish at her elopement, and his subsequent death; as also her own grief for his loss, and the vow she had so solemnly pronounced to revenge his death. Lucy wept bitterly as she listened to the painful narrative, and was naturally anxious to learn all she could concerning her immediate relatives; and as Clara had been in the constant habit of corresponding with Jane, she was enabled to satisfy her anxiety regarding them. Her father's health was daily declining; her mother, too, seemed far from enjoying her usual good health, and she alone the cause. Oh! how sad, how bitter was the reflection. She could do nothing but weep for the consequence of her own sins.

CHAPTER XVI.

"Alas! how light a cause may move
Dissension between hearts that love!
Hearts that the world in vain had tried,
And sorrow but more closely tied;
That stood the storm when waves were rough,
Yet in a sunny hour fell off,
Like ships that have gone down at sea
When heaven was all tranquillity?"

WE readily believe that the reader is by this time interested in all that concerns Walter Eardley, for which reason we desire to transport him to the interior of a genteel, though not splendid house, a short distance from London; in the parlour of which is seated a girl beautiful as a poet's dream. She seems scarce to have numbered eighteen summers; of middle height, full and beautiful proportioned; her large dark eyes are shaded by snowy lids, the long fringe of which casts a deep shadow on her cheek; her raven tresses are gathered close together and confined to the back of her head by a circlet of pearl, and her arms are clasped with bracelets of the same. In front of her stands a young man, neatly but plainly dressed; his brow is contracted, apparently with anger, and his cheek glowed with excitement. The eyes of the young girl are fixed on the carpet, and her cheek, too, was flushed, but evidently with resentment. The young man was the first to speak, and his voice was thick and husky.

"Tell me, Ada," he said, "that this story of your marriage is false; I cannot believe it possible that you will be child enough to allow a trifling quarrel so far to influence you, that you will allow it to stand in the way of your happiness."

The girl raised her eyes from the carpet for one brief moment, and fixed them flashing with anger, on the young man, as she replied—

"You may consider it a trifling quarrel, Percy, but I do not."

"Call it what you will, Ada; only, for God's sake, do not allow it to hurry you into a step you may afterwards repent having taken; I speak as much for your sake as my own."

"You are well aware, Percy," replied the young girl, "that at the very moment when I was lavishing my regards wholly upon you, even so far as to displease my uncle for your sake, you were bestowing those attentions upon another which alone were due to me."

"How often have I told you, that the lady in question possessed not the slightest share of my regard; that, being accidentally thrown into her society, I merely paid her those attentions, trivial in the extreme, and which are due to the sex."

"I know you have frequently told me so," replied the girl, "but the knowledge that I am not regarded by you, to the utter exclusion of all others, and which in the romantic fondness of my heart I once fully believed, has sufficed to restore me to a sense of my duty. I no longer deem it right to act contrary to the advice of my uncle, whom I am assured has nought but my happiness in view in proposing a marriage for me with the youngest son of Sir Richard Eardley; I have consequently told him, that for the future I am anxious to be guided entirely by his wishes."

"Then you are willing to marry this Walter Eardley?"

"I am; the young man, whose appearance is most prepossessing, is devotedly attached to me, and if I do not love him, it is of little consequence—I shall be the better able to manage him."

"Unhappy, misguided girl!" said the young man, "you will live to repent your present determination."

"I hope not," she replied, coolly, "but you must now see that it is utterly useless to urge me further."

"Alas! Ada," he returned, "I must warn you that you are casting away one whose whole life would have been too short to evince his gratitude, had you bestowed upon him your dear hand, so deeply, so highly coveted, and which you voluntarily promised should be his alone. God knows that, though I am poor and you are rich, not one thought of your wealth induces me to beg of you, even on my bended knees, to turn a deaf ear to all that my enemies have urged against me. Oh, Ada," he continued, warmly, "you drive me to despair by your unkindness, ill-deserved by me."

"It is useless," replied the girl proudly; "Percy, we must part at once, and for ever. Walter Eardley is now my accepted husband, and——"

"Enough," interrupted the young man; "this is the reward of my fond idolatry. Oh, woman! nought surely is so light, so fickle, as thy inconstant, wavering mind! Farewell, Ada; a long and last farewell—my whole soul seems changed. I despise myself for having sued to one who is wholly devoid of that gentle tenderness for which I have so long given her credit."

"Why is this wildness?" returned the girl. "Percy, you absolutely alarm me."

"You need not fear me, Ada," he replied, "I at least shall never harm you; but I will no longer intrude myself into your presence." And he hurried from the room.

Once more alone, the girl seemed for a moment moved; she was seated near the window, from which she caught a glimpse of the young man, who, with his hat drawn down over his eyes, hastened from the house—that house which had once beheld him a favoured guest, and from that very window Ada had often glanced to smile a last adieu. A faint sickness came over her as the thoughts of other days filled her heart with sadness, and she hid her face in her clasped hands and wept. Yes, strange and incomprehensible as it may appear, the spoilt beauty wept for the loss of a lover, whom, as the reader has seen, she voluntarily renounced. She was not happy, not satisfied with the part she had acted; and yet, were it possible that the interview between herself and the young man could have taken place again, there is no manner of doubt but she would again have refused all his offers of reconciliation. Her pride supported her. While in his presence, she would not have him think she was weak enough to desire to retain his affection, but when she knew he was gone, she well knew to return no more, she gave vent to her feelings in a woman's never failing resource—tears, those weapons of her weakness. Her cousin Mary entered the room shortly afterwards,

PERCY'S ASTONISHMENT AT THE REJECTION OF HIS SUIT BY ADA.

and Ada was again herself, the pretty, petulant, spoilt child. Mary Herbert was some years her senior—a girl of excellent sense and noble principle; and as she seated herself opposite her cousin, frankly enquired what had passed between her and Percy Raymond.

"I have given him his dismissal," replied Ada, with an air of affected gaiety.

"You surely are not serious," replied her cousin; "what Percy to whom you were so determinately attached, that all opposition only served to strengthen your love? You surely cannot mean me to suppose——"

"Yes, I do mean you to suppose," interrupted Ada, playfully, "that in consequence of certain rumours that reached my ears concerning this same Percy, I have dismissed him from my affections, and have even gone so far as to tell him so."

"Of course, Ada, you are the best judge of your own actions; but Percy is so devotedly attached to you, and moreover, I fully believe that you loved him in return, that I much fear you will be sorry for acting so precipitately in this affair; why not have told him all that you heard to his dishonour, and he might perhaps have been able to explain."

"Undoubtedly," replied Ada, laughing, "when are men not able to explain their actions satisfactorily—at least, as regards themselves; but if the truth must be told, Mary, I thought it wisest to be off with the old love, before I was on with the new."

"Walter is certainly very handsome," returned her cousin, "but yet I should myself decidedly give the preference to Percy. You know I am considered a good judge of character, therefore you will not feel offended when I say there is something about Mr. Eardley that I do not like."

"I am by no means offended," returned Ada, "and yet, as I am determined to marry him, it will perhaps be as well to confine your opinions concerning him to your own breast. I am convinced he is just the man for me; he thinks highly of my personal attractions, and pours the sweetest flattery into my ears;—but he will speedily be here, and this reminds me that my toilet is not quite what it should be."

And in reality, with a heavy heart that was concealed under an affected gaiety, she quitted the room. Ada's beauty had been her bane from her earliest infancy; she had been flattered, petted, and caressed. While too young to know the loss she sustained, her parents both died, leaving her to the care of an uncle, her father's brother, with a handsome dowry when she came of age. Mr. Herbert was a plain, good-intentioned man himself—a widower, with an only daughter—and he gladly received his niece into his little household. Their injudicious kindness fostered the many bad traits already manifest in the character of Ada; none were suffered to oppose or thwart her inclination, and so she grew to womanhood, proud, high-spirited, and impatient of control; while her cousin Mary, who inherited the gentle virtues of her mother, united to them the plain principles and excellent even temper of her father; and though inferior in mental endowments to Ada, she was more beloved, and was certainly a far more desirable friend and companion. About twelve months before we introduced her to the reader, Ada became acquainted with Percy Raymond, and the young man was instantly captivated with her extreme loveliness, and sought, by a course of honourable and flattering attentions, to win her affections, and ere many moons had waned, he won from her lips an acknowledgment of a reciprocal affection. This appeared to his enraptured fancy the summit of happiness; but alas! he was quickly undeceived;—Ada's temper was far from perfect, and this led to many little quarrels between the lovers; but this was not all—her vanity induced her to exact the most constant and unceasing attention, added to which, her jealousy was unbounded, and the slightest or most commonplace attention bestowed upon another, aroused her to anger and resentment. Notwithstanding the young man used every precaution against exciting her jealous feelings, it was impossible at all times to avoid giving offence to one who was so ready to take it. And a sister of one of the oldest friends of Percy, being in a measure thrown upon his care, the young lady most unintentionally awakened the jealousy of Ada. She expostulated with her lover, and the young man respectfully but firmly defended his motives; and, for the first time since their acquaintance they parted in anger. About this time, Mr. Herbert renewed an intimacy that years before subsisted between himself and Sir Richard Eardley. The baronet was immediately struck with the extreme beauty of Ada, and learning from her uncle that in a few short years she would come into the possession of large property, instantly conceived the idea of forming an alliance between her and his youngest son. Communicating this idea to Mr. Herbert, he at once eagerly embraced it, as the means of separating his niece from Percy, whom he never considered a suitable match. Arrangements were instantly entered into, for the introduction of the young persons to each other. Sir Richard plainly explained his own views to Walter, and promised to free him entirely from the consequence of his errors, on condition that he married Ada. The young man so far consented, that he agreed to see her. The introduction consequently took place, and Walter found Ada by no means backward in receiving his advances ; she was charmed with his beauty of person and his attractive manners, which never failed to secure admiration ; while on his part, he could not, of course, be blind to the extreme loveliness of her face and form, though at the same time he was thoroughly alive to her failings—the proud imperiousness of her manners was far from pleasing to him, who had been accustomed to regard gentleness as the sweetest genuine attribute. Still his creditors were to be satisfied only on condition that he married this proud beauty ; the only escape that offered itself from the horrors of a jail, was by uniting himself with her. On this condition only, his father had promised to deliver him from his embarrassments. Walter thought of this, and strove to banish all other thoughts from his mind. She was undoubtedly handsome ;—he was not required to link his fate with age or ugliness ; the more he reflected, the more advisable it appeared for him to obey the wishes of his father, and finally he proposed to the fair Ada, and was accepted.

CHAPTER XVII.

" Commerce has set the mark of selfishness,
The signet of its all-enslaving power,
Upon a shining ore, and calls it gold ;
Before whose image bow the vulgar great,
The vainly rich, the miserable proud,
The mob of peasants, nobles, priests, and kings,
And with blind feelings reverence the power
That grinds them to the dust of misery."

HENRY FERGUSSON felt deeply grateful for the tenderness he experienced from the two ladies, with whom the reader is aware he had formed an acquaintance. The time no longer hung heavy on his hands, it now only passed too swiftly ; months went by, and Henry became on such intimate terms with Mrs. Belmont, that he was constantly engaged at her residence ; dinners, evening parties, fetes passed in rapid succession ; he constantly attended the ladies to different places of amusement, and, in short, he became involved in the gaieties of a London season. This, however agreeable to the young man's taste, was not at all calculated to enhance his small finances. The money that he had received from Miss Mowbray for the purchase of his picture, had long since been swallowed up by his increased expenses, and he was again unhappily involved in debt. But how could he avoid it ? was a question he repeatedly asked himself ; he was obliged to keep up an appearance, he was conscious he could not afford, at least he conceived he was, and though his mornings were frequently spent in anxiety, his evenings never failed to remove the greater portion of his care. He still regularly corresponded with Jane, and had, on his first introduction to her new friends, informed her of the event that brought them acquainted. Free from the slightest vestige of jealousy, she had warmly congratulated him on the fortunate occurrence, and still continued to express, in all her letters, the pleasure she received from hearing that he was now possessed of friends who appreciated his talent and felt a lively interest in his welfare ; of herself she said but little ; her father she occasionally hinted was evidently fast hastening to the tomb, and her time and thoughts were fully employed in attending on his sick couch, and sustaining the fainting spirits of her mother—more she evidently forbore to say, in order to spare his feelings. At this period his letters, in reply to those of Jane, were less frequent; not, he repeatedly assured her, that she was less fondly loved and treasured, but he had so many calls upon his time, as to prevent him devoting so large a portion of it to her. So utterly free from selfishness was Jane, that the excuse was readily received; she never for a moment deemed herself neglected, on the contrary, she was pleased to hear that her lover was happy, and that he participated in the pleasures and amusements of the metropolis. In the meantime his picture proceeded but slowly, and yet he had no other means to look to, wherewith to support his present extravagance. How much he coveted a small portion of that shining ore, which is known by the name of gold. His pride would not allow him to declare the real state of his finances to Mrs. Belmont, and the two ladies innocently added to his embarrassments by leading him into expenses; he had no resource whatever to afford support. Their company had become to him so pleasant, so almost necessary, that it was with the greatest difficulty he tore himself from their society, in order to afford himself an opportunity of finishing his picture against the opening of the exhibition. Mrs. Belmont slightly remonstrated, and Miss Mowbray looked sad when he excused himself from their company; but when he frankly stated his reason for doing so, both ladies were warm in their approbation of his proposition.

"I certainly most highly approve of your project," said Mrs. Belmont, "but still I cannot allow you to exclude yourself too much."

"You may rest assured," replied Henry, glancing, as he spoke, towards Miss Mowbray, though he addressed himself to the elder lady, "that it is with extreme reluctance I resign, even for a short time, the society of those who have succeeded in rendering their company irresistibly dear to my heart. I should be ungrateful, indeed, were it otherwise, for the kindness I have experienced is, I am well convinced, far beyond my merits."

Miss Mowbray looked gratified, and exchanged a glance with Henry that might perhaps have been construed into meaning more than friendship, and Mrs. Belmont hastened to convince him that he entertained too humble an opinion of himself.

"Talents such as you possess," said that lady, "are in themselves a sufficient passport into any society, and I am proud at being enabled to number you among my friends, none of whom are more respected, or held in higher esteem both by myself and Fanny."

"The flattering attentions you have so kindly lavished upon me, serve to convince me of what you affirm," replied Henry, and his eyes again wandered towards Miss Mowbray, the colour on whose cheek deepened as she met his gaze, and a smile of pleasure illumined her countenance.

Miss Mowbray was indeed a most charming girl, and Henry had very often remarked it. There was something so extremely agreeable in her manners, so flattering to the vanity of the young artist, that she insensibly gained upon his admiration. He had never thought it worth while to enquire into the state of his feeling regarding the young lady; secure in her friendship, the affection he bore to Jane seemed sufficient to prevent even a thought that love might intrude. And yet the constant intercourse that took place between himself and Miss Mowbray, whom his heart acknowledged to be one of the most amiable and delightful young ladies he had ever known, was fraught with danger to the happiness of both. We shall see, but we fear this friendship may be prejudiced to the peace of Jane Clarence, whose amiable character and gentle loving and loveable temper render an especial favourite with ourselves. There was none to hint this to Henry, or his love for Jane would have prompted him carefully to guard his heart, to keep strict watch over every avenue, for fear the wily god should gain access to his bosom under the guise of gratitude and friendship. A man's affection is so easily diverted from an absent to a present object, that, though with women absence may make the heart grow fonder, it is one of the bitterest foes to a man's affections that can possibly exist. As yet Henry's love had undergone no sensible diminution; the portrait which he had himself painted of his beloved Jane was frequently pressed to his lips, and as fondly treasured as it had ever been. Henry was, most strictly speaking, an honourable man; it had never occurred to him as possible that Miss Mowbray's affections might, unfortunately for herself, be placed on him, or he most undoubtedly would have taken an early opportunity of making Mrs. Belmont acquainted with the engagement that subsisted between himself and Jane. He regarded Miss Mowbray, as placed by birth and fortune at an immeasurable distance from himself, he therefore exulted in her friendship, and entertained no fear for the future. Fanny Mowbray was an orphan, entrusted by a dying mother, at the age of sixteen, to Mrs. Belmont, who, with some foibles, was really a kind-hearted and excellent woman. Fanny, though a friendless orphan, came not to the house of Mrs. Belmont a pensioner on her charity, on the contrary, she was an heiress of no inconsiderable fortune, and her father's will having made her of age at nineteen, when Henry was first introduced to her, she was already in receipt of her property, with which she scattered, with no niggard hand, blessings among the poor with whom she came in contact. Frequently would she advise with Henry as to the best mode of permanently benefitting the numerous class of poor which, with sorrow be it said, were daily starving around her. Yes, in merry England, the land of hope and promise, how many—how very many, surrounded on all sides by plenty, even to luxuriousness, pass daily unpitied to the tomb, for want of the common necessaries of life. Fanny was naturally a reflective character, and though she had been brought up in the very lap of wealth, it had not made her insensible to the sufferings of others, no—deeply did she commiserate the sorrows and privations of her fellow creatures.

"It appears to me," she said, when conversing with Henry on this subject, "as if I had no right to be in the possession of some thousands of pounds, when I see so many without the veriest pittance wherewith to support life; surely there ought to be more equality in the conditions of men. I do not mean to say that every one should be in exactly the same position of life, but, that some should have more money than they can well spend, even in unbounded extravagance, while others are actually starving, is to my mind a positive wrong and injustice, that strongly resembles guilt."

"There are but few, my dear Miss Mowbray, that entertain such noble opinions. Well would it be for the millions, if all thought and acted as you do," replied Henry.

"It grieves me," resumed the young lady, "that my sphere of influence is naturally contracted, but never will I, in the most indirect manner, bind myself towards oppressing my fellows. For this reason, I feel bound to restrain myself in the indulgence of many pleasures that I should otherwise more freely participate in. I have a great desire to travel, but at present I have not even thought of it; indeed, how could I hope to enjoy myself abroad, when I should be constantly pained with the thought of the starving millions at home. And how bitter would be the reflection, that the money I was squandering on my enjoyment, might be the means of putting new hope and life into at least some anxious sorrowing breasts."

"I commend your sensitiveness, my dear Fanny," said Mrs. Belmont, who chanced to overhear the last part of Miss Mowbray's remarks. "And yet I cannot refrain from saying that I think you carry your ideas rather too far; for were you even to reduce yourself to poverty, in order to bestow on others, you would only benefit so small a part of the community, that it seems scarcely worth while to deny yourself a few trifling pleasures which cannot possibly affect the mass."

"Pardon me," replied the young lady, "but such an argument is truly a selfish one, and of which I never could avail myself; it is the use of that very argument by so many influential persons that prevents a stop being put to the present misery, instead of doing which, were all to join in the good work, we might hope for a speedy remedy."

"True, my dear, but they will not do so; it is only here and there that we meet with a person disinterested as yourself, who is willing to devote a small portion of their income towards alleviating the distress of their fellow creatures."

"Be it so," replied Miss Mowbray, "I, at least, will use all my influence, and be happy if, by contracting my personal expenses, I can in some trifling degree benefit the starving poor, and it will ever be to my mind a source of the liveliest regret, after I have done all in my power, to think that I can do no more."

Such sentiments as these could not, of course, fail to excite a warm interest in the mind of Henry for the amiable girl. He felt the deepest respect awakening in his mind on her behalf; she acted, he believed, in the same manner as he would have done himself had it been his lot to possess what is far more coveted than aught else upon earth—wealth, at whose shrine even princes bow. Henry hastened to complete his picture, now that he was for a time released from the society of his friends. And yet it was surprising even to himself, how frequently his thoughts roamed to Miss Mowbray. Her features were so constantly before him, that he unthinkingly sketched them in a figure of Faith, which was represented in his picture; and when he became aware of it, he could not resolve to make any alteration, for they were certainly the most suitable, and became the figure admirably; and then he had promised to escort Mrs. Belmont and Miss Mowbray to the exhibition, in order to view his picture, and suppose the resemblance to be recognised, the young lady would regard it as a compliment to herself, and it was one, Henry felt assured, she well merited.

CHAPTER XVIII.

First our pleasures die, and then
Our hopes, and then our fears—and when
These are dead, the debt is due—
Dust claims dust, and we die too.

All things that we love and cherish,
Like ourselves must fade and perish;
Such is our rude mortal lot—
Love itself would, did they not.

CLARA, notwithstanding the many anxieties that embittered her own lot, kindly and tenderly enquired into the affairs of Lucy; the day they spent together was devoted to tender persuasion, in order to induce Lucy to return to her parental roof.

"I urge it," said Clara, kindly; "because I am assured that both yourself and child will meet a kind reception, and you would be happier, dear Lucy, among those who are near and dear to you."

Lucy wept bitterly.

"I should indeed be happier, but oh! I cannot believe that they will be willing to receive me back; I have sinned beyond the hope of their forgiveness!"

"No, dear Lucy, you must not say so," replied Clara; "your father is most anxious to see you, in order to pronounce your pardon before he breathes his last. Jane even speaks of you in her letters most affectionately, and will be only too glad to renew all her sisterly regard."

Lucy hesitated.

"It would afford me a melancholy pleasure to draw my last breath among scenes that are so dear to my heart, but I am overwhelmed with confusion at the thoughts of meeting their reproving looks."

"You will, at least, allow me to write to Jane, and communicate the intelligence of my having seen you, and leave it to themselves to invite your return. This sweet child," she continued, caressing the lovely infant, "demands some sacrifice on your part, in order to secure its future welfare."

Lucy could hold out no longer.

"Dear Clara," she murmured, "I will be guided entirely by your advice, I know you intend kindly—most kindly."

Having thus gained her permission, Clara lost no time previous to writing to Jane, and acquainting her with the unfortunate situation of her unhappy sister. As she anticipated, her letter received an immediate reply, couched in the gentlest and tenderest terms, expressive of the heartfelt joy it would give them to receive the wanderer back, and urging Lucy to hasten her departure from London as much as possible, as her father's health was now so precarious that it was quite uncertain whether he might live to see her again. It would be difficult to describe the contending feelings that agitated the breast of Lucy as she prepared once more to visit scenes that were dear to her heart, as being connected with her early happy years, when sin and sorrow were unknown. A blight had indeed fallen upon her young heart—a blight and a bane, while he who had won her, but mocked at her shame: deep sorrow came o'er her. "Ah! what arm shall save?—one hope is before her—one refuge, the grave." And yet, though Lucy was truly thoughtful for, and fully sensible of the kindness that offered her a peaceful asylum for the remainder of her days, and she yearned, oh! how earnestly, once more to embrace the loved relatives from whom she had been so long and so painfully separated, yet a regretful feeling hovered o'er her spirit, and filled her heart with despondency and gloom as she thought of the distance that would speedily intervene between herself and him, whom, in spite of his many faults and unkind conduct towards herself, she still so fondly, so tenderly loved, that one word of kindness, one look of love, would have sufficed to change her intention of leaving London, and bind her to his side for good or ill; but the few days that elapsed before her departure, brought her no tidings from him she loved, and Lucy was compelled to quit London without seeing or hearing from Walter. With Clara she exchanged an affectionate and sorrowful adieu.

"Be true to yourself, dear Clara," were her parting words, "and do not suffer the fascinations of Walter to withdraw you from the path of duty; let the terrible sufferings that I have encountered act as a warning, should love and inclination seek to lead you astray."

Tears prevented Clara offering any reply; she strained the child of Walter to her bosom, and bending down to press a kiss upon his sunny brow, inwardly breathed a prayer for his future happiness; then restoring the babe to the arms of his mother, she endeavoured cheerfully to bid her farewell, but it was impossible, she could no longer restrain her feelings, and burst into an involuntary flood of tears."

"None, dear Lucy," she whispered, "can sympathise with your sufferings like me, or make such full allowance for your errors. I know and love Walter, and am sensible of his many attractions. Oh!" she added, warmly, "it were impossible to know and not to love him."

"I tremble for your future happiness, dear Clara," replied Lucy, tenderly. "You are daily exposed to the temptations of his presence, and——"

"Dear as it is to see and converse with him," interrupted Clara, "I feel that I must shortly deny myself that sweet delight, though the tenderness of his melodious voice, the irresistible sweetness of his smile, will be remembered by me till every vision of this changing scene shall be forgotten."

"Farewell," said Lucy, solemnly. "It is improbable we shall ever meet again on earth; I feel that my time here is short, but may you, dear Clara, yet find happiness and peace."

They parted, Clara to pursue for a short time longer her wearying avocation, and Lucy to journeying back to that spot which she had once been only too eager to quit. Jane had been apprised by Clara of the day on which she might look for the return of her long lost sister. And though she carefully and gently prepared her father for the arrival of his beloved child, yet the agitation it produced on his weakened frame was so excessive that she trembled for the result. The night previous to the expected return of Lucy, he passed in restless anxiety. Jane sat by his sick couch, vainly endeavouring to calm the agitation of his feelings. His mind occasionally wandered, and it was evident to his attendants that he was fast sinking.

"Has she come?" was a question he repeatedly asked, and which Jane was forced to answer in the negative.

At length, worn down by the anxiety of his mind, he sunk into a tranquil sleep, from which, after the lapse of an hour, he awoke refreshed and calm.

"Is she not arrived?" he asked, rather faintly, casting at the same time an earnest look at Jane, as though he anticipated, and yet dreaded her reply.

"Not yet, dear father," replied Jane, tenderly. "It is too early for us to expect her at present."

"When may you reasonably look for her?"

"Within a few hours at farthest," said Jane.

"And yet," he replied emphatically, "I shall not live to see her."

Shortly after this he calmly breathed his last. Oh! how sad, how painful a return for Lucy. As she drew nigh the peaceful village, and recognised each well remembered spot, which seemed to her distempered mind to reproach her for her unkind desertion of her home, and anon, she passed the little church-yard where her lover, who owed his death to her unkindness, slept his long last sleep which knows no awakening, what would she have given now—even life itself—could she have heard him pronounce her pardon; but it was all too late, and she could only fold her hands and weep. Presently she drew near Eardley Hall, and gazed with a reverential feeling upon its time-worn walls, with which there mingled a something of superstition. She remembered well the last time it had met her gaze, when it appeared to frown upon her contemplated desertion of home and friends. And now, as she rivetted her eyes upon the ancient structure, it looked grimly down, as if to reproach her for the little heed she had given to its friendly warning. Poor Lucy folded her infant closer to her bosom, and wept bitter tears, sobbing as if a heart-string broke with every deep heaved sob that came.

"Where art thou, faithless Walter, now?" was her inward exclamation, "thou art no more my bosom's friend—here must the sweet delusion end, that charmed my senses, and made an elysium of my life. These scenes witnessed the growth of the passion that has consumed me, and yet it seems that they should likewise witness its extinction."

Such thoughts as these flitted spectre-like across the troubled breast of Lucy, and from which she was aroused by the stopping of the carriage at her father's door, —that father who was now no more a being of earth; his spirit had taken its flight to worlds unknown. Her brothers, who had been summoned to attend the death-bed of their parent, hastened out to receive their unhappy sister. Overcome by the intensity of her feelings, Lucy had sunk back in a fainting fit, and gently disengaging the infant from her arms, they carried her into the house. Jane was waiting in the hall to receive her, but, prepared as she was to find her sadly altered, she started back in amazement, and could scarcely believe it was her once fair and beauteous sister upon whom she gazed, her whom she had parted with, but a few months before, in the very bloom and beauty of youth, whose soft blue eyes reflected the grace and purity of her soul, but now glazed and dim, her form once so round and of such fair proportions, wasted to a complete shadow, her cheeks as hollow and white as marble itself.

"Alas! what a fearful change!" Jane wept bitterly as she knelt by the inanimate form of her sister, and with her own hand administered the necessary restoratives. And when Lucy, at length, awoke once more to sensibility, and cast a look of deep despondency around her, Jane tenderly bade her be comforted, and whispered (as women only can) words of hope and consolation. After she had thus succeeded in restoring Lucy to composure, she as tenderly as possible acquainted her with the death of their parent, who but a few hours before had breathed his last, and they mingled their tears together. Not one word of reproach, or that savoured in the slightest degree of unkindness, met the ears of Lucy. Her mother received her with open arms—her sister sought by love and unwearying tenderness to win her back to peace. Her brothers never addressed her save in the gentlest tones; and had it been possible for Lucy to forget Walter, the sad cause of all her sorrows, she might have regained her lost happiness. Her child was an object of the warmest interest to all, but to Jane especially, who instantly attached herself to the infant with a maternal tenderness; she looked forward to the time when Lucy would follow their father to the tomb, and then she resolved to make the child her own. Jane was a kind and active nurse, and did all in her power to

restore the failing health of Lucy; but sorrow and privation had done their work, she was naturally of too delicate a frame to withstand the approach of disease; and though the bloom would sometimes resume its place upon her cheek,

> "Yet it spoke to those who watched its hue,
> Of sickness, death, and suffering too."

Yea, though as yet she scarcely knew it herself, death had marked her for his prey, and was hovering o'er her couch, ready to claim her for his own.

CHAPTER XIX.

" How calm, how beautiful runs on
    The stilly hour when storms are gone ;
    When warning winds have died away,
    And clouds beneath the glancing ray
    Melt off, and leave the land and sea
    Sleeping in bright tranquillity,
    Fresh as if day again were borne,
    Smiling upon the lap of morn."

WHEN Percy Raymond left Ada Herbert, his first determination was to quit London, and by travelling on the continent, obliterate if possible all trace of her from his mind.   It was, therefore, with sad and moody reflections he pursued his way towards his own home, but which gave place to a feeling akin to pleasure as he observed his two sisters, Mary and Elizabeth, anxiously looking out for his return.   Percy loved his sisters with all the tenderness of an unselfish nature; they were orphans, and he had promised his dying mother to cherish and protect them with an elder brother's guardian care, and well and faithfully had he kept his promise—they shared his every pleasure, and he shielded them as far as possible from every care.   To their bosoms had he first confided the tender passion that the fascinations of Ada had awakened in his breast, and the gentle girls loved him so dearly that they sedulously endeavoured to cultivate a warm and endearing friendship with the object of his choice ; but Ada was proud, self-willed, and haughty, and received their affectionate advances with coldness and disdain ; she was even unkind enough to be jealous of the tender interest their brother manifested in their welfare.   So exacting, indeed, was Ada, that a look even bestowed on another would suffice to spoil her temper for the entire day.   Percy, so ardently and sincerely loved her, that for a time he was entirely blind to her failings, but Mary and Elizabeth, of course, quickly perceived and bitterly mourned the many faults which were so palpable in one whom they looked upon as the future wife of their beloved brother.   Their intimacy with Ada naturally brought them acquainted with Mary Herbert, whose amiable and attractive qualities forming so agreeable a contrast to the cold and proud manners of her cousin, speedily made her a great favourite with the sisters, and often and deeply would they regret that Percy had not in the first instance given Mary the preference ; with her, they were assured, their brother might with confidence have looked forward to a future of happiness, that could scarcely be anticipated if united to one so proud and exacting as Ada.   Still they carefully concealed from the knowledge of Percy the opinion they entertained regarding her whom they well knew he passionately loved.   And hoping that in the course of time their brother's noble character and excellent mental qualifications might counteract, and happily even efface, all that was unamiable in Ada, they strove to blind themselves to her defects, and be alive only to the best traits of her character.   Thus passed a few short months, when the frequent disagreements that arose between the lovers gave evidence that Percy himself began to be sensible that she was not all his fond, warm imagination had so highly pictured her.   A sad and painful truth—but well for him that he discovered it thus early, before the indissoluble knot was tied that would have bound them together for life.   His bosom was the seat of deep and bitter emotions, and a storm of passion swelled his heart as he rushed from the presence of Ada, but the sight of the smiling faces of his gentle sisters in a measure sufficed to quell the storm of sorrow.   Wholly unprepared as Mary and Elizabeth were for the recital of the unkind part which Ada had acted towards their brother, sympathy—true and gentle sympathy—was instantly awakened in his behalf, and shown more by fond endearments and tearful eyes than by expressions of condolence or words of sorrow.   They tenderly forbore to probe the wound his bosom had received by giving vent to their sorrowful and indignant feelings. And yet they felt thankful that Percy had escaped marrying one with whom it was evident he never could have been blessed. Cheered and consoled by the affectionate assiduities of his sisters, it was no difficult matter to induce Percy to relinquish his intention of travelling, and remain at home with those who were nearest and dearest to his heart. The young girls, Mary and Elizabeth, had become sincerely attached to Mary Herbert, and the unkind conduct of her cousin offered, of course, no obstacle to their continued friendship. They refrained, from feelings of delicacy, visiting the house of Mr. Herbert; but Mary, at their earnest solicitation, frequently spent an evening with the sisters. From her they learnt that Ada was shortly to be united in marriage to the youngest son of Sir Richard Eardley, a young man remarkable for the beauty of his person and the fascination of his manners. Still Mary could plainly perceive that Ada was not happy. Walter, it is true, was a lover she might well be proud of, and his constant and devoted attentions were exclusive enough to satisfy even the heart of the imperious and exacting beauty. Yet, if the truth must be told, she loved him not; and his many attractions made but a very slight impression on her heart. She had sacrificed her happiness at the shrine of ambition, and what but misery could be anticipated as the result? She exulted, it is true, in the firm belief that Walter was truly and devotedly attached to her—not even a thought ever crossed her mind to the effect that Walter likewise might have loved another; and that, while he was whispering soft nothings in her ear, and delighting her vanity by his warm adulation of her personal charms, his heart was at that very moment reproaching him with the duplicity of his conduct. Still less did it ever occur to her that he would gladly have relinquished all claims to her hand, and have given the endearing title of wife to one, who, with all his unkindness and deception, he ardently loved. Neither was the young man so wholly destitute of feeling as it would appear. He thought often and remorsefully of his first-born son, a boy whom he might well have been proud to own; he felt the utter baseness of his conduct in so cruelly deserting that child and its mother, whose love he had once so fondly sought, and had deemed so proudly won. And nothing but the stern unrelenting mandate of his father would have induced him to act contrary to the dictates of his conscience, which whispered him full oft of his evil deeds, while remorse, that fell fiend, was constantly gnawing at his heart, turning each transient gleam of joy to anguish and sorrow; while Ada, on her part, sedulously concealed from Walter her own furious attachment to Percy, and received his attentions with an avidity that led him to believe her love was all his own. Alas! what duplicity dwelt in the breasts of these two young persons; mutually deceiving and deceived, they were about to enter into the most endearing and close relationship—a connection in which, beyond all others, it is requisite to be frank and open. Alas! Walter, what misery, what utter misery, must be the just reward of thy sins—thou hast purchased a temporary happiness by a life of sorrow. There were times, indeed, when the young man felt this so deeply, that he was half inclined to break through the bonds that enchained him, and declare to his father, the utter impossibility of his fulfiling the contract into which he had entered, but the horror he entertained of a prison, and the pressing claims of his creditors, urged him on. In regarding Ada as his future wife, Walter was not blinded by love, and was therefore fully alive to her many faults; and gladly would he have dispensed with some of her personal attractions, could he have remedied her personal defects. His long and close intimacy with Lucy, who was the very opposite of Ada, had taught him to love gentleness and amiability, far more than a pretty face or graceful figure. The proud and haughty manners of Ada offered a painful contrast to the yielding and unselfish character of Lucy; thus the more he saw of Ada, and the more closely he became acquainted with her disposition, the more he was convinced that though he might admire her personal charms, he never could feel for her that tender affection, or even that decided preference, which is so essential to the happiness of wedded life; it was, therefore, with a mournful foreboding that he looked forward to the future, and bitterly did he curse his own folly, that had thus left him no power in the choice of a wife. In the meantime, Percy Raymond was fast regaining his tranquillity. He had loved Ada with the warmest and most passionate devotion, but when thoroughly convinced of her unworthiness, he had too much self-respect to give way to inordinate sorrow—his bosom was torn and lacerated, and time alone could heal its wounds. Still he heard of her approaching marriage without one throb of regret. After the tumult of waning passions, that had raged so furiously in his bosom, he gladly welcomed the calm that now prevailed. The constant intercourse that took place between his sisters and Mary Herbert was productive of a good effect on the mind of the young man; he became sensible of the quiet gentle virtues that formed so pleasing a feature in her character; her conversation too, lively, without exuberant mirth, unaffected, sensible, and pleasing, made so agreeable an impression on his mind, that he became himself surprised that he had ever given the preference to her cousin, and still more so that he should once have thought Mary plain-looking.

"What a very pleasant, agreeable companion Mary Herbert is," Percy remarked to his sisters, when conversing of their absent friend. "I was just thinking what an egregious fool I must have been to overlook her in the manner I once did; I used to think her positively plain."

"Mary is a sweet girl," returned his elder sister warmly, "and whoever is fortunate enough to obtain her for a wife, will be undoubtedly a happy man."

Percy pondered on his sister's words, and ended in regarding her as the most discerning character, and one of the best judges of her own sex, it had ever been his lot to meet.

CHAPTER XX.

The harmony and happiness of man
Yield to the wealth of nations; that which lifts
His nature to the heaven of pride
Is bartered for the poison of his soul:
The weight that drags to earth his towering hopes,
Blighting all prospect, but of selfish gain—
Withering all passion, but of slavish fear,
Extinguishing all free and generous love
Of enterprise and daring; even the pulse
That fancy kindles in the beating heart,
To mingle with sensation, it destroys—
Leaves nothing but the sordid dust of self,
The grovelling hope of interest and gold.

ANOTHER London season has arrived, and the exhibitions are again open. By dint of close application during the last few weeks, Henry Fergusson continued to finish his picture, and forwarded it to the exhibition, and with a palpitating heart he prepared to escort his two friends, Mrs. Belmont and Miss Mowbray, to the exhibition, in order to view this effort of his genius. He was pleased to find that this time his picture had the advantage of a favourable light, but it was unfortunately placed in close vicinity to others whose undoubted merits detracted considerably from his own more humble efforts. The ladies were both warm in their encomiums, and spoke so highly in its favour, that the young artist felt his heart swell with pride.

"Why, dear me," suddenly exclaimed Mrs. Belmont, who had been intently surveying the picture through her gold eye-glass, "that female figure is the exact image of Fanny. I cannot believe so striking a likeness to be the result of accident; confess, Henry, now, that it was intentional."

The young man blushed, looked confused, and endeavouring to avoid the searching glance of the elder lady, averted his eyes, and in doing so encountered the brilliant orbs of Miss Mowbray, which were earnestly fixed upon his countenance; they exchanged but one brief glance, but that sufficed to suffuse the cheeks of the young lady to the deepened crimson of his own.

"Come, Henry," resumed Mrs. Belmont, "why should you be ashamed to confess that?"

"Pardon me, my dear madam," interrupted Henry, "I am only too proud to confess, that while absent from the society of Miss Mowbray, she has so honoured me with her friendship, her form and features so constantly recurred to my mind, that I unknowingly transmitted them to my canvas; on discovering which, I felt far too high a respect for Miss Mowbray to think even for a moment of obliterating them. No," he added, warmly, "I determined that there they should remain, a humble memento of my regard, which my heart assured me she would not disdain."

The gracefulness of this speech, and the animation with which it was given utterance to, affected Fanny even to tears, which for a moment dimmed the lustre of her bright eyes, and as she looked her gratitude to Henry, he, flattered by her evident preference for himself, pressed the small white hand that rested on his arm, without for a moment thinking that he was giving rise to hopes and feelings his long engagement to Jane Clarence would prevent ever being realised. He had never asked himself, did he love Miss Mowbray, nor had it ever occurred to him, that absence had awakened his affection for the gentle girl who so firmly relied upon his faith, and judging of the state of his feelings from what she herself experienced, that absence would only make his heart grow fonder. There surely never could be a more thoroughly unselfish being than Jane, or one more free from even the slightest shade of jealousy. And this her lover appeared to know, for his letters of late were filled with praise of Miss Mowbray; her amiability, her disinterestedness, her and noble generous qualifications were all warmly dwelt upon, and found an echo in the breast of Jane; she congratulated Henry upon the acquisition of such a friend, and delicately hinted the pleasure it would afford her, when, by becoming his wife, she might herself honour and appreciate Miss Mowbray's excellence. Never for one moment even did Jane indulge in a thought unfavourable to her lover, and never having dreamed of falsehood, she had not one word to say of constancy. When they withdrew from the exhibition, and Henry, having placed the ladies in the carriage, seated himself opposite to them, the conversation naturally recurred to his painting, and Mrs. Belmont, smiling good-naturedly, remarked—

"Upon my word, Henry, that is a very pretty compliment you have paid Fanny, and one of which she may justly be proud. It would really be a sin to allow that painting to pass into other hands. Fanny," she continued, turning to Miss Mowbray, "you must return Henry's compliment, by being yourself the purchaser of his picture."

The young lady blushed deeply as she replied, laughing—

"Something of the sort was at this moment passing through my mind; but I fear that, in purchasing the picture, I shall incur the charge of vanity."

"I cannot permit myself a second time to tax your generosity, my dear Miss Mowbray," said Henry, not altogether free from embarrassment, for he was well aware that gallantry demanded of him to offer the picture for the young lady's acceptance, in token of respect; but the many creditors who daily pressed their claims upon his notice, and the only chance he had of liquidating them lay in the sale of that identical painting, prevented him doing what he would otherwise have been only too proud to accomplish.

Alas, how much constraint and uneasiness does not poverty impose upon its victims! Henry was proud, and could not brook the thoughts of candidly stating the limited nature of his circumstances, and so suffered himself to be drawn into expenses far beyond his humble means, and for which he paid the just penalty of days of uneasiness and nights of sleepless solicitude. The exhibition was within a few days of closing, and the painting, round which so many hopes were entwined, remained unsold. His creditors became impatient of delay, and Henry, scarce knowing what to do, had half resolved to inform Mrs. Belmont of his embarrassment, when, to his utter consternation, he found himself arrested at the suit of the most importunate of his creditors. The alarm was infinite—the sum was too large for the possibility of liquidation, even had he parted with every valuable that he possessed, and in his present desperate fortunes he felt that it would be unjust, as well as ungenerous, to attempt the borrowing of it. Fortunately, the sheriff was a most gentlemanly and amiable man, and offered (to avoid any unpleasant dilemma) to accompany Henry himself to Mrs. Belmont's, with whom he appeared to be thoroughly aware he was on friendly and intimate terms. Indeed, the reason subsequently assigned for his arrest was the belief that the debt would be instantly paid by that lady. But Henry was of too noble and exalted a character to profit by the sheriff's advice. Years of incarceration would have been to him far preferable to making known his unpleasant circumstances to the friends to whom he was already indebted for many and repeated acts of kindness; he therefore signified his readiness to accompany the sheriff without delay. It happened that the day following he had an engagement to dine with Mrs. Belmont, from which he was, of course, obliged to excuse himself, as he was now deprived for the time, at least, of liberty of action; he did so, therefore, under the plea of sudden indisposition. Although Henry had unwisely allowed himself to be drawn into expenses to which he could oppose no reasonable mode of payment, yet he was too right-minded to be easily persuaded farther, and unnecessarily to increase them; he, therefore, steadfastly resisted the pressing entreaties of the sheriff's officer to remain in his house a few days, in the hope that arrangements might be entered into for procuring his liberty. The dark galleries of a prison offered a mournful contrast to the elegant and spacious apartments in which he had of late been accustomed to move, and a sad and dreary sensation filled his breast as he took possession of the apartments assigned him; he had now leisure for thought, and the events of the last few months rose reproachfully before his mind's eye.

> "Things bright or lovely in their acted time—
> But now to stern reflection each a a crime."

He thought of Jane, and conscience whispered he had grown careless of her love. How brief had his answers been of late to her kind and affectionate epistles—so brief, almost cold, that, had not Jane fondly and fully believed that he was constantly engaged in his professional duties, her love would have taken the alarm; but she reposed such implicit confidence in his affection, that there was no room in her mind for doubts and fears. But Henry felt that he had injured her, and he resolved to make her ample amends, by devoting himself for the future entirely to her happiness. He had never ceased to regard her as his destined wife, or permitted himself for a moment even to dream of wedding another, but being constantly thrown into the society of a lovely and fascinating woman, who knowing nothing whatever of his engagement, devoted herself to the task of pleasing and gaining his attentions. No wonder then, that, in the absence of Jane, his mind was favourably impressed by Miss Mowbray, and his regard for the first object of his attachment in some degree lessened. Mrs. Belmont received Henry's note, excusing himself from keeping his engagement on the plea of ill health—an excuse that was readily admitted, and sympathy and condolence expressed on his account. The evening was marked by a languidness, and evident uneasiness on the part of Miss Mowbray, that called forth the raillery of her friend.

"Upon my word, Fanny," said Mrs. Belmont, laughing, "you have long evinced symptoms of *la belle passion*, but I had no idea that you were so far gone."

The young lady blushed, as she endeavoured playfully to defend herself from the lively sallies of her companion.

"La! child, you need not blush," continued Mrs. Belmont, still laughing, "I knew that your time would come sooner or later, and you may remember I have often told you so. And now, I think that you bid fair speedily to resign your boasted liberty—the name of Mowbray will shortly be merged in that of Fergusson."

The young lady blushed again, as she replied—

"I will not attempt to conceal from you, my only friend, that I might probably be tempted to say 'yes,' if ever Mr. Fergusson should condescend to put the important question, but if I judge him rightly, I do not believe he ever will."

"That is a very pretty speech, Fanny," replied Mrs. Belmont. "And it is almost a pity that I should spoil it by any remark of my own, but, with all due deference to your opinion, I think I know Henry better, and being of a very humble disposition, I do really believe that he will some day condescend to ask you to share his brilliant fortune."

"You are laughing at me," returned Miss Mowbray, "but it is that very humility that appertains to Henry's character, which, if I mistake not, will effectually prevent him proposing for my hand."

"It may for a time," continued Mrs. Belmont, "but love, all potent love will break the spell that enchains him, and then I shall have to wish you joy as Mrs. Fergusson—he loves you, Fanny, I am convinced of it."

"I think he does," replied the young lady modestly, "though nought but his actions have ever given me reason to think so."

"And you return his affection?" said Mrs. Belmont.

"Of that I am not quite so sure," said Miss Mowbray, laughing, "so I think it had better remain for the present an open question, at least, until the party most interested thinks proper to propose it."

"Nay, Fanny," replied Mrs. Belmont, "that is scarcely fair. Nothing would please me more than to see you united to Henry. I fully believe you to be worthy of each other, and if he has but little worldly property, you have enough for both. I well know, dear Fanny, that all your desires are bounded by your own income, indeed, one half of it is scarcely expended on yourself."

In such conversation as the above the two ladies passed the evening, little dreaming that Henry was the inhabitant of a dreary prison. Miss Mowbray, it is true, retired to rest with that uneasy foreboding which frequently precedes misfortune, but Mrs. Belmont, gay and light-hearted, endeavoured to laugh away her fears, and promised the ensuing morning to call upon the young artist in order to inquire after his welfare.

CHAPTER XXI.

"Across the waves, away and far,
My spirit turns to thee;
I love thee as men love a star,
The brightest where a thousand are,
Sadly and silently."

WITH a sad and heavy heart, Clara returned once more to her irksome duties—how irksome, none may tell, save those who have been similarly engaged. Her employment had not even the poor recommendation of withdrawing her thoughts from the painful solicitude that oppressed her. Worn down with sorrows and anxieties that encompassed her on every side, in vain she essayed to fix her thoughts on the papers that were spread before her; she copied them, as it were mechanically, without once heeding the contents. Mrs. Mortimer prided herself as being a learned lady, and most of her works were dry dissertations on subjects of little or no interest to the general reader, and of much that she was obliged daily to copy, Clara was totally ignorant, which rendered her task wearying in the extreme. Still she felt the value of a comfortable and peaceful home too much to be willing easily or thoughtlessly to resign it. In the house of Mrs. Mortimer she was surrounded by every comfort, nay, even the luxuries of life were in a measure supplied. Treated in every respect as an equal by the lady, nothing that could lead to hurt the dignity of her mind, or induce her to feel herself a dependent even occurred. In the little household there were times, too, when, in the company of Mrs. Mortimer and in the rich and versatile power of her conversation, she was charmed even into forgetfulness of her sorrows. And the thought naturally occurred that if she voluntarily quitted her present employment (harassing though it was) it might be long before she could obtain the means of procuring an honest livelihood without bartering what she so dearly prized her independence. There are, unfortunately, so few means by which a young person who has been respectably educated can obtain a livelihood without becoming entirely a menial, or being utterly deprived of her self-respect, and that humble but honest independence every right-minded individual is most anxious to retain; and the few, the very few avocations that are open to young females, are without exception the most fatiguing both to body and mind, and at the same time most wretchedly paid. How often, in our walks, is it our painful lot to meet the pale face and attenuated form of the milliner's apprentice, wending her way to her day's toil, casting ever and anon a wistful glance towards the mail coach which comes dashing into London at the very hour she daily passes through the city, perhaps awakening in her mind bright visions of green fields and sunny spots that linger warm and fresh in her memory still, spite the thousand ills she is hourly exposed to. When we reflect how easily the young mind is crushed and the spirit broken, and enfeebled for ever, how painful and humiliating it is to know that youth, which should be a time of joy and sunshine, is rendered to these unfortunates a sad and dreary state of existence. At another opportunity we may, perhaps, endeavour to point out the cause of so much misery, and likewise say a word or two concerning the mode of alleviating it; at present our space compels us to keep to the interest of our tale, with the characters of which, we hope, we have succeeded in interesting the reader. The unrivalled Poet Moore might well sing—

> "There's nothing half so sweet in life
> As love's young dream!"

Yet this very bliss, that creates an elysium in the hearts of the loving and the loved, is turned to gall and bitterness when a gulf is fixed between the hearts which burn to meet. Eliza loved with all the intenseness of a first, fond, passionate devotion. Sweet, indeed, would she have deemed the humblest lot, if shared by him to whom she had yielded her pure virgin affections. The love that she so closely cherished in her young heart's core would, under other circumstances, have cast a lustre—a dazzling brightness around her path, cheered with his sustaining smile; blest with his endearing tenderness, nought would have possessed the power to harm her. Even now, to see him—to hear his voice—to listen as one entranced, while he gave utterance, in his own peculiar, loud, musical strains, to the whispered words of love, was a bliss too dear and sacred to be lightly parted with; and yet she felt the time was fast approaching when she must renounce for ever that dear and precious delight—must tread no more the flowery paths of love, but henceforth be a lone wanderer on life's thorny track. Yet, a species of infatuation seemed to enchain her soul, and prevented her declaring to Walter the cold truth, that they must meet no more; she could not even acquaint him with her knowledge of his unkindness to Lucy; no, she loved him in spite of all, and could not break to him a word that was calculated to cast a shadow on his happiness. They met, night by night, each time with renewed tenderness, to part with livelier regret. One evening, unusually dull and gloomy for the season, they wandered, side by side, their hearts closely linked to each other—their every thought absorbed in present happiness—happiness too deep and thoughtful to admit of converse. Clara clung to Walter as her heart's best treasure, while he evidently warmly reciprocated her affection.

"Clara," articulated the young man, in his soft melodious voice.

THE ARREST OF HENRY FERGUSON FOR DEBT.

She started, for silence had for some moments reigned supreme, and then turned her eyes, beaming with tenderness, on his face.

"I am so well convinced of your love," he continued, "that I do not fear to tell you that my father has designed a marriage for me with one who, in a worldly point of view, may be considered a desirable match; so strongly, dearest, has he urged me on this subject, that I have not at present dared to impart to him the state of my feelings towards yourself."

He paused an instant, but Clara made no reply, and he again went on.

"I am assured, my love, that this intelligence will give rise to no anxious or jealous feelings in your heart. You know my heart too well ever to fear a rival there; our love, dearest, is not love of yesterday, neither is it possible that either of us could be brought to doubt the faith or purity of the other."

"It is true, dear Walter," murmured Clara, "and yet my heart would never permit me to teach you to act disobediently towards your parent; rather, ten thousand times rather would I resign all pretensions to your hand, but to cease to love you were impossible."

"Time, dear Clara, I feel assured, will remove all obstacles; till then, all I ask of you, is, in silence to love me—to turn a deaf ear to aught that my enemies may perchance urge against me, and believe I could never offer to your acceptance a heart that was sullied by crime, or that had ever designed a thought injurious to the repose of another."

Clara listened as he spoke, and blessed the words as they broke upon the stillness of the night, though at a loss to reconcile them with his apparent unkindness to Lucy. Yet love is so blind to the unworthiness of the object of its attachment, that Clara began to regard her lover as more sinned against than sinning.

"Dear, generous Walter," was the inward exclamation, when, seated in her own room, she had leisure to think over their last interview; "how open, how noble has been thy conduct towards myself, and how little thou dreamest thou art nourishing in thy bosom the love that is destined to destroy thee. Alas, my brother, I shall indeed revenge thy sorrows, but it will be at the cost not only of my own happiness, but of my life itself."

A week elapsed after this interview, during which the lovers met as usual, not even the inclemency of the weather could keep them asunder—wrapped in a dark mantle, Clara fearlessly defied the storm. One evening, more tempestuous than she had hitherto encountered, Clara was preparing to start for her usual visiting place, when a servant entered with a letter, the writing of which she instantly recognised as her lover's. Her heart instantly foreboded some calamity, and tearing it open with a palpitating bosom, she read the contents; it was short, but written in the most affectionate terms, expressive of the bitter disappointment he experienced in being forced to absent himself from her side; but his father had within the last hour been seized with a fit of apoplexy; and mournful as he was to relinquish for a time her endearing society, he could not tear himself from the sick couch of his parent. Clara sought not to restrain the tears that gushed in torrents from her eyes, as she perused this epistle.

"Dear Walter," she murmured, "my heart forebodes we shall never meet again; and, alas! it were better so. On peril's brink we have hitherto met, to solace ourselves in the indulgence of a fatal passion which has been nursed in sorrow, silence, shame—a passion on my part without hope or plea, save the momentary gratification, sweet and fatal, of listening to the melody of thy voice, and basking in the sunshine of thy smile. Better, far better will it be that we meet no more."

Thoughts sad and painful banished sleep from the pillow of Clara, and she arose in the morning anxious and thoughtful; she was seated at her solitary breakfast, inwardly combating her desire once more to see her lover, and her half formed resolution to quit for ever scenes that were too dangerous and too dear, when she was surprised by the unlooked-for entrance of Mrs. Mortimer. Her face was pale, even horridly white, and her brow sad and contracted, her lips firmly compressed, and altogether she had the appearance of being the bearer of some terrible calamity. Clara trembled in every limb as she rose to receive her, fearing that she had discovered her attachment to her nephew, and was come to upbraid her with her deceit. Mrs. Mortimer, apparently without the power of speaking, motioned her to resume her seat, and when Clara mechanically obeyed, thrice she essayed to speak before she gave utterance to what she wished to say.

"I have received the most distressing intelligence," she said at length: "my poor hus——," then checking herself, she continued, "my poor brother, from whom I have been so long estranged, is ill, on the point even of death. I must hasten to him instantly."

"Sir Richard Eardley," replied Clara, greatly relieved, and scarcely knowing what she said, "was attacked last evening with a fit of apoplexy, which may well give rise to the greatest anxiety on his account; therefore, dear madam, I beseech of you lose no time in hastening to his side. I will carefully attend to every arrangement in your absence."

"Thank you, my dear," replied Mrs. Mortimer, "that is exactly what I wished to ask of you;" but she added, suddenly recollecting herself, "how came you aware of my brother's illness. I have myself but this moment received the distressing intelligence?"

Clara's cheek at these words would have matched with the deepest rose. Yet she answered with but little embarrassment, for to her mind truth was beyond all price.

"I learnt it, madam, from your nephew, Mr. Walter Eardley."

Mrs. Mortimer regarded her for a moment with an earnest and searching expression of countenance, but Clara shrank not from her gaze, as she inquired—

"Are you well assured, Miss Wilmot, that your communicant was not the elder brother, Richard?"

"Oh, yes, dear madam. I am confident it was Walter who conveyed to me the knowledge of his father's illness; his brother Richard I have never even seen, much less spoken, or otherwise communicated with him."

"I believe you," replied the lady affectionately, "and the time is now come when I may tell you that I have long since obtained a knowledge of the affection that exists between you and my nephews, though till this moment I knew not which you favoured. I love and respect you, dear Clara, and will use any influence that may revert to me (supposing Sir Richard does not survive his illness) to forward a marriage between yourself and my nephew Walter. Now, dear Clara, farewell; make yourself happy and comfortable in my absence, which will not, I dare say, extend over many days."

So saying Mrs. Mortimer affectionately embraced the weeping Clara, and left her overwhelmed by her kindness and generosity.

CHAPTER XXII.

"I joy that far from foes I wander,
    Where their shafts can pierce me more,
Yet grieve that woman's heart grows fonder
    When her dream of love is o'er.

Still, ere far from all I treasured,
    Ere I bid a last adieu,
Ere my days of pain are measured,
    Take the song that's still thy due."

LUCY drooped perceptibly day by day; her spirit was crushed and broken, and not even the smiling healthful face of her child could win her soul from the sorrow over which she constantly brooded. She had so garnered up and centered her affections on Walter Eardley, that the knowledge she was no longer dear to his heart, affected her most powerfully.

"Oh! that I had died before I made the terrible discovery that I was no longer cared for by him. Death would then have been a mercy," she exclaimed in the bitterness of her soul, while Jane was endeavouring to offer consolation to her wounded spirit.

For a long time she had fondly cherished the hope of a reconciliation, but as days and weeks wore on, and brought with them no tidings of her lover, she became reluctantly convinced of the fallacy of encouraging such a hope. Still she constantly sought news of Walter from every available source ; and at length learnt with utter despair that he was about to be married to Ada Herbert. In vain her sister sought to sustain and cheer her mind ; she resolutely refused to be comforted, abandoning herself to the most violent sorrow.

"Oh, that I could still this throbbing, aching heart !" she exclaimed in the bitterness of her spirit—

> "But soon shall its vital heat be o'er—
> These throbbing pulses throb no more."

"I shall at length find rest and peace in the silent grave."

These words were accompanied by a shower of tears that afforded some little relief to her aching heart. From this time, a deep and settled melancholy took possession of her mind ; she would frequently wander forth after the moon had risen, and all things were hushed in the stillness of the eve. Jane vainly attempted to dissuade her from exposing herself to the cool night air, which must necessarily be productive of bad effects upon her delicate frame.

"It matters not," she would reply, "death is the sweetest boon I crave— and yet he appears to fly my presence. He approaches an unwelcome guest to the happy, and summonses them forth to accompany him on their last dark unfathomable voyage ; but he shuns the wretch, who fain his blow would meet, and I am compelled to drag on a weary, miserable existence."

Eardley Hall, we have already remarked, had ever been an object of deep interest to Lucy, and this interest, from a combination of circumstances, had gradually deepened into a feeling of strong superstition. The park which surrounded the venerable building, where she had listened to the music of her lover's voice, and gazed with rapture on his manly form—where he had used every persuasive argument to lure her from the path of duty, and, unhappily, had only too well succeeded. Here she would roam for hours, forgetful of the lapse of time, and apparently living over again in memory scenes and days gone by. Often would she gaze with an earnest, mournful expression upon the turrets of Eardley Hall ; she seemed even to entertain a strong affection for the building. So long as her strength permitted, nothing would prevent Lucy indulging in her nocturnal rambles, let the weather be ever so inclement ; wrapping herself in a large cloak, she would wander forth in the direction of the park, speaking to none whom she might chance to meet ; her footsteps falling so lightly on the earth, and her face, pale and wan, with her large glassy looking eyes, startled the beholder with a feeling of superstitious fear, for her steps gave back so faint an echo that it was scarcely perceptible. Reaching the park, she would remain for hours absorbed in her own ideas, and heeding nought beyond the ancient structure, beneath whose overhanging roof she would stand for shelter, frequently when the storm was howling fiercely around her, and the fine old trees were crackling and bending under the weight and impetuosity of the resistless wind. So long, we have said, as her strength allowed, nothing could deter the unfortunate Lucy from visiting the scene of her former happiness ; but at length the fell disease that was hourly consuming her, made such ravages on her constitution, as to compel her, sore against her will, to remain entirely secluded in her chamber. Jane had a wearying and harassing task to wait upon the invalid, whom sorrow and illness made fretful and peevish in the extreme. Yet Jane permitted none but herself to perform the tender office of nurse to her suffering sister. Gentle and unwearying were her efforts to soothe the tedious hours of sickness, and awaken a hope in the mind of Lucy of meeting hereafter in a fairer land than this.

"Let us, dear Lucy," she whispered, tenderly, "look forward to the joy of meeting again where we shall join those who have gone before—where all sorrow shall for ever be done away."

The soul of Lucy melted to softness at these words, and her eyes were wet with tears, as she replied—

"Oh! Jane, tell me, shall I meet him there? Heaven were not Heaven without him—

> ' Paradise itself were dim,
> And joyless, if not shared with him.'

"Nought, even in Heaven, can I worship above him. For, oh! how wildly I do love him."

But though her lip, fond raver, burned with words of passion, bold, profane—

> "Yet was there light around her brow—
> A holiness within her eyes,
> Which showed, though wandering earthward now,
> Her spirit's home was in the skies."

Jane wept as she thought how different a being her sister might have been but for the frailty and falsehood of her lover—him, upon whom she had lavished her heart's young and prime affections; and she sighed for the falsehood of the sex, at the same moment that her heart swelled proudly as fond memory presented to her the image of Henry; him to whom she had been so long and tenderly attached, and whom she regarded as the very prototype of honour and integrity.

"If all men were like him," thought Jane, what a bright and happy world this might be; though poor in purse, how well, how noble he stands in merit."

"Draw my chair close to the window, dear Jane," said the invalid, "and let me once more look upon scenes that I have fondly loved."

Jane instantly complied, and drawing aside the curtains, they once more gazed upon scenery fair and beautiful at all times, but now rendered doubly so from being bathed in a flood of liquid light—the tall, peaked turret of Eardley Hall, aspiring, as though

> "'Twould touch the Heavens, rose, o'er all,
> And on its summit the white moon
> Rested, as on a pedestal!'"

Lucy gazed in silence from the window for a long, long time; the expression of her countenance, which at first was that of melancholy satisfaction, gradually changed into a sad and gloomy appearance, and tears trickled down her wan and wasted cheeks. Suddenly she motioned her sister to her side.

"Look, dear Jane," she said, pointing from the window, "do you observe a star to the left of the moon, shining unusually large and bright?"

Jane replied in the affirmative.

"I have often fancied," continued the invalid, "that star was the ruler of my destiny. I pleased myself with this fancy long before I left my home; and on the very night I fled with Walter, I well remember that, though the sky was particularly fine and clear, that particular one star alone looked pale and dim. I often saw it afterwards, for I could at one glance single it out from all others, no matter where I was. Of late it has looked paler and paler, as though it were gradually waning away; but to-night, see how full and bright it is."

"It is indeed," replied Jane, "and I trust that we may regard it as a favourable omen."

Lucy shook her head.

"It sparkles with increased and renewed brightness for a short time, and then it will be extinguished for ever. It has marked my wayward course, and we shall sink into oblivion at the same moment."

"Say not so, my sister," replied Jane, affected to tears. "You will be transplanted to a fairer clime. I love to think that when all your sorrows are ended, you will be in the full enjoym ent of sweet and everlasti ng peace."

" Oh ! if I could but see Walter once more," replied the invalid, without heed.ing her sister's last remark, methinks I could die content ; but—but—" and she clasped her attenuated hands before her face to conceal her emotion—" I shall never see him more."

After a painful silence of a few moments, during which Jane respected her sorrow too much to abate it by words, she lifted her face from her hands, and smiling faintly, enquired for her child. Jane hastened to fetch it from the nursery, and shortly returned with the infant, which she placed in the arms of its mother.

"Sweet boy !" exclaimed Lucy, as she pressed it convulsively to her bosom. " I am shortly about to leave thee, but with kind and good friends, love, thou wilt never miss a mother, or need a mother's care. Jane," she continued, turning to her weeping sister, " I bequeath to thee the only legacy I have to leave; receive from my dying hands this parting gift, and promise to resign the charge to none, not even if Walter should ever deem it worth while to claim his child—he is your's, Jane, by the gift of his dying mother—give me your assurance that none shall beguile you of the precious charge."

" I gladly receive the infant from you, my sister," replied Jane, " as the best and dearest treasure that could be bestowed ; he shall share my fortune, be it good or ill, and never will I forget your admonition."

" Dear Jane," said Lucy, with rising emotion, " you have relieved my bosom of the only anxiety that oppressed it." As she spoke, she pressed a fervent kiss upon the brow of her infant, whose round dimpled face, beaming with health and hilarity, offered a mournful contrast to the sunken pallid cheek of its mother.

With ineffable joy, Jane noted from this evening, a calm and more holy feeling diffuse itself over the mind of her beloved sister. She seldom spoke, unless on religious subjects, and even then with evident reluctance ; when asked if she would again wish to see her child, she faintly replied, " No !"

" Are you happy in the prospect of approaching death ?" gently whispered Jane, as she bent over the couch of her sister, whose laboured breathing betokened her time was short.

She paused for a moment, and then bursting into tears, replied—

" I scarcely know, my sister ; there is a dubious joy occasionally breaking o' my spirits, but there are earthly regrets clinging round me still ; my soul at this sad moment most ardently yearns to look upon Walter once more."

Overpowered by the exertion of giving utterance to these words, the unhappy Lucy lay for some time incapable of further speech. After the lapse of half an hour, she again spoke—

" Dear Jane," she said, " all that stood dark and drear before the eye of my strayed soul is passing swiftly by. A light came o'er me like the halo of love, or the first dawn of mercy from above. And Walter—but, alas ! my senses fail—Oh, for one minute, if my prayers prevail—

" If pardoned souls may from that world of bliss,
    Reveal their joy to those they loved in this !"

I'll come to thee in some sweet dream, and tell——Oh, Heaven. I die, dear love ! fare—well ! fare—well !"

Her voice faltered, and Jane had to bend down in order to catch the last few words that fell from the lips of her sister ; as she ceased, her face for an instant lighted up with an intense radiance, which, as it faded away, left her features pale and expressionless. Jane was alarmed, and yet scarcely thinking her spirit had taken its flight, she approached the window and drew aside the curtain, in order to throw more light upon the face of her sister. It was night, and as Jane stood for one brief instant at the window, her eye was attracted by the star that Lucy a few evenings before had called her attention to ; she riveted her gaze momentarily upon it; as she did so, she started with a feeling bordering no alarm, for it suddenly darted rapidly across the sky and disappeared. Her heart beat almost to suffocation, and returning quickly to the couch of her sister, she bent over her with intense anguish. Alas! need the truth be told?—Jane's boding fears were realised. Lucy was dead!

CHAPTER XXIII.

"Oh, too convincing—dangerously dear,
In woman's eye the unanswerable tear;
That weapon of her weakness she can wield
To save, subdue—at once her spear and shield.
Around it virtue ebbs and wisdom errs,
Too fondly gazing on that grief of her's.
What lost a world, and bade a hero fly?
The timid tear in Cleopatra's eye."

FANNY MOWBRAY, the reader is aware, retired to rest with an anxious foreboding as regards Harry Fergusson, which was by no means lessened, when on the following morning Mrs. Belmont received a second letter from him, stating that he was obliged suddenly to leave town for a short time, and though most desirous personally to bid them adieu, the nature of his business required him to make use of no delay beyond what sufficed to prepare him for his departure. This letter, which was couched in the warmest, and at the same time most respectful terms, concluded by assuring both ladies of the deep and grateful sense he entertained of their repeated and (on his part) unmerited acts of kindness, which had been showered upon him day by day.

"This is very mortifying," said Miss Mowbray, as she turned the letter over and over, carefully scrutinizing each word, as if to find therein a double meaning.

"It is indeed mortifying, my dear," replied Mrs. Belmont, " and somewhat strange likewise, when the letter of this morning is coupled with the plea of indisposition, which deprived us of his company last evening."

"I am really disposed to be uncharitable for once," said Miss Mowbray, slightly compressing her beautiful lips, and feel strongly tempted to assert that Harry's illness and subsequent sudden absence from home, is nothing more than an excuse to avoid our society.

"Oh fie, Fanny," replied Mrs. Belmont. " I did not think it possible that you could be so unjust. Henry has ever manifested the greatest pleasure in our company, has been most anxious to please and render himself agreeable, and——"

"I know all that," replied Miss Mowbray, with a little show of petulance, " and yet, as I said before, I will venture to assert that Harry, at this precise moment, is no more out of London than I am. Were either of us disposed to pay a visit to the city, we should find him in quiet possession of his lodgings, employing himself perchance on some fresh effort of his genius."

"Well, Fanny," replied Mrs. Belmont, as if suddenly struck with an idea, " that is easily ascertained. You have awakened my curiosity, and I am resolved this very morning to satisfy it; but I am convinced you are wronging Henry by your unjust suspicions."

"You intend, then," said Miss Mowbray, catching at the ray of hope that opened before her, " to call upon Mr. Fergusson?"

"Most decidedly," returned Mrs. Belmont, " have you any objection to accompany me?"

Miss Mowbray replied in the affirmative, and shortly after breakfast they equipped themselves for the walk. Arriving at Henry's lodgings, they discovered he was,

indeed, from home.   And on interrogating the domestics, found no difficulty in
ascertaining the cause.   Grieved and vexed beyond measure, they instantly
called a coach, and drove to the place of his confinement.

"I am surprised," said Mrs. Belmont, as they were proceeding to the spot
"that Henry should have conceived it necessary to conceal his difficulties from
those whom he must have known were his true and sincere friends."

"I feel that I have wronged him," replied Miss Mowbray, " and, therefore,
owe him some atonement; and his having concealed his distress from us, has
pushed him up the step or two he had lost in the ladder of my good graces; I
perceive in the part he has acted such true delicacy and innate refinement, that
I admire and revere him far more than I have ever done before."

"You speak warmly, dear Fanny," returned Mrs. Belmont; " and, as I have
said before, I know of no two persons more deserving of each other than yourself and Henry, and my heart assures me that the present crisis is favourable
to your happiness."

"We shall see," replied Miss Mowbray; "I begin to think that Henry has
been backward in declaring his affection for me, on account of the limited
nature of his circumstances.   I have wealth enough for both, therefore that need
no longer be an impediment to our happiness."

"You say truth, my love," said Mrs. Belmont, "and be advised by me,
Fanny, and allow no false delicacy to stand in the way of your mutual happiness.
But I perceive we have arrived at our destination."

Alighting at the prison gates, they were politely received by one of the officers,
and enquiring into the nature of Henry's pecuniary embarrassment, they learnt
that, beside the amount of his original arrest, detainers from other creditors
were lodged against him to a considerable amount.   Every farthing he owed,
together with all expenses, was immediately discharged on the spot by Miss
Mowbray, who, from motives of delicacy, declined making her presence known
to Henry till every arrangement was completed. When all was discharged, Henry
was informed that two ladies desired to see him.   His heart instantly warned
him whom to expect, and, overwhelmed with embarrassment and confusion,
he presented himself before them.   Astonishment chained his tongue, when he
learnt, during his progress to the apartment in which the ladies waited his
arrival, that he was free to quit those hated walls.   Miss Mowbray was the first
to greet him on his entrance.   Rising and placing her arm within his own, she
urged him towards the door.

"Come, Henry," she whispered, let us hasten from this spot; I grieve, indeed,
that you should have been subjected to this temporary inconvenience; why did
you not communicate with me?"

There was an unusual tenderness in the tones of her voice that thrilled upon
the heart of Henry, yet he could not trust himself to reply, neither did he venture
to look upon her face, till he found himself seated opposite to her in the coach
that had brought them hither.   Then, as he glanced for the first time upon her
speaking countenance, he perceived that her eyes were dimmed with tears—tears
called forth by him, and on his account alone.   If before his heart had melted at
her kindness, it now swelled with the fondest and proudest devotion; and he felt
as though he could—

> At her feet in worship thrown,
> Proffer his soul, through life her own."

"Fanny!" he exclaimed, as he took her small white hand between his own,
but she answered not.   "Dearest Fanny!"

She raised her eyes, her only answer there; he carried the hand he had
imprisoned in his own, respectfully and passionately to his lips.

> "Yet even Jano might sure forgive the bliss
> That asked from form a joy no more than this."

Sweet, unutterably sweet is liberty !   Henry had scarcely been incarcerated two
days, and yet it had seemed a month in duration; he had felt choked while he

breathed the air of confinement—now how highly his pulses beat—how glad and blithesome did the blood appear to course through his veins. He felt as though he were intoxicated with joy. How gay the streets seemed; every one seemed happy; and oh! how sincerely he pitied the poor prisoners whom he left behind him in the gaol, and how heartily he wished for riches, that he might be enabled

HENRY FERGUSSON'S TETE-A-TETE WITH MISS MOWBRAY—THE PLEDGE.

to let all the poor captives free. How large and feeling sorrow makes the heart of man; a trifling participation in the evils of others arouses all his sympathy on their behalf! He knows at once the hardship of their lot, and if he be not utterly selfish, would free them from it. The recollection of the many sorrowful hearts he left behind him, was the only bitter drop in his cup of happiness. No wonder, then, that while he rejoiced in his recovered liberty, he felt deeply grateful to her who had come, a welcome minister of mercy, and set him free.   Miss Mowbray had never looked to him one half so lovely as now; the tears that dimmed her eyes, to his mind, were purer, richer than the rarest diamonds, and enshrined in his heart for ever; her hand was still fondly retained in his own, and ever and anon pressed warmly to his lips.   Oh, that was a sweet and happy drive to two of the party, at least.   All doubts were removed from the mind of Miss Mowbray, and she revelled in the belief that she was fondly loved by Henry, Arrived at the elegant and commodious mansion of Mrs. Belmont, where wealth and luxury held undivided sway, Henry's gratitude found vent in words, though the emotions of his bosom half choked his utterance.   At this juncture something called Mrs. Belmont from the room, and Henry finding himself alone with Miss Mowbray, warmly expressed to her his grateful remembrance of her kindness.

"Speak not of gratitude to me, dear Henry," replied the young lady, with unaffected gracefulness.   "You know well my sentiments regarding wealth and poverty; those whom chance, which seldom determines right, has blest with riches, should use it for the benefit of others, who, probably far more deserving, are yet, through adverse circumstances, plunged into poverty and sorrow; regard, I beseech you, in this light the little circumstance that has occurred to-day, and then dismiss it entirely from your memory."

"Ah, that would indeed be impossible, unless I were the veriest ingrate that ever existed, dearest Miss Mowbray.   I honour and admire your noble principles as much as I love and respect yourself."

The two were seated side by side, and no wonder that, carried away by the enthusiasm of his feelings, the hand of Henry should have sought that of Miss Mowbray, which was carried again and again to his lips.   The soft yielding palm trembled perceptibly in his own, but Fanny made no attempt to withdraw it from his embrace.

"Henry," began Miss Mowbray, making an effort to speak with composure.

"Yes, love," replied Henry, gazing rapturously on her beaming countenance, which crimsoned beneath his ardent gaze, while her eyes sank modestly to the ground, and Henry was bold enough to snatch a kiss from her ruby lips.

Alas! poor Jane, thou wert at that moment totally forgotten; every thought and hope was given to the fair and gentle girl at his side.   After a silence of a few minutes, during which the arm of Henry had stolen unconsciously round the waist of his companion, and Henry had pressed her warmly to his bosom, Fanny raised her eyes, overflowing with tears of joy, and fixed them on his face, while she whispered—

"And you love me, Henry?"

"Love you!" he replied, " aye, dearer—far dearer than my very life; but dare I hope that such a feeling can be reciprocated by one in every respect so much my superior?"

"Henry," replied Miss Mowbray, "were the universe my own, and you the lowliest person that ever trod this earth, I would freely, gladly resign all to share your humble fortune; proud and noble would I deem the destiny that united me to you; let us then, love," she continued, with increasing animation, "from this moment lay aside all scruples, that I am aware are even now existing in your sensitive imagination; all mine is thine; receive it freely, as, had our situations been reversed, I am certain you would have bestowed."

"I am so utterly unworthy," began Henry.

"Hush, dearest," she interrupted, playfully placing her hand over his mouth, "not a word; where true love exists, such thoughts should never enter."

"Enough," replied Henry, fondly kissing her glowing cheek, "I will not wound your generous spirit, or give you a moment's uneasiness by again reverting to this subject, in reward for which, dear Fanny, I claim as a pledge of our future happiness one kiss from your dear lips.   You will not," he added, half reproachfully, "deny me this slight boon?"

The kiss was given, and rapturously received, and an hour of unmitigated happiness passed quickly by, which was suddenly interrupted by the return of Mrs. Belmont, whom Henry hastened to inform of the attachment that existed between himself and her young friend, which the reader has already anticipated met with her cordial approval. Thus ended this, to Henry, eventful day. How very little had he anticipated when he arose that morning, that he should so suddenly have broken his plighted faith to Jane, or given the heart that was so lately all her own into the keeping of another; but so it was, and in like manner such things daily and hourly occur. Man is most frequently a creature of circumstances, tossed about on the waves of life at the will of the combining elements—sometimes on the point of sinking in despair, but soon, "high o'er pleasure's surge, he mounts again." Sometimes indeed, in the pause " 'twixt joy and joy," he may be like a ship between two waves at sea, but there will come moments of gloom, when even pleasures pall, and he again yields himself a willing victim to its conflicting elements.

CHAPTER XXIV.

"This thought it was that came to shed
    O'er rapture's hours its worst alloys,
And close as shade with sunshine wed
    Its sadness with my happiest joys."

THE proper development of our narrative requires us at this time to introduce the reader into the lordly abode of Sir Richard Eardley. On a luxurious couch reclines the baronet, struck down in the prime of life, and in the full enjoyment of wealth and happiness; his whole appearance betokens the stupor which in cases of apoplexy frequently precedes dissolution. Kneeling by his couch, her head buried in the rich folds of damask, is Mrs. Mortimer; the smothered sobs which occasionally escaped her, gave evidence of the deep intensity of her feelings. On the opposite side of the bed are Sir Richard's two sons, watching in painful silence the last moments of their parent. A sad but sacred duty; and lost indeed must be the child who would shrink from performing it. A nurse and two physicians complete the occupants of that still chamber. Hope has entirely fled from the hearts of all, and they are waiting in mute despair the last sad moments of shadowing gloom, when the father and the friend shall be snatched away; he is even now lingering on the confines of eternity—the bow is bent, and the arrow is made ready which, with unerring aim, will fly quivering to his very heartstrings. And yet he sleeps on, apparently unconscious of his danger—heeding not the tender relatives who are gathered round his couch.

"Richard—dear Richard!" gently whispered Mrs. Mortimer, as she bent in anguish over the dying man.

But he heard her not; and dropping her head between her open hands, she murmured, half inaudibly—

"Oh, that he might recover sensibility, if only for one moment."

"It is a vain hope, madam," replied the physician, who stood by her side, and appeared deeply to commiserate her agonized feelings. "It should be some consolation to know that he is entirely free from suffering."

"It is—it is," she replied, "and yet the purest of us have sins we would fain see cancelled before we quit this world to enter upon another, and the knowledge that he suffered acute pain, would be more than atoned for by the certainty that he was enabled to seek forgiveness from that source which is never withheld from the truly penitent."

All felt that she spoke truth, and none ventured to reply. The physician would occasionally approach the bed, and place his fingers warm with life and health upon the charming wrist of the invalid, whose feeble pulse told too clearly how fast his end approached. An hour drew its slow length along, an hour of anxious suspense. Alas! how differently passed this self-same hour with Fanny Mowbray and Henry Fergusson—it was the very one we have recorded as having witnessed their confession of mutual attachment. And at the very moment when they were yielding themselves to the full enjoyment of the present, the occupants of the sick chamber became sensible that him over whom they had kept such sad and silent watch, no longer needed their fostering care—his spirit had returned to God who gave it. The agony of Mrs. Mortimer, when first convinced that Sir Richard was, indeed, no longer an inhabitant of earth, burst forth in smothered sobs and groans; with gentle force the two young men withdrew her from the room, and by dint of the kindest words, and gentlest efforts, at length succeeded in subduing the violence of her grief and inducing her to seek what she evidently so much needed, repose. A week passed in preparation for the interment of Sir Richard, which was conducted with unusual pomp and magnificence; his two sons and Mrs. Mortimer were the only true mourners, for the deceased baronet was of too proud and haughty a temperament to have secured any friends beyond his own immediate relatives. And as far as his youngest son was concerned, it was at least a question whether he most grieved for the unexpected death of his father, or rejoiced in the emancipation it offered him from his anticipated marriage with Ada Herbert. A marriage he had ever regarded with the utmost abhorrence. And he now determined at once to release himself from his engagement with her, for on the opening of his father's will he learnt to his great joy that he was bequeathed an annuity every way sufficient to supply all his wants. He retired to rest rejoicing in his freedom of choice; and remembering the long tried love of Lucy, and the fair face of his boy, who for the first time had made him a father, he resolved to do her the justice of making her his wife. He felt convinced that at his intercession she would pardon all the past, and once more bless him with her love. So happy and pleased he felt at having determined for once to act generously and honourable, that for awhile his pleasurable sensation banished sleep from his pillow, his busy wandering mind refused to rest, but looking forward into the dark impenetrable future, pictured days of happiness and joy, when himself and Lucy should be surrounded by sons and daughters, who would sooth their declining years, and be unto them a blessing. On the morrow he had resolved to see Lucy;—he had not written to apprise her of his visit. No: he would present himself before her wholly unexpected, he would throw himself at her feet, and there plead for forgiveness, while, at the same time, he unfolded his hopes and wishes for the future. The remembrance of his unkindness towards her had, ever since their separation, entirely poisoned his happiness; the thought of her pallid cheek, and sorrowful brow, had come to shed o'er every hour its sad alloy; but now he fondly hoped again to see the bloom return to her cheek, and the lustre to her eye, erst so pure and bright. Wrapt in these thoughts, which at length took the shape of dreams, Walter sunk into a soft and peaceful slumber, such as he had not known for many long weary months. He had retired early, and had not slept long before he was awakened by something apparently having startled him, and on opening his eyes, before even he was thoroughly awake, he saw, or thought he saw, the dim shadowy outline of the well known form of Lucy, who, standing in a pensive attitude by the side of the bed, was gazing earnestly and reproachfully on his countenance. She was altered, sadly altered since they last parted: her figure was attenuated in the extreme, and her face, pale as ashes, even wore the leaden hue of death. Consternation chained his tongue, and deprived him of all power of action; his breath came thick and short, and his heart seemed almost to cease its wonted action. He passed his hand across his eyes, in order if possible to clear his vision, and when he again looked upon the spot where he had seen the form of Lucy, she was gone. In vain he endeavoured to attribute what he had seen to the vivid effect of a dream, but it had appeared too palpably before his sight, plainly visible even amid the surrounding darkness; and rising from the bed he approached the window, and drawing aside the curtains, looked out upon the night. The moon was shining soft and fair, and surrounded on all sides by countless stars, that studded, like rare jewels, the dark blue sky. It was the very moment that Jane Clarence was similarly occupied, and though miles asunder, their thoughts were united; for Jane's had flown to the betrayer of her sister, and Walter, connecting Jane with Lucy, the image of her filled his mind. Suddenly, while standing at the window, he was startled by the no means unusual phenomenon of a star, that for a brief instance traversed the sky with the rapidity of lightning, and then as quickly disappeared. The young man shuddered, though he knew not why; he had often before witnessed what is termed the falling of stars, but never had it affected him like this. He absolutely felt sick and faint, and turning from the window with trembling hands, ignited his lamp, which, having carefully trimmed, he placed it by the bed side, and once more endeavoured to compose himself to sleep. But an undefinable feeling of terror filled his mind. He was vexed beyond measure with himself for giving way to such glaring forebodings as now flitted across his breast, and yet he could not cast them from him in a vague manner. He connected the falling star with the form of Lucy, which he had so plainly seen as to note even the expression of her countenance. And yet he could not perceive any reasonable manner in which they might be connected. After tossing about the greater part of the night in a state of restlessness and uneasiness, he at length fell asleep, and when he again opened his eyes the broad warm rays of the sun shed their cheering brightness into the room, and filled his heart with renewed hope.

"What an ass I must have been!" was his inward exclamation, "to allow a dream (for it was nothing more) so powerfully to affect my mind. I should blush to own even to Lucy what an egregious fool I have been."

It is surprising, indeed, what an influence the sun possesses over us mortals; it beguiles us of many cares, and sheds a lustre even on our darkest sorrows. What a dull, gloomy world this would be, were it not for its reviving rays; how dark and sad would be our destiny without it. Had not Walter, when he rose this morning, been greeted with the warmth and cheering influence of the sun, he would most undoubtedly have retained a far more unfavourable impression of the events, that had so alarmed his imagination during the night. As it was, he felt blithe and gay, and prepared for his journey with a light and gladsome heart, without the least foreboding of ill. Arrived at the little village, he wended his way once more towards the neighbourhood of Eardley Hall. Stopping for one moment to gaze with family pride upon the ancient building, he crossed the park, and proceeded towards the more humble abode of Lucy. The blinds in front of the villa were all close drawn, but then the sun shone so full and warm upon the windows, that it was by no means surprising the inhabitants should wish to exclude its searching rays. Walter hastened up the steps, and knocking at the well-known door, inquired in the first place for Jane, thinking to learn from her the reception he might expect from her sister. He was instantly shown, unannounced, into the parlour, where Jane was seated, occupied in amusing a healthful beauteous boy, whom he instantly recognised as his own, and with parental tenderness stretched out his arms to receive him, but the boy turned aside his head, and clung to the neck of Jane with convulsive tenderness. Till this moment the entrance of Walter had been so sudden that Jane had not recognised him, and now that she did so, she uttered a cry of mingled pain and astonishment.

"Do not be offended at my intrusion. I beseech of you, Miss Clarence," said Walter, in the soft persuasive tones he knew so well how to assume.

"Quit this house instantly," replied Jane, her gentle bosom roused to anger and resentment.

"Not till I have seen your sister," returned the young man.

"You surely would not be cruel enough to insist on forcing your company on those who regard you with detestation and abhorrence? Lucy is now, thank God, removed beyond your power farther to harm her, and this dear child, her dying legacy, you cannot, shall not tear from my arms."

"What mean you?" stammered Walter, his limbs trembling and a cold sw(
bedewing his forehead.   "Lucy is——"

"Dead!" replied Jane solemnly.

"God of Heaven!" He staggered back a pace or two, and with difficulty pi
vented himself from falling to the ground, but in a measure recovering his se
possession, he said—"One question more, Miss Clarence, and I will at once i
you of my hateful presence.   When did your sister expire?"

"Last night."

"At what hour?" returned Walter, trembling yet more.

"Within a few minutes of twelve."

At these words Walter was assured that the unfortunate Lucy breathed h
last at the precise moment he saw her by his side, and without breathing
word more he hastened from the house, and ordering post-horses, started i
stantly for town, his heart a prey to the bitterest emotions.

CHAPTER XXV.

" Thou art no more, my bosom's friend—
Here must the sweet delusion end,
That charmed my senses many a year,
Through smiling summers—winters drear;
And yet the dear deceit, so long
Has waked to joy my matin song,
Has bid my tears forget to flow—
Chas'd every pain, sooth'd every woe.
That truth, unwelcome to my ear,
Swells the deep sigh, recalls the tear,
Gives to the sense its keenest smart,
Checks the warm pulses of the heart,
Darkens my fate, and steals away
Each gleam of joy thro' life's sad day."

THE illness and subsequent death of Sir Richard Eardley, by separating Clan
from her lover, afforded occasion for a renewal of their epistolary intercourse.
Again was Clara charmed with the deep pathos and warm passionate eloquence
of Walter's letters; his absence was almost atoned for by the interest his
epistles excited in her bosom. She received daily repeated assurances of his
inviolable affection, and while he bitterly lamented the sad cause that detained
him from her side, he at the same time gently hinted a hope, that when they
again met all obstacles to their union would be done away, and he might
openly seek her for his bride. There was much in all this to wound the
sensitive mind of Clara; bitterly did she repent the vow she had once been so
eager to pronounce, and now there was no recall, she much and earnestly wished
she had not given such encouragement to Walter's addresses. Rather more than
a week had elapsed since the death of Sir Richard; Mrs. Mortimer had not yet
returned to her home, and Clara, as usual, was busily engaged in copying the
manuscript which had been left for her occupation, when she was surprised by
the unlooked-for entrance of her lover; so engrossed was she with her labours,
that she was not aware of his presence till he breathed her name in his own
well-known musical voice. Springing from her seat, the next moment she was
fondly clasped to his bosom.

" And, my own Clara, my dear noble girl, now I hope to make you amends
for all the anxiety you have suffered on my account."

Clara wept, and the fulness of her heart prevented her giving utterance to a
syllable. The young man kindly led her to a chair, and then seating himself by
her side, playfully closed her desk, as he said—

"No longer, my love, shall you be doomed to this fatiguing employment. I come, sweet Clara, to bid you name the day when I may claim you as my own. I have now," he continued, "an income moderate, I own, but which will suffice for all our wants."

Clara answered only by increased tears.

"Dearest!" resumed the young man with evident uneasiness. "Why these tears? It cannot be possible that so short an absence can have estranged your affections."

Clara dashed away the tears, and fixing on him a look of ineffable affection, replied—

"God is my witness that my heart, my entire affections are irrevocably yours, but the time is come when you must know all. Walter, I can never be thine!"

The young man started and turned deadly pale, and in silence looked to her for an explanation. Clara hastened to give it, that she might the sooner relieve herself from the burden of sorrow that oppressed her, therefore making a desperate effort to speak calmly, she thus resumed—

"In spite, Walter, of the duplicity you practised towards me, I love you with the fondest and warmest affection, an affection that approaches even to adoration. When we first met in the vicinity of Eardley Hall, you won from me a confession of attachment, which at your earnest request I consented to conceal from my brother; we met, as you well know, often, and each time with renewed pleasure, though at the same time you were turning the destined wife of my brother from the path of duty."

At these words the young man blushed deeply, and cast his eyes on the ground.

"Your many attractions," continued Clara with more firmness, "fascinated the youthful mind of Lucy, and the result was that she fled from her home, and my poor brother was so devotedly attached to her, that from the very moment he discovered her flight, he gradually drooped and died; what wonder, then, if I, who was doomed to witness the sorrow that consumed him, vowed from that hour to revenge his death by doing my utmost to gain your affections, and then dashing your hopes for ever to the ground. Circumstances have aided me in my purpose, and I shall indeed revenge his death, though probably, most probably, my life will be the forfeit."

She ceased, and the young man raised his eyes, which were flashing with painful excitement, and fixed them on her face as he replied—

"To keep such a vow as that you mention, Clara, would be silly and childish; believe me, it were far more honoured in the breach than in the observance, and if you persist, I cannot do otherwise than believe that you never loved me, but, actuated by a spirit of revenge, have feigned a passion you never felt."

"Could I think," replied Clara impressively, "that such a belief would lessen the pang that I am conscious of inflicting on your bosom, I would not seek to convince you of the injustice that you do me. Your love is to me the sweetest boon of existence, and fain would I consummate your happiness, even at the expense of my own, but it cannot be. Oh, Walter, can you doubt my love for you? Though it may seem madness to speak of love at such a moment as this—

"Yet it is mingled with the vital heat,
That makes my glowing bosom beat."

Nor would I change my cherished sadness for all the world could proffer now of bliss. Alas! the very mirror of despair were sweet to me, if thou wert imaged there."

"I believe you, Clara," replied the young man, his eyes filling with tears; "forgive me, Clara, if, in a moment of anguish, I were led to doubt your affection; but tell me, dearest, is it not possible to set aside that unhappy vow?"

Clara sobbed aloud, as she cast herself once more upon the bosom of him she so fondly loved, but she strove to answer calmly—

"Walter, your own heart must tell you we can never be united.

> 'Between us rolls a gulf, which ever
> Our hearts, that burn to meet, must sever!'"

He clasped her fondly to his heart, as he whispered—

"Suffer, dearest, at least this last embrace before we part for ever. One kiss —one more—another! Oh, adieu!"

> "But still so tightly did she cling to his embrace,
> That his heart heaved beneath her hidden face;
> Her long dark hair hung floating o'er his arms,
> In all the wildness of dishevelled charms.
> Scarce beat that bosom, where his image dwelt
> So full, that feeling seemed almost unfelt.

Again he fondly pressed her cheeks, then tottering to the couch, her gentle form he bore. He

> Felt that for him earth held but her alone,
> Kissed her cold lips,—turned,—alas! was gone."

Gone before Clara had recovered her scattered senses. Then gushed forth the agony of her heart in tears.

> "Large, bright, and fast, unknown to herself they fell,
> Still—still her heart refused that painful word—farewell!"

Now that she felt all joy and hope was over for her in this world, she abandoned herself unrestrainedly to the anguish of her mind. It was utterly impossible to describe the deep intensity of her sorrow; words would but feebly demonstrate the agony that oppressed her; she had for so long a time restrained her sorrow, and held her spirit in bondage, that now she gave her feelings vent, they threatened to overpower her. Suddenly she was surprised by the entrance of Mrs. Mortimer, whom, covered with confusion, she rose to receive.

"Compose yourself, I entreat of you, my poor Clara," said that lady, kindly taking her hand. "I have but this moment parted from my nephew, who has acquainted me with all that passed between you; by his desire I am now here, to soothe, and if possible, cheer your drooping spirits."

The kind words, and still kinder manner of Mrs. Mortimer did much towards composing the mind of Clara, and removing the trace of recent tears from her countenance; she strove to smile as she replied—

"I trust you will not deem me unmindful of your kindness, my dear madam, when I inform you that I must immediately quit your roof; I cannot hope even to gain peace while I remain here."

"Not so, my dear child," returned Mrs. Mortimer, "I hope to keep you with me till I see you united to my nephew."

Clara shook her head as she answered—

"It is impossible, madam. Alas! you know not my unhappy story."

"Nor you mine," replied the lady; "but deception is no longer needful. I am not the aunt, but the mother of Richard and Walter Eardley."

"The mother of Walter!" replied Clara, overwhelmed with astonishment; "as such you have even claimed obedience from me, and," she added, after a moment's hesitation, "you shall have it."

"Thank you, dear Clara," she replied, affectionately embracing her. "All I desire is, that you will encourage a hope that all will eventually end well; both my sons have promised to spend this evening with me; you will meet them, and if all that now seems dubious be now satisfactorily explained, you shall be free to go when and where you choose. Now, my love, you had better retire and endeavour to regain your wonted composure."

Clara instantly hastened to obey, and despite the bitter sorrow that oppressed her, the kindness of Lady Eardley, for such she had avowed herself, caused a gleam of sunshine to break across the darkness of her mind; she looked forward to the evening with a mingled sensation of pain and pleasure; she would once more behold him whom her heart so fondly treasured—again listen to the music

JANE CLARENCE APPRIZES WALTER EARDLEY OF THE DEATH OF LUCY.

of his voice, though for the last time, for she resolved, cost her what it might, to withstand the united persuasions of Walter and his mother. Nothing should deter her from keeping stedfast to the vow, and the only consolation she sought was the hope that she might be able to convince them of the uprightness with which she had acted.

CHAPTER XXVI.

" When the lamp is shattered,
        The light in the dust is dead—
When the cloud is scattered,
        The rainbow's glory is shed ;
When the tube is broken,
        Sweet tones are remembered not.
When the lips have spoken,
        Loved accents are soon forgot.''

So little affection had Walter conceived for Ada Herbert (notwithstanding her rare beauty) that he had not even deemed it worth while to acquaint her with the illness and death of his father, still less the change it had wrought in his own wishes for the future. The public journals first made them acquainted with the decease of Sir Richard Eardley, and Ada's bosom swelled with anger at the coldness of her lover, and she more than once determined to break off the match, but Walter was too fascinating and accomplished a lover to be easily renounced. Preparations, too, had already been made for the important event that was to unite them for life. The wedding dress was purchased, and surveyed by the proud beauty with a beating heart. Bridal presents were already bestowed, and, in short, everything had gone too far to prevent her for a moment seriously resolving to change the course of events. Vexed and indignant beyond expression then was Ada Herbert, at the continued unkindness and neglect of Walter, and for the motives that thus actuated him, she was entirely at a loss. Too proud and angry she felt to seek an explanation of his conduct herself, but her uncle deemed it proper to write to the young man, and inquire if he intended to fulfil his engagement with Ada. Great, indeed, was the surprise of the family, on receiving an immediate reply from Walter, in which he plainly informed Mr. Herbert that he had been urged into the engagement by his late father, whose death having released him from the necessity of continuing it, it was now his intention to give his hand to one who had long held undisturbed possession of his heart. The young man concluded by expressing a hope that Ada might speedily transfer her affections (supposing they had been bestowed upon himself) to one more deserving of the preference than he had ever been. To Mary Herbert was delegated the painful task of breaking the unpleasing intelligence to Ada ; and prepared as she was to witness her anger and disappointment, she had no conception of the lengths to which it might carry her. Every lineament of her fair face displayed the rage that filled her breast ; for a moment she was speechless with passion, but it ultimately found vent in bitter invectives, which she heaped upon the head of her lover. His falsehood she characterised as base and cruel in the extreme, and seizing his letter, she tore it into a thousand pieces, and trampled it under her feet. Mary, who by nature was mild and gentle, was absolutely alarmed at the passion displayed by her cousin, and which she endeavoured to allay by kind and tender sympathy.

"Compose yourself, Ada, I entreat of you," said Mary ; "I can well conceive how wretched his duplicity must make you, who so dearly loved him, but——"

"No, no," interrupted Ada, in a tone of bitterness, " it is impossible to love twice ! I admired Walter—I delighted to think that one, whose fascinating manner elicited the admiration of my own sex, was devoted wholly and exclusively to me ; but I did not love him, even while listening to his flattery, which pleased my vanity, and caused me to exult in his affection. The image of another filled my heart, and I sighed to think that, actuated by pride and anger, I had cast him from me, though even at the moment of doing so, Heaven is my witness I loved him dearly."

Mary turned very pale as her cousin gave utterance to these words, but she offered no reply. The evening of the day on which the conversation occurred, Mary had promised to spend with the sisters of Percy Raymond, who for some weeks past, had paid her marked and exclusive attention, which had filled her mind with the sweet hope that she was beloved by him. Therefore it is needless to say his intentions were even favourably received. Ada's refusal of the young man's address, and expected marriage to Walter, relieved the sensitive heart of Mary of all fear, which she might otherwise have entertained of wounding the feelings of her cousin by herself receiving the attentions of Percy, but now cold doubts and fears began to arise in her mind, and filled her once glad bosom with gloom and despondency. And she repaired to the home of Percy, sad and thoughtful; the young man with the quickness of affection instantly perceived that she was unhappy, and taking advantage of the temporary absence of his sisters, tenderly enquired the cause. Mary paused at the question, but the young man replied—

"You cannot deceive me, Mary; you are unhappy, I am certain, though you desire to conceal from me the cause. It is the more unfortunate, as I was anxious to tell you this evening how dear you have become to my heart."

Mary started at this unlooked for announcement, and faintly uttered the name of her cousin,

"Do not mention her," returned Percy. "It is of you alone, dear Mary, that I wish to speak. Can you—will you receive a declaration of love that was once made to another?"

"Can I?" replied Mary, her eyes filling with tears. "Oh! surely you need not ask; you must long have known how fondly I have treasured your love.— But," she added more seriously, "Percy, listen for one moment to what I have to say."

"Be brief, love, then," he replied, tenderly pressing her hand.

"This very morning," resumed Mary, "I made a painful discovery: it is that my cousin still loves you as warmly as ever, and most bitterly repents having engaged herself to Walter Eardley. One word from you would suffice to place you both on the same footing as formerly."

"That word will never be spoken," replied the young man firmly.

"You once loved her most affectionately," urged Mary.

"Aye; but I do so no longer," replied Percy, firmly. "I love but you. I care not how slightingly some may speak of a second attachment, but I know that the affection I entertain for you is of a dearer, purer, and more exalted character than the love I once felt for Ada."

"And if I reject you?" said Mary, hesitatingly.

"It is utterly impossible I could ever again be fascinated by the charms of Ada."

Mary listened to the tones of his voice; she gazed upon his animated countenance, and was convinced that he spoke truth.

"Dear Percy," she murmured, "I can hold out no longer. I love you, and, with the sanction of my father, will gladly pronounce the word of obedience at the altar.

When Elizabeth and Mary Raymond were informed of what had passed in their absence, their joy was unbounded—their hearts already acknowledged Mary Herbert as their sister, and warm and affectionate was the greeting they bestowed upon the future wife of their beloved and only brother. When they parted for the evening, Percy, who accompanied Mary home, declared to her his intention of calling in the morning and soliciting her hand from Mr. Herbert; but Mary loved and respected her father too highly to permit him to hear for the first time of her engagement from other lips than her own; she did not even allow herself time to lay aside her walking dress before she sought his presence, and timidly but hopefully made known all that had passed between herself and Percy. Mr. Herbert loved his daughter with the concentrated affection a widowed father may be supposed to entertain for an only and dutiful child. He would not, therefore, have slightly withheld his consent from one whom her heart had chosen, even had he not cordially approved ; but this was not the case with Percy Raymond, he knew, and sincerely respected his high moral character, and open, affectionate disposition.   He therefore freely and gladly gave his consent to the affection that existed between them. He regarded it as a far more suitable match for Mary than he had for Ada, as Percy and the former were placed in an equal station of life, and Mary was far more domesticated and retiring in her disposition, and above all, had no prospect of ever inheriting riches.   Consequently, when the young man called on the succeeding morning, he met with a kind and warm reception from Mr. Herbert.   Mary deemed it right early to inform her cousin of the engagement that now existed between herself and Percy, to which Ada manifested a strong dislike.   She assured Mary that she felt it was utterly impossible the young man could so soon and easily transfer his affections, and likewise declared her conviction that he was acting under a desire to vex and annoy herself, to all of which Mary very wisely turned a deaf ear.   Secure in the affections of him she loved, she gave no heed to aught that was urged against him.

CHAPTER XXVII.

" Canst thou forget me ?—I am not relying
    On plighted vows.   Alas ! I know their worth :
Man's faith to woman is a trifle, dying
    Upon the very breath that gave it birth.
But I remember hours of quiet gladness,
    When, if the heart had truth, it spoke it then,
When thoughts would sometimes take a tone of sadness,
    And then unconsciously grow glad again.
                              Canst thou forget them ?"

How often does it occur that in the pleasurable excitement of the evening we are led into the commission of acts, that, in the sober reflection of the morning, we deeply and bitterly deplore?   Thus it was with Henry Fergusson—carried away by the enthusiasm of his feelings, and his deep sense of gratitude to Miss Mowbray, he had broken his long plighted faith to Jane, and became the accepted suitor of another.   A few short months previously he had not believed himself capable of such unkindness to one who so fully relied upon his love ; but it was done—he who had ever abhorred such cruelty in others, had been led to practice it himself.   The evening before, he had parted from Fanny with assurances of inviolable affection, and the image of the ill-used Jane had not once intruded to disturb his peace.   But when he arose in the morning (that season of reflection, when Conscience will make herself heard) sorrowful thoughts pressed heavily on his mind, nor could he bid them thence depart.   So acutely did Henry grieve for his own falsehood to the gentle girl, who reposed such implicit confidence in his affection, that he groaned aloud in the bitterness of his spirit, as he thought upon his unkindness.   He drew the portrait of Jane from his bosom, and bedewed it with his tears.   How difficult—how painful his task, to be the herald of his own sin—to plant a thorn in the breast of one who fondly loved him : a thorn that he well knew would rankle there for ever.   Yet he had now no alternative.   Gratitude, honour, and truth bound him to Miss Mowbray, and all he could do was to write to Jane, informing her of the situation in which adverse circumstances had unhappily placed him.   He knew Jane to be entirely free from all selfish weakness ; he did not, therefore, insult the purity of her mind by words of love, at a time when he was on the point of informing her of his engagement to another, neither did he, as some men most ungenerously have done, throw the blame of his broken faith upon the innocent cause of it.   No ; his letter simply unfolded a plain statement of the circumstances that led to his declaration of love to Miss Mowbray, and besought from her to whom it was addressed a release from the engagement that then existed between them, without which he could not conceive himself free to wed another. And, although his heart throbbed with bitter regret, he gave it no vent in his letter to Jane. Neither did he attempt to exonerate himself, or extenuate his error. Jane little thought, when she received this unhappy letter, how many sorrowful pangs the writing of it cost her lover. So firmly and fully had she relied on his faith, that not even a thought unfavourable to him had ever taken possession of her heart. She loved him, perhaps not with that fond adoration a more ardent disposition might feel, but still with that self-denying truthful tenderness which induced her at all times to make any and every sacrifice for him. He was to her—her breath, her life, and light—

"His name in her ear was ever ringing,
His form to her brain was ever clinging."

And visions of future days, made sweetly blessed by being shared with him, constantly filled her mind. She rejoiced over every little circumstance that contributed to his happiness, and mourned with peculiar bitterness over the lightest sorrow that crossed his path. Jane's cup of sorrow, previous to receiving this unwelcome letter, seemed well-nigh full; she had seen her father and sister laid in the silent grave, and her mother's health now daily declined—indeed she plainly saw that ere long she must also resign this tender relative. One thought alone sustained her drooping spirit, and cheered under this accumulation of sorrow—that thought was of Henry. Jane was expecting daily to hear from him, and hopefully looking for the arrival of a letter; it came at last, and with a lightened heart she hastened to read its contents. Alas! what a terrible revulsion of feeling agitated her bosom; still she manifested no violent sorrow, no turbulent emotion, she was calm, but it was the calmness of despair, she returned to her usual duties, they were many. She did not weep—she did not speak; but day by day and week by week, she walked about like a corpse alive. Her first duty was to answer her lover's letter, which she did, freeing him entirely from herself, and not even so much as hinting at her own sorrow and despair. Her answer was of necessity short, for she had nothing to reproach or to request, and so fondly did she still love him, despite his unkindness, that she sedulously avoided saying aught that might grieve or wound his spirit; still her heart was feminine, and unwittingly a word occasionally fell from her pen, that spoke to the bitterness of her feelings. "Farewell," she said in conclusion—

"I must e'en survive this last adieu,
And bear with life, to love and pray for you."

Many—very many bitter tears did Henry shed over this epistle; now that she was lost to him for ever, he seemed as though he loved her more fondly than before; how gladly would he have undone the events of the last few weeks, but it was impossible, he must forget the gentle girl, whom till now it had been his delight and duty to treasure in his memory. Miss Mowbray, his affianced wife, claimed every thought, and he strove hard to bestow them upon her, but oftentimes, even when in her presence, and he indulged in a tender kiss, the image of Jane would rise before his mind's eye, to rob him of his bliss. Night and morning her portrait was fondly pressed to his lips, and he never failed to breathe a prayer for her happiness. In the meantime, Mrs. Belmont was busily and happily engaged in preparing for the anticipated union. A continental tour was planned by Fanny, and warmly entered into by Henry, who hoped amid other scenes to forget the regrets that still hovered o'er his spirit. Henry had always anticipated humbly walking to the little village church, in the neighbourhood of Eardley Hall, and there plighting his willing faith to Jane. How different was the reality! The ceremony that was to unite him to Miss Mowbray was arranged to take place at St. George's, Hanover-square, and a new and splendid equipage was ordered for the occasion—all the preparations were conducted on a scale of magnificence, he at one time little dreamt of. The bridal morning dawned, soft and beautiful, Henry was to meet his bride for the first time that morning at the church. He was dressed and about to descend the stairs in order to enter the carriage that was waiting to convey him to Hanover-square, when he suddenly recollected that he still wore the portrait of Jane, according to his usual custom, suspended round his neck; he snatched it from his bosom and held it before his eyes, till the tears, which fell thick and fast, dimmed its lustre, then pressing it affectionately to his lips, he cast it into the fire. Ah! how many agonised sensations filled his mind, as he watched the fire curling in wreathing circles round what had been so long and so fondly treasured. He watched it till the last atom had disappeared, and then hastening down the stairs, threw himself into the carriage, and endeavoured to compose his agitated feelings. He so far succeeded, that when he met the affectionate glance of Miss Mowbray, with the exception of being very pale, he gave no sign of recent emotion. The ceremony was quickly concluded, and after partaking of an elegant *dejune*, the happy couple, as the newspaper duly announced, started direct to the continent. Then it was that Henry, alone for the first time with his bride, felt at least a something of satisfaction, as he gazed upon her wan and blushing face, beaming at once with humidity and happiness. He roused himself constantly from his gloomy feelings, and pressing a husband's first kiss upon her cheek, discoursed rapturously on the future; Fanny's soft replies reassured his mind she was now his wife, he had voluntarily made her such, and he inwardly resolved to devote himself wholly and exclusively to her happiness; she had scattered lavish gifts around him, had blessed him with affluence, and bestowed upon him her hand, that others had striven in vain to obtain; in return she asked only for his affection, which honour and gratitude imperatively demanded him to bestow. From that instant then, he determined resolutely to cast the image of Jane from his mind. In another clime, mid other scenes, he might be happy with her who loved and treasured him in her young heart, who called him by the endearing the sacred name of husband, who from that hour was destined to share his joys and sorrows, to bear in all his after life a fond and faithful part.

CHAPTER XXVIII.

Through, through my life's short sunny dream,
    I've floated without pain or care;
Like a light leaf, down pleasure's stream,
    Caught in each sparkling eddy there.
Though never mirth awaked a strain,
That my heart echoed not again,
    Yet have I felt when e'en most gay
Sad thoughts—I know not whence or why,
Suddenly o'er my spirit fly."

IN obedience to the desire of Lady Eardley, Clara, we have already said, sought in the privacy of her own room to compose her agitated feelings. That evening she was to see Walter once more for the last time. Yet there was consolation in the hope that he would pardon her seeming unkindness, and still remember her with love and tenderness. She could have wished that this last interview between herself and Walter had been destined to have no other witness than his mother, whom, for his dear sake, she loved and respected. His brother Richard she had never seen, and therefore felt pained that he was to be present at their last sad parting. As the appointed hour drew near, her heart beat quick with expectation; she scarcely knew whether she felt most happy at the prospect of again seeing him, from whom that morning thought she had parted for ever, or sad to think that this was destined to be the last time she should gaze upon his well known form. As she sat in a pensive attitude, gazing from her window into the garden below, while sad thoughts filled her breast, she was aroused from her reflections by the entrance of Lady Eardley, who was dressed in deep mourning weeds, which well became her handsome, but pallid countenance.

"I have come, my dear Clara," she said, kindly, "to converse with you for a short time."

"It is very kind of you, dear madam," replied Clara.

"I wish, my love, no longer to have any secrets with you," continued the lady, "and I can well conceive that you feel an interest in my short but eventful history."

"I do, indeed, dear madam," returned Clara.

"Then I am anxious to impart it to you, before the arrival of my sons," replied Lady Eardley, "it will save all after explanations, and be far more satisfactory to myself."

Clara, in reply, signified the pleasure it would afford her to listen to the narrative.

"You must know, my love," she commenced, "that I was a younger and portionless daughter, and my father was therefore desirous of seeing me what he called well married, that is, to a man of family and independence. Naturally of a lively turn of mind, no thought of love ever troubled me till I had completed my eighteenth year, at which period it was my misfortune to be introduced, at the house of a friend, to Evereard Tracy—even at this distance of time my voice trembles as I pronounce his name; till that moment my heart had never received even a temporary impression from one of the opposite sex, but almost as soon as I looked upon Evereard, I learnt to love him. From that hour I became an altered being, my wonted gaiety of spirit entirely forsook me, and I would sit for hours at my window, bowered round with leaves, while down my cheek the quick tears ran, for I well knew that my stern father would never consent to my marrying one whom he would proudly deem beneath me. Yet such nobility of soul, such true generosity of spirit characterised Evereard, that he might well have ranked with the proudest and noblest in the land. We met often before he gained courage to tell me how much and fondly he loved me. I trembled while I listened to his declaration, and yet could not conceal from him the sweet satisfaction it afforded me; we mutually plighted our faith, and I lavished upon him that fond affection, life only once may know. Evereard Tracy was the son of a merchant, once wealthy and respected, but through a series of unparalleled misfortunes he was hurled into comparative poverty. This so preyed upon his mind as to cause a fit of illness, which terminated in his premature decease, leaving a widow and orphan daughter totally unprovided for. So circumstanced, Evereard thought it no dishonour to accept a situation of clerk, which was offered him by one of his father's early friends, the emolument arising from which was devoted to providing for his mother and sister; when, therefore, we exchanged vows of attachment, Evereard generously made known to me the limited nature of his circumstances, accompanying it at the same time with an earnest hope that ere long they might be considerably augmented, as he entertained an expectation of being received into the firm as a junior partner. After the lapse of a few short months, Evereard joyfully informed me that the head of the mercantile house in which he was employed was anxious for him to repair instantly to India, on important business, promising as a reward that on his return, he should be immediately received as a partner, on the most advantageous terms. My heart throbbed with sorrow at the prospect of parting from one I held so dear, but Evereard reassured me with the representation that his absence would be short, and when we again met, he should be in a condition to claim me as his sworn bride eternally. Cheered with this sweet prospect, we parted with comparative calmness, promising each other to write often and fully. Alas! we little dreamed how bitter would be our next meeting. Evereard safely arrived at his destination, and my heart began to palpitate with joy at the prospect of a speedy reunion. I cannot, my dear Clara," continued Lady Eardley, " speak of my personal appearance at this period of my life, but my partial friends were too apt to flatter me, and most unhappily I chanced to become acquainted with Sir Richard Eardley, who, pleased with my manners and appearance, a formal offer of marriage shortly followed. Alas! Clara, I cannot tell you the dreadful agony of my mind, when my father bade me prepare for the union, without so much as even consulting me on the subject. In vain I knelt, entreated, implored him not to force me into so hated a marriage. I confessed my love for Evereard, showed him the letters that I had so lately received, all of which breathed the purest and most exalted affection, and, in short, did all in my feeble power to induce him to forego the cruel sentence he had pronounced. But he was inexorable, he bade me instantly to cast all romantic notions from my mind, and prepare for a union with one whose rank and station rendered him worthy of me. Still I remained firm to my plighted faith, resolving to die rather than wed another, till my unfeeling parent threatened the future welfare of Evereard, by insinuating to his employers that he was unworthy of their patronage. Young, and utterly ignorant of the world, I doubted not for a moment that my father could thus entirely ruin my lover's prospects, and plunge not only him, but his mother and sister into the depths of poverty ; then it was that my proud heart melted, and I conceived the generous idea of sacrificing myself to save Evereard, and those who were dear to him. So long did I dwell upon this girlish and romantic notion, that I at length regarded it as a positive duty, and, unmurmuring, gave my hand to Sir Richard ; but even when I knelt with him at the altar my heart, my thoughts, my affections—all, all that was worth having—were given to another. The agony of my mind was almost beyond endurance ; but enough,

"I had not lived till now, could sorrow kill!"

Immediately after the sad, the painful ceremony, we set off for Eardley Hall. So blanched was my cheek, so mournful the expression of my countenance, that even the tenants who came to meet and give us welcome, I could perceive regarded me with sincere commiseration. After a short sojourn we returned to the metropolis. Evereard had by this time arrived home, and hastened to see and claim me for his wife. Alas! I cannot depict the intense agony that was stamped upon his manly brow, when he learnt from my lips that I was the bride of another. Sir Richard surprised us together, tore me with anger from his presence, and the very next day started with me for the continent. Here I firmly did fulfil the duties of a devoted wife, though the darkness of my heart was beyond expression drear, till at length a luring pulse beat beneath my heart, and awakened me to a feeling something akin to joy—

" I knew it could not be my own dull blood,
'Twas like a thought of liquid love,
And hour by hour, day after day,
The wonder could not charm away,
But laid in sleep my wakeful pain,

*   *   *   *   *   *

Until I knew it was a child."

Strange inmate of a living breast, which all that I had undergone of grief and shame, seemed now to atone for—to lull my care to sleep. And soon I cradled my first-born on my bosom, and then came relief in the shape of soothing tears, and a soothing warmth, as the sweet one lay, sucking the sullen milk away. Darkly forward flowed the years from this period, but on them bore another shade of gladness. Yes, Clara, I was blest with two sweet babes, delightful more in my lost soul's abandoned night, than their own country's ships may be, sailing towards mariners wrecked at sea. I did not, I never could love Sir Richard, but still I scrupulously fulfilled all the duties that devolved upon me;

my children were all to me, and I devoted myself to the sweet task of attending upon them, but, alas! my cup of sorrow was not yet full. Evereard so tenderly loved me, that on Sir Richard quitting England he instantly started in search of me. For a long while all attempts on his part to find me out were completely baffled, but fortune at length favoured him. He discovered my retreat, and

CLARA AND LADY EARDLEY.

taking advantage of the temporary absence of Sir Richard, he presented himself before me. Upon the impulse of the moment I uttered a cry of joy, and flung myself on his bosom. At that instant Sir Richard entered. Frantic with passion, he challenged Evereard to fight him on the spot. Alas! with what dreadful horror do I recall that hour? They fought;—Evareard fell. In bitter agony I pressed his bleeding form to my bosom. He died, leaving his kisses yet warm upon my lips. I looked upon him with the anguish of despair, half dreading to behold; but I was calm. I went away, though I was clammy cold, like clay. Alas! Clara, you must believe my heart was stone, for it did not break."

"Dreadful, indeed, must have been your sufferings," said Clara, who, till this moment, had not ventured to intrude upon the narrative by giving utterance to a single word.

"They were—they were," returned Lady Eardley, half choked with rising emotion, "but let me hasten to conlude this painful story.

"After the death of Evereard, I entertained so terrible a feeling of horror at the sight of his murderer, that it was no longer possible for me to reside beneath the same roof with Sir Richard, dreadful as it was to abandon the daily care of my children. I had no alternative but to demand from my husband a formal separation. In vain he besought me to pronounce upon him a milder sentence than constant banishment from my presence; the horror which he inspired in my breast kept me firm to my original intention, and we separated. Here I must do Sir Richard the justice to observe that he voluntarily granted me free permission to see my beloved children as often as I desired, and beyond that he would likewise have made me a handsome settlement, but I proudly rejected his offer. I was naturally fond of study, and I now turned my thoughts in that direction, as the means of providing for my limited wants, and in sonnets, poems, and elegies poured forth the sorrows of my mind; these meeting with a reception beyond even my most sanguine hopes, I was encouraged to proceed, and more abstruse subjects eventually engaged my attention. These studies, my dear Clara, afforded me the sole relief I have ever found from the sorrows that have unceasingly pursued me. Constant application has become necessary to keep my thoughts from preying on my own anguish. Sir Richard is now no more—God rest his soul. My father, too, has long since departed this world, therefore I would desire, as far as possible, to forget the unkindness on his part, which was the cause of all my sorrows. I am thankful," she continued, "that on me alone has all the sorrow fallen. You, dear Clara, I fondly hope ere long to see happily united to my son; I am convinced you love each other, and am truly thankful that his choice has fallen upon one so every way worthy of him. His life has, up to the present moment, been a short sunny dream, through which he has floated without pain or care. Yet, dear Clara, though surrounded by affluence and pleasures that courted his acceptance on every hand, I have repeatedly heard him say that there were moments of shadowy gloom, to which he was liable when even most gay, which came he scarce knew whence or why, and he felt like some lone bird without a mate; thus much of sorrow he inherits from his ill-fated mother, but since he has known and loved you Clara, his spirit has found a glad resting-place on your tender bosom, which I know throbs for him alone; he can repose every care, and forget in your presence every sad thought. Now, Clara, love, for my sake—for all our sakes, you must consent to become his guardian angel—do not wilfully plunge yourself and him into a vortex of sorrow."

"My dear madam," replied Clara, "I confess myself to have been much to blame in pronouncing such a vow as I have recorded, yet having done so, I do not think it possible that aught can induce me to break it."

"Well, we shall see," returned Lady Eardley, kindly; "the hour is now fast approaching when I expect to receive my sons. As you are dressed for the evening, we may as well descend to the drawing-room, where all is in readiness."

Clara willingly assented: she had always liked her companion much when she only regarded her as the aunt of Walter; but now she knew that she stood to him in the near and dear relationship of mother, her sympathy and affection were warmly enlisted on her behalf. How proud and fondly would she have rejoiced to call her mother—a name that, since infancy, had never been upon her lips. A dull and isolated being, what temptations stood in her path to break the vow she had voluntarily pronounced, and which had unhappily resulted in so much misery and sorrow to herself? Yet strong in the principle of honour and integrity, Clara firmly cast the temptation from her. Hard was, indeed, the task required of her to resign so much felicity, and abandon herself to a life of sorrow; but such she determined to do; she conceived herself rightly punished for uttering too rash and inconsiderate a vow of revenge. Henceforth she must pursue an isolated existence, not that, for a moment, Clara contemplated devoting herself to vain regret and fruitless compunction. No! she wisely resolved to seek some useful and honourable employment, by steady perseverance in which she might still become a useful member of society. It might be her delightful duty to bind up some wounded spirits, or sorrowing heart to sing for joy; to administer to the wants of the poor; to whisper words of consolation to the suffering mind; to sooth the bed of the dying invalid, and perchance make his passage to the tomb more soft and pleasant. In such offices as this Clara hoped to find some moments, if not of joy, at least of peacefu serenity; and fired with these hopes, her countenance was no longer sad, but radiant with the peace that filled her heart.

CHAPTER XXVIII.

HENRY FERGUSSON and his young bride proceeded direct to Florence as soon as the nuptial knot had been tied, to enjoy the genial air of sunny Italy, which was consonant with their elated spirits, for Henry was ever cheerful while in the society of the partner of all his joys, but not of all his sorrows; for immediately he was left to his own contemplation, the thoughts of his injustice to his former lover would crowd upon his mind, marring that which, without this reflection, would have been one continual succession of sunshine. His thoughts would revert to the village of his early home, when he was blest in the pure love of Jane, when his ambition soared no higher than to appear worthy of the esteem and love of that amiable girl; if he had not known the luxury that he had of late indulged in, and which was now at his command, but had remained contented in the village of his birth, he would not have craved for what was not in his power to possess. But now, should some evil stroke of unseen misfortune assail him, and deprive him of the means he now possessed, how degrading it would be to his manly spirit, and much more to the beloved object of his affection, whom he had bound himself to protect and guide through the intricacies of a checquered life, to sink lower in the scale of society. Although there was no probability of such being the case, for the fortune of his wife was ample to maintain them in a style far exceeding that of the nobles of the land they had chosen for a time to dwell in, Henry thought of the possibility of such an event with a feeling of horror. Ever and anon he would feel, almost instinctively, for the portrait of Jane, that had been suspended from his neck for so may months, and then recollecting that he had cast it into the flames on the morning of his marriage with Miss Mowbray, he would give vent to his heartfelt sorrow in words of the deepest self-reproach. He recalled the happy days he had spent in his dear native village; and although the place of his birth could not be compared with his present residence for magnificence of buildings, and more especially places of bustle, activity, and beautiful scenery, which are characteristics of Florence, yet there was something belonging to the old English village that had far greater charms for Henry Fergusson than Italy could present to him. The old ivy-bound church, with its massive tower, at each corner of which formerly stood four small spires that time had considerably impaired, the green tufts that covered the remains of some beloved relative, "who had gone to that bourne from whence no traveller returns," the grave deameanour of the old curate, whose delight it was to instil into his mind the divine precepts of " do unto others as ye would they should do unto you," and who first taught him the rudiments of classic knowledge, which caused the development of those talents we find him to be possessed of. The old school room with its many smiling faces, all of which were his childhood's companions, and shared with him everything that consituted his pleasure, and commisserated with him in his little troubles ; he thought of the Christmas festivities that were celebrated with glee among the openhearted village inhabitants, with whom he was not the least important, as the anticipated joys which for a long time prior to the festivity engrossed a large portion of their attention ; he recollected how Jane and he had grown up side by side together, never being out of each others society for long together ; their mutual attachment had commenced in infancy, and had only strengthened with increasing years, till it had arrived almost at its consummation ; then for him to cast from him, without any reason, the being who had remained the same mild and gentle Jane to him through all his various changes of life, seemed to rack his heart, and set his brain on fire. But, reader, what sensitive nature would not feel, even as Henry Fergusson did, if he had given up a lover so un-sullied and unchangeable—one whose only fault, if it can be called one, was to yield a free consent to her lover's withdrawal without an explanation, merely because he wished it, although the act almost broke her heart ; she bore it with-out a murmur, but her pallid cheek and the gradual wasting of her attenuated form were fearfully indicative of the inroads that were being made on the con-stitution of that fragile flower. No wonder, then, when Henry Fergusson began to reflect on his conduct towards Jane, that his mind should be troubled, and that the form of the beauteous girl appearing before his imagination, should unhinge his frame, and cause bitter tears of regret to flow down his manly cheek. Often when his bride had sought him after a protracted absence, she would ob-serve that her husband's countenance was flushed, and a settled care had the appearance of an abiding-place on his brow, which caused her a great deal of uneasiness ; but in reply to her many inquiries he would give evasive answers, and soon assume a more cheerful demeanour in her presence. Indeed, Henry Fergusson was one easily excited or easily depressed, and cheering company for a few minutes would seem to dispel all the care and gloom that had been seated on his countenance for hours ; so his wife concluded that it could not be anything very serious, as it was so easily removed, although she felt grieved that her husband should possess a secret he should deem her unworthy to share ; still she did not press the subject on his attention, trusting to circumstances to develop that which at present it seemed to be his wish to conceal. However, one morning early, one of the many of such mornings as can only be appreciated under an Italian sky, Henry, in a meditative mood, traversed the Roman pavement of the beautiful garden that was attached to his villa, which was stocked with the choicest native and exotic flowers that could be procured. Near the extremity of the garden was a grotto, composed of marble, choice shells, and portions of the same material as the paths, about eight feet high ; climbing plants of every descrip-tion grew from the interstices of the different materials that composed its stability ; behind this grotto was built a summer-house, that was the favourite resort of Henry ; here it was that he indulged in reverie—and in his lamentations respecting Jane, and here it was that his bride had seen him emerge from when his countenance has worn a gloomy aspect, and he has been depressed in spirit. One morning Mrs. Fergusson arose before her usual hour, and not finding her husband in his study, she went to the garden in search of him, and when she drew near to the grotto, which excluded all objects from view in the direction of the villa, she heard her husband's voice, as though speaking to some one. She stood, and deep, bitter sobs came upon her ear. Still she did not proceed, and instantly his voice again rivetted her attention.

"Oh! Jane," he said, "if your gentle spirit could see the pangs that are inflicted on me, by my conscience, for disregarding the holy ties that were be-tween us, and rending the cord of affection that had existed from childhood, you would pity, and perhaps forgive me. Could I be assured of your happiness, I should live in peace, And the beautiful being, whose noble heart is such a contrast to mine, and who calls me by the endearing epithet of husband, oh, how cruelly have I deceived her by allowing her to think I was free, while my most solemn promise was given to another. My destiny has been a strange one—fortunate in a worldly view, and being blessed with a loving, virtuous wife, who has my whole heart, nothing could be more blissful than our lot, if that unpardon-able folly and ingratitude did not so constantly intrude. But I must bear it—I must submit to the stings of conscience, and be subjected to the pangs of sorrow to counterbalance the joys that arise from the society of my dear wife."

He was silent, and covering his face with his hands, gave vent to another burst of grief which was heart-rending to hear. The partner of his bosom could not endure to remain any longer from him, but flung herself into his arms, her beautiful eyes suffused with warm tears, and besought him, in the gentlest accents, to explain all to her, and to harbour no secret from her, but to trust her with his heart's most treasured secrets, and rely upon her co-operation in re-moving any incubus that may be upon his mind. This gentle appeal had its due weight with Henry, for he unburthened his whole soul to her, and found great assistance in her advice, and resolved never more to make his breast the repository of any secret that his wife did not share. They resolved, as soon as they arrived in England, to go to the neighbourhood of the village of Henry's youth, and ascertain the position of Jane; and if anything could be done to the advancement of her future welfare, the lady resolved it should be done, although she purposed keeping the source from whence succour emanated a perfect secret; for if Jane were to think it came indirectly from Henry she would not avail her-self of the benefit.

CHAPTER XXIX.

" Upon my heart thy accents sweet,
　Of peace and pity fell, like dew
On flowers half dead : thy lips did meet
　Mine tremblingly—thy dark eyes threw
Their soft persuasion on my brain,
　Charming away its dream of pain."

WE have already acquainted the reader of the marriage of one of our dramatic personages; it is now our pleasing duty to speak of another, round which no magnificence or splendour is entwined. The pair, who plighted their faith at the altar of a more unpretending church than the fashionable St. George's, were not the less happy or blest on the prospect of a pleasing future. No; Percy Ray-mond and Mary Herbert's love for each other was founded on a deep respect and a high opinion of each other's moral worth; it was no light evanescent feeling, which, in a moment grows a fire, and in a moment cools again; their love had from a tender liking, grown into a warm and lasting affection, an affec-tion that would enable them cheerfully to bear each other's burdens, and lighten, as far as possible, each other's sorrows. It was a love capable of withstanding the storms and buffets of the sea of life, upon which it was now fairly launched. They expected not constant sunshine and smooth water; they knew well that they must occasionally be tossed backward and forward on a rough and stormy sea; but they were in no dread of the strength of their affection, but, on the con-trary, were well assured that it would bear them safely and happily through all. A happy man was Percy, when he gazed upon the fair face of his gentle bride, and marked the soft smiles that lighted up her beaming countenance, while a tear, sacred to the purest emotions of the breast, glistened with bright lustre in her eye. And though Ada stood by them at the altar in the full blaze of her win-ning beauty, Percy heeded it not; his whole attention was engrossed by Mary. We are sorry that truth obliges us to record that, when Percy was again a visitor at the house of Mr. Herbert in the character of Mary's suitor, Ada ungenerously strove by every means in her power to lower her cousin in his estimation, and reinstate herself in his affection. But this was impossible. Percy had once loved her with the truest regard, but when thoroughly convinced of her unworthiness, he had found it a less difficult task than he had himself imagined to cast her entirely from his mind. Vexed and angry to perceive that she had no longer any influence over him, Ada endeavoured, by assumed indifference—nay, by apparent contempt, to pique him into showing her some return of affection ; but Percy was too proud and high spirited to be moved by such palpable scheming, and the proud beauty did not even so much as gain from her former lover the slightest attention ; he was neither affected by her kindness or her disdain, it was the same to him whether she smiled or frowned. Had even any feeling of love revived in his bosom for Ada, he now loved and respected her cousin too highly to have caused the slightest anxiety in her gentle bosom, by any manifestation of it ; but, so far from this being the case, he felt nothing but contempt for Ada, notwithstanding her personal charms. Mary's gentle, cheerful mind, and affectionate heart, were to him far beyond the slight attractions of mere personal beauty. Percy felt a decided aversion to Ada's being invited to be present at their marriage, but Mary gently overruled his objections.

"It would seem so disrespectful," urged Mary ; "with the exception of my father, she is my only relative, and we therefore cannot do otherwise than invite her, on such an important occasion."

"Do as you please, dear Mary," replied Percy, "but after we are settled I shall most strongly object to receive Ada as a visitor."

"Oh, you must not say so," returned Mary, "we cannot possibly exclude her."

"But Mary, I cannot—I will not allow her to attempt to undermine your happiness, or make us less trusting to each other."

"Oh, fear not, dear Percy," replied Mary, warmly, " that she has the power to do so, and surely after we are united she will not be unkind enough to desire it."

"She is utterly cold and selfish," returned Percy, "and I believe envious enough of our happiness, to attempt by every means in her power to undermine it."

"You are really uncharitable," said Mary, smiling good-naturedly on her lover.

"Mary, dearest," replied Percy, " I know, I feel that I may safely say, my heart is so firmly wedded to you, that nothing can by any possibility estrange it. When grieved and cast down by the falsehood of Ada, so that I was led to contemn the whole sex, then it was, dear Mary, that thy soft accents fell upon my heart like dew, charming away my pain, and thy dear eyes captivated my soul, so that I fogot all ills while in thy presence, and under the benign influence of thy smile, I soon grew happy and glad again. Never, then, dear Mary, allow aught to induce you to suspect me of growing cold or unmindful of your love."

"I will not," replied Mary, firmly throwing upon him a look of unutterable affection.

"Thank you, love," returned Percy, pressing a grateful kiss upon her blushing cheek ; "and in return, I promise to be guided by you in all things. If you desire it, I will receive your cousin with politeness, though to me she can never be either more or less than the heartless coquette, who would gain admiration and flattery at the expense of the happiness of such gentle deserving beings as you, dear Mary. If," he continued warmly, "there be a being I most utterly despise, beyond all others, it is such a mean contemptible character as that possessed by Ada."

"Come," replied Mary, good-naturedly, " I will not listen to one word more against my cousin."

"Let us then forget her," returned Percy, " and, lover-like, talk of nothing but ourselves."

Ada therefore was kindly invited to the wedding by Mary, and thought proper proudly to accept the invitation. Mary on this, her important day, was dressed with extreme neatness and simplicity. Her dark hair was simply braided over a brow of unsullied purity; no jewels glittered on her arms, or costly satins adorned her graceful form. While Ada, on the contrary, was arrayed in rich and glossy silk, her white arms clasped with pearls, and her hair floating in natural curls over her shoulders. And yet with all these external advantages, she could not gain from Percy even an admiring glance, his every thought and desire was given to Mary, who in his eyes was a thousand times more lovely than her cousin. Mr. Herbert gave his only daughter to the man of her choice, and in doing so felt more happy and satisfied than if he had decked her brow with a coronet. Although he could not restrain a tear, as he saw her pass from under his roof, for though she promised after to return and devote an hour to his comfort and amusement, yet he felt that henceforth she would come in the character of a guest, not like a child at home. Mary, too, wept, as she threw her arms round her father in a parting embrace, leaving her tears wet upon his cheek. Still she loved Percy too ardently to indulge in unavailing regret. Tenderly, too, did she kiss Ada, and as she bade her adieu, entreated her as far as possible to supply her place to her father. Ada, alas! was too vexed and mortified to heed the parting admonition of her cousin, and when Percy advanced coldly to bid her farewell, she haughtily turned away, and closeting herself in her own room, gave vent to her disappointment in a violent burst of tears. After a fortnight's absence from town, Percy and his bride returned to take possession of their own home; everything was prettily and tastily arranged for their comfort by the sisters of Percy, who at Mary's earnest request had consented to reside with her. Mary warmly expressed to them her sense of their kindness, and gratified their minds by her unbounded praise of their excellent taste, which was displayed by the choice arrangement of the different rooms. Mary walked from one to the other with pleased satisfaction, and each time with renewed delight, and the sisters of Percy were pleased beyond expression to find that everything met her satisfaction. And now their friends crowded round them to give them joy, and sincerely wish them happiness, and Mary's heart swelled with joy and pride; and Percy, when he witnessed the kind sisterly feelings that existed between his young wife, and the sisters whom he so fondly cherished, exulted in his choice, and felt grateful for the events that had interposed to prevent his marrying Ada.

CHAPTER XXXI.

"Her lips were parched, and the measured breath
Was now heard there; her dark and intricate eyes—
Orb within orb, deeper than sleep or death—
Absorbed the glories of the burning skies,
Which, mingling with her heart's deep ecstacies,
Burst from her looks and gestures; and a light
Of liquid tenderness, like love, did rise
From her whole frame—an atmosphere which quite
Arrayed her in its beams, tremulous, and soft, and light."

Not long did Lady Eardley and Clara await the arrival of their expected guests. Clara trembled as they were announced, although, at the same moment, a slight feeling of curiosity filled her mind she had never seen the elder brother, now Sir Richard, and as the two young men entered she scanned the elder one somewhat narrowly. Walter instantly flew to her side, and pressed her affectionately to his bosom, and then turning to his brother introduced them to each other with an evident feeling of pride. The young man politely stretched out his hand, and Clara frankly placed her own in his. As she did so, she found time to observe, that in figure he was near as possible of the height and size of his brother. He was likewise possessed of the same handsome features, rich chesnut hair, and soft hazel eyes, and when he spoke, the low musical tones thrilled upon her ear, that had so often enchanted her in his brother. And yet, though possessing these advantages in common, in many respects they were essentially different. Richard, Clara remarked, wore upon his countenance an expression of deep and settled melancholy, while on the contrary, and which surprised her not a little, his brother appeared even in unusual good spirits.

"Dearest Clara," began her lover, as soon as they were seated. "I have come this evening to remove all doubts and anxieties from thy bosom, and entreat thy forgiveness for having so long practised towards thee a deceit, in which I can scarcely justify myself."

Clara turned upon him a look of unfeigned surprise, and then hastily glanced towards Lady Eardley, as if to seek from her an explanation of his words; she smiled kindly and encouragingly upon Clara, but made no reply to her enquiring look.

"Dearest Clara," resumed Walter, taking her hand, which he fondly pressed in his own, "behold in me no longer the portionless younger brother whom thou hast so long blest with thy endearing tenderness. It is now Sir Richard, who seeks to gain thy hand, to place thee in a situation of life, which thou art so pre-eminently worthy to fulfil. Say then," he continued in his own soft sweet tones, "that you are willing to pardon all the past, to bless me with thy tenderness, and crown my felicity by becoming mine for ever—without thee, life would be indeed a desert in which I could find no resting-place."

Clara's breath came thick and short, the burning blood rushed tumultuously to her cheek, and then as suddenly disappeared, leaving her deadly pale; thrice she essayed to speak, as she glanced with anxious countenance from one to the other, but for the time she had lost all power of articulation. Lady Eardley, with instinctive tenderness, sought to compose the agitated feelings of Clara, as she said—

"Listen to me one moment, my love, and I will explain all that seems strange, and perhaps inexplicable. This young man (pointing to him, who had long been the received lover of Clara), whom you have known and loved as Walter, I desire to introduce to you as my elder son, Richard, who from a foolish romantic notion, resolved to win your affection in the character of a younger brother, dependent entirely upon the bounty of his father. How far he has succeeded in doing so," she continued smiling, "you, Clara, must be the best judge."

Poor Clara seemed bewildered with astonishment, and it was some minutes before she could reply; at length, with faltering accents she said, looking earnestly at her lover—

"Then it was not you who won the love of Lucy, and turned it to her own destruction, who lured her from her home, and when weary of her charms, unpityingly cast her from you?"

"No, no, dearest Clara, "I never could have profaned the purity of your soul, by offering you a love less sacred than that which you bestowed. Heaven is my witness that I never wronged another, or indeed loved or cared for any but yourself."

"Then," gasped Clara, overcome by the multitude of thoughts that filled her breast, "it was not you against whom I registered the vow of revenge, and I am free to marry you."

"Bless you, dear one, for those sweet words," exclaimed her lover rapturously pressing her to his bosom; then turning to his mother with manly pride, he fondly led towards her his long intended bride. Lady Eardley received her with open arms, and Clara hid her blushing face upon her maternal bosom, while she sobbed out the fulness of her heart.

So overpowered was Clara with the sudden step she had taken from the bitterest sorrow to the very height of human happiness, that she wept loud and long, and could scarcely realise her unexpected happiness. Joy indeed frequently produces effects strangely similar to grief—tears and sighs are alike the heralds and harbingers of both ; but when the storm is hushed, and the bosom regains its wonted tranquillity, we perceive their strong dissimilarity in the different traces they leave behind. Sorrow dims the eye, pales the countenance, and stamps its

LADY EARDLEY PRESENTING THE SUPPOSED WALTER TO CLARA, AS SIR RICHARD.

devastating influence unmistakably upon the brow. Joy, on the contrary, adds renewed lustre to the brightening eye, lends a deep and unusual bloom to the cheek, and lights up the entire countenance with a soft refulgent gladness. Thus it was with Clara, when she lifted her head once more from the bosom of her whom she felt to be at once a friend and mother ; her whole face was radiant with happiness, and she gazed upon her lover with proud exultation. No sad, no bitter thoughts found a vacant place in her bosom ; all was glad sunshine ; she had remained true to herself, sacrificing nothing of her natural independence, preferring even sorrow and anguish of heart rather than purchase happiness by deviating in the slightest from the path of rectitude and honour she had marked out for herself.   True, she had suffered much and deeply, but she had remained firm and unmoved in the midst of trials and temptations that had striven to lure her fixed and unalterable determination.   How sweet and exalted, then, was her present happiness—how pure and unsullied the joy that filled her breast, and spread an halo of light and loveliness around her.   She had loved Richard Eardley, as the reader is well aware, dearly, most dearly, even when she had every reason to believe him surrounded by an atmosphere of sin ; but how much dearer was he to her warm and trusting heart, now that she discovered how erroneously she had judged of him, and he shone forth pure and sinless as her-self.   To a mind like Clara's, nothing could equal the joy that the certainty of this brought to her mind.   Bitter indeed were the pangs that her lover's apparent cruelty to Lucy had cost her ; how much and deeply she had mourned over his duplicity.   What words, then, can depict the gladness of her bosom to see all the clouds that had darkened his mental attractions cleared away, leaving his mind unsullied in its brightness, and herself free to love him with the ardent warmth of her nature, undimmed by the painful thought that he was less pure, less noble and honourable than herself.   After sorrow, how sweet, how extatic is joy ; how amply doth it make amends for all we have endured, and how much brighter and sweeter doth the present seem when contrasted with the sad and painful past.   And sweet indeed were the feelings experienced by Clara, as, seated by the side of her lover, listening with proud delight to the music of his voice, she felt that she had no longer a wish ungratified.   After a short time spent together, Lady Eardley, from a feeling of delicacy, withdrew from the room, accompanied by her younger son, and the two, whose souls were entirely wrapped in each other, were enabled to converse and open their whole hearts to each other with-out restraint.   Clara felt that she could have listened to the voice of Richard for ever, hanging, as one entranced, upon every word that fell from his lips ; his tones were always musically soft and low, but

> "Low tones to her grew lower,
>   Sweetening so his honied talk,"

that it filled up all her hearing, drowning all other sounds, and happy and glad she listened while he unfolded to her every circumstance connected with his past life.

"When I first saw you, dear Clara," he began, "my heart almost instantly acknowledged the presence of that passion, which has never since ceased to ani-mate my breast.   At the same time, I must confess I was so jealous of your affection, so desirous of being loved for myself alone, utterly independent of being the heir of a wealthy baronet, that I conceived the idea of winning your affections, under the assumed name and position of my brother, who was well-known to be entirely portionless.   This I was readily able to effect, from the circumstance of Walter being an entire stranger to you.   When we returned to town from Eardly Hall, I instantly sought my mother, whom in secret we had ever acknowledged as a parent, and for whom I have ever entertained the tenderest affection, and made known to her the attachment that existed between us, for I could not bear the idea of keeping a secret from her, with whom from earliest infancy I had been accustomed to advise on every subject.   Shortly after this, and before I had time to communicate with you again, accident made me acquainted with the flight of Lucy, who took up her residence in London under the protection of my brother, whom at the time I was personating, and my anxious and excited mind instantly apprehended the loss of your affections as the inevitable consequence of his error.   The return of my letters unopened at this period, served to confirm my worst fears ; still, by the advice of my mother, I allowed you to remain in ignorance of the truth, contriving, although you knew it not, constantly to hear of your welfare. My dear mother, whom I have said alone was cognisant of my deep attachment for you, being naturally desirous to know and scan well the merits of one, who in all probability would at some future period stand in so close a relationship to herself, proposed, one becoming acquainted with the death of your brother, and your own desire to quit the country, to offer you a situation beneath her roof. I need not say, dearest, how readily this proposal was embraced by me, who was only too anxious to see you placed under her protecting care, when I should have opportunities offered me of seeing and hearing of your welfare more frequently. And must I confess my once almost unpardonable vanity ?—I was so well assured of your love, that I doubted not an unexpected meeting would reinstate me in your favour, or at least lead to a renewal of our intimacy. In order to test well your temper and disposition, my mother, who needed an amanuensis, resolved to employ you in that capacity, and well indeed hast thou stood the test, for unrepiningly didst thou, dear Clara, labour day by day. Thy sweet temper and mild equable deportment rendering thee doubly dear both to her and myself. And now, love, can you, will you forgive us this deception?" he added tenderly.

"I am too happy, dear Walter, at this moment, to think of chiding you," replied Clara, "and therefore will at once extend my forgiveness, although, dear Walter, I have indeed suffered most acutely."

"Nay, love," he interrupted, "Walter no more—henceforth you must call me Richard, and as such, be it my sweet task to make amends to you for all you have suffered for my sake."

"I am afraid I shall make sad mistakes before I accustom myself to the change," said Clara smiling, "but I must infer, from what you have just imparted, that you never saw the truly unfortunate Lucy."

"You are right, love, I never did, though I frequently assisted Walter, in the hope that he might be induced to make her his wife. I believe, indeed, that he truly loved her, but he was unhappily—most unhappily, as it has proved both for himself and her—wedded to gaiety and pleasure, that swallowed up far more than I could at the time supply. And now that it is too late, he sincerely and bitterly repents the unkindness with which he acted towards her. Poor unhappy Lucy! her's was indeed a sad fate."

"It was indeed," replied Clara; "and Jane too, her good and gentle sister, so every way deserving of happiness, has been likewise plunged into the depths of affliction by the unfaithfulness of one upon whom she had fearlessly reposed the warmest and most undoubting confidence. Yes, Henry Fergusson, who for so long a period professed the deepest attachment to Jane, and to whom she has been long affianced, has cruelly broken his faith in favour of a more wealthy bride to whom he has been lately married, leaving Jane almost broken-hearted. If," continued Clara, warmly and overcome by her feelings, "aught could mar the happiness of my present lot, it would be the knowledge of how deep and undeservedly another is suffering."

"It is indeed sad," replied her lover; "but come, dearest, you must not allow such thoughts to depress your spirits. Soon we shall revisit together my ancestral home; you will then be near your friend, and able to offer the consolation she so greatly needs; and as her lover has proved himself so utterly unworthy of her regard, let us hope that in a short time she may be enabled to forget him, or at least to think of him without regret.'

At this moment the conversation was interrupted by the entrance of Lady Eardley and Walter, who approached Clara, and offering her his hand, affectionately greeted her as a sister, though at the same moment a tear glistened in his eye, and a pang of the deepest regret shot across his bosom, as he thought how richly blest he too might have been, had it not been for his own folly. The evening passed in quiet happiness, and pleasing anticipations for the future. Clara had borne bravely up under temptation and sorrow, never for a moment even allowing herself to be lured from the path of duty. And now that she had gained the haven of happiness she had so long sighed after in vain, her joy was tempered with calm delight; no wild expressions of gladness or over-elated hopes found vent, her happiness was rather of that calm unruffled kind, which shows itself not so much in exuberant joy, as in the beaming eye and gentle smiling face, affording an index to the peaceful serenity of a mind at ease. Richard, on his part, proudly exulted in the long-tried virtues of his chosen bride; into her keeping he was well assured he could safely give his happiness and honour. She would add but increased brightness to his name, and lustre to his long line of ancestry, and he looked forward to the future with rapturous delight. All seemed to promise a fruitful harvest of unshadowy brightness. Lady Eardley, too, appeared almost to have forgotten the many bitter sorrows that marked the early portion of her life, and in contemplating the happiness of her son, regained much that was hitherto lost of her own. Walter's heart was, in truth, the only one that was sad in that little party, but his had received a wound that only time could heal. Yet he rejoiced in the happiness of his brother, and felt that he was worthy of it all; he had himself been taught in the school of adversity, and he inwardly resolved to lay the lessons he had thus received to heart, and henceforth determined to become at once a wiser and a better man.

CHAPTER XXXII.

"Oh! grief beyond all other griefs—when fate
First leaves the young heart lone and desolate
In the wide world, without that only tie,
For which it loved to live or feared to die—
Lone as the hung-up lute, which ne'er hath spoken
Since the sad day its master chord was broken."

IT is not at the moment of renouncing a beloved object—of sacrificing our dearest and holiest wishes, our purest and long-cherished hopes, for the benefit of the one we have made for years our heart's idol, and for whom we would suffer all things in order to spare them from the pangs of sorrow, or to promote their well-being. We say, it is not at the moment of doing this, that we most feel how much we are called upon to bear; how deep and heart-rending are the pangs we have voluntarily imposed upon ourselves. No! at the moment of taking this burden of sorrow and anguish, which perhaps is destined to be our constant companion throughout life's fitful changing scene, we are borne up by a proud consciousness of our own integrity—we are animated by a martyr spirit, in thus sacrificing ourselves for the good of another, and it frequently happens that at the time of making the sacrifice, it is not felt, or, at all events, we do not experience its full bitterness, till time has cooled the ardour of our feelings, and blunted the first proud consciousness of well doing that filled our breasts with ardour, and our hearts with hopeful anticipation that our good actions might not go entirely unrewarded, or, at least, unappreciated by those for whom we have willingly encountered the rough and stormy sea of sorrow, stemming its headlong torrents, which would fain drive us at its will.

Sad fate for one, with heart and life,
And all youth's sunshine round her still.

Thus it was with Jane Clarence. When she received her lover's letter—that letter so long and anxiously expected—from which she had hoped so much, to which she had looked forward as the one well-spring of happiness, sparkling brightly and refreshingly in the desert, when all was seared and parched with the heat. When that letter at length arrived, which was destined to dash her long cherished hopes to the ground, we have seen that she unhesitatingly, and without any apparent emotion, sealed her own sad fate, in order to promote the happiness and well-being of the man she loved, and on whom she had reposed such sweet faith and unwavering confidence. No thought of her own unhappiness found even a temporary resting-place in her bosom; her lover's welfare, her lover's happiness required the sacrifice, and she hesitated not a moment in making it. Warmed and animated by the emotion of feelings that filled her mind, Jane hastened, as we have seen, to write an answer to that ill-fated epistle which had so cruelly crushed and blighted her fondest and fairest hopes. She did not then fully realise the bitterness of her lot: it seemed as though her senses were steeped in stupefaction by the suddenness and unexpected nature of the misfortune that had befallen her; but when she had time and leisure for reflection, then came the full sense of her own sorrow; not that she repented the part she had acted, in so readily freeing her lover from his engagement with herself. No; she rested with satisfaction amidst the storm of anguish that threatened to overwhelm her with its devastating power. An icy coldness appeared to settle on her heart, and preclude all her efforts to cast it off; every hope appeared to have forsaken her, and a sense of utter despondency oppressed and bore down all the energy of her character; never before, under any calamity, had she felt so strongly tempted to sit down and yield herself to the despair that threatened to consume her; still she was not unmindful of the many duties that devolved upon her. A widowed mother and a sister's orphan child claimed at once her sympathy and care, and she roused herself from the benumbing influence of sorrow, to perform the daily duties that devolved upon her; but how differently were these duties performed!—no more was her heart lightened, and her spirit made glad by the thought of the absent loved one, whom she had once believed to be toiling to procure an honourable independence for himself and her, and yet she had been so long and constantly accustomed to blend him with all her thoughts, to rest with confidence on his professed love, that, in spite of all her efforts to cast his image from her mind, she found herself involuntarily associating him with dreams of future happiness—of coming days of joy, when, as his chosen and treasured wife, they might pursue a career at once of usefulness and peace; blest in each other's love, they might, hand in hand, happily descend into the vale of life's decline, cheering each other's fainting spirits, and eventually supporting each other's tottering steps. Poor Jane! how bright and beautiful had once been such dreams as this, and, spite of all her endeavours, those dreams would recur again and again; she had so used herself to indulge in golden reveries, bright dreamy hopes, that whenever an interval of inactivity presented itself, they came back to her imagination fresh and warm as when first she painted the future in those glowing colours with which the young especially love to invest life, never thinking of, or heeding the more sombre, but true colours with which it most frequently abounds. And well was it for Jane that she had duties to perform, and which prevented her sitting down and folding her hands to weep; true, tears came often to her relief, and afforded some slight ease to her suffering mind, but they were tears which lingered not long upon her cheek; no, they were quickly dried, for she was desirous of sparing her mother the additional pain of knowing that she was so unhappy. Yet it is hard to wear a smiling face and placid brow when the heart feels breaking; and though Jane sedulously sought to conceal her inward grief, her pale cheek and sunken eye bore ample witness to the cruel extent of her suffering. Mrs. Clarence had sorrowed so much over the frailty and subsequent death of her youngest, but most favoured daughter, and repined likewise so deeply at the loss of her husband, the sharer of her sorrows and soother of her griefs, that she at length acquired that selfish feeling, by no means uncommon in persons who, like her, have been called upon to endure the most at a period of life when the buoyancy of youth has fled, and the mourner accustomed to happiness, is rendered less capable of combating the ills of life. Mrs. Clarence appeared to feel as though she alone possessed an undoubted right to repine at the misfortunes and disappointments to which all are liable, and which are felt more acutely as we descend into the vale of life; when the bright hopes of youth are departed, and the more sobered and tranquil ones of maternal age snatched from us. Yet it is surely unwise as well as wicked, to repine at the providence of God, which doubtless afflicts us for some wise and good, though hidden purpose. We cannot with our finite vision pierce the veil of obscurity which conceals the wondrous workings of Providence; let us therefore learn to be content, feeling assured, however deeply we are afflicted, the trial comes not without performing some wise mission. But not thus did Mrs. Clarence regard the sorrows and afflictions with which she had been visited. No, she murmured deeply at the stroke which had separated her from happiness; the contrast, too, which her present condition presented to the days of her youth, when all pleasures and enjoyments were spread around her path and courted her acceptance on every hand, served but the more sensibly to confirm her in her repinings for the past, and rebellious murmurings at the present, and probable anticipations of the future. Instead of feeling grateful, that though much which once bound her to life was fled, there was likewise still much left her, in the blessing of a dutiful and affectionate child, who sought to beguile her of her sorrow, and make her forget the bitterness of her sufferings—instead of this, she resolutely refused to be comforted, rejecting the sweet blessing yet left her, and, turning aside her head from the cup of happiness which was held to her lips, she refused to drink, choosing rather to indulge in her grief, and confine herself in useless lamentation over the days which were fled. And yet, strange as it may seem, though constantly bearing about with her the appearance of deep and uncontrolled suffering, she could not endure to witness the slightest appearance of it in another. No, she arrogated to herself the sole right to feel sorrow—none else she conceived had any occasion to complain—in her own person she wished to monopolise all that can be endured of suffering; not, we wish it to be distinctly understood, that she had any desire to endure more. No! she conceived she had already suffered so much, that it was impossible for any one to equal her in the amount of anguish she had borne, and consequently none else had any real cause for complaint. Jane knew this failing of her sole surviving parent, and consequently strove earnestly to conceal from her the anguish which had become so unwelcome an inmate of her breast; but there were times when all efforts proved unavailing, in the midst of her untiring efforts to be cheerful, and her endeavours to arouse her invalid mother—for sorrow and anxiety had made sad inroads upon her constitution—the long pent up anguish of her bosom would manifest itself in signs too unmistakable not to be remarked by Mrs. Clarence, although no very great observer of the inward workings of the mind.

"What! tears, Jane?" she exclaimed on one occasion, as the unwelcome moisture forced itself to her eyes. "What cause can you possibly have for tears—you, who have scarcely yet known what sorrow means?"

"Dear mother," replied Jane, stooping to conceal the emotion which shook her frame with convulsive agitation. "Do not say I have not yet known sorrow; have I not wept with you even to the tomb of a beloved father, and mourned a sister's premature decay? Oh, surely in this there is enough of sorrow to melt the hardest heart, and subdue the loftiest spirit."

"Well," returned Mrs. Clarence, "if you think you have endured so much, what must have been my sufferings. How much more have I not borne, and yet you do not see me weep."

"There are times, dear mother," returned Jane evasively, "when we feel more acutely than at others, it is thus with me this evening; but do, pray, forgive me for indulging in my own sorrowful feelings, when I ought to be endeavouring to amuse and enliven you; let us forget this painful topic, and discourse on something less calculated to awaken regretful feelings."

"No, Jane, it is impossible to-night," replied Mrs. Clarence; "it is indeed unfortunate that you should have reminded me so forcibly of my own sorrows this evening, when, strange to say, I felt them less severely than I have done for a considerable time before, but it is no matter, I cannot expect to find happiness or even peace again on this side of the grave, but it would be some comfort to know that you, at least, had escaped the blight which has fallen on our unhappy family."

Jane sighed deeply at these words, for there did indeed seem to be a blight upon the family—a blight and a bane. Had not Lucy deeply experienced this in her own unhappy fate, which had hurried her to an untimely grave, and now Jane, her sole surviving sister, was made likewise to drink deeply from the cup of sorrow, which had so early blighted the happiness of Lucy. Yes, she too was destined to experience the fickleness of man's affection, to feel how frail is the support of those who lean for succour on the love which promised to shield them from every ill. Jane felt this deeply; but she checked the rising tears, and compelled herself to lead her mother's thoughts to other subjects; but this was, indeed, a difficult task. Mrs. Clarence loved to brood over her misfortunes, and this, indeed, seemed a fitting opportunity to dwell upon them. Sedulously, therefore, as Jane strove to lead her ideas into a different channel, she descanted for the remainder of the evening on all that she had herself endured, gently remonstrating with her daughter for giving way to regret, when she had suffered comparatively so little.

"I hope, indeed," she added, "that you may never know the sorrows that I have been called upon to endure—you are young, and all the world is before you; what cause, then, can you have for unhappiness for myself? I can only look forward to the grave as a place of rest and forgetfulness, and I care not how soon I may be called upon to lay down—life is a weary load; I sometimes even think that you might be happier without me."

"Oh! dear—dear mother, say not so, think not so, I entreat of you," exclaimed Jane, throwing herself on her mother's bosom. "I have none to love or care for me but you; indeed, indeed, were you gone there could not possibly exist a more lonely or wretched being than myself—then do not, pray do not talk of dying, you, for whom alone I wish to live, or fear to die; my heart would, indeed, be a desert all lonely and sad, but for the joy of contributing to your comforts, of soothing your sorrows, and softening your regrets."

"My dear child," returned Mrs. Clarence, folding the weeping girl to her bosom, "how strange you talk—I cannot, indeed, comprehend you; you, so young to the world, and with so many happy days in store, and with so many bright prospects gilding the future, it does, indeed, seem strange to hear you talk of being lonely and desolate; for me to mourn appears natural, but you, my child, must not thus early accustom yourself to give way to vain regret; but I see how it is, you are affected with an unaccountable fit of *ennui* this evening, you had better retire early, and to-morrow, I doubt not, you will have entirely recovered your usual good spirits."

Alas! what a bitter mockery these words seemed to the agonized mind of Jane, but without venturing another word, she did her mother's bidding, and retired to her own room, but she found no rest from the thoughts that unceasingly pursued—

> " Save in dreams of troubled sleep,
>   From which 'twas joy to wake and weep;
>   Visions that will not be forgot,
>   But sadden every waking scene
>   Like warning ghosts which leave the spot
>   All withered where they once have been."

The image of him she had so long and fondly loved constantly presented itself to her mind, but not in the sweet and welcome guise it had once worn; no, she had awakened from her first fond dream of love, that sweet trusting confidence, life only once may know. In vain she sought to forget the past—the bright and happy past—fond memory would recall, in spite of all her efforts to the contrary, the days that were fled, when all things pleased, for love and life were new. And equally in vain did she shrink from the contemplation of the future, which presented itself to her disordered fancy as a dreary blank—a desert, without a single flower to bloom therein ; without one ray of sunshine to gild and brighten its darkness, there seemed no hope left to cheer her benighted mind—dimness and doubt alone seemed there, now the sole joy of her bosom was gone; the hope that had animated her spirit and enabled her to bear up under the pressure of heavy trials and sore afflictions—crushed for ever. Alas, poor Jane ! sad, indeed, and wholly undeserved was thy destiny, and more sad still the thought that he who had been thy bosom's friend, who had beguiled thy spirit of every care, through summers lone and winters drear, should be the sole cause of thy present and future misery. Jane, perhaps, felt more acutely this unfaithfulness of her lover, upon whose unblemished fate she had placed such full and unwavering confidence, from the circumstance that jealousy, even in the minutest degree, had never formed even a temporary resting place in her bosom. She had judged of his heart by the simple purity of her own, and, knowing how dear he was to her mind, how utterly impossible it would be for aught to cause her, even in thought, to stray from him, her first and only love, she had never once entertained the slightest doubt of her lover's purity ; so implicitly, indeed, had she relied on his truth, that during their long absence, in all her letters, never having dreamed of falsehood, she had not one word to say of inconstancy. Consequently, the blow was felt so much the more severe, from its having come from a quarter whence she had never anticipated misfortune. Still, as we have seen, she strove earnestly to banish his image from her breast—to forget the love that had once been her life and light—

> " And yet the dear deceit so long
> Had waked to joy her morning song—
> Had bade her tears forget to flow,
> Checked every pain, soothed every woe,
> That truth, unwelcome to the ear,
> Recalled the sigh and dried the tear,
> Checked the warm impulse of her heart,
> And gave to pain its keenest smart !"

Alas ! it is indeed a hard task to tear the image of the loved one from the breast—to check the sighs, so sinful yet so dear, which have been all too much his own. Poor Jane felt this ; and as she dwelt upon her own fond adoration of that one object of her affection, she almost conceived that her present misery was a deserved punishment for her past idolatry ; and as she inwardly murmured a prayer for his happiness, she felt as though she was willing to endure all that had befallen her, so that he was spared a participation of her sorrows.

"Alas !" she exclaimed, "if he is happy, I will learn to be content. May she whom he has chosen love and appreciate his noble qualities, as I would myself have done. May she be to him all, and more, if possible, than I once hoped to be."

Such were the pure and noble thoughts of Jane ; and had the chosen bride of Henry been less wealthy than report spoke of her, she would have experienced but little difficulty in bringing herself to believe that she must be more worthy, more deserving of the love of Henry Fergusson than herself; but when she read an account in the London papers of the splendid match which had been formed by the young and obscure artist, in the brilliant alliance he had made with the beautiful and richly-dowered heiress, her heart throbbed with a sensation akin to pity, and the tears sprang unheeded to her eyes as she mentally asked herself—

"And was it for this that he renounced my love ? Could wealth or luxury purchase the affection which I once fondly thought even monarchs would be too poor to buy, and fondly believed that nought beneath God's sky could tempt or change him ? And is it possible that wealth could exert so baneful an influence over a mind that I fondly believed to be the seat of every honourable and pure emotion ? Alas ! Henry, you have indeed destroyed my entire faith and confidence in the whole sex. Never more will I place faith in the truth of man's affection. If you could thus change, constancy must be a stranger to all ; none— none can know the meaning of the word."

Thus soliloquised Jane, as she pored over the account of her lover's nuptials ; for, although every word brought a pang to her heart and a tear to her eye, there yet seemed a strange and painful fascination that held her spell-bound to

JANE CLARENCE, THE FORSAKEN.

the page ; and when, in conclusion, she read that the happy pair had started *en route* for the continent immediately after the interesting ceremony which bound them together for life, the tears, long restrained, gushed forth large and bright, and yet unknown to herself they fell, for now she, in truth, experienced the full bitterness of affliction. Now, indeed, she seemed irrevocably severed from him, upon whom, with all his unkindness to herself, she so fondly doted. Yes, he was gone, and she was left; but ah! how sad and drear it seemed, this world, of every charm bereft, where all was beautiful with him. Yes, he was gone with his fair and happy bride to seek, and, as she believed, find happiness under the blue skies of unclouded Italy, that land of rare beauty and romance, which his mind was so well calculated to appreciate. Oh, no! she could not doubt that, while pointing out each object of attraction with admiring eyes to his fair young bride, to whom alone he was indebted for the enjoyment he experienced, he would himself find happiness and peace; while her, whose hopes he had blighted, and whose peace he had ruined, was left to pine in solitude, to weep unheeded over his broken vows. At this juncture she checked herself, for conscience whispered that such feelings and regrets were purely selfish, so, casting aside the paper, the perusal of which had caused her so many bitter pangs, she resumed once more her wonted duties, endeavouring, by a steady perseverance in these, to crush the unwelcome thoughts that would fain intrude upon her mind, robbing her of that peace which she strove to make an inmate of her breast. Ah! how little she thought, as she thus pursued her tranquil and even course, how many pangs, similar to those she herself endured, agitated the breast of her former lover. Indeed, although she knew it not, Henry suffered far more acutely than Jane; for, if her's were pangs of blighted love, the keenest pang below is to have known—and that was his—he had wronged a heart so true and pure as her's.

> "This thought it was that came to shed
> O'er rapture's hours its worst alloys,
> And close as shade with sunshine wed
> Its sadness with his happiest joys."

And but for this disheartening voice stealing amid his mirth, to say that her whom he had once made happy and glad was now, by the same arm that had once embraced her, cut off from every hope that had once budded so brightly in her bosom—ah! but for this thought, which unceasingly pursued him, he might have been happy and blest; but Jane, as we have said, knew nothing of this, and never even conjectured that he too was unhappy. No; feeling fully persuaded that he, at least, had reached the haven so long sighed after, she endeavoured to bear the burden of sorrow that oppressed her, unrepiningly; and which her sense of humiliation, at being neglected for a more wealthy bride, aided her to do, although she could not cease to love Henry—for love may, and often does, sink by slow decay, yet, by sudden wrench, hearts can never be torn away; still her pride helped to sustain her, and most probably alone prevented her sinking beneath the weight of affliction that pressed so heavily on her young heart. From the evening when unfortunately Mrs. Clarence discovered the apparent unhappiness of her daughter, Jane contrived effectually to conceal all trace of agitation in her mother's presence—whenever she wept she turned away, and shed her tears alone. Often, indeed, would she seek in solitude the sweet relief that was so necessary to her scorched and withered feelings, but from which she returned to the cares and duties of life with renewed vigour and earnestness. Never again had her parent occasion to complain of her depression of spirits. No, she was again the patient, untiring attendant—the careful nurse, and cheerful companion, beguiling the tedious hours of bodily suffering, or making more pleasant those which would have been otherwise devoted to vain regrets and useless repinings. None, indeed, who witnessed her performing the routine of duties which devolved upon her, with patient and untiring cheerfulness, would have believed it possible that she carried about in her bosom a thorn, which cruelly rankled there, destroying all happiness, save that which she experienced in contributing to the peace and repose of others. And who, with all her trials, and many sorrows, would not even be tempted to envy the noble and exalted mind of Jane Clarence? How many, with but one half the provocation of sorrow that she had experienced, have given themselves up entirely to despair—have become for the remainder of their lives one of those dread scourges of society in general, but more particularly of their own domestic circle, fretful, peevish, misanthropical, discontented beings, which are occasionally to be met with, who do nought but recapitulate their ills, and bemoan their own sorrows, construing every chance word or jest into an especial affront to themselves, and resenting the slightest injury with the bitterest malevolence. But we cannot endure for a moment even to dwell upon such characters; let us be thankful that few—but very few such exist. No, for the happiness of the world in general, for the delight of social circles and dear domestic joys, we are delighted to think and know that such pure and exalted characters as Jane Clarence are more—far more frequent. They do not shine forth pre-eminent—on the contrary, we often meet them and know it not—but all honour be to such, no matter where they dwell, be it in palace, hall, or cot—virtues such as they possess can never go unrewarded, loving hearts will gather round them, on their way, beset though it be with thorns and briers, and struggles daily, and bitter struggles, to obtain the mastery over that great foe, Despair, that grim tyrant which so oft enslaves the mind, and bears it captive at its will.

CHAPTER XXXIII.

" Oh, look not so—beneath the skies,
I now fear nothing but thine eyes ;
If aught on earth could charm, or force
My spirit from its destined course—
If aught could make this soul forget
The bond to which its seal is set,
'Twould be those eyes—they, only they
Could melt this sacred seal away."

ADA HERBERT, we have seen, met with a double mortification, in the neglect she experienced from Walter Eardley, and the subsequent marriage of her former lover to her cousin Mary. Oh ! had it been possible, at the sacrifice even of all things else which she held to be dear, to have prevented this marriage, how gladly would she have done so ! Failing in this, her most earnest desire was to render the marriage an unhappy one ; strange as it may seem, she felt as though she would willingly, nay, gladly endure any amount of suffering herself, could she also succeed in making the two, who should have been most dear to her, unhappy. In conformity, therefore, with her fixed resolution to sow the seeds of discord and jealousy between the newly married couple, who were felicitiating themselves on their fair prospect of domestic happiness, fortunately in utter ignorance that they possessed so insiduous an enemy to their peace as that of a d sappointed and envious woman, she conceived it wisest for the future to conceal her own disappointment and mortified ambition under the mask of friendship, and the guise of good and kindly feeling. Ada was consequently one of the first who hastened to welcome Mary's return to town, and to give her joy of the happiness which beamed so perceptibly on her animated countenance ; it cost Ada, indeed, a strong effort to meet her cousin—the woman who occupied the position she had once fully calculated on holding herself—who had usurped the place she once held in the affections of the only man she had ever loved ;—we say it cost her a strong effort to suppress the deep sense she felt of her own supposed injuries, in the man she had once received as her accepted suitor, presuming even, on being rejected by herself, to give his love to another, and that other her cousin, standing to her almost in the dear relationship of sister ; this was the keenest pang of all, had it been any other, she felt as though she could have borne it better, but for Mary to become his wife, to rival her in his affections, seemed almost more than she could bear. Yet, in the hope of being ultimately enabled to revenge her supposed wrongs, we have seen that she compelled herself to be present at the nuptials of him whom with all her faults and overweening self-importance, she yet fondly loved; yes, she stood beside him at the altar and heard him pronounce the vows which bound him to another. In thus doing, she had fully anticipated that her own resplendent beauty would have made a deep impression on his heart, and have wrung from his bosom a sigh of regretful tenderness that so much loveliness was lost to him for ever; in this, too, she was disappointed—Percy was devoted heart and soul to his young and gentle bride, and when all was over, and him upon whom she had once lavished the entire wealth of her affections, gone, with smiles upon his lips and sunlight on his brow, in company with the chosen of his heart, to spend the first sweet days of married life, amid sylvan scenes and blooming bowers, leaving her to shed in solitude, alone and unheeded, the bitter tears of self-reproach and wounded vanity, her whole soul seemed changed, she felt as though she had been wronged, spurned, and now must be avenged. Strange and almost unaccountable is the process by which love turns to hate, and yet it is by no means uncommon; indeed the two extremes of love and hate more strongly resemble each other than most persons imagine: the same restless, anxious fears disturb the breast in which they make their home—the same craving after the attainment of hopes full oft deferred—the same constant hovering between hope and disappointment, and the same alternation between doubt and certainty of a speedy realization of all the bosom has in secret nursed. True, the heart, where love has formed a settled and sure abiding place—where all doubts are cleared away, and the sunshine of happiness sheds its halo of delight o'er every feeling, can never be afflicted with such sensations as we have described; but we refer to the first emotions of love, when all is as yet unknown, and jealous pangs full oft afflict the mind, and doubt chills each warm and tender feeling, robbing our days of joy and our nights of peace; and in this stage of love we can fearlessly affirm that the emotions it produces in the breast are strangely similar to hate, and the change from one to the other is by no means so difficult, or so utterly at variance, as at first sight it would appear, especially when, as in the case of Ada, love has long taken the tinge of selfishness, making it less her lover than herself she loved. This was plainly shown in her persisted rejection of him, and the cruel renouncement of his love, because she conceived him wanting in that entire devotion she claimed as her due. Not, as we have seen, that she did not feel acutely in abandoning one whom she really loved, but her object and desire was to wound his feelings, and make him miserable; having succeeded in this, she heeded not her own feelings, but now that he had so entirely recovered from the effects of her unkindness as to become enamoured of another object, by whom his suit, so far from being rejected, was received with evident joy and delight, her pride had received a deep, and as she thought incurable wound—at least nothing but accomplishing the ultimate unhappiness of Percy, and making him repent the step he had taken in giving his hand to another, could by any possibility effect its cure. Ada reflected on all this, as, closeted in the privacy of her own room, she shed the bitter tears of self-mistrust and mortification.

"He shall yet suffer far more acutely," she murmured, half aloud; "I have the will, and I doubt not also the power, to wound him to the quick."

Thus musing and resolving, she dried her tears, and descended to the usual sitting-room—the very room from the windows of which she had watched the departure of her lover on the eventful day when she had renounced for ever his love; that room, too, had witnessed the anguish of Percy, as he sued to her in vain for forgiveness, and her own haughty and cold refusal to listen even to a word that he might urge in extenuation of his supposed fault. As memory brought these things once more before her mind in all the vividness of their acted time, she turned away, for she could not suppress the thought that she had sealed her own misery instead of Percy's; for was he not at that moment seated by the side of his new-made wife, descanting most probably on the bright and happy future which lay before them, apparently strewn with life's fairest and sweetest flowers ?—and would not Mary, with eager outstretched hand, pluck from his path all thorns and briers which might interpose between himself and happiness ?—while she, neglected by the man whom she had chosen in preference to Percy, was left to pine, unheeded and uncared for. The thought was more than she could bear, and for the sake of companionship she sought her uncle's room. The kind old man welcomed her with even more than his accustomed cordiality; the traces of tears were still visible on his cheeks—for parting with his only daughter he felt to be a sore and heavy trial; for, though convinced of Mary's strong affection for himself, and reposing implicit confidence in her promise of a quick return to spend some hours with him, yet he knew that henceforth she must come in the character of a guest, not like a child at home: he was no longer her sole and undivided protector, he could no more lay claim to the largest portion of her heart, and though, in taking upon herself the solemn duties of a wife, he was well aware she would never forget those which appertained to a fond and affectionate daughter, yet he also knew that her husband must naturally claim the greater portion of her time and tenderness—indeed he would not wish it otherwise—still, although as free from selfishness as most men, he could not check the rising sigh or repel the starting tear, as his daughter passed from his own into another's keeping; and not only for himself did Mr. Herbert shed the tear of anxious solicitude, for his beloved child

> "Had gone unto another home,
> Unto another's care :
> And who may say what bitter trials,
> What sorrows wait her there!"

And on her account he indulged in many hopeful, but at the same time anxious musings, for he knew by experience—

> " That love and life are mysteries,
> Both blessing and both blest,
> And yet how much they teach the heart
> Of trial and unrest."

Mary was worthy of trust and full confidence, and, blest in her husband's love and tender care, he believed that much of sorrow and anxiety would be spared her. She was worthy of happiness, and he rejoiced in the prospect she had of possessing it.

"Well, Ada, my child," said the old gentleman kindly, as his niece entered. "You miss your cousin sadly, I do not doubt, and I am myself but a poor substitute, especially at the present time, for though rejoicing at Mary's good fortune in having secured so worthy a husband, I must confess I am still selfish enough to regret the loss I have sustained in so good and dutiful a child."

"Mary is worthy of a better and more deserving man than Percy," replied Ada, as if half unconsciously.

"How so ?" returned her uncle quickly. " Percy is surely a most noble and deserving character. You cannot, my child, surely know aught to his disadvantage ?"

" I meant not to have said so much, uncle," replied Ada, half evasively, "but having done so, I will not unnecessarily arouse your fears without endeavouring to allay them; to do so, I need only refer to my own warm and long attachment to Percy, continued even against your inclination, which it was most painful to me to oppose, till, on discovering his true principles, I resolved, cost me what it might, to tear his loved image from my breast, for I knew my own disposition too well to expect to find happiness with one whom I could not respect."

"Could not respect ?" repeated Mr. Herbert in a tone of surprise, for he had never for a moment conceived that Ada's rejection of Percy arose from other motives than a desire to fall into his views, and give her hand to the man whom he conceived to be a more fitting match for the youthful heiress. " Could not respect ?" repeated Mr. Herbert; " pray explain yourself, for indeed, Ada, I am at a loss to understand you."

" As you require it of me, uncle, I shall only say, that, during our long acquaintance, I experienced on so many occasions undoubted proofs of the fickleness of Percy's character, whose attentions were given unsparingly to all with whom he came in contact, that, as I before said, I resolved on renouncing him, which I did, spite of all his efforts to induce me to alter my determination. In vain he besought me to think better of my resolve, and not doom him to perpetual misery. I remained firm to my purpose, and you see, uncle, how speedily he was enabled to transfer his affections to another. None," she continued in a tone of well-feigned solicitude, " can hope more for Mary's future happiness—at the same time, none can entertain stronger fears on her behalf."

" Why did you not tell me all this sooner ?" replied Mr. Herbert, almost sternly. " I might then have saved my child from probable misery, but now it is too late ; how could you have acted thus cruelly both to your cousin and myself ?"

" Forgive me, uncle," replied Ada, gently. " To Mary I did urge all in my power, to prevent her forming an alliance which appeared to me at least fraught with danger to her happiness, but she refused to listen to anything I could say against her marrying Percy, for whom she appears to entertain so blind an attachment, as to render her entirely indifferent to his faults."

" Then, why not have appealed to me ?" returned Mr. Herbert anxiously.

" Delicacy towards both myself and Mary prevented my having recourse to so unpleasing an alternative," replied Ada ; " but do not, dear uncle, allow this to make you uncomfortable. Mary is not naturally of a jealous disposition, and will not take offence at any display of attentions to another, and likewise reposes such full confidence in Percy's love for herself, that I am ready to believe they will be as happy as the generality of married people."

" You say right," replied Mr. Herbert, his fears beginning to dissipate as he thought upon his daughter's mental worth. " You say right, Mary's excellent disposition and noble qualities will surely counteract all the evil effects that may show themselves in her husband, and in time entirely eradicate them."

" We will at least hope so," said Ada impressively; " and now, uncle, to speak of myself, as was my original object in intruding upon your privacy, I wished to enquire whether you had heard any further tidings concerning Walter Eardley?"

" Twice I received his letter, with which I made you acquainted at the time. I learnt, through his brother, who is shortly about to be married, that the lady to whom Walter considered himself bound by every tie of honour, is no longer in existence, and though he is at present sunk in the deepest despondency, his brother yet conceives it probable that his thoughts will ultimately again turn towards yourself ; indeed, Sir Richard is desirous of seeing him form the alliance with yourself which his father was so anxious to consummate."

Ada's countenance brightened as these words fell pleasantly on her ear. She did not, it is true, love Walter—she did not even feel for him that decided preference, without which happiness cannot be expected in the marriage state ; still he pleased her vanity, his fascinations and accomplishments were such as to render him a most pleasing lover to one so proud and vain as Ada ; she desired to win his affections, to gain the entire mastery over his will, to lead him captive overawed by her own rare beauty—this she conceived would be a conquest worth boasting of, and she sighed to have him again a suppliant at her feet, to listen to the low tones of his musical voice, while he whispered words of undying love, in her not unwilling ear, yet all this she wished accomplished without the sacrifice on her part of that haughty pride which formed so conspicuous a trait in her character. Walter voluntarily returning to her side, acknowledging his error and seeking forgiveness for his past neglect, and which, after due consideration she might graciously grant, was now her most ardent wish, and which she thought would most probably pique her former lover, for she could not entirely dispossess herself of the idea that Percy still loved her, in spite of all his efforts to the contrary, and that love she desired to turn against himself, to make it poison his whole happiness, and become the means of causing an utter disunion between himself and Mary. She therefore endeavoured to conceal from her uncle's observation the satisfaction his last words had given to herself, as she replied—

"Walter has treated me with such marked disrespect, that I scarcely know how I could, consistent with my own self-esteem, receive him again into favour. I was anxious to hear of his welfare, and, indeed, as I before said, I sought you this morning purposely to enquire after him, but to look upon him again as my affianced husband would be asking too much."

"Well, we shall see," replied her uncle, "I do not intend to press you on this subject, it must rest entirely with yourself; though I do not, I cannot doubt, that Walter sincerely loves you, and that it cost him a severe effort to renounce your hand, but honour compelled him to become the husband of a lady whom he had unfortunately induced to stray from the path of virtue. But enough, my child; if need be, Walter will plead his own cause, and I do not doubt he will do so far more effectually than myself."

Ada smiled in reply. She was well pleased with this conversation, it afforded some balm to her wounded spirit, and she dwelt upon it with renewed satisfaction, sedulously endeavouring to forget the slight she conceived she had received from Percy Raymond till the return of the bridal party to London should enable her to commence her scheme for the destruction of his happiness. In the meantime Percy and his young wife were spending the honeymoon amid scenes well calculated to tune their hearts to pleasing anticipations of the future, and when the time arrived for their return to London, to take up their abode in their future home, no thought of anxiousness mingled with their glad joy. Proud and happy was Mary, as she took possession of her new home, and occupied the rightful station of mistress, receiving the warm greetings of her friends with a sweet, but blushing countenance; of her husband, too, she was justly proud, and looked up to him with that mingling of respect and tenderness so becoming in a young and new made wife. Ada, we have said, was among the first to offer congratulations to the young married pair, and so kind and conciliating were her manners, that Mary, though surprised, was not the less pleased at the change; she spoke, too, so kindly of her father, representing in tender tones his anxiety once more to see and embrace his child, and gently hinting to her cousin the necessity of removing from his mind any feeling of neglect that circumstances might have engendered, by devoting as much of her time to his society as she could well do, consistent with her present position.

"You know, dear Mary," she said in conclusion, "how pleased I am to supply your place to my uncle, but all my endeavours have not succeeded in banishing a certain despondency which seems to have settled on his spirit, and which all my efforts have not succeeded in removing. I do not wish to alarm you, dear Mary, still I owe it both to myself and you to say this much."

"Oh, thank you, dear Ada, a thousand times," replied Mary; "I know well that you have done your best to cheer my father's solitude, and I did not, indeed, think he would so much have missed me, but he has been so long accustomed to my society, that he values it more highly than it is worth, and I even now reproach myself for having been so happy away from him; but I will return with you, dear Ada, immediately—he shall not suppose for a moment that I am less anxious to see him than he is to see me."

Having thus resolved, Mary hastened to attire herself in a walking dress, and her toilet was just receiving the finishing touch, when her husband entered. At the first moment he did not perceive Ada, but regarding Mary with a look of surprise, exclaimed—

"How now, my love; what, going abroad so early?"

"Oh, yes!" replied Mary, eagerly. "I am about to visit my father. I have not seen him, you know, since our return to town, and I am afraid he will think me neglectful."

"No, my love, he can scarcely do that," said Percy, in a tone of surprise, "neither do I think it desirable that you should go to him thus early; if you will defer your visit till evening, I shall myself be happy to accompany you."

"Oh, Percy, you will not, I am sure, think me unkind if I feel obliged to decline your offer; but I have learnt from my cousin that my dear father is not either in good health or spirits, and this alone induces me to hasten to him without delay."

"I beg your pardon, Miss Herbert," said Percy, approaching the window near which Ada was standing; "but till this instant I was not cognisant of your presence; I hope, indeed, I have the pleasure to see you well."

"Perfectly," replied Ada, a sweet smile lighting up her beautiful face, "neither is my uncle so unwell as Mary's fears would make her believe; indeed, I can safely affirm that her visit may well be deferred to the evening. I know, indeed, that he is anxious to see her, but I will undertake to keep him amused till evening."

Percy's brow relaxed somewhat of its stern coldness, as he listened to the soft tones of Ada's voice, and he answered with more kindness than he usually assumed towards her—

"We are much indebted to your kind consideration, Miss Herbert, and under these circumstances, Mary will doubtless avail herself of your proposal, and you may prepare Mr. Herbert to receive us as his guests this evening."

Ada gracefully expressed the pleasure it would afford her to do so, and turning to her cousin, added—

"I think it will be better for me to return to my uncle at once, and apprise him of the pleasure in store for him; this will do more towards restoring to him his good spirits than aught else."

So far all was well, and if Mary had only fallen into her husband's views, all would have continued so, but unfortunately her fears on her father's behalf were now thoroughly aroused, and, to her affectionate mind, the bare idea of being thought neglectful or careless of his happiness and welfare, was painful and repugnant in the extreme; she could not, therefore, so easily resign her intention of hastening to him at once, but she wished to go with her husband's approval, and therefore sought to gain him over to her own views.

"I know, dear Percy," she began, "that you will not miss me for a few hours, as your sisters will be most happy to keep you company in my absence, and you will appreciate the natural anxiety I feel to hasten to my father without delay; he has never before been separated from me for an entire day, and now it is weeks since he has seen me, and I cannot help reproaching myself for remissness, in not having visited him before. You will not, therefore, object to my returning with Ada, instead of waiting for this evening."

"You are at perfect liberty to please yourself," replied Percy, with the first touch of coldness in his tones that had yet been assumed to Mary; "I thought, after your cousin's assurance, you might safely have deferred your visit for so short a period as that which I required of you, but, as I said before, I do not wish to impose the slightest restraint upon your actions—you can, therefore, act in this matter as your own wishes dictate."

Mary was too eager and delighted to receive the consent of her husband, to perceive the coldness of his tones, and never doubting that her desires were seconded with his approval, cheerfully bade him farewell, and took her departure with her cousin, who inwardly rejoiced at having thus sown the first seeds of discord in the breast of Percy, for she plainly perceived, although Mary did not, that he was far from pleased, or even satisfied with the conduct of his wife.

'Alas! how light a cause may move
Dissension between hearts that love!
A something light as air— a look,
    A word unkind, or wrongly taken.
Ah! love, that tempests never shook,
    A breath, a touch like this hath shaken."

How much, then, it behoves those who have the care of love, to keep him in rosy bondage bound—to loose not

"A single tie that round him clings,
Nor ever let him use his wings!"

ADA'S RAGE AT THE CONTENTS OF WALTER'S LETTER.

For how many have found, to their sorrow,—

"That but an hour's, an instant's flight
Has robbed his plumes of half their light!"

And those, whose prospect of happiness shone the brightest when they joined their hands and hearts at the altar, have too frequently found their love decline from the end of the honeymoon, and that instead, as they had fondly supposed, they were entering the temple of happiness on their wedding day, they made the first

No 16.

step towards the abode of misery and wretchedness.   And whose fault is this? frequently both are to blame.   They become careless and indifferent when they know that the object beloved is irrevocably their own, and, instead of keeping up the fire of affection that once burnt so brightly in their breasts, they allow it to become dull, and often to go out altogether for the want of those tender and endearing attentions without which pure love cannot exist; neither will it do so, no matter how vividly it may once have burnt, unless each are willing to sacrifice occasionally their own hopes and inclinations in obedience to the wishes of the other.   The wife has unquestionably the most difficult part to perform, because her husband is more exposed to temptations from the world, and is also frequently oppressed with cares and trials on account of the pressure and anxieties of business, and of which the wife knows nothing; great allowance, therefore, should be made by the young wife, if her husband occasionally manifests a fretfulness or ill-humour, for which she cannot account, and which it is always wisest not to heed, save by doing her utmost to charm it away by sweet and playful converse, and kind and soothing attentions; this can never fail to restore his amiability, and to dissipate the dark clouds of care from his brow. If a wife thus act, her husband, unless indeed he be something lower than man, will ever love and cherish the kind and gentle companion of his happiest hours, and never, on his part, do aught which might tend to break the chain which binds their hearts together.   This, we are willing to allow, is a difficult task, yet it is, nevertheless, one which every wife can perform, if she only put her heart and soul into it.   And why should she not? the stake is for happiness, and it is surely worth while taking pains to obtain it.   If any gay and happy bride should chance to run her eye over these lines, let her remember, that to win a man is easy, but to keep him is the difficulty, and ever will be so, unless a woman is willing at all times to sacrifice her own wishes if they interfere with his.   With much that gives promise of happiness, a young wife has yet much to contend with, and will be bitterly disappointed if she expects to meet with perpetual sunshine; clouds and storms will most assuredly threaten occasionally to darken her happiness, and destroy for a time her peace, for she has come to a new house, and with that new house there are new associations, new subjects of thought, new enjoyments, and new cares; the past, with its mingled joys and sorrows, is behind her, and the future is all hidden in the blaze of sunlight with which it is enveloped.   There is not surely a more beautiful object in creation than a young girl on her wedding day, or one that awakens so strong an interest in the heart of the beholder, as she stands at the altar, blushing and bending with the weight of her own ecstacies, tears falling from her eyes, as in the midst of her bright anticipations for the future, she thinks also of the solemn responsibility she is at that moment taking upon herself as regards the future, and of the fair and happy past, to which she is about to bid eternal adieu—to quit her childhood's home, her home no longer—to take her part in the great and busy world of active life, made up of duties and of cares, to which she has been hitherto a stranger, and consequently to which she can bring no experience to guide her through the difficult path she must henceforth pursue.   Her imagination pictures scenes of beauty and grandeur, and she hears only sweet songs of love and delight; still, a vague fear of finding only sorrow and suffering, when the brightness of the moment hath passed away, and the voices of joyful companions are hushed, embitters her thoughts, and precludes gaiety from her heart. Up to the wedding day she has fondly believed herself to be rapidly progressing towards the temple of happiness; although so many have missed their way, yet each one fully believes she at least is pursuing the right track, and that on her marriage with the chosen of her heart, the object will be accomplished, and the future be an unvarying round of enjoyment, peace and bliss; but when the long-wished-for and important day arrives, it brings with it other, and sadder thoughts—she ponders deeply upon the serious change in her position in life, and sorrows over her separation from those tender and loving hearts she leaves behind her around the parental hearth—

"And shadows o'er her brow come stealing
Like some fair temple which all day
Hath slept in sunshine, slow revealing
Its several beauties, ray by ray,
Till it shines out a thing to bless,
All full of light and loveliness."

CHAPTER XXXIV.

" 'Tis vain to strike a broken lute,
Its chords can only harm you,
Their melody's for ever mute—
Oh! how they once could charm you!
The world may clothe the cheek in rays,
But after all its wiles,
We see too plainly as we gaze,
They're desolating smiles."

THE coming on of still evening is at all times a summons from cheerfulness and gaiety to a contemplation of the past, the present, and the future. Every object appears in union with the soft pensive aspect of closing day; sadness loses something of its gloom, and joy settles into calm delight, while we review the truths and illusions of existence beneath the sunset's crimsoned glow, or the more placid grandeur of the moon and stars. At such times our musings are of good; by the fading light without and the deepening shadow within, we appear to realize the presence of angel visitants, who come in that pause from toil and sin,

"To put our senses' curtain by,
And on the wakeful soul look in."

And we wander from scenes of home, of cares, or of gladness, to sources of higher pleasures, of more ennobling and refined enjoyments. At such times, too, our minds revert to the quick fading charms of life, and how soon its promises are lost to our anticipation, even as the shades of evening veil the beauty of day. It is a fitting hour to pause upon the annals of our existence, and take note of each feeling that has animated our breasts, be it good or ill; to mourn over the errors of life, and confirm ourselves in each wise and fitting resolve to look beyond this world, and its many vicissitudes, to another and a brighter state of existence. It is then that some feeling of communion, thrown happily upon the heart, discovers its capacity to sympathise with the sorrows, and, if possible, add to the joys of another; all feelings of anger and ill-will melt in calmer and better thoughts away—

"And ere the night asserts its sway,
We bless the twilight's gentle ray."

Thus felt and communed Fanny, now the bride of Henry Fergusson, as she sat alone at the still hour of evening. The earth was bright and beautiful, the air was balmy, and came laden with a thousand aromatic scents, as it fanned her flushed and feverish brow, and the unclouded heavens formed a glorious canopy over human existence. The sunlight streamed through natural and romantic bowers and birds, trees, and flowers sent forth their purest incense and their sweetest song. Altogether the scene upon which she gazed was one of sweet and tranquil beauty, such as tunes the mind to a thankful gladness for the rich blessings so profusely scattered round even the humblest path, and Fanny, spite of the anxieties which weighed down her once buoyant spirit, felt a sense of grateful happiness stealing o'er her spirit. Since the painful discovery she had made that Henry had given her his hand in marriage solely from a feeling of gratitude, while his heart and affections were devoted to another, a change—a strange and startling change had come o'er the spirit of her young life's dream.   Up to that moment she had revelled in constant and unvarying sunshine of joyous delight, she had never walked in the deep shadows of existence, through which so many are forced to wend their dubious and unstedfast way without one friendly star to guide their course or direct their erring steps aright; never till this unhappy hour, had mirth awakened a strain which her heart echoed not again; no, she had floated, like a light leaf, down pleasure's stream, caught in each sparkling eddy there.   Not, as we have seen, that con- stant prosperity enervated her mind, or rendered her unmindful of the sufferings of others, for a more generous or noble-minded being never existed than Fanny Mowbray, or one more willing to lend a listening ear to the sorrows and trials of others, or more ready and anxious to relieve them to the utmost of her power.   Still, it is utterly impossible for one who has never sorrowed them- selves, to feel that sweet and close sympathy for the sorrows of others, which makes charity so doubly precious, so exalting and refining to the mind; and consequently, though Fanny had done her best to meliorate the sufferings and assuage the anxieties of the sick and sorrowful, she had never felt so deeply, or entered so fully into their sorrows, as now that she was herself afflicted.   She loved Henry with the fond warm devotedness of a first and only love, and it cost her bosom a severe pang to know that his love was not, as she had fondly and fully believed, all her own.

"Oh! why," she exclaimed in the first bitterness of her sorrow, "why did I not know this earlier?—all might then have been well;" for in the warm romantic ardour of her disposition, she felt as though it would have been com- paratively easy to renounce her once fond dream of bliss, and confirm Henry's happiness with another.   Yes, she would have compassed all things to gain this wished-for end.   What to her was luxury, without the consciousness of con- tributing to the happiness of the one she loved?   How gladly, even now, would she have exchanged situations with Jane Clarence, to become the loved object on which her husband's affections were fixed.   Surrounded by all that makes life a source of pleasure, her path apparently strewn with flowers, which courted her acceptance on every hand, Fanny was anything but a happy bride; she had none to whom she could communicate her sorrows, or pour out the deep anxieties of her bosom—a stranger in a strange land, an evident object of envy to almost every beholder, for her wit and sprightly manners had already secured her many so-called friends—butterflies who buz around those upon whom the sun of wealth has shed its lavish rays, but who keep aloof from poverty and suffering, shunning their very presence with horror and disgust—

"As though the poor did surely bear
Contagion in the rags they wear;"

for she possessed a mind of almost uncommon discernment, and therefore gave little or no heed to their high encomiums on her beauty and accomplishments. Their manners and customs, so different to what she had been used, frequently amused and interested her, and she sought to become acquainted with all that was deemed of interest in that land of romantic beauty; but, unfortunately, an apathy seemed to have fallen upon the mind of her husband—he became abstracted, withdrew even from her society, and, closeted in the privacy of his own studio, would remain for hours alone, and when induced by her winning and persuasive gentleness to mix occasionally in society, or visit with her some place worthy of inspection, his mind evidently wandered from the scenes upon which he gazed, and his indifferent and abstracted manners gave token of his settling into a decided and irremediable misanthropy.   Fanny deeply mourned this sad change in her husband, and frequently blamed herself as the innocent cause.   She felt that she had a painful and difficult task to perform to arouse her husband from this sad and baneful stupor, which appeared to have taken possession of all his faculties. To represent to him the unkind neglect which he manifested towards herself, and her own deep sorrow on that account, to set plainly before him the temptations to which his conduct exposed her, and the painful mortification to which she was frequently subjected by the unmistakable attentions of others, who, regarding her as a neglected wife, thought of her as an easy conquest. To do this would doubtless have been the surest mode of arousing Henry from his state of dreamy stupefaction, but not thus could Fanny resolve to act. No, her natural pride and delicacy forbade her even to hint this to her husband. No ; sooner would she see him settle into a confirmed misanthropist, than recall him to active life, by a recapitulation of her own wrongs, or the deep sense she felt of his own neglect towards herself. Fanny fortunately possessed an elasticity of mind, that rose superior to the common ills of life, and though she mourned deeply over this first sad trial, it was her lot to know she did not on that account give herself up entirely to despair. Had she known of Henry's love for Jane previous to her marriage, the natural generosity of her nature would instantly have prompted her to sacrifice her own hopes and feelings in order to bring about their mutual happiness, in the contemplation of which she would have endeavoured to find her own ; but she was now his wife, bound to him by the nearest and holiest of ties—a tie which only love should weave, and only death can part; it was consequently her bounden duty to use every effort which might tend to induce him to forget the past, instead of thus strengthening himself in vain and useless regret. And yet the task appeared so difficult, so many objects opposed themselves to all her endeavours, that she was on the point of resigning herself to despair, and giving up the task she had imposed upon herself, the performance of which seemed a positive duty. They had been absent from England six months, during which time Fanny had experienced more of real anxiety and undoubted sorrow than she had previously ever even dreamed of. The evening was warm and beautiful, the bright rays of the setting sun shed a refulgent beauty on all around, and Fanny was seated alone, gazing with fixed but wondering admiration on the beautiful objects which surrounded her. The villa in which they had taken up their abode commanded a beautiful view of the bay, on which the gondolier glided in picturesque beauty, the song of the men, as they rested occasionally upon their oars, broke pleasantly upon the stillness of the evening, all things seemed in harmony with the soft stillness of the hour, and thoughts and hopes came thronging back to the mind of Fanny, which had long slumbered in her breast. She held in her hand an open book descriptive of the sunny land which for awhile she made her home, but it rested half closed upon her knee, for busy wandering thought—which will not be enslaved, but wanders where it will o'er countless realms of space, conjuring up from the dark abyss of time, scenes and feelings long past and forgotten—had fled to other scenes. Sunk into so deep a reverie was Fanny, that she saw all the objects by which she was surrounded, as one who sees them not, for her thoughts had taken an unconscious tone of sadness ;—her husband was the first and most engrossing object of her waking dream—she mourned at this time less for herself than him ; when she pictured to her mind the deep but pent-up anguish of his bosom, so deep that it estranged him even from her, the tears which had been long gathering in her eyes, rolled unheeded down her cheeks. At this moment she was startled by the sound of a well-known voice, that came sweet and welcome to her ear, as in tender accents it pronounced her name ; she turned instantly, and beheld her husband seated by her side.

"What ails you, love," he enquired, in his kindest tones, " are you unwell, or hath anything occurred to distress or afflict your mind ?"

"Neither, dear Henry," replied Fanny, a bright smile chasing away the recent gloom from her fair face, and beaming ample testimony to the truth of her statement."

"Then why those tears ?" returned Henry. "Alas! my conscience accuses me of being the cause ; I have been cruelly unmindful of your happiness, dear Fanny—

that happiness which you confided so trustfully to my keeping. Alas! now that you know all, I fear you must hate and despise your husband.''

"Henry, love," she replied firmly, and laying, as she did so, her small white hand impressively on his arm, "you must promise me that you will not feel hurt or offended, if I open to you my whole heart, and speak those things which perhaps a false delicacy has hitherto prevented me from doing."

"Say on," returned Henry, with something of his latent moodiness. "I cannot possibly be offended, for how much soever you may blame me, you do not, cannot blame me more than I blame myself; we cannot undo the past. Oh, were it possible, then, dear Fanny, this hand—and he pressed the soft palm within his own—should be free."

"You utterly misapprehend me," replied Fanny, gently. "I had no thought or wish to chide you; indeed it was not of myself, or of any feeling connected with myself, but of you, dear Henry, I wished to speak. Have I your permission to proceed?"

"My permission! Ah! Fanny," replied her husband, "would I could yield to you the entire guidance of my destiny!"

"And is it, then, so utterly impossible," said Fanny, warmly; "believe me, no; it is far easier than you imagine. and for myself I would ask no greater boon than to be to you a guardian friend and adviser; to be allowed to steer your frail vessel through the shoals and quicksands, and guide it perchance into a safe and happy haven, where it may repose, after the buffets and storms of life, alike unmindful of the winter's snows and the summer's scorching heat."

As she finished speaking, the warmth of her feelings gave a soft glow to her cheek; her eyes shone with unwonted brightness, and her whole bearing was that of one inspired by some great and daring object; and at that moment, as the setting sun shed its last mellowed rays upon her upturned face, she appeared to Henry to assume the guise of a guardian angel, sent to pluck from his path the thorns and briers which entangled his steps, and pierced him on every side. His cheek, too, caught the reflection of her's; the deep shadow vanished from his brow, as he answered—

"And could you, dear Fanny, be all this to me?"

"All this, and more," she replied. "I will not conceal from you, dear Henry," she added, after a moment's pause, "that the tears you beheld upon my cheek were those of heartfelt sorrow, but they were not shed for myself, but you. When I saw you day by day wasting your energies in fruitless regret—when, in place of the bright hopes you once nourished, and which led you to sigh for fame—to struggle with poverty and its accompanying bitterness, suffering it not for a moment to interfere with your ambitious hopes—when your eyes shone with joyful anticipations, as your visions of fame seemed already achieved, and nothing daunted, you in your pursuit after acquirements—when, I say, in place of all this, I perceived you wasting your energies in vain regrets, burying each hope, and crushing every ennobling feeling under the pressure of your despair, I wept to think that, instead of promoting your views, confirming your happiness, and giving greater scope to your ability, I had unfortunately become the unhappy means of rendering you miserable. Oh! Henry, what would I not voluntarily renounce, even life itself, could I by so doing restore to you those bright hopes and ambitious prospects that once filled your days with dreams of bliss, and of which I have so unhappily been the means of taking from you."

Henry listened attentively as she spoke, never interrupting her, even by the slightest movement, so intently did he hang upon her words. His heart beat quick, too quick for utterance, but he warmly clasped the hand he still retained within his own. Fanny, too, dared not trust herself to say more, but sat trembling, for fear she had already said too much. While this conversation had been going on between them, the sun had gradually sank far into the west; twilight, that sweet time when day and night seem to meet and embrace each other, shed its soft influence on their minds. Henry especially felt softened, and his heart drawn more closely, more lovingly to the dear and tender partner of his days—her who, brought up in the lap of luxury, had never known what care or sorrow meant till she had united her destiny with his, scattering with no niggard hand rich blessings around his path, heeding not the deception he had practised towards her, thinking nothing, caring nothing for her own sorrows, so that she might tend to destroy, or if that could not be, at least mitigate his own. There was something so noble, so refined from the dross of selfishness in the character of Fanny, that rendered her irresistibly dear to the heart of her husband; he knew that he had wronged her tender confiding nature, that he had practised towards her the most unpardonable deception, and instead, as was his bounden duty, of seeking to make amends for his conduct by a double amount of affectionate attention, he had neglected her the more since accident had made her acquainted with the state of his feelings; while she, nobly forgetful of self, was striving to win him back to peace and joy, he had been indulging in his own selfish sorrow, and strengthening himself in vain and useless regret. He now for the first time saw his conduct in the right point of view, and while he deplored the past, steadfastly resolved to throw aside his dejection, and by mingling again in the busy world, and devoting himself to his professional studies, restore joy once more to the bosom of his good and tender wife. Alas! how utterly unmindful had he been of her happiness, how ungrateful a return had he made for her unwearying tenderness, her fond and anxious solicitude; his heart beat reproachfully as he drew Fanny closer and closer to him, and in eloquent language poured out the fulness of his breast.

"Thou art indeed my guardian angel," he fondly murmured, as he gazed upon the upturned face of his young and guileless wife, and which was now radiant with intense joy, "sent in mercy to cheer and soothe my wayward spirit, and henceforth I dedicate myself to thy happiness; thou hast indeed plucked from my path many thorns and briers, and strewn in their place sweet scented flowers, and which, when I have wantonly crushed, have only shed a more sweet and precious perfume, infusing new life and animation into my wearied and exhausted frame. Oh! Fanny, how can I sufficiently commend thy soft and touching virtues?—how attest my deep and fond adoration of the same?—the task were indeed impossible; to thy own pure heart and unsullied conscience must I leave thy reward, never doubting they will amply repay thee for all."

"And you, my husband——" said Fanny, gazing intently and anxiously on his face, while her own was bathed in tears.

"Will endeavour to prove myself worthy of so rich a treasure," replied Henry enthusiastically. "I have greatly wronged thee," he added, after a moment's hesitation, "I read it in those dear eyes," and stooping down to kiss her cheek, he mingled his tears with her own.

Sweet and hallowed were the feelings of the two fond hearts which now beat in unison, pure and sacred the emotions that filled their breasts. Twilight had given place to night, who had thrown his dark mantle over the earth, and hasted to resume his dismal reign. Yet, proud in his majesty and might, he sought to eclipse the noontide beauty of day, and, by the more subdued, yet not less beautiful light of the moon, which rose fair and majestically in the heavens, to rival even the god of day. And well might they who viewed the scene—

> "Then lit up all around them, say,
> That never yet had nature been
> Caught sleeping in a lovelier ray,
> Or rivall'd her own noontide face
> With purer show of moonlight grace."

Henry and Fanny remained clasped in each other's arms, looking out upon the lovely scenery that was spread like a beautiful picture before them—all cares and anxieties were forgotten, and they had now nought to disturb their repose. How long they thus remained it is impossible to say, hearts that beat with such fond, warm, reciprocal feelings as now animated theirs, take indeed but little note of time. The newness of their bliss forbade much converse; each was busily engaged in deep but by no means unpleasing thoughts; and when they at length retired for the night, dreams of future happiness—of coming days of bliss, made sweetly blest by mutually contributing to each other's joys, and sharing each other's cares, filled their slumbers. Henry indeed felt truly grateful to his young wife for having thus affectionately aroused him from the dread stupor that had threatened to overwhelm his entire faculties. Still, as days and weeks wore on, he could not entirely banish the image of Jane from his breast; and though he strove hard to conceal it from Fanny, and appeared cheerful and glad in her presence, there were times when sorrow and anxiety gained the mastery over him; indeed, the constant struggle he maintained with himself, soon manifested itself in his altered appearance. His health visibly declined; his form lost its roundness, and his cheek the glow of health. Fanny quickly perceived these unmistakable signs of returning indisposition, and sought the advice of an English physician resident abroad. Henry did not refuse to consult with this gentleman; though entertaining but little hopes that he could minister to a mind diseased, still, for the sake of his affectionate wife, he was content to enter into a detail of his present symptoms. The physician, with the natural acuteness that seems well nigh a part of the profession, quickly discovered that the mind, far more than the body of his patient, stood in need of the healing art, and in accordance with which he prescribed travel and change of scene as the most likely means to abate his disorder. Fanny was all eagerness to try the remedy, in which she reposed herself the greatest faith, from the hope that it might become the means of withdrawing her husband's thoughts from painful and too engrossing subjects, which she much feared, spite of his own well-directed efforts, too frequently oppressed him. Change of scene might, then, be productive of the most beneficial results, and, in order to give a still greater change to his ideas, she resolved not to pursue the old beaten track which travellers generally adopt, but to make a tour through the islands of Sicily and Malta; Henry eagerly fell into her views, and preparations were made for their immediate departure from Florence. The bustle of travelling, by giving a turn to his thoughts, had already produced a good effect upon the mind of Henry, which his young wife hailed as a fair and welcome omen, it was consequently with gay and happy hearts that they embarked on board the vessel which was destined to convey them the first part of their journey. The morning was bright and beautiful; indeed, though now late in the autumn, had it not been for the refreshing influence of the soft sea breeze, the weather would have been insupportably hot, but the wind was both pleasant and favourable, and exerted a most delightful power over the spirits of our travellers. Never had Fanny looked more lovely, or what is far better, more serenely happy, than, while hanging on the arm of her husband, she surveyed with him the splendid scenery which adorned the coast as the vessel moved slowly onward. And never had Henry looked more hopeful, or his fine features shone with greater animation, as, with a painter's eye and a poet's tongue, he directed his young wife's attention to the beautiful landscape on which they mutually gazed. And never could either painter or poet desire a more splendid view, the whole of which was so wonderfully diversified by all the riches both of nature and art, that there seemed scarcely an object wanting to render the scene complete; and it is difficult to say whether it was rendered more pleasing from the singularity of many of these objects, or from the incredible variety of the whole. Palaces reared over the tops of other palaces, and ancient magnificence trampled under foot by modern folly!—mountains and islands, that were once celebrated for their beauty and fertility, changed into barren wastes, and barren wastes into fertile fields and rich vineyards;—mountains sunk into plains, and plains swelled into mountains; lakes drunk up by volcanoes, and extinguished volcanoes turned into lakes—the earth in many places throwing out flame. In short, Nature seemed to have formed this coast in its most capricious mood—never apparently having gone seriously to work, but to have devoted this spot to the most unlimited indulgence of caprice and frolic. The palace, too, of the king formed a conspicuous and beautiful object, with many others surrounding it, all built over the roofs of those of Herculaneum, buried

LADY EARDLEY CONSOLING AND ADVISING HER SON, WALTER EARDLEY.

nearly a hundred feet by the eruptions of Vesuvius ;—the black fields of lava which have run from that mountain, intermixed with gardens, vineyards, and orchards ; Vesuvius itself, in the background of the scene, discharging volumes of fire and smoke, and forming a beautiful track in the air over their heads, extending, without being broken or dissipated, to the utmost verge of the horizon. A variety of beautiful towns and villages round the base of the mountain, thoughtless of the impending ruin that daily threatened them. Such objects as these, comprising and making up a beautiful and wondrous whole, formed the most conspicuous portion of the scenery, upon which they gazed with a feeling of entranced and strange delight. Fanny's gaze was frequently averted from these objects to the face of her husband, and when she noted the bright radiance of his eye, and the animated expression of his countenance, her heart danced with delight. They remained on deck without the wish or power to tear themselves from the contemplation of this magic scenery. Fortunately it fell calm, as if on purpose to give them an opportunity to contemplate its varied beauties, and drawing forth his pencils, Henry proposed making a sketch of the surrounding objects. Fanny eagerly seconded his wishes, and, seated by his side, watched with admiring and loving eyes the progress of his employment, occasionally suggesting some little improvement or alteration, of which Henry gladly availed himself; for though possessed of a rich genius, and undoubted skill, he did not consider himself perfect in his delightful profession; nor was he above receiving or profiting by a suggestion, even if it came from one who owned no such genius as that possessed by himself. Thus passed the first hours of their embarkation. With light and happy hearts, they continued to contemplate this delightful prospect till sunset, when the wind again sprung up, and they learnt with a feeling of pleasure that, if it continued, they might expect by the following evening to be in sight of Sicily. After descending to the cabin, and partaking of some refreshment, the weather was so fine that it tempted them again on deck. The night, though warm and fair, was not very dark, and Mount Vesuvius was flaming away at an almost fearful rate. The ship was going so smooth that they were scarcely sensible of its motion, and could plainly observe the red hot stones thrown from Vesuvius to a vast height in the air, and after their fall, roll heavily down the sides of the mountain. It was truly a strange and magnificent sight, seeming to fill their minds with a superstitious awe. At times the lava rose to the summit of the mountain, and continued without variety to illuminate the air around it; at others, a clear red flame issued from the crater, and continued to blaze without interruption for the space of half an hour, and then again it would seem as if some inflammable substance was suddenly kindled up in the very interior of the mountain; and the fire would as suddenly change its colour, and an explosion of stone take place. All this was rendered plainly perceptible with the aid of a good glass, and their fascination increased tenfold, so that they remained wrapt up in its contemplation, heedless of the flight of time and the cool night air. Henry, suddenly rousing himself from the abstracted mood into which the wonders of Nature had thrown him, turned anxiously towards his companion, and reproaching himself for his own want of thought, recommended her to retire to the cabin for the night.

"My dear Fanny," he said, with a look of anxiety, "you must, I am sure, be suffering from excessive fatigue, and which I have selfishly enhanced. Do, my love, be persuaded, and retire at once."

"Dear Henry, this has been too happy a day to allow me to think for one moment of fatigue," replied Fanny, pressing the arm upon which she leant for support.

He turned towards her instantly, as he said, in reply—

"And could you, Fanny—you, so formed for society, which has ever done justice to your wit and humour, and in which your lively manners and great conversational powers have rendered you so deservedly a favourite—could you resign all this, and devote your time and talents to the arduous task of cheering and soothing my wayward destiny?"

"Blessed task!" replied Fanny, with energetic warmth. "I ask no dearer joy than permission to share your sorrows. The charm which society once possessed for my mind is flown, and I would not wish for other joys or other pleasures than are to be found in your company. I would even shun those places of amusement wherein I once found delight, for I have found far greater and sweeter pleasure in this voyage, with only you by my side, than if I were visiting gay and giddy scenes of fashionable life, with crowds to worship at my feet."

"Then, indeed, we think and feel alike on this as on other subjects," said Henry, "and are, in truth, suited for myself, dear Fanny. I am, both by nature and inclination, unformed for mixed society; I ever felt myself entirely out of place, and could only endure it on your account alone, for it seemed unkind to withdraw you from scenes in which your many accomplishments rendered you an object at once of admiration and of love."

"Dearest Henry," returned his gentle wife, affected even to tears by the kind and affectionate words of her husband, and still more by the tones in which they were spoken; "dearest Henry, let me ever share your joys and sooth your sorrows, and then indeed I shall esteem myself truly blessed."

"Sorrows!" repeated Henry, "they are flown, for you have taught me to forget them; and how can I be sufficiently grateful to Providence for the sweet blessings conferred upon me in thy generous love and confidence, and prove to you how much I value and prize your affectionate care and tenderness; but I am doing the very thing for which I was just now blaming myself, and keeping you exposed to the cool night air; let me then, my love, lead you to your cabin at once."

Fanny willingly assented, and, rocked by the gentle undulations of the restless, murmuring ocean, soon sank into sweet and happy slumbers.

CHAPTER XXXV.

" The merry bells ring, and the merry folks shout,
    The matrons are gazing from window and door,
For a blythe wedding train the church hath poured out,
    And the green lane is crowded behind and before.
A fair blushing maiden hath promised to-day
    To love and to cherish her chosen through life,
And she walks by his side in bridal array,
    To be from that moment an Englishman's wife."

CLARA, we have seen, after many weeks—nay, months of anxious solicitude and harassing care, seemed at length to have attained to the very height of her ambition. So splendid—so far removed from all that had of late conspired to rob her of her peace, was the prospect now before her; so far above aught that her brightest and fairest visions had ever pictured, that her head turned giddy, and her heart beat with quickened pulsation, as she contemplated the dazzling height to which she was about to be raised by her marriage with the man she had so long and ardently loved, even when she had every reason to believe him unfaithful towards another, whom his cruelty had hurried into an untimely grave; and now that all shadows were cleared from his character, and he shone forth pure and sinless as herself, she looked up to him with a feeling almost of reverence, with which there ever mingled the warmest idolatry. In the fond and soft contemplation of the future, which appeared to her mind bright with hope and promise, she forgot many of the wise and useful lessons learnt in the school of adversity, and which should have taught her that no state or condition of life is exempt from its cares and anxieties, or free from those sorrows which are the common lot of humanity. She had suffered so long and unrepiningly, that she now appeared to think she had done with all human ill; that for the future she might reasonably expect to pass through life with smiles upon her lips and sunlight on her brow, loving and beloved by many; how bright to her appeared the future—how sweetly tinted were its golden rays. All sorrow and suffering seemed to fly her very presence, while domestic joys and undisturbed repose courted her acceptance on every hand. Alas! poor Clara, how mistaken are thy notions, for thou art doomed to prove that sorrows wait on every station, that neither wealth, rank, or love, that sweetest boon of all, can shield us from the troubles and anxieties of life. No matter how bright the prospect before thee, others have thought and felt as thou hast done, and yet proved that storms and sorrows were hidden in the dark future which they had pourtrayed so fair, and that anguish has frequently come from a quarter where they had never looked for misfortune, but fondly deemed themselves most secure. But we are anticipating. To return to Clara; it was perhaps natural that she should deem herself blest in having reached the goal of happiness, so long considered as beyond her most sanguine hopes, in being able to lavish the entire wealth of her heart upon the man she so fondly loved, without one pang of remorse, without one feeling of regret. There was something, too, in the character of Richard, opposed to what she had once regarded him, so noble, so pure and high-minded, that she felt as though he claimed by right her fond devotion, and she was only too happy to bestow it. He loved her, too, with a warmth, an undeviating tenderness that even rivalled her own, and blest in his endearing society, sharing his hope, his joy, his home, how sweet and precious would life prove. How quickly time flew by when hallowed by his presence, and to look forward to continued days and nights, winged with such precious, pure delights, was joy beyond compare. Lady Eardley loved to look upon Clara, and see, day by day—ay, almost hour by hour. the long absent bloom gradually resuming its wonted place upon her cheek, the lustre revisiting once more her hitherto sunken eye, which now sparkled with the brightness of days gone by, while the freshness of youth lent again its charm to her elastic step and rounded form;—how soon doth joy overcome the effects of sorrow, and obliterate all trace of its presence. Clara was again the blithe and happy being whose presence alone seemed to banish sorrow and charm away all cares. It was thus that Lady Eardley loved to contemplate her, and look forward to years of happiness that she conceived must bless and reward such virtues as those displayed by her protege, whom she already loved as a daughter. She exulted, too, in the prospect of happiness held out to her son, and rejoiced that her own sorrows were not destined to be continued in him; and while she mourned over the sorrows and blighted hopes of her younger son, she saw too plainly they were but the effects of his own misconduct. He had acted from selfish motives in withdrawing Lucy from her home and friends; he conceived he had won her upon easy terms, and thus confirmed his own happiness without the slightest sacrifice—on her alone had that fallen. She, the weaker and less able to withstand temptation, he had caused to bend to his wishes, little dreaming, while he exulted over his success, that in his pursuit after happiness he had but grasped the shadow and lost the substance. Lady Eardley was fully aware of this, and therefore judged it wisest to allow him for a time to feel the effects of the erring path he had pursued—to let him mourn over his own failings, and deplore his errors. And Walter did indeed feel bitterly, and mourn deeply over the irretrievable past. Often would he watch, unseen, the tender affection that existed between his brother and Clara, while memory recalled forcibly to his mind the happy days when he too, beloved for himself alone, owned as dear and tender a companion, one who made his griefs her own, and knew no joy unshared by him; and then the oppressive thought that she was now no more, that she had died without pronouncing his forgiveness, believing herself forgotten for another; all her loving tenderness and unwearying devotion turned against her; doomed to have her bosom pierced and wounded by the very arm which she fully believed destined to ward off all danger, to be raised firm and unyielding in her defence, her very love turned to gall and wormwood, and made the sad instrument of rending her very heartstrings. Oh! when he thought of all this, and much more, that she had endured through him, and on his account alone, his heart grew sick and his very brain dizzy; reason appeared ready to desert its throne, and he would rush from the presence of his brother, and the contemplation of his happiness, to give vent to the sorrow that oppressed him, alone and unheeded to pour forth his anguish in sighs and tears. Lucy was, indeed, destined to be avenged, for through his entire life Walter was sensibly made to deplore his early errors; and the image of the wronged and deserted Lucy would present itself to his mind in the midst of gaiety and splendour, destroying the illusions which fancy had created, and dashing his cup of happiness untasted to the ground. Lady Eardley had suffered too much herself, and was also too fond and affectionate a mother, to witness the sorrows of her son without a deep pang of regret, or seeking to alleviate them to the utmost of her power. She had her own peculiar ideas of the most likely means to remove his unhappiness and cure his sorrows; taking, therefore, advantage of an opportunity when she suddenly discovered her son in tears, and evidently a prey to the bitterest remorse, and which he vainly endeavoured to conceal from her observation, she seated herself by his side, and taking his hand in her own, said in the kindest tone she could assume—

"Walter, I have long been a silent and apparently unmoved spectator of your unhappiness, and had I not been fully aware of the true cause, and judged it best to allow time to do something towards closing those wounds which I know rank so deeply in your breast, I should not, my dear son, have kept silent so long."

Walter turned away his head, to hide from his mother, the emotion that choked his utterance, and by an impatient movement of his hand intimated his desire to be left alone.

"No, Walter," continued Lady Eardley, in answer to this signal, "I cannot leave you now; I have much to say, which I hope will influence your future conduct, and become the means of restoring to you that peace of mind which you have unhappily lost." She paused a moment, but Walter did not speak, and she again went on. "You have proved, my son, that there is no lasting joy, no real happiness apart from virtue and virtuous actions. Yes, Walter, depend upon it, even in this world, virtue never goes unrewarded, or vice unpunished; true, it may not appear so in the eyes of the world—no storm may burst over the defenceless head of the guilty, overwhelming them with its dreadful influence, and no storied page or glorious hatchment tell of the bright deeds and noble heroism of suffering virtue. This is seldom, if ever, the case, and yet notwithstanding that it is so, if we could dive into the innermost recesses of the human heart, and read with searching eye that mystic volume, tracing each strange variety of feelings which in turn impart hope, joy, and fear—doubt, dread, despair—and all that man can be or bear, we should undoubtedly prove the truth of my assertion. You, dear Walter, can bear testimony to the truth of my words, for are you not blest with competence and ease, are you not surrounded by all that could tempt the most fastidious taste, aud please the most discerning eye?—there is nothing in your outward circumstances to induce discontent or unhappiness, and yet, Walter, I grieve to say you are not happy."

"Cease, cease," exclaimed Walter, in the bitterness of his anguish; "you do but probe my wounds, and render them less endurable—leave me at least the small consolation of being permitted to sorrow undisturbed."

"No," returned his mother, affectionately, "I do but probe your wounds that I may discover their extent, and prove my ability to heal them."

Walter shook his head.

"It is useless," he replied; "never, never can I know happiness again. I am doomed to be wretched for the remainder of my existence."

"You must not speak thus," returned his mother, "or prove yourself ungrateful for the blessings yet within your reach, because those upon which you had most set your affections are gone, never to return. You have heard your mother's unhappy history, and will, I am sure, readily allow that, if any one ever had real cause to complain of the waywardness of their destiny, or deplore the sad effects of an early error, she might claim the right to do so; and yet you do not see me miserable, or vainly repining at the decree of fate. No, on the contrary, I rejoice to have experienced that duties well performed ever bring with them a sweet and sure reward. Life was not given us to waste in useless murmurings, and, though we may mourn our errors, it is not required of us to yield ourselves entirely to despair. On the contrary, convinced that we have acted erroneously—that we have strayed from the path of honour and integrity, it becomes us at once to retrace our steps; to return to the path of virtue, and all may then be well."

"I do not entirely understand you," replied Walter, growing more interested in what his mother said. "I had fully determined on doing justice to her who is now no more—of inducing her to pardon all the past, and bless me with her love and tenderness, under another name, and in a dearer and holier relationship; but she is torn for ever from my arms—my child even, doubtless, taught to hate and despise me. How then can I retrace my steps, or return to the path from whence, as you say, I have so unhappily strayed?"

"By a well and right performance of duties that are yet incumbent upon you, and which may, nay, undoubtedly will, tend to relieve your mind of its present weight of care."

"Duties!" repeated Walter, in accents of astonishment; "what duties can possibly belong to me?"

"Many," replied Lady Eardley. "There surely exists not one lone and solitary being who has a right to close his heart against the appeals of his fellow men to his consideration: each must feel himself as a link in the chain of existence, which binds one human being to another, and feel himself as necessary to the happiness and well-being of others, as they are to his. Were all who have cause for sorrow or remorse to fold themselves up in selfish neglect of everything around them; to isolate their feelings, and resolutely shut out all human sympathies from their mind, banishing all good and kindly concern for the interest of their fellows, what would this world become? How much suffering would such conduct impose upon the innocent and happy? Surely, Walter, I need not pursue this subject further; your own good sense must tell you how awful an amount of reprehensible responsibility that man must take upon himself who allows sorrow to grow into habitual selfishness—who turns a deaf ear to the appeals which are constantly being made to his feelings, to arouse himself from his neglectful apathy, and join with others in the good work of aiding and contributing to the welfare of the suffering and oppressed. Such, then, as you," she continued, warmly, "have more calls upon their time and judgment than those who have more home duties and home cares. Arouse yourself, then, my son: resolutely shake off this gloomy sloth which benumbs your faculties, and renders you but a drone in the busy hive of the world. Mark out for yourself some honourable pursuit, in the steady perseverance of which you may give as well as receive consolation and peace, if not happiness."

She ceased; but her words struck a chord in the heart of Walter, which instantly vibrated to the touch.

"Mother, dear mother!" he exclaimed, affectionately taking her hand, which he carried respectfully to his lips, "I am convinced you have not spoken thus in vain. I will no longer indulge in selfish regret: the irretrievable past shall be forgotten, or only remembered as a renewed incentive to virtue. My lot must hitherto be sad and lonely, cut off from those dear and tender ties which render life so sweet and precious; but that shall not prevent me from contributing my share to the well being of the mass. My efforts may be weak, and my thoughts too oft unsteady to their purpose, yet, in spite of all this, a glorious career appears to dawn before my eyes, and open to my delighted mind, promising a glorious harvest of good. I marvel, now, how I could remain thus inactive so long, but the past shall suffice for vain repining and useless regret; henceforth I dedicate myself to an honourable and active career."

As he gave utterance to these words, the eye of Walter brightened, his features once more became radiant with hopeful anticipation, and he no longer wore that look of remorseful despondency which had so lately set its seal upon his manly row. Lady Eardley rejoiced at this sudden change—the effect of her own wise counsel, and one of the many lessons she had herself learnt in the rough school of sorrow—which she had now so successfully inculcated in the mind of her son, and which was immediately productive of so good an effect. A word spoken in season, with kind and judicious care not to offend or say too much, is frequently, as in the present instance, the means of arousing to activity and consequent happiness the oppressed and sorrow-stricken mind, recalling once more to life and vigour energies which have so long lain dormant as to seem as though they had never been; to do this effectually is one of the most difficult, but at the same time pleasing duties which is incumbent upon us, and one from which none should shrink, though it may prove at times a delicate and painful task. Lady Eardley having affectionately embraced her son, left him to communicate the glad tidings to his brother and Clara. She found them together, a fond and happy pair, discoursing of the future, which they painted in rich glowing colours, and which they never wearied in contemplating together. They planned many interesting sources of domestic happiness, and confidently looked forward to undiminished happiness, when each, all the world to each, they should walk hand-in-hand along the bright and flowery paths of youth and joy, culling Hope's fairest flowers to charm them on their way. Sweet indeed was the trust and confidence they reposed in each other's affection, never dreaming of doubts or fears, which might eclipse even love like theirs, or cares and sorrows came between their hopes and every fairy scene. They saw or feared nothing of this in the future, which cast no shadow before it—gave no omen that might warn them to look for storms and clouds, where all appeared so brightly beautiful. Lady Eardley looked upon the two as they thus sat together, conversing on their future plans with such bright and hopeful faces, and for the first time a feeling of sadness hovered o'er her spirit in connection with those two beings so justly dear to her heart. But she cast the unwelcome warning from her mind as she murmured—

"No; it cannot be—they will at least be spared the sad heir-loom which brings grief and despondency where we have most looked for happiness and joy. They, so young, so loving, and so full of hope. No—no; it cannot be; or I, at least, shall not survive to see."

So painful were the thoughts that at this time weighed down the usually serene and placid mind of Lady Eardley, that, instead of joining the pair, by whom she was unobserved, she turned away and sought in seclusion to recover the buoyancy of her spirits. In this she succeeded so well, that when they again met, no trace of anxiety was visible on her countenance. Richard and Clara both listened with pleasing satisfaction to the account she gave of Walter's renewed animation, and whose appearance shortly afterwards, with a calm and brightened aspect, fully confirmed all she had said concerning him. The day appointed for the marriage was now fast approaching, and, by all looked forward to with a feeling of almost unmixed delight. Walter's spirits had regained their usual elasticity; he had determined to pursue a course of usefulness, and no longer waste the precious hours of existence in useless lamentations and vain sorrow. True, he could not entirely tear the image of the wronged and lost Lucy from his heart. Often would it arise before his mind's eye to rob him of his transient joy or dream of future happiness. His child too, whom he fondly longed to acknowledge as his own—to take entirely under his fostering care, was probably taught to despise, if not hate him. He too well remembered the reproachful eye and upbraiding accents of Jane, when she made him acquainted with the death of her sister, to hope, for a moment, that she would teach his child to pronounce his name, which would have been some consolation to his mind, although the care of a parent he must consent to forego. Still, Walter, in spite of all these depressions, regained much of his wonted animation; his mother's words had sunk deep into his heart, and given rise to the most ardent desire to devote his talents and energies to the welfare of others. To do this, as he conceived, most effectually, he resolved on endeavouring to secure a seat in parliament, where, by sedulously advocating the cause of the people, and entirely devoting himself to the promotion of the liberal interest, he might not only usefully employ his time and talents, but likewise in some humble measure contribute to the good of thousands.   No sooner had he conceived the idea than he communicated it to his beloved parent, who highly applauded his resolution, and confirmed him in his intentions.   Sir Richard, too, who was possessed of great parliamentary influence, and was too much engrossed with the sweet prospect of a quiet domestic life, to have the slightest desire to embark on a public career, however gratifying such might have been to his ambitious views, promised to use it entirely on behalf of his brother.   This arrangement beguiled Lady Eardley of many cares and anxieties for the future ; she rejoiced that Walter had been induced to cast off the lethargy that had so much oppressed his faculties, and doubted not that his maturer manhood would atone for the errors and sins of his youth, and in the warm affection that existed between Richard and Clara, she reposed hopefully for the happiness of her elder son ; indeed, could she herself have chosen him a companion for life's ever-changing fitful scene, Clara would have been the very one upon whom she could have placed the greatest confidence, both as to her natural strength of mind, her great power of endurance, and the firm unyielding integrity of her character ; she had likewise been sorely tried in the sad school of adversity, and her good qualities had shone out conspicuous amidst the surrounding gloom.   As far, therefore, as Clara was individually concerned, she could not reasonably entertain any fears for the future happiness of Richard, and yet as the wedding day grew near, a dark and settled gloom hovered o'er her spirit, and which she with difficulty concealed from her home circle.   It was arranged that immediately after the ceremony which united them for life, the bridal pair should proceed to Eardley Hall to spend the honeymoon in undisturbed repose, and Clara looked forward with pleased satisfaction to again beholding the sweet scenes among which her earliest and happiest years were spent. Lady Eardley declined accompanying them, urging the well received plea, that to view again the ancestral home of her late husband would be only to recall sorrows and painful feelings she would wish to bury for ever in oblivion.   Walter, too, desired for the present to shun the spot in which he had first learnt to love, and which had so often witnessed the meetings of himself and the hapless and ill-fated object of his boyish passion.   Alone, therefore, Clara and Richard were to take possession of their future home—the home of Sir Richard's forefathers, and which had descended to him from a long line of noble ancestry, and of which he was now the youthful proprietor.   The servants and villagers were apprised of their expected arrival, and all things were made ready to receive and do honour to the new married pair.   Clara had written to her only friend, Jane Clarence, communicating her own unexpected happiness, and bidding her repair to the hall in order to meet her on her arrival.   It being the mutual wish of all concerned to have the nuptials celebrated in as private a manner as possible, consistent with the rank and station of Sir Richard, but few friends were invited to be present at the ceremony ; but among those few was numbered Ada Herbert, who at the request of Lady Eardley was asked to officiate as bridesmaid.   And here, perhaps, it may be as well to remark that Lady Eardley wished to become acquainted with Ada, in order to test as much as possible her temper and disposition, with the ultimate view of forwarding a marriage between her and Walter, being anxious as far as possible to promote the wishes of her late husband, whom, she well knew, was most desirous that such a marriage should take place.   She, moreover, commisserated the supposed feelings of the young lady, and was solicitous to show her every mark of respect in her power, so that the world should not suppose that her son's relations approved of or even countenanced his neglect.   Ada felt flattered by this attention, and was nothing loth to avail herself of the invitation.   She was anxious, as the reader is aware, to marry Walter, and consequently resolved to ingratiate herself into the favour of his mother; no difficult task, as Lady Eardley was all ready prepared to like her, and espouse her cause.   The day—the eventful day at length arrived; the morning sun shone bright and beautiful; a gentle breeze just rustled the foliage of the trees, and scattered the searest to the earth, for it was now autumn, yet so fair and soft, that it might well have been mistaken for spring. It was one of those delightful mornings when all nature seems in harmony, and sunk in that sweet, soft repose so pleasing to a contemplative mind, as affording an opportunity of viewing the wondrous works of God under the most tranquil and, at the same time, the most beautiful aspect, when each little flower raises

THE NUPTIALS OF SIR RICHARD EARDLEY AND CLARA.

its tiny head, and sheds its grateful perfume on the balmy air; when the night dew sparkles brightly in the lily's cup, and a purer, though hidden sweetness seems to breathe from the violet's leaves; and the rose, the sign of joy and love young blushing love, in its earliest dawn opens wide its petals, and sends forth its richest and purest fragrance; and the myrtle's snowy flower, that emblem of chaste and unobtrusive worth, looks yet more fair and lovely, while the glossy leaf of the bay seems to tell of Fame's bright star and Glory's swell. And even the cypress, that darkly shades the grave-like sorrow that mourns its bitter lot, puts off in a measure its look of gloom, and in the freshness of its appearance reminds us of the renewed life, when spring shall revisit the mouldering urn, and day even dawn on the night of the grave. Such was the fair and lovely morn which witnessed the betrothal of Sir Richard Eardley and Clara Wilmot—which saw united two hearts long and silently attached, and never did pair pledge faith at the altar under more auspicious circumstances, or with a more reasonable prospect of happiness. Clara's eyes were moist with tears, as yet unshed, when tearing herself from the encircling arms of her friend and mother, she suffered Sir Richard to lead her to the carriage which was waiting to convey them to their destination; but no sooner was the carriage in motion, and the blind down, which concealed her from the prying eyes of the curious, than leaning her head on the bosom of her husband, she gave free vent to her feelings, and suffered the tears, long surpressed, to course each other down her cheeks. It has been often asked why should a woman weep on her wedding-day—a day that must undoubtedly be considered by her as the happiest and brightest of her life? The question may be answered in a few words. Of all the popular fallacies, and there are a great many, none certainly is more fallacious than that which connects the idea of gaiety exclusively with a wedding-day. If the newly married couple entertain a sincere and warm affection for each other; and if they possess minds of noble and generous susceptibility, the happiness of the moment will not assume a character of boisterous mirthfulness, but will most naturally be qualified by serious, if not anxious thought. The bridegroom cannot fail to meditate upon the serious responsibility he has incurred in assuming the sole guardianship of the fair being whom he has just made his own; and on her part the bride will ponder upon the important change she has made in her position in life, and remember that, though she may now possess new joys, she must also perform many new and important duties, and take upon herself many fresh anxieties, for though

A wife hath joys, yet she hath cares,
For she must strive to soothe
The worldly paths, and calm the brow
Of him she's sworn to love;
Must watch his glance, and court his smile
When in his gayest vein,
And with attentions kind beguile
His hours of care and pain;
Must ever be to him e'en as
The sun is to the day,
To shed sweet light to cheer his soul,
And point the future way.

Sir Richard knew and felt this, consequently he did not chide the apparent weakness, or seek to check the falling tears of his young bride; no, he only pressed her fondly to his bosom, and kissed the pearly drops away. Clara felt grateful for the consideration thus shown to her feelings, and soon tears were banished from her eyes, and her smiles returned again more bright and radiant than before, as the sunbeams, after a storm, shine forth afresh more brilliantly upon the dreary plain. The morning, as we have already said, was soft and fair, and soon it beamed brightly and beautifully over scenes that were endeared by tender and long associations to the mind of Clara, and as she welcomed each well-known spot, and memory haunted shades, they seemed smilingly to greet her as old familiar friends. The busy, crowded town was far behind them, and as the carriage slowly ascended an eminence, she turned to gaze on the mighty mass of dwellings which composed the hallowed abodes and consecrated hearths of its countless multitudes, with the dim and somewhat misty haze of an autumn morning's sun settling over them, and listened to the drowsy hum which, softened and mellowed by distance, stole half insensibly on the ear. How greatly contrasted was all this with the spot she was now fast approaching, all clear, lovely, and serene, where every bush and every flower seemed to put forth some hidden sweetness. And now the carriage is once more in rapid motion. The city, with its bustling walks, its splendour, and wealth, and power, is entirely lost to view. The bright and much loved scenes of early youth are again around her, as fair, ay, clothed as it seemed in richer beauty than when their quiet loveliness first inspired peace and happiness. The brook to which she had so often listened, still murmured along its course of melody and verdure. The very wild flowers seemed to seek the same shades their fragrance had perfumed in other years. And now the old mansion appears in sight, rising from out the close and beautifully tinted foliage, half hidden by its leafy vale, its fine old turrets just surmounting the hill top, and rendering itself the first object that becomes visible to Clara as she enters once more her native village. Sir Richard glances from the face of his fair and now smiling bride, to the noble hall of his ancestors, which for the first time he now beholds himself master of; a smile of pardonable and grateful pride lights up his manly and expressive countenance as on a still nearer approach the fine old building stands boldly out appearing to disdain competition with surrounding objects, while it claimed admiration and homage from all. The time-honoured walls were peculiarly dear to the heart of Richard—they were hallowed by bright visions. And the remembrance of his youthful fancies threw over all concerned with them the enchantment of imagination and hope. And while the shadows of the past swept over him, he turned to Clara, and warmly pressing her hand within his own, directed her attention to the time-worn turrets of Eardley Hall, and with a look of proud triumph, bade her welcome, as its new mistress. Sweet indeed and touching was the smile of mingled hope and pleasure with which Clara met her husband's glance, but that sweet smile was all her speech, for her quick and sensitive mind was again busy with the future, and she could not refrain from mentally asking herself the question, will it ever be thus?—will this warm and early glow of heart live in years to come, undimmed by remoteness and, unsupplanted by other thoughts and attachments?—will the tie that now binds our youthful feelings never fade, or grow weak? And as the remote possibility of such an event swept across her mind, she felt that better, far better would be adversity and sorrow, even the morbid sensibility excited by the contemplation of the happy past, than the cold heartlessness of extinguished feeling or the hollow merriment of absorbing dissipation; for if borne down for awhile by sorrows and anxieties, with feelings still sensitive and hearts not yet closed against the affection that so fondly enchained them in the morn of life, spite of all else that might befall them, the pliant mind would arouse itself from its passing weakness to seek for purer sources of happiness, and find in the sweet virtues of philanthropy and social life, a balm for its griefs, a refuge for its affliction. Clara was roused from such contemplations as these by the loud and merry welcome pealing from the lowly village church. And now the tenants of Sir Richard, all in trim and holiday attire (among whom Clara recognised many familiar faces), made the air re-echo with their glad shouts of welcome. " Long live your honour and your honour's lady !" resounded on all sides. And while Sir Richard kindly acknowledged and returned their greeting, giving orders that substantial fare and foaming quarts of ale should be dispersed to all who chose to partake of his hospitality, Clara leant back in the carriage, and again gave vent to her feelings in tears, but they were tears sacred to the best emotions of the breast, tears of gratitude and joy—the sweet dew of the mind, watering and refreshing the parched feelings and bidding them bloom in renewed and continuous beauty. And now the great gates are thrown open to their fullest extent, and the carriage is rolling leisurely through the richly verdent park, skirted on either side by fine old trees, (for no axe had ever been permitted to profane their sanctity, whose thick foliage meeting and entwining high over head formed a complete and beautiful avenue from occasional openings, in which the eye rested with pleased satisfaction on the soft verdant lawn, with the beautiful transparent lake in its bosom. Clara was enraptured with all she saw, and warmly expressed herself to that effect.

"How beautiful a spot is this," she exclaimed, as she gazed upon the tranquil scene, and constellated flowers before her, the last roses of summer twining fantastically among flowers of less beauty, and the majestic dahlias towering in the distance above them, all over which the blue unclouded sky formed a glorious canopy."

"You say right, dear Clara," replied her husband, "this place is indeed rich in beauty, and I rejoice that it is so, and it shall henceforth be our mutual care, dear love, to retain, and, if possible, enhance its luxuriance ; but we have still other and higher duties and more ennobling pleasures. For if meadows and trees in their cheerful verdure—if flowers in their bloom, and all nature smiling around us can inspire our hearts with gladness, and make us join in the universal chorus of joy, what superior pleasure it should give us to see those by whom we are surrounded, whose welfare in a measure depends upon ourselves, happy and flourishing. And how much must that pleasure be heightened if we ourselves have been instrumental in contributing to their happiness—if we have helped to raise a heart drooping beneath the weight of grief or reviving a dry and sterile mind, with refreshing showers of love and kindness. I envy not the feelings of the man," continued Sir Richard, warmly, as he proceeded, "whose estates flourish while his tenantry fell into poverty and decay—whose land is cared for, and whose domains are rich in beauty—where the most refined taste is gratified by the choice gardens, and magnificent conservatories—where the inanimate parts of the creation—the meadows, flowers, and trees, are all in a flourishing state, while the more wondrous portion of God's works, the more noble and rational portion of creation, are suffered to live in poverty uncared for, unattended to die in sorrow and neglect, for want only of a small portion of the care and money so lavishly bestowed by the rich man on his garden, his parks, and conservatories. Be it ours then, my own love, to study at once the happiness of ourselves, and those who are in a measure committed to our keeping, and no more suffer one among them to stand in need of comforts that we can supply, or bend under a weight of anguish that we can remove, than we should allow this noble park and fertile vegetation to become an arid waste or barren desert."

Clara warmly coincided with the husband's remarks, and for a few moments they drove on in silence, when Clara, falling again into the same train of thoughts which had previously taken possession of her mind, exclaimed—

"Pity that all this brightness—all that was ever bright and beautiful, should fade and perish, that flowers which look so glorious, which breathe such delicate odours, should, with the eye that gazes upon them—the cheek upon which bloom roses we could fain think eternal, the lip which breathes love and tenderness, after a few short years—fade and perish."

"It is, indeed, sad," replied Sir Richard, "to contemplate the decay of youth and flowers, but more sad—far more blighting is the decay and loss of love. Affection is the sunshine of existence, and when it is gone, the rest is all darkness. The flowers of life, the beauties of being, are all obscured, and we wander blindly on through an unseen world, which might, as far as we are thus individually concerned, as well be a desert as a garden. But these thoughts are too sad for so joyous a day as this," continued Sir Richard ; "surely our destiny will be a happy one—although marriage may be, as many aver, a lottery, yet I feel convinced that we shall draw a prize."

"Marriage is to a woman," replied Clara, "at once the happiest and most important day of her life ; buoyed up by hope—by the confidence of requited love, she bids a fond and grateful adieu, to the life that is past, and turns with high hopes and joyous anticipation to the happiness she believes in store, shared with him to whom she has rendered her destiny, and whose fortune she is happy and blest in being permitted to share, be it good or ill."

By this conversation, it will be seen that Clara and Richard commenced their new career, animated by those principles and feelings which most tend to ensure happiness, and without which no true enjoyment can be found on earth. Richard had no time to give an appropriate reply to the last words which fell from the lips of his young wife, for as she ceased speaking the carriage stopped in front of the broad stone steps which led to the entrance of the hall, the massive oak door of which was already thrown open, and the assembled servants stood ready to receive and pay their respects to their new master and mistress. Among these Clara instantly recognised the familiar face of Jane Clarence, who, standing a little in advance, was waiting to receive and embrace her friend. With a mingled feeling of joy and pride, Sir Richard handed Clara from the carriage, and led her up the broad stone steps of the noble building which in future was to own her for its mistress. Clara heeded not the assembled servants, nor the restraint which their presence would seem to impose, she saw only the pale face and attenuated form of her best and only friend, so altered—so sadly altered, that her own joyous and animated countenance, must offer, she feared, as great a contrast, and seem as great a mockery to the pallid brow and sunken eye of her friend, as her gay attire and bridal ornaments offered to her plain and mourning habiliments.

"Dear—dear Jane," she exclaimed, as she threw herself upon her bosom, "after so long a separation, how sad and painful must this meeting be to you."

Jane was deeply affected at this consideration on the part of Clara, on a day when she might naturally be supposed to be engrossed with her own new position and duties, to the total exclusion of all other thoughts; true, from what she had long known of Clara's affectionate disposition, and the sisterly regard that had for years existed between them, she might have expected such an evidence of her friendship, but Jane was one of the most unselfish beings in the world, one who was ever eager to give, but never claimed the right to receive sympathy and consideration on the part of others; she had not, therefore, expected this outbreak of affectionate interest, and we repeat, it affected her deeply. Never before had she felt so inclined to give way to the feelings which oppressed her, but she mastered them, nevertheless, and in her usual quiet gentle tones, warmly expressed the joy she felt at this reunion, and the high hopes she entertained for the future happiness of her friend. Sir Richard now approached, and taking her outstretched hand in his, claimed to be looked upon in the light of a friend, if not on his own, at least on Clara's account. Jane gracefully expressed the pleasure she felt at this meeting, and hastened to lead the way to the drawing-room, whither the housekeeper, in her old-fashioned mob cap, and lawn apron of spotless purity, with a huge bunch of keys—her badge of office—jingling from her waist, was already waiting to precede them. Having lingered so long with Clara on her journey from London to Eardley Hall, we must for the present take our leave, as other dramatic personages claim, for the time being, our attention.

CHAPTER XXXVI.

" Some difference of this dangerous kind,
By which, though light, the links that bind
The fondest hearts may soon be riven—
Some shadow, in love's summer Heaven,
Which, thorgh a fleecy speck at first,
May yet in awful thunder burst."

AFTER Percy had watched the departure of his wife, accompanied by her cousin, he descended to the drawing-room, in by no means the best possible humour either with himself or her; he thought himself neglected for the first time by his young wife, for whose society he would have abandoned every other object, and heeded not the sacrifice. And thus had he—as he now thought—too fondly judged of her, he felt more hurt and grieved than he liked to acknowledge even to himself, at the deep anxiety Mary had manifested for the comfort and happiness of her father, regardless, as he considered, of his own more prior claim. It was not so much this one particular instance that he lamented, as the breaking up of that strict seclusion in which they had hitherto lived, while absent from London, and the friends who were so eager to gather round her. Mary had been entirely devoted to himself, there was none to share with him the sunshine of her smile, or listen to the playful converse that seemed destined to cheer and amuse her husband alone. And though by no means what is understood by the expression of a jealous man, he was yet possessed of a shade of that selfishness which forms so conspicuous a trait in some men's characters. He wished to keep his young wife entirely to himself, to be alone the object of her constant and unceasing attention, to live in the mutual exchange of fond and warm endearments, undisturbed by the bustle and cares of life. Such was the home of love he had pictured to himself, they were to be all in all to each other, as in the first days of married life; he had learnt to regard Mary as the very acme of perfection, and never even dreamed of the possibility of her hesitating to sacrifice her fondest wishes, if for a moment they interfered with his own. It was therefore in no pleasant mood that he joined his sisters in the parlour, who, unapprised of Mary's absence, were waiting to partake with them of the evening meal. Percy had suffered himself to be so annoyed at the absence of his wife, that the dinner-bell had failed to attract his attention, and as he entered, he for the first time became aware of his negligence. Hastening, therefore, to apologise for his unintentional disrespect, he proceeded to take his usual place at the dinner table. The quick eye of sisterly affection, instantly detected that something had occurred to vex or annoy their brother, whom they had from infancy been accustomed to study and respect, so much so, that they never enquired into the source of any anxiety that he appeared to wish to keep unknown to them, but the absence of Mary was too strange and unexpected an affair to be passed over in silence, and after waiting a moment to see if Percy made an illusion to the circumstance, Elizabeth, the elder sister, enquired if she would not dine with them as usual.

"Not to day, at any rate," replied Percy, in a tone so moody and discontented, that both sisters involuntarily raised their eyes to his face, grieved and astonished at the expression of vexation which was plainly visible there.

Percy remarked this, and the affection he had so long entertained for his sisters, and which had caused him of late somewhat to forget, now returned, with redoubled interest, their evident solicitude for his happiness, and the anxiety so plainly manifested on the present occasion, when he appeared before them for the first time since his marriage, with a clouded brow and the thoughtful delicacy which prevented them even enquiring into the cause which had occasioned it. All this, as we have said, awoke a doubtful interest in his mind, and the slight feeling of dissatisfaction which he felt as regards Mary, swelled into real and undoubted discontent, as he placed her conduct in contrast to that of his sisters.

"Would they have insisted on leaving me for an entire day against my expressed wish?" was a question he mentally asked himself, and which he found no difficulty in answering, for Percy had for years been so accustomed to be studied, and his lightest wish attended to by his affectionate sisters, that though naturally of a most kind and generous disposition, it had encouraged a growth of that selfishness which, as we previously remarked, seems almost inherent in all men; and from being accustomed to have others yield unhesitatingly to his desires, he grew in time constantly to expect it, and think himself really ill-used if any one ventured to contradict him.

This was the only failing in Percy's character; and if his young wife only knew it, her generous disposition and uncommon stability of character would doubtless suffice to counteract this one great fault. But Mary has not yet made this important discovery, and much evil may befall her, that might otherwise have been prevented. So important is it that the new made wife should be thoroughly aware of the bad as well as good qualities possessed by her husband, in order that she may, as much as possible, counteract and correct them—not that she should ever take upon herself the office of censor, or on any account lecture him, even when she may suppose there is sufficient cause; a woman should never employ any other power over the mind of her husband than gentleness, and the force of love, to which even strength will yield. When we look upon a rose, we feel assured that its odour is sweet and grateful to the senses, and should turn away sad and sorrowful if we did not imbibe the sweetness of its perfume. And thus men naturally look for everything that is soft and amiable in a woman, and it is painful indeed that they should ever be deceived; it is a positive duty every woman owes, not only to herself, but to her sex, to emulate not only the delicate beauty of the blushing rose, but what is far better, its rare and undying perfume. How sweet to pass through life loving and beloved, winning all hearts and drawing that tender interest towards ourselves which love and gentleness never fail to awaken in the breasts of all towards whom it is exercised. How much happier as well as wiser is it to push our way through the thorns and briers of life with smiles upon our lips and kind and gentle words upon our tongue, making light of each difficulty, and, battling uncomplainingly with the waves of adversity looking hopefully forward to brighter days and happier hours; than sitting down to bemoan every little ill, and lament the difficulties we cannot withstand. But we fear we are too prone to turn moralist, and hasten to take up once more the thread of our narrative. Percy sat silent some time, drawing in his own mind a comparison between his sisters and Mary, a comparison by no means favourable to the latter; while they, in their turn, regarded him with anxious countenances, feeling assured that something had occurred to disturb his usual serenity. Their brother at length spoke: he considered them worthy of his entire confidence, and resolved that they should have it. It was some relief too,—a relief that he needed—to tell his source of uneasiness to those whom he well knew would sympathise and feel for him. And yet his sisters, so fondly, so devotedly attached to Percy, were the very last, as well as the most unfitting persons to whom he could have breathed a word of distrust concerning his young and new made wife for the very love that they entertained for their brother, rendered them more keenly sensible of any apparent slight which might be unintentionally shown him; consequently their indignation knew no limit, as they listened to his account of Mary's anxiety concerning her father, and which would not permit her to defer her visit even for a few hours, although he had earnestly requested her to do so.

"I could never have thought it possible that Mary would have acted so unkindly," said Elizabeth, the elder sister.

"Nor I," replied the younger, "especially when Ada, as you say, assured her there was no necessity for hastening to her father, had he been really indisposed, it would have made a material difference."

"You say right," returned Elizabeth, "but Mary is in many respects a very different sort of girl to what I expected to find her."

Percy said nothing, but those words of his sister sank deep into his heart. "A very different sort of girl to what I expected to find her." Was Mary then aught, but what his fond imagination had so brightly pictured her, could it be possible that he was deceived? Ada had once appeared to him all that was fair and beautiful, not only in person but in mind; but, alas! he discovered that he had thought her not what she in truth was, but what his fondest wishes would have made her. And might it not be thus with Mary; might not his judgment, so prone to err, again have deceived him. The thought was torture, and yet he could not cast it from his mind. His sisters in their well meant efforts to soothe and sympathise with his supposed uneasiness, only added to the unhappiness which oppressed him. Suspicion, that bitter foe to the peace of the breast wherein it has become an inmate gnawed remorselessly at his heart, and destroyed for the time those sweet hopes which had given promise of so much happiness, he became restless and uneasy, so much so, that he could not bear even the presence of his sisters, to whom he had ever been so fondly attached; he could not bear to hear them cast the lightest reflection on the conduct of Mary, although deeply vexed and displeased with her himself. Dinner therefore being ended, he excused himself from attending at the tea-table, and the evening being warm and beautiful he sauntered into the garden, and pacing up and down the smooth cut lawn, busied himself with endeavouring to think Mary less kind, less gentle, and less amiable than he had fondly supposed her. It is strange how much trouble people will sometimes take in order to render themselves miserable—one half the pains bestowed on the more laudable as well as more pleasing object of making themselves happy, would doubtless go far towards accomplishing it. And yet how frequently it happens, that persons turn aside their heads and refuse the cup of joy when it is proffered to their lips, while they eagerly seize on the ills of life, and brood over the sorrows that will at times assail even the brightest lot. It is often a matter of astonishment to ourselves to perceive the facility some people appear to possess of extracting troubles and misfortunes, even out of the very materials from which happiness is formed, and who never seem contented or satisfied even when surrounded by all that is supposed to render life desirable. We cannot but pity such persons, at the same time we regard them as beacons to warn us from the dangerous road into which they have unhappily wandered. We do not say that, by nature, Percy was thus constituted, but most certainly at the present time with every incentive to happiness, with every reasonable desire gratified, while the future dawned fair and bright before him with all these blessings, he yet refused the happiness within his reach, and sought to find some reasonable excuse for being miserable, till, as he continued pacing to and fro on the smooth green grass he began to persuade himself into the belief that he was one of the most unfortunate and unhappy beings in existence. In the meantime Mary was by no means free from anxiety herself; having arrived once more at her childhood's, the home of early happy days, ere she had known what sorrow meant, but had sported in joyous freedom, gay and wild, a gush of fond emotions filled her breast and shed a halo of gladness over her heart. How happy, too, she felt on entering the old-fashioned parlour where her father occupied the chair whereon he had daily sat as far back as her memory extended, and as he raised his eyes to fix them once again on the face of his darling child, how radiant and bright—how full of joy and happiness was the smile that illumined his countenance. And proud and happy was Mary, as she clasped her arms round his neck, and assured him of her continued and fondest love. And when the first, fond, warm greeting was over, and seated once more in her old accustomed place by her father's side, Mary looked up into his face from time to time, and watched the tide of gladness again stealing over it as he listened to her conversation in which she detailed all that had befallen her since their last meeting, and which she well knew, however dull and common-place to another, would nevertheless interest and amuse her parent, who rejoiced alone in the happiness and well-being of his child. Thus past the early part of the day, Mr. Herbert recovered his usual gaiety, and his fears concerning the happiness of his daughter were beginning to dissipate, and he exulted anew over her acquired good fortune. Ada, too, was in excellent spirits, and so kind and attentive to her uncle, that Mary felt grateful and happy, and expressed it in affectionate terms to her cousin. Thus past the early part of the day; but as it drew to a close, Mary's heart began to grow heavy, although she scarce knew why. Her thoughts fled back to her husband, whom she was anxious again to behold; she was vexed with herself for not having yielded to his request, and a deep sense of uneasiness filled her mind. So true it is, that coming events cast their shadows before them. She hoped that, at all events, Percy would call for her in the evening, and regreted now that it was too late that she had not requested him to do so; she could not, however, for a moment doubt that he would come, and therefore resolved to await the hour when she might reasonably expect him;

but, alas! that hour arrived and passed away. Another drew its slow length along, but nought with it: no token of the absent one, and Mary, now really uneasy, stated her intention of returning alone. Ada offered to accompany her, but Mary gently yet firmly declined her offer, for she could not think of depriving her father of his sole companion. Having, therefore, succeeded in inducing

THE FIRST MISUNDERSTANDING BETWEEN PERCY AND MARY.

Ada to remain with him, she started on her journey back; this was the first time since her marriage that she had ever been out unattended by her husband, and she felt unreasonably low and depressed. She could not help thinking it in her unkind of Percy not to come and meet her; still she blamed herself the most for having in so trifling a matter opposed her own wishes to his, and re-sov'd for the future to study him more closely. Wise resolution!—and well would it be for many others, if they thus early became sensible of their faults, and resolved to counteract them. With a heart somewhat lightened by this determination, Mary entered the house. Percy's two sisters alone occupied that sitting room. Mary saluted them with her usual friendly greeting, but, to her surprise and mortification, they did not return it in the same good feeling; there was a coldness in their tones, which Mary, although she did not resent, felt at once to be unkind and disrespectful. She, therefore, merely inquired if Percy were from home, and having received for answer that they believed him to be somewhere about the grounds, without waiting to lay aside her walking dress, she hastened to join him.

"My dear Percy," she began in her tenderest tones, as she approached within speaking distance of her husband, "I am afraid I have given you cause to feel displeased with me; if so, I will not apologise for the past, but content myself with promising for the future to be more circumspect."

These words, which were spoken half serious and half in playful gaiety, were surely well calculated to dissipate all suspicious feelings from the breast of Percy; but, alas! doubts had arisen in his mind—doubts that filled his heart with anguish and his bosom with regret. He gazed into Mary's upturned face; so open, so pure and ingenuous was its expression, that it would have convinced any other than a suspicious husband that all his doubts were entirely unfounded, and that her heart was the throne of virtue and of truth; but he remembered Ada, and the sweet trustful look she had so long worn. He remembered, too, his own unbounded confidence in her almost child-like simplicity—in her blushing confession of the fondest and truest love for himself, ere his eyes had been opened to the duplicity of her conduct, and he had learned that all her supposed truth was falsehood, and her innocence but an assumed charm, which could be worn or laid aside at will. Yes, Percy thought of all this, as he gazed upon the face of his young wife, which now beamed with the purest love and tenderness, and the remembrance of it caused him to answer not as his heart, but as his sense of anger dictated.

"Make no excuse," said he, gloomily. "I wish you to study your own happiness. You have done so to-day, and I hope you have enjoyed yourself."

"Do pray excuse me this once," continued Mary, without heeding his last remark. "I have been very unhappy these last few hours. I thought, indeed, you would have called for me."

"As you never expressed the slightest wish to that effect, I could not, of course, be expected to know that my company would be agreeable; indeed, you seemed so eager to leave me this-morning, that I could not help thinking you preferred being alone."

"Oh, Percy," replied Mary, now really hurt, "how wrong, how unkind are such thoughts."

He only shook his head, as he replied—

"I believe my sisters have been waiting tea these last two hours, in expectation of your return."

"My dear Percy, do not be displeased with me, I entreat; indeed, I should have been home much earlier, but I fully expected you at my father's this evening; but we will not keep your sisters waiting longer. Let us hasten to them at once. I am sorry, indeed, that you did not take it in my absence."

"It shall be so, in future," said her husband, anticipating, in a sort of gloomy despair, the total destruction of all that had given so sweet a charm to the short interval of his married life.

"Indeed, indeed it shall not happen again. I am very sorry that it should have occurred this once," she replied, with persevering sweetness. "It must be extremely painful to you to have the regularity of your life disturbed. Will you not forgive me this once?—I am sure you will."

Alas! how much misery doth not suspicion engender! His heart ached as he looked at her—as he listened to her words, and yet he would not suffer himself to be convinced. He made no reply, but turned towards the house. Mary walked in silence. She was hurt, more hurt than she had ever been before. She knew not, it is true, the doubts and suspicions that had been aroused in her husband's mind: she only knew that he was vexed and angry with herself for having left home to visit her father, without his free consent, and yet he had expressed a wish that she would act entirely in consonance with her own wishes, and, consequently, Mary could not help regarding his present resentment as both unkind and unjust. Still, most fortunately, her natural sweetness of temper prevented her offering any remark which might tend to widen the breach which already existed. In silence they entered the sitting-room, where the grave looks of Elizabeth and Mary sent a chill to the heart of the young wife. She saw too plainly they regarded her brother as unkindly treated by herself, and while they sought to cheer and amuse him, she was for the first time entirely overlooked. Percy scarcely noticed the attention bestowed upon him by his sisters; he sipped his tea, but was perfectly unable to swallow a morsel of the tempting cake they forced upon him. He was brooding over what he considered the entire breaking up of the sweet social intercourse that, till this unfortunate day, existed between himself and Mary. He sighed heavily as he thought upon this, and hastily pushed his plate with its untasted delicacies aside. Again Mary ventured to speak.

"Dear Percy, what is the matter? You are ill."

"I have got a head-ache," he replied, shortly. "I would rather be left alone."

Again she was silenced; she turned aside her head to brush away unheeded the first tear Percy had ever caused her to shed. Mary could not say more, for the presence of his sisters offered a painful restraint; she therefore affected to busy herself with the tea equipage. The meal was scarcely finished when Percy rose and left the room. Mary heard the door of the library close behind him, and after waiting a short time she succeeded in conquering the little irritation his manner and repulses had occasioned, and joining him in the library. He was sitting in his chair, absorbed in the most gloomy reverie. He held a book in his hand, but it was plain to perceive he was by no means interested in its contents. He just lifted up his head as she entered the room, and then bent it again over his book, without seeming to notice her. She approached him, kindly laid her hand on his shoulder, and said—

"My dear, dear Percy, you are ill; tell me what is the matter?"

He gently moved his shoulder, as if to throw off her hand, and looked up in her face, but did not speak.

"I am sure I grieved and offended you," she continued. "I am so extremely sorry. What more can I say? I would not be wilfully negligent or unkind to you for worlds. Indeed—indeed"—she added, and the tears stood in her eyes—"indeed I would not."

He looked at her again.

"You are very kind; but do you really love or care for me?"

She started back wounded at the injurious suspicion these words conveyed; she felt how deeply he wronged her, and upon what slight cause; and for the moment she was too much mortified and indignant to speak, but her candid and generous disposition quickly gained the mastery over these feelings, and stepping forward she said, gently but firmly—

"I do not know, Percy, what I have done to give you reason, with justice, to suspect me of having deceived you with a profession of love. I did not give you my hand without my heart. I have always endeavoured—whatever, and many faults I have had—to be at all times truthful and sincere. And this is the first time I have ever been accused of attempting to deceive. I do not deserve it now. I see," she added, with some emotion, "by the expression of your face, that you do not believe me, therefore it is useless to say more. Time, and time only, can undeceive you. Time can and will prove the injustice of your present feelings."

And she turned to leave the room.

"Mary," said Percy.

"Did you speak?" she said, returning.

He took her hand, gazed for a moment in her face, then dropped it, and turned away. Again she was deeply moved, but she did not know what to say or do. She stood silent, hesitating, and uncertain. Percy walked to the window, scarcely less affected, but he soon recovered himself, seemed ashamed of his weakness, and turned and abruptly left the room.

"Percy!" exclaimed Mary; but he heard her not—he was gone. She longed to throw herself at his feet, and beseech him to forget the past—to bless her again with his love as in days gone by—to confess she had been wrong—to implore his forgiveness, and assure him of her undying love and tenderness. But her pride still held out—she conceived he had wronged her by suspicion; he had wounded her in the tenderest point, and though she yearned to call him back the words she would have spoken died upon her tongue, for her lips refused to give them utterance. Sad that it should have been so—much better at all times is the sacrifice of pride, when it comes between us and our holiest feelings, separating us from those dear and loved ties, without which life can possess no charm to bind us to existence. It is painful to know how light, how trivial a cause may at times suffice to awaken distrust and dissension between hearts that love—hearts that the world in vain hath tried, and sorrow but more closely tied; that stood the storm when waves were rough, yet in a sunny hour fall off, like ships which have gone down at sea, when Heaven was all tranquillity. Mary thought she had done all in her power to conciliate her husband, and even now, were he again by her side, her natural sweetness would have prompted her again to entreat his forgiveness, and assure him of her love. She was agitated and unhappy as she paced the floor of the library, and would have given all else she held dear could she have recalled the events of the last few hours. And yet, when she asked herself what she had done, she could not satisfactorily answer the question. She remembered the cold look of his sisters, and while she was convinced she had done nothing to deserve it, she could scarcely suppress a feeling of resentment that rose in her breast. Still Mary's wonted gentleness prevailed, and she resolved to endeavour to cultivate anew the good will and sympathy of her sisters. Percy, she well knew, loved them with the truest affection: how necessary, then, did it become to stand high in their good opinion, if she would be beloved and treasured by her husband? Henceforth she determined to make his will her law—to study his happiness, to promote his wishes, and then she hoped to secure her own.

CHAPTER XXXVII.

"And youth's wild hopes and warm desires
    Come thronging to his troubled breast;
And love began to kindle fires
    That blazed more fiercely than the rest.
The stolen kiss, the plighted word,
    The whispered spell, when none were nigh,
The voice, that trembling to be heard,
    Gave answer in a modest sigh."

Who has not experienced the deserted sensation, the utter loneliness and despondency of the breast, when those we have been accustomed to see are gone, when the agitation, the interest of parting is over? Oh! how melancholy, how lonely does the house appear, where, but a moment before, all has been interest and hurry? What a contrast doth not the stillness present—the forlorn empty nook of the apartment, where all has been so lately hilarity and bustle? The work-box, the drawing materials, the music—all gone; or, perhaps, one single thing left to remind us how all once was. A flower that had been gathered and cast aside; the cover of a letter which had been scribbled over in the forgetfulness of a happy conversation; a glove, a handkerchief dropped in the moment of parting; any or all of these tend forcibly to remind us of the loved one who has left us perchance for ever—left us to seek another home—to shed the glad sunshine of her presence o'er other hearts—to enliven another dwelling—to have new sources of joys and sorrows, such as we cannot share as we did in days gone by; and with these thoughts what a rush of agonised feelings fill the breast—what an utter sense of despondency settles on the mind, overwhelming us with that depression of spirits so difficult to bear, when we feel left in the wide world alone, without one friendly hand to guide our tottering steps, than which nothing can be conceived more desolating. Oh! who would dwell alone amidst a crowd. Better to be where willows wave above the marble shroud, than live to feel that dreariness of heart—that aching void which wounds the soul more than the keenest dart. To be alone!—oh! better far a living grave would be, upon a lonely raft upon a stormy sea; or on a burning desert sand, and meet the fierce siroc, than live amidst our fellow men, and feel we are forgot. Something of this desolation was experienced by Lady Eardley after the departure of her son and daughter. She had now known Clara a considerable period; she had availed herself of the ample opportunity afforded by their respective situations to become intimately acquainted with her temper and disposition, both of which had convinced her she was every way worthy to fill the exalted position in life she now occupied; she knew that her son's honour and happiness might safely be confided to her keeping. She had, therefore, no doubts or fears concerning their future welfare, save those vague forebodings which the sadness of her own wayward destiny, and the blight which seemed to rest upon the family, brought vividly to her mind; but for the time she gave way to the selfish sorrow of deeply deploring the loss she had sustained in Clara. She had become so accustomed to the cheering influence of her presence, which had served to throw an almost indescribable charm over her hitherto sad and solitary home;—she had tasted once more of the sweets of social intercourse, from which she had been so long debarred, and which had been to her wearied mind sweet as the well springing up in the desert is to the tired and thirsty traveller, and now she felt that this was at an end for ever. True, she had secured her son's happiness, and for this she desired to be thankful; but then, it was a happiness with which her superstitious feelings told her she must have nothing whatever to do. Great as she felt the desire within her to watch over the happiness and welfare of those most beloved —most deservedly treasured in her heart—she must separate herself from them, keep aloof from the happiness of those, the contemplation of which would have been balm to her wounded spirit. Such thoughts as these filled the mind of Lady Eardley, as, immediately after the departure of the newly married pair, she paced up and down the apartment which had lately been known as Clara's. Frequently would she check the train of thought into which she had fallen, and enquire of herself if it were not possible to forego so great a sacrifice. At such moments the cloud of despondency cleared from her brow, and the light of joy danced momentarily in her clear dark eyes, only to vanish, leaving her more sad and desponding than before.

"No, no," she murmured, "it must not be; I should but poison the happiness I would willingly lay down my life to confirm. Thus it has been before—all who loved or cared for me, all upon whom I ever cast a thought of tenderness, have been doomed to wretchedness and misery; it was this alone that compelled me to separate myself from my children, even while they yet required a tender mother's care—to forego the dear delight of watching over their infant years, and inculcating the sweet lessons of truth and love; this—this I did, and shall I hesitate now?—No! I must, I will be firm. I linger only that I may see Walter united to one worthy of him, and then I will quit for ever scenes too dangerous and too dear."

It was a strange and unwonted power this unhappy lady appeared to possess over herself; it would seem that she had only to say to each agonised feeling, " Peace—be still !" and they instantly obeyed her mandate ;—thus when she said " I must, I will be firm !" all trace of her recent agitation disappeared; she was again the calm, gentle, apparently unmoved being that we first presented to the reader; the same quiet grace sat upon each feature of her countenance, and betrayed itself in her equable deportment—the struggle was at an end; she had gained the mastery over her feelings, and resolved on her future career. Having taken her seat at the table so long occupied by Clara, she opened her desk and began to write, and none who might have looked upon her as she thus sat occupied with her pen, fully intent upon the abstruse subject on which she wrote, could for a moment even have guessed at the deep struggle which had so lately taken place in her breast, so completely had she succeeded in suppressing the slightest sign of emotion.   In the meantime Walter and Ada were left alone, not unintentionally by Lady Eardley, who had been much pleased with the appearance and manners of Ada during the day, and consequently was anxious to promote the wishes of her dead husband, by doing all in her power to forward a marriage between that young lady and her son ; to this end, after commending her to the care of Walter, she left the young people to amuse themselves, while, as we have seen, she retired to quell the tumult of feelings which agitated her breast.   At first, Walter was sensible of a slight diffidence on finding himself alone with Ada for the first time since he had severed the bonds which had apparently bound them together; but his natural self-possession soon returned, and feeling himself bound by politeness and gallantry to do all in his power to amuse and interest his guest, as the weather was fine, and the shrubbery thickly planted, so as to afford a pleasant shade, invited her to walk with him round the garden, which, though not extensive, yet possessed a variety of attractions, not always to be found in those of larger dimensions. Ada readily assented, but her hand trembled as she laid it on his arm, and for a few minutes they walked in silence ; at length Walter spoke—

"You are very kind, Miss Herbert," he began, " not to resent my conduct, which I candidly own to have been such that you might have been well justified in refusing me the honour of your company at the present time. I have frequently wished for an opportunity to apologise for my apparent disrespect, and yet, now that it is afforded me, I know not how to commence."

Ada made no reply, the wished for moment had arrived when she might hope to win back the love of Walter Eardley, supposing it had ever been her own, and if not, to dazzle, to bewilder, to captivate him by her extreme loveliness, and bring him a willing, anxious suppliant to her feet. All this was possible—she had long considered it probable—but never till this moment had she thought of the possibility of failure, but now she actually grew pale and trembled for the result, she could not trust herself to speak for fear of saying aught that might break the spell she trusted her beauty had cast around him.

" I fear," resumed Walter, after waiting an instant for the reply—" I fear I have offended you by alluding to this subject—painful, doubtless, to yourself as to me ; believe me, I would not have done so, but I had a wish, a vain, perhaps, and foolish wish of standing as high in your estimation as it is possible to do. I wanted to tell you that I had made proposals for your hand in obedience to the wish of my father ; I had promised him this before I saw you, when my heart, my affections, all that was worthy of acceptance, was given to another."

" And that other ?" faintly enquired Ada.

" Is since dead," returned Walter, solemnly. " My own unkindness—my neglect—my desertion," he continued, bitterly, " was the chief cause of her premature decease. Oh ! Miss Herbert, have you not reason to thank God that you escaped so fearful a fate as that of linking your destiny with such a wretch as I am."

" Hush," replied Ada, trembling yet more. " I cannot bear to hear you speak thus, I cannot think so ill of you."

" I have told you the truth," returned Walter, " not to shock your feelings or to terrify your mind, but to reconcile you (in case it were possible you should regret the past) to the loss of one every way unworthy to win and wear so bright a gem, I trust to the gentleness and amiability of your character, the glorious attributes of your sex, to pardon the unkindness, the duplicity with which I acted towards yourself. You know not—you never can know how deeply my bosom was torn and rent by contending emotions, at the time when I promised my father to offer you my hand ; at that period I had never seen you—you had been represented to me as cold, imperious, and selfish, and I flattered myself that if my manners and appearance were fortunate enough to please you, you would accept my hand without troubling yourself about my heart—need I say how much I was deceived ? Alas! what a cruel mockery it seemed to offer to your accept-ance so worthless a boon as I had to bestow. I scarcely knew, Miss Herbert," he continued, " when my father's death left me free to renounce the engage-ment that then existed between us, whether I rejoiced most on my own account or yours."

"On your own account you might well rejoice," replied Ada, averting her face from her companion's gaze, " for it opened to you a prospect of being united to one whom you had long loved, but on my part there was room for nothing but regret. I have tried to forget the past, to remember no longer those days when I was vain and foolish enough to suppose myself beloved by you, but the memory of those hours clings to me still ; indeed—

> " The withered heart, and vain regret,
> Are things we seldom can forget."

And as she spoke she turned aside her head to hide the tears which were swim-ming in her eyes. Walter started and turned pale as he gazed upon her half averted face—

> " Oh! too convincing, dangerously dear,
> In woman's eye, the unanswerable tear ;
> Avoid it—virtue ebbs, and wisdom errs,
> Too fondly gazing on that grief of her's.
> Yet be the soft triumvir's fault forgiven—
> By this how many lose not earth—but Heaven ;
> Consign their souls to man's eternal foe,
> And seal their own to spare another's woe ?"

Her hand still rested on his arm—

> " He pressed that hand—it trembled—and his own
> Had lost its firmness, and his voice its tone.
> He watched her features till he could not bear
> Their tearful aspect and averted air."

"Ada," he murmured in his low musical accents. But she replied not ; she raised her eyes, her only answer there ; he read in them, as he believed a love such as he had once felt—such as he believed he could never feel again—he commiserated her sufferings, and was anxious as far as possible to alleviate them. He led her to a seat in a small but fragrant bower, and having placed him-self by her side, took her small white hand within both his own, as he said—

"Miss Herbert—Ada—dearest Ada, will you listen patiently to me for a few moments ?"

Ada, by a gesture, signified her willingness, but she did not speak.

"Till this moment," resumed Walter, " I had not a thought that my unsteadi-ness, my cruelty had rendered you unhappy ; on the contrary, I conceived, when you knew my character, and became acquainted with the baseness of my conduct to one, young, pure, and happy as yourself, that you would only feel cause for rejoicing that you had escaped linking your destiny with one so vile as I am. Have I been deceived ? Speak, Ada, and relieve me from this torturing suspense ; can I have been unhappy enough to have inspired aught beyond a transient feeling of affection in your breast ?"

"I will be candid," replied Ada, after apparently struggling for a moment with the feelings that oppressed her. " I accepted your proffered hand ; I listened to your words of love, and yielded myself blindly to the joy of thinking I was beloved by you, and all I can ask of you is—

'Can things like this be once believed,
And leave no pang in hearts deceived?' "

"Oh, Ada!" exclaimed the young man, as he knelt beside her and pressed her hand. "Oh, pray forgive, though Heaven itself detest. Reproach me, but not yet. Oh! spare me now; my brain appears bewildered. Do not madden me quite."

Thus spoke Walter, and thus did he upbraid himself for the cruel part he had acted towards the apparently confiding girl at his side; he could not at the time say more. He was silent, but not the less did he feel—

"Though speechless all—damp, dark and unexpress'd,
They bleed within that silent cell, his breast."

Ada imitated the silence of her companion, and for the time, no voice stole on the stillness of the air—that sweet soft stillness which we have frequently observed during the sweet season of song and of bloom, when the lark, high poised in the air, pours forth its sweetest melody, and the bee goes singing by, extracting the sweets from each fair flower, which invites by its fragrance, and sheds its grateful perfume over every sense. Walter was again the first to speak; he had been musing deep and thoughtfully, and had fully resolved upon the wisest course.

"I have deeply wronged you, Ada," he said, in his full clear manly tones, "and am anxious to offer you the only recompense in my power. Her whom I once fondly, madly loved, is dead. No thought of her, therefore, can mar your future happiness. I have but a crushed and broken heart to offer to your acceptance—this, and my entire respect, my constant and unceasing desire to render you happy, is yours, if deemed worthy of acceptance; all that I could ever feel towards one of your sex is yours. The rest," he added, solemnly, "is laid in ashes, which no breath could ever recall again to life and being. Think of all I have said, Ada; if you love me, think well. The home to which I would carry you, will most probably be a dull and gloomy one for myself. I have dedicated my energies and my talents to a parliamentary career; this will take me much and often from your side; this will chiefly occupy my thoughts, to the total exclusion of other and lighter subjects. Ask yourself then, seriously, Ada, if you love me well enough to cheerfully bear all these inconveniences (to call them by no lighter name) for the sake of becoming my wife."

"For the sake of becoming your wife," replied Ada, averting her blushing face, "I would cheerfully bear more—much more of the ills of life than those you have enumerated."

"You consent, then, to be mine?" said Walter, pressing the hand he held to his lips, though none of that warmth was visible in his manner which a lover generally manifests on such an occasion. "I trust," he continued, and as he spoke a cloud came over his brow, such as she had never seen before, and she felt the hand which clasped her own move with a slight convulsive tremor. "I trust that the love you now feel for me may never turn to hate; but there is a strange fatality about our race, that all we love seems to turn against us. Some wild story of an ancestress is said to be the cause; something wild and fearful of her marriage, but of which I have never been able to ascertain the entire truth. It is said that she married against her heart's consent, her affections being bestowed upon one too poor to meet the ambitious views of her parents, though of high, indeed I believe noble rank, and her marriage with the then existing Sir Richard Eardley was reported to have been almost by force. After the priest had pronounced the benison (for our family were Catholics in those days) a figure, who had been watching the proceedings, advanced towards the bride, and in a voice loud enough for all present to hear, exclaimed—'Mark me, false woman!—nor thee nor thine shall ever know requited love that leads to happiness.

Even thy descendants shall be cursed before the altar. I pray to Heaven to curse them. I pray that they may love as I have loved, and then bring a curse on all, and leave their hearts a sad desolate blank, that the fairest flowers may tempt them with their rich perfume, but only lure them to betray.' The man would have proceeded, but at the sound of his voice the bride had turned towards him, faintly exclaiming—'Mercy! mercy! spare me this!' And overcome by her

WALTER EARDLEY IMPLORES ADA'S FORGIVENESS OF PAST CRUELTIES.

feelings, she fell forward, fainting, against the bridegroom, who, unprepared, allowed her to fall to the ground; her forehead struck against the stone steps of the altar, and her bridal dress was covered with blood, and in the confusion that ensued the author of the mischief was allowed to escape."

"It was a fearful marriage," said Ada, the growing darkness of evening which now began to gather round them adding gloom to the story; "it make s m quite shudder."

"The curse was on our race," replied Walter, gloomily, "and a sad one it has been.   We never loved a thing, but in time it was sure to turn against us; did we even rear a dog, it would in time tear the hand that fed it; all things that have shown us affection have turned to hate us—all, down to the present time.   Witness my father's unhappy marriage with my mother; how much of sorrow did he not endure from one whom he most fondly loved; in myself, too, the curse has been long working—

> ' Oh! ever thus from childhood's hour
> I've seen my fondest hopes decay ;
> I never loved a tree or flower,
> But 'twas the first to fade away !'

And as I grew to manhood, and fixed my affections on one every way worthy of my fondest adoration, how short a time was I permited to enjoy the dear delight of loving and being loved. No! the curse was still working through, under the silence and darkness of night; soon, too soon, alas! her love turned to hatred; she shunned my very presence as the insidious destroyer of her peace.   Nor was this all; when at length I found myself in a position to do her justice, and fondly hoped to win back that confiding tenderness she had once placed in me, I sought once more her parental roof, fully believing that she might be induced to pardon all the past, and bless me again with her love. I went, as I have said,

> ' —— with quivering lip and tearful eye,
> But strong in truth, and arm'd for her reply !'

I went in the full belief that all would yet be well, and, alas! alas! discovered, to my utter bewilderment—to my almost maddening sorrow, that her whom I had so cruelly wronged, and to whom I would have knelt for pardon, was re- moved for ever beyond my reach—nor good, nor ill could ever touch her more; she was dead! Oh, who shall say that the curse is not still working ?—was not this a dread fulfilment of its bitterest power ?"

Again Ada shuddered.

"It is indeed fearful," was all that she could say.

"So fearful that you would not link yourself to so ill-fated a family; say, Ada, is it not so ?—fear not to speak the truth."

"Oh, no," she replied, hastily, " I meant not that ; if I can in any way tend to confirm your happiness—if my presence may in the slightest degree charm away your sadness, and make you less unhappy, then, Walter, I am willing to become yours for good or ill."

Walter thanked her with a grateful kiss, as he replied—

"For ill, I hope not ; it shall be my care to preserve you at least from the effects of that curse which has been the bane of all who have ever loved or trusted us, so as to turn their love to hatred and distrust ; still it cannot be so for ever; it must end somewhere. Ada, you will never learn to hate me ?"

"Never," she replied fearlessly.   "Your brother has not hesitated to contract a marriage with one to whom he is ardently attached ; if he fears not the future, why should we ?"

"You are right," replied Walter, " my brother has so far escaped the curse; may we not, then, reasonably entertain a hope that its influence is over—that it will no longer possess the power to harm us ?"

"Yes, yes," replied Ada, eagerly, " it must—it will be so."

"We will at least hope it," said Walter.   "And yet I feel that I cannot give you that warm, trusting love which I know to be your due.   My heart is seared, my affections blighted and scattered to the ground. Alas! can respect—can constant and unvarying attention, and care for your happiness requite you for all you must sacrifice in becoming my wife ?"

"Yes, Walter," returned Ada, endeavouring to smile away the fears which oppressed her to a sense of suffocation; " I am willing to sacrifice all this, and more, to become your wife—to possess the right to cheer your hours of sadness, and share your moments of joy."

Again Walter kissed her polished forehead, and expressed a hope that he might be able to make her happy; and yet, even while he spoke, sorrow rankled severely in his breast, and deep despondency settled on his spirit; he asked himself what he had done, and trembled at the weight of responsibility he had incurred; he had engaged himself to marry one whom he did not—could not love;—true, he did not love another: the only one for whom his heart had ever breathed responsive to that fond warm passion, was no more; the grave had closed over her, and with her was buried likewise his own once ardent affection, which he felt nothing on earth could ever recall to renewed life. The past, with its bright halo of sunshine and glad delights, was gone for ever, and the future had no joy for him : it appeared one sad scene of desolation;—his hopes were withered, his fond expectations blighted, and nothing seemed left him but the memory of the past, on which his conscious heart yet dwelt with the only joy his spirit ever knew. He did not love the proud beauty to whom he was now affianced, and marriage without love, seemed indeed a sad and mournful affair; but Walter strove to comfort himself with the conviction that all he had to give of love and respect, was given to Ada, and though he well knew it was but a poor exchange for a faithful and loving heart, such as he fully believed, in the warmth of her affection ,she had given to himself, he still found solace in the statement he had made to her, touching his own affections. She had expressed herself content with the respectful attention and anxious solicitude for her welfare which he had proffered to her acceptance; she had assured him that such would suffice to ensure her happiness. Why, then, he asked himself, need he tremble for the future, or dread the fulfilment of that contract he had now entered into ? Still, spite of his own endeavours to the contrary, he could not contemplate the future without a shudder, or look forward to his marriage with Ada, with anything like satisfaction. On her part, too, Ada felt restless and uneasy; she had now attained the summit of her ambition. She had seen Walter again a suppliant at her side, pleading for forgiveness of the past, and a renewal of those bonds which had previously united them. She was now his affianced bride, not the lonely deserted being she had so lately been. And yet she was not happy. How seldom, indeed, is unmixed pleasure the lot of mortals ! How seldom does the attainment, even of our brightest hopes, bring with it that satisfaction we had so vainly and heedlessly desired ! How often, in the midst of the enjoyments we had long and foolishly coveted, do we sigh for the simple pleasures and untainted desires of the past ! All, we are sure, have felt this—all have known the sense of weariness which attends the fairest pleasures, and palls the brightest joys. And now, as we have said that Ada had reached the goal of happiness she had so sighed after, she felt more sad and depressed than she had ever done before; the wild story which Walter had imparted to her, and the bitter curse which appeared to rest upon the family, making it the forerunner of some dire calamity to love or wed with an Eardley, had decidedly some share in the gloom which hovered over her spirit, making her at times well nigh resolved to tell Walter that she could not accept of half a heart, even though the remainder was buried for ever in the tomb of his beloved; but no, she seemed impelled by the unseen hand of Fate itself, to link her destiny with that of Walter's. She had so long coveted to be his wife, to hold that position in society she looked upon as her due, that she could not now prevail upon herself to resign the dear delight. And yet, when she looked upon the clouded brow and gloomy aspect of her lover, something whispered to her that, in accepting his hand, she would be only sealing the misery of both. Alas ! how truly painful was the position of these two young persons, both so richly blessed in personal charms, so highly cultivated in mental attractions, so fully possessed of those influences which most tend to secure happiness, blindly pursuing a course of action which would, in all probability, lead to their utter misery and sorrow. Mutually deceived in their opinion of each other—wilfully resolved to contract a marriage, to which neither could bring those fond and united feelings, without which there can be no happiness. A marriage without !—love can aught be conceived more painful? Without love, how can either husband or wife perform their relative duties? how bear the many little anxieties and trials which they must occasionally meet with? how bear the infirmities of each other's temper and disposition? if—

> "The fondest and the happiest pair
> Will find occasion to forbear,
> And something every day they live,
> To pity, and perhaps forgive."

How will those do who have no trusting affection—no devoted love wherewith to enable them to battle with the ills of life, and withstand the storms and buffets that will at times beset them on their onward career? Oh! it needs love—fond and devoted love, to enable us to bear each other's burdens, to share each other's sorrows, as well as the pleasures of existence! The shadows of evening had gathered deeply around before Walter and Ada returned to the house. No smile of gladness shed its brightness over their countenance; on the contrary, an unusual sadness seemed to have settled on their spirits—they were engaged. Alas! what of happiness, what even of content or satisfaction could be expected from such an engagement? And yet how often are such engagements formed! How seldom, comparatively, is love made the basis on which to rest the foundation of happy marriage? How much oftener are the minor considerations of wealth, station, and rank, swelled into that importance which love alone should hold, in so serious an affair as marriage?—a contract which exists, not merely for weeks or years, but for a lifetime; a contract which nought but death can break, and which seals the happiness or misery of those who enter into it. . Oh! when we think of this, when we remember the solemn and binding vows which are pronounced by those who consent to unite their destinies, to share each other's fortune, be it good or ill; we repeat, when we think, we cannot refrain from impressing upon the minds of all who may chance to read these pages, that nothing short of love can ever bring happiness in the marriage state. We do not say that nothing but love is requisite; still happiness will bless the humblest home where love resides, while it will shun a palace, if love be not a constant guest. Walter knew this by experience, and yet he hoped to secure the happiness of one whom he fully believed fondly loved him. Indeed, this was the sole reason for resolving to unite himself to Ada; he knew too well the maddening power of love, voluntarily to consign her to the sad fate of hopeless attachment; it never occurred to him that it would have been both wiser and better to have allowed time to heal the wounds he had himself inflicted, than to have confirmed her unhappiness by giving her his hand: while his heart was free, he hoped to secure her happiness—his own, he believed to be crushed for ever. Lady Eardley had some time previously returned to the drawing room, where Walter and Ada found her, on their arrival, awaiting their return to the house.

"You have taken a long ramble," she observed, smiling as they entered. "I hope you have succeeded (turning to her son) in making it a pleasant one to our young friend."

Ada blushed deeply at these words, and Walter, who desired to have no secrets from his mother, hastened to explain how matters stood between them; and leading Ada to her side, concluded by saying—

"My brother has this day given you one daughter, whom I am convinced is every way worthy to stand in that close relationship to you. Will you also permit me to claim your love and interest on behalf of another, whom I hope ere long to call by the endearing name of wife?"

Lady Eardley drew the blushing girl closer to her, as she bent down and tenderly kissed her cheek.

"I warmly congratulate you, my dear Walter," she said, " in thus fulfilling the last wishes of your father. Had he lived, you would have been already united to Miss Herbert; it is, therefore, a source of the sincerest pleasure to me to see you thus obeying his last mandate—the more so, as you were not bound by any tie save that of honour. I have never, my dear son, pressed you on this subject, as I wished it to emanate with yourself, and it having done so, has gratified me more than I can say. I had, indeed, a superstitious feeling regarding it, and could not have rested with any feeling of satisfaction, for your future happiness. Walter looked pleased; he felt thankful that his mother approved of the part he had acted. He was more than confirmed in his previous belief that he had done well in offering his hand to Ada, whom he felt assured truly loved him, and to whom he inwardly resolved to dedicate every effort to promote her happiness and well being; in short, to do all in his power to prevent her feeling the want of that which he could not bestow, and which nothing could ever make amends for, for what could ever atone for the want of love—that sweet solace which makes even troubles and sorrows light? But Ada had expressed herself willing to accept his hand, though unaccompanied by the heart, and he, therefore, strove to be content; and yet, though pleased that the course of action he had adopted had met with the warm approval of his mother, Walter felt sad and depressed: his thoughts fled back to his lost Lucy, her whom he had once fondly hoped to make his bride. He thought of her gentle and unobtrusive worth; her cheerfulness under adversity; her quiet grace and uncomplaining tenderness; of all her good and estimable qualities, which shone more conspicuous in the days of sorrow and anxiety than they had ever done in those of glad sunshine and of joy. He gazed upon the fair face of the blushing girl at his side, and while he acknowledged her superior loveliness to that of his first and only love, he could not help fearing that she was greatly her inferior in mental qualifications; but he checked himself, for he felt the comparison was not a fair one. While Walter was thus engaged, Ada, on her part, was likewise thinking of another, and drawing in her own mind an equally unfair comparison between her present and former lover. Walter, her heart acknowledged to be the very type of manly beauty; but then he lacked the warm feelings and passionate devotion that had formed to her mind so pleasing a trait in the character of Percy; she had loved him, as far as it is possible for a character so devoted to self, to love; and though she admired Walter, and was proud of having attracted the observation of one so well qualified to ensure the admiration of her own sex, she yet did not, could not feel for him that affection which Percy alone had inspired in her breast. Thus, each thinking of another, even while seated side by side, what a sad prospect did the future present to these young people; could they have seen each other's hearts, and read the thoughts that were passing in their breasts, they never would have been unreasonable enough to expect happiness in a marriage so utterly opposed to those principles from which it is extracted. Nothing, surely, is more painful, or fraught with more dangerous consequences to the peace of all who practise it, than habitual deception; well might the poet beautifully and truthfully say—

> "Oh! what a tangled web we weave,
> When first we practise to deceive."

The very knowledge that duplicity tends, not only to undermine the happiness and peace of others, but likewise renders miserable and friendless the persons who practise it, must surely do more to induce perfect openness and candour, in our relative positions of life, than aught that our feeble pen could write in praise of it. Ada, alas! thought by a system of deception to secure her own independence, and, she hoped, happiness. Alas! what a mistaken idea!—how utterly impossible it is to find happiness apart from perfect sincerity and candour! Walter was sincere, and consequently possessed the greatest chance of securing to himself that brightest and best of jewels, happiness. He had not attempted to deceive the fair being whom he believed fondly loved him, but had unflinchingly told her of his own blighted affections—his buried hopes, and increasing love for one who had been snatched from him by the remorseless hand of death ere the meridian of life had come—whose sun had gone down at noon, and left him—like some lost bird without its mate—all lonely, sad, and desolate. But Ada had not emulated his candour; no, on her part, the connection had ever been carried on under a system of constant and unvarying deception—a deception which must inevitably bring with it, in time, its own punishment. Walter, more happy and self-satisfied, from the approval his mother had manifested of his conduct, before they parted for the evening, took from his breast a black riband, that fastened something round his neck.

"Wear this, dear Ada," he said, giving her a curiously worked gold cross, "it was the gift of my lost Lucy. Wear it for my sake; think of her who once so fondly loved me, and if ever yours should turn to hate, return it to me."

"I accept the pledge," replied Ada, smiling. "When I turn to hate you, you shall receive your token back, and that will be when——"

The sentence remained unfinished by the entrance of Lady Eardley into the room, and no further opportunity offered for resuming the conversation.

CHAPTER XXXVIII.

"The scene on which we gaze
    Recalls life's summer morning dream,
The music of departed days
    Still murmuring in the stream;
While love and friendship's voices long
    Have passed to silence, like the strain
Breath'd in some sweet heart-touching song
    We never hear again."

WHEN Henry and Fanny appeared once more on the deck of the vessel, the morning sun, warm and beautiful, shed its cheering brightness on the lovely scenery which was spread before them, while its beams gaily danced on the clear waters, whose gentle ripples washed the sides of the vessel. They were now within half a mile of the coast of Sicily, which is low but finely variegated, while on the opposite side lay the coast of Calabria, which is very high, and the mountains covered with the finest verdure. It was almost a dead calm, the ship scarcely moving half a mile an hour, so that our travellers had time to get a complete view of the famous rock of Scylla on the Calabrian side, Cape Pylorous on the Sicilian, and the celebrated straits of the Faro, that run between them. Whilst they were still some miles distant from the entry of the straits, they heard the roaring of the current, like the noise of some large impetuous river confined by narrow banks. This increased in proportion as they advanced, till they could see the water in many places rise to a considerable height and form large eddies or whirlpools, while the sea in every other place was as smooth as glass. On nearing the straits, as the current was directly against them, they were obliged to lie to for some hours till it turned. The motion of the water ceased for some time, and they lay just opposite to Cape Pylorous, where the lighthouse is built. From here they had an opportunity of observing a pretty large portion of Calabria, which formerly constituted a considerable part of that celebrated country known by the name of Great Greece, and looked upon as one of the most fertile in the empire. Henry gazed with delightful surprise on these beautiful hills and mountains, covered with trees and brushwood to their very summit, and to judge from the appearance they presented in the distance, pretty much in the same state as some of the wilds of America that are just beginning to be cultivated. Fanny fully participated in the pleasure of her husband; the past, with its many sorrows and sources of anxiety, was now forgotten in the new delights—the fond warm joy that filled her days and nights. She felt herself blest in the returning health and happiness of Henry; there was now no cloud upon his brow, no sign of anxiety on his animated countenance; on the contrary, his eye was bright with intelligence and hope, and he looked, as indeed he felt, happy and content; and Fanny had the satisfaction of knowing that this pleasing change was in a great measure to be attributed to herself. She had planned the present tour for the express purpose of giving a turn to her husband's thoughts, and relieving his mind of those gloomy feelings which so heavily oppressed it. How wise had been her conduct; instead of enacting the part of the jealous wife, and increasing her husband's gloomy despondency by bitter upbraidings and vain repinings at his conduct, she had done her utmost to alleviate his sorrow, and win him from brooding over the loss of one he had fondly loved, but had resigned from a feeling of gratitude and pity to herself. Fanny, as we have said, had acted well and wisely in subduing each angry and jealous feeling, and for this she was amply rewarded by seeing the light of joy revisit once more the cheek of her husband; to hear him address her by the tender and endearing epithets that she well knew emanated from the warmest and tenderest regard, and to know that she had weaned him from his sombre thoughts, and bade happiness and peace become once more an inmate of his breast. After the vessel had remained stationary for some hours (affording them, as we have said, an opportunity of seeing and admiring the beautiful coast which was stretched on either side of them, inviting their admiration by its extreme and versatile beauty), the current changed in their favour, of which they hastened to take advantage, and as soon as the ship entered the current, they were carried along with great velocity towards Messina, the approach to which is the finest that can be imagined; it is not, perhaps, so grand as that of Naples, but it is infinitely more beautiful. Henry and his affectionate wife had remained on deck, wrapped in wonder and delight, nearly the whole morning, and at four in the afternoon they cast anchor near the centre of the quay, the beauty of which greatly delighted them. It is built in the form of a crescent, and is surrounded by a range of magnificent buildings four stories high, and exactly uniform for the space of an Italian mile. The street between these and the sea is about an hundred feet wide, and forms one of the most delightful walks in the world, at least Henry and Fanny thought so, when, having landed after their short and pleasant voyage, they promenaded for a short time over this delightful walk, which enjoys the fresh air, and commands the most beautiful prospect, and possesses likewise the additional attraction of being, even in the warmest seasons, delightfully cool, as it is only exposed to the morning sun, being shaded all the rest of the day by the buildings we have described. It is, besides, constantly refreshed by the cooling breeze from the straits, for the current of the water produces likewise a current in the air that renders this one of the pleasantest habitations in Sicily. So delighted and gratified with all that met their gaze were our two travellers, that they were entirely insensible of fatigue. What most particularly interested Henry, was a fine fountain of pure white marble; which stands on the quay, representing Neptune holding Scylla and Charybdis chained, under the emblematical figures of two sea monsters, as represented by the poets. The beauty of these he pointed out to Fanny, discoursing eloquently on their respective claims to admiration. The extreme magnificence of the harbour likewise attracted their attention, in which there was a number of gallies and galliots, which added greatly to its beauty. Three of these were just sailing, in order to cruize round the island, and to protect it from the sudden invasion of the Barbarians, who are often very troublesome on the south coast. These vessels made a very picturesque appearance as they went out of the harbour, their oars moving all together with the greatest regularity. All this was at once so new and pleasing to Henry, that he felt as though he should never be wearied, but consideration for his most delicate companion induced him to propose their immediately seeking accommodation for the night. In this they experienced no difficulty, for they easily obtained lodgings, though certainly in the most wretched of inns, yet said to be a first-rate one for Sicily; but our travellers were in no

humour to be discontented, on the contrary, they were so happy and
self-satisfied, so delighted with all that met their gaze, that they only laughed
at the inconveniences they were forced to put up with.   Henry, it is true, was
somewhat solicitous on account of Fanny, but she appeared so happy and
cheerful, and made so light of every little inconvenience, that his anxiety was
quickly dissipated.   The following morning they arose early ; the weather was
still fine, and the sun shone so beautifully that it tempted them to walk out.
They found some fine shady walks running along the sea shore, and fanned by
the cooling breeze from the straits, and here Fanny was delighted to observe
many of the flowers growing wild, that are held in high esteem in our English
gardens, and others, too, with which she was entirely unacquainted, particularly
one, which grew all over the mountains, and bore a beautiful looking round
fruit of a bright shining yellow, and which upon enquiry she found was
called " Il pomo d'oro," or golden apple.   In addition to these attractions,
all the fields were covered with the richest white clover, intermixed with a
variety of aromatic plants which perfumed the air, and rendered their walks
most delightful.   Having dined and rested themselves during the heat of the
day, Fanny expressed a wish to visit one of the convents.   Henry was only too
happy to meet her views, and having in the course of the day made the
acquaintance of a Sicilian gentleman, through his instrumentality they gained
admittance to several, and were received by the nuns with the greatest politeness
and affability, with whom they conversed for some time through the gate.
They all appeared to be happy and contented, and declared they would not
change their prison for the most brilliant situation in life.   However, Fanny
imagined that some of them had a soft melancholy in their countenances, which
seemed utterly at variance with their words.   Several of them were extremely
handsome, but perhaps their simple attire gave an additional grace to their
charms, indeed we incline to think that there is no artificial ornament, or
studied embellishment whatever, that can produce so strong and pleasing an
effect on the mind as the modest and simple attire of a pretty young nun
placed behind a double iron gate.   Indeed, to see an amiable, unaffected, and
unadorned person, that might have been an honour and ornament to society,
make a voluntary resignation of her charms, and give up the world and all its
pleasures for a life of fasting and mortification, cannot surely fail to move a
contemplative mind to pity.   From these and the like reflections, neither Henry
or Fanny felt in such good spirits after conversing with the nuns.   Indeed,
it seemed utterly impossible to leave the gate, that inexorable and impenetrable
barrier, without a sad and heavy heart.   On leaving the convent, they
observed a great concourse of people on the top of a high hill, at some distance
from the city.   They were told it was the celebration of a festival in honour of
St. Francis, and well worth their going to see.   Accordingly they immediately
bent their steps in that direction, and arrived just as the saint made his
appearance. He was carried through the crowd with great ceremony, after which
he was again lodged in his chapel, where he performs a number of miracles every
day to all who have abundance of faith and no lack of money.   After this
ceremony had been performed, the young people assembled began to dance in
soft Sicilian measures till after sunset, when they retired.   Many of the young
girls were very pretty, and danced with much grace.   The young men were
all in their holiday clothes and made a good appearance.   The assembly room
was a fine green plain on the top of a high hill, the view from which was
beautiful beyond description, the straits appearing like a vast majestic river,
flowing slowly between two ridges of mountains, and opening by degrees from
its narrowest point, till it swelled to the size of an ocean ; its banks at the
same time adorned with rich corn-fields, vineyards, orchards, towns, villages,
and churches, and the prospect terminated on each side by the tops of high
mountains covered with trees.   All this pleased them very much, and reminded them of Theocritus's descriptions of the Sicilian pleasures.   One part
of the ceremony, however, somewhat alarmed Fanny.   The whole court before

the church, was surrounded with three rows of small iron cannon, about six inches long; these were charged to the muzzle, and a train laid that completed the communication through the whole number, which must have exceeded two hundred. Fire was set to this train, and in two or three minutes the whole was discharged, the reports following one another so quick, that it was impossible for the ear to separate them. The effect

SIR RICHARD AND LADY EARDLEY CONTEMPLATING THE BEAUTIES OF THEIR DOMAIN.

was very grand, but would have been nothing without the fine echo from the mountains on each side of the straits, which prolonged the sound for some considerable time after the firing was finished. Fanny, we have said, was at first somewhat alarmed by the suddenness of these reports, but she quickly recovered from the effects of the surprise, and joined with Henry in praise of the beauty and grandeur of all they saw.

"This would, indeed, appear the land of enchantment," she said, smiling, "and I seem absolutely bewildered, both by the novelty and grandeur by which I am surrounded, for wherever I chance to turn my eyes, I am certain of discovering some fresh object of wonder and delight."

"It does, indeed, surpass description," replied Henry, energetically, "I had till now no conception of the wondrous and diversified beauty of Nature; how tame and dull our own country appears by comparison."

"And yet," said Fanny, warmly, "I confess, notwithstanding its cloudy skies and November fogs, I love it well. Yes, dear native England! I would not exchange thy varying climate and shadowy skies, for even this delightful and fertile country."

"Dear Fanny," said Henry, smiling in his turn, "you are enthusiastic in your love of country."

"I acknowledge it," replied Fanny, "and never did I feel how dear to me were my own native fields and flowers, till I became a wanderer from the loved scenes of my childhood; and though none can admire more this beautiful country, with its splendid views and soft lovely scenery, yet, aught that reminds me of my native land is a thousand times more dear and treasured; for instance, these flowers," she continued, glancing at a small bouquet she held in her hand, and which she had gathered during her morning, walk composed entirely of flowers that bloomed as brightly in her garden bower at home. "For instance, these flowers are inexpressibly more dear to me than the more rare and perhaps more strictly beautiful blossoms that surround us in this land of enchantment."

"I admire and appreciate the good feeling that dictates such a preference," replied Henry, glancing affectionately at the animated countenance of his young wife. "The love of country," he continued, "I fully believe pervades all breasts, and it is wisely ordered that it should be so. I agree with you, my Fanny, that though it is pleasant for awhile to sojourn in other climes, and make ourselves acquainted with the varied beauties of nature, yet it would cost me a severe pang to bid an eternal adieu to our native shores. But we had better now return to the inn, for as we purpose resuming our journey to-morrow, you must, my love, stand in need of rest and refreshment."

Fanny readily assented to his proposition, though at the same time assuring him that she was perfectly insensible of fatigue. Early the following morning they left Messina, in excellent spirits, having engaged the attendance of a guide and several native servants, all of whom, as well as themselves, were mounted on mules. Fanny, who was an excelent horsewoman, greatly enjoyed this novel mode of travelling, and kept up an agreeable and animated conversation with Henry as they passed along. The road they pursued was extremely romantic. It lay the whole way along the coast, and commanded a view of Calabria, and the south part of the straits, covered with chebees, galleys, galliots, and fishing boats. The view on the right hand was confined by high mountains, on the very summits of which are built several large towns and villages, which with their churches and steeples, make a very picturesque appearance. The sides, too, of some of these mountains are highly cultivated, and present the most agreeable aspect that can be imagined—corn, wine, oil, and silk, all mixed together in the greatest abundance. The sides, too, of the road along which they journeyed, were covered with a variety of flowers and flowering shrubs, some of them exceedingly beautiful. Many of the inclosures were fenced with hedges of the Indian fig or prickly pear, all of which was new and pleasing to the tourists. Towards evening they arrived at their present destination, and in full view of Mount Etna, which made a glorious appearance from the spot whence they beheld it in all its magnificence. It was throwing out volumes of white smoke, which did not rise in the air, but seemed to roll down the sides of the mountain like a vast torrent. While they were gazing, rapt in wondrous awe, on the majestic spectacle before them, their guide advanced to inform them that he had succeeded in procuring them excellent accommodation at a village, a the foot of the mountain on which it stands. They instantly obeyed the welcome summons, and found an excellent supper and good wine already waiting their arrival, and which the exercise of riding, and the fresh air they had inhaled from the mountains, made them nothing loth to do ample justice to the fare so temptingly set before them. After partaking of the evening meal, Henry and Fanny sat for some time at the open window, looking out with admiring eyes upon the beautiful and apparently magic scenery that was spread before them.

"How sweet and precious a blessing is it," began Henry, "to possess a companion who does not shrink from sharing our sorrows, or the more pleasing duty of alleviating our anxieties! Had it not been for your undeviating love and constant attention, I tremble to think what I might have been, instead of feeling grtaeful to Providence for the rich blessing I possessed in you. I was fast sinking into a gloomy misanthrope, discontented and unhappy, because one boon I had coveted was denied me. Alas! Fanny, can you forgive my ingratitude, my unkindness to yourself?"

"Oh! never let this subject be renewed between us," replied Fanny; "if I have in any manner tended to beguile your sorrows, or alleviate in the slightest degree your anxieties, I am well repaid by your love and tenderness; this was all I coveted. For this, I confess I would willingly have endured any amount of suffering, and deemed myself blest, if, in the end, I attained that which was the summit of my ambitious hopes—your love."

"And that, my beloved Fanny, is now all your own. I have no thought—no care—no love for any but yourself."

"Then I am indeed blest," replied Fanny, turning her beaming face, radiant with joy, full upon her husband, "Oh! Henry, may you ever thus feel, or may I never live to experience that bitter revulsion of feeling which must be my portion, were it possible you could again brood sorrowfully over the memory of the past—that past which I was the innocent cause of blighting, and shedding over the sunshine of another's life, the terrible influence of grief and sorrow. When I think of this," she continued, "I do not wonder that my very presence was once painful and distressing to you; indeed, I have at times almost wondered that you did not hate me."

"Hate you! Oh! Fanny, how could you, even for a moment, allow such unjust thoughts to find a place in your heart? But I cannot chide you, my love—the fault lay entirely with myself: indeed I cannot recall my long-continued unkindness and neglect, without a severe pang of regret; but it can never be thus again. No, I love you, Fanny, with no light or evanescent passion, but a love founded on the deepest and truest respect; on a warm admiration of your numberless virtues and excellent qualities—thus I love you, Fanny; and never again, from love's shining circle, can the gems drop away."

The tears glistened brightly in Fanny's eyes as these words fell from her husband's lips—they were tears of gratitude and joy; and yet, in the midst of these joyous feelings, she thought of Jane Clarence, once so fondly loved by Henry, and her gentle heart ached with pity for the fate of one she had never seen, yet had unintentionally and irretrievably injured, by coming between her and her fondest hopes, chasing each joy away, crushing her fairest wishes, and strewing her withered and blighted affections to the ground. She thought of all this, and, had it been possible, would have resigned part of her present happiness to restore once more the light of joy to her heart, to have cancelled that deep despondency she felt assured must be her portion. Henry, too, had loved!—yes, she was his first and earliest love; she had realised his first fair dream of bliss by his side; she had wandered whole days amid mossy green and forest glen, while she listened to his whispered words of love, so inexpressibly dear to a woman's bursting heart, and now she was bereft of this first pure joy her bosom knew. Henry had renounced her love, even at the moment he most fondly and fervently returned her affections. As Fanny thus mused, she gazed earnestly on the expressive face of her husband, and asked herself, could she ever love him too well—could she ever sufficiently study his happiness, who had sacrificed so much for her? She knew well that, in giving her his hand, no sordid or selfish feeling had induced him thus to act. No, she entirely acquitted him of all such motives. She was thoroughly aware that he had discovered the secret of her own but half-concealed affection for him, and gratitude and pity had conspired to compel him to sacrifice his own feelings, in order to spare her's. This raised Henry in her estimation so highly, that she entertained a feeling almost of reverence for his character, and while she commiserated the sufferings of Jane, she did not, could not blame the author of them. While Fanny thus mused for awhile in silence, Henry's thoughts were similarly engaged; the foregoing conversation had vividly brought back to his memory the image of the wronged and forsaken Jane Clarence. He thought of her, not as he had last seen her in the bloom and freshness of requited love, when the world seemed to her filled with joys, and she was anxious to resign them all—to leave the world with him; when she looked forward with full certainty to one day sharing his fortune, however humble; when the smile beamed brightly on her cheek, and joy danced in her eye as she anticipated the glad hour of his return to his native village to claim her as his bride. How sweetly had she discoursed of the future, and pictured in glowing colours how blest it would be when shared with him; how trustfully, too, had she relied upon his plighted faith, never for a moment doubting his constancy, or allowing herself to think of his love as less pure, less constant, or true than her own. Oh! not thus did Henry's imagination now picture her, but sad, sorrowful, and unexpressed each feeling, that had once been sweet to cherish—all changed, even to the confiding gentleness that formed so pleasing a trait. Alas! he thought she must hate, she must contemn the entire sex, she placed such full reliance on my love, and yet I deceived her fond expectation, wounded her in her tenderest point, and through her holiest and purest feelings, that never again will she put faith in man. And then he pictured her pallid face and reproachful aspect—her days of unceasing sorrow and nights of bitter anxiety; for he well knew that Jane's love had not been lightly won, and consequently would not be soon forgot, though the chords of sweetest melody had from silent harp been torn, yet he was well aware she would mourn long and deeply over its broken strings, and though it would remain the whole of her after life mute, never again to give forth those sweet and touching strains which had so lately charmed her senses and whiled away her hours of sadness, she would yet weep over its departed melody, and mourn that its master chord was broken. This was the one dark spot in Henry's otherwise bright and happy destiny. Blessed with an adoring wife, and all that makes life sweet and precious—with the means of gratifying his most fastidious taste, and dispensing rich bounties to his fellow men, without in the least impoverishing himself—in short, with every incentive to happiness, his prospect and position in life doubtless the cause of envy to many, yet Henry had one secret source of uneasiness, that in a great measure poisoned his happiness, and prevented him enjoying to the full, those gifts which Providence had so lavishly bestowed upon him. And how often is this the case—how seldom should we find, if we could dive into the inmost recesses of the human breast, that those who are the most envied, who are looked upon as possessing the utmost incentives to happiness—we repeat, how seldom, if ever, should we find those persons blessed above their fellows; on the contrary, how frequently should we prove, that under the smiling exterior lay concealed some dark sorrow or frowning calamity. Let us, therefore, pause ere we envy the state or condition of another. For every heart knows its own bitterness, with which a stranger meddleth not, and we may ever rest assured that no station in life is exempt from cares and anxieties which are the common lot of mortals; let us, therefore, learn to be content with the situation in which Providence has wisely placed us, repining not over the little ills and minor sorrows which will occasionally perplex and annoy us ; rather let us rejoice that so much good, so many sources of the purest happiness and sweetest delights, are open to all who choose to avail themselves of them, while at the same time we bear in mind, that all paths alike are checquered more or less.

CHAPTER XXXIX.

My boyhood's home !—oh, welcome sight !
　Green spot of memory, ever dear—
In youth my subject prayer at night,
　And now a joy no time can sear ;
My boyhood's home !—I see thy hills,
　I see thy valley's changeful green,
And manhood's eye a tear-drop fills,
　Tho' years might roll since thou wert seen !
I come to thee from Sorrow's school—
I come with pride o'er thee to rule ;
But while I gaze on each lov'd plain,
I feel I am a boy again.

HAVING been conducted by the housekeeper into the room already prepared for their reception, Clara, with a few words of kindness, spoken in her own peculiar tones of consideration, dismissed her for the present, and approached the large bay window, which was thrown open to admit the sweet refreshing breeze which rushed into the apartment, laden with the sweet perfume of the jasmine and honeysuckle. The window commanded a fine view of the noble park, with the small glassy lake in its bosom, which reflected on its polished surface the dancing rays of the autumn sun, and lent an additional beauty to the scene.

"And this is the home of your forefathers !" said Clara, turning to her husband, while a bright and happy smile illuminated her countenance. " Oh, how beautiful it is."

"And you will love it for my sake," replied Richard.

"For your sake," returned Clara, " I would love the meanest habitation, and think it sweet if shared with you ; but this is so fair and beautiful, so far surpassing my highest expectations, that I shall love it also for its own ; look, Jane," she added turning to her friend who had followed her to the window, "see what a woody appearance these fine old trees present, forming so sweet and shady an arch with their overhanging boughs, that even now I feel tempted to seek the welcome repose their deep shadows offer while wandering beside yon purling stream. Oh, is it not beautiful ?"

"It is indeed " replied Jane, " and to a contemplative mind, nothing could be more beautiful than to rest for hours under the friendly shade of those willows, whose long pendant branches dip deep into the stream, as though mourning over the mortality of human things—hopes long nourished only to be crushed ; affections, which like the flowers around, bloom brightly while the spring and summer lasts, but whither and fade in autumn's rougher day, leaving the spot all sad and lonely where they once have been."

These words were spoken in a tone of the deepest melancholy, and a tear rose to the eye of Jane as she concluded. Clara moved closer to her side. She understood and sympathised with the feelings of her friend too deeply to offer consolation, otherwise than by the mute pressure of her hand, which she gently took within her own. " How happy and blest am I !" was her inward exclamation as she glanced affectionately at the approving countenance of her husband, " and poor Jane is equally as miserable, while, at the same time, so amiable and good, so every way worthy of happiness." As these thoughts passe through the mind of Clara, her face assumed an expression of melancholy strongly resembling that which sat upon the countenance of her friend. Richar instantly observed this, and a deep pang of anxiety shot across his breast, melancholy foreboding of ill. Up to this moment he had allowed no fears fo the future to take even momentary possession of his breast; he had smiled in credulously at the family superstition, that to love an Eardley was the sur forerunner of some heavy misfortune, and so far he had been confirmed in hi unbelief, for as his mother had told Clara, that, through his life's short sunny dream, he had floated without pain or care—still there had been times, thoug brief their stay, like summer clouds which shine themselves away—moments o gloom, when every pleasure palled—still they were but summer clouds, and, with this exception, he had entirely escaped the curse which was said to rest so heavily on his family;—consequently, as he had never felt its pressure, he had never feared; but now, as he remarked the melancholy expression that sat upon the fair face of his young bride, he for the first time trembled with apprehension for the future. Oh, could it be that there lurked indeed some truth in that prevailing creed, that the family were destined to bring sorrow and destruction on all who loved them? The bare thought of the remote possibility of such a catastrophe filled his heart with the deepest despondency; how could he endure the maddening thought that in time the love of that one being, upon whom he had so fondly lavished the entire wealth of his affections, might turn to hate?—that those eyes, which were now bent down in order to conceal the deep revelation of her own tenderness as she met his look of fond devotion, might one day coldly meet his glance, or, what was still worse, be turned from him with aversion or contempt? "Oh, why," he asked himself, "had he not thought of this sooner?—now, alas! it was too late." Too late!—how often have those words been given utterance to under the deepest paroxysms of despair?—how many have folded their hands in bitter anguish, as they enquire of themselves—"Oh, why did I not think of this sooner?—now—now, alas! it is too late!" There is something indescribably painful in the sound of the words—"too late!" How great is their signification—how wide their meaning, for none can say how much they may be intended to convey to the mind of the hearer. For ourselves, we can truly say we never heard them breathed without a feeling of ominous dread —that they imparted more than met the ear. We may make wise resolutions for the future—a future, perhaps, that we are never destined to behold; our resolves may be all too late, and in bitterness of spirit we may be forced to exclaim—"Oh, why did I not think of this sooner?" We may be lured to do that which our conscience whispers is wrong, but we turn a deaf ear to its wise and faithful pleadings, and when we suffer from the consequences of our error, as all must sooner or later, how bitter—how heart-rending is the feeling that we cannot recall the past—that it is now too late! How full of the keenest remorse is the exclamation—"Oh, why did I not think of this sooner?" The knowledge of this should stand us in good stead in the hour of temptation, and induce us steadfastly to persevere in the path of virtue, for one false step, and it may be all too late to return; and in bitterness of spirit we may utter the desponding enquiry.—Oh! why did I not think of this sooner?"—But we are doing that to which we are too prone, diverging from our subject, and for which we beg the reader's pardon. Sir Richard Eardley, we were saying, for the first time, began to reflect deeply, and in consequence sadly, on the curse which was said to rest upon his family. Still he possessed that natural buoyancy of spirit that prevented at least imaginary evils from troubling him long. Jane, with that instinctive good feeling which appeared natural to her, quickly perceiving the melancholy aspect of her friend, and the anxious air with which her husband regarded her, roused herself from the contemplative mood into which she had fallen, and endeavouring to smile with her once wonted gaiety, said, turning to her friend—

"Come, dear Clara, you must not allow this romantic scenery to affect you otherwise than with joyous anticipations of the many happy hours that you may reasonably hope to spend in this delightful spot—the future doth indeed appear to dawn with increasing brightness for yourself."

"It does," replied Clara, glancing once more with affectionate kindness at her husband. "And you, Jane, must promise as much as possible to share it with me. I know," she added, kindly, "that I but give utterance to Sir Richard's sentiments, when I entreat of you to make use of these grounds in every respect as though they were your own."

Sir Richard warmly reiterated the injunction of Clara, and as the hour was now growing late, the little party separated to dress for dinner. Jane undertook to conduct her friend to the apartments assigned to her especial use, and Clara, with a feeling almost of awe, followed her up the massive oak staircase, for she thought upon the time when Lady Eardley, her friend and patroness, was first introduced into this noble hall, as the chosen bride of its master. The rooms destined to be occupied by Clara, were situated in the left wing of the building, and had been chosen by Jane, chiefly on account of the fine view which the windows commanded; they were large and commodious, and new furniture, and light draperies, took from them much of that heavy and sombre cast which formed a marked and somewhat unpleasing feature in the others. Music, too, and books, added to the cheerfulness of their appearance, and gave them more the air of the apartments of a modern fashionable lady, than they previously presented."

"You like these rooms," said Jane, as she noticed the smile of pleasure that illumined the animated countenance of Clara, as she gazed round the apartment into which she had last introduced her, and which was fitted up as a boudoir."

"Like them!" repeated Clara; "why, Jane, I must be the most ungrateful creature in existence, were I not absolutely charmed with the elegance and good taste you have so lavishly displayed in preparing them for my reception."

Jane looked pleased.

"I think," she said, as she walked towards the window, "in consulting my own ideas of what is beautiful in nature, I shall also have the satisfaction of knowing that you approve my taste;—the view from this window I consider to be particularly fine."

Clara stood by her side gazing in silent and rapt admiration. On the right, hills, with their soft green sloping sides dotted with snow-white sheep, who cropped the verdant grass; while, by the edge of a glassy stream, the cows were stretched in drowsy satisfaction under the friendly shadow of the elm which sheltered them from the noon-day sun. On the left, the village church, with its tall spire glittering in the sunbeams, formed a conspicuous object, and here and there, between the thick plantations of trees which surrounded the park, glimpses might be caught of the quiet churchyard, where slumbered the dead in undisturbed repose; while before the window lay the magnificent park, with its fine old trees and rich meadow land, the bright autumn flowers, and the last roses of summer shedding their sweet perfume upon the air, lending additional beauty, to the landscape. Oh! sweet is Nature!—wise and good are the lessons which it inculcates in our breasts, whether viewed in its most soft and tranquil aspect, or when storms and clouds eclipse for a time its lustre, and fill our minds with rapt and wondering awe. Cold must be the heart, and lost to every pure and noble feeling the breast of him who can contemplate the fair scenery of hill and dale—the wonderous and soul-inspiring works of God, unmoved; who can live surrounded by the bright and beautiful, and feel no thrill of praise within his breast; no high and ennobling emotion, which would induce him to look from Nature up to Nature's God; who can view the simplest flower, and feel no sense of gratitude to the bountiful Giver of all good, no sense of pride and joy as the sweet reflection crosses his mind—my Father made them all! Not such a one was Clara. Accustomed from early infancy to the fair scenery upon which she now again cast her enraptured gaze, constant association had not even for awhile destroyed its charm. She loved her hills—

her native hills, where oft, a child, she played amidst the wild flowers bright, the meadow green, and each soft sylvan glade, and it was with unbounded joy that she again hailed the spot she had so loved in other days; but as her eyes turned towards the quiet churchyard, the last sad resting-place of the hallowed dead, a change came over her countenance, for busy memory recalled scenes and days long past and gone. She thought of her brother, and the many happy hours they had passed together at the farm. How little had she then anticipated ever becoming mistress of the noble mansion in which she now resided, or the premature decease of that loved and only brother.

"Jane," she said, as these thoughts passed rapidly through her mind, and raising her hand she extended it towards the churchyard—"that spot reminds me of the loss of those we once held so dear, and whom we fondly anticipated seeing united in life, but it was otherwise ordained; it was the lot of each to know much of sorrow and bitterness, and death hath early united those whom sin and suffering widely separated in this world."

"This is a painful subject—a very painful subject," replied Jane, impressively, without venturing to raise her eyes to the face of her friend. "You have suffered much, I well know, from one who, with all her faults, was still my sister, and whom (you will pardon this, I am sure) I cannot bear to hear mentioned in terms that sound like reproach; she is gone to a better and purer world. Oh! could you have seen her as I did, and heard her last sad parting words, which breathed at once sorrow for the past, and hope for the bright future, into which she was so soon about to enter, then you would believe as I do, that she was far more sinned against than sinning."

As Jane gave utterance to these words, her eyes filled with tears—tears that were sacred to the pure sisterly affection which filled her breast.

"My dearest Jane," returned Clara, "you misunderstood me, indeed you did. I had no thought, I assure you, of casting the slightest reproach on the memory of your sister, whom I, of all others, can most fully extenuate. I know to what temptations she was exposed. I know, too, the fascinations of the man she loved, and the persuasive eloquence of his person and manners; indeed, when I say that he strongly resembles Sir Richard, whose addresses I could not refuse or withstand, even when I thought by so doing I was not only injuring another, but bringing sorrow and disgrace upon my own head, I repeat, when I say this, you will no longer conceive it possible that I could wantonly cast the slightest reproach on the memory of your dead sister, whom living I long loved and looked upon as the affianced bride of my only brother, to whom you well knew I was fondly and devotedly attached."

"I do, indeed," replied Jane. "Pardon me, love—I fear that my sorrows have made me fretful and selfish; and knowing the deep injuries you have received from my unhappy sister——"

"Say no more," replied Clara, affectionately interrupting her, "you will not love myself or Richard less, because we are so closely related to the man who so deeply wronged your sister—you will promise me this."

"Indeed, I could not be so unjust," returned her friend; "none, dear Clara, can more warmly rejoice at your present felicity, and the almost certain prospect of continued happiness which the future presents, than I do and ever shall."

"It is pleasant, indeed, to find that all men do not prove false, cruel, and ungrateful, wringing with sorrow the hearts they have wooed and won, casting carelessly aside the flower whose modest worth had long been treasured, blessing them with its faint perfume, and cheering them under every anxiety—casting, I repeat, this humble flower aside, for the first fairer and richer blossom that chances to court their acceptance. And yet how often is this done!—how regardless are men of wringing or breaking a heart already to sorrow resigned."

"Dear Jane," replied Clara, eagerly, "believe me, you wrong the sex, indeed you do"—seeing that her companion shook her head incredulously—"with sorrow be it said, there are men such as you have described, but believe me, they form the exception, and not, as you suppose, the rule."

"It is well for you," replied Jane, "that you can thus think, but you are wrong." Here it was Clara's turn to look incredulous.

"You," continued her friend in the same tone, "have never experienced the bitterness of knowing yourself deserted, not so much for a fairer as a richer bride. Poverty is indeed a curse, when it can cause such an utter breaking up of hope long nourished, of trust and confidence warped to wrong, betrayed too early, ans

SIR RICHARD EARDLEY, CLARA, AND MISS CLARENCE IN THE GROUNDS

beguiled too long; all this I have experienced, both for my sister and myself. Yes, spite of all she had endured of the cruelty and oppression practised towards her by one whom she had only loved too well spite of all this; I was yet mad enough to put trust in man, to lend a willing ear to his flattery, falsehood, and deceit. Yes, I believed, though all others were base and deceitful, there was one at least free from guile. Yes, I was weak enough to place the warmest reliance, the fullest confidence on one, who lured me on, who sought to confirm me in my faith, who professed the fondest devotion, the warmest love, but only the more cruelly to blight my hopes and crush my fond expectations. But enough, it is better so, far, better than if in continued blindness I had married one whose character I could neither respect or love."

"Oh, ever regard it in that light," replied Clara; "that surely will reconcile you to the disappointment you have sustained."

"And yet," continued Jane, "it is a difficult task to tear his image from my heart—to teach myself to forget one whom I have so long treasured in my memory; but," she added, checking herself, "I am infecting you with my own gloomy feelings on a day when you have every reason to rejoice, and consider the most fortunate of your life."

"I do look upon it in that light," returned Clara, "and whatever of misfortune the future may have in store for me, of this I feel assured: I shall never look back with a feeling of regret to this day. Oh, no," she continued, in an animated tone, "I shall always rejoice in having secured the love and respect of one whose esteem and good opinion I so highly value."

"And this reminds me," returned Jane, "that we have been wasting our time, I will not say in idle conversation, but certainly, on my part, in giving way to vain regret for the past, while Sir Richard is anxiously expecting our return."

"We will not keep him waiting much longer," replied Clara, eagerly. "But let me thank you once more, dear Jane, for the good taste you have displayed in the arrangement of this apartment; it is, indeed, charming."

A smile of gratified pleasure lighted up the pale features of Jane at these words. The two friends hastily laid aside their walking dresses, and in a few minutes again joined Sir Richard. After dinner a walk was proposed round the park, and Clara delighted her husband by her warm praise of all she saw.

"You must naturally feel proud," said Jane, who had been walking for some time in silence, "as you look upon these beautiful grounds, and know yourself, like Alexander Selkirk, 'monarch of all you survey.'"

Sir Richard, to whom these words were addressed, smiled at the playfulness of the remark, as he replied—

"There is, Miss Clarence, an undoubted feeling both of pride and pleasure in the ownership of what is fair and beautiful, and this feeling more particularly applies to houses and lands that have descended to us from one generation to another. There is something hallowed in the home of our forefathers, and in the associations of our childhood's remembrance; and yet a sensation akin to pain will at times cross the mind, when we reflect that we only attain to the brief delight of calling these our own by the death of our nearest and dearest friends. For myself, though the greater portion of my life has been spent abroad, amid the beautiful and varied scenery of more sunny lands, yet I must in truth confess that this spot of ground is more endeared to my heart, more treasured in my memory, than any other. It may be, indeed it most probably is, from the circumstance of being able to call it mine, and associating it with those long dead and passed away, who doubtless once exulted, as I now do, in calling themselves, as you remarked, Miss Clarence, 'monarchs of all they surveyed.' But, be that as it may, I would not exchange the cloudy skies and varying climate of my own native valley for the brighter skies and more sunny land in which my earliest years were spent. No; I love the home of my ancestors, the land of their birth, far more than any other."

"I am pleased to hear you say so," replied Clara, "for I cannot imagine any spot of earth more beautiful than this. I know," she added, playfully, "that you are going to say this arises solely from my never having visited other countries; but you know where ignorance is bliss, 'tis folly to be wise.

Sir Richard kissed the fair cheek of his young wife, as he replied—

Far be it from me, dear Clara, to instil into your mind the lightest dissatis- faction to this place, so greately endeared to me, so treasured in my memory, as the home of my ancestors.

"And yet," returned Clara, "I have sometimes doubted whether there be anything in the tie of birth, to endear us to a spot of earth, and for myself have always felt—

> 'No matter where my steps may ream ;
> If friends be near that place is home.'"

"I entirely concide in your opinion," said Jane, "but it seems the peculiar privilege of our sex, to be able to resign, without even a sigh of regret, home, friends, fortune all, and enlist our best sympathies and feelings on behalf of others, whose love is as yet untried, to make their joys and sorrows our own, and forgetful of the past, look forward to the future with hopeful anticipa- tion."

"I believe you are right," rejoined Sir Richard. " 'Tis woman alone with a firm heart, that can separate herself wholly and solely from her home and kindered, to bless with happiness and love the lot of him upon whom she has bestowed her best and purest affections, and which cannot be too highly prized or cherished ; she is, indeed, man's guardian angel, and

> "From the hour of Eve's sorrow, when sin had its birth,
> Fair woman appears to have lingered on earth,
> To pluck from our path all the thorn's that she can,
> And strew with sweet flowers life's trifling span."

"The compliment is a a pretty one," replied Clara, smiling, "but I am afraid, that in all candour we must disclaim some of the merit you so kindly give us credit for ; we leave, it is true, the home of our childhood, and the friends who guarded our youth, voluntarily resigning all that has once been dear ; but there," she added, gazing affectionately on her husband's face," in so doing, we consult our own happiness, for when love takes possession of the breast, it masters ever other feeling."

Sir Richard returned her affectionate smile, and they continued the walk with renewed interest.

"I think," he said, after they had been out for some time, " I think you have now thoroughly inspected the grounds, and exerior of the building ; to- morrow you shall view the interior, under the guidance of the old housekeeper, who is more acquainted with the differentsuites of apartments than I can myself at present boast of. Your friend, Miss Herbert, will consent, I hope, to remain with us for a few days at least."

"Thank you," said Jane, eagerly, "did I study my own inclination, I should need no second invitation, but I have other and more pressing claims upon my time and attention. My mother, I fear, will even now think herself neglected, if I do not immediately hasten my return ;" she hesitated a moment, and then added, " I have also another claimant on my time and care, the sole legacy and dying gift of my lost, but never to be forgoten sister."

"Your little nephew," said Clara ; "indeed, Jane, I had not forgotten him. You must be with us early to-morrow, and bring him with you ; I long to renew my acquaintance with the dear little fellow."

Sir Richard too, having warmly expressed his desire to see the child, Jane was easy prevailed upon to give the required promise, and with warm expressions of sympathy, the friends separated. The following morning, accompanied by her husband, and under the guidance of the old housekeeper, Clara commenced her inspection of the building. Many of the rooms presented a curious mixture of the modern, the more showy and luxurious articles of domestic comfort, afford- ing a strange contrast to the cumbrous and more costly ones of days gone by. But this strange disparity was only apparent in a few of the apartments, and was perhaps rather the effect of accident than design. Others, long disused, were regarded as curious specimens of the past, and remained undisturbed by the hand of improvement, or the desire for modern luxury and refinement. Among these was a suite of apartments, the furniture of which, though more than a century old, retained its original lustre, undimmed by time. Attached to these apartments was a small chapel, through the oval window of which (as Clara for the first time stood beneath its roof) the red beams of the sun seemed faintly to stream.

> " Now tinging with light yon holy shrine,
> And now on the gorgeous altar shines,
> Though scarcely illuming a sculptured tomb,
> But dimly seen in the chapel's gloom,
> On which was carved an image fair,
> Some said a saint was buried there ;
> And some that a bride of the Eardley's line
> Had perished by a false kinsman's crime.
> One thing was certain, the marble cold
> Was cast in the sculptor's choicest mould."

And Clara stepped towards it, admiring at once the exquisite workmanship, and the beauty it so perfectly revealed.

"You would wish to know the history of this tomb?" said Sir Richard, rightly interpreting the glance of inquiry Clara threw upon him.

"I should, much," she replied eagerly. "I feel sure there is a tale connected with it which will interest me much."

"There is a tale connected with it," returned Sir Richard, "but it is a sad and fearful one, and though it may interest you, yet I think it will of necessity, pain you more."

"Nevertheless, allow me to judge for myself," said Clara, pleadingly. "My curiosity is fully aroused, and it rests alone with you to satisfy it."

"I will gladly do so, my love," replied her husband, "at least, as far as possible. That tomb," he continued, resting his hand impressively on the stone, "is said to have been reared to the memory of one who died a virgin bride ; perished even at the altar, having fallen dead at the feet of her new-made husband, almost instantly after the marriage ceremony was performed, at whose command she was buried within this chapel, and as the legend goes—

> " On that same eve a passing bell
> Was heard through rocky gorge and dell ;
> Within the chapel was a light,
> So strangely, so unearthly bright,
> That all repaired in haste to see
> What flame so marvellous could be."

"But," he continued, checking himself, "to be more explicit. You must know, my dear Clara, that more than two centuries ago, one of our ancestors, who bore the name and title which has now descended to myself, while travelling in Spain, became deeply enamoured of one of her dark-eyed daughters. I need scarcely repeat that she was beautiful, when I tell you that this marble figure is said to be an exact counterpart of the fair original, while her dark sparkling eyes were bright as the sun of her own cloudless skies.

> " Her brow, proud and calm, no feeling expresst
> Whatever the tumult which raged in her breast."

His addresses were favourably received by the parents, and apparently so by the daughter. My relative loved with such devotedness, that he was blind to the utter coldness with which he was regarded by the object of his ardent adoration, who only received him as an accepted suitor, in obedience to the command of her parents ; and yet there were times when he remarked a strangeness in her manners, for which he could not account, and while he sat by her side, and poured forth his impassionate feelings, in language warm and eloquent she would scarcely smile as she listened to his words, and it would seem as though her spirit had fled to other objects, and she would become fair yet pale as this image of stone—

> ' Her hand as cold as the hand of the dead,
> From whom the spirit—the life, hath fled.'

At such moments he would tremble with a feeling of unaccountable dread—

> ' Yet the fancy would quickly pass away,
> And the lady be radiant and bright as before ;
> So sweetly she smiled, he could but deem
> It was all the illusion of a dream,
> Yet strange to say, even at such an hour
> Divided thus could be love's power.'

He thought of his father's halls—youth's happy time—the holy vesper's warning chime, and longed once more to return to his native land, to behold once more the home of his childhood. And anxious as he was to make the loved one his wife, a superstitious feeling prevented him having the ceremony, which was to unite them for life, performed in a strange land. He, therefore, hastened his return home, accompanied by his affianced wife, and immediately on his arrival at the Hall the marriage was solemnized within this chapel. The day was a holiday to the whole of the tenantry ; a festival in which all care and toil was for the time set aside to welcome the return of its heir.

> ' The tapers were lit on yonder shrine,
> Round which bright nuptial garlands twine.'

for

> ' The youthful heir had brought a bride,
> Meet flower to grace his home and side ;
> And when they gazed upon her face,
> The ladies prais'd her courtly grace ;
> Though others gravely shook their head,
> And thought—far better had he wed
> Some maiden of his native isle,
> Less lovely perhaps, yet free from guile,
> Than thus have madly courted danger,
> For what ? a wild-eyed, dark-brow'd stranger.'

Thus far, my dear Clara," continued Sir Richard, "I have ventured to quote from the legendary rhyme which endeavours, in its own way, to solve the mystery of the tomb, which has succeeded in attracting your attention."

"And which has greatly interested me," replied Clara ; "pray go on, I am eager to hear the conclusion of your tale."

"It is well nigh told," replied her husband. "The long-desired day had at length arrived which was to unite Sir Richard to the chosen of his heart. Since their arrival in England, to his great joy, much of the mysterious melancholy which had previously appeared to hover over the spirit of the lady had vanished, and though she gave no farther sign of reciprocating the warmth of his feelings, he loved her, as I have already said, with such mad devotion, that to call her his own—his bride—he would willingly have sworn by cross, by bead, by shrine, heart, body, soul, for ever her's ; thus the sad uncomplaining sorrow which evidently gnawed remorsefully in her bosom entirely escaped his observation. They stood together before the altar, for admittance to the chapel was granted to all who chose to avail themselves of the circumstance ; in consequence, a vast number of persons were assembled to witness the ceremony, which proceeded without interruption to the close, when immediately after the priest had pronounced the benediction, a tall figure, muffled in a dark cloak, evidently a foreigner, stepped forward and whispered some words in the ear of the trembling bride, who, overcome by her feelings, tottered, made an ineffectual attempt to save herself by catching at the railings of the altar, and fell senseless to the ground. The bridegroom bent down and took her hand ; it was icy cold. Alas! the trembling bride lay lifeless at his feet ; the attendants gathered round and raised her veil, believing she had only fainted from excess of terror ; but no sooner had they done so than all shrank away, for cold and white as a marble statue lay the late warm and animated bride.

'They turn'd to Sir Richard, but he stood
In madness' most ungovern'd mood ;
Alone and sad doth Eardley's chief
Mourn for his bride ; yet more than grief
Rankles within, and leaves dark trace
Upon each feature of his face.
Now on that tomb doth the statue lie,
Above doth Sir Richard Eardley sigh ;
And many hath said that he would not tell
Of that lady's fate, what he knew too well.'

Thus, my dear Clara," said her husband, "does the legend end. I have told it you because you expressed a wish for me to do so, not that I place any reliance upon the truth of it ; indeed, a legend that has been handed down through so many generations, you may be certain, has lost nothing of the marvellous in its transmission."

"You are doubtless right,'" replied Clara ; "and yet the tale has made me sad. So beautiful and so young—so fondly loved, too, by one pre-eminently worthy of her regard, surely she was deserving of a brighter and happier destiny."

"Be that as it may," returned her husband, "years have now rolled their slow course away, and swept with them, to the dust, all who were in any manner connected with that painful affair ; this monument alone survives a mute witness to the truth of the tale, so far that a Spanish lady died, as I have stated, at the altar immediately after the ceremony which united her to one of my ancestors." And as he spoke, he directed Clara's attention to an inscription on the marble which set forth, in few and simple words, that the lady whom the figure represented had fallen dead at the altar in the manner described by Sir Richard. And this was all, leaving the imagination of any who might be attracted to the spot to fill up the painful narrative, as the fancy of the moment might dictate. Clara eagerly inspected the inscription, which remained clear and unmarred by the defacing influence of time, though the hand which carved it had long since forgot its carving, and all who had existed at that remote period crumbled silently to dust, while other faces, fresh and new, occupied their place, and in their turn became possessors of the old hall and its adjoining estate. "And thus it must be again," thought Clara ; "a few short years, and we, too, shall have passed away ; others will fill our place, and we shall soon become as though we had never been." These ideas naturally gave a sadness to her thoughts, which was increased by the surrounding objects—mute emblems of sorrow and decay ; and yet there seemed a fascination about the spot which drew her towards it ; and it was not till Sir Richard had twice spoken, inviting her to leave the chapel, and pursue her inspection of the remaining portion of the building, that she was enabled to command herself sufficiently to reply in her usual quiet tones ; but though she mechanically followed him from room to room, it was impossible for her to take an interest in anything she saw ; her mind was engrossed with the marble image in the chapel, so beautiful—so wondrous fair. She longed to look upon it again, and resolved to do so at the earliest opportunity.

CHAPTER XL.

" For if this scene be overcast,
    'Tis woman's first dream and her last ;
Then better far the grass so green
Above her early tomb were seen,—
Then better far the new-turn'd sod
That said her spirit was with God."

ADA returned to the home of her uncle after her renewed engagement to Walter, sadder, but not the wiser, for all that had passed between herself and him to whom she was now affianced—whom she was soon to call by the tender name of husband. The proud and self-willed beauty felt somewhat humbled at knowing that with all her attractions she had failed to eclipse the light of a dead rival, or awake even a passing emotion of love in the breast of him to whom she was shortly to be united—who had proffered her his hand from a feeling of commiseration for her supposed attachment to himself, not from any sentiment of love, or even respect on his part. This he had not hesitated to avow, in terms so plain, that it was impossible for her to mistake his meaning, or gladly would she have attributed his renewed offer to his utter inability to withstand the charms and graces of her person; and her vanity had received a deep and rankling wound at the impossibility of putting this flattering construction upon his proposal. It was, indeed, deeply mortifying to her self-love to feel herself indebted to the pity of Walter for the prospect she now entertained of becoming his wife; and, but for her long determination to accept his proposal, let it come from whatever source it might, she would have renounced his offer; but she wished to show Percy that she was capable of forming a more advantageous alliance in a worldly point of view than she would have done had she continued her engagement with him. Walter's fascinating appearance, too, charmed her eye, and rendered him in her own ideas worthy of becoming her husband. His father's death, too, had put him in possession of a handsome income, which, united with her own fortune, would enable them to command an establishment of a superior description. These considerations, combined with the dread of being regarded in the light of one who had been forsaken when almost a bride, confirmed her in her resolution to accept of his hand, even though his heart were wanting. Mr. Herbert was equally as pleased as Lady Eardley with the proposed match, and though the old man felt that he would now be left alone without one companion to cheer or share his solitude, he would not for a moment allow any selfish feeling to mar the pleasure he experienced in the contemplated settlement of his niece—a settlement so exceedingly advantageous that it afforded him almost unmixed pleasure. After having acquainted her uncle with Walter's renewed offer, and her own acceptance of the same, Ada proposed visiting Mary, in order to impart to her likewise the pleasing intelligence.

"Do so, my dear, by all means," replied her uncle, " and, if possible, induce Mary to return with you ; it is a long while since she was here, and yet the distance between the houses is so short that——"

"My dear uncle," interrupted Ada, "you forget that Mary cannot at all times act as I am sure her heart dictates. You should remember that she must now bend to the will of her husband."

At the mention of this magic word, poor Mr. Herbert's countenance changed.

"Yes, yes," he muttered to himself, " I am too forgetful—I must remember that Mary has a husband whom it is her duty to endeavour to please, even at the sacrifice of the comfort and happiness of her father. Well, well, I shall get used to it in time, I dare say."

Having so entirely succeeded in making her uncle think himself neglected, and unkindly treated by Mary, Ada, like many other persons of her temper and disposition, made a great show of attending to his comfort and preventing the time hanging heavy on his hands during her temporary absence. Assiduously wheeling the arm-chair to the fire—for, though the weather was warm and beautiful without doors, Mr. Herbert liked the sociality of a glowing fire, and held as part of his creed, that there were but few days even in the middle of summer that a fire was not only endurable, but comfortable and pleasant in the extreme; wheeling, therefore, his large arm-chair to the most cheerful corner, where the bright rays of the sun shed a transient ray of gladness to the dull room and heavy old-fashioned furniture, Ada placed a small side-table before it, on which she arranged, with due care, the luncheon, of which her uncle invariably partook, consisting of cold fowl and ham, with a bottle of the finest old port. Having thus provided for his bodily comforts, she carefully folded and arranged the morning papers, and placed them within reach of his hand. This done, she affectionately inquired if he wished anything else, to which the old man with a dejected air, replied by the monvsyllable, "No." Upon which Ada tripped merrily out of the room, and presently returned equiped for walking.

"Good bye Uncle," she said in her own lively tones; and stepping up to his chair, she imprinted a kiss upon his cheek. "I shall not be gone long," she continued, "and if possible will induce Mary to return with me."

These words were not calculated to inspire Mr. Herbert with any great amount of cheerfulness; on the contrary, the doubt they conveyed of the possibility of inducing Mary, his only and tenderly loved child to pay him a short and passing visit, filled his mind with melancholly, which he in vain endeavoured to cast off by murmuring to himself—

"Well, well, it can't be helped; she must of course study the wishes and happiness of her husband."

Without, however, finding much comfort in this reflection, Mr. Herbert sedulously applied himself to the disposal of the good things which were so temptingly placed before him. With this and the papers, he found employment enough for the present time. And yet, though he looked forward to the marriage of his neice with Walter Eardley with feelings of almost unmixed pleasure, he could not help contrasting his present situation, with what it must inevitably become when this last prop of his declining years was taken from him. How dull the old house would be when the young and fair had passed away, with no light and merry voices to enliven it with their gladsome tones, with no smiling faces to wish him good morrow, or give him a parting kiss at night. He pictured to himself how sad and sombre would be the change from light and life to darkness and despair. It is indeed sad for the aged to be called upon to renounce ties and habits which are close woven round the heart, to snap the links in the chain of existence which has for years close bound them to others who have so losely woven their affections with their own, that to tear them asunder seems but little less than death itself! To the young, change is natural; their mind speedily accustom themselves to its influence; and they can easily form new ties and new associates, which the old cannot, however much they may desire to do so. Mr. Herbert felt this for years; his sole care and anxiety had been expended on behalf of his daughter and niece. Early deprived of his wife, his affections had never again been called forth, or rather they had diverged from their original source, into another channel, and settled themselves entirely upon his motherless child, to whom he had in a great measure supplied the loss she had so unhappily sustained; for with almost maternal tenderness and assiduity he had watched over opening years; and as she grew to womanhood, she found in this her sole surving parent, a firm friend, and wise counsellors. Sweet and close had been the affection which bound the widowed father, and orphan child together. They had but one hope, one joy, one sorrow which up to the period of her marriage, had never known the slightest interruption. But now a change, and as far as Mr. Herbert was concerned, a sad and desolating change had come to pass. Mary had passed into another's home, into another's care; and though he strove to think it was for the best to hope, to almost believe that Mary was happier there, he could not help feeling that he at least was the sadder and more uncared for by the change. "Tis true that the constant presence of Ada, who really loved her uncle, had prevented him feeling this so much as he would otherwise have done; but now she too would soon be removed from his care. She, too,

THE CONVERSATION BETWEEN MARY AND HER FATHER.

had formed other friends, and would shortly contract new ties that must seperate her for ever from his side. As he thought of these things, Mr. Herbert glanced round the vacant apartment, anticipating, as he did so, the time near at hand when he would indeed be left alone, not for a few short hours or even days, but for the remainder of his existence. The paper dropped from his hand as the thought passed through his mind, and the tears glistened brightly in his eyes.

At this moment the door of the apartment opened, and Mary hastened to his side.

"My dear father !" were the only words to which she gave utterance, as she threw her arms fondly round his neck, and kissed his cheek.

"My darling child," returned the old man, tenderly embracing her, and the tears which were swimming in his eyes rolled unheeded down his cheek.

"My dear father," said Mary, with much anxiety, "you are unhappy. Tell me, I entreat you, the cause;" and sitting down by his side she took his hand within her own, and gazing affectionately on his face, entreated him to impart to her the cause of his apparent uneasiness.

"It is nothing, my child," replied the old man evasively. "Your cousin being absent part of this morning and the whole of yesterday, I have been thrown more upon my own resources for amusement than I have been as yet accustomed to, and these failing," he added with a smile, "I was actually working myself up into a fit of low spirits."

"But it is wrong of Ada to leave you so much alone," replied Mary, evidently vexed with her cousin for her apparent neglect.

"You must not think thus unkindly of your cousin, my love," said her father striving to force a cheerful smile, "for may she not be inclined to follow your example and marry ?"

"Ada, marry ?" repeated Mary, in a tone of unfeigned surprise.

"Why not ?" asked her father, smiling this time with more sincerity. "Surely stranger things than that have come to pass before now."

"They have," said Mary, still hesitating ; "and yet, my dear father, I cannot bear to entertain the idea, it is so extremely painful to me."

"In spite of all that, my love, you must hear the plain and simple truth—which is, that Ada does intend to get married ; and no wonder either that she should prefer the society of a young and handsome husband to that of a foolish, and troublesome, though, perhaps in the main, a good-natured old uncle. Why, Mary," he added, smiling still more broadly, "surely your own experience of marriage has not induced you to regard it as a misfortune ; but you look as sad and serious as though you had been listening to some terrible piece of ill news."

"No, no, father," replied Mary hastily, and blushing deep as she did so, "it is not that I do not regret the prospect of Ada's marriage on her account, but what will become of you, left alone in this large and gloomy house by yourself. Indeed, indeed, I cannot entertain the idea ; it is positively intolerable."

"You must not think of me, my child," replied the old man, affected to tears again by the warm feeling and duteous affection manifested not only in Mary's words, but in the evident uneasiness and anxiety which was depicted on her countenance. "You must not trouble yourself about me," he repeated; "I shall contrive to get on very well, I dare say, without two selfwilled girls constantly troubling me ; besides, Mary, you are now a wife, and have other cares and duties."

"I have," replied Mary, gently ; "but new ties cannot sever old ones."

"Well, well, my girl ! have it your own way ; but in a very short time, see if I do not manage to live very merily in the old house, though unenlivened either by your presence or that of your cousin."

Mary shook her head.

"It will not do, father," she said ; "we must contrive it better than that if Ada really intends to be married."

"You still appear to doubt my assertion, just as though I was in the habit of telling you stories," replied Mr. Herbert, endeavouring to assume a gaiety he could not for the moment feel. "Why, I tell you it is all arranged ; and as soon as settlements and other such things are got over, she will become Mrs. Walter Eardley."

"She will marry Walter, then, after all ?" said Mary, in a tone of surprise.

"Yes, so it seems," replied her father. "The young man, last evening, as

Ada informed me, apologized for his past conduct, and pressingly renewed his offer, which she accepted."

"And where is Ada, now?" enquired Mary, lost in surprise at what she had just heard."

"She left me a short time since," returned Mr. Herbert, "in order to convey these tidings to you."

"Then we must have passed each other on the road," said Mary, in a musing tone. "Well, it cannot be helped. I am grieved, on your account, my dear father; but of course I cannot blame Ada."

"I should think not," returned Mr. Herbert; "why, girl, it is natural she should wish to get a fair start in the world for herself—very natural; and I hope she will be happy." And as he spoke, he poured out a glass of wine, and hastily drank the contents.

"But, my dear father," began Mary, who had for some minutes been silently thinking over in her mind the best course of action to be adopted in the present emergency, for up to this moment she had never calculated on Ada's marrying, and the consequent loneliness of her parent. "But, my dear father, I never will consent to allow you to live entirely by yourself; for servants, however willing, can never render you those little attentions to which you have been so long accustomed; and even if they could, without society—the society of those who know and love you—you would be lost. No," she continued, shaking her head emphatically, "it will never do."

"Nonsense, girl," said the old man, turning aside his head to brush away a tear; "I tell you I shall do very well. Give me a bottle of good wine, and I shall want for no other society."

Mary again repeated her words.

"No, father, it will not do. I can persuade Percy and his sisters to share this house with you—it is surely large enough for us all; and if our society is at any time troublesome, you can retire to this apartment, which has ever been exclusively your own."

Mary saw by the glad sunshine which lighted up her father's countenance, how agreeable this proposition was to his mind; but he offered no remark, and she again went on.

"I repeat, if I can persuade Percy and his sisters to share this house with you, I shall once more gladly return to my parental roof, where so many of my happiest years have been spent; but if they will not consent to my wishes on this subject, then, my dear father, you must waive all scruples, abandon this house entirely, and for the future live with me."

This idea Mary was quick-sighted enought to perceive was far from being so agreeable to the mind of her father as her former proposition. She well knew that from constant association he had grown attached to the old house, and that it would cost him a severe pang to be forced to leave. Still, to allow him to remain there alone and unfriended, was so repellent to her mind, that she inwardly resolved to combat every objection he might urge against quitting it.

"You know, my dear father," she urged, pursuing the subject, "that it was not the house or the surrounding objects which made us so happy and cheerful. No, it was simply the pleasure we felt in each other's society, and which will render us just as happy under any other roof as it did this. Will it not?" she added, with an half playful smile, but which met with no encouragement on the part of her father.

"You will think I have grown selfish, my love, and indifferent to your society," he said seriously, "when I tell you that I think nothing on earth could induce me to quit the shelter of this roof; it seems as though we had grown old together; and I have conceived an attachment for the place which may seem weak and frivolous to you, my child, but which I cannot conquer. You will understand this feeling, Mary, when you are as old and have lived as long in one house as I have," he added, endeavouring to speak cheerfully; "but we will not discuss this painful subject any longer, my child."

" But," urged Mary, " you will not refuse to admit Percy and his sisters to share this house with you, if I can induce them to do so ?"

" I cannot expect so great a sacrifice from your husband; indeed, I have no right to expect it," said the old man, smiling kindly and encouragingly on his daughter; and then, as if determined to give her no further opportunity of renewing the subject, he started a variety of other topics, on which he kept Mary in full converse during the remainder of her visit, which was brought to a termination by the sudden recollection of Mary, that she had already exceeded the time she had fixed for her return home. They parted with mutual regret, Mary promising shortly to renew her visit. She walked home more sad and sorrowful than she had done on the former occasion of her visit to her father. The idea of Ada's marriage was extremely painful to her, on her parent's account; and though she firmly resolved in her own mind not to allow him to remain in the sad solitude to which he endeavoured so cheerfully to resign himself, she yet felt that she had promised more than she might be enabled to perform. Between herself and Percy's sisters there had existed a coldness ever since her last visit to her father, and which had been productive of such unpleasant consequences. It was clear, too, that Percy regarded any little attention or anxiety she manifested on her fathers account with a jealous eye, as though it interfered with his own more prior claim. There was a formal sort of politeness likewise about the manners and conduct of his sisters, more difficult to be borne by such a girl as Mary than open rudeness or expressed dissatisfaction. In vain Mary (with her usual sweetness of temper) endeavoured to conciliate and win their good opinion; in spite of all her efforts, they maintained a rigid coldness in their demeanour, mingled with an air of lofty politeness, which at once distressed and perplexed her. She saw too that Percy was always more willing to abide by their decision than his own. This she was willing to attribute to force of habit, and consequently entertained no unkind feeling towards him on that account; indeed, up to the present time, she had never felt disposed to contest any point after his sisters had given their decision; but she trembled now, for the result of a petition, which she was convinced would depend on their favourable consideration. Still, the affection she entertained for her father, made her resolve to broach the subject without delay. Immediately, therefore, on her arrival home, she sought a private interview with her husband, feeling that she could more easily prefer her position in the first instance to himself alone, but unfortunately Percy was sitting in the drawing-room in conversation with his sisters and Ada, who had not as yet taken her leave.

" I am glad you have returned, my love," said Percy as she entered; " we want you to add your persuasions to ours, and induce your cousin to remain with us the entire day; and yet she is so anxious to quit us, that we have found the greatest difficulty in keeping her till you return; but I doubt not she will yield to your solicitations what she denies to ours."

" I should be very pleased with my cousins's company," said Mary in a faltering tone, " but my father is entirely alone, and his spirits do not seem so good as usual this morning."

" Then that shall decide me at once," said Ada, " and I will hasten to him immediately."

" But," urged Elizabeth, joining in the conversation at this point, " you know he must get used to being alone, or how will he manage when you are gone altogether ?"

" The thought of that has distressed me much," said Mary, thinking this a favourable opportunity of opening the subject on which she was so solicitous.

" He will naturally feel somewhat dull and low spirited at first," said Percy, " but I do not doubt that he will soon get used to it; it is strange, indeed, how soon we accustom ourselves to change."

" I agree with you, Percy, entirely as far as young persons are concerned; but it is different, very different with persons of my father's age," said Mary, "and I do not believe he will find it an easy matter to accustom himself to the sad change in his household arrangements and domestic comforts, which will inevitably take place, if he is left entirely by himself; on the contrary, I think he will feel it so severely, that it will really become the means of shortening his existence.".

"You must not take so painful a view of the case," replied Percy; "really Mary, you seem of late to have become quite an adept at gloomy forebodings. You must endeavour to throw off this tendency, my love, or it will have the effect of rendering you miserable, especially when, as in the present case, the misfortune you so deplore cannot possibly be avoided; unless," he added, smiling archly, "you can persuade your cousin to give up her matrimonial views, and settle down into a good and quiet attendant on her old uncle, for the remainder of her days."

"Indeed it would be scarcely fair," said Ada, "to doom me to old maidenism, especially when she has shown so great a distaste for it herself."

Percy's sisters laughed loudly at this sally; but Mary was in no mood for jesting; she therefore answered seriously—

"I had no desire, I am sure, to put a burden upon my cousin that I would shrink from bearing myself; on the contrary, I should be most happy to relieve her by having my father entirely under my own care; indeed," she continued, growing bold by the earnestness she felt in the cause she was so anxious to espouse, "if we were all living together, I could devote a portion of my time to attending to his comfort without detracting from my other duties."

There was a silence of a few moments, and then Percy replied—

"Certainly, my love, if this could be managed it would be more pleasant for all parties. We will consider the subject again; in the meantime, perhaps you can persuade your cousin to favour us with her company for the remainder of the day."

Mary's eyes glistened with delight.

"Oh! thank you, love, that is so kind—so like yourself," said Mary, with glistening eyes, for a weight seemed removed from her breast. She already saw in perspective the return of herself, accompanied by Percy, to her father's roof. Much that at present conspired to vex and annoy her would then be done away with; she would be able to attend to her father's comforts without incurring the annoyance her absence from home invariably occasioned, and all would then be well. These thoughts lighted up her face with a beaming smile of gladness, as she cast a look of grateful joy upon her husband, who, pleased that he had the satisfaction of seeing that he had pleased her, returned her smile with one scarcely less joyous.

Pleased with the prospect of a bright future, Mary endeavoured to conceal the dissatisfaction she felt when Ada yielded to their united entreaties and consented to remain; and, though she strove her utmost to appear cheerful throughout the day, her thoughts wandered frequently from those by whom she was surrounded to her father, whom she pictured anxiously expecting the return of Ada, and endeavouring to while away the tedium of her absence as he best could. As the afternoon was fine, the little party amused themselves after dinner by walking round the garden. It so happened that Ada was the companion of Percy; and walking somewhat in advance of the others who, stopping behind to examine some objects, which at the moment attracted their attention, they were accidentally separated from them.

"I think," said Ada (as if suddenly recollecting it) "I heard Mary mention to my uncle that you had a small alcove somewhere in your grounds, fitted up with the sweetest regard to tasteful elegance; and as I should much like to have something of the sort, by and by, myself, I should like to look at it, if it is not troubling you too much to ask you to conduct me there."

"By no means," replied Percy, "although I think when you have seen it, you will willingly allow that it is on no account deserving of the high encomiums Mary seems so lavishly to have bestowed upon it," replied Percy, with an air of affected modesty, for in truth he prided himself upon the beauty and good taste displayed in the adornment of this alcove, whose appointments he regarded as nothing short of perfection ; and with a feeling of gratified, pride he prepared to lead Ada to the spot.

"It is, indeed, tasteful and pretty it the extreme," said Ada, as they entered together a small but light and graceful bower, whose delicate hangings of sky-blue silk harmonised with the soft green of the climbing plants, which peeped in at the open lattice and mingled their sweet perfume with the more rare and delicate exotics which were tastefully ranged round the walls. "It is indeed beautiful," repeated Ada, as she inspected more closely the different appointments ; "this would seem to be exclusively the bower of love."

"And beauty," said Percy, almost involuntarily as he gazed upon the fair face of his now blushing companion.

"You should devote it to the Muses," continued Ada, without apparently having heard the words of Percy ; "you should indeed."

"I have in a measure anticipated you," replied Percy, taking from the book-stand a small volume, which he opened, and smilingly presented to her. It was one of Byron's most exquisite poems.

Ada half sighed as she received it from him.

"You have, indeed, anticipated my ideas on this subject ;" she said, "here is, in truth exquisite poetry ; but the sister muse is wanting. I do not see any music."

"If you would condescend to sing," replied Percy, "the want would be instantly supplied."

A smile, bright and gladsome, passed over the beautiful face of Ada, in acknowledgement of this compliment ; but without otherwise heeding it, she replied—

"I feel really disappointed to find that music, which seems the very soul of poetry, should be wanting in this sweet retreat, where all of superior enjoyment seem to court acceptance ; where we may cast away all earthly feelings and associations ; and thoughts and aspirations are inspired which make us feel how inadequate is human enjoyment to the wishes of the soul painting for the music which is divine, and the love that is pure and death-less, in which there is no deceit ;" and here she stopped abruptly, covered with blushes and confusion, as though she had been led by her feelings inadver-tently to touch upon a dangerous subject.

Percy regarded it in this light ; and commiserating her apparent confusion, and wishing if possible to relieve her from her embarrassment, without betray-ing his observation of it, he replied to the first part of her speech—

"I cannot allow you, Miss Herbert, to entertain so poor an opinion of my taste, as to suppose me insensible to the charms of music, which has ever pos-sessed a peculiar fascination to my mind ; indeed, I could not, as you say, con-ceive my bower perfect without it lent its aid to soothe and charm."

"You are right," returned Ada. "I remember now having heard Mary mention a piano, which doubtless occupied this recess (pointing towards it), and which was shaded like the windows with sky-blue draperies, whose silken folds were gracefully arranged."

"Yes, you are right," replied Percy, "that was the position it occupied before I consented, at Mary's earnest solicitation, to have it removed."

Ada turned to him with a look of unfeigned surprise, as she enquired—

"And Mary really wished to have it removed ?"

"Yes," replied Percy with some hesitation, "she imagined that the damp was likely to injure it."

"There cannot surely be sufficient damp here," returned Ada, "to do it any harm ; and, indeed, I would seriously advise you to have it replaced."

"I certainly regret its removal at the present time," said Percy, "since it deprives me of the gratification I should otherwise have solicited at your hands."

At this moment Mary and her sister entered.

"I think, my love," said Percy, turning eagerly towards his wife, "we will have the piano replaced in its orignal position. I have just taken your cousin's opinon on the subject, and she assures me that she does not think there is sufficient damp materially to affect it."

"It was sadly out of order, before we decided on removing it," said Mary, quietly, "which we all attributed to the dampness of the situation in which it stood; besides," she added, "that is not all, for we find it so much more useful within doors, were we can play it at all hours, and in all seasons; whereas it is only in the fine weather that we can enjoy the pleasures of music in the midst of the garden, even if we could reach the alcove without inconvenience, which is impossible in the winter months."

"And yet," said Ada, "with all these serious disadvantage, I should much prefer, were I in your situation, having the instrument here, at least during the continuance of this lovely season; indeed, at the present moment, I selfishly regret its removal, for we might have had quite a sweet little concert in this romantic bower."

"Here is a guitar," said Elizabeth. "If that will server in lieu of a 'better instrument, we shall be delighted to hear you accompany yourself."

"Oh, do consent to oblige us," said Percy, who was an ardent admirer of music. Ada possessed a sweet voice, and was an admirable performer; and in days gone by, the two frequently amused themselves for hours, by singing duets, and performing pieces of music on different instruments. Ada full-well remembered these hours of tranquil gladness, and would have given worlds, had she possessed them, to to recall the past—the bright and happy past, when Percy was held captive by her charms, and a willing slave to her slightest wish; she did not, therefore, require much pressing to induce her to sing. But why does her fingers tremble as she touches the strings, or her voice for a moment lose its tone, ere it sends forth its gust of sweetest melody, "stealing on the senses like a May-day breaking?" Percy stood near her chair listening like one entranced as he hung upon the notes. Yet he trembles likewise, and the expression of his face changes as the well-remembered words steal upon his ear, accompanied by the most exquisite harmony—

> "Who can chain the heart's affection,
> Who can banish its regret?
> If you blame my deep dejection,
> Teach, oh, teach me to forget."

Mary, too, trembles and turns pale for the first time in her life. She covets not the beauty, but the gift of song so richly possessed by Ada.

"Oh, would," was her inward exclamation, "that I had the power thus to charm and interest him;" and though she did not doubt the purity of his love for her, she doubted her own worthiness of possessing it, till the thought grew pain, and she almost mistrusted her own power of retaining a love she so highly prized, yet possessed in her own opinion so slight a claim to deserve. The song was ended; the last notes died away in the distance, and the lovely song-stress sat mutely bending over the instrument from which she had called forth such sweet strains, as though entranced by the intensity of the melody she had herself created. Percy stood near, and was the first to break the silence, by a warm expression of the pleasure he had experienced in listening to her performance.

"But you will sing again, Miss Herbert?" he said in canclusion; "do not leave us anxiously wishing for a prolongation of our enjoyment; come, Mary," he added, "join your persuasions to mine, and they will surely be effective."

As he spoke, he turned towards the spot where his wife stood; but in her he observed no fellow-feeling, no sign of pleasure; on the contrary, her face was paler than usual, and she looked sad and depressed.

"Are you unwell, Mary?" he said, in a tone of suprise at this unwonted change in her appearance.

"No, thank you," she returned. "I am perfectly well."

Percy felt annoyed; he could not avoid observing that Mary regarded his admiration of Ada's musical talents with no pleasant feeling; and conscious of his own entire devotion to herself, he was vexed with her for apparently doubting him, or showing the slightest symptom of displeasure at the attention politeness and good breeding imperatively demanded of him to show his guest, the cousin and only near relative, too, of his wife; but as he thus reasoned, Percy forgot to take into account that he had once been not only devotedly attached to Ada, but was likewise her promised husband; and this might well excuse any painful forebodings in the mind of Mary, arising from the fascinations of his companion. Percy had ever prided himself on his good breeding, and was one of the most zealous devotees at the shrine of etiquette. He did not, therefore, show in the slightest degree that he observed anything uncommon in the appearance of Mary; neither did he abate in the least the attentions he considered due from himself to his guest. Turning, therefore, to Ada, he again entreated her to continue her performance. She shook her head.

"You will excuse me, I know," she said, rising and turning aside her head, but not before Percy had perceived that her blue eyes were swimming in moisture. "You will excuse me, I am sure; for I cannot sing again to-night."

Percy pressed her no farther; but rising in his turn, inquired if it would be agreeable to her to continue their walk? Ada answered by placing her hand once more within his arm; and, followed by Mary and his sisters, the little party again set forth. The garden, which was large for a London one, was terminated by some fields, which branched off into a thick and woody plantation, so pleasant and shady in its appearance, that Ada expressed a wish to walk in that direction. Percy was happy in having it in his power so readily to meet her views, and hastened to conduct her to the spot indicated. Mary, with her sisters, followed half mechanically, as none of them had expressed any inclination on the subject. They had not proceeded far, when they observed a female figure seated on the ground. She rose as they approached, and turning towards them, displayed features singularly handsome. The deep bronze of her complexion betrayed her at once as belonging to the strange and wandering class known as gipsies. Her dress was of the commonest description, and yet it was disposed with a sort of natural coquetry, that gave an appearance of interest to the wearer; this was especially to be remarked in her head gear, which was composed simply of a scarlet handkerchief, tastefully wound over her raven hair, forming a most pleasing contrast with its shiny blackness. She arose as the little party approached, and addressing herself to Ada, said, in a low persuasive voice—

"Lady, shall I tell you your destiny?"

"You cannot tell me more than I know already," was Ada's reply.

"Will you put my knowledge to the test, lady?" said the gipsy. "Come, there is no one that can overhear us, if it should be some love tale that I read upon the lines of your hand."

Ada, with her usual impetuosity, felt for the moment inclined to humour the gipsy; and holding forth her hand, exclaimed—

"Well, then, let me have proof of your skill."

"'Tis a fair hand," said the stranger, taking it in her own; "but there have been fairer than this, where there have been likewise false hearts."

"You do not surely mean to infer that I have a false heart?" said Ada, pettishly withdrawing her hand.

"Lady, look up," said the gipsy; "the sun is now unclouded (and she pointed with her finger emphatically towards the setting sun) and it is beautiful; there is a joy even in looking at it in its dazzling brightness and glory; but in a moment clouds—dark stormy clouds—may come across it, and in the place of the bright sun, we may have only gloom and tears."

There was something in the mournful and touching tones of the gipsy's voice that fixed the attention of Ada, and filled her bosom with sad thoughts, as she replied—

"Do you think, then, that my life will end in gloom and tears?"

"Not so, lady," said the gipsy hastily, "for I perceive two lines upon your

MARY HERBERT.

hand which, meeting at one point, separate quickly: the one leads to happiness the other terminates in despair."

"Then my life will be exactly according to the line I may chance or choose, to follow?"

"You guess right, lady. Ah!" she added, again taking the hand, and carefully examining the palm. "A bride, too—wealth, title, and honours. It is a rare hand; jewels and gold, princeless gems, and—but where's the heart? I look in vain for that. Lady," she continued, in a tone of increased mournfulness, "thy heart is not here."

"What mean you?" exclaimed Ada, startled, and half frightened by the pointed remarks of the gipsy, which brought strange things to her recollection; "my heart not here? Do you imagine I carry my heart in my hand?"

"No; but the hand should go with the heart—and here," she added, gently striking the small white palm with her own bronzed fingers, "here there is no heart to match the hand."

"You talk in riddles," replied Ada, affecting to laugh at the words of the gipsy. "Do be so good as to explain yourself, or it will be wiser to break up this grave conference."

"I will tell thee thy fate, then," said the stranger sternly, gathering her cloak around her, as if preparing to depart. "Listen, lady. The serpent," she began, speaking in the metaphorical language to which the tribe are so much addicted; "the serpent with its glossy scales is beautiful—ay, how beautiful, how fascinating the reptile seems. Before it has been clasped to the heart of beauty, it has been loved, it has been adored; but how did it repay the love that warmed and sheltered it?—by inflicting a poisonous and deadly wound in the bosom on which it reclined. But beware, lady, again I say, beware!"

"Beware of what?" inquired Ada, in tremulous accents.

"Of thy own heart's treachery."

"Of my own heart's treachery?" reiterated Ada, in indignant accents.

"Yes, lady, those were my words. The gates of despair are of pure gold studded with diamonds; and you prepare to go up to them rejoicing, and the serpent that lures thee there seems very fair—yet he has destroyed fairer flowers than thou. If you enter, the gates will be closed upon you, and there will be no such thing as returning. Think, lady, well before you resolve to enter there."

"This is worse than folly," said Ada, moving as if to depart, though she trembled and turned pale with a boding fear that shot across her heart, as she listened to the words of the gipsy.

"Stay one moment longer," said the stranger, stretching out her hand, and laying it on Ada's arm, as if to arrest her steps, and force her to hear what else she wished to say. "Remember, ere you determine to link your destiny with one who comes of a fated race, with the curse branded on his forehead. Remember, I say, the days that are past. Ere thou layest thy head upon thy pillow, bethink thee of past happiness beyond recall; then act as thy conscience dictates. Shun a cursed and fated race—crush the serpent ere he encircles thee with his envenomed fold; think of the fair flower his love has already blighted. Remember, I say, and beware!"

The gipsy waited for no reply; but hastily folding her cloak around her, turned away, and was soon lost to sight amid the trees. In vain the whole party (whose tongues had appeared chained while in the presence of the strange woman) endeavoured to rally Ada on the absurdity of giving the slightest heed to what had been said by the gipsy. Ada strove to laugh; but a cold chill ran through her veins, and she trembled so much that she could scarcely sustain herself, and was forced to lean upon Percy for support.

"We will return at once to the house," he said, kindly. "I am grieved, indeed, that this unfortunate circumstance should have affected you so deeply;" and he regarded his fair companion with an expression of the deepest commiseration and anxiety.

Ada was gratified. The pleasure she now felt was cheaply purchased by her previous fright; and, leaning affectionately on his arm, she prepared to return to the house. At this instant the gipsy re-appeared. Ada scarcely suppressed a shriek as she encountered the wild dark eyes of the stranger fixed upon her face, as she uttered the words—

"Think not that the lamp of love which has once gone out can ever be re-lighted again. I have need, lady, to repeat my warning—again I say beware!" and she held up her hand menacingly.

The words were scarcely spoken, before the gipsy was again gone. Indeed, so sudden had been her re-appearance and the manner of her second departure, that none knew from whence she came or in what direction she went. Ada, more and more affected by this second and unlooked-for appearance of the stranger, begged Percy to hasten homeward. The remainder of the little party were nothing loath to follow their example; and they were soon once more seated in the accustomed parlour; but a damp had fallen upon the spirits of all, which they found it difficult to shake off, and which indisposed them for conversation.

"I declare I never felt more alarmed in my life," said Elizabeth, who was the first to speak.

"Nor I," said her sister Mary. "Indeed, were I in your place," she added, turning to Ada, "I should most certainly profit by the warning so gratuitously given. There was a depth of prophetic meaning in the wild dark eyes of that strange woman, which convinces me she spoke truth."

"It is strange," remarked Percy, "but her words have certainly made a deep impression on my mind. Indeed," he said, looking at Mary, who seemed entirely unmoved by the incident, and addressing himself to her, "you, my love, appear to be the only one amongst us entirely unaffected by this strange adventure."

"That may possibly be attributed to my entire disbelief in her power of pro-phecy, and consequently the want of credence in a single word she uttered," said Mary, smiling.

"And yet," said Elizabeth, "I feel certain she is not a common imposter, for not only did she never hint at receiving any remuneration for her supposed pro-phecy, but put it intirely out of our power to offer any by departing before we had time to recover from the state of stupefaction into which she had thrown us."

"True," said her sister, "I never thought of that before; and it is certainly an additional and powerful reason for giving at least some credence to what she said."

"It is certainly a most romantic adventure," observed Ada, joining for the first time in the conversation.

"And that is all that can be said of it," replied her cousin, smiling incredu-lously. "If this woman is not a common imposter, she was certainly actuated by some motive which we cannot at present fathom, for wishing to alarm and annoy us, and in which she appears in a great measure to have succeeded."

"Well, I hope that Mary may prove correct; she may be a better judge of this affair than either of us," replied Ada, looking an appeal to the opinion of others.

"It may be so," said Elizabeth, doubtfully; "and yet I do not know—Mary is so entirely matter-of-fact."

Percy, smilingly, coincided in the opinion of his sister, and the others laughed approvingly. Mary was silenced; and though the strange *rencontre* with the singular woman, whose prophecy weighed heavily on the heart of Ada, formed the subject of conversation for the remainder of the evening, she did not venture to offer any other remark, convinced in her own mind of the truthfulness of the opinion she had formed. Mary listened in silence to the remarks of the rest, secretly retaining her own ideas on the subject.

CHAPTER XLI.

" How silently the moon's soft ray,
   Just waked from sleep,
Steals, like a spirit, far away
   Along the deep.
And see, the bark, whose brighten'd sail
   Hangs carelessly,
That kisses ev'ry gentle gale
   That fans the sea.
There is a time of calm delight,
   'Tis at this hour,
For those who love the silent night,
   And feel its power."

WHEN love lights up a home, no matter where that home may be, it is a Paradise, wherein frail humanity enjoys a sweet foretaste of Heaven. And yet what is love, what is this pure light which makes such happiness, which elevates us so far above our fellow creatures, which so brightly irradiates our path, scattering roses before the footsteps of youth, smoothing the furrows and wrinkles of age, and giving peace and resignation to the bed of death? We are all of us conscious of perpetually desiring a something which seems beyond our attainment, for in the beautifully expressed words of the poet,

" Man never is but always to be blest."

And thus are we constantly following shadows ; our wishes are no sooner gratified than new wishes spring up ; we go on through our brief pilgrimage, our wants and desires increasing every day, till old age overtakes us, and we are induced to cast a retrospective glance at our career ; then we are lost in amazement at the folly of the game we have been pursuing. There is, indeed, but one bright spot in human existence, an oasis in the desert of light, which could we but discover its brightness and value while it is ours, we might throw care behind us and be supremely happy. This is love, true, pure, and constant love, which every human being feels in all its truth and purity once in their existence, which every one has the power to perpetuate if they choose, but which too many do not see the value of till it is gone, and once gone it is lost for ever ; for when love once goes out, nothing on earth can revive it—it dies, passes away, and is known no more. It was this pure and constant love, which lighted up the home of Henry and his young wife. Yes, though travelling in foreign climes, surrounded by entire strangers, yet they found a home, a double home, which, though the cold-thinking world might despise and suppose to be two distinct and seperate abodes, is nevertheless, and notwithstanding appearances, but one connected and inseperable abode, to those who happen to be under the same influence as Henry and Fanny. And, oh ! how happy was that home, how brightly was it irradiated. What costly furniture was it filled with, what dazzling genius studded its walls, and what strains of music divine, and what sweet odours was it filled with ! Their home was each other's hearts. Together as they explored the mountain height, cr wandered in the deep shades of romantic valleys, they were equally happy and blest, so true it is—

" No matter where our fate may guide us,
   If those we love are still beside us."

So eager was Fanny to contribute to the enjoyment, and share the pleasures of her husband, that she bade defiance to all difficulties, seeming insensible to fatigue, although they were forced to encounter much in their ascent up to Mount Etna. They travelled, it is true, by easy stages, frequently stopping to admire and explore. Henry, too, would frequently tarry, to make sketches of the scenery; on these occasions Fanny was invariably at his side, ready to hold his pencils, or assist in arranging his portfolio, never weary—never dull, or out of spirits; the same bright smile ever encouraged him to proceed; the same gentle cheering words ever blest him with happiness and peace, or lent their soothing charm to bind him to existence, as being blest, if shared with her. Notwithstanding the fatigue and difficulties they were forced to surmount, Fanny frequently expressed herself delighted with the tour. Having arrived at Nicolosi, an hour and half's travelling, over barren ashes and lava, brought them to the confines of the Regione Sylvosa, or as it is otherwise called "The temperate zone." As soon as they entered these delightful forests, they felt as though they had got into another world. The air, which had previously been sultry and hot, was now cool and refreshing, and every breeze was loaded with a thousand perfumes, the whole ground being covered over with the richest aromatic plants. It seemed one of the most delightful spots on earth, and they could resemble it to nothing short of paradise; and, to their minds, it was a no less curious consideration that this mountain should unite at once every beauty, and every conceivable terror, and, in short, all the most opposite and dissimilar objects in nature. On one side they observed a gulph, which once threw out torrents of fire, now covered with the most luxuriant vegetation, and changed from an object of terror into one of delight. And again they gathered the most delicious fruits, growing on a spot which was but lately a barren rock, but now covered with flowers and fruits, and presenting an aspect of the most inviting and pleasing description, alluring and gratifying at once by their delicious taste and sweet perfume. Still all this, wonderful as it at first appeared to our travellers, sunk into nothingness as they reach the higher regions of the mountain, and beheld, in perpetual union, the two elements which are usually in perpetual war—an immense gulph of fire for ever existing in the midst of snows, which it has no power to extinquish, and immense fields of snow and ice for ever surrounding this gulph of fire, which it is powerless to extinguish. Lost in wonder and astonishment at all they saw, frequently beguiled on their way by some new and beautiful objects, they preserved in their ascent, and at lenght reached the highest summit of the mountain, having so timed themselves as to arise there in full time to see the most wonderful and sublime sight in nature. But here description falls short, for no language can depict so glorious and magnificent a scene. The immense elevation from the earth, raised on the brink of a bottomless gulph as old as the world, discharging rivers of fire and throwing out burning rocks, with a noise that shook the whole island. Add too this the unbounded extent of the prospect comprehending the greatest diversity and the most beautiful scenery in nature, with the rising sun advancing in the east to illuminate the wondrous scene. As they stood side by side, gazing with entranced delight, the whole atmosphere by degrees kindled up, and showed at first, dimly and faintly, the boundless prospect around them; both sea and land looked dark and confused as if just emerging from their original chaos, and light and darkness seemed still undivided; till the day by degrees advancing, completed the seperation; the stars were extinguished, and the shades disappeared. The forests which before seemed black and bottomless gulphs from whence no ray was ever reflected, began to show their form and colour, and look like a new creation rising to the sight, catching fresh life and beauty from every increasing beam. Gradually the scene still enlarges, and the horizon seems to widen and expand itself on every side, till the sun, like the great and glorious creator of all around, appeared in the east, and completed the wonder and beauty of the mighty scene. All seemed the work of enchantment; the view was abolutely boundless on all sides; nor was there a single object within the circle of vision to interrupt it, so that sight was everywhere lost in immensity of space. But the most beautiful part of the scene, Henry regarded as being certainly the mountain itself, the Island of Sicily, and the numerous island lying around it, which, from their elevation, they looked down upon as on a map, and could trace every river through all its windings from its source to its mouth, and could thus embrace the whole island, and see all its cities, rives, and mountains, delineated in the great chart of nature, all the adjacent islands, and the whole coast of Italy as far as the eye could reach—for it was nowhere bounded, but everywhere lost in space.   On the sun first rising, a curious sight presented itself to their notice—the shadow of the mounting extending across the whole island, and making a large track visible even in the sea and air; but by degrees, this was shortened, and in a little time confined only to the neighbourhood of Etna.   It was with a mixture of pleasure and pain, that Henry and Fanny quitted the spot; but the wind having become very high, and clouds beginning to gather round the mountain, which had the curious effect of producing as it were another Heaven below them, similar to that above, they judged it best not longer to delay their descent.   Henry heaved a sigh as they turned away, but did not speak.   Both were silent for some time; their senses, unaccustomed to the sublimity of such a scene, were bewildered and confounded with its beauty and splendour; their meditations were elevated in proportion to the grandeur and sublimity of the objects which surrounded them. All nature lay expanded below them in her gayest and most luxurant dress, and they beheld, united under one point of view, all the seasons of the year, and all the climates of the earth; indeed the prospect as they descended was little inferior to that from the summit.   From the regions of the most rigid winter, they soon arrived at those of the most delightful spring.   On first entering the forests, the trees were all bare as in December, not a single leaf to be seen, but after they had descended a few miles, they found themselves in the mildest and softest of climates, the trees in full vendure, and the fields covered with all the flowers of summer.   The course of the Semetrus, the ruins of Hybla and other towns, the rich corn fields, and vineyards on the lower region of the mountain, and the amazing number of beautiful mountains below, made up a delightful scene.   The rich and stately oaks, orange and citron tree in full blow, all added to the beauty of the the prospect, and formed a fair and wondrous whole. They were surrounded too on all sides with a variety of fine evergreens and flowering shrubs, of which the palmeta and the arbutus or strawberry tree, Fanny though decidedly most beautiful, and gathered a bunch of each to preserve for botanical purposes.   She likewise greatly admired a blue everlasting flower which she regarded as rather curious, the stem rising about a foot high, and crowned with a large cluster of small blue flowers, the leaves of which were of a dry substance like the globe amaranthus.   As they walked side by side, oecassionally stopping in their walk to call some fresh specimen or admire the beauty of the scenery that surrounded them, its romantic nature would at times be greatly heightened by the sudden appearance of a roebuck or stag, which would rapidly dart across their path and plunge into the thickest part of the forest.   Occasionally, too, an eagle or vulture would soar above their heads, clapping their large out-spread wings, and making the air re-echo with their discordant cries.   As they descended, Henry remarked and pointed out to Fanny that it was easy to trace the progress of vegetation from its utmost luxuriance, to where it is checked by the extremes of heat and cold; for the different regions of the mountain are distinctly marked out by their different colours and varied productions, exposing at once to the delighted eye, every climate, and every aso n, with all their variety, or in the words of the poet—

> " Blossoms, fruits, and flowers together rise,
> And the whole year in gay confusion lies."

The first region exhibits every object that characterises summer and autumn, l those of the most delightful spring, and the fourth, to complete the contrast, the regions of unextinguishable fire.   And through the whole of these they passed in succession, experiencing a change of climate at almost every other mile.   Somewhat fatigued with the expedition, though far more entranced and delighted by all they had witnessed, they arrived once more at the foot of the mountain, and they were glad again to take possession of their apartments at the little village of Giardini, were they resolved to stay for a few days to be devolved, Henry insisted on Fanny's part, to entire rest, in order to enable her to recover from the fatigue she had undergone, not so much from the travelling as the bad roads leading to Mount Etna, and the variety of changes, she had gone through in so short a time. Fanny was nothing loth to profit by the suggestion, and the three succeeding days were spent in complete retirement. Henry was her constant companion, never leaving her side for an instant, and together they conversed on all the wonders they had seen, and the fresh cities they yet intended to visit. Neither of them possessed the slightest desire for other society, or experienced the least weariness; they were only too happy in being together. All regrets were banished from the mind of Henry; he ceased to think of Jane, or only thought of her, as hoping she had, like himself, found a dear and treasured companion to share her joys and soothe her sorrows. He hoped this so much, that he half persuaded himself it would, it must be so; and more and yet more charmed with the rich blessing he possessed in Fanny, he yielded himself to the delight of her society and the happiness of the present without regret for the past or fear for the future. Fanny, too, looked forward to days and nights winged with such precious pure delights as only those can experience who, like her, have made a home of love and happiness in the breast of a beloved and cherishsd object. Having sufficiently recovered from their late fatigue, they resolved to resume their tour, and consequently embarked on board a vessel, and set sail for Syracuse. The wind was favourable, and for some time they went at a great rate. The view of Mount Etna during the whole of this voyage was wonderfully fine, and the bold black coast, formed for nearly thirty miles of the lava of that common volcano, gave them the most awful idea of its eruptions. For there is no part of this coast nearer than thirty miles to its summit, and yet there has scarcely been any great eruptions where the lava has not reached the sea, and driven back its waters to a great distance, leaving high rocks and promontories that for ever set its waves at defiance, and prescribe their utmost limits. They all agreed in the opinion, that the view of the mountain from the sea is more satisfactory than any where on the island; the eye takes in a greater portion of the circle; and they could observe, with more distinctness, how it rises equally on all sides, from its immense base, overspread with beautiful little mountains. There was nothing else of an interesting nature worthy of remark in their voyage to Syracuse, for the coast lies low, and with the exception of Etna, there are no very striking objects. The voyage being short, was easily accomplished; and a few hours brought them within sight of Syracuse, the remembrance of whose glory, magnificence, and illustrious deeds, fired the breast of Henry with ardour; but, alas! they discovered, as they approached within a short distance of it, that this proud city, which once vied even with Rome itself, is now reduced to a heap of rubbish. They rowed round the greatest part of its walls which still remain standing, those very walls which were the terror of the Roman arms. On landing, they found, to their increased disappointment, that the interior of the city agreed but too well with its external appearance. There was not an inn of any sort to be found, and it was with the greatest difficulty they could procure accommodation even of an inferior description; but as travellers, they were already used to put up with inconvenience, and were consequently far from complaining; indeed, the very novelty of being forced to make their own arrangements, and prepare what was necessary for their own comfort, possessed a charm for Fanny; and never had she laughed more merrily or seemed more free from care, than when superintending the preperation for their mutual repast. Notwithstanding the want of proper attendance and accommodation, our tourists resolved to make a short stay at Syracuse, in order to inspect that ancient city, now fast falling to utter ruin and decay. Yet, not wishing to devote more time to this object than was absolutely necessary, they set out early the following morning, and began their exploring expedition without any needless delay. Of the four cities that composed the ancient Syracuse, they found there was but one now remaining. The ruins of the other three are computed at twenty-two miles in circumference, and nearly the whole of this space they discovered to be converted into rich vineyards, orchards, and cornfields ; and the walls seperating these, Henry observed to be every where built with broken marbles full of engravings and inscriptions, but most of them entirely defaced and spoiled. The principal remains of antiquity they discovered to be a theatre and amphitheatre, many curious sepulchres, the Latomiæ, the catecombs, and the famous Ear of Dionysius, all of which they determined to visit in turn, and gratify the expressed wish of Fanny. Henry resolved to make the Latomiæ the first place they visited, and which well repaid their trouble. Fanny, indeed, was loud and warm in her expressions of admiration of the noble and subterraneous garden, which goes by that name, and was, indeed, one of the most beautiful and romantic spots they had yet beheld ; most part of it being about one hundred feet below the level of the earth, and of an almost incredible extent, the whole hewn out of a rock as hard as marble, composed of a concretion of shells, gravel, and other marine substances.   The bottom of this immense quarry, (and from which Henry conjectured it was probable the greatest part of Syracuse was built), was covered with an exceeding rich soil, and as from its situation no wind from any point of the compass can touch it, it was filled with a great variety of the finest shrubs and fruit trees, which appeared, to judge from their present appearance, to bear with great luxuriance, the oranges, citrons, burgomots, pomegranates, and figs, all being of the very finest quality and of a remarkable size.   Some of these trees, they observed, (but more particularly the olive,) grew out of the hard rock, where there was no visible soil, and exhibit an uncommon and very pleasing appearance.   There is, too, a variety of wild and romantic scenes in this curious garden, which greatly pleased and attracted the admiration of Fanny, who having arrived with Henry to about the middle of the gardens, they were surprised by the unlooked-for appearance of a tall figure under one of the caverns, that added considerably to the dignity and solemnity of the place.   The figure they found, on approaching the cavern more closely, to be that of an aged man, whose looks were venerable in the extreme. His long flowing white beard reaching half-way to the ground—his wrinkled face, and scanty locks, whose whiteness might rival the purest snow, bespoke him a member of some former age, as well as of this.   His hands, which shook and trembled with apparent weakness, held a pilgrim's staff, and round his waist he wore a girdle, composed entirely of large beads, with a crucifix suspended to the end of it. This figure, together with the scene in which it appeared, were admirably adapted to each other, on which they respectively reflected a mutual dignity. Fanny was anxious to address the stranger, whose venerable appearance had created an interest in her mind, and was about to consult Henry on the best mode of doing so, when he relieved her from all embarrassment by telling them he was the hermit of the place, having originally belonged to a convent of Capuchins, on the rock above them ; but that he had long since bid adieu to the upper world, and was determined to spend the remainder of his life in this solitude, in prayer for the wretched mortals who inhabit it.   He concluded by inviting them to walk into the cavern and rest themselves. They instantly complied with this request, gladly availing themselves of the opportunity of viewing the interior.   Fanny started with surprise at its uninviting aspect, and yet there was a neat simplicity about the arrangements that could not fail to attract her attention, as she seated herself on the stone bench, which, to judge from its appearance, served the double purpose of a bed by night, and a seat by day. There was not the slightest vestige of furniture of any kind, and the delicious fruits which the hermit spread before his guests were carefully arranged on the broad leaves gathered from a tree that grew close beside the cave, affording a pleasant shelter from the mid-day sun. He likewise presented them with a glass of water, which he fetched himself from the crystal spring hard by. Fanny gratefully received it from his hands, and forcing him to sit on the stone bench by her side, entered into conversation with this aged recluse.

"Do you not feel very dull," she enquired, "shut out from all companionship, at an age, too, when you must necessarily require affectionate care and attention?"

"My wants are few," replied the hermit, "and the means of supplyin those are close within my reach; nay, more, I have dainties which court my acceptance. The most delicious fruits 1 can at any moment pluck without the slightest inconvenience; and my drink is of the purest crystal stream—my home

THE GIPSY BARKLY FORWARNING ADA OF THE FUTURE.

is situated in a garden filled with the choicest plants, the sweet odours from which I constantly inhale. I live in an atmosphere of perpetual summer, and under the fairest and most unclouded skies. What more can I desire? So far from coveting the lot of others, I think there must be many who would gladly exchange the world and all its cares, for the enjoyment of the simple pleasures and unalloyed happiness that is constantly mine."

"So far, I believe you are quite right," replied Fanny, thoughtfully; "but it is the want of communion—the want of affection," (she continued, glancing at Henry, who smilingly signified that he understood and appreciated her feelings), "that you must feel."

"You forget," returned the hermit, stretching out his withered hands, "that such feelings have long been a stranger to my heart. The only communion—the only affection, my breast can know, is to be found in the exercise of our holy and blest religion." And as he spoke, he raised the crucifix to his lips, which he devoutly kissed.

As Fanny regarded the venerable pilgrim, and remarked the serene and peaceful smile which lighted up his countenance, she almost envied the calm unruffled feelings which evidently filled his breast. For years he had pursued the even tenor of his way—

> "Ne'er roughened by those cataracts and breaks,
> Which human interposal too often makes."

And now he had reached the vale of life's latest decline, and could look forward with peaceful resignation to the arrival of that hour when he must yield his spirit into the hands of his Maker, while his body returned to its original dust.

"Have you no dread of being seized with, perchance, a long and painful sickness, and being left lone and untended to combat it as you best can?" said Fanny, as these thoughts passed through her mind.

"God is good," replied the hermit, bowing his snow-white head, "and I do not dread any visitation with which he may see fit to purify me of my sins, and render me more meet for Heaven."

Fanny was charmed by the fervour and devotion of this religious recluse. Henry, too, observed with pleasure the glow of gratitude and affection that animated the countenance of the old hermit, as he spoke of the goodness of God, and felt pursuaded that the warmth of enthusiastic devotion he felt must have something extremely delightful in it, and for the moment, at least, envied his feelings, and in his heart cursed the pride of reason and philosophy, with all its cool and tasteless triumphs, that lulls into a kind of stoical apathy those most exquisite sensations of the soul, stealing those feelings of the human heart, which are most worthy of it, and for which of all others it seems by nature most fitted, but which, steeled over with the hard and impenetrable temper of philosophy, the fine spun threads of affection that were so pliable, and easily enchained, become hard and inflexible, and for ever lose the sensibility that put them into a kind of union with every object around them.

"You are happy and perfectly content in this retreat?" said Henry.

"More happy than it is possible to be surrounded by worldly objects and human affections, which only serve to withdraw the thoughts and affections from higher and firmer aspirations. Here I am, separated from all that could by any possibility tend to withdraw my soul from the contemplation of heavenly things. My days are spent in sweet devotion, and my nights are past in peace."

"I believe you," replied Henry, "and can scarcely help envying the purity and calmness of your life, passing from youth to age unsullied by evil thoughts, and, if it is possible to be so in this world, free from sin."

"My son," replied the hermit, "we have all of us sufficient reason to seek atonement; we have all sinned, but the same gifts, the same religious ardour and enthusiastic feelings are not bestowed on all, neither is it required of all to abandon the world, and in perfect seclusion devote himself in service to God, and in prayer for his fellow mortals, who may be forced to combat with the world, encounter its ills, its cares, and strife. Of such, my son, are you, and my poor prayers shall not be wanting on your behalf."

"Call them not poor prayers, father," replied Henry, modestly, "for such prayers as yours must assuredly avail much."

"They must, indeed," said Fanny. "And though I, too, envy (if that word is applicable : I use it for want of a better), the holy fervour of your devotional feelings ; yet I cannot leave you in this lone and dreary retreat without a sensation of regretful sadness. When I am far from here I am confident there will be times when my imagination will picture you in this lonely cave, suffering from bodily weakness and disease, with no friendly hand to administer to your wants, or smooth the bed of death, but dying alone, unheeded, and uncared for. The thought is so extremely painful that I cannot bear to entertain it, and yet it will force itself upon me."

Again a radiant glow of animation overspread the features of the aged pilgrim, as he replied again, devotely pressing the crucifix to his lips.

"Do not, my daughter, allow any such thoughts to disturb your repose ; we part now to meet no more in this world, but we shall meet again in Heaven. A few short years, at most, and I shall gladly lay down this weary load, and rest in peace."

Both Henry and Fanny left the cavern with a feeling of regret ; they were alike charmed with his devout religious feelings, and the simple purity of his life. Before they took their leave, the hermit inquired if they would like to visit the convent on the rock above, to which Order of Monks he belonged ; and having received an answer in the affirmative, he furnished them with credentials to the superior, who he assured them would gladly admit them on his recommendation. Having thanked him for the pleasure the stay in the cavern had afforded them, they hastened their departure, and left the Latomiæ, with which they were much delighted, with the deepest regret.

" I have been thinking," said Fanny as they walked towards their temporary home, " I have been thinking that much which has been urged against the Catholic religion in our own Protestant country, has arisen from want of a due consideration of the effect it produces on the mind, especially on those of an inferior order."

" True," replied Henry, " for the mode of worship is decidedly calculated to produce a strong, and sometimes even a startling effect ; but at the same time, my love, we should remember, that the doctrine it inculcates is fatal and delusive in the extreme."

" Yet who would not like to be deceived, when the deception inspires such pure and exalted feelings, as are experienced by many of its professors—for instance, the aged man whom we have just left ?—who could observe the glory of an enthusiastic adoration, that lighted up his withered countenance, as he pressed the holy symbol of his religion to his lips, and not envy the feelings of his breast ?"

"I certainly agree with you so far," replied Henry, " that I think this personal kind of worship is more adapted to the capacities of the lower classes, than the more simple, but infinitely more sublime, modes of it, which only distracts and confounds their simple understandings, unaccustomed to speculation, and which appears to require something material, some object of sense to fix their attention ; and this would even seem to be the opinion of many of the sacred writers, who frequently represent the duty under some material form ; and hence it happens that among the lower orders, we find much more religious feeling in those who possess the Catholic religion than in Protestants."

"I entirely agree in your opinion," said Fanny ; " in this country, for instance, where all are Catholics, there is certainly a far greater outward appearance o religion than in Potestant countries."

Henry having concurred in this opinion, which was drawn from close observation, and therefore admitted of no controversy, they conversed on other subjects, the beauty and fruitfulness of the Latomiæ engrossing Fanny's thoughts, and on which she dwelt with delighted admiration. The following t rning early they went to visit the celebrate convent of Capuchins. They found it contained nothing very remarkable, except the burial place, which ed they considered a great curiosity. It was a vast subterraneous apart-mant, divided into large and commodious galleries, the walls on each side of which were hollowed into a variety of niches, as if intended for a vast collection of statues; these niches instead of statues were all filled, with dead bodies, stood upright and fixed to the niche. Their number was about three hundred, and they were all dressed in the costume of the Order to which they had belonged while living, and formed an unusual and strange assembly. To this burial ground they were informed, the monks made frequent visits, and recall with pleasure and regret the scenes of former days in which their lost companions once took a part. Here, too, they familiarise themselves with death, and choose the company they would wish to keep in the next world. It is a common thing likewise to make choice of their niche, and to try if their body fits it, so that no alteration may be needed after they are dead; and sometimes (by way of a voluntary penance) they accustom themselves to stand for hours in these niches, or even sleep in the galleries the entire night. These visits Henry thought must prove admirable lessons of humility, though they were by no means such objects of horror as he would have conjectured, for they are said even for ages after death to retain a strong likeness to what they were when in life; so as soon as Fanny had conquered the feelings excited by these venerable figures, she only looked upon it as a vast gallery of original portraits, drawn after the life of the justest and most unprejudiced hand. True, it must be owned that the colours were rather faded, and the pencil did not appear to have been the most flattering in the world; but no matter, it was evidently the pencil of truth, and not of a mercenary who only sought to please. Henry thought, too, that they might be made of considerable use to society, and that those dumb orators could give the most pathetic lectures on pride and vanity.

"This is a strange country," Fanny remarked as they quitted the Convent; "what a strange way of disposing of the dead."

"I am not sure," replied Henry, "that it is not a better method than our own. The visit we have just made, must serve admirably as a lesson of humility of whoever becomes vain, or assumes an haughty and supercilious air. I would send to visit, as we have done, the monks in the gallery; and if these arguments did not bring them to a proper way of thinking, I would give them up as utterly incorrigible."

Fanay laughed. "I am afraid," she said, "you would find many whom your lesson would fail to convince."

From this spot they directed their steps to the next object deemed worthy of inspection; this was the Ear of Dionysius, a monument, no less of magnificence and ingenuity, than of the cruelty of that tyrant. It is a large cavern cut out of the hard rock, in the form of a human ear, and which, as an object of curiosty, Henry regarded as one of the wonders of the city, the height of the cavern being computed at eighty feet. Having examined this gigantic cavern, and likewise the ancient Amphitheatre, which they found much ruined, though the theatre was entire, most of the seats being still remaining, and which they regarded with some curiosity—they had now seen all worthy of inspection in the once opulent and powerful city of Syracuse, whose former magnificence makes a dismal contrast with its present meanness. However, they did not regret the time spent within its walls. Although during their stay they had been forced to put up with much inconvenience, performing the most menial offices for themselves, the difficulty of procuring attendance being so great, still they were by no means sorry to leave the mighty city, so reduced that it could scarcely afford beds and lodgings to the two weary travellers, who, in consequence, abridged their stay in it. They accordingly hired a Maltese Sparanoro to carry them to that island. This is a small six-oared boat made entirely for speed, to avoid the African pirates, and other vessels, with which those seas are said to be infested. It was a little after nine in the evening when they embarked; the wind had died away about sun set, and a soft calm prevailed, so that scarce a ripple ruffled the surface of the water. The coast of Sicily quickly began to recede from their sight, and in a short time they found themselves once more farely launched upon the ocean. There was a profound silence, only broken by the noise of waves as they rolled in upon the distant shore, which served to render the scene more solemn. It was a dead calm, and the moon shone bright upon the waters. The scene naturally sank them into a calm and meditative mood, and they sat side by side clasping each other's hand in silence for nearly an hour without speaking a word, when the sailors began their midnight Hymn to the Vrgin. The music was simple, solemn and melancholly, and in perfect harmorny with the scene, and with the feelings of the two who listened with pleasure to this melancholy concert, feeling, as they did so, the vanity of operas and oratorios. There is often indeed a greater solemnity and a sweeter pathos in the modulation of these simple productions, that causes a much stronger effect than the compositions of the greatest masters, assisted by the boasted rules of counter-point. At last they sang our travellers to sleep; and when they awoke, they found themselves forty miles from Sicily. They were now on the main ocean, and saw no land, but Mount Etna, which is the perpetual polar star of these seas. Fanny, who had become an excellent traveller both by land and water; greatly enjoyed this little excursion. A fine breeze had sprung up, and in a very short time they were able to perceive the Island of Malta, and in a few hours more they reached the city of Valitta. The approach was fine, although the shore was low and rocky; the entry into the port was very narrow, and commanded by a strong castle on either side;—they were hailed from each of these. On landing, Fanny was astonished, and seemed to feel herself in a new world. The streets were all crowded with well-dressed people, who bore about with them the appearance of wealth, which formed a pleasing contrast to the place they had just left, where scarce a creature was to be seen, and even those few had the appearance of poverty and wretchedness. They were immediately conducted to an inn, which had more the appearance of a palace, and where every comfort and every luxury courted their acceptance.

"Let people say what they will," said Henry, as he sat down with Fanny in an elegantly furnished apartment to an excellent supper, which had been hastily prepared for their refreshment, and to which was added a bottle or two of choice wine; "let people say what they will, there is no true enjoyment in living in perpetual ease and affluence;—true luxury can only be obtained by undergoing a few hardships."

"Such as we have lately endured?" replied Fanny, smiling archly.

"Even so," said Henry. "Come, Fanny, do not laugh. Have we not encountered a vast deal of fatigue in order to gratify our love of adventure?"

"It will be your turn to laugh," she replied, "when I confess that I felt so much pleasure in performing for you, myself, the many little offices we deligate to servants, that I have often been tempted to wish that it was always so, that, in fact, we had no more wealth than would suffice to keep us in an inferior station, so that I might have the delight of preparing your refreshment after the toil of day, and attending to your comfort entirely myself."

"I cannot laugh, dear Fanny," said her husband, "at such proof of your fond devotion, unworthy as I feel myself of possession such true wealth as you bestow in your constant and unwearying affection—an affection that it shall henceforth be my earnest endeavour to deserve."

"Say not so, Henry," she replied; "for the words imply that you are not yet deserving; whereas, I am sure, you are worthy of all, and more than I can give."

"That is so like yourself," replied Henry, pressing a fond kiss on the glowing cheek of his young bride, inwardly resolving to make her happiness his first and dearest care, and wondering however he could have been insensible to the worth and nobility of her character.

After partaking together of the evening repast, they drew (according to their habitual custom in Italy) their cushioned chairs to the window, and were delighted with the beauty of the setting sun, much superior to what they had ever before observed. The whole of the eastern part of the hemisphere was of a fine deep purple for more than half an hour after the sun had sank to rest, and made a most beautiful appearance. And this, upon inquiry, they learnt to be the case every evening during that season of the year. The window of the inn at which they sat, commanded a fine view of the harbour, and from which they witnessed the departure of a Maltese squadron, consisting of three gallies, the largest consisting of several hundred men. These gallies, large as they were, were all worked by oars, and moved with the greatest regularity, the admiral going first, and the rest in order according to their dignity. The sea was crowded with boats, and the ramparts and fortifications were filled with company. The port resounded on all sides with the discharge of heavy artillery, which was answered by the gallies and galliots as they left the harbour. As the echo at this spot was uncommonly great, it produced a very noble effect. There were about thirty knights in each galley, making signals all the way to their mistresses, who were weeping for their departure upon the bastions. This show formed a very imposing sight, and our travellers considered themselves fortunate in having arrived at Valetta in time to view it. So pleased, indeed, were they with their present resting-place, that they resolved to make a longer stay in the island than they had previously intended. The climate was certainly hot, but it had, notwithstanding, many attractions, and the houses were admirably contrived to procure, what of all things was most desirable, shade. And there were sweet walks of orange groves, though the aspect of the country was far from being pleasant, the whole island being a great rock of very white free-stone, which rendered walking in many instances unpleasant ; but, as we were saying there were sweet shady walks in orange and citron bowers, in which Fanny loved to roam, musing on the beauties of nature by which she was surrounded. The country, too, a short distance from the city, was delightful, and a drive over it afforded her the greatest satisfaction. The sweet perfume from the fields, covered with a variety of her finest fruits, such as oranges, lemons, pomegranates, almonds, pistachio nuts, &c., delighted her at once by their odour and splendid appearance ; the bright colour of the fruits contrasting agreeably with the rich green foliage, and varying the tints which might otherwise have wearied the eye with their excessive brightness. Shortly after their arrival at Valitta, our tourists visited the church, which was a handsome noble building, elegantly finished and adorned with statues of the finest marble and exceeding rich tapestry, as also a quantity of silver plate. The pavement in particular, they were told, was reckoned the richest in the world, being composed entirely of sepulchral monuments of the finest marble, together with a variety of the most valuable stones, curiously wrought and joined together, so as to form a kind of Mosaic, and presenting both a rich and singular appearance. They likewise visited the catacombs, which are considered a great work, the guides assuring them, that many of them extended for fifteen miles under ground. This they were perfectly willing to take on the credit of the guides, thinking it would be risking rather too much to put it to the test. They also discovered several other places of curiosity and interest, such as the Bosquetta, (a wood, which, being the only one on the island, is considered a great curiosity), the Palace of the Grand Master, the horse races and the like. They were confirmed in their original idea of remaining for some time on the island. The weather gave promise of a long continuance in its present state, being perfectly clear and serene ; and every evening after sunset, the heavens exhibited the beautiful appearance they had observed on their first arrival, the eastern part of the hemisphere being of a rich purple, and the western of a perfect yellow glow ; the season was likewise warm, without being too hot, and appeared to agree with Fanny, whose health was now somewhat delicate, and excited all Henry's sympathy on her account. As rest and retirement, she assured him, was all she needed to thoroughly confirm her in the sweet expectation she began to entertain of ere long becoming a mother. Henry resolved to remove into a private establishment. Fanny concurring in his wishes on this subject, he sought from among the different villas on the island one about which there was nothing great or magnificent, but admirably contrived for a hot climate, where shade is the most desirable object. There was some pleasant grounds attached to this villa, containing some beautiful fruit trees, among which the Maltese orange was at once the most beautiful to look upon, and the most delicious to eat. The villa was prettily situated, commanding a pleasant view of the harbour, and affording them likewise an opportunity of observing, that one half of Mount Etna was clearly discernible from their present abode; the thundering of the mountain, too, they could at times hear with the greatest distinctness. The garden in front of the villa was bordered on each side by a row of exceedingly large Armenian aloes; the flower stems of these noble plants being twenty and thirty feet high, and were covered with blossom from top to bottom, forming a beautiful kind of pyramid, the pedestal of which being the fine spreading leaves of the plant. These, together with some beautiful flowering shrubs, they learnt were esteemed the greatest curiosities of the vegetable tribe that the fertile island produced. Everything was speedily arranged, and in a few days after their arrival at Valetta, they removed to the pleasant villa which for the time they called their home. And here, in this sweet retreat, blest in each other's love, surrounded by the fair and beautiful, resting themselves after the fatigue of travelling and giving to each other, every day, fresh proof of the fond devotion which animated their breasts, and looking forward with anticipated delight to the arrival of the time when their joy would be enhanced by the birth of a child, the only link wanting to render their happiness complete—we will for the present leave them, and give our attention for a time to another portion of our dramatic personages, whom we fear we have too long neglected.

CHAPTER XLII.

When the white cliffs of England are fading to view,
    And objects grow dim on her shore;
When the waters around thee, shall deepen their blue,
    And the parting of friendships are o'er:
When the wind woos the sails that shall bear thee along,
    Far away from the land of thy birth;
When sad silence usurps the gay place of her song,
    And sorrow is seen 'stead of mirth:
When those by thy side may affect a glad smile,
    While for sorrow their hearts are in tone;
Like the sunshine of April, it may dazzle awhile,
    But when past—thou wilt think of thy home.

Love is poetically described as the highest and most enobling of human passions. If this be true, and no one can doubt that it is so, we must also allow that it is omnipotent mastering all other passions revealing the true temper and disposition of all who are under its influence; for according to the different operations of love in our bosoms, we are furious or tame, compassionate or revengeful, animated with hope, or tortured with despair. By love, the proudest and most arbitrary of men are converted into abject slaves—by love, those who have hitherto had the meanest opinion of their own imaginative and creative powers are inspired with towering ideas, and exalted aspirations. Love leads all ranks—does away with all its distinctions, and makes those who swelled high with their own self-importance, humble and postrate at the feet of the object who has inspired the first emotions of love within their breast. Love can even thaw the icy heart of the miser, and cause him to throw about his wild profusion, utterly regardless of his cherished and worshipped gold. Love is certainly productive of the greatest happiness in life, if the individuals in whom it is comprised be capable of keeping alive the fire from which it proceeds; for if that fire be suffered to go out, it can never be relighted. But this precious boon, intended for the greatest solace of our lives, to counteract the many ills and cares to which we are all exposed, is frequently, more frequently, turned to gall and wormwood; and instead of confirming our happiness, sealing our misery and despair. The love Jane Clarance had felt for Henry Fergusson made up by its constant truth and perfect confidence, what it might appear to some to have wanted in warm and self-devotion; she had refused, in the first instance, to unite her destiny with that of her lover's, resisting all his importunities and most pressing entreaties to become his wife, before his departure to the metropolis; she had acted from a feeling of integrity, and possessed sufficient strength of mind to remain firm to the resolve, not to quit her parents so long as they required her care, never doubting that at some future period her filial duty would be rewarded by a life of happiness with him to whom she was so fondly attached, that she resolved never to become a burden upon his slender resources. We commenced this chapter, by remarking that love affects every individual according to their different tempers and disposition; and thus Jane, ever kind and gentle, considerate of others rather than herself, wept in secret the falsehood of her lover, seldom speaking of the grief she nursed in the inmost recesses of her bosom, unless when at times she would occasionally open her heart to her friend and sister. Clara and Sir Richard had now been at the hall for some weeks. Jane was Clara's constant companion and associate; together they had visited the little church-yard, where the brother of one and the sister of the other rested in eternal repose—death and the grave uniting those whom in life fate had doomed to separation. The weather continued fair and mild for the season; true, autumn was now far advanced, and set its sombre hue on the plants and trees, telling so truly of decay and death; the chilly winds of fast-approaching winter would occasionally rustle the leaves of the trees, casting the searest to the ground; still, save these remote signs of coming winter, all was so fair and beautiful that the season might have been taken for early summer. One unusually warm morning, Clara was seated with her friend at the open casement, whose folding doors led out into the lawn, on which the child of Lucy, now a tall fine boy, pursued his sports with all the hilarity and buoyancy of youth. The two ladies, who employed themselves with the work-table, conversed with each other on some subject which seemed of deep interest to both, to judge from the expression of their countenances.

"You are, then, positively determined, Jane," said Clara, looking up from her work, and regarding the face of her companion steadfastly.

"Yes," replied Jane, endeavouring to assume a cheerful air, while a faint smile passed over her pallid features. "And I am sure you will neither blame my resolution or attempt to shake it. My mother, you know, is far from rich, and even the little she possesses dies with her, and her health has so long declined, that I cannot but anticipate her early decease," and as she gave utterance to these words, the smile vanished and a tear resumed it place. "If," she continued after a moment's hesitation, "if aught can prolong her life, the physician says, it can only be effected by a warmer climate. She is herself willing, nay, anxious to avail herself of the only remedy that can by any possibilty lengthen out the threads of life, and has frequently urged our departure for a warmer clime. The only impediment is now removed: I can comply with her wishes without encroaching upon the liberality of my friends, or risking the possibility of being left entirely friendless and unprotected in a strange land, without perhaps even possessing a sum of money sufficient to enable me to return to my own country."

"The picture you have drawn is frightful," replied Clara, "but it is impossible you could ever be reduced to so fearful an extremity; at least," she added, with a little hesitation, "you wrong me, your first and earliest friend, not less, dear Jane, than you wrong yourself, could you hesitate a moment in receiving from my abundance sufficient fully to provide against so sad a catastrophe."

A slight blush crept over the face of Jane, as she answered with her usual frankness—

"You say right, dear Clara; you are not only my earliest, but my best and truest friend, and if ever I needed your assistance, I would not hesitate or feel

MRS. CLARENCE'S PEEVISH OBJECTIONS TO JANE ON THEIR INTENDED JOURNEY.

myself lowered in my own estimation by receiving it. But the present opportunity of visiting a land, with whose habits and customs we are wholly unacquainted, is so very advantageous, that to allow it to pass without profiting by it, would be on my part worse than folly."

"But Jane," said Clara, deprecatingly, "think well before you positively decide."

"I have thought well," she replied firmly, "and feel sorry that I cannot induce you to regard it in the same light as myself."

"You will have to encounter so much," urged Clara; "there will be so many difficulties to surmount."

"Pardon me," replied her friend, "but I cannot see them; there can surely be no hardship or difficulty in becoming the instructress and guardian of those little girls whose motherless state will give them a double claim to my love and care."

"That is the very thing," returned Clara. "It is an arduous task to perform at once the duties of mother and governess, especially when no kindred feeling claims your sympathy and love."

"My dear Clara," replied Jane, warmly, "what are the ties of kindred or family? I reckon them almost as nothing. Look at we two; could we love each other more, could we feel a deeper or more tender interest in each other's welfare, if we were in truth sisters, and the same blood circulated in our veins, than we do now that we have no tie of birth and can claim no other kindred than the warm sympathy induced by a similarity of taste, feeling, and pursuit?"

"I acknowledge," replied Clara, "that you are in a great measure right; but those children—you know not their temper or disposition; they may be gentle and amiable, but they may be utterly the reverse, stubborn, headstrong, selfwilled, perhaps too foolishly indulged by their widowed father, whom you tell me is so devotedly attached to them as to prohibit for a moment the probability of his ever marrying again."

"Mr. Carlton is a very different person to what he has been represented to me, if he allows his affection for his children to get the better of his judgement," replied Jane; "and as for the temper or disposition of my little charge, I hope to carry with me so good a stock of patience that it will suffice to overcome all obstacles. Consider, too, how very handsome Mr. Carlton has behaved, proposing, even of his own accord, that my dear little nephew should share my care and instruction equally with his own children; my mother, likewise, to be received as a member of his family, her comfort cared for, her wants attended to, in short, to be regarded by the entire establishment as its mistress; in return for all this I have only to take charge of three little girls, for the education of whom I am to receive a most liberal remuneration. Oh! surely Clara you cannot further urge me to renounce so excellent an opportunity of ensuring my mother's comfort and happiness in a foreign land, and my own present and future independence."

"I am afraid my Clara is selfish in her wish to keep you by her side," said Sir Richard Eardley, who had entered unperceived by both ladies, and overheard a portion at least of their conversation. "Come, you must plead guilty to my accusation," he continued, laying his hand kindly on the shoulder of his wife, "or you cannot seriously wish Miss Clarence to refuse so eligible an offer."

"What Richard, and would you counsel her removal?" replied Clara, somewhat reproachfully.

"Yes, my love," said Sir Richard, "and so would you, did you regard it in the same light as myself; it is indeed in every respect so entirely advantageous, that it would be unkind and selfish on our part to wish Miss Clarence to do otherwise than accept it."

"Which I shall do most gratefully," said Jane, with one of her old bright smiles for a moment irradiating her countenance.

Clara would say no more; she was grieved and sorry to lose the companionship of Jane, to whom she was sincerely attached. Yet, when she marked the peaceful and happy look which Jane wore, and which had of late been a stranger to her countenance, she could not regret the determination she had come to, the more especially as it met with the entire approval of Sir Richard, whose opinion she never for a moment questioned.

"As the vessel in which you are about to embark will sail in a few weeks, I fear we shall be forced to resign you sooner than I anticipated," said Sir Richard, addressing Jane, after they had sat for awhile in silence.

"I have no desire to make any stay in London," she replied, "and, therefore, shall not leave here till the latest moment, as I have stipulated that my duties should only commence with the voyage."

"I think you named Malta as the place where Mr. Carlton holds a government appointment?" replied Sir Richard.

"Yes, he has settled there for several years, and only obtained leave of absence in order to visit England, on account of his lady's health, her native air having been strongly recommended by the faculty; but it unfortunately proved of no avail, for she died a short time after her arrival, leaving a family of three little girls, for whom he was anxious to procure a suitable person as governess and guardian, but found great difficulty, on account of the sacrifice it required of a residence in a foreign clime, when it opportunely occurred that the physician (whom I consulted on account of my mother's health, and who strongly recommended a sea voyage, and a warmer climate for the coming winter) was an intimate friend and distant relative of Mr. Carlton's, and through whose instrumentality the present arrangement has been brought about, and for whose services I shall ever feel deeply grateful."

"You have not as yet seen Mr. Carlton," said Clara, "and can scarcely form an opinion of his merit. I hope, indeed, that your expectations may be fully realised."

"I do not doubt it," replied Jane, eagerly. "The gentleman I before mentioned assures me that his character stands high in the estimation of the world at large, but more particularly in the small circle of his private friends, as Mr. Carlton shuns all unnecessary display, living in a quiet and unostentatious manner. His lady, too, to whom he was most fondly attached, is represented as being a most amiable and accomplished woman, devoted to himself and their children so much so, that since her death, he has become in a great measure an altered man, secluding himself entirely from society, and even shunning the company of his children, whose presence reminds him too strongly of his lost wife, to enable him to endure the sight of them for more than a few minutes at a time; but all this, it is fully hoped, will disappear when he returns once more to his active duties."

"Doubtless," replied Sir Richard, "time will heal the wound which now rankles in his breast; and for the sake of his children, he will endeavour to exert himself."

"Oh, yes," returned Jane, whose generous heart induced her to enter warmly into the interest of the motherless little ones. "Oh, yes; and I hope ere long to see him desire the company of children as his greatest solace, and enter again into all their little amusements with the interest he has hitherto done."

"Dear Jane," said Clara, affected by the earnestness of her friend, "I will no longer oppose your departure. I feel that the new interest awakened in your mind will, in a great measure, dissipate your past sorrows, and enable you once more to feel that your existence is not altogether a pain. Yes, my dear Jane," she continued, "we shall some time meet again; then I hope to see the smile of happiness resume its place on your countenance, and the light of joy again revisit your eyes."

"Oh, thank you, dear Clara," replied Jane, rising and warmly embracing her friend; "now I shall go happy—the only drawback to my satisfaction is removed. We shall correspond frequently," she added in a more lively tone, "and you must promise to acquaint me with all that concerns or interests you."

Clara smiled through her tears, as she gave the required promise. She felt acutely at being forced to part from this her only and early friend; yet she too truly appreciated the noble mind and disposition of Jane to attempt further to shake her resolution. She felt, too, assured that change of scene and occupation, more than aught else, would tend to recover the health and spirits of her friend; she would not therefore give way to selfish regret, or mourn the loss she must herself sustain. Jane, pleased and self-satisfied with the line of conduct she had adopted, busied herself in active preparation for their departure. Mrs. Clarence, with all the nervous fretfulness of an invalid, complained loudly of the slightest inconvenience; and frequently deplored the necessity that in a measure compelled their removal.

"I don't know, I am sure," she remarked as she watched the progress of packing actively superintended by her daughter; "I don't know, I am sure, why I should put you to so much trouble on my account—I might just as well have remained here; I can but die."

"Oh, pray do not talk in that manner, my dear mother," replied Jane, raising her face, beaming with smiles, towards the couch on which Mrs. Clarence reclined. "You know," she continued, "that anything I can do for you is always regarded as a pleasure, a sweet and dutiful pleasure."

Mrs. Clarence sighed.

"I know, my dear," she returned, "that you are always very kind and attentive. I have nothing to complain of on that scene, I am sure; but you always seem to think I am finding fault."

"Oh! no mother," replied Jane, eagerly, "nothing, I assure you, was further from my thoughts."

Mrs. Clarence sighed again. Jane resumed her employment, and there was a silence of a few moments, which was again broken by the elder lady.

"I declare," she began (having just glanced at her watch), "you grow quite thoughtless, Jane, not to call it indifference. I ought to have taken my draught full half an hour ago, not that it is of any consequence; I do not suppose it will do me any good."

"My dear mother," returned Jane, "you must excuse me this once; I am, indeed, very sorry, but it really escaped my memory."

"Yes, that is always the way," said Mrs. Clarence, with her usual peevishness; "but, as I said before, it is of no consequence."

"That is not my opinion, very far from it," replied Jane, tendering the glass into which she had poured the medicine

"I am sorry I said any thing about it," returned her mother, "as it seems to annoy you so."

"That I have unintentionally laid myself open to the charge of neglect does annoy me," returned Jane, with her accustomed gentleness; "indeed, I cannot think how I could be so thoughtless, and unmindful of you."

"I am sure I never accused you of neglect, or called you unmindful," said Mrs. Clarence; "but you always misunderstand me, and interpret all I say into fault-finding; a thing to which I have ever been opposed, so much so, that I frequently allow things to pass without remark for fear of being thought peevish or ill-tempered."

"No one, I am sure, could think so of you, dear mamma," replied Jane, tenderly kissing her cheek, as she took back the empty glass; and then anxious to divest her mother's thoughts, and give them a more agreeable turn, she began to talk of their appraoching voyage.

"The weather bids fair to be fine and beautiful, and how pleasant and delightful will be the voyage; we shall have, too, such sweet companions in the little girls that are about to be consigned to my care, that the time will pass away quite cheerfully."

"It may be as you say," returned her mother doubtfully; "but I greatly dread that bane to travellers, sickness; and in my weakened state, too, I really think I should be totally unable to withstand its effects; and then to die at sea would be dreadful in the extreme. Mind, Jane," she continued, with more animation than she had hitherto manifested, "if it should happen thus, do not allow me to be thrown overboard. I am sure I could never die easy if I thought it possible you would permit such a thing."

"Oh, pray do not give way to such gloomy forebodings," replied Jane; "I declare, dear mamma, that you make me quite miserable, in the anticipations of a voyage I have hitherto regarded with the greatest delight. I thought, indeed, that it would greatly tend to restorate your health, or I would never have consented to undertake it."

"In the event of my death," returned Mrs. Clarence, musingly, "it will be a great thing for you to be under the protection of such a man as Mr. Carlton; and having secured to you his interest and influence, will ever be to me a source of the greatest satisfaction. I would not, therefore, mar your future prospects by refusing to undertake this voyage; no, not even were I certain of its bad effects hastening my death;" and Mrs. Clarence smiled complacently.

It is strange what facility some persons possess of actually persuading themselves, and endeavouring to persuade others, that everything they undertake is done, not for their own good, but for the good of others. This was one peculiar characteristic in the mind of Mrs. Clarence; she regarded herself as a continual martyr to her own anxiety to benefit her "darling Jane," for thus she ever spoke of her; she cared not for herself—it was of little importance, as she remarked to Clara, who called to bid her farewell—very little importance what became of her; but for her darling Jane, she was willing to make every sacrifice; and to procure her the countenance of a man of such high-standing in the world as Mr. Carlton, she would even expose herself to the inconvenience and danger of a long sea voyage; although, in her weakened state, it was impossible to tell what might be the consequence of such temerity; at her time of life, too, it was exceeding painful to be forced to quit your native land and the companionship of old and esteemed friends, and embark on an expedition which was fraught with perils; and for no less would she ever have been induced thus to act; but the welfare—possibly the future happiness—of her darling Jane required the sacrifice, and she was therefore ready and willing to make it.

"But, my dear madam," urged Clara, who had listened with great astonishment to these remarks, "if I recollect right, your physician strongly recommended a sea voyage as being the most probable means of reinstating your health; can it be that I am mistaken?"

"Not in supposing that my physician strongly recommended this voyage, but he also wished to procure the services of Jane on behalf of Mr. Carlton."

"Then I am to infer that the voyage was only recommended as an inducement for Jane to accept of the situation Mr. Carlton was desirous to have filled in his establishment?"

"I should not like Jane to know this, of course," replied Mrs. Clarence; "but that is my own impression."

Clara was sensible enough to take this in the right light; she saw through the selfish littleness of Mrs. Clarence's character, and in proportion as she sunk in her estimation, Jane rose still higher; indeed, she could scarcely find words sufficiently to commend the noble and exalted character of her friend, rising superior to her own sorrows and anxieties, in order to alleviate the self-created sorrows of her mother, and if possible mitigate the virulence of her disease, and ward off from her the approach of death, casting aside all selfish feelings, and devoting herself entirely to the welfare and happiness of her parent. Jane was, indeed, no shining star in the hemisphere of fashion; no admiring crowds bent the knee to worship at the shrine of her beauty and talents; no voices even applauded her virtues, or encouraged her to persevere; and yet she was happy, blest with the encouragement of that "small still voice within," which, if it speaks approval, we need fear nothing, though all the world denounce us and frown upon our actions. It was this that enabled Jane to bear patiently with her mother's continued ill-temper, to pursuade with words of gentleness and love that sometimes won a smile of approval, even from her invalid and fretful parent. Mrs. Clarence, on the contrary, though satisfied in her own mind that she was a perfect martyr to her parental affection, was far from happy, constantly complaining of her own sufferings, murmuring at the slightest inconvenience, even at the very time she was loudly extolling her own heroism, in being so willing to sacrifice herself for the good of her daughter. Mrs. Clarence was neither happy herself, or allowed, could she by any means prevent, any other person with whom she came in contact to be so; it required, indeed, a vast amout of patience and forbearance on the part of Jane to bear the constant complaining of her mother, not only with gentleness, but with kind words and conciliatory actions; she never, indeed, allowed herself to dwell on this weak point in her parent's character, unless when at times the thought would force itself upon her mind, that Mr. Carlton might not be gifted with the like forbearance, especially as he would not be called upon to exercise it as a bounden duty; and then she would question herself as to whether her services would be deemed equivalent, so as to form a counterbalance in favour of herself, and in consequence of her mother also; at all events, she resolved so entirely to devote herself to his orphan children, as must in a measure secure his good opinion. Yet, there was a difficulty even here. Mrs. Clarence began already to entertain a jealousy as regarded the attention of her daughter.

"I must learn to think for myself now," she remarked one evening, as Jane, thoughtful of her mother's comfort, spread before her the accustomed wine and biscuit. "I must learn to think of all these things myself, as, of course, your time and attention will be given entirely to the Miss Carltons."

"Not so entirely as to exclude my still being able to attend to your little wants," replied Jane. "They will, of course, engross much of my time," she added; "but you, my dear mother, will ever be my first and dearest care: every moment that I can snatch from my young charges will be devoted to you."

"I do not doubt it," replied Mrs. Clarence. "I am sure I never thought of you otherwise than as kind and dutiful. I know I am a great deal of trouble to you; but it may not be for long—that is one comfort."

Jane could scarce reply to these unkind remarks; tears long suppressed swam in her eyes; but she drove back the unwelcome visitants, and smiling kindly on her parent, replied—

"Long—long may you live, my dear mother, to be a source of comfort and happiness to your child."

"Ah! I wish it were possible," returned Mrs. Clarence, with a sigh; "but I know I am a trouble—a burden to every one."

"Not to me, dear mamma," said Jane, eagerly. "Never otherwise than a comfort and happiness to me."

"You are a good girl," replied Mrs. Clarence, something moved by the gentle and tender accents of her child. "You are a good girl, I know. I am sure, indeed, I never thought you otherwise: but you are so apt to mistake me—so much given to think that I am finding fault when it is far from my intention to do so."

Jane knew from experience that it was best to keep silent when her mother addressed her thus; she therefore made no reply till a fitting opportunity arrived for adroitly turning the conversation. The weeks that had intervened previous to their departure for London fled rapidly by. Jane devoted a portion of each day to visiting her friends, from whom she was so soon to part. And now that the time drew near, she felt acutely, and now fully realised, how much she was about to resign. The village (her dear native home, from which she had never strayed) had witnessed the happy meetings of herself and Henry. They had strayed together in its mossy dells, and over its sweet blue hills, giving them a feeling almost of sadness in her eyes, and from which she could not part without a feeling of regret. With a mingled sensation of joy and sorrow, she visited every spot that was endeared to her either by association or from the beauty of its prospect. The little church-yard, where two graves, not far seperate, each covered with the fairest flowers, over which a simple tablet told the name and age of the departed, was a frequent place of resort. By the grave of his dead mother, Jane had taught her child to love and respect her memory, for she would not for worlds allow him to know how deeply and irretrievably that mother had sinned; and thought there were times when her heart swelled with anguish, as the boy inquired for his father, asking if he too were dead, yet] she checked the rising sob, and answered with forced calmness—

"Yes, love, dead; worse than dead to you."

Again and again did she lead the boy to this sacred spot, increasing her visits more and yet more often as the day appointed for their departure drew near; to leave the grave of her sister seemed like parting with her anew; and it was with the utmost difficulty that she concealed her anguish from her mother. To her friend, Lady Eardley, alone she fully opened her heart, and poured out the secret feelings of her breast. Clara fully sympathised with her emotions, and encouraged her to look forward to happier days, when they might again revisit together their favourite spots. Thus the days and weeks flew by, till the day of their departure arrived. Clara had determined, with the consent of Sir Richard, to accompany her friend to London. They accordingly set out, in one of the baronet's private carriages. Mrs. Clarence was, as usual, fretful and complaining, which, perhaps, was at the present time beneficial to Jane, inasmuch as it served to prevent her thoughts dwelling too tenderly on the past, as her undivided attention was given to her mother, who continued, during the entire journey, to manifest so much ill-humour and peevishness, complaining loudly of the fatigue of travelling, and her own delicate health, as to keep Jane in a constant state of uneasiness, and almost made Sir Richard remonstrate with her on the unkindness of her conduct towards one so amiable and deserving as Jane. Clara, too, felt annoyed and vexed with Mrs. Clarence; but for the sake of her friend, bore it patiently, and even lent her aid to sooth her wayward spirit. It is painful to think how frequently the bad temper and discontent of one person may discomfort, and render miserable a whole party, who might otherwise have been happy and comfortable, making sometimes a whole party met for the purpose of enjoyment, and disposed to mirth and relaxation, restless and ill at ease. Such persons are a bane to society, of which they should never form a part, but live in total isolation, where their ill-temper and humours can affect none but themselves; for it is hard indeed that one should disturb the equanimity of the whole, as in the case of Mrs. Clarence, who contrived to render a journey that would otherwise have been pleasant and agreeable, so irksome and uncomfortable, that all were glad and conscious of a feeling of relief when it was terminated. It had been previously arranged that Jane and her mother should remain for the few days previous to their embarkation with Sir Richard and his lady, thus affording Clara an opportunity of enjoying the society of her friend to the last; in consequence, they all alighted at the town residence of the baronet, where Clara vied with Jane in affectionate attention to the comfort of Mrs. Clarence.

"I hope, my dear madam," she said, as she conducted that lady to the apartments prepared for her reception; "I hope you will not scruple to order of the servants anything that you may stand in need of while under this roof; in short, both myself and Sir Richard will feel highly favoured if you make use of this house as though it were your own."

Mrs. Clarence thanked her ladyship for her kind consideration, and assuring her that at present she needed nothing that was not already anticipated. Clara left her and repaired to her own room, where she was shortly afterwards joined by Jane.

"My dear Clara," began that young lady, as soon as she entered the apartments of her friend, "I cannot, I assure you, sufficiently express my deep sense of your kindness;" but she was interrupted by Clara, who, with a bright smile of welcome, invited her to take a seat by her side, saying at the same time—

"I want to have a little quiet conversation with you, Jane, for I have something to impart that I know will surprise, but I hope not vex, you. Do not be alarmed," she continued, seeing that her friend trembled and turned pale, "as my intelligence does not intimately concern you, unless it is through the dead."

" It relates then to my lost sister ?" replied Jane faintly.

" You are right love," said Clara ; " I wished to tell you, because that Water is shortly about to be married to the young lady to whom he was engaged previous to the death of his father, but which engagement he broke, under the full determination of doing justice to your sister."

" The recompense came too late," returned Jane, while a flush of indignation coloured her usually pale cheek.

" This is a subject," said Clara, without heeding her last remark, " that up to the present moment we have mutually avoided ; and believe me I should not have broached it now, if I had not have been solicted by Walter to prefer a request at your hands."

" He is about to be married," said Jane firmly, " and I can ask of Heaven in my faltering prayer to hallow his new connection. I can, as the representative of my dead sister forgive the past, and hope tnat he may find happiness in renewing the ties once so cruelly broken ; it is soon, indeed, to think of another, and convinces me that he cared but little for poor Lucy, as a fleeting twelvemonth scarce has past since she mingled with the living. But enough; you have my permission to tell him that I forgive him as Lucy would have done, and hope that he may yet ,find happiness and peace. Now, my dear Clara, the short time we are together, never again let this subject be renewed."

" But you have not yet heard the favour he desires to crave at your hands," said Clara.

" A favour from me ?" replied Jane, turning paler than before. " Ah! now my conscious heart devines the truth ; he would rob me of the child ; but no! that can never be. My solemn promise was pledged to Lucy on her death-bed, never on any pretext to allow Walter to gain possession of her child ; that promise I hold sacred, so that nothing on earth should force me to yield its guardianship to another, more especially to him."

" You are alarming yourself unnecessarily, I assure you, dear Jane," replied Clara. " Walter has never for a moment so much as hinted at a wish to deprive you of the child ; on the contrary, he has ever expressed his satisfaction, that it was so well provided for under your fostering care. The only favour he wishes to solicit, is one that he has almost a right to claim."

" I am utterly at a loss to conceive what favour he can, by any remote possibility, possess the right to claim from me," said Jane in a clear but dignified tone.

" It is simply this," replied Clara, " that he may be permitted to see and take leave of his child, previous to its quitting England, perhaps for ever."

" It is a favour which I would much rather be excused granting altogether, and can only be induced to do so conditionally," returned Jane with her wanted firmness.

" Name your condition," said Clara, " and I will endeavour to act as mediator.

" In the first place," began Jane, " I cannot admit Walter to an interview with the child, unless it takes place in my presence ; and as it would be painful to me to see him alone, I should prefer the meeting taking place in the presence of us both ; and in the next place Walter must pledge me his word of honour not to make known to the child the near relation he bears towards him. He can represent himself as a friend of his dead mother's, and that may sufficiently account for the interest he may manifest in his welfare."

Clara listened attentively to all that Jane urged, and in reply said she would endeavour to persuade Walter to abide by her conditions. Nothing more was said on the subject for a day or two, when Clara informed her friend that she had communicated with Walter, who was willing to avail himself of the interview on her own conditions, and had appointed the following day for it to take place, if convenient to herself. Jane expressed herself perfectly satisfied with this arrangement; and accordingly Walter was admitted at the time appointed. The meeting was a painful one both to himself and Jane. Clara, too, was affected, as she saw the wondering child clasped for the first, and in all probability, the last time to the heart of his father—that father whom he would henceforth be taught to shun, who did not even now dare to declare his relationship, but must pay the penalty of his own sins, by foregoing for ever the dear delight of rearing his son to manhood, of watching over his infant years,

JANE'S FIRST RECEPTION WITH MR. CARLTON'S CHILDREN.

and instilling those smeet lessons of truth and virtue, which becomes so exclusively the duty of a parent. Walter thought of this, and would have given worlds could he have recalled the past, as he gazed into the deep blue eyes of his little son so wonderingly, and yet so lovingly, upturned to his.

"Dear boy, how strongly he resembles his lost mother," he said, as he laid his hand caressingly on the golden ringlets.

Jane sighed, but she made no reply; indeed, gentle as was her nature, she entertained a feeling of resentment against Walter, which she could not wholly suppress, though she struggled hard to do so; yet the memory of her sister, once so bright and happy, till lured by him to sin, and afterwards left with her helpless infant to suffer the pangs of sorrow and remorse, aggravated by poverty and disgrace—Oh! when she thought of this, she could scarce endure to see the boy resting (with all the fond trusting confidence that forms so sweet a trait in the character of a child ere it has learnt the hard lessons of distrust and deceit) on his bosom, his face fondly upturned towards his own, as he listened to the low musical tones of his voice, little dreaming in his unconscious innocence that those very tones had lured his mother on to sorrow and to death.

CHAPTER XLIII.

The foam of the billow how it gaily rolls on,
   O'er the tremulous ocean's dark-heaving breast,
Adora'd by the smiles of the broad fiery sun,
   As he slowly declines in the bright crimson west.

O'er the dark foaming waters how swiftly it glides,
   As it gildeth the crest of the high curling wave;
The couch of some Naiad, where softly she rides,
   To protect from intrusion the seaman's cold grave:

But how soon is its life's dreamy phantasy o'er;
   Its wild fleeting visions, how swiftly they fly;
For it beats 'gainst the rocks of the rude tow'ring shore,
   And then curls in dark vapour to fade in the sky.

THE time had now arrived when Jane must bid adieu to her native land—must take an addition to her already multiplied duties, foreging the sweets of solitude, and the treasured contemplation of the past, to take upon herself the duties of active life. She had willingly undertaking the charge of Mr. Carlton's motherless children, and consequently did not shrink from the anxiety of mind, and fatigue of body, the guardianship of such young children would naturally impose upon her; but now that the time had arrived for her introduction to the family of Mr. Carlton, and the consequent commencement of her duties, she was conscious of a feeling of deep anxiety, which had never before given her uneasiness. Should she find in him a cold stern man of the world, wrapped in his own self-importance, and regarding the governess of his children in the light of a menial, whom he could not condescend to notice, unless it were to find fault, or point out errors; should this be the true picture of the man (whom, up to this moment, she had loved to endow with the noblest and best of qualities) she might find her situation more irksome and painful than she had hitherto anticipated. Such thoughts as these pressed heavily on the mind of poor Jane, as, accompanied by her mother and Clara, she proceeded in one of Sir Richard's carriages to the abode of Mr. Carlton; so deep, indeed, was her anxiety, to find favour in the eyes of that gentleman, to obtain a kind reception both for her mother and herself, that when she alighted from the carriage she trembled with apprehension, and lost, for the time-being, her usual quiet self-possession. At the hall door, they were met by a servant in plain mourning livery, who conducted them up stairs into a large and well-furnished library. There was a table in the middle of the room literally covered with papers, at which was seated a gentleman of fine and commanding exterior. He rose to meet them on their entrance, and slightly apologising for the confusion which the apartment betrayed, begged them to be seated; and then turning to Mrs. Clarence, kindly inquired after her health, hoped that she would find the voyage beneficial, assuring her that he doubted not for an instant that the climate of Malta would agree with her constitution, representing it as warm and beautiful in the extreme. All this time Jane had leisure to observe the manners and appearance of Mr. Carlton, without herself attracting attention; there was a quiet grace—a gentle and unobtrusive air about his person and address that at once pleased her, and set her mind at ease. He was as we have already observed, tall, and of commanding exterior, and though evidently somewhat past forty, still retained sufficient youthfulness to counterbalance the effect of a dark complexion, evidently rendered more bronzed by frequent exposure to the sun and air; his eyes were large, dark, and expressive; and though an occasional grey hair might be found, contrasting with the glossy blackness of the others, it did not sufficiently detract from his appearance as to prevent him being still styled by many persons a young man. His manners, although that of one who is accustomed to command, seemed yet more remarkable for their propriety and good breeding. A pensive sombre air sat upon his features, for which Jane was at no loss to account, and which seemed far from being their prevailing expression, which an occasionally gleam of playful gaiety, as though struggling to resume its wonted place upon his countenance, fully testified. Jane had sat in an obscure corner of the apartment silently remarking all this, but without heeding much of the conversation that was passing around her, when she was suddenly aroused from her abstractive mood by the voice of Mr. Carlton, as he, for the first time, addressed her by name.

"You will allow me, Miss Clarence," he said, "to tender you my warm thanks for having so readily undertaken the charge of my motherless little ones. I feel that I can, with confidance and satisfaction, entrust them entirely to your care."

Jane answered by assuring him of her deep anxiety to benefit the youthful objects so soon to be entrusted to her charge, and expressing a hope that she might be be permitted to see them.

"With pleasure," replied Mr. Carlton; and ringing the bell, ordered the servant to introduce the children immediately.

In a short time they entered, accompanied by their nurse, a coloured woman, who had come with them from Malta, and whose long and faithful services had rendered her a privileged and favourite servant. The two eldest, aged respectively seven and five, immediately flew to their father, clasping their little arms around his neck, while they affectionately kissed his cheek, while the youngest, a beautiful infant of eight months, clapped her dimpled hands, and stretched out her arms, in vain attempts to gain the envied place upon her father's knee. There was something beautiful and holy in the little group, of which Mr. Carlton formed the centre. The bright happy faces of the children, wholly unconscious of the loss they had thus early sustained, forming a marked contrast to the mournful expression of the father's countenance, as he fondly caressed the little ones with almost maternal tenderness.

"My dear children," he said at length, leading the two eldest to the side of Jane, "this young lady has kindly promised to come and live with you, to devote herself entirely to your happiness, to teach you many things with which you are as yet unacquainted, but which it is necessary for you to know, in order that you may grow up clever and accomplished women. You must, therefore, promise me to be very good and attentive, and always mind everything she says to you; for you must remember, if she is at times forced to chide you, it is entirely for your good. You will promise me this, my children?"

"Oh! yes, dear papa," replied both the children, eagerly.

"And I hope you will soon learn to love me," said Jane, bending down to kiss the fresh rosy cheeks of the little girls.

"I am sure I shall," said Lucy, who, althought the youngest, possessed more self-confidence than her sister, "for you look so kind, and good tempered, that I almost love you now."

"And you will love me, too, will you not?" said Jane, taking the hand of the elder child within both her own. There was a look of confiding tenderness in the soft blue eyes of the little girl, as she raised them timidly to her face; and then, as if satisfied with the effect of her scrutiny, replied—

"Oh! yes; I will love you dearly, as dearly as I used to love mamma, if you will let me," she added, with the timidity that seemed natural to her.

Delighted with having gained so much favour in the good opinion of the elder children, Jane turned toward the infant, anxious likewise to make friends with the little creature.

"I am afraid, Miss," said the nurse, "that she will not be good with you (seeing that Jane stretched out her arms to take it); she has been so little used to strangers, that she will seldom, if ever, go to any one with whom she is not well acquainted."

"Let me try her," replied Jane, gently, "and if she is not good, I will give her back to you immediately."

The nurse replied, by placing the infant in her arms, who, contrary to the expectation of all present, displayed no symptom of dissatisfaction, but, on the contrary, laughed, and seemed well pleased with her new nurse.

"I though we should soon be good friends," said Jane, smiling kindly and affectionately on the child. As she spoke, she caught the eye of Mr. Carlton, lighted up with pleased satisfaction, and her heart was instantly relieved of a weight of anxiety. She felt assured, that by securing the affection of his children, she would possess a passport to his favour, and secure his continued good-will and favour for her mother. Her heart, too, seemed drawn towards these motherless little ones, their happy merry faces contrasting painfully with their mourning dress. The baby especially attracted her love, so joyous, so utterly unconscious of the loss she had sustained, and yet wearing the outward insignia of sorrow; and the little thing, usually so wild and unruly, laid her little face on the bosom of this new friend, and nestling closely to her heart, soon fell into a sweet and gentle slumber.

Ah! sweet unconscious innocent. You have indeed chosen a true and tender resting place, a blest heaven from whence you may fly the cares and trials of life. Oh! rest in peaceful slumbers; nestle closer and yet closer to the affectionate bosom on which you repose—a bosom all tenderness, truth, and puriety—one that will ever shelter thee from the rude storms, and stand in the place of they lost mother.

Jane looked tenderly down upon the little creature sleeping so sweetly and confidingly on her bosom, and felt happier, far happier, than she had done for many a long and dreary weeks. A new path in life was now open to her, one in which (though she must expect to find some cares and trials) she might be useful; and consequently, happy to rear these children in the simplicity of truth and virtue, to impart instruction and mould their pliant minds, seemed a blest and holy task, and to which she inwardly dedicated all her energies, resolving steadfastly and perseveringly to pursue the line of conduct, she marked out as her duty. The visit, which had been somewhat prolonged, was at length brought to a close by Mrs. Clarence rising to take leave. Since the introduction of the children, Jane had devoted herself exclusively to them, while her mother and Lady Eardley conversed with Mr. Carlton.

"It is all arranged, then?" said that gentleman, as he received the parting adieus of his visitor; "yourself and Miss Clarence will join us on board the vessel at Portsmouth the day after to-morrow?"

Mrs. Clarence hastened to assure him that she perfectly understood and concurred in the arrangements; while Jane turned aside to conceal a tear which rose to her eyes at this undoubted confirmation of their speedy departure. The next day was devoted entirely to the society of her friend, whom she was about so soon to leave, perchance to meet no more on earth. Both felt this—yet neither had courage to make the slightest allusion to the subject; on the contrary, each spoke almost with confidence of again meeting in happiness and joy.

"Dear England, noble country !" said Jane—

> " ' From hall and lowly cot,
> A voice speaks forth of happy days
> That may not be forgot.'

No; roam where I may, amid fairer climes and richer scenes, the bright and happy past will remain engraven on my memory for ever. No country will ever be so dear to me as England—pleasant, happy England! How often shall I pine in exile for its sweet shady lanes and bright green fields. Methinks," she added, smiling, "that I shall even sigh for its cloudy skies and ever-varying climate amid the richer beauties of the sunny-south."

"I do not doubt it, my dear Miss Clarence," replied Sir Richard, who entered at this moment; "I have done the like myself. Indeed, there is no land so sweet, so precious to the sensitive and refined mind, as the land of our forefathers—the home of our youth—in whose language we have been first taught to lisp our thoughts, and express the first pure feelings of our breast. There is a pride of birth inseparable from a properly constituted mind; so that each one loves the land of his nativity dearer, far dearer, than all others—indeed, I can scarce believe

> ' There breathes a man with soul so dead,
> Who never to himself hath said—
> This is my own, my native land.' "

"And in the hour of parting from any cherished or beloved object," said Clara, " we feel more than at any other period how much we have loved them ; we are even surprised at the intensity of our own feelings—not knowing how much we clung to the object from which we are about to be separated. It is thus that I feel now, dear Jane; I cannot endure the thought that the waves are so soon about to bear you from my sight."

"We must not, in this our last evening together," replied Jane, " dwell upon painful topics, or sadden the pleasure of our meeting with vain regret; for though we are so soon about to part, we shall still enjoy the sweets of intercourse by constant epistolatory correspondence. I shall duly record the events of each day for your perusal; and in reading your letters shall rejoice to hear that you are happy—and weep if sorrow should ever enter your home."

Thus passed the last evening of Jane's stay in England; her mother had early retired, to prepare herself for the fatigue of the morrow, and she consequently was enabled to enjoy the sweets of unrestrained intercourse with her friend.

"My dear Jane," said Clara, emphatically, when, after a lengthened converse, the two friends were about to separate for the night, " you will grant me one promise before we separate ; it is this—if the time should ever come (sooner or later it matters not), but if the time ever should come, that my love, my services, my purse, can in any way, however remote, assist or befriend you, you will not hesitate to claim them as part of a debt of gratitude which has long been due ?"

"I will gladly, proudly apply to you," said Jane, firmly, " if the hour of sorrow arrives, and places me in need of your friendly services, either on my own or my mother's account. And now, dear love, farewell—a long and last farewell !" And Jane, no longer able to restrain her tears, sobbed on the bosom of her friend.

The following day was one of much bustle and anxiety. Jane busied herself apart from all others till the moment of departure came, as she wished to conceal how much she felt, and could not even command her feelings in the presence of her mother. Lady Eardley sympathised with her friend, and for that day took her place in attendance upon her parent. Mrs. Clarence was by no means pleased at this apparent neglect on the part of Jane; and when she came forth to join her in the dining-room (where lunch was spread), pale and agitated, loudly exclaimed against her unkindness.

"I am sure I have not seen you the whole morning, Jane," she began as soon as she entered; "at the very time, too, when I most required you services, feeling, as I do, low-spirited and nervous in the extreme; to be sure, Lady Eardley has been kind enough to see that I wanted for no care or attention, but still I cannot help feeling hurt that you should so entirely have neglected me."

"Forgive me, dear mamma, this once," replied Jane. "I have not been quite well myself, or I should not have left you so much alone; but it shall not happen again."

"Well, you need not say any more about it," replied Mrs. Clarence; "you always seem to think I am finding fault with you, and I am sure I cannot bear to do so; indeed, I have always said that you were kind and dutiful in the extreme, and yet you always think me discontented, and pleased to have an opportunity to complain and show my dissatisfaction."

Mrs. Clarence was here fortunately interrupted by the announcement of Sir Richard that it was quite time they should start for Portsmouth; and in a few minutes they were all seated in the carriage. Mrs. Clarence's ill-temper found vent during the drive in constant complaints; first, of her own bodily weakness, and secondly of the sacrifice she was about to make in exilling herself from her native land. Lady Eardley was no longer able to attempt the task of reconciling her to herself; but Jane (from whom all trace of agitation had disappeared), endeavoured, by every means in her power, to divert her mother's thoughts, and if possible atone for her apparent neglect in the morning. In this manner the time passed till they reached Portsmouth. Jane, with an almost bursting heart, hurried on deck, accompanied by her friend, Lady Eardley. Mrs. Clarence followed, leaning on the arm of Sir Richard. Mr. Carlton received them on deck with his infant children. There was but little time for parting adieus; a few tender and consoling words passed between Jane and Clara, and some polite ones on the part of her mother and Sir Richard, and they were gone; the ship speedily weighed achor, the large sails flapped lazily in the wind, the sailors gave their parting shout, and the broad vessel moved slowly and gracefully through the waters. Mrs. Clarence had hastened to her cabin immediately after the departure of Sir Richard and his lady, where, after seeing her comfortably provided for, Jane left her and returned to the deck. And as the tall ship slowly moved along, she espied her friend Clara and her husband affectionately watching its movements; she waved her handkerchief in token of recognition, which greeting was returned by Clara; the gallant vessel continued its course, and the two friend were parted, perhaps for ever. A melancholy stole over the mind of Jane, as she stood leaning over the side of the ship, watching the waves as they dashed against its sides, so strangely resembling human hopes, which rise bright and glistening with the fairest promises, but are presently dashed to pieces against the rocks of despair. There was something, too, in the ceaseless roar of the ocean, which harmonised with her present feelings; and the fast receding shore in the distance reminded her of all she had left behind; and as she thought of the many hours she spent with him she so dearly loved, and of his subsequent falsehood and deceit, she repeated to herself the following lines—

"Bounding billows, cease thy motion,
　Bear me not so swiftly o'er;
Cease thy roaring, foaming ocean,
　I will trust thy waves no more.

Fare-thee-well ungrateful rover,
　Welcome now a foreign shore;
Now the breezes waft me over—
　Now we part to meet no more."

So filled was Jane with her own sad thoughts, that she did not observe that the little timid Amelia was standing close beside her, till the child ventured to place her tiny hand, within her own. Jane instantly started and turned round.

"What, you here, my love?" she said kindly.

"Yes; I have been watching you a long time," replied the child.

"Indeed, I was not aware of your presence," said Jane. " Why did you not speak to me, my love."

" I did not like to disturb you," returned the child : " but you looked so dull that it made me feel dull too ; and when I told this to Lucy, she said perhaps you were leaving some dear kind friend in England on purpose to go to Malta with us, that you might teach us how to become clever and accomplished like yourself; and when I told papa what Lucy thought, he said so too, and told us to be sure and be very kind to you and mind everything you said to us, and to love you as we did our own dear mamma, that is dead and gone to Heaven."

" It is indeed very kind of your papa," replied Jane ; " and I do not doubt that we shall be very happy together."

" But," began Amelia with the frank confidence that is so peculiar to children, " will you tell me, dear Miss Clarence, if you have any one in England whom you are sorry to leave ?"

" Yes, Amelia," replied Jane, " I have a dear, I may say an only friend, whom I have loved almost from childhood ; and it has grieved me much to be forced to part with her ; still, it will not prevent me being happy—I hope and expect, very happy—with you and your dear little sisters."

" Then it was the thought of that dear friend which made you look so sad just now, my dear Miss Clarence ?" said the child.

" No, Amelia, it was not that, but other and still more painful thoughts, such, my child, as you cannot at present understand. When you are older, I will tell you my little history ; it may serve to warn you from an error which proved fatal to myself."

The attentive child listened as she spoke, and seemed gratified at the confidence reposed in her. At this moment their conversation was interrupted by a summons to dinner. Jane instantly repaired to her mother, whom she conducted to the dining-room ; and seating herself by her side, carefully attended to all her little wants, supplying her plate from time to time with her own hand from her favourite dishes. Yet, in spite of all this attention, Mrs. Clarence was out of temper and dissatisfied, continually declaring she could not eat a morsel of anything, and yet as continually emptying her plate of the delicacies her daughter so kindly piled upon it. Jane, forgetful of herself, thought only of the happiness and comfort of her mother, whom she strove by every means in her power to enliven and amuse ; and though Mrs. Clarence seemed wholly insensible of her kindness, and marked not the gentle attentions of her daughter, there was an eye that saw it all, and whose heart was touched by her tender patience and forbearance. Mr. Carlton, not having recovered from the effects of his recent deprivation, had conceived a dislike for mixed society, and, in consequence, had engaged a handsome private cabin for the sole use of himself and family ; thus there were no strangers present, and while affecting to be busily engaged with the duties of the table, Mr. Carlton had ample opportunity of observing, unheeded, the kind and gentle manners of Jane. He marked her earnest, though unostentatious, anxiety for her mother's comfort, her kind and conciliatory manners, and, above all, the evident sweetness of her disposition, and amiability of her temper; and felt thankful that fortune had so far favoured him as to enable him to secure such an apt preceptress for his motherless little ones—to place so bright an example daily before their eyes. Dinner ended, according to his invariable custom, the children were introduced. They came on this occasion, for the first time, accompanied by little Walter, who had already succeeded in making himself agreeable to his new associates. Immediately on their entrance, Jane arose and took the infant from its nurse's arms, and, carrying it to the side of her mother's chair, endeavoured to interest her in its little gambols. In the mean-

time, Mr. Carlton called Walter to his side; and the boy, nothing abashed, but
on the contrary, proud of the notice, readily entered into conversation with him.
Mr. Carlton, pleased with the quick perception and cultivated mind of the
child, inquired of Mrs. Clarence if he had as yet studied under any master;
to which she hastened to reply in the negative, assuring him that Jane had been
his sole instructress.

"Which greatly redounds to your honour, Miss Clarence," returned
the gentleman, addressing her daughter; "your nephew is one of the most
sensible and intelligent boys of his age I have ever met with, either at home or
abroad."

Jane smiled and slightly blushed, as she replied—

"But trifling credit is due to myself, as the child's natural love for literature
led him to pursue as an amusement studies which, in most cases, are only
acquired as a positive duty."

"Indeed, you greatly interest me," returned Mr. Carlton. "You and I,
my little friend, must become better acquainted," he added, laying his
hand kindly on the golden locks of Walter; "and if you still preserve
the same love for learning which you have hitherto manifested, nothing shall
be wanting to enable you to prosecute your favourite studies."

Although these words were ostensibly addressed to the boy, the eyes of Mr.
Carlton rested on Jane as he spoke; and he was pleased to observe that her
mild features became radiant with delight, as she thanked him with a grateful
smile for the interest he so kindly manifested in one so dear to her. The
weather was fine and warm; scarce a cloud floated over the blue expanse of
Heaven—scarce a ripple agitated the surface of the calm and beautiful ocean—
the light breeze but gently kissed the snowy sails, which wooed its fickle embrace, and then pressed rapidly onward and was gone. Jane gazed and gazed
again at the broad expanse of sea which surrounded her, wrapt in wonder and
awe at the still soft beauty of the scene. There was a tranquil gladness in
her heart, which whispered her that—after the storm of sorrow had passed
away, and the falsehood of him she once so fondly loved no more possessed
the power to wound her heart, and rob her of her peace—she might hope to
find happiness, that sweet and quiet happiness she was conscious of so ardently
desiring, in the bosom of the family with whom she was now so closely associated. The thought, too, of rendering herself a kind and tender monitor, a
wise and affectionate friend, to those whom death had deprived of their
natural protector, and thus thrown upon the good-feeling and right principle
of an entire stranger for early guidance and gentle precept, filled her heart with
joy; all things seemed conspiring to render her happy and content. Mr.
Carlton's evident and undisguised interest in her darling nephew—the treasured
gift of a departed sister—the fondness the children began strongly to manifest
towards herself—the improvement which was rapidly taking place in her
mother's health—all swelled the tide of gladness which filled her breast, and
gushed from her eyes in welcome tears. As day after day glided peacefully and
rapidly away, the wound her heart had received began gradually to heal, and
the flood of grief to stem its torrents before the hand of time. Again her smile
began to return, and, like the sunshine after rain, beam forth afresh more
pleasantly upon the dewy plain; and though Henry Furgusson was not less
thought of, he was regarded more in the light of an affectionate and absent
brother than he had hitherto been; as such it was no sin to think of him,
and as such she could hope for and pray for his happiness. She even began to
think that her love was entirely conquered—that she could look forward without sorrow, and backward without regret, and to believe that the separation was
ordained for some wise and good purpose, and to which she would willingly
subscribe. But here, alas! Jane knew not her own heart, or the depth of her
affection. It is true, she sorrowed not; but her love was not dead—it only
slumbered. A breath, a touch would suffice to rekindle the fading embers, and bid
them blaze forth brightly again; but Jane knew it not; neither was she aware

that she was fast hastening towards the very spot where Henry and his young wife had taken up their temporary abode. No; she conceived they had long since returned from their wedding tour, and had most probably settled in London, on account of Henry's profession; for though no longer forced to pursue it as a livelihood, she judged him right in supposing he would still

LADY EARDLEY'S PENANCE FOR HER SON'S WELFARE.

desire to prosecute for fame that bright phantom which had so long and so successfully eluded his grasp. Her mind was consequently at ease. She feared not the future, or entertained the slightest expectation of again seeing her half-forgotten lover; time will heal the deepest wounds, and Jane's, as we have said, had lost much of its former bitterness. The infant, who from the first had manifested a strong predilection in her favour, grew more and more attached to her each day; and often would she pace the deck of the vessel, carrying the baby in her arms (for whom she felt an almost maternal tenderness), and listening to the soft music of the waves, which seemed to lull her sorrows to eternal repose; musing, as she walked, on the mutability of human hopes, and the perishable state of human affections. Oh! never again would she murmur to herself at such times, "Will I put my trust in man, or rest for happiness on his false delusive words—words which, when spoken, mean nothing? Why, then, should I have relied on the promises of one whom I only loved too well? Oh! never again will I trust his plighted vows. Alas! I know their worth. Man's faith to woman is trifling, dying upon the very breath that gave it birth. Yet I remember hours of quiet gladness, when, if his heart had truth, it spoke it then; when thoughts would sometimes take a tone of sadness, and then unconsciously grow glad again;—can he forget them?" Here she checked herself; she felt that she was treading on dangerous ground; her heart was pure and honest, and she felt she would rather be forgotten, than aught of sad though vain regret should lead him, now that he was irrevocably another's, to bestow even one stray thought on her; she would rather, ay, a thousand times rather, be forgotten, and know him entirely devoted to the woman of his choice, to be enabled to think of him as making amends, by his honourable and upright conduct, for his early falsehood and duplicity to herself. And now she reaped the rich harvest she had herself sown in sorrow and in tears. Now she began to eat of the sweet fruits of obedience and uncomplaining tenderness, for her heart (the seat of every noble and tender virtue) experienced the peace she had so long sighed for in vain. Her mother's improving health removed, in a great measure, her only source of anxiety, and the duties appertaining to her situation prevented the slightest weariness or approach to ennui during their long and, in some respects, tedious voyage. Mr. Carlton likewise appeared in better health and spirits than on their first embarkation. He would frequently enter the little cabin which Jane had set apart for the youthful studies of the little charges assigned her, and, begging her not to disturb herself, listen attentively to the course of instruction she was imparting to his offspring; little Filias (such was the baby's name) frequently made one of the number. On these occasions, nestling lovingly on the bosom of Jane, she would rest for hours, in undisturbed repose. Sometimes Mr. Carlton would suggest that the infant should be consigned to its nurse, but the little one would cling so entreatingly to her new friend, and which, seconded by a gentle remonstrance on the part of Jane against her removal, never failed to draw a willing acquaintance from her father. Mrs. Clarence was not only improved, but (though still at times fretful and complaining) never felt herself more happy or contented in her life. Mr. Carlton was most assiduous in his attention to her comfort, even evincing an anxiety on her account which almost rivalled that of her daughter. At dinner she was the first attended to; the richest delicacies was heaped upon her plate; such a thing was ordered because he thought it would be pleasing to Mrs. Clarence, or another countermanded because she had expressed a dislike towards it; the servants were desired to do her bidding in everything; and, in short, Mrs. Clarence was entire mistress of the household. For any or all of these, the grateful smile of Jane seemed a full and sweet reward; but whenever she attempted to express her gratitude, he stopped her immediately.

"My dear young lady," he would say, "not a syllable, not a word; we are in every sense of the word the obliged party. My children owe you much. Let me, if possible, repay at least a portion of the debt we are still contracting."

Thus silenced, Jane could only show her gratitude by her still more devoted and unceasing attention to the children, whom she thus early taught herself to love, and who repaid her affection with full interest. Thus, the time past sweetly on, and the gallant vessel rapidly neared the shores of Malta, where new and unlooked-for events were about to befal her, and for which she was perhaps preparing, during this sweet and tranquil voyage—a portion of her life to which in after years she ever looked back to with a feeling of calm and pleased satisfaction. But her life was not destined thus early to reach the haven of happiness; she was doomed to be again tried by affliction—cast down by sorrow to the very verge of despair. She needed an interval of quiet repose to prepare her for the scenes of active life in which she was destined to become an actor, and to encounter the storm of sorrow which was yet to burst over her devoted head. This interval she was now enjoying, indulging in bright day-dreams for the coming future, and happily unconscious of the painful vicissitudes which, as yet, cast no shadows before them.

CHAPTER XLIV.

One only thought, one lingering beam,
Now broke across his dizzy dream
Of pain and weariness—t'was she,
His heart's pure planet, shining yet
Above the waste of memory,
When all life's other lights were set.
And never to his mind before
Her image such enchantment wore ;
It seemed as if each thought that stain'd,
Each fear that chilled their loves, was past,
And not one cloud of earth remain'd
Between him and her glory cast.

WALTER EARDLEY had seen his boy, the child of his departed Lucy, for, as he fully believed, the last time in his life ; the sea would soon roll between them, and then every vestige of she he had loved, and yet so cruelly wronged, would be lost for ever. It was strange how fondly his heart clung to this child, how warmly he responded to the parental tenderness which at one period seemed closed for ever in his breast; how he would have parted with all else, had it been possible, rather than with this child ; would have made any and every sacrifice to be permitted to keep the boy near him; but, no ! he was not even allowed to see him, save in the presence of Jane, as though his very company might prove baneful or injurious to his future peace. When he thought of this, his pride was wounded, and for the time he was sensible of nourishing a feeling of resentment against the gentle and unoffending Jane ; but this quickly past away ; he was too generous long to entertain so unkind a feeling. And yet, seeking, if possible, to extenuate his own error, and attribute the blame to anything in preference to himself, he turned once more (with that moodiness which had of late become habitual to him) to the curse which had been pronounced upon his family.

"It is useless to contend," he murmured, half aloud. "It needed but this to complete my misery. The prediction is indeed fearfully working. All who have ever loved me have changed to hate—even my child is forbid to know the relationship which exits between us, and will doubtless be taught to hate and contemn me. Well, it is no matter : there is nothing for it but patient endurance."

"You must not talk thus sadly, my son," said his mother, speaking as she entered the room, having overheard the last words of Walter. "A course is yet open to you, noble and sublime ; you may now devote your talents to the good of your country. Ever, my son, espouse the cause of the suffering and opprest, make the poor man's wrongs your own, and endeavour, by a steadfast adherence to the true and just principles I have striven to inculcate, to wring from the hard hand of the oppressor a moiety of justice and tenderness towards those whom he has long trampelled in the dust."

Lady Eardley's fine expressive features were lighted up with enthusiasm as she gave utterance to these words ; and Walter, to whom she had ever been inexpressibly dear, caught at least some of her enthusiasm, and his handsome features were radiant with joy, as he replied—

"My brother, then, has succeeded in obtaining for me a seat in parliament?"

"Yes, Walter," returned Lady Eardley, "and I am happy in being the bearer of such glad tidings, as also to be the first to wish you joy on the occasion; nor can I hesitate in offering you the counsel which has ever been so well received; be careful then, my son, in what manner you use the power which is intrusted to you; the interest of the suffering man is consigned to your care. Those who have returned you for this borough, consist chiefly of the inhabitants of your own native villages. To use their own words, they have fearlessly placed their interest in your hand, nothing doubting that you will as fearlessly espouse their cause. Through you they will seek redress and protection. Oh! never let them seek it there in vain. Rather than allow their cause to suffer, freely resign all things else, if even your own personal comfort; ay, even if your own happiness must be the sacrifice."

She ceased speaking, but her face glowed with excitement. Walter, too, was fired with animation as he replied—

"My dearest mother, carefully, oh! how carefully, will I treasure your counsel in my breast, and ever seek guidance from one who has for so many years espoused the cause of the suffering masses."

"My dearest Walter," said Lady Eardley, while the excitement, which had lent a bright yet transient glow to fine features, subsided, leaving her unusually pale and wan, so that even a sickly pallor overspread her countenance; "my dearest Walter, what has been, can, alas! be no more. I have endeavoured, as you observe, to use the talents which have been entrusted to me, for the good of my countrymen. In all my writings I have striven, as far as my humble power lay, to improve and strengthen the condition of the working classes; and while I pointed out the errors of those who governed them, I did not foolishly conceal from them their own. This I have done; but my work is now ended. From the hour of your marriage, it is my firm resolve to retire entirely into private life. Seek not," she added warmly, "to alter my determination, or turn me from my purpose; for, once for all, I warn you it would be useless, My resolve—my firm and unalterable resolve—is taken, and not even your persuasions or entreaties could move me."

"But, mother," said Walter, turning towards her, with surprise plainly depicted on his countenance, "you surely do not intend——"

"Ask me not, my son," she replied, "of aught concerning the future. Rest assured that, whatever my plans or intentions may be, they tend towards your ultimate good. I can have no motive, no hidden purpose, save your happiness, your welfare. Think of my words. Remember the counsel I have given you, for most probably the last time, and follow it, so far as I trust it may prove beneficial not to yourself only, but through your instrumentality to others. And now Walter, my dear son, farewell. Persevere in the path of life you have chosen, and do not be lightly beguiled to renounce the trust you have voluntarily taken upon yourself."

"You are surely not about to leave me, perhaps for ever?" said Walter, somewhat awed by the solemnity of his mother's address.

"No, no, not yet, my son; we shall meet again," replied Lady Eardley, in trembling accents. "Seek no explanation, ask no questions, but obey, as far as possible, my last injunctions, and you will yet be happy."

And before he had time to make any reply, she left the apartment as hastily as she had previously entered it. Walter, left once more to his own meditations, his thoughts naturally recurred to his own fast approaching marriage; and now that it was too late to retract, he nervously asked himself if he had done well in offering his hand to the fair and volatile Ada? He mourned, too, deeply that he was about to take upon himself duties which he was powerless to fill, and ties which he had no love to bind; he could not even bring himself to regard Ada with that decided preference which might have made amends for the want of love. No, his heart was like a ruined tower, around which the ivy still clings for support, but with the frail tenement on which it leant for succour, is crushed and trampled to the dust. Thus it was that his morbid imagination pictured the fair and fragile flower he was about to transplant to his own cold and cheerless hearth. Yes; he conceived he should soon see her beauty wither; her gay and buoyant spirit fade, and her heart, like the ivy, crushed and broken beneath the weight of the very temple on which she leant for support. His mother's words, too, re-echoed mournfully in his ears, and sent a boding chill through his heart; she evidently contemplated withdrawing from him at the very moment he felt the greatest need of her guidance and counsel. Left alone to pursue his sad and solitary destiny, how should he be enabled to ward off from Ada the baneful effects of the curse which was pronounced upon his race, and which had, even up to this remote period, been fearfully fulfilled? In the midst of this dingy dream of coming pain and weariness, with which he appeared to feel a morbid satisfaction in torturing himself, one thought of past joy—one gleam of sunshine—broke across his mind. It was evening, and in the midst of his conflicting thoughts, he had, as it were, half mechanically approached the window, and looked out upon the night, which was fair and beautiful; the stars shedding their soft light, and seeming to look down upon the earth, as it were, more in sorrow than in anger. Walter turned his gaze upon these mild planets, sad and silent, as if he sought some mournful secret in their light.

> "And asked them, 'mid that silence, why
> Man, glorious man, alone should die,
> While they, less wonderful than he,
> Shine on through all eternity?"

As he thus gazed—"Oh, that from yonder orbs," he thought, "pure and eternal as they are—

> 'There could to earth some power be brought,
> Some charm with its own essence fraught,
> To make man deathless as a star,
> And open to his vast desires
> A course as boundless and sublime
> As lies before those comet fires,
> That roam and burn throughout all time.'"

While thoughts like these absorbed his mind, firing his breast with that romantic enthusiasm, which formed so peculiar a trait in his character, he was startled from his reverie by the star on which his eyes were particularly rivetted suddenly traversing the sky at a rapid rate, and then wholly disappearing from his view. As this by no means uncommon phenomenon attracted his attention, he could scarce suppress a shudder; it vividly brought back to his memory the image of his departed Lucy. He remembered the last time he had witnessed what is termed a falling star; when full of hope and joy, he had conceived the possibility of inducing her to pardon all the past, and bless him once more with her love, in a nearer and dearer relationship; while, at that precise moment, he was well assured, her spirit was winging its flight to worlds unseen, that star had been perchance her herald from another world. At all events, he associated the phenomenon he had just witnessed with his lost Lucy; and never before had she appeared to his mind so fair and lovely, so gentle and full of trusting confidence; it seemed—

> "As if to charms before so bright,
> New grace from other worlds was given,
> And his soul saw her by the light
> Now breaking o'er itself from heaven."

The thought brought a ray of comfort to his disconsolate breast; it seemed as though a voice spoke near him, and it bore the tone of a loved friend—the only one to whom his heart had ever warmed with that fond affection, which makes this earth so much resemble heaven, whispering of hope and rest in those far off regions, on which his finite gaze could not penetrate, but where he would at length assuredly join her, who was called thus early from the cares and sorrows of existence. This thought animated his mind with renewed ardour; he resolved steadfastly and wisely to pursue the line of conduct his mother had pointed out; and the hope of ameliorating even in the slightest degree the condition of his countrymen, filled his heart with joyful anticipation. In the meantime, after quitting Walter, Lady Eardley repaired to her own apartments, and having secured the door, gave vent to her feelings in that sweet relief to the weary and overcharged mind, tears, without which many a grief " would whisper the o'er-fraught heart, and bid it break." But not long was even the bitterest sorrow permitted this transient indulgence in the mind of Lady Eardley, who—as we have already had occasion to remark—possessed, in an extraordinary degree, the power of controlling her feelings.

"Shall I weakly indulge in vain regret?" she murmured half aloud, as she dashed away the unwelcome moisture from her eyes; "I who have ever prided myself on my power to crush each bitter thought, to trample on each tender feeling, and keep down the remembrance of past happiness? To stay would be destruction, not to myself—that I should little heed—but I must not expose others to the temptations and subsequent anguish I have myself endured. Suffice it, the curse is on our race; would to God it might fall alone on me, or that my sufferings might be received in mitigation of others. It may prove so—I have almost acquired the faith to think it will; but it can only be accomplished by my removal to a distance from these scenes. It would be asking too much of Providence to permit me to view the happiness of my children, from infancy separated from me, freely resigned, because I saw how much the sacrifice was needed; and shall I hesitate now, or shrink from the fate which awaits me, while I foolishly indulge in remorseful regret? No! never shall it be said that I shrank from completing the sacrifice. My children's welfare, their present peace, perchance even their eternal repose, imperatively demand of me to keep aloof from them; to see them no more on earth, unless—but I will not conjure such painful thoughts; they will, they must be happy; and for myself, ' now all is o'er on earth, save some few short years to hide my grief and sorrow deep in my heart's core.' It is well; it is better so; and I will strive to be content. At a distance from them, I may yet, unseen, watch over their happiness, and, if need be, lend my feeble power to stay the shafts of adversity, bareing my own bosom to the storm, if by so doing I can shield them from its baneful effec's. On me, on me alone may sorrow fall, for I can brave its rude blasts, so that my beloved children escape the bitter curse which is the sad heirloom of their family."

Thus it was that the unhappy lady reasoned with herself, and strove to accustom herself to the separation which she contemplated. She undoubtedly possessed a strong mind, and was ever animated by a species of moral courage, which enabled her unflinchingly to perform what she conceived a portion of her duty; still she was not the less susceptible of the finer and more delicate feelings of our nature; of which a strong and ardent attachment to her children formed a most pleasing trait; and at one period she had fondly contemplated spending the remainder of her days in the sweets of social intercourse, and the dear exchange of mutual affection.

> " Severe, then, her task, this blessing to forego,
> And feed her heart with voluntary woe."

Yet this she resolved to do, cost what it might, in the same manner as she would have submitted to the amputation of a limb, had it been necessary. She determined to cut herself off from those ties which were so closely woven round her heart; and having thus determined, she conquered, as it were, by the exertion of some magic power, the feelings which a few moments before seemed well-nigh to obtain the mastery over her. All trace of agitation disappeared from her demeanour—she was again the calm, cold, proud lady; and proceeded to the disposition of her affairs with that perfect equanimity which so peculiarly marked her character. Seated at her desk, she wrote directions for the management of her affairs, as one may do who contemplates an immediate and sudden removal from their present scene of action. While thus employed, no one would have credited it was the same person who a few minutes before had given way to such an extremity of sorrow. No sigh heaved from her breast to tell of recent agitation—no tear-drop whispered of inward, though suppressed, anguish. No; all was calm without, and, to all appearance, the same within; the storm was hushed—the mighty spirit had prevailed over the frail body, and left no trace of its late presence. Thus, when the mother and son again met, she conversed with him with her usual fluency on indifferent topics, making no allusion whatever to the subject which had engrossed them when they last met. Indeed, it was evident to Walter that she purposely avoided that subject; he did not, therefore, allude to it himself on this or any subsequent occasion. It was tacitly understood between them that they must part, yet nothing was said on the subject till a few days prior to the one fixed for the wedding, when Lady Eardley called Walter's observation to the circumstance of her having made over to Ada, as a marriage present, the house and grounds, which were now her own.

"I have been induced to do this," said Lady Eardley, "from a feeling which is strong within me, that the time will come when she may be glad to avail herself of it as a residence; in that case, I can only pray that she may spend her life in the same calm and blest retirement which has for years been so sweet and pleasant to myself."

"But, my dear mother," replied Walter, "why doom yourself to a voluntary exile from your family—those to whom you are so dear, and who would esteem themselves blest if they could in any manner contribute to your happiness?"

"Walter," returned his mother, and he again observed the tremulous, nay, almost convulsive movement of the lip he had remarked on a former occasion, "you must not urge me on this subject; believe me, my son, when I assure you I am actuated by an ardent desire for your welfare in thus resolving to withdraw myself from you. When I am gone (and she seemed to speak the words with difficulty) think of me often as from a distance watching over your happiness, eager to turn aside the poisoned dart, should it threaten to sheathe itself in your breast. Think of me as your firm defender, if foul calumny should dare to assail your character; and as being ever ready to fly to your assistance, should you stand in need of counsel, succour, or reproof."

"But for yourself, my mother," said Walter, in low persuasive tones, "if you should need aught, or all of these, where can you look for it? if cast down by despair, or assailed by sickness and disease, who will assuage your sufferings, or tend your fevered couch? Removed from all who are near and dear to you, how sad will be your lot. Oh, think better, mother, of your determination; or, at least, explain to me this seeming mystery; tell me the need, if need there be, for this painful—this cruel separation."

Again she trembled yet more convulsively than before, as she replied—

"Be satisfied, Walter, to know that there is a need—a strong and powerful need—for this separation, or I would not thus resolutely tear myself from the society of the only beings on earth with whom I can claim affinity, or deny myself the dear delight of witnessing the happiness, I feel assured, must be their portion, and partaking with them of the sweets of constant and reciprocal affection; but it may not—must not be, Walter. To you alone will I confess that I have struggled long with myself, mastering each rebellious feeling, and quelling each anxious thought; how well I have succeeded, let my present composure bear witness."

Walter started, as these words fell from his mother—she, so calm and proud, to confess so much—to declare how deep had been her feelings—how much she had endured ere she had come to the determination to separate herself from her children—at once surprised and grieved him. And now doubly did he regret her fatal resolution; and yet he felt himself wholly powerless to change it; her calm and unmoved demeanour vouched for the truth of her words when she declared her resolution to be unalterable; he sat, therefore, in silent sorrow, inwardly grieving for the separation that was so soon to take place. Lady Eardley was the first to speak. She was now perfectly composed—not a muscle of her countenance moved—not the slightest variation was perceptible in her manner, as she spoke in her usually low musical tones, so strongly resembling those of her son.

"I trust that I have now convinced you, Walter, of the utter fallacy of supposing it possible you could by any remote possibility turn me from my purpose. I must go, Walter—your own and your mother's repose imperatively demand of me this sacrifice, and I am prepared to make it."

"But the motive, mother?" replied Walter; "having imparted to me so much, why should you shrink from telling me all?"

For the first time Lady Eardley betrayed an emotion which alarmed her son; it seemed as though some painful spasm contracted her entire frame, and she scarce suppressed a cry of anguish; but it was only momentarily. Indeed, so soon did it come and go, that Walter half doubted the evidence of his senses; but when she spoke, the low tremulous accents of her voice betrayed how much she had felt.

"I entreat of you, Walter, the short time we are together, never again to speak on this subject if you would respect and esteem your mother. Never—oh, never, seek an explanation of this seeming mystery."

Walter was deeply pained by his mother's words. Eagerly did he bend forward to take her outstretched hand, and press it warmly to his lips.

"My dearest mother," he said, "never will I seek, either by direct or indirect means, to penetrate a mystery you deem it right to conceal from my knowledge; but of this, rest assured, you can never be otherwise than loved, respected, and esteemed by your son, proud to owe his birth to so pure an origin."

"Not one word more on this subject," replied Lady Eardley, with quivering lip and tearful eye. "Not one word more, Walter, if you love me."

Walter was silent; and after a few moments, his parent spoke again.

"I have confided in you, Walter," she began, "all I dare confide to any one. Indeed, I fear I have almost said too much; but enough of this. Your brother, I would say, knows nothing of my intended departure; let him remain in ignorance of my intention; his persuasions, united with yours, though they could not possibly shake my resolve, yet they might—indeed, they would—so deeply affect me, as to make me almost repent of having formed it. And now," she added, rising as she spoke, "our conference is ended. Remember my parting admonition, and seek not to penetrate the motive which at present actuates my conduct, as you would desire to continue to love and respect your mother." And without saying another word she hastily quitted the room, leaving Walter overwhelmed with astonishment and confusion.

There was, doubtless, some painful mystery concerning his parentage which thus drove his mother into a voluntary banishment from home, friends, fortune, all. Yet he was forbid to entertain the slightest hope of ever being able to penetrate it; nor in truth did he wish to do so. No, he would rather it should remain for ever thus shrouded in obscurity; better—far better—that it still remain an impenetrable mystery, than the truth should be discovered only to involve his already over-charged heart in a greater weight of woe. Reconciling himself, therefore, as well as he best could, to the speedy separation of himself and his much-beloved parent, Walter turned his thoughts more than ever to the parliamentary career which was now open to him. His return, as his mother had informed him, was already secured, and he waited only for a few preliminary settlements previous to taking his seat. Full, therefore, of these engrossing cares, Walter had

but little time to devote to A da, who piqued, more and yet more by his apparent coolness and utter indifference to her feelings, notwithstanding her attractive manners
and rare beauty, inwardly resolved to force him to do homage to her charms,
and bow before her absolute sway. There was something peculiarly attractive
rom the very circumstance of its novelty (to such a mind as that possessed by

THE GIPSY FOREWARNS ADA OF HER DESTINY.

Ada), in thus forcing an homage she had hitherto only been induced to receive
b.y a long course of adulation and personal flattery. And yet, though inwardly
nd firmly resolved, spite the warning of her own conscience, to consummate
at the altar the tie that bound her to a man, who openly avowed he entertained
ao warmer feeling for her than a desire to secure her happiness, even were it
necessary at the expense of his own ; yet, as we were about to say, Ada was

not happy. She was no longer the proud exacting beauty, at whose shrine all were eager to bend the willing knee, and to gratify whose lightest caprice many would have sacrificed their all. No light song or gay remark enlivened the home she was about to leave for ever; on the contrary, an unusual gloom hung over the spirits of its inmates. Mr. Herbert mourned in secret that this last stay of his declining years was so soon to be removed from his parental care; and Ada, once so merry and light-hearted, had become by turns moody, capricious, and either extravagantly gay, or utterly the reverse. To be sure, she smiled brightly, and seemed supremely happy, while trying on her wedding-dress and selecting appropriate ornaments; but at other times she would shut herself up in her own apartments, and sob and cry like a spoilt child who has been denied some coveted gift or forbidden pleasure. Thus did this wayward girl, this creature of impulse, resolutely rush upon her fate. She did not love —she well knew that she was likewise not beloved; yet she would neither listen to reason or affection, which might have warned her of her folly, stifling even the voice of conscience, that strove hard to make itself heard; she wilfully pursued her headstrong career, and impetuously hurried on to almost certain destruction. Her love for Percy continued unabated, and she flattered his self-love by constantly asking his advice, and deferring to his opinion on all occasions. His sisters, too, were frequently consulted on household matters, and the slightest information received with apparent gratitude. Poor Mary alone was the only one who was deemed too insignificant to impart either information or advice, and who saw with sorrow the increasing influence Ada was rapidly obtaining over the entire family—an influence she well knew to be baneful to her own peace. Yet, how could she hinder or stop the growing evil was a question she frequently asked herself, and on each occasion felt a greater difficulty in procuring a satisfactory reply. To speak to Percy seriously on the subject, would doubtless have been Mary's wisest course; but who is at all times wise? and Mary had the greatest horror of being thought jealous of Ada's influence over the mind of her husband, and consequently did not so much betray the uneasiness she so deeply felt; besides, the day appointed for Ada's marriage, was rapidly drawing near, and she hoped, till she almost believed, that after she became a wife, her new and more important duties would engross her mind, to the entire exclusion of all meaner things. She would not think so unkindly of her cousin as to suppose it possible she was desirous of awakening in the breast of Percy the love that he had himself avowed to be incapable of starting to renewed life; and, yet, why did Ada make him so constantly her friend and counsellor? It might be that she regarded her lover with a pure sisterly affection, which could in no way interfere with the nearer and dearer claim Mary possessed of his love; but she more than doubted the wisdom of Ada's present line of conduct, which, in her opinion, boded no good either to her own happiness or that of her cousin's.

CHAPTER XLV.

"Bring flowers—bring flowers for the bride to wear,
The snow-white pearl and lily fair;
But keep away the mourning wreath,
Which tells of sorrow, pain, and death."

WOMAN, in her natural purity and lovliness, ere she has mixed with the world, and become in a measure contaminated by its blighting influence and withering associations, is truly said by the poet, to be the choicest object in creation. It is, indeed, a pleasing sight, and one worthy of our liveliest contemplation, to see a woman in the flush of youth and innocence, just stepping out of girlhood, and standing on the threshold of the world, of which she is shortly to become the ornament, or the disgrace ; for it is a true, though, at times, a painful thought, to know that the best and the worst, the most pure and virtuous, and likewise the most debased, have each equally had their time of innocence and glory ; when, full of angel-thoughts and holy desires, their aspirations have arisen from the warmth and purity of their young hearts, bearing the very love of Heaven. There is glory surrounding a woman at this stage of her being, the mere contemplation of which makes the happy heart happier, and the sad one sadder ; throwing the one into momentary forgetfulness of the nature of all perishable and earthly things. and causing it to dream of eternal life and a love that shall never die. And a thousand bright and beautiful fancies take possession of it, picturing the lot of that fair creature, as happiness and peace, all forgetful of the fierce temptations which are waiting to lure her steps astray—of the bright roses, which covet her acceptance, only to wound her with its thorns. While, on the other hand, the sad heart becomes sadder ; for the contemplation inspires sorrow for the perishableness of youth and beauty, and awakens that intense yearning for the purified state of existence, where there shall be no death—where all that is bright and beautiful shall never fade or perish, but the angels' faces, and the sweet voices of glad music, arising from the warm overflowing of a pure and innocent heart, shall exist for ever in the full glory of lovliness ; and divested of the base material part, the enjoyment of this life and light will be the pure and hallowed enjoyment of the soul. Thus fair and beautiful to look upon was Ada, but not thus fair and lovely was her heart; she had past that bright stage of her existence, and had allowed herself to be overpowered, and her brightest qualities warped to wrong through the false adulations, and still falser homage of the many who had bent before the shrine of beauty rather than of worth. From constantly having her own beauty made the theme of praise and fulsome compliment, she learnt to set an undue value on her personal charms, and to neglect those sweeter and more attractive qualities which sheds so bright an halo round the path of youth, making them far more lovely, far more highly admired by those whose love and admiration are worth securing, than all the meretricious charms of mere personal beauty. Oh, let the young think of this —let them remember it ever rests with themselves to secure, by a cultivation of those pure and ennobling virtues, with which they are by nature so richly endowed, and which all may perpetuate if they choose. Why, then, for a moment's gratification, barter those priceless gems, without which the richest beauty fails to please, or the most dazzling complexion to charm the eye of the beholder. Ada, with all her beauty and rich endowments, was far from being happy, notwithstanding she was on the point of marriage with the man whom she had long desired to fascinate, and who possessed the power, if he chose to exert it, of securing her future welfare and independence, perhaps even of restoring to her the sweet feminine virtue of gentleness, and amiability of temper which, coupled with a modest self-distrust, a delicacy of wounding the feelings of others, and a humble sense of her own worth, form the brigtest ornament of the female character; these are the jewels with which she should adorn herself, and which, thank God, require no purchase-money, but are free gifts to all who choose to avail themselves of the bright endowment, and which constantly worn, must win the hearts and love of all with whom she may be brought in contact. Walter knew not that Ada had expended these pure treasures—he regarded her as a capricious child, that had been somewhat spoiled by fortune, yet still retained those inestimable qualities which he, of all men, prized as the most glorious attributes of woman, gentleness and amiability. He saw her at all times to the best advantage. She was mortified by his too evident coolness, and piqued by his indifference into a determination, if possible, to win his love—to force him to acknowledge the potency of her charms, and humbly sue for that love which now thinking entirely his own, only awakened on his part a feeling of pity. The lovers, if such they might be called, seldom met. Walter desired Ada to make what preparations, and give what orders she might think necessary, without in any way appealing to him ; and Ada was nothing loath to take upon herself the entire management of everything, consulting only, as we have seen, the opinion of Percy and his sisters.   A large and handsome establishment was formed in the most fashionable part of London, and which, in its apartments and adornings, rivalled even that of Sir Richard's town mansion.   All this was done, and even an alcove fitted up in precisely the same style as Percy Raymond's, without Walter being even apprised of the circumstance, save by the vast amount of bills which poured in upon him from all quarters; these were immediately discharged with the same indifference he manifested to all things appertaining to his fast approaching marriage.   So far, all was well, but on paying a short visit to his betrothed a few days previous to the one appointed for their nuptials, Ada informed her lover that she had that day received a letter from Sir Richard, kindly offering the use of Eardley Hall, in which to pass their honeymoon. Walter was thoughtful and abstracted, and scarcely understood the purport of her words ; and when she concluded by enquiring if he had any objection to avail himself of his brother's kind proposal, he replied—

"Oh dear, no—certainly not.   You know all places are alike to me."

"Then," returned Ada, " I will answer your brother's letter, and inform him that having resolved to profit by his kindness, we shall proceed to Eardley Hall immediately after the ceremony."

"To where?" asked Walter, starting hastily from his reverie, and regarding Ada with a stedfast and surprised look.

"To Eardley Hall," she repeated ; " did you not understand that your brother had been so polite as to place it entirely at our disposal so long as we chose to make use of it."

"And did you suppose it possible that I could for a moment entertain a thought of visiting that spot—a spot," he continued, raising his voice, "which of all others I would most desire to shun, haunted as it is by dim memories of the past, and the image of one loved and lost for ever.   No, Ada," he added, again sinking his voice to its usual quiet melodious tone, " I shall be happy to accompany you to any other place that you my deem convenient for a short stay from Town, but to Eardley Hall I never go again."

"I am sorry," she said, allowing, for the first time, a little vexation to make itself apparent in her intercourse with Walter, "that you should so resolutely refuse your brother's offer ; he will doubtless think it unkind."

"Let him think what he pleases," he replied ; "it matters but little.   Yet I am surprised that he should suppose it possible that I could ever visit again that once loved and valued spot."

"I have heard so much of the beauty and magnificence of Eardley Hall," returned Ada, petulantly, "that I have conceived a most ardent desire to see it, and judge for myself; indeed I have every reason to believe that your brother was chiefly induced to place it at our disposal, in order to afford me an opportunity of gratifying my (I think not very unreasonable) curiosity."

"I am very much obliged to him," replied Walter, ironically ; "but you may inform him that I can decline to avail myself of his politeness, which, as far as I am concerned, I should much rather had never been offered."

"It is uncommonly vexatious," returned Ada, unwilling to give up the contest. " I thought that for once you would have been willing to resign your own gratification, in order to insure mine, but——"

"There is no such thing as gratification in the matter," interrupted Walter, hastily ; "and it is absolutely weak and childish in the extreme, to swell so minor a circumstance into one of vast importance ; it can signify little to either of us where we may take up our temporary abode, for the time we devote to ruralising, must of necessity be very limited, as parliamentary duties will compel me speedily to return to town.   Of course you will be entire mistress of your own actions, and if you wish to remain for a longer period in retirement, you will be at perfect liberty to do so."

"I do not suppose that it signifies much to you where we may decide to go;

and for that very reason, thought you would not oppose my wishes on the subject, which you know tend to Eardley Hall."

"In one word," said Walter, vexed beyond measure at the perseverance of Ada, in pressing her wishes on his notice, even after he had somewhat peremptorily decided the matter. "In one word, Ada, if you are resolved to visit Eardley Hall you go alone; for never again will I re-visit scenes so painful, yet so dear."

Ada was silenced, but not convinced; she was sorry to have annoyed Walter yet still more sorry not to have obtained her point. Had she gained this much from him, she might have entertained a hope that he was at least not indifferent to her happiness. And like a spoilt child, that casts aside all the glittering toys which are heaped around him, and stretches out his hand to grasp some fancied treasure which he can never hope to obtain, did Ada yearn to touch the heart of Walter—to awake to renewed life the love that was cold and dead within him. Never, in her brightest and happiest days, when Percy fondly loved her, and sought to gratify her lightest wish, had she prized the love of one being then fondly, madly devoted to her so much as one kind word—one tender smile from Walter. To win his love seemed to be her highest aim; not so much from any kind affection or love for him, as from that strange feeling which leads us to prize and value most those things which are rare or difficult to obtain; and this it was that made her determine to win the love of Walter, cost her what it might. Ada was by nature proud and ambitious; she had high aspirations and exalted hopes: she longed to be raised in society, and to have unbounded wealth at her command. She had pictured worlds of happiness, which wealth might procure; and all her fairy dreams seemed now on the point of realisation; for a few days after the foregoing interview with her lover, she received a letter from him, informing her that his mother, by a deed of gift, had made over a large amount of property, to be mutually divided between them. It also conveyed the intelligence of the house and grounds, which was entirely freehold, having been set apart by Lady Eardley for her exclusive benefit. The letter concluded by a few words of more tender import than he usually addressed to her; she read and re-read the letter each time with increased delight, and was thus employed, when a domestic entered, announcing a female, unattended, wished to speak with her; she would disclose her business to no one but Miss Herbert. Ada, vexed by the interruption, rose pettishly from the couch on which she had been reclining, and still retaining Walter's letter in her hand, proceeded to an ante-room, where the female was waiting. Wholly unprepared for this second meeting, Ada started back in utter astonishment, with which there mingled a feeling of horror, as she recognised in her visitor the gipsy, whose warning voice had often rung in her ears, when she would willingly have excluded the boding sounds, but could not, so powerful an impression had they made upon her mind. No wonder, then, that she started, as her eyes fell upon the tall commanding figure of this singular woman, whose very presence seemed to chill her blood, and fill her mind with awe; so that she felt herself incapable of uttering a sound, but stood motionless and statue-like, silently confronting her for some seconds; and then, in the same deep melancholy tone in which her predictions had been last delivered, the gipsy broke the silence by saying—

"The lamp of love which has once gone out, can never be relighted again."

Ada's heart failed her—she gazed for a moment in speechless wonder upon the mysterious being before her; but at length, gaining courage, and calling up the semblance of a smile to her cheek, she said—

"To what circumstance am I indebted for the honour of this visit?"

"You know the cause of my visit," replied the gipsy. "I see it in your eyes —I read your knowledge of it in your convulsive clutching of that folded serpent in your hand."

"Serpent!" exclaimed Ada, looking with an ominous fear upon her hand, in which she held Walter's letter.

"The serpent," re-echoed the gipsy; "how beautiful—how beautiful are its glossy scales, how alluring the aspect it assumes to fascinate its prey. But listen, lady, and beware. The lamb who forsook its kind to mate and play with lions, only repented of its error when preparations were set on foot for its slaughter for the lions' food.''

"This is absurd," replied Ada, endeavouring to rally her drooping spirits; " my time is too important just now to be wasted thus—I cannot, therefore, listen to this folly any longer."

And having thus spoken, she was proceeding out of the room; but her steps were arrested by the gipsy, who, stretching out her hand in a manner at once authoritative and impressive, exclaimed—

"Yet stay one moment—think ere it be too late. I have braved much danger in order to come here, and give you this last warning; it is not now too late—bethink thee, ere thou repliest to that letter in thy hand, of past days —remember the fate of one pure and lovely, but who was lured from her home of innocence and bliss by the very serpent whose smooth and glossy scales now attracts thy heart, and leads thee to unite thyself to a cursed and fated race. But act as thy conscience dictates, and the serpent may yet be crushed. This, lady, is my last warning—let the words ring in your ears, and persuade you to hesitate, ere it is too late; for if once thou enterest in at the golden gates of despair, they will be closed upon thee for ever; and how much thou mayest repent, there will be no returning. Consider, then, whether thou doest well to enter there—lady, remember my words, and beware !" And without waiting for a reply, the gipsy immediately quitted the room; and presently after Ada heard the hall-door closed.

Now that the strange woman, who thus so strangely forewarned her of her destiny, was gone, Ada for the first time felt capable of action; rousing herself from the almost stunning effect of the last words of the gipsy, she rang the bell violently, and summoned her uncle; but when the old gentleman hastened to her apartment, she was so overcome by terror that she sank well-nigh fainting in his arms. Mr. Herbert was alarmed, and wholly unable to account for her emotion till he learnt from the servants that a strange woman had been conversing with her, when he ordered the domestics instantly to go in search of her, and if possible induce her to return; but vain were all their inquiries, and utterly fruitless their search—the gipsy was no where to be found.

When she recovered, Ada informed her uncle of the particulars of the two interviews which had taken place between herself and the mysterious female who had just quitted the house; and Mr. Herbert, instantly concluding that his niece was sought to be made the victim of some of those wandering adventurers who practise upon female credulity, gave orders that if the gipsy ever presumed to call again, she should be driven from the door. Ada, naturally of a light and volatile mind, was easily induced to listen to her uncle's representations concerning the strange woman, and readily gave credence to his words, when he spoke of her as having some ulterior designs upon her purse, in thus endeavouring to arouse her fears, and strove as far as possible to dismiss the subject from her thoughts; and yet it would at times intrude itself upon her notice, and banish peace from her pillow—for it was in the quiet and solitude of her own chamber in the night season that the prediction of the gipsy made the strongest effect upon her mind. At such times she would rise from her couch, and, seating herself at the window, seek to calm her agitated mind by gazing upwards at the myriads of stars shining in all their placid glory upon the sleeping earth. There was one particular star, bright and large, which on these occasions she loved to single from the rest, and amuse her fancy by supposing it might hold some power over her destiny. The more she thought of this, the more the fancy pleased her : and she loved to gaze upon it in the silence of the night, and, either by its dimness or its glory, trace some shadowy imaging forth of her own fate.

Thus time sped on ; all was in readiness for the bridal. Another spot more congenial to the mind of Walter had been fixed upon, in which to spend the first few weeks of their married life—the wedding itself was to be celebrated at the house of the elder Lady Eardley, and which Sir Richard and his young wife had promised to grace with their presence—having purposely remained in town for a much longer period than they had originally intended, in order to be present at the nuptials. Percy, too, with his sisters and Mary, had promised to attend her to the altar—the two unmarried ladies in the capacity of bride's-maids. Thus all was done; the white satin dress, with its rich, yet delicate folds, was placed in readiness for the morning toilet, and close beside hung the bridal veil, with its accompanying wreath of orange blossoms, wearing upon their snow-white bloom the shade of coming years.

> " Once, only once, that wreath is worn—
> Once only may she wear
> The snow-white wreath of orange flowers
> Within her shining hair."

It may be that such thoughts as these flitted through the mind of Ada, as she sat for the last time in her accustomed seat by the window, gazing, as was now her wont, upon the star she had pictured to her mind as being the guider and ruler of her destiny. She was deeply absorbed in her contemplation, and did not therefore observe a shadowy figure flit past her casement, which she had thrown open to its fullest extent, till the well-remembered voice of her late mysterious visitor fell upon her ear. She started and turned pale, as she heard her words, which, though spoken in a low tone, were yet so distinct and clear that they thrilled her very soul; there was likewise a plaintiveness in the tones, which struck mournfully to her heart.

"Lady," said the gipsy, looking upwards to the chamber window, and her tall well proportioned form stood out in the pale moonlight, and cast its lengthened shadow upon the ground, while her thick mass of black hair was thrown back from her face, and hung in sweeping folds over her shoulders, giving her the appearance of an inspired prophetess of old, while one hand drew the cloak over her bosom, and the other was stretched impressively forth."

"Lady," she said, " you have despised my warning. Two paths were open for your footsteps; the one leading to happiness, the other to despair. You have made your choice, to-morrow you pass through the golden gates, and enter the region of despair. Thus the gipsy's prediction will be fulfilled, and your life end in gloom and tears."

And again the gipsy was gone; in vain Ada strove to ascertain in what direction she went; bewildered, speechless with fright and astonishment, she lost for the time all power of motion, and remained rooted to her seat, till she accidentally raised her eyes to the vaulted arch above, and encountered the star which a moment before was shining clear and bright, but now seemed shrouded in vapour, and looked dim and obscure. This comparatively insignificant circumstance, coupled with the warning voice of the gipsy, made so deep and painful an impression upon her mind, that she felt on the verge of fainting, and with difficulty mastered her feelings sufficiently to gain composure to close the window, and hastily seek her couch, where sleep soon weighed her eyelids down, and steeped her senses in forgetfulness. When Ada again opened her eyes, the morning sun shed its cheering influence on all created things, and refreshing sleep had banished from her mind much of the discomposure which had oppressed it some hours before, and she indulged for awhile in pleasing and hopeful meditations on this, the last morning of her maiden life. But she was quickly aroused from these reveries by the glad voices of Mary and Elizabeth Raymond, who, in their capacity of bridesmaids, had come thus early to attire her for the ceremony, and they then were soon deeply engaged in performing the mysteries of the toilet. Ada's love for dress and personal appearance always made this a pleasing occupation; and on this particular morning it is by no means surprising that she should find it unusually interesting, as likewise a work of time and patience. At length all was done, even to the adjustment of the rich lace veil, which reached well nigh to the ground, and the crowning chaplet of orange-flowers, which were weathed around her high and noble brow. The attendants and the domestics retired a short distance to admire their own work, and Ada, blushing at the reflection in the mirror of her own charms, was overpowered by their praise. While thus employed, a gentle tap was heard at the door, and being opened by one of the attendants, a jeweller's parcel was given to Ada, which she pushed towards her bridesmaids, while she hastened to read the note which accompanied it. It was, as the reader may conceive, from Walter, but it contained only a few lines begging her acceptance of the jewellery, as a bridal gift, which he concluded by expressing a hope would meet her approval.

"I must wear these ornaments in compliment to Walter," said Ada, as she laid aside the letter, pained that its contents were not of a warmer character.

"They are pearls, doubtless," said Elizabeth, "and will become you greatly. Shall I open the parcel?"

"By all means," returned Ada, "we have but little time to devote to their adjustment. I wish, indeed, on this occasion, it was not necessary to wear them. I thought our arrangements had been perfect."

"Oh! but pearls are at all times becoming," said Mary, "and these are as a bridal gift. I doubt not, are particulary, so indeed. I quite long to deck you in them."

There is at all times something charming to the mind of young girls in looking at rich jewellery, at all times and under all circumstances, but never perhaps might such a feeling be regarded as more excusable than at the time of which we are speaking. To Elizabeth, as the eldest, was delegated, the task of opening the casket, while her sister peeped over her shoulder, anxious to gain the first glance; the waiting-maid, too, eagerly watched her movements, as conscious of her own importance. Elizabeth deliberately removed the paper in which it was carefully folded, and disclosed a richly embossed casket; the key was quickly fitted to the lock, and the next instant the lid was raised. At the same moment all started back, and a cry of astonishment escaped them. Elizabeth hastily dropped the fatal casket from her hands, and its contents rolled out upon the dressing-table; even Ada's brow contracted, and her cheek turned pale as she looked upon those strange gifts to bestow upon a bride; no white orient pearls were there, no delicate blossoms wherewith to deck the gladsome form of youth and beauty, going forth to pledge her troth, and to take upon herself, from that hour, the solemn and responsible duties of a wife; not either or both of these did the casket contain, but a complete set of mourning ornaments.

"There is some strange mistake, here," said Elizabeth, who was the first to recover from her surprise; "we had better send the parcel back, instanly."

"Decidely," replied Mary, "for of course they cannot be meant for Ada," and she began to hurry the ornaments back into the casket.

"Stay," said Ada, stretching out her hand, and arresting the movement of her friend. "Stay, my determination is taken. I intend to wear these ornaments; let us, therefore, adjust them, for we are losing time, and we have none to spare."

All looked at her with unfeigned astonishment.

"Impossible," said Elizabeth, "it would be worse than folly; do not, I entreat of you, persist in such a strange line of conduct, rendering yourself the subject of general remark. Your dress is perfect, you require no farther ornament; let us therefore hasten down stairs immediately."

"Had these ornaments been pearls," replied Ada, firmly, "you would have exhausted all your persuasions to induce me to wear them, thinking, no doubt, they would greatly improve my appearance, whereas I should have worn them only because they were the gift of Walter; and for the very same reason I intend to wear these; it matters not whether they are bridal, or funeral ornaments, he has presented them to me as a wedding present, and on that account alone, I m determined to wear these ornaments."

"Your argument is a good one so far as it goes," replied Elizabeth, " and I should decidedly commend your resolution, and were it necessary, confirm you in it under any other circumstances than the present ; for of course a bridal gift should be worn on such an important occasion, even if not entirely appropriate, out of respect and in compliment to the giver."

ADA PREPARING FOR HER NUPTIALS.

" You but anticipate my thoughts," said Ada ; " that is decidedly my reason for resolving to adorn myself with the strange insignia of sorrow on my wedding day ; giving myself the appearance of a mourning bride, perhaps not altogether unappropriate."

And as she spoke, she clasped one of the jet bracelets round her snowy arm,

"Wait one instant, dear Ada," said Elizabeth, persuasively; "you did not allow me to finish my remarks, or I should have concluded by saying, that were these mourning ornaments really the wedding present of Walter, I would not attempt to dissuade you from meeting his evident, though unexpressed wishes, by wearing them; but it is too absurd to suppose for a moment that he intentionally sent you this utterly inappropriate present."

"Impossible," echoed Mary; "it is clear there is some mistake."

"It matters not," returned Ada, "my resolution is taken."

And she proceeded to dispose the ornaments about her person.

Although feeling it entirely useless to attempt to dissuade her from her purpose, yet no one offered their assistance; and when Ada at length finished her strange toilette, by encircling her brow with a tiara of jet, all started back with a feeling almost of horror; but she only smiled sadly, more sadly than she had ever done before, and hastened down stairs to join her uncle, who was engaged in conversation with his daughter and Percy. Great was the surprise of them all at the unlooked-for appearance Ada presented, and which was by no means diminished when they learnt the strange cause which led her to adopt the emblems of mourning on so glad and joyous an occasion; but though all united in their persuasions to induce her to lay aside such unfitting ornaments, Ada remained firm to her original intention, and as the hour was now late, the party proceeded in two carriages to the church appointed for the ceremony. On entering the porch of the sacred edifice, Ada gently raised her eyes from the ground, and the first object upon which they fell was the mysterious gipsy, who humbly curtsied to her as she passed. Ada trembled violently, and leant for support upon the arm of her uncle, who was walking by her side. Mr. Herbert marked his niece's emotion, but ascribing it to the peculiarity of her situation, offered no observation, and they proceeded at once to the altar. At this moment Walter came forward to take her hand, but as his eye suddenly encountered the jet ornaments, which everywhere mingled with her bridal attire, he started, and let it drop; but almost instantly recovering himself, he again took her hand within his own, raised it respectfully to his lips, and then led her to the altar without any further sign of emotion. But Walter's eye was not the only one that noticed the strange ornaments apparently chosen by the bride; his cheek was not the only one that grew paler as he gazed. Lady Eardley was at least equally afflicted as her son; indeed, her emotion was far more palpable; her hand trembled, and her cheek assumed the hue of death, as she fixed her dark searching eyes on Ada's face, as if she sought to read the secrets of her soul depicted there. Ada accidentally raising her eyes, encountered the earnest look of Lady Eardley; and though her lip no motion made, but that fixed look was all her speech; she understood and fully appreciated the evident anxiety of her future mother; her bosom laboured with the sigh that she strove in vain to repress. And on this, her long desired Bridal-day, she was more sad and depressed than she had ever been before; the presence of the mysterious stranger added a deepened gloom to her already overchanged heart; for though she had not seen the gipsy, save for that one instant in the porch, she felt certain she made one of the numerous persons assembled to witness the ceremony, and scarcely dared to raise her eyes from the ground for fear they should encounter the dark portentious glance of the stranger Walter was calm and self-possessed, and pronounced the few simple vows which the service required of him in a clear and emphatic tone, but without betraying the slightest interest in the fair being to whom he was thus uniting his destiny. Ada, on the contrary, was pale and spiritless, her voice was weak and tremulous as she pronounced her part of the service; this, combined with the singular ornaments she had adopted, led many who were present to remark that she looked anything but a happy bride. At length the ceremony was ended, and the spectators who had crowded the church to witness the nuptials made way for the bridal party, whose progress was suddenly arrested by the mysterious exclamation, so well understood by one of the party at least.

"The lamp of love that was suffered to go out, is not relighted here." The whole of the persons assembled heard the words, but no one could tell whence they came. Ada raised her head, and gazed wildly round, but in vain her eyes sought the well known figure of the gipsy—she was no where to be seen; a convulsive shudder ran through her frame, and she could scarcely suppress a shriek; she felt assured now that it was too late—that she had passed the golden gates, and entered into the region of despair, and that thus the gipsy's prediction was verified; leaning on the arm of her new-made husband, she passed on to the carriage which was in waiting to convey them to their destination, and Walter having placed her therein, entered and seated himself by her side; thus, for the first time alone, it was but natural that Ada should expect some outbreak of affection, or at least a manifestation of tender regard on the part of Walter; in this, however, she was doomed to be disappointed, he merely raised her hand to his lips (not with the warmth of an impassioned lover, but with the habitual coolness of one who would respect if he could not love), and whispered a few words of passive happiness which died away upon his lips, ere he could give them utterance, and throwing himself back in the carriage, yielded himself to, evidently, gloomy reflections. Ada was more than hurt by this utter want of sympathy on the part of him who was now her husband; she was appalled—an icy chill struck to her heart—she remembered the words of the gipsy who had so mysteriously warned her of her fate; and with the conviction that she had wilfully chosen the path that was destined to close in gloom and despair, tears, she could no longer suppress, chased each other quickly down her cheeks; large and bright, though half unknown to herself, they fell, as her busy wandering mind waned over future scenes, depicting everywhere gloom and sorrow. While the new made bride was thus indulging in sad thoughts, Walter was by no means more pleasantly engaged; the image of his dead Lucy seemed to rise reproachfully before him, upbraiding him with his past conduct, and forbidding him to find peace in this, his new connection; he, too, looked forward to the coming future with sad and painful apprehensions that all would not be well; the curse long pronounced upon his race had ever been fulfilled, and he did not dare to hope that it would yet cease.

"No, no!" he muttered, half aloud, "the time is not yet come—it may end with my existence; but before, never. I do not, will not expect it."

As he gave utterance to these words, a slight movement made by Ada attracted his attention, and rousing himself from his reverie, he made some remark on the beauty of the morning. Ada made no reply, but raising her handkerchief to her eyes, buried her face therein, and Walter thought he heard a sob; surprise for a moment checked the power of utterance, but quickly regaining his self-composure, he inquired if she were unwell; still no reply, save by a smothered sob; Walter, yet more surprised, and annoyed beyond measures, endeavoured to remove the handkerchief from her face, as he said—

"Ada, hear me patiently, for I must and will speak."

At the sound of his voice, so cold, not to say harsh in its tones, Ada raised her head, and gazed sorrowfully and intently upon him.

"I thought," he said, contriving to speak calmly, and averting his eyes from her stedfast gaze. "I thought that in consummating this marriage, I was securing your happiness, or I never would so far have sacrificed my own feelings."

"Sacrificed!" said Ada, faintly, and the tear drop quivered on her eyelid.

"Yes," replied Walter, endeavouring to speak firmly and composedly. "I made no secret of my real feelings when in obedience to an impulse which led me to think your love and happiness was entirely in my keeping. I offered you my hand; I told you then my love was dead for ever, that I had loved once, and could not under any possibility ever love again; you cannot therefore blame me or complain if I manifest an indifference I have never attempted to disavow. If," he continued, warming with animation as he spoke. "If I have mistaken your feelings, do not, I entreat you, from a mistaken delicacy, conceal it from me; let me at once know what I have to hope or fear."

"Oh, Walter," replied Ada, speaking for the first time with truth and sincerity, "if I cannot possess your love, let me at least have your respect, your esteem,—let me feel that I am in the least degree necessary to your happiness— your well-being—and I shall be content."

"I have already told you," returned Walter, "that those you do and may possess; but the lamp of love, having once gone out, can never be re-kindled."

An involuntary shudder passed through the frame of Ada at these words, so strongly resembling those spoken by the gipsy; but she did not reply.

"Are you satisfied and content?" resumed Walter, after a moment's silence. "I have made your happiness and welfare my peculiar care—it is, and ever shall be, my study to promote it, as far as possible. If my presence should ever be unpleasing or distasteful to you, I would——"

"Oh, stop, Walter!" exclaimed Ada; "I ask for no more than permission to be ever near you—to watch over all your happiness—to weep if you but sigh—to mourn if paler be your cheek, or lustreless your eye. You shall never know," she continued, her eye sparkling with animation, "how much and how truthfully I am devoted to your happiness from this moment—

'My anxiety, my anguish shall ne'er be shown;
    And if I weep, I'll turn away
And shed my tears alone.'"

"Yet why," said Walter, something moved by the earnestness of her manner, and the deep, tender tones of her voice; "why should you ever have cause to weep?"

"Can you ask," replied Ada, half-reproachfully, "when you tell me it is impossible I can ever possess your love?"

"You knew well," returned Walter, "the terms of our engagement, and might, if you chose, have refused to ratify them—that you did not, I can only attribute to the full belief in your own mind that you would be happier as my wife. Do not, therefore, I intreat of you, ever give me cause to repent of the step I have taken, actuated by the firm, though perhaps fatal, conviction that I was confirming your happiness."

Again Ada was silenced. Gladly would she have thrown herself on the breast of Walter, and sobbed out the fond warm feelings she was conscious, for almost the first time in her life, were gathering round her heart; but there was something in the cold tones of his voice that repulsed her efforts, and, as it were, froze up the current of affection, which strove to flow bright, clear, and free. The conversation between the new-married pair was ended—each had fallen back to their former reveries; and it is at least questionable whether either would have again spoken, had their journey comprised as many hours as on this occasion it did minutes. Arrived at the present residence of Lady Eardley, Walter handed out his bride in silence, and, drawing her arm within his own, entered the house. Lady Eardley took the hand of Ada, and, drawing her towards her, imprinted a fond kiss upon her polished brow, as she said, in somewhat faltering accents—

"Long, long may you live, my dear children, to be a blessing and a comfort to each other;" and then, disengaging herself from her circling arms (for Ada had fondly clung to the mother of him whom she now called by the endearing name of husband), she hastened from the room.

Others now approached to offer congratulations, and express their kind feelings and warm hopes, which was received by Ada with silent gratitude and respect, and by Walter with a few slight expressions of thanks. A sadness appeared to creep over the whole party; none were inclined to mirthful conversation or cheerless discourse; Lady Eardley sent a message, begging the bridal party to excuse her from farther attendance, as she had been suddenly seized with indisposition. Thus the breakfast passed over, and Ada having changed her dress to one more suitable for travelling, the adieus were soon made. Lady Eardly, secluded in her own chamber, having refused Ada's request for admittance, threw a gloom over the entire party, and Mr. Herbert, especially, bade his niece farewell with a feeling of despondency, wholly unsuitable to the occassion. Ada clung tightly round his neck, and lifting up her face from his, pale and bedewed with tears; she likewise warmly returned Mary's parting embrace, and gave her hand to Percy, who pressed it slightly in his own; with Clara and Sir Richard, to whom, though now related, she was but little known, she felt no difficulty in exchanging the farewell embrace; and she was shortly again led forth by Walter to the carriage, which once in motion, he roused himself from his seeming apathy, again to address her.

"Will you permit me to inquire," he said, "your motive, in mingling mourning ornaments with your bridal attire; I ask, believe me, from no idle curiosity, but——"

"Dear Walter," she interrupted, hastily, " do not, I entreat of you, apologise to me for asking any question, no matter of what import soever; as regards the ornaments, I wore them simply because they were your gift."

"My gift," returned Walter, in a tone of astonishment.

"Yes," repeated Ada. " You sent them to me, accompanied by a note, this morning."

"There must be some strange mistake altogether," said Walter, thoughtfully. "I ordered my jeweller to furnish you with a set of pearls, and by some fearful fatality, he has sent you funeral, instead of bridal ornaments."

"Alas! it must be so," replied Ada, " but you are not offended with me for wearing them ?"

"Not in the least," returned Walter; and he again relapsed into silence, which continued uninterrupted the remainder of their drive. And thus ended their cold and cheerless nuptials.

CHAPTER XLVI.

" For now thou'rt gone, I feel as some
    Lone boat upon the sea,
 Whose consort's gone, whose rudder's lost—
    And in uncertainty
 Doth speed to find a home to rest
    Upon the watery waste,
 Wafted by winds, which seeming fair,
    My dire destruction haste.

THE opening of Mary Herbert's married life had been bright and beautiful, but a change speedily came over the path of her existence, and the once cheerful, light-hearted Mary, was now oppressed with care and anxiety, solicitous to secure at once the happiness of her husband and her father. She could not, as we have seen, endure the thought of leaving him in his old age entirely to the care of menials, and yet when she ventured to open her heart to Percy on the subject, and express her fervent wish to return with him to her childhood's home, in order to soothe and cheer the declining years of her parent, she was hurt to perceive that he did not enter into her feelings with that warmth she had been previously led to anticipate. Yet this did not prevent her persevering in what she perceived a point of duty, and with her natural sweetness, she ventured to press the subject yet more closely.

" You know, Mary," said Percy, in answer to a remark made by his wife, "that it would be exceedingly inconvenient for me to leave our present residence, which I have especially had fitted up entirely after my own taste; at the same time I admire and greatly respect your feelings, so much so that I shall be pleased to receive your father as an inmate. This will be the most pleasant arrangement for all parties, and can divide your love and attention between us."

"I am sure it is very kind of you," replied Mary, "so readily to strive to fall into my wishes, but my father has lived for so many years under one roof, that he is prejudiced in favour of it, and will not, I fear, be easily induced to abandon it for another."

"Then I am at a loss what to propose," said Percy, "but, however, Mary, do not make yourself uneasy, as I will speak to my sisters on the subject, and I dare say it will all be pleasantly arranged, to the entire satisfaction of all concerned."

Mary thanked him with her usual sweetness, but in spite of his injunctions to the contrary, she was conscious of feeling a deep anxiety on her father's account; she knew too well the character of Percy, to place much reliance on the prospect he held out of all being pleasantly settled, and with a sad heart, she waited his ultimate decision. Often, indeed, have we had occasion to remark the great changes which frequently takes place in the opinions and feelings of married people, when all that seemed good and alluring in their mutual dispositions is forgotten, or lost sight of, and their faults and errors (hitherto unobserved, or if observed, regarded only as of slight and transient importance) alone are kept in view. And as often have we endeavoured to solve the query, which naturally arises in the mind, as to why should such things be ? and for this reason have exercised our pen, in the developement of some of these courses of estrangement, and have endeavoured to set forth from time to time brief admonitions, by the attention to which, we fondly hope that much of the unhappiness which so frequently overtakes young married persons, may be avoided. Thus our present tale is almost exclusively one of married life, in which we have endeavoured to set forth the line of conduct, which in all human probability must necessarily lead to happiness. It is sad to think, that there are too many persons in this world, whose views upon entering the marriage state do not extend beyond the wedding day, that day the most important, and fraught with either happiness or misery for our entire lives, be they long or short. All their thoughts and feelings are fixed upon that day, and on nothing beyond it; they prepare for the marriage ceremony, and seem to expect that happiness, as a matter of course, will follow of its own accord. Alas! what a fatal error; a rock on which many a fond heart hath made eternal shipwreck of happiness. Husbands too frequently are to blame, for wilful or unintentional neglect of the fair and fragile being they have made their own, and to whom, during the honied days of courtship, they were willing slaves, dreading to give the slightest offence, lest they should lose the coveted treasure for ever, but when once the indissoluble knot is tied, and they have no more occasion to dread the loved ones loss, then they begin by little and little, perhaps half unconsciously to themselves, to relax those tender and endearing attentions which first captivated the fond heart which is now their own and which is as necessary to keep alive the lamp of love, as it was absolute at first to kindle it. The bridegroom gradually returns to his old courses, lounges once more at his club, and interests himself more in the mirth and good fellowship of companions of his own sex, than in that of his young wife, who is thus made sensibly to feel the difference between courtship and marriage, and soon learns deeply to mourn the loss of that entire and devoted attention, which possessed so sweet a fascination to her youthful and romantic mind. This is in itself painful to contemplate, but well and happy is it if the estrangement go no farther. But it often happens that the persuasions and entreaties of his male companions, draw the husband from home at the very time when an intellectual and affectionate woman most feels the want of a companion, we allude, of course to the evening, that sweet portion of the day, when the various trials and ills of life are forgotten, and we can hold free commune with those we love, opening our whole hearts and pouring out the pent-up feelings of the breast. Who does not rejoice in the quietude and calmness of dreary eve, the time of all others most exclusively dedicated to love and peace?

> " The labourer who, at early dawn,
> Oft rises with the peep of morn,
> His toil renewed, his work begun,
> Scarce glances at the rising sun ;
> But when eve shades the silent plain
> He seeks his lowly cot again.
> His children run his steps to meet,
> His wife her welcome doth repeat ;
> His toil is o'er, his work his done,
> He blesses the declining sun."

And yet, as we have already remarked, at this soft tranquil period, when hearts should be knit more closely together, and the hours especially devoted to domestic happiness, and the sweet exchange of thought and feeling, man too frequently absent themselves from home, in order to participate in pleasures and amusements which his wife cannot share, and the new-made bride is left to while away the tedium of his absence with her books, her music, or her pencil, as she best may—her condition being by no means an enviable one. At such times, too, she cannot refrain from drawing comparison of her past and present lot, necessarily unfavourable to the latter ; nor is this all—for the heart like a tendril, accustomed to cling, let it grow where it will, cannot flourish alone. And if the husband, who should be the oak to which it might cling, deriving at once support and protection is not there, some other and less worthy love may usurp its place. To a young and sensitive mind, especially is neglect baneful, one whose ideas are all poetical, who during the days of courtship has walked in the air and built castles there, and is even disappointed at finding husbands are but mortals. She has married with a head full of poetry, and a heart full of love, which but a continuation of the tender affections and fond endearments which first won it, might seal his own for ever, but withered by neglect, and blighted by the prevailing thoughtlessness of her husband, who leaves her to amuse herself in his absence as she best may ; and it can be no matter of surprise, if the attentions she is compelled to receive from others, be productive of a baneful effect upon her mind. This much have we said, not from a desire to throw entirely the blame of unhappy marriages on the opposite sex, although most unquestionable they frequently arise from the neglect to which we have referred. Yet much rests with a woman, in order to secure happiness. Marriage is a circumstance of life, which in its actual course involves the feelings and fortunes of human beings—more, much more than any other event in their life. And yet it is a connection generally formed by inexperience under the blindness and caprice of passion. Yet the conduct and fate of a woman is so intimately blended with that of her husband, that it is a well-known thing utterly beyond the power of controversy, that a man, however neglectful or ill inclined by nature, is never ruined if he is possessed of a kind, faithful, and loving wife, while he is lost to comfort, fortune, and even to hope, who has united himself to a weak-minded, frivolous, or unprincipled one. And thus more rests with the wife, (and whose duties we have more than once averted to in these pages already). Yet neither should even relax their energies to promote their united happiness ; and where such constant endeavours are observed, no sorrows or unhappiness ever can approach. Mary Herbert possessed a strong and powerful mind, coupled with a firm and innate principle, which never permitted her to swerve from the path in which she conceived her duty lay. If she had one fault, it was that of being perhaps a shade too matter-of-fact, at least to suit the ardent and romantic mind of Percy. He had loved Ada for her beauty and talents, admired the versatile powers of her mind, and reckoned too highly the gifts she possessed both by nature and education ; but when he discovered how deeply and bitterly he had been deceived by this first object of his love, he blindly rushed into the opposite extreme, and united himself to Mary for the very reason that she was deficient in those qualities he had so loved and prized in Ada. And, as might easily have been anticipated, after the first fresh feelings of novelty had worn off, he almost regretted the precipitation with which he had acted. Not that he less appreciated the excellence of Mary's character, or failed to admire the simple integrity of her character, but he felt the want of more kindred feeling, and sighed for those fascinations which Ada had flung around him; and in consequence, he sought amid other companions, (companions it is true of his own sex), that excitement he did not realise in the society of Mary. The constant presence, too, of his sisters's seemed to preclude the possibility of her feeling herself neglected, or treated unkindly, if he occasionally sought amusement at his club, or interest himself more with the concerns of the turf, or parliamentary business, than in domestic matters, which he left entirely to the superintendance of Mary. And yet, with wilfuness which a man only can display, he was hurt and offended, if ever Mary absented herself from home, even on the most reasonable errand of visiting her father, and was therefore easily induced to offer Mr. Herbert a home under the same roof as his daughter, nothing doubting that it would meet the views both of Mary and her father. He was not, therefore, altogether pleased at being solicited to abandon his own home, in order, as he conceived, to humour the weak prejudice of a silly old man, who, if he did not like to change his residence, might do very well by himself. But not so thought Mary: emboldened by the cause of him so nearly and dearly related to herself, she warmly espoused it; and as after a few days she found that Percy made no further allusion to the subject, she ventured once more to jog his memory.

"You know, Percy," she began, after his sisters had left the room one evening, and Percy, under the plea of ill health, had stretched himself on the couch to sleep away the effects of dinner. "You know, Percy, I cannot endure the thought of being troublesome, but you have not as yet decided on a subject which is nearest my heart."

"You allude," replied her husband, mildly, "to your father."

"Exactly, dear Percy," returned Mary, in her usual quiet tones; and she hesitated a moment.

"Well, I thought that was all settled," said her husband. "I told you I should be glad to receive him as an inmate."

"I know it, Percy," returned Mary, with her accustomed sweetness, "but if you remember I mentioned at the time, my father's antipathy to change, and you were good enough to express your determination to consult your sisters on the subject, and which led me to hope might lead to an more pleasing arrangement."

"True," said Percy, "I have not forgotten that circumstance. I did mention it to my sisters, but their opinion coincided exactly with my own."

"Might I be permitted to inquire," resumed Mary, after a short pause, and glancing uneasily towards her husband, who ivinced decided symptoms of drowsiness. "Might I be permitted to inquire the nature of that opinion?"

"Certainly. Oh, yes! by all means," replied Percy, languidly rousing himself from his dreamy reverie. "We have all of us as much dislike to quit this house, as your father can possibly feel at the prospect of quitting his; consequently, as he is entirely the obliged party, we think it nothing but right, if there is a sacrifice to be made, that it should be on his part;" and having delivered himself of these sagacious remarks, Percy turned on his couch and composed himself again to sleep.

Mary's heart sank within her; she saw that this decision admitted of no appeal; and bending her head once more over the book, from which she had previously been vainly endeavouring to extract amusement, she yielded herself to the painful feelings which opprest her. In the first place, she felt the difficulty of inducing her father to abandon his old home, and with it the many associations connected therewith, hallowed by memory and the hopes and fears of other and happier days, when love and life were new ; and in the next it was apparent that in receiving her father, Percy considered he was conferring a favour, which might perhaps hereafter tend to destroy his happiness ; and she questioned herself as to whether she would be acting wise and well, by inducing her father to break up his establishment in order to share her own.

MARY EXPERIENCES A FEELING OF SLIGHT FROM PERCY.

She glanced towards the couch on which her husband was stretched, utterly regardless of her presence, emitting at regular intervals that unpleasant and discordant sound, which is not inaptly termed snoring. Under any circum-stances, few noises are more disagreeable to female ears, possibly owing in a measure to the utter indifference which admits of sleep in their presence ; at all events, a woman even of an amiable and gentle temper, never fails to be ruffled by hearing a man snore in her company. Mary was certainly as free from all selfish or unkind feeling as it is possible to be, yet she felt indignant and vexed with Percy, for so composedly going to sleep, during a conversation of so much moment to herself, and the red blush dyed her cheek, as book in hand she turned and left the room. The subject was not again renewed between herself and Percy, for when they again met, with his usual careless forgetfulness, he entertained her with a particular account and description of the last winner at the Derby, together with his own prior impressions, and speculations on the same, which, being all in favour of the wining horse, raised him mightily in his own opinion, and as he conceived it ought to do in that of all others. Mary compelled herself to listen to her husband, and feel, or at least feign, an interest in all he said ; and Percy having started a subject on which it was his pleasure to be eloquent, he kept her in converse for a much longer time than he usually assigned to the drawing-room.

"By-the-bye," he said, suddenly recollecting himself. "I had forgotten that I have an engagement this evening with Dick Fenton. Capital fellow Dick. You know him Mary? a good judge of horse flesh generally, but lost considerably last Derby, although betting on the favourite, though I told him at the time it was a bad speculation."

"And you have an engagement with this gentleman for the evening?" inquired Mary.

"Yes; I know you will excuse me."

"By all means," replied Mary; "the more especially as I am desirous of spending a few hours with my father, in the hope of inducing him to accept your kind proposal, and take up his residence with us."

"Oh, yes, I had forgotten that," said Percy ; "well, go Mary, if you please. I shall not be late to-night. Good evening."

"Good evening," repeated Mary, and thus they separated. Percy to find amusement with his male friend, and Mary to hasten to the side of her parent, and with kind and persuasive words to induce him to accede to her husband's proposal. She found this a less difficult task than she imagined, for Mr. Herbert had been now left by himself for more than a week, and to use his own expression, felt lonely and out of sorts. "I did not think," he remarked in reply to Mary's suggestion, "than ought would ever induce me to quit the old house ; but I find it, my child, a more arduous thing to part with you ; and with the pleasant prospect of being again united to you, my darling, I will, even cheerfully, bid adieu to these old wall. I could not of course expect your husband to relinquish his home to gratify the whims of a weak doating parent."

This was a great relief to the mind of Mary ; and smiling brightly and kindly, she applauded her father's resolution. Thus one great point was gained ; and Mary proceeded to arrange with her father everything necessary for his removal.

"How happy I shall be, my dear father," said Mary, "to have you entirely under my own care ; wealth could not yield, or power command, aught that I have yearned for, like the dear delight of having you ever near me; to live over again those bright and happy hours, when your smile was the sweet reward of every exertion, and I coveted nothing beyond thy fond approval; and thus it shall be again. We shall once more be all-in all to each other."

"Nay, Mary," replied her father, smiling kindly, "you must not allow me to trespass too much upon your time, or lead you to forget that you have now other and dearer ties to bind you to existence."

"Never dearer!" returned May, pressing her lips fondly to her father's cheek; "what tie could be dearer than that which unites the widower and orphan?"

"You are right, my child," said Mr. Herbert, while a shade of sorrow passed over his countenance ; "we are nearer and dearer to each other than all the world beside."

Mary instantly blamed herself for having awakened painful recollections in the bosom of her parent, and strove, by light and mirthful converse, to bring back his accustomed cheerfulness; nor were her efforts in vain. She had speedily the pleasure of observing her father's spirits rise even beyond their usual eleva-tion. The evening was quickly spent; and bidding her father farewell for the last time, she promised to come early on the morrow, and fetch him to her own home. Mary was happy in many respects—happier this evening than she had been for some time. Ada was now a wife, and removed—she hoped and believed entirely removed—beyond the power to exercise (supposing she desired to do so) any influence over the mind of Percy, who was thus disen-thralled of the fascination her extreme beauty and accomplishments seemed to have thrown over him. Her father, too, had consented to remove one great source of anxiety by sharing her home, and dividing her cares with Percy. Still, with all these provocatives to satisfaction, Mary was not entirely content: a tear-drop dimmed her eyes, as she pursued her solitary walk along the streets of London, for him to whom she had given her first warm pure affection was not by her side. The novelty of married life had passed away, and with it the happiness of which years and years had been fondly anticipated, at least by her. Mary's disposition was perhaps, in some respects, a peculiar one, not (as we have already remarked) inaptly termed matter-of-fact by Percy's two sisters; and as such, she failed to render herself so agreeable to them as she would otherwise have done; for as close communion discloses facts and errors which we should never have discovered in a partial friend, or less intimate relationship, so does it likewise require a certain command of feeling and pursuit to keep alive the warmth of friendship, which is too frequently accorded without a due consideration of the merits or demerits of the objects which called it forth. And for this very reason, Mary and her sisters-in-law discovered many, very many subjects on which they essentially differed; and the youthful sister's of Percy, though they had liked Mary much on a more slight acquaintance, when they became more closely and intimately connected, found much in her mind and disposition, so utterly at variance with their own ideas, that it soon became to themselves a matter of perfect surprise how they could once have thought so highly of her. There was something in the plain, honest, and open heart of Mary, utterly opposed to the ardent romantic ones of her sisters, whose minds were all poetical, warm, and imaginative; while Mary, on the contrary, possessed but little imagination. She never indulged in idle day-dreams: her life was all reality. If her sisters ever spoke to her passionately in discussing poetry—or works of art—or of mighty nature itself, there was no kindling of the eye, or flushing of the cheek. If even Percy thus addressed her, and who was by nature ardent and romantic as his sisters, before the fatal day when Ada, in a fit of jealous caprice, had blighted all his hopes and long-cherished dreams, and from giving his mind a false impression of the instability and fickleness of her sex, forced him for a time to renounce all womankind, and rendered him an easy dupe to the wiles and artful designs of the bad and unprincipled of his own, whose assumed airs of easy and careless gaiety induced him to regard them as lively, good-hearted companions. But to return from our digression: We were remarking, that if even Percy thus addressed her, Mary would listen with great composure, and placidly reply (if at all) without any corresponding animation, or apparent participation in his feelings; and if, as it sometimes happened, he was keen-eyed enough to detect a slight—very slight smile, seen in the eyelids rather than the eyes, it was at least as likely to be at, as with, his earnestness about a matter which to her seemed of very little importance, one way or the other. This naturally had a tendency to alienate the affections of those who thought and acted so differently; and it was doubtless this want of sympathy that induced Percy so soon to return to his old courses, and prefer the company of his gay associates to that of his wife. Still Mary was utterly unconscious of all this; and sooth to say, while everything about her seemed calm and wanting in that depth of tenderness which characterises a warmer temperament, Mary was yet capable of strong and lasting affection, that was destined to shine out more bright and clear from the dark clouds of sorrow and adversity, than under the more promising and fairer skies of worldly prosperity and ease.

CHAPTER XLVII.

" The woodland wild, where the d.n de«r roam,
    And the song-birds build them a happy homo;
Where the grass is green, and the turf so sweet
Seems shorn by the tread of fairy feet.
Where the daylight comes so richly dim,
    And the cushat's coo seems a fairy hymn;
The careworn-heart might be beguiled,
    To forget its woe in the woodland wild."

SWEET indeed, and touching, are the intervals that passion and busy excitement allow to us, while yet in the morning of life, the fair and glowing flush of
hope.   With feelings still sensitive, and hearts not yet closed against ti e whispers that enchain the mind, memory has a peculiar and overwhelming power over
us; the more especially if dimmed by remoteness and supplanted by other
thoughts and attachments, the tie that bounds our youthful feelings has b.en
weakened or subdued; if the perishableness of earthly affections has been
brought forcibly to our minds by the inconstancy or unkindness of one upon
whom we had placed our first and purest hopes, but who rent the crown of
glory from our head, and trampled our best and holiest feelings in the dust.
Then better the grief which admits of no control—better even the morbid sensibility excited by the contemplation of the past, and the yearning murmurs of
the evil from an heart—far better than the cold heartlessness of extinguished
feeling, or the hollow merriment of absorbing dissipation.   For once roused
from its passing weakness, the heart will seek for better and purer sources of
happiness, and find the virtues and duties of an active and social life, a balm
for its griefs—a refuge for its afflictions.
    What though our young affections may run to waste, have we not higher and
more enobling ones to supply them? And if they may not, like those bright and
early blossoms of our hearts, be the soul's satisfying wealth, yet if we cherish
them as we ought, they will ever be to us a hiding place from the storm, a cover
from the tempest.
    It is good at all times to turn from our deprivation, and our heart's deep
griefs, and look on the wide field of the world spread before us, for the exercise
of our holiest and least selfish emations; to look around over the bright earth,
which in our unthankfulness, we frequently turn from and despise in the reckless
thoughtlessness of youth, with the heart's bright vision of happiness continually
evading its pursuit, till the dazzling meteor vanishes in gloom and despondency.
How sweet, then, to turn from all this and look abroad over the wide scenes of
action, in which our time, our talents, and our hopes, may be exercised for the
ultimate benefit and well-being of others. Who that regards this transitory state of
things in the light of truth, would not resign all the hollow pleasures, the
satiating delights, which too oft allure our minds, to gain feelings which must
of necessity bestow such pure enjoyment?
    The death of the heart's first blossoms, the strivings of crushed affections,
the yearnings of our social and kindred customs, when nature in her revealed
loveliness, hath touched the spring from whence these flow—how desolately
the heart turns from the petty world it hath made for itself, to worship the
glorious universe of God and nature, that it loved in early days.
    Some such feelings as these animated the breast of Jane Clarence, as the
gallant vessel, in which she had been so' long a prisoner, rapidly neared the
shores of Malta.
    It was night—silence, calm and beautiful, reigned supreme, only broken by
the ceaseless hum of the many waters, as they washed the sides of the ship, and
died away into foaming sparkling ripples in the distance.   Night—solemn night
--fair and beautiful is thy chastened and shadowy reign; deep are thy mysteries,

and potent the spell wherewith thou callest from their slumber parted years, to bid—

> "The unliving past revive and bloom!"

and fling o'er memory's shadowy scenes the hue of life's own witchery; thou hast, indeed, a voice more potent far than gorgeous day, waking remembrance which hath darkly slept; touching the deep springs of feeling, and opening the hidden founts of being. Thought, by thee, doth grow more thoughtful, and the lonely heart doth hold deep commune with things on high, linking the present with eternity.

Jane loved to watch the restless ocean, when all else was hushed and still, and listen to its musical murmurings as it pursued its endless career; and now that the night was far advanced, she still kept her place on the deck of the vessel, and leaning over the side, yielded herself to the deep thoughtful musing which the tranquil beauty of the scene inspired; the night so fair and lovely; yet it were difficult to describe its sweet serenity. But 'twas a night to make earth's meanest slave regret leaving a world so pure and bright.

> "On one side, in the dark blue sky,
> Lovely and radiant was the eye
> Of Jove himself; while on the other,
> Mid stars that came out one by one,
> The young moon, like a Roman mother,
> Among her living jewels shone."

On the calm bosom of the ocean was reflected, like a polished mirror, a thousand worlds outflashing from the centre of the dark expanse above, till the sea and sky seemed linked in one sweet vision blest of silent calmest beauty.

Jane gazed upon the silence of night, and her thoughts turned upon the past, and the bright youthful fancies which had at one time thrown over all things the enchantment of imagination and hope; but now a change was in her heart, and as she looked up to the spacious firmament, cloudless and unsullied, a deep and burning intensity of thought burst from the caves where they had slumbered, and she wept as the shadows of the past swept before her.

So deeply was she engaged by her own meditations that she had not once perceived the tall commanding form of Mr. Carlton, though he had been for some time pacing the deck close to the spot where she was seated, occasionally stopping abruptly as he approached her side, as though desirious of attracting her attention, failing in which, he would again resume his walk, again to pause as he drew nearer to her side.

At length, as if in despair of drawing her observation to himself, otherwise than by a direct announcement of his presence :—

"The night is fair and beautiful, Miss Clarence," he said; "but the air is somewhat cool. Do you not fear the effects of this exposure on your constitution ?"

Jane started abruptly, for till this moment she was unaware of his presence; but instantly recovering her usual self-composure, she replied, in her own gentle tones—

"I thank you, sir, for your kind consideration, which, however, I hope to prove entirely needless. It is seldom, indeed, if ever, I take cold, though constantly in the habit of indulging my taste for moonlight rambles."

"You are a great admirer of fine scenery," said Mr. Carlton, more in the tone of an inquiry than of asserting—a fact of which he was cognisant.

"Romantically so," returned Jane; "indeed, I cannot conceive anything in art one-half so beautiful as Nature; so bright—so changeful in its view, and yet so glorious—so beautiful in all its attributes."

"I am glad to hear you speak so warmly," replied Mr. Carlton. "You will admire Malta much, and I shall feel proud to point out to you the chief beauties of a spot which is dear to me, as being connected with home associations, and hallowed memories, and which I hope, my dear young lady, you will likewise learn to love; for though I cannot expect that you will ever forget the land of your birth, for well I know that the ocean with its billowy foam can never check the wanderer's dreams of home. No," he continued, as if musing with himself rather than addressing her—

> " 'No; there are moments, hallowed—blest,
> Sweet moments to the exiled breast,
> When visions of an early home
> Across his throbbing bosom come.'

But," he added, checking himself, "I was speaking to you of Malta, which I may well call a fair gem on ocean's southern breast, where Nature, in her most sportive mood, hath many a scene of beauty dressed ; and there, my dear Miss Clarence, you may indulge your romantic taste to the fullest extent, by roaming in quiet glades, surrounded by the beautiful leafy shades of the orange and citron groves. Yet even there," he added, smiling, "I cannot promise that—

> ' Pensive memory shall never stray
> To scenes of beauty far away ;
> Or that the fears,
> The hopes, the joys, and love of years
> Were vainly spent, or like the gem
> On ocean's bosom cast,
> Once sparkling in the diadem,
> Be forgotten all at last.' "

The manner in which he gave utterance to the last words, greatly pleased and delighted Jane ; passionately fond of poetry herself, she was quick to perceive undoubted signs of it in another ; and the musical emphasis with which Mr. Carlton repeated the lines above quoted, convinced her that he too was a reader and admirer of those works she so fondly treasured herself. Too modest and diffident, however, to give utterance to the thoughts which filled her breast, with animation, she replied only to the first part of his speech.

"That I shall ever love and treasure the memory of my native land beyond that of all others, I cannot doubt," she said ; " at the same time I can admire and love another sufficiently to enable me to pass the rest of my life in happy exile from its shores, content and thankful for my lot."

"I am pleased to hear you thus express yourself," replied Mr. Carlton ; "we are now rapidly nearing the shores of Malta, and to-morrow I hope to introduce you to my home. You will allow me," he added, after a moment's hesitation, "to take this opportunity of expressing the satisfaction I feel at having secured so apt a preceptress for my motherless children, from the knowledge drawn by close observation, during the time we have been together, I have obtained of your excellent character and disposition. I feel assured, my dear Miss Clarence, that I shall ever have to look back with gratitude to your kind offices on behalf of my children, in return for which may I entreat of you to regard me in the light of a friend and guardian ; indeed, the difference of our years is such that I might lay claim to even a parental interest. Will you, then, at all times, fearlessly apply to me for assistance, advice, or protection, whenever you stand in need of the same ?"

"I have no hesitation in saying I will," replied Jane, warmly and gratefully, for it was much to her to have secured the friendship and esteem of Mr. Carlton; a friend, whom the difference in their respective ages, as he had himself remarked, might well entitle him to be regarded with the affectionate respect of a parent.

Now her heart was indeed lightened of much that had once so heavily weighed her spirit down, and forbade her to taste of that sweet boon to the weary, peace and content. After returning for a few hours to her cabin, Jane rose and again hastened to the deck, which was speedily crowded with the passengers, anxious to obtain the first glimpse of land, so sweet and refreshing to those who have been for some time hemmed in on all sides by the sea. Mr. Carlton was among those already on deck, and took great pains to point out to Jane the dark speck on the horizon, which they were now fast approaching.

"There, my dear young lady, is your future home. God grant that it may prove to you one of happiness and peace," he said in a low and melancholy tone, as if musing on past happiness, when he had brought to this spot a bright and happy bride she who now rested in the silent tomb, of joys nipped in the bud, and hopes crushed for ever. Alas! time has an iron pen whose point is cold.

> "'Tis made of hopes o'ercast ;
> Of youthful eyes grown dark and cold,
> Of friends entombed beneath the mould ;
> Of glorious visions darkly rolled
> Before misfortune's blast ;
> Of ashes from the silent urn ;
> Of passions that have ceased to burn."

Jane respected the feelings of her patron, and did not therefore intrude upon the silent workings of his breast, by any word or remark ; contenting herself by straining her eyes in gazing towards the land, which was as yet, but a mere speck upon the ocean ; soon, however, as they rapidly neared the coast, by the aid of a glass, Jane could distinctly perceive the shore, though they were still some miles distant from the desired haven.

Jane continued on deck ; there was a fine breeze stirring, and in less than two hours, she discovered the Island of Malta plainly visible to the naked eye. She instantly ran down to her mother's cabin, anxious to impart the joyous intelligence.

"Dear mamma," she exclaimed, "thank God, our voyage has happily terminated ; we are now within sight of Malta ;—do come on deck mamma, the air is so sweet and fresh, that I am sure it will quite revive you, and we shall soon be in sight of the harbour."

"I can't think," replied Mrs. Clarence, with her usual peevishness, "how you feel so rejoiced at knowing that we are so many miles distant from our own country. I am sure the very thought that we are in all probability eternally separated from our home and friends, fills me with gloom and despondency."

"Dear mamma," returned Jane, in a deprecating tone, "I can but feel most deeply the separation ; at the same time I rejoice in the speedy prospect of again beholding land—a land where I hope to spend many happy days with you, and whose beneficial climate will, I hope, restore you to full health and strength."

"Why, child, how strange you talk," said Mrs. Clarence ; "one would think that we were returning to our native land, instead of disembarking in a foreign country, and being about to mingle with persons, of whose manners and customs we are totally ignorant ; and, for anything we know to the contrary, may have to put up with the worst usage from their hands—for foreigners are always hated and insulted."

"I think, at all events, we have no occasion to entertain the slightest fear on that account," unwilling to controvert her mother's statement, though in her own mind thoroughly assured of its inaccuracy ; "under the protection of Mr. Carlton, we are certain to meet consideration and respect."

"And, then," continued Mrs. Clarence, pursuing her own remarks, without heeding those offered by her daughter ; "and, then, I feel sure that the climate will not agree with my constitution—how should it, when I have ever been accustomed to England all my life? I am certain if my own native air would not benefit me, nothing on earth would."

"But you have been in better health during the voyage," said Jane, with persevering sweetness and good temper.

"Yes," replied her mother, in the tones of one who unwillingly admits an indisputable fact; "I have been better I know; and if we were now returning to England, I think my health would be thoroughly re-established. But I am confident that Malta will not suit my constitution—not that it is of any importance—the hastening of my death by a few short years is as nothing when I reflect that I have secured you a friend and protector; in so doing, I feel that I have fulfilled my duty; it required, it is true, a sacrifice—a great one at my time of life—and no less object than your happiness and welfare would have induced me to make it; but it is done, and I congratulate myself on the effort I have made."

Having reached this point of self-satisfaction, Mrs. Clarence became somewhat more cheerful, and suffered Jane (who knew from experience that it was wisest to offer no remark) to lead her to the deck, where, seated in a chair provided for her accommodation by the kind consideration of her daughter, sh inhaled the sweet pure air; while Jane, standing by her side, sought to interest her in the fertile island they were now fast approaching. The children, too, who were now upon the deck, pressed closely to her side, and, with bright smiles and happy hearts, hailed once more the shores which were associated in their young minds with all that they had ever known of earthly bliss. The approach to the island was very fine, although the shore is rather low and rocky, and everywhere made inaccessible to an enemy by an infinite number of fortifications; the rock in many places being sloped into the form of a glacis, with strong parapets and intrenchments running behind it.

On the arrival of the vessel at the side of the quay, they were visited by an officer from the health office, and obliged to give oath with regard to the circumstance of their voyage. Immediately after which ceremony, the little party in whom we desire to interest the reader, landed, and Jane, gazing around her with admiration and surprise, found herself in a new world; indeed, she knew not whether most to admire the verdant banks covered with flowers, and the lofty trees, brilliant in blossom, appearing to lose their heads in the clouds, or the rich and splendid scenery of hill and dale — mountain and valley—all covered with the richest verdure, and interspersed with country houses, and villas, all of the prettiest and most picturesque aspect, and diversified occasionally by a noble church, the structure of which was by far the handsomest Jane had ever seen; but small time had she to remark the beauty by which she was surrounded; her mother, together with her young charge, claimed her undivided attention.

Mr. Carlton's arrival having been expected, carriages were in waiting to convey the family to his residence which was situated near the top of a mountain four miles distant from the harbour, and about eleven hundred feet above the level of the sea. The drive was a most delightful one, the road on each side being bordered by a row of large American aloes, the greater part of them being in full blow, and presenting the most beautiful appearance that can be imagined; while the splendid country, seen to advantage as they slowly ascended the eminence, and the rich fields on either side covered with a variety of the finest fruits, and the beautiful trees growing in rare profusion by the road-side (among which, as the most curious, Jane noticed and pointed out to her mother the cotton-plant, rising to the height of about a foot and a half, and covered with a number of nuts or pods full of cotton), all combined to make up a scene of perfect beauty in which not one object seemed wanting.

"This would, indeed, seem to be the Garden of Eden!" exclaimed Jane, in a burst of admiration as she gazed abstractedly from the carriage window.

"I hope indeed you may prove it such," said Mr. Carlton evidently gratified at the pleasure expressed by Jane. "And you, too, my dear madam," he continued, turning towards Mrs. Clarence, "I hope you are pleased and satisfied with the aspect of this fertile island, which I hope you will for many, very many, years make your home."

"It would be impossible," replied that lady, "not to be pleased with the delightful scenery and fertile vegetation, by which we are surrounded; at the same time, no spot of earth could by any possibility ever become so dear to my heart, or so fondly treasured in my memory, as that of England; and the exiled heart might well pine to view again its shores."

PERCY ENGAGES MARY'S ATTENTION ON HIS DERBY SPECULATIONS.

"Doubtless, madam," returned Mr. Carlton, "there is much in the tie of birth to bind us to the land of our nativity; but it is not I assure you altogether impossible to become attached, through the ties of kindred feeling, and association, to another clime, to love it as our home, and cease to pine for a return to our own; this I hope you will prove; indeed I am almost bold enough to expect it."

Mrs. Clarence smiled faintly as she shook her head with an incredulous air; but Jane's countenance was lighted up with a beaming smile of gratitude, and Mr. Carlton was content. And now the carriage, winding up a steep ascent, they fast approached the summit of the mountain on which Mr. Carlton's villa was situated, and the children began to recognise each object on the road, and with childish delight, congratulate one another upon their return; but their father's brow grew dark, and a deepening gloom settled upon his countenance, when a sudden turn in the road brought them in sight of the villa, the approach to which was very fine, commanding an extensive view of the country, all clothed in the richest verdure, and covered with a variety of the finest fruit trees, bending beneath the weight of their own luxuriance. Jane gazed around her with unmingled delight, for the beauty and richness of the country increased in proportion as they advanced; the valleys and mountains likewise, to a considerable height, being of a delicate shade of green, which grew deeper and deeper till the whole upper region was covered with a dark rich verdure. The villa, from being built on the summit of the hill, commanded at once the most extensive and diversified views of the surrounding scenery, that it is possible to imagine. And when alighting from the carriage, Jane cast a hurried glance at the beautiful scenery that was spread like a beautiful landscape before her admiring eyes, she could scarce suppress an exclamation of pleasure. But Mr. Carlton looked sad and dejected, and her mother complained bitterly of fatigue, and the children, unconscious of the pain they were inflicting in the bosom of their father, were calling her attention first to one object and then to another, fondly treasured in their young hearts, from sweet associations and hallowed delights.

"And this was mamma's favourite walk, and here mamma used to bid us sit by her side, while she read or talked to us," broke from their lips, and it required the greatest effort on the part of Jane to prevent these remarks from being overheard by their parent, and thus add to the sorrow he must naturally feel at returning to the abode which had so lately been the home of love. Suppressing therefore all expressions of surprised delight, that the beauty and novelty of the scenery by which she was surrounded was calculated to draw from so ardent an admirer of nature as Jane, she hastened with the children into the interior of the villa, where a servant was in waiting to conduct the new-comers to the rooms assigned for their occupation. The villa was a plain but noble structure, and evidently built with more study for comfort than magnificence. There was nothing great or showy about its exterior, but it was admirably contrived for a hot climate; and while fanned by the fresh sea breeze, was likewise sheltered from the scorching heat of the sun by a grove of trees, which completely encircled the building, among which Jane observed the orange and promegranate, mingling with the delicate leaves of the palmetta. A great number of beautiful statues were placed on either side of the large hall, and upon her first entrance they appeared to Jane like a little army drawn up for its defence. The great staircase which led to the principal apartments, and lighted by a beautiful oval window of stained glass, which shed a soft and mellow light, as it reflected the last beams of the setting sun, struck Jane, as being the most broad and noble in its dimensions she had ever seen. The rooms too which were set apart for her own and her mother's use, were spacious and magnificent, with high arched roofs and paved with fine marble, richly polished; the windows were mostly of stained glass, and opened on to a verandah, graced with the most beautiful flowering and aromatic plants. The tables in each of these apartments were composed of the finest tortoiseshell, and inlaid with mother-of-pearl and ivory. Jane was delighted with all she saw, and even Mrs. Clarence expressed the pleasure the contemplation of so much affluence afforded her.

"It is really a very charming place," she said, in answer to some remark of her daughter's; "very much so, indeed; but the heat is so suffocating, that I feel sure I shall never be able to bear up against it, and would gladly dispense with much of the beauty with which we are surrounded, to fell the sweet fresh breezes of our native hills."

"I allow it is very warm," replied Jane, "but then you must remember, dear mamma, that this climate was recommended to you solely on that account."

"I remember nothing of the sort, Jane," returned Mrs. Clarence pettishly. "I only know that this intense heat oppresses me with a sense of suffocation; not that I repent of the sacrifice I have made, in leaving my home and friends for your sake; on the contrary, I feel more and more thankful that I have been able to make it; still I cannot refrain from an earnest longing after the sweet mild season of spring, so soft and warm in our dear old England."

"But dear mamma," urged Jane, "spring only lasts for a short, a very short time, and winter, with its chilling blasts, and damp cold fogs, used to try your constitution severely; indeed, I could not endure the thought of exposing you to another trial of its influence."

"It is very well to talk Jane," replied her mother, "but I would gladly have braved its utmost rigour in preference to this scorching heat, not that it is of any consequence."

"Oh, do not say so, dear mamma," returned Jane; and then endeavouring to turn attention to something else, threw open the casement, and directed her attention to the grove of orange trees which surrounded the house. "These, dear mamma," she said pointing to the spot, "you will at all times find a pleasant shade; and see what a beautiful and almost boundless prospect this window commands."

"I have no doubt," returned Mrs. Clarence, "that it appears very delightful to you, for the young ever like change; but it is far different with me; I cannot bear the thought of dying so far from all I have held dear, and nothing but your welfare, Jane, would have induced me thus to have wandered from my home."

At this moment the children entered. Jane, anxious to divert her mother's thoughts, encouraged them to talk, thinking their innocent and lively remarks would beguile her sadness; but Mrs. Clarence seemed determined not to be pleased. In vain her daughter strove to interest her with the playful gambols of little Lilias, whom she placed upon her knee; and a summons to dinner at length afforded them some relief. As this was a matter of no small interest to Mrs. Clarence, Jane hastened, therefore, to conduct her to the dining-room, where they found Mr. Carlton already waiting their arrival. He rose to meet them, as they entered, and extending his hand to Mrs. Clarence, conducted her to the head of the table.

"I hope, my dear madam," he said, "long—very long, to see you fill this position, not only at my table, but in my household. If it is not trespassing too much upon your kindness, will you allow me to express a wish to secure your excellent arrangement as the head of my family?"

Mrs. Clarence smiled complacently, as she expressed her deep sense of his kindness, and her own desire to do all in her power towards promoting his comfort and the well ordering of his household. If the marked attention and polite respect shown towards her by Mr. Carlton was calculated to please the mind of Mrs. Clarence, the dinner was no less likely to gratify the most fastidious appetite; though only three at table, there was scarcely less than twenty dishes, containing various delicate viands, all dressed with the richest sauces; nothing was wanting that could be invented to stimulate and flatter the palate, or to create a false appetite as well as to satisfy it. The dessert consisted of a variety of fruits, such as figs, pomegranates, pistachio nuts, and very fine strawberries, together with a still greater variety of ices, disguised in the shape of peaches, oranges, and the like, and which the warmth of the climate rendered most acceptable. These Mr. Carlton particularly recommended to her notice, as being likely to prove beneficial to her complaint.

"Indeed, he remarked, in conclusion, "I have known persons in a very short time cured of a threatening consumption only by a free indulgence in the use of ices; and I feel persuaded, that in skilful hands, few remedies would be more effectual, as scarcely anything has a stronger or more immediate effect upon the whole frame. Perhaps," he added, " it is from the great benefit I find from the use of ice myself, that has induced me to speak so much in its favour—for I am fully persuaded that if I had not a quantity of it constantly placed by my side during the hottest months, I should never be able to fulfil the duties which my position calls upon me to perform; but whenever I begin to flag, a glass of ice-water is sure to set me to rights again, and I have thus learnt to regard it as a perfect luxury."

Mrs. Clarence professed herself anxious to put the proposed remedy to immediate test, at the same time expressed her fears that the intense heat of the weather might greatly retard her progress towards perfect health.

"Pardon me," replied Mr. Carlton, in answer to this observation, "but I must, in this point, differ from you. There is one thing I have invariably observed in southern countries, that, although the degree of heat is much greater than in England, yet it is not commonly attended with that weight and oppression of spirits which is so general during its sultry days in summer."

"I think I must entirely agree with you," said Jane, modestly, "for I am sure on such a day as this in England I should be panting for breath, and perfectly unable to give my thoughts either to reading or writing; but such is not the case now—for I was never in better spirits in my life."

" I am glad to hear you say so," replied Mr. Carlton ; " and, if the atmosphere should at any time produce a contrary effect, I can fearlessly recommend a draught of ice-water as the greatest cordial to the spirits—not only from the cold it communicates, but from the suddenness of that communication, it braces the nerves, and gives a new tone to the spirits."

After dinner, according to custom, the children were introduced, among whom was Walter, who was cordially welcomed by Mr. Carlton; and whose expressions of warm delight at the beauty of the island, and childish wonder at the magnificence with which he found himself surrounded, seemed at once to please and amuse him. The following day, Jane took the earliest opportunity of writing to her friend Clara, acquainting her of her safe arrival and the improved state of her mother's health. She then arranged the course of studies she intended her young charges to pursue, and, having submitted them to Mr. Carlton, had the satisfaction of meeting his entire and cordial approval of every arrangement.

Thus days glided sweetly and swiftly on ; Jane dividing her time between the tuition and care of her pupils, and affectionate attendance on her mother. Mr. Carlton continued likewise to manifest a warm interest in behalf of Mrs. Clarence, and frequently relieved Jane from the tedium of too constant attendance upon her parent, and inducing her to seek recreation and amusement among the variety of wild and romantic scenes with which the beautiful island abounded. Her affectionate heart attached itself closely and fondly to the motherless children—but little Lilias had become the favourite ; and, holding her tenderly in her arms, Jane would frequently pace the broad avenue singing some low, musical strain, while the cool sea-breeze fanned her cheek, and the sweet aromatic perfume from the orange and citron groves delighted her senses, and the beautiful and picturesque scenery with which she was surrounded, afforded the most pleasurable as well as soothing reflections. And now, indeed, she could look back to the past without feeling so very sick at heart; new objects of affection, and new scenes, did much towards chasing away the gloom which blighted love had caused to settle on her once buoyant and happy heart. Her respect—nay, almost reverence—for Mr. Carlton increased yet more and more as she became more intimately acquainted with his temper and disposition; and she rejoiced to perceive that the violence of his grief gradually abated as he again resumed his wonted duties; and, though there were still times when sorrow and regret would usurp the place of content and gladness, they became, like angel visitants, few and far between. Jane knew and respected this secret grief of her friend and patron, and did her utmost to charm away its evil influence, without allowing aught to remind him of his loss. Never, indeed, did she, even in the most distant manner, allude to the sad cause which would frequently shadow his brow with deepening gloom, for

> " The portrait of the fair and young
> Still hung upon his walls;
> But the husband's brow a sadness wears—
> On his heart a shadow falls.
> A herald from the spirit-world
> May tell its spirit tale,
> Why cheek and lips, once bright and red,
> Are livid now and pale."

Mr. Carlton, on his part, felt deeply grateful to the kind interest so strongly manifested by Jane, both on account of himself and his children; his recent deprivation precluded him receiving much company, but he so far relinquished his own wishes, as to encourage the visits of the neighbouring gentry, especially that of young persons; but on Jane these kind intentions were intirely thrown away, not that she seemed ungrateful for his kindness; on the contrary, every fresh instance of his attention to her, was met on her part by the warmest gratitude; but in this respect his anxiety for her appeared needless, for Jane had extended towards him all the affectionate respect she had so long manifested towards her mother, and when she walked with him and the children over his grounds, where the orange and the myrtle flung their sweet perfume, or sat with him and her mother, reading aloud some book descriptive of the sunny land in which they dwelt, or listened while he discoursed on some topic of mutual interest; none could be more tranquilly happy than Jane. Mr. Carlton, too, was delighted to contribute to her amusement or interest, frequently accompanying her in her walks, in order to point out some object either of curiosity or interest; her most favourite spot, and one which they often visited in company, was a delightful walk called the Marino, boanded on one side by the walls of the city, and on the other by the sea, from whence—even in the hottest season, there was always an agreeable breeze.

In the centre of the Marino was erected an elegant kind of temple, which during the summer months was made use of as an orchestra for music, and as in that season, from the intense heat of the weather, they were obliged to convert night into day, the concert did not commence till the clock struck midnight, which was the signal for the symphony to strike up, and at that time the walk was crowded with carriages and people on foot. Mr. Carlton on several occasions escorted Jane to this novel concert, but though much pleased, and even fascinated with the melody of the performance, and the richness and beauty of the scene, yet she infinitely preferred a quiet walk in a more sequestered spot, the bustle and gaiety which was manifested at such times possessing no charms for her; a solitary ramble, with only Mr. Carlton for her companion, was far more delightful. Still she appreciated his kindness, and felt grateful for the good feeling which prompted him thus to sacrifice his own taste, in order, if possible, to contribute to her enjoyment. And she longed to tell him how much her own ideas were in consonance with his, and how much happier she felt in the companionship of himself and her mother, enjoying the sweets of social intercourse and cheerful conversation, than when surrounded by all the gaieties and external pleasures of the world. One evening as they were sitting over their wine and fruit, Mr. Carlton, addressing Jane, informed her that the feast of St. Rosolia would shortly take place, and as it was regarded as perhaps the most remarka-

ble one in Europe, he should be happy to afford her an opportunity of witnessing
and partaking in its festivities.

"You are very kind, sir," replied Jane, "but I assure you, sir, I have not
the slightest desire to mingle again in the gay world, which has of late too
often removed me from my mother, that I am fearful indeed of having justly increased the accusation of neglect."

"I am sure, Jane," returned Mrs. Clarence, "I have never accused you either
of unkindness or neglect; I am, indeed, only too happy to contribute to your
amusement; but you constantly persist in not understanding me. But as to this
feast of St. Rosolia, if you really have no desire to go, I do not see that there
is any necessity for you to do so; on the contrary, I have a natural antipathy to
such heathenish rites. I think, therefore, your resolution a wise one. I am
sure we are all very happy, and do not require other sources of amusement than
are to be found within these walls."

"No, indeed, dear mamma," returned Jane, "I have not the slightest wish to
avail myself of Mr. Carlton's kind offer, though deeply grateful for the generosity which prompted it."

"That is quite right," said Mrs. Clarence. "I knew that you could not
possibly wish to mix with such absurd festivities, and which, in truth, I think
positively sinful. We will, therefore, consider the matter settled."

"Pardon me, madam," said Mr. Carlton, who had been a silent observer
of the selfishness and littleness of Mrs. Clarence, and the amiable self-denial of
her daughter, as shown in the foregoing conversation. "Pardon me, but I
cannot, under any pretext, consent to profit by the self-denial of Miss Clarence.
It is but natural that young persons should like occassionally to see a little of the
gaieties and amusements of the world; and as I have been at the trouble
of procuring an introduction for her into a family of the highest re-
spectability, it would be a pity not to allow her to avail herself of the opportunity of witnessing one of the finest sights in the world."

"You are very good," returned Mrs. Clarence, "and were it anything but a
matter of conscience, I would not withhold my consent; but I regard all such
heathenish rites as positively wicked."

"But, my dear madam," urged Mr. Carlton, "your daughter will only be a
spectator not an assistant in the ceremony, which is conducted on a scale of
grandeur and magnificence which is never surpassed, if equalled, by any other
in the world; therefore, under existing circumstances, you will not, I am sure,
deprive your daughter of the pleasure I have been the means of procuring for
her."

Mrs. Clarence still hesitated, and Jane hastened to assure Mr. Carlton, that
though she felt truly grateful for his kindness, she had no desire to avail herself
of it, and with his permission begged leave to decline the projected amusement.
Mrs. Clarence eagerly seconded this proposal, and added that as she had no
desire to go herself, she did not conceive it possible that Jane could do so.

"We must not, my dear madam, judge of Miss Clarence's feelings on this
subject by our own," said Mr. Carlton; "we are no longer animated by the
buoyant spirits of youth, which finds pleasure and amusement in the bustle and
gaiety of fashionable life. Yet I remember the time when I looked forward with
delightful anticipations to this very scene of amusement, to which I desire to
introduce your daughter; nor was I dissappointed in my expection, for I assure
you, that for splendour and magnificence, it even surpassed my expectations;
and so anxious do I feel that Miss Clarence should have an opportunity of
judging for herself, whether or not I have coloured the representation too highly,
that had I not succeeded in procuring her suitable protection, I would, contrary
to my own wishes, have visited once more the scene of festivity; but having
done so, I shall be happy as far as possible to supply, during her absence, the
loss you must necessarily sustain."

Jane sighed as she listened to these remarks.

"Alas," she thought, "I have lost the buoyant and elastic spirits of youth, though yet new to the world, and would ask for no greater enjoyment, than permission to spend my days in quietude and retirement." But not to appear ungrateful, she compelled herself to seem pleased with the arrangement, and express a desire to be present at the forth-coming feast. Mrs. Clarence, of course, could offer no further objection, and the matter was thus settled.

CHAPTER XLVIII.

" Yet now he comes, brighter than even he
E'er beamed before; but ah ! not bright for thee !
No—dread, unlooked-for, like a visitant
From the other world, he comes as if to haunt
Thy sad'ning soul with dreams of lost delight,
Long lost to all but memory's aching sight.
Sad dreams, as when the spirit of our youth
Returns in sleep, sparkling with all the truth
And innocence once ours, and leads us back
In mournful mockery o'er the shining track
Of our young life; and points out every ray
Of hope and peace we've lost upon the way."

THE honey-moon hath quickly passed, and Ada has taken possession of her town residence, and by plunging at once into all the gaieties and follies of fashionable life, endeavoured to forget the past visions of happiness which had once so brightly illuminated her life; but it was impossible ; there was a canker gnawing at her heart, which constantly destroyed her peace. Walter had commenced his parliamentary duties, and Sir Richard, with his young wife, returned to Eardley Hall. Lady Eardley had disappeared immediately after the marriage of her youngest son, gone no one knew whither, and Ada was thus left alone to pursue her giddy course, without one warning voice to bid her take heed how she walked in the slippery path which she had chosen. In vain she sought by every means in her power to win the love of Walter, or touch his heart ; so cold and obdurate did it seem, that there were times when she felt all efforts were useless, and half determined to yield herself to despair ; but yet the more difficult appeared the task of gaining his love, the more resolutely did she resolve to win it. Her personal charms, upon which she had once set so high a value, appeared as nothing to her, so long as they failed to attract the only heart she now desired to win. Such thoughts as these filled the mind of Ada, as, attiring herself for an evening party, she surveyed her unrivalled form in the mirror before which she was seated.

"He surely cannot be entirely indifferent to my attractions," she murmured, as now, full dressed, she prepared to descend to the dining-room, resolved to overpower him with the full blaze of her beauty.

And in truth Ada had never looked more lovely than on the present occasion ; the rich folds of delicate satin displayed the symmetry of her figure, and her snowy arms rivalled in whiteness the pearls with which they were adorned. Her high and polished brow shed lustre on the almost regal diadem with which it was encircled ; her eyes flashed with unwonted animation, and the hope of conquest, combined with the self satisfaction she experienced, coloured her cheeks with a beautiful crimson glow, as she presented herself before her husband. Walter was seated on a sofa, intently engaged with a book, which he held in his hand; so much so, that he did not even raise his eyes as she entered. Vexed and mortified at this convincing proof of utter indifference, and yet anxious, if possible, to attract his attention, and force him to do homage to her charms, Ada walked to his side, and coquettishly laid her small white hand over the book. Walter started, and with a look of impatience pushed it off, and again resumed his studies. There was no smile—no approach even to the most distant gallantry in this action—that Ada's eyes filled with tears, and for a moment she turned away. Still, however, anxious to attract his attention, she presently returned to his side, and playfully looking over his shoulder, as if to read the title-page of his book, made an attempt to snatch it from him, and which resulted in its falling to the ground. Walter's brow flushed with anger as he stooped to pick it up.

"I wish, Ada, you would leave me alone," he said, pettishly. "I never interfere with your amusements, however absurd they may be, unless, as on the present occasion, they take the form of annoying myself."

"Interfere with my amusements?—absurd? Annoying you?" repeated Ada, while the crimson flush mounted to her temples, and anger took place of every other feelings. "But enough; I know that you hate and despise me."

"I do neither," replied Walter, as he turned over the leaves of his book, in order to find the lost page, which having done, he threw himself back on the sofa, and again commenced reading. Again was Ada mortified, and this time more deeply than before; the words of the gipsy seemed to wring mournfully in her ears—"The lamp of love that has once gone out can never be relighted again;" and for a moment her heart re-echoed the fatal words; but she so ardently yearned for the love of Walter, that she determined not thus soon to despair.

"He cannot be so cold—so utterly indifferent as he would have me imagine," she murmured to herself, as she paced with impatient steps the elegant dining-room, and her eye turned from all its costly appointments to rest upon the handsome form of her husband; as, utterly regardless of her presence, he reclined on the soft downy cushions of the couch, his attention wholly engrossed by the book.

Ada could keep silence no longer; but once more approaching to his side, said, with the petulant air of a spoilt child—

"Do, Walter, put aside that stupid book, and tell me what you think of my dress. Come, I know your taste is excellent; tell me if mine is not perfect;" and she laid her delicate hand on his shoulder.

"I am no judge of a lady's attire," he replied, as he impatiently moved his shoulder, on which her hand still rested, "neither do I wish to be interrupted by such frivolous and childish questions."

"Childish!" repeated Ada. "Yes, it is always thus; whatever I may say or do, is invariably termed weak and childish."

"Then why do you persist in a line of conduct deserving such censure?" inquired Walter, raising his eyes momentarily from his book to fix them on the face of his young and beautiful wife; but her charms awakened no sentiment of love; his heart gave no response to the eloquent appeal that shone from her beaming eyes. She was not the treasured companion of his happy hours, or the soother of his secret griefs. Her mind charmed not his own; they had no feeling or cares and joys in common. No; though bound together by the tenderest of all ties, they were as much separated as though seas rolled between them; divided in disposition, sentiment, and pursuits.

Ada saw and felt this as she met the gaze of her husband, and sought in vain to catch at least some stray beams of love. Her heart sank within her, and turning away with an emotion of bitter anguish, burst into tears.

"This is really most foolish and absurd," exclaimed Walter, as he glanced angrily towards her; "because I did not care to be annoyed by your weak caprice and silly behaviour, you must vex still more by this expression of anger."

Indeed, Walter had a settled dislike to tears. He considered it as an evidence of a weak mind and ungovernable temper. In short, Lucy had never been given to weep over every little ill or vexation that crossed her path, and consequently Walter had no sympathy with such a display of Ada's feelings. While she in her turn, mortified and irritated to the last degree by the cold and as she thought, unfeeling indifference manifested by her husband, replied in a tone of resentment—

"I am wretched and miserable in the extreme; and when I give way to the bitterness of my heart, and seek the sole relief which is left me—tears—I am called foolish and absurd. But it matters not. I will no longer humble to seek your notice. I," she added, proudly, and drawing herself up to her full height, "I who am courted, caressed, and flattered by all others, why should I make

WALTER COMMANDS ADA TO SHOW TO HIM THE LETTER.

myself miserable, because, forsooth, you are careless and indifferent, both of my welfare and happiness?"

Walter dropped his book, and surveyed the proud form of his wife, now dilating with anger and disdain; there was much of pity, but more of displeasure, in the glance which he now cast upon her, as he said—

"I have suffered you, Ada, hitherto to pursue your own career without the slightest interruption or interference on my part; never for a moment thinking (although it was evidently one of folly and frivolous gaiety) it could by any possibility degenerate into inconsiderate rashness, or more ungovernable weakness. Your last words have convinced me how much I have been mistaken. I give you warning, then, that henceforth I shall narrowly watch your conduct; and if I consider it reprehensible, withdraw you entirely from scenes which may become dangerous to my peace and honour."

"Ah!" exclaimed Ada, a look of triumph lighting up every feature of her countenance, and shining in the lustre of her large dark orbs, which appeared to dilate and flash fire, as she spoke. "Ah, then I do possess the power to move you? You are not so utterly indifferent as you would make me believe."

"I have no wish to make you believe anything that is unpleasing or disagreeable to yourself," replied Walter; "but at the same time, I would advise you, if you love your present mode of life, to be circumspect, and avoid all occasion to give me offence."

"It is easy to give advice," returned Ada, still in the same triumphant tone, "but example is at all times better than precept; and in return, I would advise you, if you prize your boasted peace and honour, to spare at least some portion of your time to devote to the amusement of your wife, and the consequent enlivenment of her home, or you may find them in danger of total destruction."

"Ada," said Walter, and a dark frown gathered on his brow, "I have long discovered you to be weak and childish in the extreme, but I did hope, nay, I fully believed, that your folly went no further; indeed, even now I cannot think that your words have any meaning. For your own sake, I am willing to attribute them wholly to the thoughtlessness of your character. Could I do otherwise, I should not speak to you thus calmly;" and once more he resumed his reading.

Ada, conceiving she had gained some power over the mind of her husband, resolved to raise it to the utmost, and continued to walk up and down the long dining-room, with a proud disdainful step.

"I will let him see," she murmured to herself, "that I am neither weak nor childish enough to be intimidated by his threats. I have at length discovered the point in which he is vulnerable. I possess the power, as I have long had the will, to rouse him from this seeming apathy, this pretended indifference."

At this moment the carriage was announced.

Ada turned towards her husband. "Walter," she said, "I have an engagement this evening at the Marchioness of Lansdowns; will you call for me on your return from the house?"

"I have neither time or inclination to devote to fashionable amusements," he answered somewhat moodily.

"Of course you are at liberty to please yourself," returned Ada, with a proud and haughty air. "You refuse to perform the office of cicerone, and I must of necessity depend upon the kind feeling of others, for those attentions which most naturally belong to you."

And without waiting for a reply, she went out of the room, and descended to her carriage, which was in waiting to convey her to the scene of festivity. And as she gracefully reclined on the cushioned seats, yielding herself to the reflections which her last conversation with Walter was so calculated to inspire, it would be difficult to say whether she rejoiced most in the power of knowing herself able to wound the mind of her husband, and destroy his peace, or grieved at the utter indifference he had shown towards her; he had not even manifested the common politeness of handing her to her carriage—no words even of doubtful tenderness had escaped his lips; it seemed all the same to him whether she smiled or frowned. As she thought of this, her brow contracted, and angry feelings took possession of her mind, as she inwardly resolved to make him suffer the same jealous pangs which had so often agitated her own breast.

A few mornings after the foregoing conversation, as the self-willed beauty was seated in her elegant breakfast-room sipping her chocolate, which was served in an elegant service of Dresden china, Walter (whose parliamentary duties had detained him abroad late the previous evening) entered; and, seating himself opposite to his wife, folded the morning paper, and commenced reading. Ada surveyed him for a few moments in disdainful silence.

"I hope you are quite well?" she said at length, in a tone of satire; "really, it is an age since I have seen you—indeed, it seems so long since you have mingled in the society of ladies, that you appear totally to have forgotten the politeness due to the sex."

"You know well enough," replied Walter, "that I have no time for such idle ceremonies, and I wish you would content yourself with lecturing the servants, and leave me to do as I please; I hate this silly and childish mode of expressing your discontent."

Ada's lips curled contemptuously.

"It is easy to term everything I say weak and childish," she replied, pushing aside the cup from which she had been drinking with so impatient a movement that it fell to the ground, and the delicate china was broken to fragments.

"If that is not childish," said Walter, glancing towards the broken pieces, "I know not what you would term it."

Ada disdained to reply, but turned impatiently away—in so doing, a letter dropped from her bosom. Walter stooped to pick it up, but Ada's movement was more rapid, and in an instant she had recovered her lost treasure. Walter eyed her somewhat intently for a moment, as he said—

"Ada, that letter was in the handwriting of a gentleman. May I inquire if you received it from your uncle?"

"No," replied Ada, "certainly not."

"Whom, then, do you favour with your correspondence?" he returned.

"That is a question I do not conceive you have any right to ask," she replied.

"We differ, then, greatly on that, as on many other subjects," said Walter. "As your husband, I conceive I have a right to know with whom you correspond, and insist upon doing so."

Ada laughed scornfully.

"You insist?" she said; "and pray how do you intend to satisfy your very reasonable curiosity? for I assure you I have no intention of revealing the name of my correspondent. Suffice it, that all men do not regard me as the weak childish creature you are constantly representing me; though you are so cold and indifferent, it is pleasurable to know that I am capable of inspiring a deep and ardent attachment."

"What mean you by those words?" demanded Walter, sternly.

"Oh, nothing—of course, nothing," she replied. "You need not be the least uneasy concerning the conduct of one whose greatest faults are vanity and childishness!"

And again her clear satirical laugh resounded through the room.

"It is useless," replied Walter, "to attempt to turn me from my purpose, either by scorn or satire. Your words may have no hidden meaning, and it is possible you may be only actuated by caprice and folly in thus opposing your will to mine. I say it may be thus, but it is necessary that I should be convinced of it before I can again entrust my honour to your keeping. If, therefore, you value my trust and confidence, I command you to show me that letter."

"Command?" repeated Ada; "how indeed it is likely I shall gratify your whims, especially as you have ever shown yourself so indulgent to mine? Well, I never thought to see you enacting the part of the jealous husband."

"Jealous," returned Walter, "I could never be; but I owe it to myself to watch well and narrowly the conduct of my wife, and prevent, if possible, her bringing disgrace both upon herself and me."

"You are at liberty to do whatever you please," said Ada. "And under existing circumstances, I do not consider it entirely out of place to arrogate a small share of the same privilege to myself."

"Be careful, Ada," replied Walter in a warning voice; "you may go further than you intend, beyond even the power of my endurance."

"Stuff, nonsense," replied Ada, drawing closer to her husband's side. "What if I should be inclined to grant for tenderness, that which threats could never extort from me, and confess that I have done all this on purpose to tease and aggravate you into bestowing a greater share of your love and time upon my poor little insignificant self—I repeat, what would you say to all this?"

"I would tell you," returned Walter, "that you were treading on dangerous ground. I would advise you, for the sake of your own peace, your own happiness, to avoid a line of conduct so fraught with danger."

"How strange and serious you talk," said Ada, half frighted at the storm she had herself raised. "It was really so delightful to be able to torment and vex you—you who exercise such subtle power over my mind—that it really seemed not only pardonable, but perfectly right to retaliate when I possessed the opportunity."

"And now for this grand affair," she continued, drawing the letter from her bosom. "Why, it comes in truth from no less a person than my cousin's husband, Percy Raymond. Now confess how easily I have succeeded in arousing your jealous fears."

"But on what subject does Mr. Raymond think fit to correspond with you?" replied Walter, by no means entirely satisfied.

"Oh, merely a matter of some little alteration in the grounds on which (knowing his uncommon good taste) I wrote to consult him;" and as she spoke, she tossed the letter into the fire. "There," she continued laughing, as the last fragment was consumed, "there is an end of this grave business."

"You mistake," replied Walter; "the beginning you mean, for the end must not be. Yet, let me give you at least one word of caution :—never for a moment entertain the absurd idea that you can in any way advantage yourself by endeavouring to arouse in my mind, fears for your moral conduct. If ever I have occasion seriously to suspect you, either of duplicity or double dealing, that moment, Ada, we part, part for ever. I married you entirely from a firm conviction, that your happiness wholly depended upon my doing so : beware, then, how you give me reason to suspect. I have been deceived ; for could I think it possible you were actuated by other motives, or other feelings than those I have always assigned to you, I should no longer entertain the slightest respect for your character. I know you to be weak and frivolous ;—let that be the extent of your feeling—difficult at all times to endure with patience : more difficult than I believe that you are aware of."

Ada moved pettishly from his side.

"Always thus," she murmured. "Never thought capable of inspiring aught beyond pity and forbearance. Why should I be thus constantly reminded of what he knows to be most painful, most repellent to my mind ? But he cares not for me : it is vain to hope for love or confidence from him. Yet I can touch him to the quick : he is sensitive at least on one point, and through that I will yet make him acknowledge my power—he shall yet bow before my shrine. I will have it thus. Not always shall he regard me as childish and incapable of aught beyond folly ; he shall see that I can act a part that shall make him tremble for his boasted honour." And as she thus thought, the rich blood mounted to her cheek in a deep and crimson glow.

In the meantime, Walter, convinced that Ada's greatest fault was a weak and foolish pride, pursued his own course, utterly unmindful of the guidance he had imposed upon himself in the charge of a young and volatile wife. No, he was too fully engrossed with his parliamentary duties to bestow a thought upon the giddy and neglected Ada, who, left solely to herself, plunged anew into every species of fashionable dissipation, carrying to balls, routs, and assemblies, a gay countenance, and sparkling eye; but a sad and weary heart. Fortunately for herself, her every thought, her every desire, tended towards the cold and apparently heartless being to whom she had united her destiny. We say fortunately, as this, more than ought] else, preserved her from the snares and temptations which are expressly employed against those whom society regards as a neglected wife, too often an easy victim, and ever looked upon as such by the butterflies who buzz around the young and unwary, ready to mark them for their prey. Ada was in no danger from the attentions of such as these; one look from Walter was worth to her more than the most insidious attentions and captivating manners of all others; and the more cold, the more careless he became, the more she was confirmed in her resolution to inspire him with jealous fears and tormenting doubts. Unhappy girl! she was bent on her own destruction. Alas! into what a fatal error had she fallen, to suppose for a moment, that by leading her husband to doubt her truth—her purity—she could by any possibility succeed in awakening his love. And yet how many like Ada have thus deceived themselves, how many have raised the storm which destroyed themselves. Jealousy is at once one of the most painful and fatal passions, which can be roused in the human breast; how much of wretchedness, how much of madness, and even crime, may be traced to this baneful power, which it is easy to raise, but difficult, if not impossible, to quell. Never, then, should any feeling of vanity, or a wish to raise their self-importance in the eyes either of the lover or the husband, prompt the young and thoughtless after the young and thoughtless to awaken in their breasts the baneful influence of jealousy, the bitterest foe to the peace the of mind, wherein it becomes an inmate..

CHAPTER XLIX.

"The face may seem devoid of care,
    The placid brow, eyes sparkling bright,
Speak peace within; and yet 'tis there
    Affliction spreads her with'ring blight.
While from the world we would conceal
    Our suffering, nor our woes impart,
A bursting sigh will oft reveal
    The anguish of a breaking heart!"

THERE is a beauty—a rich and fertile beauty—in green tree, as in all the silent workings of nature: a beauty upon which it is both wise and sweet to look upon, and trace the hidden or but half-revealed glories of Him who doth teach himself in all things, and hath stamped beauty and utility over the entire universe. There is nothing more beautiful than a fine old tree, towering with majestic dignity far above the earth: a tree which hath been old a century, standing firm and unrooted amid the blasts of nature, the forest's pride and glory, yet receiving the first rays of the uprising sun, like a crown of glory encircling its head, and the dews of night shining like diamonds amidst its foliage. Trees are ever the resort of the young and fair, when hopes are young, and hearts are fond, and all the poetry of existence breathes audibly from human lips. Under the shade of green trees, happiness pure and untainted, may be realised; among whose pleasant shades, lovers so often wander, darting light into each other's eyes, and fondly dreaming that the world is all bright and beautiful, as their young hearts, imagining that their path though life must necessarily be as brilliant as the green-sward, bathed in the glorious sunlight, before them. Ah! who does not love green trees? In whose memory are they not associated with days of childhood, of bright and happy hours, when the dark sycamore, the luxuriant chesnut, the graceful beech, and beautifully yellow-tinted elm, formed a glorious canopy, under whose green boughs we sought shelter from the noon-day sun, with a sky over head as soft, as blue and radiant, as the eye of infancy, while streaks of sunshine, scattered hither and thither in the soft grass, gave an appearance of deep interest, as their mysterious glimpses we caught through the gentle waving of the trees ? How deep, how solemn, did the silence at such times seem to our young hearts, when there floated no breeze amongst the over-hanging branches, when even the song of birds were hushed, and there waved not a single leaf to disturb the deepened silence. The influences which then appeared to be showered down by every gentle zephyr, was, even at that early period, soothing and salutary ; and we looked upon trees as replete with high and beautiful inspiration as the true and genuine spirit of poetry. And even now, what tree is there among all we have loved, and upon each of which our thoughts have rested, and still rest with such happy memories, that does not seem ready to tell us some tale of pleasure, or of sadness ? that does not seem, while it waves over our heads, as if it (like us) had memory of the past, and was ready to whisper of days long gone by—to tell us of past joys and childish sorrows, responding to the secret feelings of our breast, and greeting us with the warmth and truth of undying friendship, still the same, though unexprest sympathy hovers round every branch, and the gentle rustling of the leaves, just moved by the breath of Heaven, bid us dream over again those blissful dreams of the past, when the world appeared one bright and glorious garden, filled with sweet ordous and unfading blossoms ! How sweet even (and how fondly we cling to such thoughts in maturer years) are the very fallacies that blessed our childhood !

> " I remember, I remember, the fir trees dark and high,
> I used to think their slender tops were close against the sky:
> It was a childish ignorance ; but now how sad the truth,
> To know I'm further off from Heaven than in my earlier youth."

There is something in the face of nature at all times beautiful to look upon—in the varied scenery of hill and dale, skirted here and there with fine old trees, now forming a sweet grove with their overhanging foliage, inviting, by their depth of shade, a pleasant resting place from the scorching heat of the noon-day sun. Those who love such scenes as we have attempted to describe, who have learnt to look upon the open book of nature, and call therefrom wise and useful lessons, storing the mind with good and unerring preceipts, by which they may safely steer their way even amid the rock and quicksands with which the world abounds in the shape of temptations and trials, which seek to lure them from the path of honour and integrity—such, we have said, who love such scenes, we would invite to accompany us to one of those sweet and fertile spots, which, spite all that is urged against it, are yet to be found in our own loved island home. It is indeed a sweet spot : the sun's heat has blent itself with the cool morning air, and not a tree nor a shrub, nor a blade of grass, but sparkles up with an aspect clear and glittering, full of cheerfulness and gratitude. A grove of fine old trees, round whose trunks surviving frame is covered many a long forgotten name, and doubtless " many youths and lovers in their shade," had " their vows of truth and rapture made." The music which murmurs from every bough seems a voice that celebrated the glory, or bewailed the departure, of by-gone days. In the distance mounts a rich amphitheatre of green hills, in all the varied colours of fertile beauty. Around is a deepened silence ; and the whole scene is one of soft and quiet grandeur, with nothing to disturb the tranquil stillness, which gives it almost the appearance of solemnity. But hush ! what stirs behind the underwood ? There is no one to be seen ? Yet there is a murmuring sound suddenly breaking upon the stillness of the air, and falling upon the ear, in tones low, yet earnest and passionate.

" The love of man," said the speaker, " is fasle and evanescent, like the bright blaze of sunshine in the noon of day, decreasing as the day declines, and lost when night is come."

" Not so," another low, but fuller voice replied. " Rather, man's love clings to its object, even as the ivy clings round the tree ; and when the night of life approaches, clings all the closer, that its warmth may compensate for the absence of the noon-day sun."

"'Tis a perilous venture," rejoined the first speaker, "and may crush other hearts and blight other hopes, without in the least benefiting ourselves."

"It is impossible," returned the other; "will you calmly see another reveling in wealth and luxury, which is by right your own?—will you consent to toil for your daily bread—or will you humbly sue for charity, and become a prisoner on the bounty of those who enjoy wealth and honour, to which you are by birth the rightful heir?"

"No—no," said the one who had first spoken to this. "I could not submit; but have you sufficient evidence of this first marriage, so as to make the second one invalid."

"I tell you I have every proof; for this purpose I have brought you here—it is entirely in my power to place the broad lands of Eardley Hall in the hands of the rightful owner; others have for years enjoyed your inheritance, while you, reared amid more humble scenes, were looked upon as worthy of no higher title than the mistress of the man whose family, by a system of heartless duplicity, have succeeded to the property they have no right whatever to enjoy."

"Enough—enough," repeated the other, in quivering and half suppressed accents. "I hesitate no longer; for years have I mourned the loss of one whom I fully believed would eventually redeem the pledge he voluntarily pronounced, to make me his wife, but it is ended—the struggle is over; I hate myself, that for a moment softer thoughts should have swayed my breast; from this time I dedicate myself wholly to revenge. Why should a sickly fancy keep me back, or induce me to spare those who from infancy have heaped wrongs upon my head, blighted every prospect, and shut out every hope from my young heart?"

"Now you speak like yourself," returned the other. "Laura, you shall yet be rich and great."

A scornful laugh re-echoed through the grove, but oh, what a mockery of mirth was in those sounds; how utterly the reverse of the light joyous laughter, which should have escaped from the lips of one so young and fair, for at this juncture the speakers emerged from the grove—one of whom, as we have intimated, was in the very heyday of youth and beauty, her tall commanding form, and lofty polished brow, seemed to speak of high birth; indeed, spite of the almost meanness of her attire, there was in her whole bearing a stamp of nobility, utterly at variance with the course materials which formed her dress. A cloak was loosely thrown across her shoulders, and but partially concealed the symmetry of her form; a close bonnet lightly thrown back, revealed a face of undoubted beauty, though a physigonomist might have detected in the lines about the mouth, and in the quick contraction of the brows, evidence of strong and violent passions, over which she had evidently accustomed herself to hold but slight control; her raven hair was folded in thick masses and drawn towards the back of the head, thus leaving her forehead bare; her eyes were large, dark, and intricate, and appeared at times to emit lightning from their glance, so deep and flashing were their rays. Her companion was a man of middle age, with a face that had evidently once been handsome, but time and sorrow had made sad ravages in his countenance, and turned the once raven hair to grey, while it indelibly stamped its presence in deep furrows on the brow; there was likewise a look of deep-seated sorrow plainly depicted in the expression of his countenance, and which strongly resembled that of the young female who moved by his side, and which might have led the observer to mistake them for father and daughter, but for her sudden observation as she stopped abruptly in her walk, and addressed her companion by the name of uncle, inquired whither they were proceeding.

"Our day's journey is well nigh ended," he replied; "put implicit confidence in me ; it is necessary that after having obtained suitable accommodation, that I should leave you for a time—a very short time ; and when I return, I doubt not that I shall be able to give you such information as will greatly facilitate our plans."

She made no answer, save by a silent gesture of her hand, and again the mysterious strangers resumed their way. They had not proceeded far ere they stood before, half hidden by the grove of trees by was which it surrounded, a small, but pretty and unique-looking villa, the whole appearance of which bore ample testimony to the good taste of the proprietors. The garden was well stored with a choice collection of rare and beautiful plants, and gave evidence of being richly cultivated, not so much, it would appear, from the ostentatious vanity of attracting the admiration of the passing traveller, as from a pure love for those rich gifts to man. This was the more apparent from the marked simplicity of the arrangements, and the vast number of pretty though humble blossoms, which are too frequently exploded from the gay parterre, and left only to grace the cottage of the labouring man—such as the simple daisy, and delicate white convolvulus, together with the modest violet, which shed its sweet perfume on all around.

Leaving the travellers to pursue for the present their own route, we will, with the reader's permission, take a peep into the interior of this abode, which is furnished with strict neatness and simplicity—no gaudy trappings or gay appointments detract from the beauty of the building, which, though styled a villa, was strictly a cottage residence ; not one of the commodious London houses, which are occasionally to be met with in the country, defacing the beauty of the scenery, and causing a smile of pity from the lovers of nature for the bad taste of those who cannot even enjoy the country unless they surround themselves with the luxuries and comforts, which may in a measure be necessary to the enjoyment of a town life, where there is naught without doors to fascinate the eye or charm the mind ; and which conseqently demands a far greater amount of in-door comforts to compensate for the loss of those sweeet incentives to happiness with which the country so richly and lavishly abounds, and which, thank God ! restricts itself not to the opulent or high-born, but spreads its charms far and wide, inviting the careworn sons of toil, the humble artisan, and still more humble labourer—to come forth from the crowded cities, where pestilence and death is so often inhaled in every breath they draw, and breathe the fresh pure air of the country, instilling new life and vigour to the vital organs, and at the same time raising the mind to high and ennobling thoughts—sublime and beautiful inspirations—as they wander through the green fields and shady hedge-rows, while a feeling of quiet gratitude pervades the breast, as the thought crosses his mind, that, though full oft oppressed by his fellow-men, worn down by toil and hardship, suffering frequently from the most cruel privations ; yet amidst all this, there is still as sweet, as pure a source of enjoyment open to him, as to the most highly-favoured among his fellow-mortals.

Though six days of unremitting toil draw their wearied length along, uncheered by one kindly smile or soothing word, yet, blessed be God ! the welcome seventh must yet dawn—a welcome day of rest and refreshment—when the poor man, released for a short time from the shackles which held him in bondage, is free to wander where he will. And happy and blest are those who employ this sweet interval of rest among the beautiful works of nature—the gifts of a wise and good God, who made the hills and dales to be covered, with a rich green verdure that it might refresh the weary eye—who planted the trees, and bade them spread their branches far and wide, that they might afford a sweet shelter from the noon-day heat—who bade the fragrant air shed its balmy influence on the earth, and gave to each little rivulet a music of its own.

Alas ! that man should so often turn from these rich blessings with no hallowed feeling in his breast—no words of praise and thanksgiving upon his tongue ; while the feathered songsters daily pour forth their song of gratitude, and more mindful of His mercies, shun the crowded cities, in which man hath made his home, and dwell among the often deserted, but beautiful, scenes of nature.

It is delightful to see the labouring man, forgetful of his week's toil—heedless of the morrow, which must again call him to renewed activity—leading his

EVERARD'S INTERVIEW WITH THE LADY EARDLEY.

children far from the dull alleys and busy streets, to spend the sabbath (that day of rest and refreshment) among the sweet green fields, inhaling the soft pure air of the country, and teaching their young hearts early to love and treasure the memory of the sabbath, from the sweet associations with which it is connected. Who is there that has not, at times, been tempted to envy the feelings of such a man?—who has purchased this sweet enjoyment by six days of unremitting industry, who has counted each hour as it past, as bringing him so much nearer to the promised indulgence ? With the happiness of such there can be no alloy, no shadow of disappointment. How different with the wealthy, where pleasures fall, and the noblest delights weary from the very want of that incentive to perfect enjoyment, occasional hardship and privation, which causes any extra indulgence on the part of the poor to be so much sweeter, so utterly devoid of any slight drawback, which is seldom, if ever, the case with those who are regarded as fortunes favourites, who are courted by pleasures on every hand, till they sigh (and sigh in vain) for some fresh source of happiness, some new and unwearied excitement. But to return to our tale : we were saying that though styled a villa, the residence to which we desire to introduce the reader wass trictly a cottage, elegantly but neatly furnished—simplicity and good taste were everywhere perceptible. A small room on the ground floor was fitted up as a kind of study or library, well stored with books, and at an open desk is seated a lady of middle age, whom from the calm and polished brow, the pale, but intellectual features, the reader will have no difficulty in recognising as Lady Eardley; her pen moves, as it were, half mechanically across the paper, and she occasionally raises her head to glance at the open window, near which she is seated; and as her eye looks on the beautiful, yet varied scenery, it lights up with an expression of enthusiastic delight, but which speedily passes away, leaving a dark shadow on her countenance, and displaying in sterner characters, the habitual melancholy which is seated on her lofty brow. She appears struggling to keep down some painful thoughts, which mars, for the time, her peace; and as hour after hour passes by without the slightest interruption from any one, anxiety appears to predominate over every other feeling; pushing her desk aside, she rose and paced the room with rapid, uneasy steps.

"He will come," she murmured. "Oh, yes, he will surely come; but after all these years how shall I meet him, how suffer the agony of my soul, how endure his too just indignation? Can it be possible that I shall succeed in turning him from his scheme of vengeance, in appeasing his resentment? Alas! I fear not; were it possible by the sacrifice of myself, or everything connected with self to do so, how gladly would I make it; but if in spite of all that I can urge of every remonstance, though I condescend to implore him to have mercy on mine, on me, if he should still hold out, then have I humbled myself in vain, shall have endured the additional anguish of this dreadful and dreaded meeting." Here her emotion appeared to gain the entire mastery of every other feeling, for she drooped her head between her clasped hands and wept, and sobbed aloud; but this did not last long. We have already had occasion to remark the wonderful power possessed by this extraordinary woman of suppressing her feelings, and in a very short time she raised her head, the storm was hushed, and she betrayed no sign of the recent agitation which had shaken her frame. "It is worse than folly thus to allow my feelings to overcome me." she murmured, "I must prepare myself for this meeting; the hour is fast drawing nigh—the sun is already on the decline—and when he shades yon silent hill, I shall once more stand face to face with him whom I never thought to meet on earth again; to aid me through that meeting, I must collect all my self-command; my habitual firmness will surely not desert me, now that I have most need to use it. No! I will quell this violent emotion, and let him see that neither threats or fears have power to intimidate me."

Thus resolving, this truly unhappy lady reseated herself at her desk, and having closed the window, prepared herself for a meeting she evidently so much dreaded. As she thus sat, the last rays of the declining sun, brightly illuminated her pallid countenance, and which, even by that strong light, betrayed no sign of the emotion which was working in her breast. No! her brow was soft and placid, her demeanour quiet and tranquil in the extreme, and when, after the lapse of an hour, a servant entered to inform his mistress a gentleman wished to speak with her, in a clear and gentle voice, whose tones evinced no trepidation, she bade him instantly to be shown into her presence. Twilight had now for a brief season resumed its tranquil reign, shedding soft lustre on the balmy hour, and soothing all creatures and all things, to quiet and repose.

> "Sweet hour of twilight, calm the feeling,
> That gently on our senses stealing—
> Bright thoughts of other days revealing,
> We bless thy pure and tranquil gleaming,
> Which comes with soft, and gladened tone,
> To make a world of bliss our own,
> And thoughts, and hopes, till then unknown,
> With sacredness around them thrown."

But not thus did it appear at the present time to Lady Eardley, not thus did she greet and welcome its presence, for it brought no hope to her bosom, no glad tidings to cheer her wayward destiny; still she was calm, and when the servant again returned—ushering in a man of middle age, whose dress, even in the dusky twilight betrayed a plainness, bordering almost on eccentricity, he simply bowed to the lady with whom he had sought an interview, who preserved the same ceremonious mode of greeting till the servant had retired, closing the door behind him, when Lady Eardley motioned her visitor to be seated, (though she remained standing herself) waited without displaying the slight-est trepidation for him to break the silence, which seemed almost ominous, so profound was the stillness which reigned around. It is perhaps worthy of remark, that in motioning her visitor towards a chair, Lady Eardley had taken the precaution, that it should be on that side of the room nearest the window, consequently the last lingering rays of daylight fell full upon him, while remain-ing on the opposite side herself, she was almost hidden in its depth of shade: at all events, the expression of her countenance was entirely concealed. There was a silence of a few moments, which neither seemed inclined to break; not even a breath disturbed the serenity of that hour. At length the stranger spoke—

"Lady Eardley," he said, " I have sought this interview, not from any desire to upbraid you, with the enormity of your sin against myself, neither do I desire to wound your feelings by recurring to the past further than is abso-lutely necessary for the attainment of an object upon which I have fixed my hopes—my fairest wishes; at least all that is left me of either, that one great object obtained, I shall leave to Heaven the just punishment of your sins, and rid you for ever from my hateful presence. You shall never again have cause to fear the slightest intrusion on my part, think of me as dead, and enjoy, if possible, that happiness and peace which you so cruelly denied to me."

Lady Eardley heard him calmly to a conclusion, and then in her own clear, musical tones, replied—

"I gathered something of this from the note I received from you yesterday, but I must confess, I am entirely at a loss to comprehend to what you allude; I see only in this subterfuge a fresh source of annoyance and aguish to myself. Was it not enough," she continued, raising her voice and warming with indig-nation as she proceeded, " was it not enough that in obedience to your mandate I separated myself from my children, from all who were near and dear to me, and in solitary isolation resolved to spend the remainder of my existence, in the hope, as it appears, the vain hope that I might be permitted to drag on life's weary load without farther molestation or interruption from you ?"

"Nay, Lady Eardley," returned her visitor, and he laid a bitter empasis on the words, " say rather, to save your reputation—to prevent your children look-ing upon you with horror and detestation, to enable them to retain their legiti-macy in the eyes of the world, to induce them to think of you with respect and affection. Say, rather to compass all this, you freely resigned yourself to a voluntary exile."

"Beware !" returned the indignantly lady, "your threats of exposure, to use your own words in your written communications, (for till this hour you have had the grace to spare me the pain of a personal interview)—your determination to tear aside the veil, which at present conceals the deformity of my character, and reveal to my children the cruel duplicity of my conduct; because all this, on your part, drove me to adopt such a course, in order to preserve to my children their unblemished honour—their most cherished riches, a good and spotless name."

"It were a pity then," replied the stranger, in a cold sarcastic tone, "that their mother did not transmit to them as their right so priceless a treasure, especially as she appears to value it so highly."

"Enough—enough !" returned Lady Eardley. "I cannot think it possible, after I have unmurmuringly acquiesed to all your commands, under the full assurance, that by so doing I should spare my beloved children all the mortification and anguish I have so long endured, I repeat, after all this I cannot conceive that you can possibly possess the refinement of cruelty to force your presence upon me, simply for the gratification of witnessing the torments you so needlessly inflict."

"You say right," returned the other. "I did not come here with any such intention, far, very far from it, though deeply wronged and injured. I was content with compelling you to sacrifice your childeen, if you desired to preserve at least the semblance of virtue. I was resolved to make you feel something of the anguish and isolation you had mercilessly cast upon me, dooming me to perpetual celebacy, for I could not, like you, perjure myself in the sight of God and man. I could therefore never hope to be blest with an affectionate wife, or soothed by infant voices ; no—the joy of children was denied to me, I could never hope to hear them pratling round my knee in early years, or blessing with affectionate attention my life's decline ; why then, I asked myself, should you, who so cruelly blighted my hopes, revel in joys that I could never know ? The though that you were thus blest was torture to my mind, and I resolved to sever you from those tender relatives, to reduce you to the lonelinsss and utter isolation of my own condition."

"And having entirely succeeded in this cruel project, why do you farther molest me ?" inquired Lady Eardley. "You have no more occasion to be jealous of my superior happiness ; better had I never been a mother, than thus have suffered for my children ; the dread too, the cold dark dread, that all my efforts have been useless, that in spite of all your assurances to the contrary, you may yet reveal to those beloved objects the bitter truth that they have no claim, not only to the estates—that indeed they would bear with the moral courage they inherit from myself, but to know that they have no right to the name they bear, would be to humble them to the dust, to force them to hate, to contemn their mother. Alas ! alas ! the very thought is maddening, and yet what can I do, what further sacrifice would you require of me, if I can do or suffer more ? Name your conditions, the price of your secrecy, and if it be possible I will abide by them."

"It is possible still to perserve your good name unsullied," replied the other in the same cold, sarcastic tones, utterly unmoved by the sufferings of the unhappy lady to whom he addressed himself ; " no greater sacrifice is required on your part, but an act of justice is due from another ; that justice performed, I leave you for ever, only binding you to the life of solitude I am myself forced to endure."

"You speak in mysteries," retured Lady Eardley, "which I cannot comprehend."

"Listen, and I will solve them to you," replied the other. " My conduct em the commencement of our unhappy connexion must have convinced you that I entertain no animosity or ill-feeling towards the innocent offspring of your guilt. I was even willing to confirm them in the respect and affection they evinced towards their mother ; having therefore withdrawn you from the pleasure you must naturally have felt in their society, and forbidden you under any circumstances again to taste of the sweets of social intercourse, I should have been content to leave them in blissful ignorance of the deceit you had so long and successfully practised, had not a circumstance of a most painful nature come to my knowledge, involving the misfortune and anguish of one near and dear to me; for this reason I sought the present interview, to impart to you the cruel wrongs heaped upon the head of one who has been dear to me from infancy, treasured as the sole legacy of a dead sister, and whose wrongs shall yet have ample vengeance; whom do you think," he added, rising from his seat, and approaching the spot where Lady Eardley was still standing, but who shrank back as he advanced. "Whom think you brought the ruin and destruction of your niece and mine for such in truth is Laura. Why he who enjoys the wealth the name, the tittle, that is by right her's alone. And by Heaven she shall have it."

Lady Eardley shuddered; still her voice preserved its clear, calm tone, as she replied—

"I cannot understand to what you allude; if you infer that either of my sons have acted in the manner you describe, I have no hesitation in casting back the foul aspersion, for they are incapable of dishonour."

"Think you so?" returned her unwelcome visitor; "then listen while I undeceive you; fear not," he added, "that I am going to enter into details; I will be as brief as possible. You may remember, that at one time I had a sister to whom I was fondly, tenderly attached, some few years after, the now somewhat remote period, when the late Sir Richard Eardley, believed me killed in a duel by himself, that sister suddenly left her home, leaving behind her a letter, in which she assured my mother that she was not actuated in the step she had taken by any feeling of shame or disgrace, for she was honourably married to a man of family and consideration; but that for the present she was forbid, for reasons which it is needless to assign, to acquaint us either with the name or rank of her husband; she farther stated that she was going abroad, and on her return hoped to be at liberty to abandon all secresy for the future. Some years after this occurrence, while staying in Switzerland, my attention was drawn by my landlady to the circumstance that a country-woman of my own was at that moment dying in the house, with no one to tend or cheer her, save a little girl, whose age rendered it inadequate to the task. I immediately sent to the unfortunate lady, soliciting an introduction, in the hope of being able to offer my services to one evidently in distress; my desire was met with gratitude and pleasure, and I was accordingly admitted to the sick chamber; a pale and attenuated countenance was just visible above the bed-clothes; yet strange to say, that sallow and sunken visage reminded me of my lost sister: the eyes of the invalid were fixed upon me with a deep and searching gaze, and then making an effort to raise herself in the bed, she stretched out her arms, and having with difficulty given utterance to the words 'My brother!' sank back fainting; the shock had been too severe for her weakened nerves, and though I sat for hours by her side, anxiously expecting a return of consciousness, it was in vain, she died, and made no sign; her infant daughter of whom I endeavoured to gain some information, could only tell me that her name was Laura, that papa had gone away to India, and by her description of his dress, I entertained no doubt of his being in the East India Company's service; this was all I could learn, for I searched in vain among her boxes for some clue to the discovery of her husband. Being, therefore, compelled to leave chance to clear up the mystery, I took the little Laura under my protection, educated her in the very spot where your sons were living in affluence, though in a far different manner, for my humble means precluded the possibility of anything approaching to luxury. For years we lived together, this child and I, being the one little being to whom I was dear— the only one in the wide world to feel the slightest interest in my welfare. Thus she grew to womanhood, fair and lovely, when business suddenly called me to England. I was unwilling at that time to subject Laura to the inconvenience of a sea voyage. Having, therefore, procured for her such accommodation as my limited means permitted, I departed alone, promising a speedy, and, I hoped, happy return. Alas! during my temporary absence, Laura had attracted by her grace and beauty the admiring eyes of a libertine, who, by specious words—by falsehood, flattery, and deceit, succeeded in robbing her of the bright jewel which had hitherto been preserved with unsullied purity. Lady Eardley, that libertine was your son!"

"Impossible! I cannot, will not believe it!" she exclaimed, in a burst of passionate indignation.

"It is true," replied the other; "but this is not all. I did not at the time discover the frailty of her whom I loved as a child, but attributed the deep dejection of her manners to ill health. In the meantime, Sir Richard and his family returned to England, and after the lapse of a few months, Laura became unable any longer to conceal the truth. Throwing herself upon my bosom, she told me all, and shortly after gave birth to a daughter, which, thank God, survived but a few short weeks. I will not," he continued, "dwell upon my own anguish and resentment when I discovered that my child was doomed to be struck down by well nigh the same hand which had inflicted so much injury upon myself. Yes, her sorrows and indignities flowed purely from the same source, and I resolved on vengeance; yet in what way to procure it I scarcely knew, till a few weeks back, when, looking over the writing-desk which had formerly belonged to my sister, I discovered a secret drawer, which had hitherto escaped my notice, concealed in which was a document of more intrinsic value to myself than all the wealth of the Indies, for it opened to me a plan of vengeance, deep, sure, and certain; it was the certificate of my sister's marriage with Frederick Eardley, the only brother of Sir Richard, him whom you called by the name of husband."

Lady Eardley started and turned deadly pale as these words fell upon her wondering ear, and spite of her habitual self-control, she betrayed too palpably how much they affected her. Her strange visitor was quick to perceive the advantage he had thus gained, and hastened to follow it up, and as much as possible turn it to his own ends.

"You must now fully appreciate the object of my present visit," he began in his cold sarcastic tones, "and I trust to the instructive good sense, equally as to the desire of Lady Eardley to bury the past in oblivion, and preserve untarnished her spotless name, (a name of which she has every reason to be proud), to offer no opposition to the plan I am anxious to lay before her, and which approval on her part cannot fail to secure both."

There was a peculiar and bitter irony in the tone with which he gave utterance to these words, that sent a severe pang to the heart of the unfortunate lady to whom they were addressed. In vain she struggled to suppress the rising emotion; her efforts to do so caused a sensation of suffocation, her head swam, and she was forced to cling to the marble mantle-piece to prevent herself from falling. But brief was the struggle, short though severe the conflict of contending emotions. Like clouds which ere we've time to say how bright the sky is, shade the sky: so did this emotion come and go. In a moment she was again the calm self possessed woman, wearing an appearance of outward placidity that was utterly at variance with the anguish which rent her heart.

"Your words," she replied, "are so strange, your information so incredible, that I am utterly at a loss how to comprehend you. Nevertheless I am a mother, and as such would willingly make any sacrifice to secure the happiness, the future welfare, the peace, of my children."

"This can only be done," returned the visitor, "by uniting the destinies and fortunes of Sir Richard with those of his cousin Laura, who can at any moment lay claim to the estates he now inherits in such fancied security as her own. Yes," he continued, for the first time during the interview warming into something like animation; "the wronged and forsaken Laura is now the only heir to the property so long enjoyed by you and yours."

"It is impossible," returned Lady Eardly. "Monstrous. I cannot, will not believe such a tissue of fables, cunningly contrived I allow, but which will not work upon my fears to the extent you vainly appear to suppose."

The stranger replied by drawing from his bosom a small bundle of papers, which he laid upon the table as he said—

"There, Lady Eardley, are the proofs. You are at perfect liberty to examine them in my presence; indeed I would wish you to do so, in order that you may be the better enabled to determine what line of conduct it would be wise and best for you to pursue."

Lady Eardly made no reply, but touching a bell, ordered the servant to bring lights, which being done, she drew her chair towards the table, and quietly commenced an examination of the papers. Her face, though thoughtful, expressed no anxiety; her smooth and polished brow showed no sign of care. And as she calmnly turned over the different certificates of birth, marriage, carefully examining each document with the strictest scrutiny, ere she laid it aside to commence upon another, no one could by any possibility have imagined that these papers were of the most momentous import, not only to herself, but to those still more dear, whom to shield from the slightest ill, she would willingly have sacrificed all selfish and less sacred feelings. No, there she sat, the mellowed light of the lamp reflected in her calm and still beautiful features, engaged (for aught that the most minute observer could have detected) in perusing those documents soley for her own amusement or curiosity.

On the opposite side of the table sat her strange and unwelcome visitor, watching well and narrowly each movement of her countenance, seeking, if possible, to read thereon what was passing in her mind. The two formed a strange contrast to each other: the one so calm, so apparently almost indifferent, even to the weighty matter which now engrossed her mind; the other quick, yet cold in his demeanour, evidently anxious and ill at ease. Thus they sat, for well nigh the space of an hour, in perfect stillness; no sound, save the occasional rustling of paper, disturbing the perfest quietude of the room. At length Lady Eardley spoke; her voice was clear and even musical in its tones, as she said, laying aside the last sheet—

"It is enough, sir; I am so far convinced that these certificates are genuine. Now, all I wish to be informed further, is to what purpose you intend to turn them?"

"Under other circumstances," replied the stranger, "it would be most natural in me to answer that I intended to make use of them to prove the legitimacy of my niece, and assist her in attaining her own. This, I repeat, under other than existing circumstances, would be my most probable, as well as most natural, course of action; but the unfortunate circumstance of her having early fallen a victim to the falsehood and deceit of Sir Richard——"

"Richard!" interrupted Lady Eardley. "This, indeed, I cannot believe—it s impossible."

"That I am likewise enabled to prove," returned the other, in his cold calculating tones, so utterly opposed to the low musical ones of his present companion. "You see, Lady Eardley, I have come fully prepared for any suggestion on your part, and ready to act upon it. In proof, therefore, of your son's cruelty and falsehood towards my niece, she has in her keeping letters written by himself, and which will fully establish his guilt. You are also at liberty to appeal to him in truth of my assertion, which he will scarcely deny; but should he thus act, the letters I have spoken of shall be placed at your disposal."

"Then God help us!" exclaimed Lady Eardley, in the bitterness of her feelings, "for there does indeed seem to be a curse upon our race. In vain have I endeavoured to shield my children from its baneful effects—in vain have I struggled with my feelings, and sacrificed my own happiness on the altar of parental affection."

"I am glad you view this subject in the right light," interrupted her visitor, "as I hope to induce you to lend your assistance in furthering my present plans, which is to unite the fortunes of our children. Let Sir Richard give his hand to Laura (who in right of her dead father, is heiress of Eardley Hall) and she is willing to forego her claim, or I should rather say merge it in that of her husband. By this means he will retain his title and honours, and preserve to his parent continued security."

"Alas! then," returned Lady Eardley, "you are not aware that my son is already married?"

"No, I am better informed than your ladyship appears to imagine; but the circumstance of his marriage is by no means an impenetrable barrier. Divorces are not altogether uncommon, and wealth can procure all things."

"What!" exclaimed Lady Eardley, firing with indignation. "You would recommend me to advise my son to break the heart of a sweet and inestimable girl whom he has voluntary made his wife; to bid her live the remainder of her days for the finger of scorn to point at; to cast her from him without the slightest provocation on her part, for such a refinement of cruelty?"

"It is to this he has doomed my niece, his cousin, although he knows it not; after wearying of her charms, which pleased but for the passing moment, he left her unheeded—uncared for, to struggle with poverty and affliction, while he revelled in luxury and wealth, which is by right her own : seeking new sources of pleasure, and making a newer bride grace his home, and cheer him with her smile; thus he has acted towards my unfortunate Laura. Why, then, need he shrink from thus acting towards an ther? If there must be a victim, it cannot, shall not be my child."

"Would you, then," inquired Lady Eardley, "have my son perjure himself at the altar for the sake of gold? Can wealth, honours, or titles, think you, purchase affection, or enslave a heart which disdains bondage, and pants alone for freedom?"

"These are questions," returned the other, "which Lady Eardley had better put to her own heart, and read the answer there. If," he continued, without noticing the increased pallor of Lady Eardley's expressive countenance, "Sir Richard agrees to my proposition, he will not be the first member of his family who has thus perjured himself."

"And you would punish my fault—my crime, if you will—through my child, making him the instrument to wring my soul with torture? This you may call ustice, but my whole being rebels against it, and to this indignity my son shall never submit. No, far better to welcome poverty, in all its most hideous forms, than to procure wealth and honours at the expense of the noblest feelings of the soul."

"You are willing then to permit me to establish the claims of Laura in a court of justice?"

"As willing," replied Lady Eardley, "as the prisoned bird is to remain within the limits of its narrow cage. So far I may be termed willing, but no farther."

"Then our conference is ended," returned the other, taking up his papers and preparing to depart.

"Yet stay," exclaimed Lady Eardley; "is there no middle course? must I of necessity involve my children in my own ruin, leave them without even a name, save one which they must blush to own, as avowing the guilt of their mother? Oh, Evereard," she added, addressing the stranger for the first time by name, "can you not spare me this for the sake of my children? I cast off all pride, and condescend to implore you to act with less severity towards me whose youthful sins have been deeply punished by years of agony, by days of unceasing sorrow, and nights of unseen mitigated anguish; when, could you have seen the tears which bedewed my pillow, the groans which have burst from my agonised bosom when none were nigh to witness my emotion, could you have seen and heard all this—Oh! surely—surely you would acknowledge that my sins were expiated, and would spare me this last bitter struggle. Bethink you, then, could no other course be found, if wealth, or power, or both combined?"

"Stop—stop, Lady Eardley," interrupted the other. "Laura is proud and high-minded, as the proudest of you all, and would never consent to be a pensioner on the bounty of your son. Nothing but marriage will satisfy her; that

EVERARD'S SURPRISE AT LADY EARDLEY'S MASTERY OVER HER FEELINGS.

accomplished, she consents to waive her right and confirm your son in the belief that he alone is the legal heir."

"That can never be," returned Lady Eardley. "Alas! alas! what an unhappy family is ours, to bring sorrow and misfortune on all who ever loved us. Yet," she continued, after a moment's hesitation, "you must doubtlessly possess some power or influence over the mind of your niece;—could not your persuasions or entreaties induce her to demand something less than the utter separation of two hearts which now fondly beat in unison?"

"I have, as you say," returned the other, "some power over the mind of Laura; but she is revengeful as she is proud, and is resolutely determined to make your son feel some of the misery she has herself endured through him."

"Oh! Evereard," exclaimed Lady Eardley, "what would I not give to avert so terrible a calamity; my own existence would be as nothing placed in the balance. Let me then beseech, implore of you, for the sake of past days of happiness, to exert the power you acknowledge to possess over the mind of your niece, in order to induce her to forego this scheme of vengeance. Say," she continued, with increasing animation, and extending her hands beseechingly towards the stranger, "is there nothing that will induce you to pity and to spare? Though perjured and forsworn, my bosom has yet ever been the seat of virtue—my name spotless; if, then, the treasures of my heart, which you once so highly coveted, can avail to alter your determination, or relent your stubborn will, from this hour it is your's—your's for good or ill."

"I can well understand," replied the stranger, "the extent of the sacrifice you are thus generously inclined to make; but you will pardon me, if I decline to avail myself of the honour thus intended. There was a time when I implored the boon of your love, as the greatest blessing Heaven could give, when to call you mine, I would have renounced all else; but that time is past, never to return. You might now sue in vain for a return of those fond warm feelings, which I once so richly, yet madly lavished upon you; the lamp of love is gone out, and nothing on earth can relight it. You were perhaps right in preferring wealth to comparative poverty—a title to a name, which had nothing beyond the love of its owner to recommend it to your notice. How you answered to your conscience to procure these at the expense of honour, worth, and purity, you must be the best judge; suffice it, a woman whom I could not respect—I could never love."

"You might well have spared me this additional humiliation," replied Lady Eardley; "but let it pass, only listen to my suit. I ask no mercy for myself, but for my children I would entreat you, even on my knees, to spare them the bitter mortification of knowing their mother's guilt."

"It rests with yourself to do that." said the stranger. "I have shown you how it may be accomplished, and however distasteful my proposition may be, I would strenuously advice you to accept it."

"But the proposition is so monstrous—so almost impossible for me to accede to," urged Lady Eardley.

"I am sorry that I cannot offer you other and more pleasing terms," replied her visitor; "but I will not press you on the subject; you are of course at perfect liberty to accept or decline my terms."

"At liberty?" repeated Lady Eardley her pale cheek glowing with excitement, as she rose and paced the room, with quick and agitated steps; "at liberty, when you leave me no choice of action, hedged in on either side by shame and sorrow, forced to use my maternal influence to induce my son to act with dishonour, or bring disgrace on the head of him and his, by declaring my own! You may call this perfect liberty, if you please, but it is an utter perversion of the word, for it is nothing but cruel, sordid bondage, which chafes and irritates my proud and restless spirit."

"Years, ay, years ago," said the stranger, as he watched with a light sparkling eye the hurried anxious steps of Lady Eardley, as she continued to pace the room, "I warned you that the time would come, when you would sue to me in vain; I swore to be revenged, though at the time I knew not how it was to be accomplished; but Heaven, in its own time, and in its own manner, aided me with its just and wise decrees. I could never have foreseen that I should thus hold, not only yours, but your children's happiness in my keeping. Heaven is indeed both wise and good."

"Talk not thus impiously," replied Lady Eardley, stopping abruptly in her walk and confronting her visitor with a stern and angry brow. " See, I am calm ; I feel, I know the utter inutility of appealing to you, either for mercy or justice. I ask only for time to consider your proposition ; give me a month to think it over ; at the close of that period you shall have my resolve."

" It is rather a long period ; but——"

" You are disposed to grant it ?" interrupted Lady Eardley. " I thank you, sir, for so much consideration, it is more then I dared to expect."

There was a quiet dignity in the tone with which she gave utterance to these words ; her brow had once more resumed its habitual serenity, her manner was calm and wholly unmoved. Again the master spirit had prevailed over the frail body—not a muscle moved, not the slightest agitation was perceptible in her demeanour, as after a moment's pause, she again spoke—

" Our conference is now ended ; you will have the goodness to leave me ; I have no longer need to endure your presence," and she moved to the opposite end of the apartment. The stranger gazed at her with astonishment. The extraordinary power she possessed over her feelings, had never been apparent to him before, and he knew not whether most to admire or wonder at the change a few seconds had sufficed to produce over her mind. But he had no longer any farther excuse for intruding on her presence ; therefore, without any other leave-taking than a simple bow, which meet no return on the part of the lady, he hastily quitted the apartment. Lady Eardley removed not from the position she had taken up, but stood firm and erect, like some fair and beautiful statue ; indeed, so still, so calm, and wholly unmoved was her bearing, that she might well have been mistaken for the work of the sculptor, rather than a being warm with life and breath.

CHAPTER L.

" Then weave the web of the mystic measure,
    From the depts of the sky, and the ends of the earth,
Come, swift spirits, of might and of measure,
    Fill the dance and the music of mirth,,
As the waves of a thousand streams rush by,
To an ocean of splendour and harmony."

THE skies are still blue and bright in the sunny land of Italy. The flowers are exhaling their richest perfume, and the birds are singing their sweetest song ; all is in bright and beautiful harmony ; or if for a short time a summer cloud passes over the face of a mountain, it is but a transient one, fitfully heightening its already beautiful tints. And sweet and fair indeed are the scented flowers, making the air with their pefume fit for angels to inspire ; and the dew-drops glittering, as the rays of light fall upon them, look like orient pearls ; and the many tints, though ever varying, ever beautiful, some in their delicate whiteness, bearing the appearance of alabaster ; others again, before the flower has expanded, or when its petals are fully unfolded to the view, present from the first blush of beauty, to the gradual unfolding of the softened hue of its prime, when the tints become fainter and fainter, until the flower has performed its allotted office, when like everything earthly it dies, and we all know how short-lived it is. Alas !

" How small a part of time they share,
    That are so wondrous sweet and fair."

Indeed, it seems the peculiar property of beauty to be evanescent, whether in flowers or in mortals. How many roses of earthly mould have we seen snatched away, even before maturity was attained ! perhaps nipped in the bud, by the frosts of adversity, or perhance through its confiding unsuspecting innocence, deceived and betrayed. Since we last left Henry and his fond young wife, six months have elapsed ; a short space, yet to the two with whom we are

at present interested, brimmed with happiness and joy, Fanny's heart still
beats responsive to the fond warm affection, which had never been lavished
on any but the one chosen of her heart. She had said, and said truly, that—

> " With him she had no cares, if skies were bright and blue,
>   Or hidden by the tempest-cloud, a vault of gloom might show ;
>   For then the balm of love would shed its fragrance round her form,
>   And not a drop should touch her wing, however rude the storm."

And well might all who knew her gentle, tender worth, reply—

> " Oh fairest, rarest of the gems the fav'ring clouds drop down,
>   That young Aurora's coronet upon the world has thrown,
>   Oh, meetest, sweetest of the things, the powers above have given—
>   Were all of womankind like thee, sure this had been our heaven."

Henry, too, is happy. How indeed could he be otherwise, while blest with such
a fond and devoted companion ? But she is not his only source of happiness, for
some few months back, Fanny presented him with a fine and beautiful boy. And
already has the father's heart beat with rapture, as he watched the first dawn
of reason lighting up its fair and beaming face, putting the coral lips into
that bright smile of joyousness, which belongs alone to infancy—

> "Ere yet upon its years,
> The soil of human vice appears,
> Ere passion has disturbed its cheek,
> And prompted what it dares not speak,
> Ere little it recks of this sad store—
> Would it might never reck them more."

This sweet pledge of affection has done more than aught else, to bind his
heart to Fanny ; and when she pressed the first kiss of love upon its downy
cheek, and witnessed the heart-felt joy of Henry, as he gazed upon his first-
born child, she inwardly gave God thanks and breathed a prayer for their
united happiness.   And when returning health enabled her once more to resume
her wonted duties, a proud and happy wife, a fond and thankful mother was
Fanny, her cup of joy now seemed full ; she had no fears or cares for the future;
her husband and her child were all the world to her, as she fully believed she
was all the world to them.   She had no longer the slightest desire to mix
again in the festive gaiety, which had once possessed so sweet a charm ; her
love even for exploring was over, and though constantly surrounded with
fetes and curious ceremonies, neither herself nor Henry felt in the least disposed
to avail themselves of the repeated invitations they received, either to witness,
or take part in the same.   They still retained possession of the villa, and the
weather being so propitious and entirely agreeing with the constitution of Fanny,
they resolved to remain at Valetta during the winter months, purposing to return
to England the ensuing spring.   One beautiful afternoon, as they were seated
together in the dining-room, the windows of which opened into a verandah,
which Fanny's excellent taste had caused to be filled with the choicest aromatic
plants, the conversation accidentally turned upon the wonders of Mount Etna.
" I have often thought," observed Henry, " that it would be an almost
endless task to recapitulate all the various commodities, and curious productions
of this island, as Etna alone affords a greater number than many of the most extensive kingdoms, and is no less an epitome of the whole earth in its soil and
climate, than in the strange and opposing varieties of its productions.   Besides,
the corn, the wine, the oil, the silk, the spice and delicious fruits of its lower
region, the beautiful forests, the flocks, the game, the tar, the cork, the honey,
of its second, the snow and ice of its third, it also affords from its caverns a
variety of mineral and other productions, such as mercury, sulpher, alum,
nitre, and vitrol, all of which we have explored together, and can therefore say
of our own knowledge that this wonderful mountain produces at one and the
same time every necessary, and every luxury of life.   Its first region covers

our tables with all the delicasies that the earth produces ; its second supplies us with game, cheese, butter and honey, and not only furnishes wood of every kind for building, but likewise an inexhaustible store of fuel ; and as the third region with its ice and snow keeps us fresh and cool during the heat of summer, so I am assured (upon good authority) it contributes equally to keep them warm and comfortable in the cold seasons."

"It is indeed wonderful," returned Fanny, "and prevents me feeling any surprise at the attachment of the people to this mountain, so that all its terrors have not been able to drive them away ; for although he sometimes chastises, yet like an indulgent parent, he mingles so many blessings along with his chastisements, that their affections can never be estranged, for at the same time that he threatens them with a rod of iron, he pours down upon them all the blessings of gold."

"Your words would lead me to infer," replied Henry, "that you would not object to spend the remainder of your life in this beautiful and fertile place."

"If such were your wish," returned Fanny quickly, "I would willingly submit to such an exile from my native shores. Still the manners and customs of the inhabitants are so utterly at variance with those of our country, that it entirely does away with that unanimity of feeling, without which we cannot feel ourselves at home."

"You are perfectly right, dear Fanny," returned her husband, "we have made a long stay from home and friends, and I shall not be sorry when the time we have fixed upon for our return arrives, although I shall not be able to quit this island without a feeling of regret, for we have passed so many happy days here, and on this spot I have received so many convincing proofs of your affection, and it is moreover the birth-place of our darling boy ; still," he continued, smiling kindly at the earnest expression pourtrayed on Fanny's countenance, "change of place, I am convinced, will produce no corresponding change in your love and tenderness."

"Oh, never, dear Henry," returned his wife, fondly pressing the hand which Henry had laid upon her shoulder while speaking. "And as we have seen everything that is considered worthy of observation or interest, upon quitting the island we shall have no room for regret."

"This reminds me," said Henry, "of a somewhat curious ceremony which will shortly take place ; it is called the feast of St. Rosolia ; it has been described to me as being the most remarkable, as well as magnificent in Europe, so much so, that it has impressed me with a great desire to witness it ; and as I ever wish you near me, particularly when I am happy (though you know it is by no means shows or feasts that can make me so), I should feel gratified, if you could prevail upon yourself to leave home for a short time, in order to participate with me in the forthcoming festivities."

"Dear Henry," returned Fanny, affectionately, "you know I an never so happy as when contributing, even in the slightest degree, to your's ; for though I love our child dearly, yet, Henry, I love thee more."

"I know it—I know it," replied her husband, eagerly ; "my own Fanny, if ever woman was free from fault, it is you."

"Stop," returned Fanny, playfully placing her hand over his mouth ; "do not give me credit for more virtues than I really possess. Besides," she added, smiling, "I have no desire to be thought perfect, neither do I think it possible you would love me so much if I could, in truth, lay claim to it ; a few failings act as a kind of piquant suace to rich viands, tempting the fastidious appetite to a more full enjoyment of their dainties."

Henry smiled as he listened to her playful remarks.

"Then we will consider it settled, my love. You consent to accompany me to this feast ?"

"By all means," replied Fanny. "I should be sorry, after having seen so much, to leave Malta without witnessing a ceremony so highly spoken of, though I am half inclined to believe we shall find the representation has been too highly coloured."

"That remains to be seen," returned Henry. "For my own part, I must confess that I am on the very tip-toe of expectation."

"Well, I hope you may not be doomed to be disappointed," said Fanny, smiling.

And now for preparations, as so young a mother cannot leave her child, even for a few days, without due caution and care as to his well-being in her absence. And Fanny said truly, for it cost her some anxiety and not a little amount of self-denial to separate herself from the darling of her heart ; but her husband, who was still the first object in her affections, requested the sacrifice, and for his sake she was not only willing to make it, but what is. a far more arduous task, to make it cheerfully ; so that he knew not the effort it cost her to relinquish her own desires in obedience to his. But we grieve to say that on this particular occasion it would have been better otherwise, far better for all concerned, had she declined the pioposed expedition, which was unfortunately destined to involve them once more in sorrow and anxiety ; but Fanny knew nought of this, as, a few days after the foregoing conversation, she took her departure from Valetta, accompanied by her husband, leaving the port in a small sailing boat, which they hired to convey them to the city of Palermo. As they coasted along the island, Henry took the opportunity of viewing the north part, its fortifications and lazaretto. All these they found very great, and more like the works of a mighty and powerful nation, than of so small a state. The mortars cut out of the rocks, were, in particular, a tremendous invention, at least so thought Henry, who pointed them out to Fanny. There were about fifty of them near the different creeks and landing-places around the island, directed at the most probable spots wher e boat s would attempt a landing. The mouths of some of these mortars, the men who accompanied them in the expedition, assured Henry were as much as six feet wide, and would throw a hundred cantero of cannon ball or stone to a considerable distance. As they proceeded, they found the coast everywhere bare and barren, but covered over with towers, redoubts, and fortifications of various kinds. After coasting round the island for some time, Henry desired the sailors to pull out to sea, and they soon found themselves once more at the mercy of the waves, and in the course of an hour were out of sight of all the islands, and saw only a part of Mount Etna smoking above the waters. The wind sprung up fair, and after a short, and, in every respect, pleasant voyage, they arived at the famous city of Palermo. Here they found everybody full of bustle and confusion ; the feast of St. Rosolia was to begin on the morrow, and all the world (that is, of course, the Palermo world) seemed filled with expectaton and interest. The place, indeed, was so crowded with visitors, that it was not without some considerable difficulty that Henry succeeded in procuring suitable accommodation for himself and Fanny. The following day, about five in the afternoon, the festival began by the triumph of St. Rosolia, who was drawn with great pomp through the centre of the city, from the Marino to Porto Nuovo. The triump hal car was preceded by a troop of horse, with trumpets and kettle-drums, and all the city officrs in their gala uniforms. The car was, indeed, a most enormous machine, measuring seventy feet long, thirty wide, and upwards of eighty high ; ard as it passed along, overtopped the loftiest houses in Palermo. The form of the under part resembled the Roman gallies, but it swelled as it advanced in height, the front assuming an oval shape, like an amphitheatre, with seats placed in the theatrical manner. This was the great orchestra, which was filled with a numerous band of musicians, placed in rows, one above the other. Over this orchestra, and a little behind it, there was a large dome, supported by six Corinthian columns, and adorned with a number of figures of saints and angels ; and on the summit of the dome, there was a gigantic silver statue of St. Rosolia. The whole machine was dressed out with orange-trees, flower-pots, and trees of artificial coral. The car stopped every fifty or sixty yards, when the orchestra performed a piece of music, with songs, in honour of the saint. It appeared a moving castle, and completely filled the great street from side to side. This was, indeed, its greatest disadvantage, for the space it had to move in was in no wise proportioned to its size, and the houses seemed to dwindle away to nothing as it passed along. This vast fabric was drawn by fifty-six huge mules, in two rows, curiously caparisoned, and mounted by twenty-eight postilions, dressed in gold and silver, with great plumes of ostrich feathers in their caps. Every window and balcony on both sides of the street was filled with elegantly-dressed persons, and the car was followed by many thousands of the lower sort. The triumph was finished in about three hours, and was succeeded by the beautiful illumination of the Marino. There was a range of arches and pyramids, extending from end to end of this noble walk; these were all painted, and adorned with flowers, and were entirely covered with lamps, placed so very thick, that at a little distance the whole appeared like so many pyramids and arches of flame. The whole chain of this illumination was about a mile in length, and to both Fanny and Henry was more splendid than they could possibly have conceived, there being no break or imperfection anywhere, the night being so still that not a single lamp was extinguished. Opposite to the centre of this great line of light, there was a magnificent pavilion, erected for the viceroy, and on the part of this at some little distance in the sea, stood the great fireworks, representing the front of a palace adorned with columns, arches, trophies, and every ornament of architecture. Ranged round this palace, and forming a kind of amphitheatre in the sea, enclosing it in the sea, were all the chebicks, galleys, galliots, and other shipping. Then began the show by a discharge of the whole of their artillery, the sound of which, re-echoed from the mountains, produced a very noble effect. They then played off a variety of water rockets, and bombs of a curious construction, that often burst below the water. This continued for nearly half an hour, when in an instant the whole of the palace was beautifully illuminated. This was the signal for the shipping to cease, which it did, with almost the appearance of enchantment, so instantaneously and altogether was it accomplished, and without the visibility of any agent. At the same time the fountains that were represented in the court before the palace, began to spout up fire, and made a representation of the great *jet d'eaux* of Versailles. As soon as these were extinguished, the court assumed the form of a large *parterre*, adorned with a variety of palm trees of fire, interspersed with orange trees, flower pots, vases, and other ornaments. On the extinguishing of these, the illumination of the palace was likewise extinguished, and the front of it broke out into the appearance of a variety of suns, stars, and wheels of fire, which in a short time reduced it to a perfect ruin. And when all appeared finished, there burst from the centre of the pile, a vast explosion of two thousand rockets, bombs, serpents, squibs, and the like, which seemed to fill the whole atmosphere. The fall of these made great havoc amongst the clothes of the poor people who were not under cover, but afforded admirable entertainment to the nobility who were. During this exhibition, there was a handsome entertainment provided for the guests in the centre great pavilion, consisting of coffee, ices, and sweatmeats, together with a variety of excellent wines. As soon as the fireworks were finished, the viceroy went out to sea in a galley richly illuminated. It was rowed by seventy-two oars, and indeed made one of the most beautiful objects which could possibly be imagined, flying with vast rapidity over the waters, as smooth and as clear as glass, which shone round it like a flame, and reflected its splendour on all sides; the oars beat time to the French horns, clarionets and trumpets, of which there was a numerous band on the prow. The great street was illuminated in the same magnificent manner as the Marino. The arches and pyramids were erected at little distances from each other on both sides of the street, leaving a broad promenade in the centre; and these illuminations, when seen from either of the gates, appeared to be two continued lines of the brightest flame. The promenade was crowded by the nobility and gentry; and the beauty of the ladies, the richness of their dress and brilliance of their jewels, were displayed in the most advantageous manner. The company appeared all joy and exulta-tion; scarce two separate parties passed, without some mutual acknowledgment of affection or respect, and the pleasure that sparkled from every eye, seemed to be reflected and communicated, by a kind of sympathy, through the entire company. In such an assembly, it was impossible for the heart not to dilate and expand itself; and Fanny being naturally of a warm and generous nature, felt hers often so full that she could hardly find utterance; and frequently had she viewed a tragedy with much less emotion, than she did this scene of joy; for the universal gaiety seemed really to spring from the heart, brightening every countenance, and speaking affection and friendship from every face. There was no stately airs, no supercilious looks; all appeared friends and equals. And the beauty of the ladies was not one half so much heightened, either by their rich dresses or splendid jewels, as by that air of good humour and kind feeling with which they were evidently animated. Fanny was com-pletely overjoyed, and warmly expressed to Henry the pleasure she felt at this delightful sight.

"If," she said, in conclusion, "superstition often produces such pleasing effects, I only wish we had a little more of it amongst ourselves at home. I declare, at this moment, I could positively throw myself down before St. Rosolia, and bless her for making so many people happy."

"You speak warmly," replied Henry, "and I will even own to you that I have never myself beheld a more enchanting sight;" he stopped abruptly at this moment, for a small party approached whom they had already encountered several times in the course of the evening, and which, for some reason scarcely definable to himself, filled Henry with a vague and indescribable interest.

The party consisted only of six persons—a lady and gentleman of middle age, and moving, to all appearance, among the higher circles, to judge from the number of bows and acknowledgments which constantly greeted them, and the blaze of jewellery that adorned their persons; a young lady and gentleman, evidently their son and daughter; a still younger lady, whose dress and ap-pearance were those of a foreigner, and a handsome, noble-looking boy, whose golden ringlets, floating loosely over his shoulders, clearly proclaimed his English birth. There was nothing peculiarly attractive in this little party to call forth either the admiration or distinct notice of Henry. There were many females more beautiful than the Italian girl who leant upon her father's arm, but whose beaming face was lighted up with pleasurable emotions, and whose graceful and unaffected demeanour might nevertheless have entitled her to the greatest consideration. Still it was neither the charms of her person, or those reflected from her mind, that caused Henry's heart to beat quicker as the little party drew nigh. No, it is almost questionable whether he even bestowed so much notice upon her as we have done. For there was another there that claimed his undivided attention—one on whom the light had not yet shone, or—

> "Shone but partly, so downcast
> She held her brow, as slow they passed;
> And yet to him there seemed to dwell
> A charm about that unseen face—
> A something in the shade that fell
> Over that brow's imagined grace,
> Which took him more than all the best
> Outshining beauties of the rest;
> And she alone his eyes could see,
> Enchained by this sweet mystery;
> And she alone he watched, as round
> She glided o'er that magic ground."

In vain he strove to catch a glimpse of that as yet unseen face; she still remained so placed between the lamp's strong glow and him, that he but saw, in outline traced, the shadow of her symmetry.

"Yet did his heart, he scarce knew why,
Even at that shadowed shape beat high!

and brought to his mind the recollection of other hours, which still dwelt upon his mind in all the vivid colours of reality, and imparted a pleasure no earthly

JANE SWOONS AFTER HENRY SAVES WALTER FROM THE SEA.

power of ill could throw a gloom over, and caused his enraptured fancy to revert to the scenes which he loved as a youth, with all the ardent pleasure of that bright though brief period; to the long-remembered spots which returned upon his mind, loaded with the remembrance of boyish pleasures and fancies, with pure and unmixed feelings of delight; those scenes which in life's early hours he most dearly prized—most fondly loved; when his was "the gay sunshine of the breast," and his heart glowed in all the lightness of youth and joy and

> " Again he seemed to breathe the heartfelt vow,
> And feel its seal imprinted on his brow ;
> Then in imagination fond retrace
> His steps o'er every well-remembered place,
> Wander delighted o'er each hallowed spot,
> Which, while life lasts, can never be forgot !"

But, oh ! how changed the scene, when, rousing himself from his passing reverie to reply to some lively remark of Fanny's, the dear deceitful dream was dispelled.

> " Alas ! joy turned to sadness—hope to deep despair,
> An emblem of what life's best pleasures are—
> An airy nothingness—a vapour's light,
> Which dazzles brightly to deceive the sight."

Although delighted—nay, almost entranced by the extreme beauty and magnificence of the spectacle they had witnessed, Fanny had on more than one occasion remarked the abstraction of her husband ; and now that the little party we have already described again approached them, she could not fail to observe that their presence seemed in some mysterious manner powerfully to affect him.

"Is that young lady known to you, Henry ?" she inquired, observing, for the first time, that the one whose appearance seemed peculiarly attractive to her husband, was evidently one of her own countrywomen.

"No," replied Henry, with some little hesitation ; " why do you inquire ?"

" Simply because I remarked that she drew your attention more than any other person in this vast assembly."

"May that not be accounted for," returned Henry, endeavouring to rouse himself from his abstracted mood, "by the mere circumstance of her being (with the exception of ourselves), as far as I have been able to discover, the only English person present ?"

"There is surely something pleasing," returned Fanny, " in meeting far from home, and friends, one upon whose lips there hang the accent of the mountain tongue, whose feelings, like our own, must go back far from these festive scenes to the less magnificent, but more sweet, pleasures that England can afford. I admit all this, but will you pardon me if I add, that I thought the sight of that young lady recalled other, and perhaps still dearer, associations ?"

" My dear, Fanny," replied Henry, " you are in a measure right, so far, that the form of the stranger forcibly reminded me of one whose image I would gladly banish from my mind."

Fanny was generous and high-minded, possessed by nature of the most beautiful and attractive virtues, without which the most splendid talents are desecrated or lost, and even high and lofty actions fail to inspire love ; still she could not endure this allusion to a rival in the affections of her husband entirely unmoved.

" Let us leave this brilliant assembly, dear Henry," she said, pressing yet more fondly the arm on which she leaned for support. " I declare the glittering scenes, and gaudy objects by which we are surrounded, have already exhausted me so much, that I feel sure it is utterly impossible to keep up the excitement much longer. The pleasures must necessarily flag; indeed, from what I can observe, they have well-nigh exhausted the stock of amusements prepared for the occasion ; how, therefore, they are to keep up the festivity for many hours longer, I own I cannot at all comprehend."

" We shall see, my love," said Henry, smiling, "for I really feel disposed to tax you patience to the fullest extent ; this is a sight which in all probability we shall never have an opportunity of witnessing again. I am, therefore, desirous to view, if possible, the entire exhibition."

Fanny did not further urge their departure ; still she felt restless and uneasy her eyes constantly followed those of her husband's, which seemed entirely drawn towards the spot which the stranger might for the moment occupy. And again she would be lost amid the crowd, and in vain she strove to catch a glimpse of her features, till suddenly

> " Wide open flew
> The temple's gates, and from them threw
> A flood of light, and as though the same
> Rich source gave birth to both, there came
> A swell of harmony as grand
> As e'er was born of voice or hand ;
> Filling the gorgeous place around
> With that mixed burst of light and sound.
> Then was it by the flash that blazed
>   Full o'er her features—oh ! 'twas then,
> As startingly her eyes she raised,
>   But quick let fall their lids again,"

that Henry recognised in a moment the never-to-be-forgotten features of his first and earliest love. He scarce suppressed an exclamation of wonder and astonishment; but short time was allowed him for reflection on the strange and unlooked-for circumstance of thus meeting her in a foreign land, in close association with the wealthy and high-born dames of Italy ; it seemed an impossibility, and yet he could not mistake that well-know form. Love—such love as he had felt for Jane—could never err—" No, sooner might the rose of May, forget her own sweet nightingale."

While thus deeply musing, Henry was roused to action by a wild and piercing scream, which broke from the lips of the very object of his secret thoughts. Lost in astonishment, forgetful for the moment of all else, Henry suddenly relinguised the arm of Fanny, and pressed forward to ascertain the cause of that shrill cry of agony ; he had to contend with but slight difficulty in reaching the spot, where the cause was soon made manifest, for the brilliant light quickly enabled him to discern at a short distance from the land, a boy struggling convulsively in the water, which threatened every moment to entomb him for ever ; close to the brink stood Jane, wringing her hands in the anguish of terror, and vainly endeavouring to escape from those who forcibly held her back, in order to prevent her precipitating herself into the sea, in the wild hope of saving the child of her sister, who through some unfortunate accident had fallen into the water.

Henry hesitated not a single instant, but being an excellent swimmer, at once plunged into the stream, and made towards the object of her earnest solicitude. In a very short time he succeeded in reaching the boy, whom he firmly grasped with one hand, and with the other impelled himself towards the shore. This was a more difficult task than he had imagined, inasmuch as the tide was fast running out, and each successive wave drove him farther back into the sea. Nothing daunted, however, and not for an instant even losing his presence of mind, Henry steadily battled with the waves ; and persevering in his efforts, encouraged likewise by the shouts of the people on the shore, who were fast maning a boat to put out to his assistance, Henry sustained both himself and the boy on the surface of the element, which seemed yawning to engulph them in its bottomless abyss, till such time as the boat reached them, when they were both safely conveyed to the shore. Henry heeded not the congratulatory shouts of the vast number of persons assembled, saw not in the admiring eyes, and glowing faces of those by whom he was surrounded, their warm and full appreciation of his gallant conduct. No, he saw only the pale and agonised face of Jane, as she knelt upon the ground beside the inanimate form of little Walter, chafing his hands and temples, and vainly endeavouring to assure herself that the vital spark had not fled for ever. Wet as he was, Henry essayed to assit her in this labour of love, and gently raising the head of the boy, drew back the golden ringlets, now heavy with moisture, and parted them over the fair and polished brow.

"He is dead," exclaimed Jane, frantically clasping her hands in anguish, as the boy gave no sign of returning animation.

"Not so," replied Henry, "believe me, you alarm yourself unnecessarily. He will soon and easily be restored, if the proper means are resorted to without further delay."

Jane started at the sound of his voice. Till, this moment she had been so entirely engrossed with the child as scarcely to bestow even a passing glance on his deliverer; but at the sound of his voice she started, and turned even paler than grief and terror had made her. That voice could not be mistaken: throughout the breathing world's extent, there was but one such voice for her—so soft, so kind, so eloquent. She looked wildly at him for a moment, and scarcely articulating, "Great God 'tis he," fell forward, and would have sunk fainting to the ground, had not Henry sprung forward and caught her in his arms. Almost at the same instant the young man who had been her companion throughout the evening pressed forward, and officiously offered to relieve him of his burden. Henry looked at him sternly for a moment, and felt strongly disinclined to relinquish his precious charge; but a glance at his own wet clothes, and the necessity of immediate exertion on behalf of the child who lay inanimate at his feet, decided him, and he consented (though not without reluctance) to resign her. As he did so, he raised his eyes and encountered those of Fanny, mournfully fixed on himself, though there was more of sorrow than of anger in the look which she cast upon him.

CHAPTER LI.

"Now in my heart there is a source of tears,
    Which the imperious hand of fate hath nurst,
Distilling o'er my path of future years,
    And poisoning all sweet flowers that there were nurst.
And though this is a world where years estrange
    The soul from its affection and its truth,
Where guilt may conquer, and deception change,
    Oh, still I love thee as in earliest youth."

THERE is not perhaps in the wide world a more melancholly object for human contemplation than a fair and fragile girl, deserted by him upon whom she has placed her heart's fondest affection, clinging around him like the ivy for support and confidence, and which, when they are rudely disunited, lie perishing in neglect and loneliness. And numberless are they brightful and good whose excellence of heart and mind might have spread happiness and bliss on all around them, and have made the earth they inhabit somewhat to resemble paradise, but who, by the perfidy—the cruelty of one loved not wisely, perhaps, but too well, remain in solitude and grief, bowed down to the grave, with tears upon their eyes, and anguish and sorrow in their hearts. And yet how sad—how strange it seems that the votaries of a mutual passion should ever grow cold or neglectful; that the hour should ever arrive when both, or either, should meet each other with indifference—almost with unconsciousness—and only, with an effort, recal their vanished scenes of felicity that quick, yet profound sympathy—that ready, yet boundless confidence—which once was so inestimably dear, leading to an an utter abandonment of self, in order to anticipate each others wants and wishes; in truth, it makes the heart ache only to picture such sad vicissitudes.

The knowledge that such changes can and do occur flits over the mind like the thought of death, obscuring all our gayer fancies, and tainting our brightest happiness with its bitterness. There is nothing, indeed, not even ruined cities that were once among the glories of the world, or mouldering temples breathing with oracles no more believed, or arches of triumph, which are triumphs no longer, having even forgotten the heroes names they were piled to celebrate; not any or all of these fill the mind with half such mournful impressions as the sad spectacle of exhausted affections, and the unstability of human hopes.

One of these was Laura Eardley, who had trusted—who had trusted in vows, subsequently, alas! proved to be false as the sands of the fair-seeming sea—who had fondly relied upon the love of one, who, after basking in the sunlight of her eyes, and opening the secret recesses of her heart and soul, feeling convinced that he only was enshrined there, forsook—abandoned her. Unlike her, he, perhaps, loved variety; and when the novelty of her affection had worn off, no longer felt a charm or fascination in her society; or it might be attributed, and probably was, to his being of an age when a man scarcely knows what he loves, and often spurns a treasure which might become his own in his vague and undefined aspiration for something of greater value than is to be found in humanity; when he forms an idea of perfection, which has more affinity to the angels in Heaven than to any creature of earth's mould, and treats with scorn all who do not reach up to it. But be that as it might, after some months of that pure and exquisite enjoyment, which is obtained when heart communes with heart, and each feels confident of the other's sincerity, he grew gradually cold and distant in his manners to Laura, and eventually she was forsaken.

Woman's heart is never inclined to doubt where it loves; and Laura, though she felt deeply the increasing reserve of her lover, yet formed excuses for it to her own heart, and shut out from her mind the supposition that he could be unfaithful; consequently when he quitted Italy for his native land, she buoyed herself up with the hope of his quick return, till she could no longer deceive herself; and his continued absence, and the neglect even of epistolatory correspondence, stamped conviction upon her mind, and reduced her to the lowest depths of despair. What could she do now on the very point of becoming a mother? Clinging to hope, she wrote to him, beseeching him with all the earnestness of which she was capable, to prevent her bringing disgrace and sorrow upon the only relative or friend she had in the wide world. She waited anxiously—oh! what words can tell how anxiously!—for an answer. Day after day she expected some tidings of the loved one, whom she fondly imagined would yet prove true to himself and her, but no letter came; and then, and not till then, could Laura believe that the ties which had united their hearts were severed—that she was no longer beloved. Proud and high-minded in the extreme, Laura's heart sickened, and her whole soul revolted at the cruelty of her lover's conduct; she became stern, haughty, and inflexible, while schemes of vengeance haunted her dreams by night, and her thoughts by day; to compass which, she would willingly have encountered all difficulties, braved all dangers, careless of self, and all things else, so that she might bring sorrow and remorse to her lover's heart. Yet the distance between them seemed to render all ideas on such a subject more than improbable. Still her injuries were deep; and time, so far from cooling her desire for vengeance, but added fuel to the fire which consumed her.

Thus months and even years rolled on; the once ardent lover of Laura Eardley had contracted new ties, and new affections. Accompanied by her uncle, Laura had been for some considerable period in London, when the certificate of her birth was suddenly discovered, and which led to the conviction that she alone was the rightful heir of Eardley Hall. Now, then, the long-wished for, but scarcely expected hour of retributive justice had arrived. Now she possessed the power to wound him to the quick—to inflict such pangs upon his wandering mind, as she had herself so long and hopelessly endured.

And yet there were moments when her woman's heart was melted even to pity her lover, and half doubt her own power to carry out schemes of revenge; but such moments were few and far between; and when they did come, easily and effectually subdued. She had but to think of her own wrongs—her own

unrequited affection, which struggled even yet (amid the utter desolation of a
other feelings) to raise its drooping head, and plead with her, to pity and t
spare. Such thoughts would send the burning blood mantling to an indignan
glow upon her cheeks, and nerve her heart with strength and fortitude to per
severe.

In the meantime, Sir Richard Eardley and his young wife, happily un
conscious of all that was plotting against their happiness, continued to preserv
the even tenor of their way in such sweet tranquil happiness, that none bu
those whose beings are wrapt in each other, could understand or appreciate
They lived in perfect retirement at Eardley Hall; saw no company; paid no
visits; each was all-sufficient society for the other, and they were never apart
Together they rode or walked, calling occasionally at the cottages of the tenantry
and always on some errand of kindness or of mercy; so that bright smiles, and
rough, though well-meant words of welcome ever greeted their coming, and
poured down blessings on their heads. Together they read works of instruction
and amusement, or planned slight alterations or improvements in their little
domain. Thus their days glided sweetly and swiftly along. To some there
might have appeared a dull monotony in a constant succession of days, thus
spent without variation or change, save in the books they read, or the employ.
ment with which they busied themselves; but not so thought Richard or Clara.
Blest in each other's love, constantly exchanging those sweet endearments which
make life so sweet and precious, and cause us to feel how blessed a thing it is
to love and be beloved, they knew no weariness. Dulness was a stranger to
their breast: they sighed not for the so called pleasures of the world, which
would have been no pleasure or joy to them. No; they experienced that
pure and exalted happiness which has its fount deep in the inmost recesses of
the heart, and will constantly be as a sweet well springing up even amid the
arid desert of all other feelings.

Thus time had sped on, for happiness such as enjoyed by them is not to be
counted by days or weeks, when one fine evening for the season—for winter had
now resumed its sway, yet the country was still fair and beautiful, though clad
in its winter garb—Richard, accompanied by his young wife, took their usual
walk round the grounds; the clear, frosty air imparted a bracing effect to their
frames, and made their spirits still more light and joyous. Clara gathered with
her own hands such flowers as yet lingered out their latest day, in spite of the
chill cold air.

"I have been thinking, Richard," she said, "that these flowers are more
sweet and beautiful than those by which we were lately surrounded, but which
have drooped and withered under the very first blast of autumn; and most
truly can I appreciate the language of the poet, when he says—

'Oh, bring me roses—oh, bring me roses!
That bloom in a wintry day;
But do not bring the roses of spring,
For their bloom passes quickly away.'"

"I fully appreciate your sentiments, my love," replied Sir Richard, "and the
same poet has well compared flowers to friendship, when he says—

'When clouds of misfortune
Most drearily bend,
How changed from life's sunshine
How rare is a friend.
Give me not the flowers
That bloom for a day,
And in the storms of the winter
Quite wither away.'"

"I cannot bear to regard love or friendship in that light," returned Clara
"it seems to take entirely from it that pure divine essence with which we are
all so prone to invest it."

"Yes, and very frequently err in so doing," returned Sir Richard.

"I cannot think so," replied his young wife. "For instance, dearest, would the love we bear each other grow cold or less ardent, if poverty and misfortune should at any time overtake us? Oh! surely no, would it not rather resemble these flowers that bloom more, far more bright and fair under a wintry sky, and raise their heads fresh and unflinchingly before the winter's storm, which though it may bend the delicate stem, is powerless to uproot the plant, which still remains firm and undaunted 'midst Nature's stroke?"

"I believe you, my own love," said Sir Richard, taking both her hands within his own. "Thus would your love prove true and tender; but you must not judge other hearts by the truth and purity of your own. There are but few, my Clara, who love as you have loved."

"Few, indeed!" echoed a voice that seemed close beside him; "and among those Sir Richard Eardley need not reckon himself. He hath already blighted hopes, and crushed the fondest and most devoted heart; but the worm will turn if trampled too cruelly, and may even, base, mean as it is, retaliate the cruelty which has been practised upon it."

Clara started, and clung to her husband as if for protection, as these words fell upon her ear; and at the same moment the speaker emerged from behind a small clump of trees, where she had been a silent listener to the foregoing conversation, and presented to the astonished eyes of Sir Richard the image of the injured, and till now almost forgotten Laura!

She was dressed with a singular mixture of coquetry and neatness: a small cloak still partially enveloped her form, but in lieu of more suitable head-gear, she had a handkerchief of scarlet silk tastefully wound round her head, and which formed a pleasing contrast with the raven blackness of her hair, whose shining folds, having partly escaped from the band which confined them, fell in thick masses over her shoulders.

"Lady, you need not fear me," she said, impressively stretching forth her hand, as she observed that Clara clung yet closer to Sir Richard. "Poverty, misfortune, and sorrow may chill the heart's best affections, and harden the love that once warmed them into life and being, far more than the frost and snow chills and destroys the bright flowers of summer. Some have already proved the truth of what I say, and it only remains for you to do so."

"For me?" repeated Clara, faintly, and retreating a step or two behind her husband.

"Yes, lady," returned the other, "those were my words. Thou art fair, and pleasant to look upon; so have been others—but this did not save them from the hand of the spoiler, who has destroyed fairer flowers than thou."

"Alas! what does she mean?" exclaimed Clara, in trembling accents.

"Do not alarm yourself, my love," replied Sir Richard, recovering his self-composure; "it is clear she has lost her senses, and has wandered in these grounds, not being aware that they are private property. I do not wish to use unnecessary violence, but, if needful, I will call the servants to conduct her to some temporary place of safety."

"I am not mad, Sir Richard," returned the stranger; "though your cruelty and oppression were well calculated to render me so. Suffice it, you took the most likely course to produce a result so favourable to yourself—therefore, I owe you no thanks that I am still in possession of my reason."

"It will be wisest to humour her," said Sir Richard, aside to Clara; and then turning towards the stranger, said aloud, "since you appear to regard us in the light of your enemies, will you have the goodness to quit these grounds, which are entirely our property?"

"You may call it what you please," returned the other, "but lands may change owners sooner than you anticipate; then it will be my turn to warn you off as a trespasser on private grounds. In the meantime, remember that the lamp which went out in a far away land, can never be relighted here; wait till poverty, despair, and anguish, is the portion of your bride, till even her good name is taken from her—and by you; then see if she will 'love thee then as now,' if her heart will remain true and tender when all joy, all happiness, is flown for ever. It is easy to bind summer garlands, but will they, think you, bind her to your side? No; you are yet doomed to experience, as I have done, that it is not flowers that can bind a love of yesterday. I see you tremble and turn pale at my words, which are no vain boasting, but true and prophetic as you shall be forced to acknowledge. Again, I say, beware! the day of retribution has come, and nothing can aid you in escaping from it."

"Richard, dear Richard!" exclaimed Clara, half fainting with alarm and astonishment, "come away, I entreat of you; do not stay to bandy words with that dreadful woman—leave her, and fly with me, I beseech, I implore of you."

"One moment, my love," returned her husband, endeavouring to support her trembling frame. "Woman!" he exclaimed, in a voice harsh and discordant with anger, "will you quit these grounds before I call my servants to drag you forcibly from them? Think you that threats or violence will extort money from me? If you are poor and need assistance, apply to my steward, and you shall receive it to the utmost; but do not taunt me with your presence, or strike me through one so inestimably dear."

The breast of the strange woman heaved convulsively—her brow grew dark and contracted, while the burning blood rushed to her very temples, as she replied—

"Think not, Sir Richard, I came hither to seek your charity, or ask for a mouthful even of the fragments which daily fall from your table. Were I, indeed, the lost forsaken wretch you would fain believe me—had I not a crust of bread or a drink of water to sustain my fainting steps—think you I would receive them at your hands? No! were I dying, and you proffered a glass of water to my parched lips, I would dash it untasted to the ground, even though one drop might restore me to life and health! May my bitterest curse rest upon you and yours! May all upon whom you cast your affections be left to pine in neglect, and at length sink unpitied to the tomb! May the very love which has been lavished upon you be turned to gall and wormwood! May death at length overtake you ere you may imagine that half your glass of life is run! This," she added in the bitterness of her feelings, "is my parting benediction—these my parting words. May they constantly ring in your ears, and poison every joy!'

As she thus spoke, she turned towards the brushwood, which soon concealed her from their sight.

"Clara, dear Clara, my own love!" exclaimed Sir Richard, as he fondly bent over the inanimate form of his wife, and endeavoured to restore her to consciousness.

Finding all his efforts ineffectual, he raised her gently in his arms, and carried her towards the house. Here he was met by the servants, who assisted him in conveying her to a couch. It was evident that Clara was very ill; and in an agony of alarm, Sir Richard ordered a surgeon to be instantly sent for. The presence of this gentleman succeeded in a short time in allaying his fears, as far, at least, as her life was concerned, which he repeatedly assured Sir Richard was in no danger; but alas! the alarm she had sustained threatened to deprive them of the sweet hope they had for some months nourished, of ere long having an heir to their estates. This the surgeon assured them was the extent of the calamity, and all he need fear as regarded the result of her illness. Thankful as Sir Richard felt on learning that the life of his beloved Clara was in no danger, he yet bitterly deplored the loss of his expected child, which it soon became manifest would be inevitable.

At last, when all was over, and the surgeon informed him that Clara had recovered consciousness, and was doing as well as could be expected, and extremely anxious to see him, he repaired to the sick chamber with a sad and heavy heart Seated by the bed-side of his wife, who leaned her head on his bosom and sobbed aloud, Sir Richard vainly endeavoured to subdue the bitterness of his own feelings, in order, if possible, to mitigate the severity of hers.

"My own Clara—my dear love,' he said, as he bent down and affectionately

SIR RICHARD EARDLEY IN THE SICK CHAMBER OF CLARA.

kissed her cheek, "thank God you are now out of all danger, and will soon I trust, be fully restored to your accustomed health."

"I know it, dear Richard," replied Clara; "but alas! my weakness, my folly, in allowing myself to be so overcome by the words of that strange woman, has deprived you, for a time at least, of the hope over which we had so fondly exulted."

"Name it not, my dear Clara," returned her husband, gently; "consider your own delicate health, and dedicate all your thoughts and energies towards the perfect recoverment of the same; for your well-being is far more precious to me than all else."

"I know it, dear love," returned Clara; but at the same moment a sigh escaped her bosom, for the words of the stranger had made a deep impression on her mind; although, fortunately, the state of insensibility into which she had been thrown, had prevented her hearing much that had passed between her and Sir Richard. Still she had heard sufficient to fill her mind with anxious forebodings; and when returning health enabled her to seek an explanation from her husband, his evasive replies and evident uneasiness were from being calculated to subdue it. She was restless and ill at ease; a vague fear of some impending calamity pressed heavily on her spirits, and made the hours of convalescence dull and tedious in the extreme, notwithstanding the constant and unvarying attention of Sir Richard, who allowed no other person to perform for her those offices which he considered by right devolved upon himself. Her constant companion, he endeavoured by every means in his power to prevent her feeling the slightest weariness. Selecting from the library those books he thought would be most pleasing, he read them aloud for her amusement, and frequently contrived to beguile the tedium of the sick chamber.

They were thus employed one afternoon, the one in reading, and the other in listening, when a letter was brought him by the servant. Sir Richard had but few correspondents, and it was consequently with some feeling of surprise that he glanced at the address, not expecting a letter at the present time. The writing was familiar; and yet, strange to say, it filled him with gloomy apprehensions, and he cast a look of anxiety towards Clara, as he hesitated to break the seal; but conquering this feeling, though evidently not without an effort, he hastily tore it open, and read the contents. His brow contracted as he did so, and his cheek flushed, either with anger or excitement; but presently turning towards Clara, who had been anxiously watching his countenance during the perusal, said, in his kindest and most considerate tones—

"I fear, my love, that I shall be obliged to leave you for a short time."

"Leave me?" echoed Clara, faintly, and turning pale.

"Only for a very short time, my love," replied Sir Richard, "and even then, believe me, with the greatest reluctance. My mother," he continued, "is in delicate health, and particularly requests an interview, which I cannot, under existing circumstances, well refuse; still you, my dear Clara, shall decide for me; say, then, can you spare me for this purpose, or shall I write and decline the interview?"

"Oh, no," replied Clara, eagerly, "go, go by all means; my friend, my benefactress, would not I am sure call you from my side, were it not absolutely necessary."

"Be it so, then," returned her husband, "my absence shall not be one moment longer than I can possibly avoid. In the meantime you must promise me to take additional care of yourself, guard your health carefully, and believe that my heart's best affections will dwell yet more fondly on you during this first, and I hope last separation."

"You think of going early?" said Clara, after a moment's pause.

"That I may the sooner return," said Sir Richard, "I will, if perfectly agreeable, start to-day."

"So very soon?" returned Clara, faintly.

"Not, my love, if you would prefer a farther delay."

"Oh, no," replied Clara, eagerly. "It is hard to be forced to part; but as it must be, I will endeavour cheerfully to submit."

"That is like yourself, my own dear love," returned Sir Richard, tenderly embracing her. "I shall count each hour that intervenes between our renewed meeting—separation even for a short time being so extremely painful to me, that were it not for your recent severe indisposition, I should have asked you to accompany me; as it is, we have no resource but to submit, which you have assured me you will do cheerfully."

The few preparations that were needful, for a contemplated absence ifrom home, were soon made, and with many tender words and gentle admonitions both given and received, Richard and Clara separated. Weak from recent illness, sad and low-spirited at the sudden and unlooked-for departure of her husband, it would be impossible to describe the feelings of Clara, now for the first time left alone in the ancient hall, of which she was the present mistress. A strange presentiment of trouble weighed down her spirits, and coming events cast their terrible shadows before them, saddening every waking scene, like warning ghosts which come and go we know not whence or where, leaving the spot all desolate where they once have been. She thought of the curse which had been pronounced upon the race to which she had allied herself, till the very thought grew pain, and trembled with a vague and undefined feeling of dread, as she looked forward to the future, where all seemed drear and full of gloom. There was something too strange and mysterious in the very circumstance of Lady Eardley thus suddenly calling her son to her side, after having so sedulously concealed from them her present abode, withdrawn herself too from their society without the slightest allusion as to the cause of so doing, without even having previously intimated to Sir Richard her intention.

"There must surely be some powerful reason for her thus acting," thought Clara; and yet the more she thought upon the subject, the more difficult did she find it to solve the seeming mystery; still a sense of danger to her own happiness and welfare was the most predominant feeling, and filled her with alarm and despondency.

From a sense of delicacy, she had forborne to question her husband as to the contents of Lady Eardley's letter, so that she was totally ignorant even of the route he was about to take. She could not, therefore, if it were necessary, correspond with him by letter, unless he first communicated with her; which now that he was gone, she bitter regretted having in the hurry of departure neglected to request of him. This added a more deepened tinge to her already sombre spirit, and she felt that the time would indeed drag on heavily until his return. While such thoughts as these pressed heavily on her mind, it suddenly occurred to her to visit once more the chapel, where the beautifully chiselled marble figure had so attracted her attention. She felt as though she would like once more to muse on the strange tale she had heard from the lips of Sir Richard, on the day when she first became mistress of Eardley Hall. It was now evening, and feeling that the presence of her attendants would be a restraint, she dismissed them, and proceeded to the chapel alone. It was, as we have already remarked, a small, but handsome building, fitted up with the most costly appointments and rich specimens of art, among which the beautiful statue might well be said to be cast in the sculptor's choicest mould; the setting sun shed its last and most brilliant rays through the oriel window of stained glass, making the faded crimson bright, and gilding the fringe again. And as Clara gazed with a feeling of awe around her, she thought that

> " Since these trappings first were new,
>   How many a cloudless day,
> To rob the velvet of its hue,
>   Had come and passed away.
> How many a setting sun had made
> That curious lattice-work of shade.
> Crumbled beneath the hillock green,
>   The cunning hand must be,
> Which carved the fretted door, I ween,
>   Acorn and *fleur-de-lis*.
> And now the worm hath done its part,
> In mimicing the chisel's heart."

As she thus thought, her contemplative mind returned to tread again o'er the flowery, though slippery paths of more early youth, to dream over again the wild sunny dreams of childhood, when the world seemed all before her, where to choose, and she pleased herself with the possibility of grasping life's finest flowers without the accompanying thorns ; when joy and life were one, and no sad thoughts had power to cast even the semblance of a shadow over her light and sunny brow. It is oftentimes wise and good to revert to the past, to talk as it were with by-gone hours, comparing the present with what it might have been, and gathering fresh confidence and hope to cheer us on our way, beset though it may be with cares and trials. Retrospection is always a duty, and frequently a pleasing one., How many a sad and heavy heart hath gained fresh courage and renewed strength to battle with the waves of adversity, "Though clouds and darkness round them lower, and all forsake them in that hour"," though calling to mind past memories, and taking as it were a retrospective glance at the past—

> "When the rainbow's tints divine,
> Give promise joy again shall shine ;
> Foretells the sun will shortly rise,
> In fairer, bluer, brighter skies."

Thus Clara felt somewhat comforted, as, within the hallowed precincts of the chapel, she looked backward to the past, and remembered that—when she had given way to the wildest sorrow, folding her hands in anguish and despair—even in that hour, " when grief seemed the searest, yet joy was in flushing, and hope was the nearest." And she asked herself, might it not be thus now, had she not allowed herself to swell a matter of but trival importance into such magnitude? Smiling at the sadness which had so greatly troubled her, Clara resolved to banish the unwelcome visitor from her bosom. Having thus in a measure succeeded in recovering her usual placidity, she once more approached the tomb, and bending down, examined yet more closely than she had hitherto done the exquisite beauty and workmanship of the sculptured figure which rested on the marble monument. At this moment some writing, which she had not before observed, caught her eye, and stooping down she endeavoured to decipher the characters ; but time had rendered them well-nigh illegible, and she could only make out the following couplet :—

> " Rigid and cold, for life had flown,
> And Eardley's lord is now alone."

While engaged in striving to read more of the inscription, Clara was startled by a sigh, which seemed breathed close to her ear. Knowing herself perfectly alone, and her mind already saddened by the painful events of the day, it is by no means a matter of surprise that she trembled violently, and was conscious of a feeling of extreme agitation ; indeed, for the moment was even overcome by superstitious terror. Rousing herself with a violent effort, she gained courage to glance round the chapel, when her eye suddenly encountered those of the strange woman who had accosted Sir Richard in the grounds. She was dressed exactly the same as when they last met, and her large dark eyes, seemingly lighted up with triumphant excitement, were fixed full upon her face.

"It is well," she murmured, as soon as Clara became conscious of her presence. "The curse pronounced in this very chapel, more than two hundred years ago, is still working fearfully, and will continue to do so till the time (not far distant) shall arrive when the race shall be at an end ; and from its baneful influence, not one shall escape."

Clara scarce suppressed a scream of terror, as she listened to the words of the strange being whom she had thus again so singulary encountered; but she strove to answer calmly.

" I cannot comprehend what your purpose may be in thus endeavouring to alarm those who have never injured you.'

"Never injured me ?" returned the stranger, her eyes appearing to flash fire ; so deep and powerful was her resentment, that Clara trembled yet more, and turned to leave the chapel, or at all events call for assistance; but her steps were arrested by the other, and as if anticipating her intention, she said in tones that seemed more those of command than entreaty—]

"Yet, stay lady, one moment. Mine," she continued, in more mournful accents, "is a tale of shame and suffering. Once you might have read it on my cheeks, in burning characters; shrinking shame was their beseeching looks. Painful humility! But the time for these is past, and the hour of revenge and retribution draweth nigh. Still, lady," she continued, seeing that Clara shrank from her with trembling and agitated looks, "you have nothing to fear form me: nay rather would I willingly spare you the terrible misfortune which is even now impending over this house, shaking it to its very foundation; so that all who are in the remotest manner allied to it must participate in its downfall, and consequent ruin. All in vain are admonitions and remonstrances, or the gipsy's warning, though darkly given, had not been treated with so lightly."

"It was you then," said Clara, who, though trembling with apprehension of she scarce knew what, yet began to feel a strange interest in her companion. "It was you, then, that so repeatedly forewarned the wife of Walter Eardley of sorrow and despair."

"Yes, lady, you have guessed rightly. Knowing the shame and misery which must inevitably so soon befal this unhappy family, I repeatedly warned her, if she valued her own peace, not to unite her destiny with that of a cursed and fated race; but she heeded not my words; indeed how could she, when urged on by the unseen hand of fate itself to the accomplishment of her destiny, which is as yet but half fulfilled?"

"Your language is strange and unsatisfactory," replied Clara. "If you know of any conspiracy or base design plotting against the happiness and peace of a family, of whom I am proud to acknowledge myself a member, why not declare at once all you are able to disclose on the subject, that we may take measures to prevent the design, or, if that may not be, prepare ourselves to meet the misfortune with becoming fortitude?"

"If," continued Clara, increasing in self-composure as the silence of her companion seemed to auger favourably to her wishes, "if you cannot, or dare not do this, better to leave us still in blissful ignorance of coming danger, never doubting that from whatever quarter the blow may descend, we shall meet it with calmness and resignation!"

"Lady," began the other, without replying to Clara's last words, "I once loved, fondly, truly, as you do now; indeed I doubt whether one apparently so cold and unimpassioned can love with that madness which once characterised my feelings towards Sir Richard Eardley."

"Richard?" repeated Clara, in faltering accents. "Impossible,"

"Ay, call him Richard," returned the other, "for the time of which I speak is years ago; he was not then possessed of title, lands, and fortune; but these would not have endeared him to my heart. I loved him, but for himself alone; and had he been sunk into the very abyss of infamy, I should have loved him still."

"Oh, then," returned Clara, her cheeks colouring with the excitement which filled her breast; "oh, then, you did not love with that purity, that truth, which makes love so dear. If, as you say, we both loved the same object, how differently have the like sentiments affected us. I love Richard, my husband, for his noble qualities, his excellent and manly worth."

"Speak not of noble qualities or worth in connection with one who has outraged them all, who has for ever forfeited his claim to the consideration, the respect of others. I loved him, as I have said, with the most passionate devotion; not shame or infamy could lull the affectionate beatings of a heart which throbbed for him alone, till he acted the still baser part of the betrayer, and left me in solitude to mourn over his broken faith, to prove the worth of blighted vows; his child, too, forsaken and abandoned with its mother, even before it saw the light, to suffer the stings of contumely, at once an object of pity and contempt—held up as an example of the workings of sin, which others might look upon and avoid. All this and more have I endured for his sake. Spurned, wronged, crushed, and trampelled on, my whole soul was changed. I thought, nay, brooded on my wrongs, and his guilt, till revenge took entire possession of my being. For this alone I lived, contending with every difficulty, waiting patiently till the time should come when I could strike to his very heart. I could have injured him long ere this; but I was above all meaner revenge, and thus permitted him to go unscathed by the scorching withering fire which burnt so fiercely in my breast. But fortune at length favoured me, disclosing a scheme of vengeance, sure and terrible, such as I had long panted for in vain. Yes," she continued, stretching forth her hand, as she was wont when excited, and erecting her tall well-proportioned form to its full height, while her large dark eyes seemed to emit fire, so deep and sparkling were their rays; "yes, the time for revenge is come—the hour of retribution is fast drawing nigh, and neither prayers nor entreaties can turn me from my purpose—both are alike vain and useless. No, though he knelt at my feet for pardon—for pity, if not for himself, for you, I would spurn him from me, and rejoice at the ruin I had worked—a ruin in which all who claim kith or kin with his accursed race must be involved!"

She would have proceeded, though it is impossible to say how much longer, had not Clara, weak from recent illness, and overcome by the terrible words of her companion, sank fainting on the statue, which had so attracted her attention.

Laura approached and gazed upon the inanimate form of Clara with something of womanly pity and compassion depicted in her looks; stooping down, she gently loosened her dress, and chafed her cold hands and forehead, murmuring as she did so—

"Another victim to the falsehood and depravity of man! Would that I could strike without injuring her; but it cannot be. Neither can I withhold the blow; an imperious destiny urges me on—fate has willed that by and through me the curse shall be again fulfilled—deeply and bitterly fulfilled—till none of the race shall remain unscathed by its blighting influence. Yes," she continued, raising her head and gazing round the vacant chapel with a look of proud exultation, "a glorious and soul-inspiring revenge will be mine; and if in after years my name should be mentioned coupled with shame and sorrow, the same tongue shall tell how deeply and surely were my wrongs avenged."

At this moment Clara showed signs of returning consciousness, and Laura, instantly abandoning her self-imposed task, withdrew to the farthest corner of the chapel, so that Clara's opening eyes might not light upon a form so calculated (after what had passed between them) to fill her mind with terror.

CHAPTER LII.

"The evening sky flung golden light
    On hill and glade and fountain bright,
And earth lay calm in sunset's smile,
    And radiant in its sweet repose;
Could aught below deep care beguile,
    Sure might that daylight's close.

*   *   *   *

His lofty brow had shade of care,
And woe had traced her furrows there;
The piercing eye had lost its light:
Yet as some fearful withering blight
Had swept across his hoary years,
It flashed amid o'ermastering tears."

EVER-RESTLESS busy Time, never retarded in his progress by the most ardent wishes of the happy and joyous, or induced by the prayers and hopes of he careworn and anxious to speed more rapidly in his flight, but with one unwearying steady motion stedfastly pursues his endless course, heeding no more the bright flowers and sunshine of summer, than the frosts and snows of winter; but still speeding onward, bearing on his wing the sighs of the aged, together with the warm aspirations of the first glow of youth!

Ever-restless busy time had thus sped by since the marriage of Mary to Percy Raymond, bringing to the young wife many new cares and duties, but not, as it should also have done, new joys and brighter happiness to form a counterbalance in her favour. She had, as she conceved, removed one considerable source of anxiety in inducing her father to take up his abode under the same roof as herself; and certainly in so doing, she secured to him the satisfaction of having her ever near him, anxious to promote his comfort and happiness to the utmost; but she had not taken into account the anxiety he must of necessity feel, at witnessing the constant neglect of Percy, shewn not by apparent unkindness or cold demeanour, but in constant absence from his own fireside, which should have been his dearest and most desired resource for intellectual enjoyment, and relaxation from other and more engrossing pursuits. Mary had not calculated for the anxiety this state of things must of necessity produce in the mind of her father, who, being an inmate of her home, could not of course fail to remark the repeated absence of his son-in-law; and when questioning Mary on this subject, it was in vain that she strove to make excuses favourable to her husband, urging, as she frequently did, the plea that it was but natural he should like to visit his club, and chat with the old companions of his bachelor days.

"You are no doubt perfectly correct, my love," returned Mr. Herbert, affectionately, "while surrounding your husband with all the comforts and happiness of a married man, at the same time, to allow him the perfect freedom and liberty of action, that more properly belongs to a single one; neither do I blame Percy for feeling at times inclined to profit by your kindness; but this freedom, innocent, indeed, praiseworthy as it is in a right point of view, may be carried too far, as I have no hesitation in pronouncing it to be in the present instance; believe me, Mary, it augers unfavourable for the happiness of both, when home is not the dearest and most desired spot. A wife, too, should ever be a man's sweetest and most treasured companion, whom, if he ever leaves for a short time time, it should only be that he may come again with livelier zest. You should then, my love, exert all your powers to render both yourself and your home irresistably dear to you husband."

"Oh, father," replied Mary, raising her face covered with blushes, "do not, I entreat of you, for a moment suppose that I have been neglectful of my duties, or ——"

She stopped suddenly, feeling that in thus exculpating herself, she was rendering Percy still more indefensible in his conduct. Mr. Herbert saw and understood her confusion.

"Forgive me, my child, if I have unintentionally wounded your feelings, but you have never known a mother's care or tenderness, and in consequence my love for you has assumed a maternal character, and I have spoken to you, Mary, as I know your mother would have done, had she been spared to see you grow to womanhood; and the advice I have given you is founded upon the wise precepts which she daily practised during the few years of our wedded life. I am proud to say we enjoyed perfect freedom; no fretful peevishness bewailed the tedium of my absense when business called me from her side; on the contrary, I was ever received with a cheerful smile of welcome; her conversation was at all times sensible and unaffected, and she reposed the most perfect confidence in my love, so that if at times I was tempted to seek amusements which she could not share, I had no fear of fretful pinings or unkind upbraidings on my return. This of course bound me still closer to her, and home was ever a treasured spot, and my wife the sweet companion which shed a lustre on all around; and bidding care disappear from my bosom, nothing disturbed me but her many disorders; and these she bore so cheerfully, never complaining or giving me the most remote idea that she anticipated an unfavourable termination, that for a long time I was entirely unapprehensive for the result; indeed, almost to the last I clung to hope, not bearing to anticipate so speedy a close to so much happiness; but her illness proved fatal, and I was obliged to resign a treasure so inestimably dear. She died, leaving me an orphan child to love and tend for her dear sake. From that time up to the present moment, you have been my only care, my solace under affliction, my support and succour in old age; indeed, words cannot express all thou hast been to me, Mary," continued the old man, throwing his arms affectionately round his daughter.

"And ever will be my dear, dear father," returned Mary, tenderly kissing his cheek.

"I know it—I am sure of it," replied Mr. Herbert. "I am anxious, not on my own account, but yours. I cannot endure the thought of your being undervalued by one who should most prize your worth."

He stopped out of consideration for his daughter's feelings, whose glowing face plainly evinced that the subject was painful to her, and for the very same reason forbore to mention his uneasiness to Percy himself as he would otherwise have done; still Mr. Herbert was far from feeling satisfied; he asked himself if it were possible he had set too high a value upon the noble qualities and mental endowments of his daughter; still, making every allowance for parental tenderness, he found the balance preponderate greatly in her favour; and yet, as he became by degrees on a more intimate footing with the entire household, he could not fail to remark that neither Percy nor his sisters appeared to yield Mary that precedence and respect to which he considered her entitled. He, of course, threw the entire blame of this upon Percy, and felt naturally indignant against him in consequence; nor was this all, for Ada having, since her marriage, kept up a constant intercourse and exchange of friendly feeling between herself and Percy, they were more often together (planning and arranging alterations, or improvements that Ada was anxious to effect, either in her house or grounds)—they were, as we were saying, more frequently together than Mr. Herbert thought quite consistent with the position in which they both stood.

Often, too, Ada would come to spend what she called a quiet happy day with her cousin; at such times Percy was always at home. Music, on these occasion, was always resorted to as a source of pleasurable amusement, and Ada, being an excellent performer, was always the chief musician; indeed, she and Percy amused themselves to the entire exclusion of all others. Together they played and sang, as in days gone by; and Mary, who was possessed of no voice, and but a very indifferent performer, felt at such times wretched and uncomfortable in the extreme.

Yet what could she do? To evince a jealousy of her cousin she felt would be far from raising herself in the estimation of her husband; and were it even probable that her so doing might have a favourable result, the innate delicacy and good-feeling of Mary would have forbade her to profit by it. And now, indeed, she began almost to repent of having so successfully combated her father's resolution not to quit the old house, where they had passed so many happy years together. In inducing him to reside beneath the same roof as herself, she had placed before her eyes the only one object of being able to render him more comfortable—to attend to all his little wants herself, and soothe and cheer his declining years. And this she made her most sedulous care—a labour at once of love and duty; but alas! she felt this did not compensate for the anxiety he suffered on her account.

"Oh, no," she murmured to herself, "better had he have remained apart from me, than thus be subject to so many cares on my account."

And with the conviction that she had acted erroneously in persuading her father to quit his own home, came the bitterest pang Mary had ever known.

Still she pursued her career in that quiet even manner, which could not fail at times to attract Percy. Mary had never been a discontented, love-sick girl ; still she loved her husband with the best and most devoted affection, and acted as a wise and sensible woman, never for an instant chiding Percy for his repeated absence from home, or permitting how much she felt his neglect to

become apparent in her demeanour. True, in her own heart, she acquitted him o t nourishing even the slightest regard for Ada, incompatible with her own honour and happiness. Still it pained her to witness those constant attentions which Ada seemed to claim as a right. Indeed, had she consulted her own feelings, she would more often have excused herself from attendance in the drawing-room, while Percy and Ada were thus engaged ; but for the sake of her husband, she put a constraint upon her wishes, and constantly compelled herself to make one of the number. Added to all this, she had continualy to defend the conduct of her husband to her father—a difficult and painful task, especially when she felt how little Percy deserved such forbearance on her part.

"Shall you return to dinner, Percy?" she inquired, one morning, as he prepared to leave the house.

"I scarcely know," he returned; "however, do not wait. I am going to call upon Dick Fenton, to get him to accompany me on a visit to the owner of the horse your cousin has commissioned me to procure for her, if possible, and I should like Dick's opinion of its merits. A capital judge of horse-flesh, generally, though he did lose considerably last Derby, as I daresay you remember, Mary."

"Perfectly," she replied, with a smile visibly playing round the corners of her mouth; "then I am to understand that it is probable this gentleman will engage you the entire day?"

"Yes, it is not unlikely that we may take a chop together at the club; so, as I said before, do not wait, as I intend to side with him at the next betting, and shall probably look in at the jockey club."

At these words, Mary was sensible of an anxiety on a subject which had never before affected her; and, looking earnestly in her husband's face, she ventured to remark, without, however, allowing her uneasiness to become apparent —assuming, indeed, an air of gaiety similar to his own—

"I do not altogether agree with you, Percy, as to the merits of your friend, inasmuch as you observed just now that he lost considerably last year; I would not, therefore, advise you to back his opinion in preference to your own, which proved so much better in judgment."

Percy felt flattered by the implied compliment to himself, and smiled good-humouredly, as he replied—

"For all that, Mary, as a rule, Dick is a far better judge of such matters than myself; it was accident, mere accident, that favoured me, and which Fenton has repeatedly proved to my perfect satisfaction. I intend, therefore, on the present occasion to side with him."

"Oh, pray do not!" returned Mary, hurriedly. "I am certain he is no judge, and in all probability will only involve you in his own losses."

Percy laughed outright, as he replied—

"You really quite amuse me, Mary. Why, when, and where did you become conversant in matters of the turf to set up your opinion against Dick, who, I tell you, has a thorough knowledge of the business, and is the best judge of horses going?"

"He did not prove so last year," said Mary, quietly.

"That is nothing at all to do with it," replied Percy; "but how should you know anything of such matters?"

"How, indeed!" thought poor Mary; and fervently, though inwardly, she hoped that she never might become better acquainted with such things than she was at present; yet her husband's careless, thoughtless good temper filled her mind with despondency.

While she was thus occupied in painful forebodings of coming ill, Percy had been busily engaged in adjusting his dress, and gazing with something of satisfaction at his own reflection in the opposite mirror. Having at last settled his cravat to his entire approval, he turned round, and gaily wishing her good morning, quitted the room humming the air he had sung with Ada on the previous evening, leaving Mary more lone and desolate than she had ever been before, while he sought once more the company of his gay associate, whose influence over a mind so constitutionally careless might well awaken fears in the bosom of his young wife, and who, although she knew it not, had already involved him in speculations hazardous to the small fortune he jointly inherited with his sisters.

Poor Mary felt more sad from the very circumstance, that she had none to whom she could breath her fears, or speak of the painful distrust Percy's words had given rise to in her mind. The day passed drearily on, and as Percy did not return, Mary sought the apartment of her father, and seating herself by his side, endeavoured to engage him in conversation.

"I have been thinking, my dear child," he said, in answer to some playful remark, "that I did wrong when I allowed you to overcome my scruples, and persuade me into abandoning the old house. We are neither of us, Mary, treated with that respect which I think our relative position deserves."

"Oh! pray do not say so, my dear father," replied Mary, hastily; " you are mistaken—indeed you are. Percy, I grant, is thoughtless, but nothing more : he means most kindly, I am convinced."

Mr. Herbert was silenced; he would not pain Mary by any farther remark, or by appearing to doubt the truth of what she said; still he was far from feeling reassured, and sat in the soft still hour of eve, thinking on days and years long past and gone. Mary, too, did not urge anything farther, but sat still and silent, thinking of the great change a few short months had worked in Percy, once so fond and attentive, so anxious for her society, and now willing to withdraw himself from it on the slightest pretence. In vain she endeavoured to trace the cause to herself; she was perfectly unconscious of having afforded him the smallest reasonable excuse for his present conduct, so altered, so entirely estranged from her; there was no longer existing between them that close association and sweet interchange of feeling, that made her married life so sweet; no, a coldness had settled on the manners of Percy, and true it was that he thought much more of the turf and the company of his gay associates, than of his young and affectionate wife, who should have been his first and dearest care; and Mary was left to mourn the departure of those bright hopes she had once so fondly cherished, and she, too truly, began to think that a young bride's joy in her bridal hour was frequently but ideal. Poor Mary! and also may we not say, poor Percy? for his habitual carelessness and unthinking temperament may well render him an object of commiseration. And how many such characters are to be met with in the daily walks of life, regarded by all but their immediate relatives, as good fellows, gay, noble, generous spirits, who are nobody's enemy but their own. Alas! how different are the sentiments of the neglected wife, left in solitude to mourn over the thoughtless extravagance of her husband, who dissipates the fortune which should be devoted to home comforts and enjoyment, among profligate acquaintances, who in return (when the day of need comes, and come it must sooner or later) would not extend a helping hand to save him from positive ruin.

It is indeed a painful truth that these choice spirits, gay, and light-hearted boon companions, often pitied for possessing a wife who does not understand or appreciate their good qualities, are more often than not petty tyrants in their own homes ; enslaving in the most cruel bondage, and estranging from them the love and affection which they should most desire to cultivate. Those, then, who so much admire these gay fellows who shine so pre-eminently in society, should see them by their own firesides, and mark the effects of their thoughtlessness in the saddened looks and distrusting anxiety of their nearest and tenderest relatives ; let them witness the fretful pevishness and nervous instability of these choice spirits, and after that term them nobody's enemy but their own—if they can.

Percy, it is true still appreciated the quiet unobstrusive worth of Mary, and consequently his neglect of her could only be attributed to a part of the utter thoughtlessness of his character, and thus it was that possessing a small independent fortune he contrived to spend the greater part of it himself, frequently reducing Mary to the greatest inconvenience in order to make up for the deficiencies which his own extravagance solely occasioned ; this, however, she had always borne, not only uncomplainingly, but cheerfully, as having brought Percy no fortune, she felt with an intuitive delicacy (not always to be found even in minds which boast a greater degree of refinement) that she had no right to offer any remonstrance as to the sum he chose to appropriate to his personal expenses, however deeply they might act upon the necessary comfort of her own. Up to this period therefore she was content with contracting as far as possible all her household matters, and even curtailing her expenditure to the utmost limits, in order to counterbalance the thoughtless extravagance of her husband. But now a new and unforeseen calamity appeared hovering over her. Should Percy be led by his gay associates to incur debts to which he could oppose no reasonable mode of payment, might not his entire ruin be the consequence? His sisters fortune, too, while they remained under age, was in a measure at his entire disposal, and if urged on to forfeit that also (and she foresaw the possibility of such a misfortune) what would become of them? Inheriting a portion of his thoughtlessness, they ever placed the most unbounded confidence in their brother, without the slightest suspicion that the career which he had of late pursued, was calculated to involve them all in utter ruin; and Mary had too much delicacy to hint to them the probable consequence of his meddling in matters of the turf, and of which in truth he understood but little, which circumstance, combined with his habitual carelessness, rendered him an easy victim to the artful and designing, who are ever ready to take advantage of such characters. Mary's heart ached with gloomy apprehensions for the future, and yet there was none to whom she could pour out the sorrows of her breast, or hint at the anxiety which had taken possession of her mind; all she conceived she could do to avert so terrible a calamity, as that which now seemed hovering over her, she was by no means slow in accomplishing, and this was to speak to Percy himself, kindly and affectionately, representing in true colours the losses which were frequently sustained by persons who took bets on such uncertain grounds, and the sorrow he would necessarily feel, if by any unfortunate circumstances, it were possible for him to involve his sisters in misfortune. But Percy, as she had too surely foreseen, only laughed at her anxiety, and repeated his former question in tones of unmistakable sarcasm—

"How should she know anything about such things?"

"I know this," replied Mary, "that the turf has brought ruin and desolation on hearts and homes, equally as innocent and unconscious of all such matters as me and mine."

"Pooh, pooh, Mary," returned Percy, "I am sure I meant no unkindness, but women, of course, cannot understand things of this sort; and if a man ventures to launch into a little additional expense, are always ready to foretell ruin and sorrow as the necessary consequence."

"On the contrary," replied Mary kindly though firmly, "I am ever pleased to afford you an opportunity of enjoying yourself, and have never sought to prevent you participating in pleasures which I could not share; but this betting can scarce afford you much gratification, and may involve others as well as yourself."

"Enough," said Percy petulantly; "do you take me for a fool, that I cannot manage my own affairs. Once for all I beg of you to mind your household concerns, and leave all others to me."

Mary was silent, but not less sad; she felt satisfied in having performed her duty, though convinced of the utter inutility of attempting to remonstrate with such a character as Percy, who resolutely turned a deaf ear to one who would have counselled so wisely and so well. While Mary was thus beset with anxieties and cares, her cousin Ada, though in a far different manner, had equal cause for uneasiness; the distance between herself and Walter seemed sensibly to widen each day, spite of all her efforts to the contrary; her company, she too well knew, had no charm or fascination for him. Wedded in thought, feeling, and pursuit to his parliamentary career, his wife was unheeded, uncared for, and he seldom addressed her, save to point out some error, which he wished to see corrected, or to dissent from some line of conduct, she had thought proper to adopt. Ada had by this time discovered, that tears and frowns were the most unlikely weapons to oppose to his cold and inflexible temper, and which fenced him round like a coat of mail, from which anger and vexation (on her part) harmlessly rebounded. Yet she had not likewise failed to discover, that there was one point on which he was vulnerable, and on that she resolved to touch him to the quick. Walter possessed in common with many others, a quick and sensitive delicacy on all points touching his honour, which he had thoughtlessly entrusted to the keeping of Ada, without taking the necessary precaution to guard her from the snares and temptations to which the young and unwary are exposed, especially when left to pursue a giddy round of pleasure, amid festive scenes, unprotected by the love and care of one dear or tender relative, who might have warned her erring footsteps where alone it was safe to tread, and though Walter never mingled in the gay world himself, yet his position brought him in frequent contact with those who did, and consequently the knowledge of Percy's attention to her in public soon became known to him. At first, rumour with its hundred tongues, though busy with the name and fame of his wife, was unheeded, or at most treated with silent contempt by Walter. But some still more painful reports touching the conduct of his wife having reached him, he resolved to use the power he conceived appertained to him as a husband, and strictly forbid the habitual intercourse, which now constantly existed between her and her formerly discarded lover; not, be it understood, that he entertained the slightest suspicion that these rumours had any more solid foundation, than such things upon proper sifting are usually found to possess, but the bare idea of having his wife's conduct impeached by the breath of scandal, or her name made the subject of censure, was repellant to his mind in the extreme, and such a state of things could not be allowed further continuance. He thought that nothing beyond his own authority was necessary to do this, and therefore determined to exert himself. To this end therefore he sought his wife's apartment, not in a kind and gentle spirit to reason with her, on the impropriety of making so constant a companion of her cousin's husband, and which would, far more than all else, tend to claim the attention and respect of Ada's restless and wavering mind, but with his usual stern inflexibility, which refused for a moment even to yield to the pleadings of affection or restraint.

Now, it so happened that Percy, who had been one of Ada's morning visitors, passed out of the room at the very moment that Walter was about to enter, and who, scarce replying to the light-hearted greeting of Percy, felt yet more amazed by the presence of the very man he conceived he had every reason to dislike. Ada, as we have already intimated, had some time since discovered that frowns and tears were by no means calculated to make a favourable impression on such a mind as Walter's; she had, therefore, adopted in lieu of such weapons an air of extravagant gaiety and carelessness, which she most frequently assumed when her heart was saddest. Thus it was at the present time, that, affecting not to observe the entrance of her husband, she continued gaily humming to herself the fragment of some lively song, and which appeared to afford her unqualified pleasure. Walter hesitated a moment; and then seating himself near the fire, for the morning was cool, said—

"If you are at liberty to attend to me, I wish to have five minutes' serious conversation with you, Ada, on an important topic."

"Indeed I am highly flattered," she replied, smiling, "and shall be most happy to attend to you."

"You are pleased to be facetious," he returned, "and have lately acquired an unhappy knack of turning everything into ridicule."

Ada answered only by continuing the song her husband's remarks had interrupted.

> "If sighs could make us sin the less,
> Perchance I were not glad—
> If mourning were the sage's dress,
> My garb should still be sad;

> But since the angels' wings are white,
>   And even the young saints smile;
> Since virtue wears a brow of light,
>   And vice a robe of guile—
> Since laughter is not under ban,
>   Nor goodness clad in grey,
> Believe I'm happy when I can,
>   And merry while I may."

These lines were sung by Ada with perfect sweetness, but they made no impression whatever on the mind of Walter, who, yet more and more vexed by the apparent levity of her manner, replied, in a tone of increasing severity—

"I have every reason to feel dissatisfied with your conduct of late, and am resolved, Ada, no longer to permit you to lay yourself open to the censure of the world."

"The opinion the world may think fit to form regarding my conduct, is a matter of perfect indifference to me," she replied, carelessly.

"I do not doubt it," returned her husband, sarcastically; "and since you no longer manifest any regard, either for your own honour or mine, you will permit me, I hope, to interfere on behalf of us both; and believe that I speak with due consideration and earnestness, when I say that the present state of things must not continue."

Ada's brow flushed with anger, as she repeated the words—

"Must not?"

"Ay," returned Walter, "must not. The visits of Mr. Raymond are unpleasant and distasteful to me; and in consequence, I desire their discontinuance."

"Indeed?" she returned, with a slight curl of the lip, and the smallest possible elevation of the eyelids. "Indeed?"

"You hear me," replied Walter, "and I doubt not, fully understand my wishes on this subject. I do not, of course, desire to cause a separation between yourself and your cousin; but the constant attendance of her husband, who, I am credibly informed, is your companion, not only in private, but to places of public entertainment, is at once lowering to yourself and unpleasant to me. I leave it, therefore, with yourself to explain my wishes to Mr. Raymond, or not, as you may think fit, but at all events to discontinue the piquant intercourse which now exists between you."

"And if," said Ada, with crimson brow and flashing eyes, "if I cannot see the necessity for all this, what then?"

"What then?" repeated Walter, and his voice was stern and cold.

"Yes," replied Ada, delighted that she possessed the power thus much to move him. "What then?"

"I cannot suppose it possible," said Walter, "that you will venture for a moment to oppose your will to mine; but if such should ever be the case, we part at once and for ever. I have repeatedly warned you of this, and if you value your present position, would advise you to be careful how you tread on dangerous ground. I have quietly permitted much that I was far from approving; but there are limits which I will not suffer you to pass; remember this, and all may yet be well."

And without pausing for an answer, he hastily rose, and quitted the room. During this brief conversation, there had not been the slightest manifestation of affection on the part of Walter; not the most distant approach even to gallantry, either in his words or in the manner with which he gave them utterance; and Ada paced the room with a proud step, convinced that she had at length succeeded in awakening in the mind of her husband some symptoms of that passion she was so eager to kindle in his breast. Unhappy, misguided girl! she inwardly resolved to do the very thing against which Walter had so impressively warned her.

"He thinks," she murmured to herself, "that I fear him, and must of necessity do his bidding; but he shall see I have a will of my own, and sufficient firmness to use it; and when he has felt the full extent of my powers, and sued to me for that love which, esteeming his own, he once held so lightly, then, and not till then, will I pity his sufferings, and forgive him."

As she thus spoke, a smile of triumph lighted up her countenance, and there was something proud and disdainful in her whole bearing. Alas! how sad to see her thus resolutely bent on her own destruction, impetuously pursuing a course which could only redound with sorrow and misery to herself. Walter, on his part, was for the present content, not for a moment supposing that his words would fail in conveying to the mind of Ada his fixed and unalterable resolve. And, as a matter of course, he conceived he had only to express his commands in order to have them obeyed. And, in truth, so much power rests in the authority of a husband, that a noble and generous-minded man should be careful how he uses it, for a young and sensitive mind is often wounded (thoughtlessly we allow) by wishes and desires being expressed in tones that sound more like commands than requests; and there is in almost every mind a spirit of rebellion which cannot brook the words—"I will," and which ever tempts them to resist a ruling, unless it be by the gentle force of love, and the tender chords of affection; then, indeed, it is a pleasure and a happiness to obey the authority of a husband—not otherwise.

CHAPTER LIII.

"'Twas vain to speak, to weep, to sigh;
Oh, more than tears of blood can tell,
When wrung from guilt's expiring eye,
Are in that word—Farewell, farewell."

It was night, and the broad expanse of heaven glittered with myriods of stars, and the moon threw its soft light over the dark hills (covered with trees like a rich woody plantation). The country, fair and beautiful to look upon by day, seemed scarcely less fair and lovely by the mellowed light which now shed its lustre on all around. And well might they who viewed the scene, now lit up all around them, say—

"That never yet had nature been
Caught sleeping in a lovelier ray,
Or rivalled its own noontide face,
With fairer show of moonlight grace."

A sweet soft repose pervaded all things, and not a foot-fall broke the stillness of the night, as Sir Richard Eardley approached the cottage residence of his mother. So fair and tempting was the night, with the silvery moon shedding its soft and balmy influence on all around, that the youthful baronet, on alighting from his carriage at the little town, preferred, as the distance was but short, prosecuting the remainder of his journey on foot, the more especially as by doing so he would rather hasten than retard his progress, as the carriage-way was some miles round. Desiring his servants to remain at the inn, Sir Richard started on his little journey; the road lay through fields and hedgerows, comprising some of the finest scenery in England; and the softened light by which he viewed it, yet still more enhanced its charms. Stopping frequently in his walk to admire the fair propect by which he was surrounded, and wishing each time with increased earnestness, that Clara was there to participate in his enjoyment, Sir Richard at length reached his destination.

Ever since the memorable interview between himself and Laura, his mind had been filled with a vague feeling of apprehension: doubts and fears constantly beset him; and in this unlooked-for summon from his mother, he already foreboded some fresh source of anxiety; it was consequently with a new dread of some impending misfortune, that he presented himself before his mother. Lady Eardley rose to meet him, and folding him in a warm embrace, affectionately bade him welcome.

"I rejoice to see you, my son," she said, in her usual quiet musical tones, "although the meeting is in many respects a painful one to us both."

"I am here, mother, at your bidding," returned the young man; "yet I will frankly own it cost me an effort, both deep and painful, to leave home at the present time; but I judged, both from the tenor of your letter, and what I know of your disposition, that you would not thus command my presence unless some imperative necessity compelled you thus to act."

"You are perfectly correct in your conjecture," returned Lady Eardley, in the same calm unmoved tones in which she had before spoken. "But you have travelled fast and far, and must greatly stand in need of rest and refreshment," saying which, she took her son by the arm and led him into an adjoining apartment, where covers were already laid for dinner.

Sir Richard had never felt less inclined to eat; and notwithstanding the dinner (which was served immediately on their entrance) consisted of the choicest and most *recherche* viands, but little justice was done them, either by himself or Lady Eardley. Conversation during the attendance of the servant, was confined entirely to the common-place topics of the day, but no sooner was the cloth removed and the dessert spread, than turning anxiously to his parent, Sir Richard requested her to releeve his anxiety, by immediately acquainting him with the object of their present meeting.

"To-morrow," said Lady Eardley. "You have partaken of some refreshment; rest is likewise needful, in order to enable you to hear patiently what I have to impart."

"No—no, mother," replied the young man, hastily, "do not, I entreat of you, tax my patience further."

"You will sleep the better for it," said Lady Eardley.

"Pardon me, dear mother, but indeed I should not. I am so perplexed and beset with doubts and fears, that to sleep with all I am so anxious to learn, as yet untold, is a moral impossibility."

"Think you so?" replied his mother, still in a doubtful tone.

"I am sure so," returned Sir Richard. "Dear mother, I beg, I entreat of you to tell me all."

"Alas! my son," replied the unhappy lady, "it is for me to beg—to implore of you to save our family from impending ruin and disgrace, by the sacrifice even of all you hold most dear."

The young man trembled and turned pale.

"Mother," he said, after a moment's hesitation, "I cannot understand your words."

"Richard," she said, still in the same low tones, "I have calculated the extent of the sacrifice I desire you to make. I know it to be immense; yet the pride of family, of birth, and fortune, which you inherit from myself, induces me to believe, that great as it is, you will not refuse to make it, for your own—your brothers—for all our sakes."

She paused to note the effects of her words upon her son's countenance, but it gave no clue to his thoughts, and she again went on—

"I had no means to prepare you for the information I am about to impart; still I do not dread its effects, for I well know you possess sufficient moral courage to meet reverse of fortune with fortitude and patience; and yet the threatened loss of title, wealth, and honours, is no trifling matter."

"You would tell me, then," began the young man——

"That another claimant has arisen to the broad lands of Eardley Hall," interrupted his mother, "one whose prior claim even I have been forced to admit, though with the utmost reluctance."

Sir Richard turned still paler than before, and his brow momentarily contracted, but it quickly passed away, and making a strenuous effort to smile, he replied—

"You see, mother, you have not mistaken my wonted firmness, which might now even rival your own. Though wholly unprepared for such startling news, I am by no means so easily overcome as many would naturally suppose; and if I have so long enjoyed these estates illegally, I shall not hesitate freely, and I hope cheerfully, to resign them to the rightful heir."

CLARA'S INTERVIEW WITH LAURA IN THE CHAPEL.

"Spoken like my own noble-minded boy," said Lady Eardley, while the rapture which filled her bosom tinged her cheek with a crimson glow, "and confirms me in the belief, that you will not hesitate to sacrifice your own feelings, in order to secure to your family wealth and title, the loss of which is now threatened."

"Name the conditions, mother," replied Sir Richard, "and if it is possible to further your schemes, rest assured you will find me ready, nay, anxious to do your bidding."

"I come now, my dear Richard," returned his mother, "to the most painful part of this business, and for your sake will touch upon it as lightly as possible. The claimant of whom I made mention just now, I must inform you, is a lady, one too, I believe (if my information is correct) not entirely unknown to you; she even claims relationship with our family of a near and tender kind; but this of course is unknown to you, as she made your acquaintance under the name of Laura Tracy."

At the mention of this name, which he had, indeed, such terrible cause to remember, Sir Richard scarce suppressed an exclamation of grief and astonishment; indeed, it needed all his habitual self-command to conceal from his mother how deeply he was moved; but Lady Eardley was quick of perception, and though she affected not to have remarked the uneasiness of her son, she was nevertheless convinced of the truth of Evereards communication in their ast interview; and as though she was replying to some admission on the part of Sir Richard, she said—

"Then my information was correct, so far, that this lady is not entirely a stranger to you."

"Some years ago," he replied, "I met her frequently; indeed, some love passages passed between us at the period to which I allude; but I was then too young and thoughtless to be able to entertain a serious affection, and in truth, I had long forgotten even the existence of such a being."

"And yet," replied Lady Eardley, "the lady's memory is far more retentive, for I am assured she still entertains a lively regard for you."

"I am sorry to hear it," said Sir Richard, coldly.

"Nay, my son," returned his mother, "you should rather rejoice that this very regard opens a door by which you may hope to escape the impending calamity which is even now hovering over our house."

"Not through her—never by her means, mother," returned the young man eagerly.

"Say not so, my son," replied Lady Eardley, "the star of Laura Eardley (for such is her real name) is in the ascendant, while ours is fast declining into oblivion; consequently she must be humoured, and, if necessary, even courted and caressed."

"Mother," said Sir Richard earnestly, "your words are so strange, so unwelcome to my ears, that I cannot understand them. How is it that this stranger can lay legal claim to estates which from infancy I have been taught to consider myself the heir? My father too, and his father before him, enjoyed them for a long succession of years unmolested and unopposed. How does this tally with the pretended illegality of my inheritance?"

Now it was Lady Eardley's turn to change colour, and betray other and evident symptoms of alarm; still she struggled with herself, and contrived to speak in a calm, clear voice, as she replied—

"Your father, Richard, was legal heir to the title and estates which he enjoyed, but," (and she seemed to give utterance to the words with difficulty) "but, you are not."

"Speak plainly, mother," said Sir Richard, and his voice was thick and husky, while his brow contracted, and a dark portentous shadow, seemed to have fallen on his spirit. "Speak plainly. Am I, or am I not, the son of the late Sir Richard Eardley?"

"Yes, yes," replied his mother, "you are his son, his acknowledged and undoubted son, but——" she hesitated a moment, and her very lips became as marble, so white and rigid was her entire countenance, "but I was not his wife."

Richard started back with horror and amazement, as he listened to this confession. Had a thunder-bolt rent the ceiling at that moment, and fallen at his feet, it could not by any possibility have filled him with the alarm and bewilderment which these few words occassioned in his bosom ; and with it all there rushed through his mind, with the rapidity of lightning, so many attesting and convincing circumstances as regarded the truth of his mother's words, that he could not for a moment even entertain the slightest doubt concerning them, however much he felt disposed to do so. Shame, sorrow, and anger, struggled for the mastery in his bosom, each reigning by terms, and rending his heart with sorrow and despair. Lady Eardley saw all this, and watched an opportunity to take advantage of a calmer mood, but long she waited in vain. At length her son spoke—

"Mother," he said in the same husky voice he had before spoken, "it would ill become me to upbraid the source from which my being flows, yet your confession has affected me more deeply than words can ever tell. Poverty and sorrow I could have borne as a man, but infamy and disgrace are hard indeed to endure; to know myself a child of sin and shame, from my very cradle, to think that derision sneers upon my birth, and yields me scarce a name on earth. This is more, far more dreadful than I once conceived it possible I could ever endure. But enough : these tears shame my manhood," and as he spoke, he dashed the unwelcome moisture from his eyes.

"My son," said Lady Eardley, and her voice seemed to issue from between her livid and compressed lips, for they did not part, to allow what she wished to say free vent. "My son, you have drawn a dreadful picture of the sin and wrong heaped upon your defenceless head, yet all these shall not even one hope destroy, if you consent to abide by my counsel."

"No, no, mother," replied Richard, "suffice it, I am not the legal heir to these estates ; be it my first duty then to resign them to their rightful owner. This I am resolved to do, at any cost to myself."

"To do this," returned Lady Eardley, "you must make your own illegitimacy known to the world, must hold up your mother to contempt, and link her name for ever with dishonour. Will you, can you act thus cruelly ?"

"My mother," returned Richard deeply affected, "I would not. I do not mean to upbraid you, but you should have thought of this somewhat earlier."

"Listen, Richard," she replied, "while I unfold to you a true statement of the painful circumstance to which I have alluded."

Richard slightly signified his acquiescence, and his mother thus began—

"Early in life—indeed, while yet little more than a girl—I conceived a most ardent and romantic attachment for a young man, of birth and station somewhat inferior to my own ; but who at that period returned my affection with at least equal warmth. This love I was compelled to nurture in secret, for it was not

> ' A pure, open, prosperous love,
> Pledged on earth, and sealed above,
> Which grows in the world's approving eyes—
> In friendship's smile, and home's caress ;
> Collecting all the heart's sweet ties
> Into one knot of happiness.'

No; mine was a love nursed in sorrow, silence, and shame—a passion without hope or pleasure—for I knew that my father would never countenance my marriage with Evereard. After we had for some months contrived to keep up a mutual correspondence, and occasionally see each other, though at long and repeated intervals, Evereard found himself suddenly compelled to quit England for a short period. He wrote acquainting me with the circumstance, and soliciting a farewell meeting. It was granted ; and while we mingled our tears together, Evereard besought me to grant him one convincing proof of my affection. I hesitated. He pressed me yet more strongly, and at length gained my consent to a private union. I was too young to think of the solemn responsibility I was about to take upon myself. I thought only of Evereard, and was pleased to have an opportunity of giving him so convincing a proof of my devotion. But I must not dwell upon this painful subject; suffice it, I met him on the appointed day, and we were married. Immediately after the ceremony, we separated, alas! to meet no more as his in love; for during the absence of Evereard from England, I was compelled by my father, a stern, cold unfeeling man, to give my hand (though never my heart) to Sir Richard Eardley. I had none of whom I could seek counsel, or impart the secret of my breast. My mother, long since dead, and no other relative near me at that time, my sufferings were indescribable. And yet what could I do?— Young, thoughtless, and inexperienced, I suffered myself to be led anew to the altar, spite of the sorrows and conflicts of my bosom. Now, my son," she continued, "you know my unhappy story. Much as I blame myself, I am not guilty to the extent my first words might have led you to believe."

"No," replied Richard, and his voice had lost something of its harsh discordant tones; "no, your fault was but comparatively a light one; and, though it has cost me the loss of honour and of fortune, it is not for me to blame. Mother," he added, after a moment's silence, "I must return to Eardley Hall immediately; I may not stay here another hour. Do not," he continued, "seek to turn me from my purpose—I know your firmness, and you must now know mine."

"But you will not resolve to make my shame known to the world? Think for your brother, if not for yourself, and do not, I entreat, I implore of you, consign us all to infamy and sorrow."

"But what can I do?" said the young man.

"Everything rests with you," returned his mother; "you can save us all. Had it not been so, I should not have imparted to you my painful story. Listen. Your cousin, Laura Eardley (heiress to Eardley Hall, in right of her dead father, who was brother to Sir Richard), consents to waive her claim, and thus confirm you in your present position, on condition that you set aside your present marriage, and give your hand to her."

"Mother!" said the young man, hastily, "you cannot ask this of me?—You who know Clara—who have ever loved her as a daughter—you will not, cannot counsel such baseness?"

"What can I do?" replied the unhappy lady; "it is no longer a question of feeling or affection, but a choice of infamy and dishonour on the one hand, and name, title, fortune, all, on the other. Can you hesitate, when even on my knees I implore of you, to make this one great sacrifice?"

She would have prostrated herself before him, had he not divined her intention and frustrated it.

"Kneel not to me," he said, endeavouring to lead her to a seat, "you do but rend my heart with anguish, and tempt me to swerve from the only path I can with honour pursue."

"You will consent then to save us all from destruction?" returned his mother; "you must, you will consent? Indeed, indeed, I will not quit this spot, till you have given me your promise, your solemn promise to be guided in this matter entirely by me."

The young man made no reply, but took two or three hurried turns up and down the room—his heaving breast and contracted brows, plainly evincing the conflicting feelings which rent his breast. At length he stopped, and confronting his mother, said in a firm and even commanding voice—

"I must have time to weigh well every circumstance, before I stir in this matter. I must have time for cool reflection, and not suffer myself to be led on by the heat of argument to decide at once on so weighty an affair. I shall return at once to Eardley Hall, and thus remove myself beyond the power of your influence, for in this matter, I must and will decide entirely for myself. It is utterly useless," he continued, seeing she was about to speak, "to attempt to dissuade me from my purpose—fear not to trust me, resting assured that I shall act as becomes your son. Mother," he added after a moment's pause, "farewell; give me your parting blessing. I have lingered here even now too long; it is no time to sit idly down lamenting the irretrievable past. I must up and be going. Once more farewell."

Lady Eardley passively received the embrace of her son; she felt that it was vain to speak, to weep, to sigh; and though her heart was rent with anguish, she was silent; yet who might tell what deep thoughts dwelt in that silence of heart? And yet, when he was gone, and the time for speaking was lost for ever, she roused herself from her seeming apathy, and bitterly reproached herself for not having strenuously opposed the departure of her son.

"Oh, why," she exclaimed in the bitterness of her feelings, "did I thus submit to his will, instead of exerting my maternal influence to compel him to do my bidding. Alas, alas! all is lost for ever! My shame and sorrow, which I have so long concealed, sacrificing my best and purest feelings in order to hide it from all eyes, must now become known to the world, and I be held up as an object of derision, for the finger of scorn to point at. I know this boy's stubborn will apart from me. There is no hope for either of us. Had I kept him by me, I might, I must have succeeded."

She paused and remained silent for a considerable time, when suddenly her face lighted up with a transient ray of sunshine, and she murmured to herself—

"Yes, I must follow this self-willed youth, and compel him, if need be, to comply with my request. I know it is no light thing I ask of him, to resign the love of one so pure and noble as Clara hath always proved herself; but it must be done: our family must be saved from shame and dishonour, at any and every cost."

While his parent thus held commune with herself, Richard had by rapid strides succeeded, in an incredible short period, in reaching the Inn where he had left his servants; ordering post-horses without a moment's delay, he was soon whirling away at a rapid rate towards London; so great, indeed, was the young man's impatience to reach Eardley Hall, that he stopped not one moment on the road, save to change horses, and this was accomplished in as short a space of time as possible. He passed through London with unabated speed, and once more in the open country, soon began to recognise each object he passed upon the road. He was now fast nearing scenes, dear to him from earliest youth, and of which he had long looked upon himself as the rightful heir; the dream, alas! had passed away, and with it how great an amount of happiness. Up to this period he had never once permitted himself to reflect upon the line of conduct it would be most fitting for him to adopt; but now thrown back in the carriage, he closed his eyes and yielded himself to deep and painful thought. There was still one bright spot shining amid the arid desert of all other feelings, one halo of gladness shedding its lustre, and speaking of hope and promise over his dark and benighted mind. Yes, now that all life's meaner joys were set, his heart still beat responsive to the fond warm passion, the worth and virtues of Clara had so deeply inspired in his breast. And as he thought upon her love for him, her tried and gentle worth, he felt assured that loss of fortune and of honours would make no difference in her affection, unless it was to make him yet more dear, more treasured in the hour of trial and vicissitude, than she had ever been in the brightest days of prosperity. This thought it was that came to shed its sweet and soothing influence over his sad and troubled spirit, hushing the storm of passion, and saying to each rebellious feeling, "peace be still." And yet as he momentarily drew near and more near the home of his forefathers (his home no longer), his heart throbbed anew with anguish; but again the thought of Clara came like an angel visitant to speak peace to his agonised mind, and cause him to bid defiance to all ills, so long as she was spared to share and cheer his darkened fortune.

So intrinsically dear, so highly prized at this moment was the thought of his young wife, that it seemed as though he had never loved her till now. How solicitous he felt to behold her once more, to assure himself of her continued and unalterable affection. The rapidity with which he travelled did not keep pace with the restless anxiety that filled his breast; and yet, when at length the carriage stopped for a moment at the park-gates, which being thrown open, he entered once more upon the little domain he had been so proud to call his own (teeming as it did with alterations and improvements, projected and carried out by the joint taste and exertions of himself and Clara), he felt more sad and dejected than even he had anticipated.

Closing his eyes to exclude objects so familiar and so dear, he yet found it impossible to banish them from his mind. No, faithful memory pourtrayed them as clear and vividly as though he saw them all in the bright and cheerful glare of a noon-day sun. And now he has reached the entrance of the noble hall, and, alighting from the carriage, ascends the broad stone steps, and stands once more within the home of his forefathers. Hastily inquiring for Clara, whom he half expected would have flown to his embrace the moment he set foot within the hall, he learnt that, still being very much indisposed, she had retired to rest some hours previously.

Without waiting for a word more, he hastened to her apartments, and entered softly—so softly that he did not disturb the quiet repose of his wife, who, all unconscious of the troubles that were gathering so thick about her, was sunk into a sweet and tranquil slumber.

Richard stood for some moments gazing upon her with a sad and heavy heart. She looked so calm and beautiful in her unruffled sleep, that for a time he dreaded the awakening, which must inevitably be the herald of grief and sorrow. It is, indeed, sweet to gaze upon those we love while sleeping, and all unconscious of our presence, and the hopes and fears that take possession of our mind on their behalf.

" An infant, as it gazes on the light—
    A child, the moment when it drains the breast—
A devotee, when soars the host in sight—
    An Arab, with a stranger for a guest—
Feels rapture; but not such true joys are reaping
As they who watch o'er what they love while sleeping.
For there it lies, so tranquil, so beloved;
    All that it hath of life with us is living,
So gentle, stirless, helpless, and unmoved,
    And all unconscious of the joy 'tis giving;
All it hath felt, inflicted, passed, and proved,
    Hushed into depths beyond the watcher's diving.
There lies the thing we love, with all its errors
And all its charms, like death without its terrors. '

Thus Richard stood for some minutes gazing on the sleeping form of his young wife, when suddenly she unclosed her eyes, and instantly becoming conconscious of the presence of her husband, uttered a cry of joy, and threw herself into his extended arms. Richard fondly clasped her to his heart, as he listened in silence to the glad welcome she so fondly poured out.

"So soon returned ?" exclaimed Clara, affectionately; "indeed, I had not dared to expect you so early," but suddenly checking herself in her joyous exultation, as she glanced anxiously at his pale and haggard face, "but you are fatigued in your anxiety to return to me—you have travelled too hurriedly, not allowing yourself sufficient time for rest and refreshment, and glad as I am again to behold you, I must yet chide you for thus endangering your own health, so precious, so inestimably dear to me."

"My dear Clara," returned Richard, "I am perfectly well in health, but mental prostration is far more difficult to endure, than even the most acute bodily sufferings; tell me then, my love, have you sufficient fortitude to enable you to bear up under the pressure of misfortune for my sake ?"

" For your sake," she replied eagerly, while a bright smile illuminated her countenance, " for your sake, I could bear all things cheerfully."

" Even comparative poverty and loss of honours ?" said Richard.

" All this, and more," returned Clara, affectionately kissing his cheeks.

" Then my sole cause for sorrow is forgotten," he replied, warmly returning her embrace. " My own Clara," he continued, " I am no longer the wealthy baronet, capable of surrounding you with every comfort, and even some of the luxuries of life, but poor, love, and friendless, depending entirely upon you for comfort and for succour."

" Then," replied Clara, more eagerly even than before, " then are you a thousand times more my husband, more dear, more treasured than you have ever been. Why," she inquired gazing sorrowfully yet hopefully on his anxious countenance, " why need we fear poverty, while spared to cheer and share each other's humble fortune ? Think of that, dear love, oh, always think of that, and we shall yet be happy. I have no care," she went on still smiling brightly, ay, more brightly. " no anxiety so long as I possess your love and confidence; who knows," she added, " but that loss of fortune may prove to us great gain, for shall we not yet be more closely bound together, more deeply and truly devoted to each other ? If, dear Richard, you had come to tell me that you had farther advanced in worldly prosperity, that higher rank and power were now at your command, methinks I should have trembled with apprehension for fear these should in a measure have disunited us, and drawn you from my side ; but now, I have no dread, I feel capable of no anxiety, for I shall henceforth be your all."

Richard's heart throbbed with the keenest anguish, as Clara rapidly poured forth these disjointed sentences, smiling upon him all the while with such sweet and trusting tenderness, as rent his bosom with conflicting emotions to behold : but struggling with these feelings till he had in a measure conquered them, he contrived to speak calmly, and repress all outward sign of the inward anguish of his spirit.

" My poor Clara," he said, " you have not yet heard the worst. It is true title and fortune are lost to me for ever, but this is not all. I am surrounded by enemies, cruel and unrelenting enemies, who, if such a thing were possible, would exult to tear you from my arms, to part us, sweet love, for ever. Oh, now I see you tremble and turn pale."

Richard spoke truth, for as he gave utterance to these words, Clara did indeed turn pale, and shook with apprehension. Now the words of the mysterious stranger (whom, during her husband's absence, the reader will remember she had encountered in the chapel) recurred to her with redoubled force, and which in the joy of again beholding him, she had for the time forgotten ; but quickly recovering her composure, she clasped her arms yet more tightly round him, as if in defiance of all the powers on earth to separate them, and said with the same bright smile again irradiating her countenance—

" Fear not, dear love, they cannot harm us or prevent us clinging to each other, so long as life shall last."

" I know not that, my Clara," returned her husband ; " they have the will to do all things, and with the power they undoubtedly possess, much may be compassed ; still, do not alarm yourself unnecessarily, or tremble with fear of what shall never come to pass," he added, pressing her lovingly to his bosom ; " believe me, there is one hope left us. I see you anticipate my meaning—yes, it is flight, instant and secret flight."

" Oh, yes !" returned Clara, with renewed eagerness, " let us go at once, far —very far from here, and seek out some lovely quiet spot, where we may live and die unseen—unknown ; let us lose not a single moment, dear love, but leave here now this very moment,"

Richard was affected even to tears, by the earnest and fond devotion of his wife ; for some minutes he essayed to speak in vain, but when at length words found utterance, he gently soothed her fears, assuring her that at present they were free from all danger, and might with perfect safety remain at Eardley Hall for a few days; but Clara's fears were now thoroughly aroused, and she would not hear of the proposed delay.

"No—no, go at once; I feel as though I could not breathe free till we are far from here," she said, in reply to all his remonstrances, urging this plea so successfully, that Richard was at length forced to yield to her tender persuasion, which he did the more willingly from his own anxiety to remove beyond the influence of Laura and Lady Eardley, whom he regarded as conspiring together to rob him of his peace.

"Early to-morrow, love," he said, "we will leave here without one regretful feeling, dear and hallowed as the days have been that we have spent within these walls; but they are no longer a shelter from the blasts of adversity, and with you for my friend and companion, I shall have no fears for the future, dark and gloomy as it appears."

"Never dark—never gloomy to me," replied Clara, "while we are together; your presence alone is all sufficient to banish every sad or sombre thought. When with thee, what ills can harm me? Thou canst every pang assuage."

"My own Clara," returned Richard, again and again embracing her, "you relieve my bosom of all its weight of care, which was felt alone for you; but the hour is late, and we must be stirring early to-morrow; let me entreat of you then, my love, to seek the repose which is so needful for you, that you may have strength to prosecute our intended journey."

Smiling kindly upon him, Clara rested on her pillow and closed her eyes (in order to feign slumber, she well knew would not, for that night at least, refresh her exhausted frame); and yielded herself to deep and thoughtful musing. She loved her husband so fondly, so truly, that in spite of all the strange woman had urged against him, she still believed him the very soul of honour, still invested him in the same bright colours he had first appeared to her young imagination; with him, therefore, she considered she had no cause of anxiety; so strong indeed was her faith in him, that she never suff red herself for a moment to question the uprightness of his conduct. Still she trembled with anxiety; and longed—oh! how earnestly!—to be far away, as she thought upon the dread curse which rested on the family, to which she was so closely allied, and the present sad fulfilment of the words which had been uttered in the chapel by her strange and unlooked-for visitor. Yes, they were now bitterly fulfilled—wealth, and title, both gone, (she had never asked or cared to know why), and themselves driven from their home to become wanderers, none knew where. As she thought upon these things her head grew sick and dizzy, and her mind became perfectly bewildered.

In the meantime Richard busied himself in preparation for immediate departure; determined, on renouncing the estates, to take with him nothing that was not strictly his own. He selected from among the valuables a case of jewels which had been presented to him by his father; the great value of which he was well assured would prevent them heeding other aid for at least some considerable period, by which time he hoped to be able to turn his talents to account. It being Richard's desire to depart as quick and as secretly as possible, he roused his servants at the first faint dawn of day, and ordering the carriage to convey himself and Clara to the nearest railway-station, hastened to her room, and to his great surprise found her already dressed for travelling.

She greeted him with a sweet and happy smile as he entered, and never to his eyes had she looked one half so beautiful as now; gentle, yet courageous, tender, yet firm, rising superior to the weakness of her sex, even while she betrayed evident symptoms of the softest feminine attributes. Richard clasped her fondly to his heart; felt that for him the world held her alone, as he kissed her cold lips and felt her tremble with eagerness to depart.

"Now, now," she said, clinging fondly to him, "do not leave me again; let us leave without another instant's delay. I have been waiting for you a long, long time."

"All is in readiness, my love," replied her husband, "the carriage is even now at the door, and nothing need longer oppose our departure."

These words afforded a sweet relief to the aching heart of Clara. For the last few hours she had been in the momentary dread of having him torn from her ; this great fear swallowed up every other feeling, and she was conscious of no

RICHARD EARDLEY'S ASTONISHMENT AT HIS MOTHER'S CONFESSION.

other source of uneasiness. She had risen directly Richard left the room, and hastily dressing herself waited his return with feverish impatience ; and as the tedious hours drew their slow length along, frequently had she crept on tip-toe to the door of the library (where Richard had been closeted the greater part of his absence from her) to listen to his heavy breathing ; and having thus assured herself of his presence, with a lightened heart, stole cautiously back to her own apartment.   How much mental suffering she had endured during this time it would be utterly impossible for words to depict, and yet, as we have said, she greeted her husband with a bright and happy smile, and which was not merely assumed, to console and encourage him, (kind and worthy of herself, as such a motive would doubtless have been) ; for never had she felt more truly happy, than when, still leaning on his arm, she passed down the grand staircase and took her seat in the carriage, which was to convey them for ever from scenes which had been rendered so dear and precious to both ; but they were still together bound, even yet, more closely than of yore, and would carry to a more humble home the same trusting love and confidence that had so richly gilded the one they were about to quit.   And now the carriage is in motion, and one parting glance is all that Richard can spare for the ancient structure, which seems to look grimly down upon him ; a dark cloud is hovering over its summit, strangely resembling the cloud of adversity, which now rests more or less on every member of this ill-fated family.   He was glad to see it thus surrounded by a dark haze, which soon excluded it entirely from his view ; it seemed as though mutely mourning the sad change which had befallen him, and he loved the old walls dearer than ever, for thus apparently sympathising with his sorrows.

It was strange, indeed, how differently the like affliction affected the two, who were now flying from all that once was dear.   Richard, stern and unbending, yet deeply and bitterly deplored the loss he had so recently sustained, and parting from this treasured spot rent his heart with anguish, and forced the burning tear to quiver on his eyelid.   For the moment, even Clara was forgotten, or only remembered to increase his misery for an outcast from home and friends, dependent upon his own untried powers for obtaining the very means of subsistence ; the thought of his cherished companion, who had voluntarily become the sharer of his lot, dark and desolate as it now appeared, but rendered his sorrows yet more acute, and as he glanced downward on the tranquil face which was resting on his bosom, his heart heaved with anguish, and he experienced, for the first time, the full bitterness of affliction ; while Clara, on the other hand, now that the time for active preparation was over, and she felt that they were, in truth, fast hastening from bitter foes, and friends untrue, thought not, even for a passing moment, on the wealth and luxury so freely resigned, nor of days and hours too bright to last ; free from the slightest taint of selfishness, she thought of none of these.   Her husband was still besides her, and with him to cheer and comfort, and the world before them, happiness, calm, sweet, and tranquil happiness, was still within their reach ; and it is at least questionable, whether she mourned most for the terrible misfortune which had overtaken one she so dearly loved, or rejoiced at the opportunity it afforded her of proving to him the warmth and utter devotion of her heart.   She had no cares——no fears for the future, which her sensitive imagination still pictured as bright and sunny in a far off clime.

"A cottage, lifting to eternal summer, whose walls should peep from out a glassy bower of coolest foliage, musical with birds, where they might sit together beneath the arched vines, and feel that naught could render them unhappy, while heaven still left them youth and love."   Thus Clara's affectionate mind pourtrayed the future, and in so doing gave sweet relief to emotions too powerful to be restrained ; and a softened feeling sprung up from the depths of her heart, giving renewed freshness to the journey of life, and bidding flowers to grow and blossom even by the wayside of toil.   And sweet, indeed, is domestic love, such as she fondly looked forward to ; and not in proud palace halls

> " Is often seen its beauty to abide.
>   It's dwelling is in lowly cottage walls,
>   That in the thickets of the woodbine hide,
>   With hum of bees around, and from the side
>   Of woody hills, some little bubbling spring,
>   Shining along through banks with harebells dyed,
>   And many a bird to warble on the wing."

CHAPTER LIV.

Forget the past? 'twere vain to try,
My thought will dwell on scenes gone by;
The time—the place—where first we met,
Are things I never can forget.

Can I forget that calm still night,
When by the moon and stars so bright,
You told me all your hopes were set
On one you never could forget?

But you are changed, and I must bear
The trials others may not share;
The withered heart, and vain regret,
Are things we seldom can forget.

IF there be anything thoroughly lovely in the human heart, it surely is affection; for all that makes hope elevated, or fear generous, belongs entirely to the capacity of loving. What a divine guide would be human reason, if love were, indeed, the power of the one and the inspiration of the other! But unfortunately love is too frequently perverted, and deprived of its divinest and purest essence, without which it degenerates into selfish littleness, or partakes of a vain and frivolous character.

Woman, in her first love, is too prone to invest the object of her adoration with a feeling almost of divinity. With man it is not so; there is not that purity of feeling—that abstract devotion, raising it to something higher than the feelings of common life.

With woman, love is often like a vision, an unreal shadow never to be converted into a reality, and like a dream it vanishes, leaving only a resting place in the imagination where it was created; for man exists not in nature as woman in her love paints him; the bright tinged feelings of her fancy forms a being that has no existence elsewhere. Such love is consequently evanescent in the extreme. But not thus had Jane Clarence loved Henry Fergusson; never, not even in their brightest days, had love rendered her blind to his faults, or glossed over the imperfections of his character; still, (though her feelings were not of that high coloured romantic kind which frequently characterises a first and absorbing passion), her love was a real not an ideal feeling. She worshipped no perfect creation of her own imagination, but bestowed her warmest affections upon one with whom she hoped to tread the world's thorny maze, to aid with her counsel, to soothe in adversity, and make still brighter his days of prosperity and peace; yet, on discovering his unworthiness, she had sought, and in a measure succeeded in banishing his image from her mind. Absence, long and apparently interminable, had likewise done much towards subduing a passion from which all hope was banished; but when, after so long a lapse, they again met, the sight of the once idolised Henry, recalled again to life and being a love that she fondly deemed was dead for ever. Yet so short had been their interview, for like a spectre, Henry had to her imagination come and gone, for on recovering her sensibility, Jane looked in vain for his well known face among the crowd who gathered around her; but he was gone, leaving her heart all sad and lone, that for one brief moment had been lighted up with happiness, happiness too pure and exquisite to be of long duration.

Jane sighed heavily as she dropped back into the recumbent position from which she had hastily arisen to look among the assembled persons for the form of him she had loved so true and tenderly, and questioned herself whether or not she might have mistaken some other face for his; but no, she felt she could not have erred, all things else were possible, but that never before had her imagination cheated her, and she was convinced it had not done so now. No, she had seen Henry, had rested for a brief space in his arms, and felt his breath warm upon her cheek; he it was who had rushed forward to save the life of

Walter, even by perilling his own; but that was like him, noble, generous, and exalted above his fellows. But how came he there, and whence had he flown so hastily? These were questions she could not solve, and the more she endeavoured to do so the more involved in mystery did it appear. But anxious as Jane felt concerning all this, she was too unaccustomed to consider herself or her own feelings to allow it long to engross her mind. Resolutely, therefore, banishing such thoughts, her first care was for Walter, whom she learnt with indescribable joy, had already evinced symptons of returning animation.

"Let me go to him," she exclaimed eagerly, "let me see him at once;" and having entirely recovered from her own illness, no opposition was offered to her expressed wish, and Jane was instantly at the bedside of Walter, who was sufficiently recovered to recognise her with a smile of pleasure.

"Dearest Walter," she said, tenderly taking his little hand within both her own, "thank God you are safe and will soon be well;" and she bent down to kiss his cold and pallid cheek. He smiled and feebly returned her tender embrace, but that was all, and Jane for the first time observed that the face of the attendants wore an expression of anxious sadness; and turning towards a gentleman who, from his appearance, was evidently a surgeon, inquired if the child was so very ill.

"My dear young lady," he returned kindly, "you have fallen into a very common error in supposing that after animation as been once restored, all danger is over, whereas it not unfrequently occurs, that a long immersion in the water, produces so great an amount of weakness, that the patient gradually sinks from utter exhaustion. I do not say," he continued, as he observed the anguish his words evidently produced in the mind of his hearer, " it will be so in the present case; at the same time it would be well to prepare your mind for the worst."

Jane could hear no more, but turning away gave vent to her feelings in a flood of bitter tears, which afforded some relief to her agonised heart. But quickly subduing her emotion, she was again at the bedside, tending with her own hand to all his little wants; and as in a few hours he was so far recovered as to admit of removal, Jane carefully enveloped him in a large cloak, and having seen him comfortably placed in the carriage, seated herself by his side, anxious to be once more at home. Yet, deeply as she regretted having been induced to participate in the late festival, she forebore to give expression to the slightest allusion to the subject, out of respect for the feelings of her friend and patron, who had so kindly insisted on her witnessing the gorgeous spectacle, but which had unhappily been productive of such a painful result. But Mrs. Clarence was not gifted with the like forbearance; and no sooner was she made acquainted with the accident which had befallen her grandson, than she indulged in loud and bitter invectives against her daughter's having been persuaded to join in what she termed a wicked and heathenish rite.

"I knew how it would be from the very first," she exclaimed in a burst of indignation. "I was quite certain that no good could possibly come of such doings. You were not satisfied, Jane, even in persisting, against my repeated remonstrances, to mix yourself up with such absurd festivities, but must likewise drag that poor child to scenes wholly unfitted to his years; and if anything happened to him—as I was quite positive it would—I told you before you went that you alone would be answerable for the consequences. There is one comfort," she added, "that no blame whatever can be attributable to myself, as, from the very first mention of the subject, I strenuously opposed it. You remember that, Jane?"

"I do, indeed," replied her daughter, as the bitter tears coursed each other in quick succession down her cheeks; "I know that I alone am to blame; but, dear mamma, do not reproach me now—do not speak unkindly—or my heart will break."

Mrs. Clarence immediately replied, that she really believed no person was ever tried to the extent she was; but, she thanked God, she was able to bear it, and would do so without uttering a word of complaint; though, to be sure, it was very hard, after doing all in her power to promote the happiness and comfort of those around her, to be constantly reproached with everything that went wrong, and told it was all her fault. She might be very weak and foolish, and she daresay she was, still she could not help feeling these things, especially when her own daughter, for whom she had sacrificed so much, as good as told her every day of her life that she was a trouble and burden to her. But it could not possibly last much longer, for she felt herself rapidly sinking, and her strength constantly giving way—there was some comfort in that.

And having arrived at this consolatory conclusion, she folded her hands, and smiling with affected resignation, bade Jane dry her tears; as to be continually crying (as she did) over every little misfortune, evinced symptoms of a very fretful and repining spirit, which she was sorry to observe, inasmuch as it was wicked and ungrateful in the extreme, considering the many blessings which were so profusely scattered round her path.

There is no knowing how much longer Mrs. Clarence might not have continued in this strain, had not Mr. Carlton interposed at this juncture.

"My dear madam," he said, respectfully but firmly, "we must not be too hard upon Miss Clarence—indeed, in the present instance, the whole censure should fall upon myself. It was I alone who projected the late visit, and succeeded, though not without difficulty, in overcoming your daughter's scruples, and prevailed upon her to leave you to my care in her absence; and as to the unlooked-for accident which has befallen little Walter, none could possibly have foreseen so painful a catastrophe. So be comforted, my dear young lady," he continued, approaching Jane, and taking her hand with the affection of a parent; "I am so entirely convinced that no particle of blame can attach itself to you, that if the like accident had occurred to one of my own children, under exactly similar circumstances, I should equally as soon have reproached myself as the cause."

Jane did feel comforted by this assurance, and forcing a smile, thanked him from her heart for his kind consideration; and then hastened to her little nephew, who by this time had been put into a warm bed, and every arrangement made for his comfort. Seated by his side, she soon forgot all else in her anxiety for his recovery, which the surgeon, who had just arrived, appeared to consider at least doubtful.

"He must be kept perfectly quiet, and constant restoratives administered," was his parting injunction, and which Jane undertook wholly to superintend; but her heart throbbed with anguish at the prospect of being forced to resign one who had become so inestimably dear, and whom she had promised her dying sister to love and cherish.

"Alas!" she murmured half aloud, "that this unhappy accident should have menaced the life of one I would have parted with all other things to spare. Had he been struck down with disease, I could have borne it better; but this accident, which a little more care on my part might have prevented, seems almost more than I can endure."

"You must not reason thus," said Mr. Carlton, who entered at the moment and unintentionally overheard some of the expressions which had fallen from her lips. "You must not reason thus, for believe me the decrees of fate, though inscrutable, are nevertheless unerring, and it is at all times wrong to permit ourselves to question the wisdom of any dispensation that may visit us, knowing that nothing can happen by chance, and an all-wise providence at all times determines right; and when the rod of affliction seems to be heaviest upon us, there is a wisdom in the stroke, such as our finite vision cannot penetrate."

"I know it," replied Jane, mildly, "and yet—" she paused, for tears choked her utterance.

"And yet," returned Mr. Carlton, "you would say, it is hard to bear it patiently; and I can deeply sympathise with your feelings, having been myself severely tried; far then, be it from me to chide your grief, or entreat you to recall the tears which fain would flow; on the contrary, I would rather encourage the evidence of such feelings, and beg of you at all times to give your sorrow vent.   And for the dear child," he resumed, after a short pause, "if early called away, who can tell how much sorrow and anxiety he may escape? Think of the many ills, the temptations of the world, its hollow falsehood and deceit, and let such thoughts reconcile you to the loss of one, to whom you have been the best and kindest friend the child ever had."

Jane sobbed aloud, as she replied—

"And is he then so very ill; is there no hope of his ultimate recovery?"

"I fear not," returned Mr. Carlton; "his constitution, naturally delicate, has received so severe a shock, that I do not think it possible he can survive it. You feel this deeply, I know, I am sure you do," he added, as Jane sobbed yet more bitterly than before; "yet do not, my dear young lady, I beg—I entreat, allow it thus to overcome you; summon your wonted fortitude, and think— not for yourself—for your mother, who has been accustomed to your tenderest care and devotion, that were she to see you thus, I should tremble for the consequences."

Those words were not without their due effect upon Jane: she did think of her mother, and quickly dried her tears.   And yet she felt that it was hard to part with Walter. Her best affections (since the loss of Henry) had been given to this boy, round him every hope and wish of her heart was entwined; and had it been possible, she would gladly have laid down her own life, in order to preserve his. Yet she steadfastly repelled the rising tear, and checked the emotion which struggled to vent itself in sighs. Mrs. Clarence, on the contrary, indulged in the noisiest demonstrations of grief, constantly reminding Jane, she had no one but herself to thank for this unfortunate accident; and repeating, that had her own wishes on the subject been attended to, it never would have occurred, inasmuch as from the very first she had opposed the proposed expedition.

"Not," she would observe, on such occasions, "that I for a moment expected my wishes would be attended to; no, I knew well enough that they would not have the slightest weight with you; but foreseeing, as I did, that some lamentable occurrence must be the necessary consequence of a participation in such heathenish rites, I thought it nothing but right to declare my sentiments on the subject, and which I am truly thankful I did, notwithstanding it vexed and annoyed you so much at the time."

"Indeed, dear mamma, you mistake," Jane would reply; "I assure you I had no desire whatever to avail myself of Mr. Carlton's kind proposition; but he pressed it so strongly, that I could not, without appearing rude and ungenerous, refuse to do so."

"Now really, Jane," returned her mother, "I am, indeed, surprised you should endeavour to through the blame of this misfortune upon one who has proved himself in every respect so good and amiable, so anxious to promote your happiness, that it was on that account alone he so successfully combatted my scruples, and wrung from me an unwilled consent to your mixing yourself up with such absurd rites and festivities."

"I am sure," replied Jane, "I had not the slightest intention of attributing to Mr. Carlton anything but what was kind and generous in the extreme. I merely wished to free myself from the imputation of having had the least desire to avail myself of his kindness. Could I, under the circumstances, have acted otherwise than I did? But I am well aware there is no one to blame in this matter but myself."

"I am glad, indeed," said Mrs. Clarence, "that you see it in that light, and trust it may act as a warning to you, and teach you for the future to pay more attention to my opinion, and above all, make you careful not to expose the poor child to such sad accidents."

"Alas!" replied Jane, "for him I fear all will soon be over on earth; and I shall constantly carry about me the bitter reflection that, but for this calamitous event, he might have been spared to manhood."

"Really, Jane," returned Mrs. Clarence, indignantly, "you do take the most absurd ideas in your head that any one ever heard of ; and, without the slightest consideration for my feelings, talk in a manner calculated to increase my nervous affection, and make me dull and low-spirited in the extreme. But it is always the way," she added, in a tone of resignation. "Thank God, I am used to it—there is some comfort in that ; but if ever I feel a little more cheerful or talkative than usual, I am always thrown back and rendered gloomy and apprehensive in the extreme."

"Dear mamma," replied Jane, affectionately, "indeed I did not mean to give you pain ; it was thoughtless of me, I allow, to speak to you so abruptly of the child's death ; yet, as it appears next to impossible that he can recover from the shock his constitution has received——"

"Nonsense, Jane," interrupted her mother, "your fears have magnified the extent of the misfortune ; the child is doing very nicely, and he will soon be erfectly well."

"Oh ! would, indeed, that I could think so," replied Jane, earnestly ; "Heaven only knows how thankful I should be. But it is very different, indeed, mamma—do not buoy yourself up with hopes that can only prove delusive."

"You will allow me, if you please, to be a better judge of illness than yourself," said Mrs. Clarence, in a tone of lofty dignity. "I am perfectly aware that there is not the slightest occasion for uneasiness, or you may be sure I should be the first to observe it."

And contenting herself with these sagacious remarks, Mrs. Clarence rested perfectly satisfied, being firmly convinced in her own mind that the child was in no danger. Only, as she remarked to Mr. Carlton, Jane was so highly sensitive, that she imagined danger when none existed.

"I have endeavoured," she continued on, "to induce her to cast from her mind all groundless fears ; but she appears to experience a gloomy sort of pleasure in indulging in them, and which, indeed, I am very sorry to observe."

"I must on this subject differ from you, my dear madam," said Mr. Carlton, respectfully, "for I do not believe Miss Clarence entertains the slightest apprehension beyond what may be reasonably anticipated. The child's constitution is naturally delicate ; and you will pardon me if I say I do not dare to anticipate a happy termination of his present illness."

"Really !" returned Mrs. Clarence. "Well now, you do surprise me. I am sure if you could only know what I have gone through myself, though always delicate in health, as you see me now, you would not so soon give way to despair, but feel emboldened—as I do—to place the greatest reliance on his ultimate and perfect restoration."

Mr. Carlton was silenced, for he clearly saw the utter uselessness of attempting to convince Mrs. Clarence of the fallacy of entertaing hopes which all but herself well knew could never be realised ; and yet, though the child gradually grew weaker each day, and was perceptibly hastening to the tomb, she still persisted in her own opinions—indeed, clung to them the more tenaciously as all apparent hope grew weaker. Yet spite of all this, the fiat had gone forth, and grim death was hovering over the couch of little Walter. His mind, at all times bright and unusually clear and vigorous for a child, seemed to expand yet more, and unfold its beauties, as he rapidly approached the confines of eternity ; as the frail body became weak and helpless, so did the mind of the dying boy grow strong and full of confidence.

"Dear aunt," he said, one evening, as Jane occupied her accustomed seat by his bedside, "I have been thinking of my mother. I dreamt of her last night, and thought she told me I should soon come to live with her in heaven. Do you know," he added, "that this, at first, made me very sad, and I cried when

I awoke, and felt glad that it was only a dream, for I thought it would be so dull to leave you, and never again take those pleasant walks which delighted us so much, or listen while you sung those sweet songs I so love to hear. I could not bear the idea of leaving you, dear aunt, and all other kind friends, to die by myself, and I tried to think that though I was very ill, I should be sure to get quite well in time, or, at all events, be no worse for a long, long while; but though I tried very hard to think this, I could not do it, for something seemed to tell me that my strength was failing fast, and though I longed to live, I must leave you all and die. Does not this seem sad?"

"It does, love," she said, in her tenderest and gentlest tone. "Yet do not let it make you unhappy, darling; we must all die; and though it is early for you to be called hence, yet, believe me, you will escape much sorrow and unhappiness by dying while young, and uncontaminated by the wickedness and sins of the world."

"I should not like you to die, aunt," said the boy, thoughtfully, "and I love you so dearly, that I do not like to leave you. I think you will be so dull without me."

"I shall, indeed, my love," replied Jane, affectionately, "but I shall rejoice that you are safe-landed on that happy shore, where nothing shall have power to harm you, and where in a few short years we shall assuredly be reunited, never to part again."

The child's eyes glistened brightly as he answered with renewed eagerness—

"Oh yes, aunt, we shall meet again. I thought of that, and was going to tell you how happy it made me; but the hours will seem long and dull till you are with me. I wish we could go together, aunt."

"In heaven, love," she replied, kindly, "there is no space—time is as nothing; neither can sad thoughts enter there to destroy or mar the peace of the blest; all is happiness and joy, compared to which the pleasures we have experienced together is of no account."

"And yet," returned the boy, more thoughtfully even than before; "and yet I think, among the glittering crowds, I shall seek in vain for you—though angels' faces smile upon me and welcome me to heaven, I shall sigh for the love to which I have been so long accustomed, and long to be back again to this place, though dull compared with heaven, yet sweet when shared with you."

Jane soothed him as she best could, talking of the quick flight of time, and the happiness of the blest, till he sank in a sweet and tranquil slumber, from which he awoke refreshed and strengthened, and asked to see Mr. Carlton, who, obedient to the summons of Jane, was instantly at the bedside of the sufferer.

"Are you better, Walter?" he said, kindly taking his hand within his own.

"Thank you, much better," replied the child. "You have been very kind to me," he added, after a pause, "and I wished to see you, not so much to tell you how proud and grateful I always felt, as to ask you always to be kind and good to my dear aunt, whom I love so very much. I never," he continued, with increasing animation, "knew my mother, and, therefore, cannot tell how kind and full of love she might have been; but of this I am sure, I could never have loved her more, or felt that she was dearer to me than my aunt Jane, who never in my whole life has said one cross or angry word to me, though I have deserved it often."

"I am certain, dearest Walter," interrupted Jane, "you have merited my entire love, and returned it as child scarcely ever did before."

He smiled affectionately, as he returned the kiss she stooped down to press upon his cheek; but again addressing Mr. Carlton, who, with tearful eyes, had in silence contemplated them both, said—

"You, sir, are rich and powerful, yet not less kind and good; when I am gone, love her as I have done, if that be possible: it will make her happier, I know, and she will miss me less."

These words, spoken with the pure guileless innocence that only belongs alone to childhood, powerfully affected Mr. Carlton, and he hastened to assure the boy that his dying wishes should be respected.

"From this hour," he replied, solemnly, and turning to Jane as he spoke, "I look upon you as appertaining exclusively to myself; not even the love I bear towards my own children shall excel in the slightest degree my love for

CHARD AND CLARA'S FLIGHT FROM EARDLEY HALL.

you. Regard me, my dearest Jane, as a parent—a fond and affectionate parent, to whom you may fearlessly confide the dearest secrets of your breast; who will ever love and cherish you as though you were in truth his child;" and bending down, he tenderly embraced her.

Jane felt, as she had ever done, truly grateful; and yet, when she again raised her face, it was covered with a burning blush, and she was conscious, though she scarce knew why, of a feeling of increased sadness. It could not be that she was too proud to receive Mr. Carlton's proffered friendship. Oh, no; when she asked that question of her heart, it answered her truthfully that she was not only grateful, but thankful and pleased at having secured so kind a friend and protector; one whose character she esteemed and respected beyond all others, whose amiability of temper and excellence of disposition she had ample opportunities afforded of proving to be all her most sanguine wishes could have desired in a parent. Why, then, that trembling of the heart, which seemed for a moment to stop its pulsation, and the next to cause it to beat with a rapidity which sent the burning blood in a crimson glow to her cheeks and temples? She shrank with instinctive delicacy from pursuing such a turn of thought, and busied herself in arranging the pillows of the little invalid, in order to conceal her emotion from the observation of her friend and benefactor, while Walter poured out his childish gratitude, and heaped blessings on his head. But it needed not this; Mr. Carlton was too deeply affected himself to remark the confusion of Jane. From the first mement of becoming acquainted with Walter, his heart had been drawn towards the boy, and he had by no means been slow in cultivating his affection; and he now reaped the rich harvest he had sown; and as he listened to the lisping words of the child, the expression of the warm feelings of his breast, he felt a source of joy, deep, pure, and abiding. And it is indeed sweet to be blessed by infant voices, in whom there is no guile, and feel that we have, in some slight measure, contributed to the happiness and peace of one of those little wayfarers, whose blessing is of more worth—of far more intrisic value than the priceless gold at whose shrine so many bend the knee. Jane was the close and constant attendant of little Walter, while Mrs. Clarence seldom visited the sick chamber more than once a day; it had' she averred, too much effect upon her nerves to allow her to remain long in the apartment of the invalid, greatly as she desired to share with Jane the fatigue of attending upon the little invalid; and Mr. Carlton relieved Jane of all anxiety on her account, by devoting the greater portion of his time to the amusement of Mrs. Clarence, thus enabling her daughter to give hers entirely to Walter. Each day since the festival had been marked with so great an amount of anxiety and mental suffering, that the image of Henry was entirely banished from her memory; she had even ceased to marvel at the strange and painful vicissitude which had brought them momentarily together, and parted them as suddenly. No; she thought of none of these things.

Great, then, was her surprise at receiving one morning an intimation from the servant that a gentleman wished to see her. At first Jane peremptorily denied the request; but a still more pressing message induced her to comply, and giving the nurse strict charge to watch over the child in her absence, descended to the receiving-room, and, to her utter astonishment, beheld in her unexpected visitor the well-known form of Henry! So great, indeed, was her surprise—so deep and absorbing the emotions of her breast, that for the time it deprived her of the capability both of speech and action. Henry, too, seemed deeply affected, as, advancing to meet her, he took the hand she had no power either to give or to withhold.

"Jane," he said, kindly, but his voice trembled as he spoke, "after so long a separation, this is a sad and painful meeting to us both."

"So much so," she returned, with quivering lip and tearful eye, "that you might well have spared me its painful effects."

"Say not so," returned the young man, warmly; "neither attribute to me other than pure and generous motives in thus seeking an interview. Our first meeting," he continued, in firmer tones, "was entirely the result of accident, (or rather let me attribute it to a merciful Providence, since it enabled me so save the life of one so dear to you), since which period I have earnestly desired to behold you once more; to hear from your own lips that you freely forgive my past unkindness, and likewise.—But this," checking himself, "is a more delicate subject. Yet, Jane, I will be plain with you, nor suffer myself to be withheld by a false delicacy from declaring my wishes and sentiments, and which indeed is the object of my present visit."

"You have my permission to speak freely," said Jane, seeing that Henry still hesitated, and glanced anxiously towards her. "I owe you much for the generous impulse which prompted you to risk your own life in the hope of preserving one so inestimably precious to myself; and that one act," she added, raising her eyes (beaming with gratitude) for the first time in his face, "that one act has cancelled all past injuries, and I would promote your happiness and peace at the expense even of my own, if such a thing were possible."

"You encourage me," returned the young man, "to speak plainly, without the fear of incurring your displeasure. I would say," he continued, though still with something of hesitation in his tones, "that I am now rich and independent."

"Yes," replied Jane, with a flushed brow and burning cheek, "yes, I am already aware of that; and I can say with truth, that I sincerely hope you are happier for its possession. Poverty, indeed, is often sorely tried and afflicted, and you have undoubtedly escaped much by uniting yourself to one who had it in her power to scatter influence around your path."

"You will not then," rejoined Henry, eagerly, "refuse the united wishes of myself and her who, whatever my faults may have been, is free from all but the most kindly feelings towards yourself, who, knowing your dependant condition, sent me hither to entreat, nay, to implore you to regard her in the light of an affectionate sister; and as such, scruple not for an instant to abandon your present position of toil and dependence."

"Stop, I beg of you!" replied Jane, with flushed cheeks and sparkling eyes.

She hesitated a moment, for pride was busy in her heart, prompting her to reject with scorn and indignation the proposed kindness; but she quickly mastered these feelings, and answered with her accustomed gentleness—

"I thank you, indeed, for what I am sure is meant kindly—most kindly; but indeed, under any circumstances, I could not, without the sacrifice of my self-esteem, consent to profit by it; but no such need as you imagine, does or ever did exist. My present situation is one of happiness and peace—such peace as a few short months ago I never expected to know or feel again. I am surrounded by kind, affectionate, considerate friends, whose good opinion I value, I cannot tell you how highly——"

She stopped abruptly, for at this instant Mr. Carlton entered. He observed Henry, who politely returned his salutation; then stepping up to Jane, he drew her arm within his own.

"You will pardon me," he said, as he gazed upon her half-averted face, "for having unintentionally overheard a portion at least of your conversation, which has produced the effect of raising you still higher in my estimation. I had already regarded you with so deep an interest that I did not think it possible that aught could increase it; but I was mistaken, and feel renewed thankfulness in having secured so bright an example for my children, who, with the constant contemplation of such true virtue, cannot fail to become all my heart can wish."

He gently pressed the hand that rested on his arm; but the pressure, gentle as it was, sent the warm blood to the cheeks of Jane; and then turning to Henry, who had been a silent, but not unobservant witness of all this, said, in a polite yet distant tone—

"I trust sir, you will allow me to set you right on a point whereon you have perhaps naturally, yet greatly erred. You see in this young lady," he continued, drawing Jane still more closely to his side, "no hireling dependant on her own exertions for the means wherewith to support existence, and who can be hired or discharged at will—but the dearest friend, the treasured companion of my motherless children, who, I am proud to say, evince towards her the affection and respect due to an elder and affectionate sister; and for my self, my heart acknowledges a feeling of tenderest love, for one who generously devoted her warmest influence on behalf of me and mine. The difference in our respective ages, is such as to warrant me in assuming towards her the character of a parent; and were she in truth my daughter, I could not love or prize her more highly."

As Mr. Carlton gave utterance to these words, Jane was again conscious of a feeling of deep sadness, though she scarce knew why. They were surely calculated to reassure her mind and make her happy and thankful, instead of producing so opposite an effect. Alas! there are strange chords in the human heart, which will at times vibrate though touched ever so lightly; and susceptibilities we had long deemed crushed, start anew to life and vigour; a breath even will suffice to awaken the dormant passions of the breast which have slumbered so long; we thought them dead and withered, but who can search that mystic volume of the heart, and trace the strange variety of conflicting and opposing feelings with which it abounds? Jane in truth knew not hers, but love is quick and sensitive, and Henry saw or thought he saw, symptoms of a new love springing up in the breast of Jane—a love whose chief characteristics were those of deep and abiding gratitude and respect, a love founded solely on the perfect knowledge of the high and the noble worth of the object which called it forth. Consequently he took leave with a troubled heart, without having received the slightest encouragement to repeat his visit. His brightest hopes were now dashed to the ground, for since his unexpected recognition of Jane at the festival of St. Rosolia, he had conceived the romantic idea of becoming the best and truest friend she ever had, of inducing her to share his wealth and splendour, of seeing her and Fanny close and constant companions, of loving her still, though with the tender affection of a brother. He had never imagined her love for him diverted to another object, and he felt more pained by the discovery he had made, or fancied he had made, than the occasion warranted. But the noblest and best of men are more or less selfish, and Henry, though capable of the most generous devotion, was more disturbed than he liked to acknowledge even to himself.

CHAPTER LV.

Her voice was like the wildest, saddest tone,
    Yet sweet, of some loved voice heard long ago !
I wept: Shall this fair woman all alone,
    Over the sea, with that fierce serpent go ?
His head is on her heart, and who can know,
    How soon he may devour his feeble prey !

LADY EARDLEY we have seen, immediately on the departure of her son, deeply regretted having suffered him to leave, without first extracting from him the promise she was so anxious to obtain. To remedy this misfortune, she resolved with that energy of character so natural to her, instantly to follow him to Eardley Hall, nothing doubting that she would regain her lost influence over his mind, and force him to do her bidding; or if by any possibility this could not be, she determined to entrust Clara with the secret, and thus throw herself entirely upon her generosity. In accordance, therefore, with this resolution, Lady Eardley left home early the following morning, and hastened with all speed towards the ancient hall she was so desirous to secure to her children.

"I will not despair," she murmured to herself, as doubts and fears occasionally crossed her mind; "up to this period I have succeeded in overcoming every obstacle, why then should I permit the obstinacy of this self-willed boy to vex or depress my spirit? I must, I will bend him to my purpose; all else must be sacrificed to secure our good name, to keep my sin a secret from the world."

And yet when she thought of Clara—her long and tried worth—a pang at once of pity and regret shot through her mind; but it was quickly quelled: she permitted herself to dwell alone upon the necessity which existed; for rending asunder two hearts so inexpressibly dear to each other. She loved Clara with the tenderest affection, and while she was thus resolving to wring her bosom with anguish, and crush the fairest blossoms of her heart, at the same time she was mentally engaged in anticipating various schemes for her future happiness: so strange and so conflicting were the feelings of this extraordinary woman! Kind and gentle by nature, she was cruel only, as she deemed, by necessity, and was imbrued with an amount of moral fortitude, that enabled her unshrinkingly to pursue the course she judged it wisest and best to pursue; heeding not in her impetuous career, how many pure and blessed emotions were repelled, or what tender and loving natures rent with the keenest anguish. No! she thought not, cared not, for aught beyond the purpose she resolved to achieve at any and every cost.

The journey indeed, though performed with the greatest celerity, did not keep pace with her deep anxiety to be again with her son. At length the park gates were reached, and alighting from the carriage, Lady Eardley proceeded on foot along the path which had so lately been traversed by Richard and Clara. She had not walked far before she encountered a somewhat singulary dressed female, who, standing full in her path, did not attempt to turn aside as she advanced, but remained perfectly motionless with her eyes fixed upon the ground, and her brow contracted as though with deep and painful thought. Unwilling to intrude her presence upon an entire stranger, who was evidently unconscious of her near approach, Lady Eardley attempted to pass her unobserved; but at the very instant (apparently attracted by the rustling of her dress), the stranger raised her eyes, and fixed them full upon her. There was a wild and glassy look in those orbs, dark and brilliant as they were, that attracted the attention of Lady Eardley, and she hesitated a moment whether or not to address her; but the stranger anticipating her intention, said, as she drew her cloak closer round her form, for the morning was cold, and in her abstraction she had suffered it to fall aside—

"Lady Eardley, I know you; there is in those features too strong a resemblance to one I have loved, not wisely I own, but too well, to permit me to pass you unheeded by. I should have know you anywhere, but in these grounds, the meeting is at once strange and retributive. I was drawn towards this spot by a singular fatality which has forced me to keep in the close neighbourhood of one whom I hate and despise."

"I see in you, then," replied Lady Eardley, "the rightful heiress of this domain. Your features, too, represent those which are most painful, I will not say most repellant, to my mind; suffice it we are doubtless here for the same purpose. I came to enforce obedience from my son, and compel him to do you late, yet ample justice."

Laura, for it was indeed she, laughed loud and scornfully.

"You are too late to do either," she returned in mocking tones; "the bird has flown, taking with him the dove who fled for shelter to his bosom, who even now has carried with her the olive branch of peace, and for whom he forsook his early mate; but the curse is working on every member of your ill-fated race, and soon sorrow and discord will be the portion and inheritnce of all. You lady," she continued, "have long drank from the poisoned cup, yet you must drain it to its very dregs. None shall be spared, no, not one, and you less than all."

"Talk not thus wildly," returned Lady Eardley; "remember that we espouse one and the same cause. If my son has indeed taken advantage of my absence to quit this place, he cannot be far distant; let us therefore unite our power to track him out; and once found, fear not that I will force him to do my bidding."

" I fear nothing," said Laura, " neither would I consent to save my life even to unite in any measure with one of your accursed race. No wonder revenge is tardy when such as you pretend to lend a helping hand to its accomplishment. But I waste time idly here, time that should be devoted to active pursuit."

" What mean you," said Lady Eardley, " and whither would you go?"

" To the world's end," returned Laura, " if need be, to find your son—to blast him with my continual presence—to be ever a bane to his peace in his fanced hours of security and happiness—to rise before him and rob him of his bliss—to spread sorrow and desolation around his path! This," she continued, " is my mission. Poverty, shame and sorrow would be as nothing, if I were not by to taunt him with my presence. Revenge, deep and abiding, fills my breast, swallowing up every other feeling in its absorbing power. For this have I lived, for this have I hoped and trusted, knowing that though slow in coming, the day of retribution was sure."

" And for yourself," said Lady Eardley, " what will become of you?"

" Oh, me," replied Laura, and though her voice was still wild, there was also a sadness in her tones that touched the heart of her listener, recalling those she had once so loved to her, but now lost to her for ever. " It is long since one of my own sex hath put that question to one ruined and forsaken as I have been, and it matters little indeed how my span of life is destined to pass. I feel," she continued, in still more mournful tones, " as though its few remaining sands were fast ebbing away, and this more than aught else urges me to complete the work of vengeance ere it be too late."

Lady Eardley's heart sank within her, as she listened to these words. The proud beauty of the strange being, yet so scornful, so utterly regardless of her own charms—the wildness of her demeanour—her avowed thirst for vengeance—and, above all, the burning wrongs which had thus driven her an outcast from all the nearest and dearest ties of life, made a deep and painful impression on her mind; and the tear-drop quivered on her eyelid as she though—" Shall I allow this frail woman to depart without one kind word, without one effort to withdraw her from this vain and vague pursuit?" And as the thought passed through her mind, she resolved to do all in her power to turn her from her purpose, and induce her to forego her fancied scheme of revenge.

" Laura," she said, emphatically " listen to me, I entreat of you. I know your wrongs, and also the source from when they flow. You have been greatly injured by one nearly allied to myself. He has refused, even at my intercession, to do you justice—flown from here purposely to escape my influence; he is, therefore, no longer my son. From this moment I disown him. Let me pray of you then to fill the vacant place in my heart: be unto me a daughter, and I solemnly promise to fulfil towards you the duties of a parent. Share my house; and as both have tasted deeply of the cup of sorrow, let us then dedicate the remainder of our lives to soothing and cheering each other. There is happiness yet, oh! believe me, sweet tranquil happiness in a country life, among the green fields and trees, in the song of birds and all the sweet and silent workings of nature; these are mine, and may also become yours, if you consent to share my solitude. more sweet and blessed than words can tell, where those who have sinned like you and I may learn to forgive the injuries we have received, and even pray for those who have wronged us."

She ceased speaking; and Laura, with an impatient movement, turned away her head, and endeavoured to pass Lady Eardley, but who, frustrating her intention, hastily caught her hand, which she warmly pressed within her own.

" You consent?" she murmured. " I knew, I was sure you would. Let us hasten from this spot, hateful alike to us both."

" Yes, yes," replied Laura, still averting her face. " I must from here: delay may ruin all. Lady Eardley, your intention is meant well, but I would lay me down and die gladly with the work of vengeance still incomplete, rather than receive aid from one of your accursed race; and yet," she added, in a softer tone, " our paths in life are utterly distinct and separate; we have no one feeling in common; and yet," she continued, turning her wild dark eyes full upon Lady Eardley; "and yet I do not hate you, though I despise myself for the confession which has been thus wrung from me. Tears?" she murmured, after a moment's pause, as they stood quivering on her long dark eyelashes; "'tis long, very long since these eyes were last wet, and long may it be ere they are moist again; a strange and unwonted feeling has taken possession of my breast. I feel that I look upon this place for the last time, that I am going far from here to die on a foreign shore, to perish in a strange land, away from all that can claim kith or kin with me."

"Then why go?" inquired Lady Eardley, moved still more to pity.

"I go," replied the other, "to fulfil my destiny; an imperious fate urges me on, and I have no choice but to obey its mandate. Lady," she continued, impressively, "we part for ever; I have no word of encouragement to give, neither can I receive one from you; and yet I feel as though I valued your good opinion—I who have set all others' respect at defiance. Had we met sooner, we might have had different, very different feelings. Suffice it—I was not always what you see me now."

"If, indeed," said Lady Eardley, "you are determined to follow my unhappy son, who, I doubt not, will instantly quit England, let me be your friend and companion. You have been deeply injured through me; it it but meet then that I should endeavour to heal your wounds, and as far as possible bid your sorrows cease."

"Urge me no farther," replied Laura; "my fate is sealed. I go alone to breast the strong world, to complete my scheme of vengeance, or perish in the attempt;" and impatiently waving her hand, she passed Lady Eardley, and pursuing her walk with a rapid pace, was soon lost to view, leaving her companion to meditate on the strange chance which had brought them together.

Lady Eardley turned, and watched her retreating footsteps till the last fold of her mantle was lost to view.

"It is useless," she murmured, "to attempt to detain her strange infatuation; and yet my heart was drawn towards her so deeply that even now it prompts me to follow, and induce her to return; her voice has revived feelings long buried in oblivion, and I would rather have parted with my right hand, than know that Richard has acted the base part of the betrayer, throwing aside the toy when the gilding was worn away. Alas! alas! I placed such faith, such undoubted confidence in his honour, that it rends my heart with anguish to know I have been deceived, and she above all others to be his chosen victim! My cup of misery is now indeed full."

While thus musing, the unhappy lady resumed her walk, and soon reached the noble edifice, to retain which in her family, she would have sacrificed so much. Having entered, she learnt from the domestics the departure early that morning of Sir Richard and his lady, as likewise the return of the servants with the carriage which had conveyed their master and mistress to the nearest railway station, from which they took the train to London. On hearing this, Lady Eardley instantly divined the intention of her son to leave England without delay, and as instantly foresaw the utter inutility of her attempting to follow him; her mind was, therefore, immediately made up, and she resolved to retain possession of Eardley Hall, at all events for the present. Yes, painful as it was to reside even for a short time within those walls, teeming as they did with mournful memories, calling up the past from the deep abyss of time, and bidding her live over again days and feelings she had so long struggled to forget, yet spite of all this, she resolved to quell her own morbid sensibility, and for the sake of the peace and honour of her children, to retain possession of the estates of her late husband, till they were torn from her, hoping even against hope, that some fortunate occurrence might yet enable her to conceal from the world her own early error, and thus secure to her children the legal inheritance. Her secret was indeed known to but few, and this confirmed her in the cherished thought, that it was still possible to keep the knowledge so fraught with danger, from all who might endeavour to turn it to their own advantage, and the consequent ruin and downfall of her family. Upon cool reflection, she even derived comfort from the very circumstance of Richard's premature flight; and not for a moment doubting that he contemplated a long residence in some foreign country, considered that circumstance, as augering favourably to her own schemes, as during his absence she was, at least, free from all counterplotting on his part. Laura, too (who she now rejoiced had not availed herself of the offer, which in the warmth of her feelings she had so pressed her to accept), would likewise ere long be removed beyond the power to molest her, and without her aid, Evereard could not injure her through her children, or turn their secret marriage to his own account. As she thought of all these things, the dark shadow cleared from her brow, and she was again the calm unimpassioned lady, as when the reader first made her acquaintance. There was something, too, in her habitual self-complacency, and the quiet, though dignified manner in which she issued her commands, that induced the servants without the slightest discontent to submit to her rule, as though she had been for years their mistress, and they her hired dependents; not one amongst the number ever even thought of questioning her authority, or felt disposed to murmur at the strange manner in which she had so suddenly come among them, and taken the reins of government so adroitly in her own hands; and though not a word to that effect had on any occasion been dropped by their 'new mistress, they all concluded she had been commissioned by Sir Richard to take charge of the household arrangements in his absence. Confirmed in this opinion by the thorough knowledge the lady evidently possessed of the entire mansion, and in which they were seconded by the old housekeeper, who always spoke of her as a kind and amiable lady, who must have been long accustomed to command, and though somewhat cold and proud, yet one whom it was a pleasure to serve—all went well; and when week after week passed by without aught occurring to disturb her possession, Lady Eardley became more and more satisfied with the course she had adopted, living in strict retirement, and seldom going out, save for a quiet walk in the grounds. Walter, to whom we must turn in the next chapter, was utterly unconscious of the near vicinity of his mother, or the startling events which had driven his brother into exile.

CHAPTER LVI.

" From that dread hour entirely wildly driven
From him, and, she believed, lost maid ! from Heaven,
Oh, then, the look—ah ! where's the heart so wise,
Could unbewildered meet those matchless eyes—
Quick, restless, strange, but exquisite withal,
Like those of angels just before their fall ?
Now shadowed with the stains of earth, now crost
By glimpses of the heaven, her heart had lost,
In every glance there broke, without control,
The flashes of a bright but troubled soul;
Where sensibility still wildly played,
Like lightning round the ruins it had made."

ADA, bent upon the wild project of rousing the jealous feelings of Walter, and thus (as she hoped) securing his love, which, as the reader is aware, she was so solicitous to obtain, turned a deaf ear to his repeated admonitions, and in utter defiance of his expressed mandate, continued to make Percy her constant companion, consulting him on every arrangement, and following his advice against the known wishes of her husband. Percy, in his turn, reckless and careless in the extreme, had seriously involved himself in gambling speculations, from which he had no means of extricating himself, save by an appeal to Ada

for the loan of a few hundreds, which, with natural generosity, she instantly
granted, though he could offer no more probable mode of payment than the
doubtful dependance on some hazardous speculations which he contemplated. In
the mean time, Walter, though more and more dissatisfied with the conduct of
his wife, was yet convinced, by past experience, of the inutility of attempting to

WALTER'S MEDITATIONS AFTER BEING LEFT BY ADA.

reason or expostulate with her, till an unfortunate occurrence made him acquainted with the obligation then existing between her and Percy.   Fired with
anger and disdain, he instantly sought the apartments of Ada; nor was this all,
for Percy's pecuniary difficulties having been noised abroad, his gay associates
had hesitated in accepting his bets, till with his constitutional carelessness he
had avowed his obligation to Ada, accompanied with the boast that the rich

and beautiful Mrs. Eardley would willingly accommodate him in the like manner for any amount he chose to name. All this was evidently repeated to Walter, with a pretended anxiety for his honour, by one of those miscalled friends, who are ever ready to sow the seeds of discord, and appear to find a malignant pleasure in arousing the evil passions of the breast, and under the guise of good and tender feeling, too often wring the heart with sorrow and remorse. Walter, already mortified and suspicious, was enraged well-nigh to madness by this (as he thought) convincing proof of his wife's dishonour, and, as we were saying, instantly sought her apartments, with all the deep and burning sense of his injuries full upon him, allowing his passions no time to cool, or he might have acted with less precipitation.

Now it so happened that this very evening Ada had returned home early from a gay assembly, disgusted with the fulsome compliments and unmeaning flattery which was constantly showered round her path, and which, deprived of their only charm, novelty, wearied and oppressed her. How gladly would she have exchanged the beauty she had once so highly prized, for the fascinations of an amiable and well-ordered mind, such as might have charmed and delighted the only man whose heart she wished to win! On this particular evening she was so deeply oppressed by the dark shadows which appeared to flit around her footsteps, warning her of coming ill, that, contrary to her habitual custom, she stole from the brilliant company and returned home; the hour, though early for a London season, was yet late enough to warrant her in the idea she at first conceived, of retiring instantly to rest; but an indefinable sense of approaching trouble forbade her to seek that sweet boon to the weary—rest and sleep. She inquired if Walter was at home; and learning that he had not returned from the House, resolved to await his arrival.

"He cannot be much longer absent," she murmured, as she threw herself on the soft cushions of her couch; "and I shall feel happier when I know he is at home."

Hours drew their slow length along, and sleep gradually weighed down her eyelids; but it was anxious, troubled sleep, from which she was at length aroused by the well-known step of Walter ascending the stairs; she listened attentively, and her heart almost stopped beating. No, she was not mistaken; his hand was on the lock: the door turned on its hinges, and the next instant her husband confronted her. She hastily rose from the couch, and with an exclamation of delight, said—

"Oh, Walter, I am so glad you have come!" And then remarking, for the first time, his dark and angry brow—"What ails you, Walter?—Are you unwell, or has anything occurred to vex you?"

"Much—much," he replied, "though I come not here to reproach or upbraid you."

"Reproach, upbraid me?" repeated Ada, in tones of astonishment.

"You hear me," replied her husband, making a strong effort to repel the rising passion; "though, I repeat, I come not here to reproach you for your baseness; the time for talking is past, and the hour for action has arrived."

"I do not understand you," replied Ada, endeavouring to rally her wonted spirits, and speak with her accustomed gaiety.

"Be content, then," said Walter, "with the knowledge that, thanks to the good feeling of a friend, who could no longer endure to see me the dupe of an artful and designing woman, I am in full possession of your guilty secret—ay, you may well tremble and turn pale. I marvel that you dare even to confront me!"

"I dare anything," replied Ada, "that innocence may dare; for I cast back the foul aspersion, and ask you rather how you dare address such language to me?"

"This assumed indignation," replied Walter, "rest assured, will not serve you. I tell you I have discovered all."

"And I!" said Ada, drawing herself up, while the warm blood mounted to her temples, "and I tell you that whoever gave you such information as you speak of lies, and with base and cowardly meanness takes advantage of the weakness of my sex, which alone withholds me from forcing him to recant his words, and confess how vile and abject a being he is, if need be, even at the dagger's point."

"Enough—enough," replied Walter. "I have borne with you long, too long for my own peace. You have falsely, shamelessly betrayed my trust and confidence; but I will vindicate my honour, and show the world that I am no vile panderer to the evil passions of my wife; duped and betrayed I have been, but I am now no longer blind to the depravity of your conduct. I see it in its true colours, and marvel that you should once have possessed the power to deceive me."

As he gave utterance to these words, Walter's voice was hoarse with suppressed passion, and his breast heaved convulsively; while Ada, though conscious of her own innocence, trembled so deeply, that she sank back upon the couch, unable to give utterance to a word in her own defence.

"To-morrow," resumed Walter, in the same hoarse voice in which he had before spoken, and which offered a strange contrast to his habitually low musical tones, "to-morrow you quit this roof for ever. Thanks to the generosity of my mother, you are well cared for. For the future, you are entire mistress of your own actions; and I have only one request to make, and which I cannot force upon you too strenuously"—he paused a moment, as if for a reply; but Ada had dropped her head between her clasped hands, and was weeping bitterly; but without heeding her emotion, he again went on.—"I have said," he resumed, "that I had one request, but I should rather have said one command, to enforce before we part for ever. It is that you will never, under any pretence, attempt to intrude your presence upon me, for neither tears or entreaties can ever disarm my too just resentment, or induce me to regard you otherwise than as the greatest foe to my peace—my most cruel and unrelenting enemy, who has wounded me in the dearest point—who has probed my sorrows to the quick; and under the mask of tenderness, and in the guise of affection, has torn from my bleeding bosom the only consolation or joy it knew, holding me up to the contempt—the pity of my fellow-men, till my very heart grows sick and faint at the thought of entering again upon the world. But why should I open these hidden founts of anguish? rather let me conceal them, if possible, even from myself."

Ada answered only with renewed sobs; she longed—oh! how earnestly—to throw herself upon his bosom, to pour out the long pent-up feelings, and tell him how cruelly he was mistaken, and how much and deeply she loved him; but one glance at his dark and angry brow was sufficient to repel her half-formed resolve to obey the dictates of her heart, and cast aside that withering pride which threatened to consume her with its intensity.

Alas! what a vain and false feeling is the pride that forbids us to confess our errors, and seek forgiveness of those we have injured! What an obdurate thing is the human heart, when hemmed about with this weak and hollow feelings, causing us to seal our own misery, and add renewed and increased bitterness to our sorrows, rather than own our faults, and acknowledge how far we have sinned! How much it behoves us then early to struggle with such pride, to accustom ourselves to crush all such feelings, and at the cost of a little self-denial in the first instance, spare ourselves and others a far greater amount of anguish. Ada held but trifling command over her own feelings, and though she wished to open her heart to Walter, and tell him how far she was innocent, and how greatly she had erred—pride, a weak, foolish pride sealed her lips, and kept back the confession at the very moment she was so solicitious to make it. As Walter ceased speaking, she raised her head, and while the tears still hung in pearly drops upon the long fringed lids, her eyes flashed with anger and resentment, the demon pride was busy at her heart, prompting her to summon her habitual scornful satire to her aid.

" It is well," she said at length, tearing the costly jewels from her dress, and casting them in a confused and glittering mass upon the floor. "It is well to forge an excuse for ridding yourself of me, whose presence has become hateful to you; neither do I wonder at such hatred, for men usually hate those whom they have neglected and illused. Take back your costly gifts," she added, spurning the confused heap with her foot, "they are still gay and bright, and may serve to win the love of some fond weak girl. For myself,

> ' Treasures so splendid I could not impart;
> My poor return was a faithful heart;
> Yet now that our griefs we each resign—
> Alas! how sad an exchange is mine.'

Your glittering gems are still pure and unsullied, and may yet please some high-born maiden's sight; but the simplest love would spurn a token like the heart your treachery has broken;" and without waiting for a word in reply, she opened the inner door and disappeared from his sight.

It would be impossible to convey an adequate idea of the biting and withering scorn with which Ada gave utterance to these words, or the stately and dignified manner in which she swept from the room—not a look, not the slightest sign was perceptible of the inward workings of her breast, and Walter surveyed the proud form of his wife with anger and disdain. As the bitter and satirical words fell from her lips in rapid succession, his passion nearly mastered every other feeling, the veins in his forhead stood out like thick cords, while his chest rose and fell, in evident and painful throbs, while the fire that shot from his eyes, seemed to threaten annihilation to the object on which he gazed. Still he quelled the rising storm, forcing himself with a deep and mighty effort to be calm. And when she was gone, and he was left alone gazing upon the vacant spot she had so lately occupied, a deep sigh heaved from his breast, and he was conscious of a feeling of relief; and as he sought his own apartments, he muttered to himself—

" I have done right in casting her from me; she is more debased even than I anticipated;" while Ada in her turn being once more alone, tore open the casket of rich jewels, the splendid gifts of Walter, and strewed them recklessly about the apartment. Her wardrobe too, with its costly contents, was emptied, (utterly regardless of the delicate satins and laces) and formed a strange and unwonted heap as they lay carelessly strewn upon the floor. While thus employed, Ada's pride still maintained the mastery over every other feeling, and she murmured to herself that she had done well—quite well, in meeting his anger with scorn and indignation.

Thus the two so soon about to separate for ever, to tear asunder the cords which had bound them so closely together, were each actuated in their conduct by that false pride which has broken so many hearts, and caused more misery perhaps than any other feeling. Each were buoyed up by the reflection that they had done wise and well, and were willing to sever the holy tie that linked their destinies, to recant the vows they had uttered at the altar, and forego the sacred duties they had voluntarily taken upon themselves. And yet, it is scarce possible for two who have been so closely united, by sudden wrench to tear away all kind and tender feeling, which must at times have animated their breasts, and caused their hearts to beat in unison. All other ties may perchance be lightly severed, but there is something so pure and sacred, so akin to immortality, so deathless and exalted in its very existence, that we much question whether (under any circumstance) the marriage knot has ever been disunited without a deep and remorseful regret gnawing at the heart, and bidding the severed hearts yearn again to be united. And thus it was both with Walter and Ada—the morrow came, and the bright light of morning shed its soft sunny rays upon the vacant apartment laden with its strange and unwonted freight; rich jewellery blazed from beneath the costly satins which were heaped upon the floor, and seemed to reflect anew the scorn and indignation of her, who had been once so proud to wear them; while she, the late mistress of the elegant apartments, who had trod the floor with such dignity and grace, was gone, and gone for ever, leaving behind her every ornament that might remind her of him so nearly and dearly related. Yes everything was left, the smallest present she had received from him, together with the lavish luxury his wealth had procured, all cast aside as worthless, at least to her, all, save one little gift which was pressed to her bleeding bosom yet. She had struggled hard to remove it—thrice had she attempted to dash it with the others to the ground; but no, she had pledged her word when she received it, and that word was sacred still; in spite of every effort, her conscience told her she did not hate him; there was one pulse beating near her heart, a pulse yet true to him, and the golden cross—sad ill-omened gift—was still retained, now that all others were renounced. Walter remarked this, as, on hearing of her departure, he entered the vacant room, which seemed to breathe her very presence, and recalled her so forcibly to his mind, that her proud and disdainful form seemed to stand before him, and reproach him for the past. Among the rich jewellery he sought in vain for the golden cross, and his heart sank within him as he became assured that it was not there.

"Then her love has not yet turned to hate!" he murmured to himself; and, spite of his inward conviction of her guilt, he more than half repented the precipitation with which he had acted. But it was now too late! Ada was gone—gone to mourn in secret over their broken faith—to shed the bitter tears of remorse and anguish alone and unheeded.

Availing herself of the marriage gift of Lady Eardley, Ada had for the present taken possession of the house that once belonged to her mother-in-law; and now that time had cooled the warmth of her indignation, she bitterly repented the part she had acted.

"Oh, why," she murmured in the bitterness of her feelings, "did I not confess the extent of my error, and seek his pardon? He could not, would not have withheld it when he learnt how innocent I was in all but my mad opposition to his wishes—and even that he would surely have forgiven, when he knew I was actuated by no worse motive than a desire to raise myself in his estimation; but now, alas! it is too late—we are separated forever!"

And with this terrible thought, she threw herself upon a couch, and, burying her head in her clasped hands, wept as though her heart would break.

CHAPTER LVII.

"Oh! rapturous Hope, thy cheering voice
  Doth soothe us through life's thorny path,
And strew with flowers of virtue's choice
  Those dreary ways till life be past.
Who to the drowning wretch lends aid?
  Say, who can lighten slavery's yoke?
And who can soothe desponding age
  Like thee, sweet Hope?"

WE have already intimated, that spite the warning voice of Mary, Percy had seriously involved himself. And though the loan, which had cost Ada so great an amount of misery, sufficed for a short time to free him from his difficulties, he was speedily again embarrassed; and this time without the slightest chance of freeing himself from his liabilities. Unwilling to be the first to communicate these unpleasant tidings to his wife and sisters, and yet conscious that it could not much longer be kept from their knowledge, Percy became nervous and irritable in the extreme—every kind word or manifestation of tenderness wounded him to the quick, and seemed to reproach him for the little care he had taken of the interest and welfare of those so near and dear. Frequently would he absent himself from home for long intervals, dreading to meet the smiling cheerful faces of his wife and sisters—for never now did he

look upon them without a shudder, for he thought upon the fast approaching
period when tears and sorrow must usurp the place of every other feeling.
Mary saw the sad change which had come over her husband, and was at no
loss to divine the cause, though never for a moment dreading the extent of the
calamity, which was even then hovering over them. In vain she questioned
Percy on the subject; he ever on such occasions adroitly turned the conversation to some other topic, and appeared so agitated and depressed if she
ventured to recur to it, that she eventually discarded the matter entirely from
her conversation, seeking by every kind and tender attention to improve his
spirits, and render him, if possible, happy.

Thus weeks passed on; when one evening returning from a walk, Mary, on
entering the drawing-room, perceived to her utter astonishment that it was
occupied by two strange and vulgar-looking men, who were sitting with
her husband, whose pallid countenance and darkened brow betokened
the unwelcome reception of his guests. Glasses, which had contained spirits-
and-water, stood in confusion on the table, while the whole room bore marks of
disorder.

Mary, overcome with terror and confusion, not knowing how to interpret
this strange occurrence, stood on the threshold of the apartment, utterly
unable either to advance or retreat, till one of the men, rising and advancing
towards the spot where she stood, said, in tones meant to re-assure her, though
they were productive of exactly an opposite effect—

"Don't be alarmed, ma'am; it's a mere nothing, I assure you, only for a few
hundreds. Why, bless me, if there aint well nigh enough of finery scattered
about this room to pay our demand."

The hour of man's adversity is that of woman's conquest over all the petty
feelings that take from the heavenliness of her nature. To dart forward and
clasp her arms fondly round the neck of her husband, beseeching him at the
same time to take comfort, was the work of a moment, while her own tears
gushed forth and bedewed his cheeks. The bailiff (for such he was) stood
looking upon them in mute astonishment, awed into silence by the intensity
of her distress, as with convulsive sobs Mary threw herself upon the bosom
of her repentant husband. None are all evil—and from that hour the seeds of
virtue, which had never been quite extinct in the breast of Percy, sprang up to
a goodly harvest. Thus from the very depths of affliction, Mary dated the commencement of true substantial happiness—for from that moment Percy and his
wife were all the world to each other.

As soon as the first emotions of her sorrow was past, Mary, raising her head,
inquired of Percy the amount for which he was thus inconvenienced; and on
learning that it did not exceed five hundred pounds, declared her intention of
immediately soliciting that sum from her father.

"It is useless," replied Percy, "and would only injure him without in the
least benefiting ourselves, as this is but a moiety of the debts I have so foolishly
—madly incurred. Oh, Mary, can you, will you forgive me?"

"Say no more, dear Percy," she said, tenderly kissing his cheek; "keep
your mind at ease till to-morrow, when I will consult with my father as to what
had better be done."

The following morning early, Mary held a long consultation with her father,
concerning Percy's debts, which resulted in the determination on the part
of Mr. Herbert, to draw from the bulk of his own property a sum sufficient to meet the entire demands of his creditors. This generosity on the
part of his father-in-law, drew tears from the eyes of Percy, nor did he seek
to conceal the genuine feelings from the dear home circle who gathered round
him, to mingle their tears of gratitude and love with his own. Elizabeth and
Mary pressed affectionately to the side of their sister, blessing her for the
kind part she had acted towards them all, and entreating her forgiveness
for every little manifestation of disrespect or neglect which might at any
period have been apparent in their manners towards her; this was readily

granted on the part of Mary, who, affectionately kissing them, expressed a fervent hope, that for the future they should be better friends than ever; this kind wish was warmly seconded, not only by Percy, but by both his sisters likewise. Thus was this cup of sorrow in which they are alike participated, made the means of ensuring their future peace and felicity. Ah, who shall say that afflictions are not sometimes blessings in disguise! Mr. Herbert, too, was happy and thankful at having been enabled to secure the comfort and happiness of his child, even at the sacrifice of nearly his entire funded property. Percy knew this well, and was loth to receive such munificent aid from one towards whom he was conscious of having, up to this period, been wanting in that true respect which his age and position demanded; but Mr. Herbert silenced his scruples, assuring him that the money would all have descended to Mary at his death, and her availing herself of the property some few years earlier, was at the worst even a matter of but second importance. But the sorest trial was yet to come: the alteration in their circumstances rendered it absolutely necessary that they should quit their present residence, and seek a more humble abode elsewhere. This to Percy was worse than all. Could he have endured sorrow and privation alone, it would now have seemed but a trifling ill; but to know, to feel that through his own thoughtless, selfish extravagance, he had brought ruin on all who were near and dear to him, was painful and heart-rending in the extreme; but it was nevertheless a useful lesson, and was productive of a wholesome effect upon his mind, for though a sadder, he was now a wiser man. And Mary was so kind and gentle, so studious, as not to wound his feelings even in the remotest manner, and withal apparently so cheerful and light-hearted, so desirous to make the best of everything, that when they took possession of their new home, her sisters, who, on gazing around the apartments, and missing the various comforts and luxuries they had lost, were at first disposed to look sad and sorrowful, took courage from her example, and smiled even as brightly as herself. Mr. Herbert likewise, though subject to much inconvenience, both on account of the narrowness of his income, and the lack of those comforts, which had become, by long usage, well-nigh necessaries, generously refrained from making the slightest complaint; on the contrary, affected to be amused by the novelty of their present mode of life. Thus encouraged on every hand, Percy sought some means of augmenting their slender income, and after some little difficulty obtained a situation in a mercantile house in the City; but the income arising from this source was so trifling, that Mary suggested to her sisters that they should likewise endeavour to procure some employment. They immediately expressed their willingness to profit by the suggestion; but a difficulty arose as to what means they could resort, in order to obtain a livelihood without reducing themselves entirely to menial service.

"As far as I am myself concerned," replied Mary, "I have already decided. I have thought over, since our misfortune, how I could by any means obtain employment. I scarcely cared in what manner my services might be made available so that I could procure for my dear father some of the comforts he has lost. I was saying, I thought of this a long time, and yet could not decide. I felt that I was incapacitated by the want of musical talent, for almost the only recognised mode of gaining a genteel livelihood. I refer of course to that of imparting instruction. To learn any business would require some outlay at first, and could only be doubtful dependance afterwards; still, spite of every difficulty, I was unwilling to forego my warmest wishes, when accidentally glancing over a paper, an advertisement caught my eye, stating that good fancy braiders for robings of ladies dresses' were wanted immediately, and to whom the highest wages would be given. Is not this fortunate?" she continued smiling, "for you both well know how clever I am with my neeble. I shall apply for work at once, and if either of you feel inclined to assit me a little, I shall be very thankful to accept of your services." Both sisters wormly expressed the pleasure they should feel in aiding her to the utmost, and with hearts lightened, and hopes revived, they repaired in course of the afternoon to the place indicated, which was in the immediate neighbourhood; and on Mary having given proof of her skill in the branch of art in which her services were required, was immediately supplied with three robings to be braided in a given pattern down each side. Bent upon her kind and amiable project, Mary commenced her labour that very evening, but though she worked hard and was dexterous in the extreme with her needle, she found that each robing took her nearly or quite five hours to complete. Still she worked on, encouraged by the munificent promise of the highest wages; and at length having finished them all, much to her own satisfaction, hastened to return, thinking, as she walked with her little parcel in her hand, of the best means of investing her first earnings. Judge, then, of her utter bewilderment, when on handing in her work and finding it entirely approved, she was paid, with the greatest nonchalance, by the munificent advertiser of the highest prices—one shilling!

Yes, start not, gentle reader, nor accuse us of exaggeration, or straining a point to give effect to our writings, for each of those robes—which had taken Mary five hours unremitting and tedious toil—fourpence was considered by the liberal employer not only a fair remuneration for the time and dexterity expended on the work, but, by his own showing, the best possible price that could be expected for the labour!

Poor Mary was so overcome with astonishment, that she stood for some seconds balancing the little coin in her hand before she was capable of expressing a doubt, which had naturally arisen in her mind, that there must be some mistake. A smile of pity for her ignorance in such matters, accompanied with an assurance that it was more than was paid at other warehouses, was the cool and self-complacent reply of the proprietor of the establishment; and then, seeing that Mary still hesitated, hastened to inquire if she would take any more? She indignantly replied in the negative; and quitting the shop with a more sad heart and depressed spirit than she had ever felt before, quietly slipped her shilling into the hand of a fair, but emaciated woman, on whose hectic cheek consumption had already set its deadly seal, (and who was waiting with many others to receive the scanty pittance doled out to them for their close and painful toil,) and wended her way towards her own home, both sadder and wiser than she had been but a few short minutes before, musing as she walked, on the sad experience she had gained. Alas! she thought how little the purchasers of such articles can be aware of the trembling fingers, the weary eyes, and what is still worse, aching hearts, with which their gay dresses are too often prepared by those who are compelled, by adverse circumstances, to earn their bread in this manner, or their womanly feeling would make them shrink from purchasing such things, save at a price that must ensure the workwoman an ample remuneration. Oh! never again shall I look upon them without recurring in thought to the poor victims of needle slavery, who, to earn even the means of a miserable subsistence, must ply their calling when all, save them and such as them, are seeking rest and refreshment. Many had purchased wisdom, and well would it be for many others if they had done the like, as it might prove the means of bettering the condition of thousands who may aptly be termed the white slaves of England—yes, if our British Isle, vaunted for its glorious freedom, famed and extolled in lyric poem and storied page, with the proud boast of its free-born sons, that all who touch its shores participate in its glorious attribute. Would we had space to dwell upon this painful topic, in the bright hope of aiding in some small measure the interest of those who must claim sympathy with every feeling heart; but the interest of our tale compels us, for the present, to abandon it. Mary, fortunately, was not reduced to the terrible necessity of thus toiling for her daily bread, and abandoning from that moment all hope of turning her talents in fancy work to account, she sedulously devoted herself to the comfort and happiness of her father, contenting herself with curtailing to the utmost all personal and household expenses. With her sisters she was now on more happy and affectionate terms than ever; and

Percy, though deeply mourning over his own selfish and thoughtless extravagance, was yet made so happy in his returning love and confidence in Mary, that there were times when he half forgot the sad change which had taken place in his fortune, and ceased to sigh for the comforts he had lost. Entirely separated from Ada, and engrossed with their own new duties, none of them were

LADY EARDLEY'S INTERVIEW WITH LAURA IN EARDLEY PARK.

acquainted with the separation which had taken place between her and Walter, or Percy would have felt that he had yet more to answer for, from his constitutional carelessness, than the misery he had brought upon his own home circle ; but in happy ignorance of this, he devoted all his energies to the promotion of the interest and prosperity of his employer, and blest by the tender love of Mary, and a cheerful, happy home, was for the time content.

CHAPTER LVIII.

" A soul, too, more than half divine,
    When through some shades of earthly feeling,
Religion's softened glories shine,
    Like light through summer's foliage stealing ;
Shedding a glow of such mild hue,
    To warm, and yet so shadowy too,
As makes the very darkness there
    More beautiful than light elsewhere."

SINCE we last called the reader's attention to Jane Clarence, many sources both of joy and sorrow had been opened afresh, and though she has been called upon to weep over the early tomb of little Walter, her sorrows have been mitigated by the presence of her loved and early friend, Clara. Yes, removed as they fully hoped and believed from bitter foes and friends untrue, Richard and his treasured companion had sought out Jane, from whom they received the warmest welcome ; upon the bosom of Clara she had sobbed out the bitterness of her own feelings, when conscious that Walter was torn from her for ever; and aided by her counsel, cheered by her tender words of consolation, Jane had dried her tears, and listened in return to the strange and painful news her friend had to impart.

" Thank God," replied Jane, when Clara had finished her relation. " Thank God you are here where nothing can harm you more."

" Oh, how happy we shall be together, we shall indeed," replied Clara, affectionately returning her friend's embrace.

Mrs. Clarence, too, was pleased to have an opportunity of manifesting her respect and lively interest in Sir Richard (as she still persisted in calling them) and Lady Eardley. In vain Jane strove kindly to point out to her the necessity which existed for an ardent desire on the part of her friends to drop the title, which they could no longer claim by right. Mrs. Clarence persisted in her own opinion, and she was quite convinced that Sir Richard was the legal heir.

" Pardon me, dear mamma," Jane replied on one of these occasions ; " but I think you do not quite understand——"

" I dare say," interrupted Mrs. Clarence, angrily ; " I have no doubt that I am very weak and foolish—indeed, I must be, as it seems I cannot understand a circumstance so trifling, that a child even might give an opinion on the subject."

" Oh, no, dear mamma—indeed, I did not make any such remark."

" Well, it is of no consequence ; I know you do not pay the slightest attention to my opinions, or that poor dear child might now have been alive and well."

" Oh, dear mamma, pray do not renew that painful subject," replied Jane striving in vain to suppress the tears that rose to her eyes.

" I am sure," returned her mother, " you have no occasion to shed tears. I have said nothing that need vex you ; and as regards dear little Walter, if any one has a right to give way to the selfish indulgence of their feelings, it should be myself; for no one knows how fondly and dearly I loved him, or the dreadful state of my feelings when forced to resign him. However, I am perfectly free from all blame in this matter, and did my best to prevent the sad catastrophe."

Mrs. Clarence was about to wind up with her usual consolatory remark, that "there was some comfort in that ;" but the entrance of Clara gave a new turn to her thoughts, and she instantly went off to some other topic, which she pursued with her usual volubility, till in its turn it likewise gave place to another.

As soon as the first violence of Jane's grief for the loss of her beloved nephew had abated, Mr. Carlton endeavoured by kind and soothing attentions to dissipate her grief, and so far relinquished his own retired habits as to encourage the visits of the neighbouring gentry. To Richard and Clara he was kind and attentive in the extreme, entreating them to make his house their home. This, however, they politely declined; and having been fortunate enough to secure a small but pretty villa in close vicinity to Mr. Carlton's abode, had frequent opportunities of enjoying the society of Jane, who spent some portion of each day with her friends.

When Mr. Carlton perceived this, and remarked the affectionate feeling which existed between her and Clara, he gradually resumed his old habits of retirement, and generally spent the greatest part of the day in his library. Jane was not long in perceiving the change, and her gentle heart feared some unintentional offence on her part had made him less kind and attentive than usual; and to make up for her imaginary fault, she redoubled her respect to him when they met—but the result was the same.

Mr. Carlton, unconscious of the uneasiness he was giving her whom he was so desirous of making happy, still spent his time among his books, while poor Jane was wandering alone about the grounds, thinking of past times, and sighing over the change. At length she became by degrees entirely altered; she was no more the cheerful companion, but thoughtful and melancholy. And when company came to the house, she was silent and reserved, if she could not (as she was evidently desirous) avoid seeing them; and it was with the greatest difficulty she was prevailed upon now and then to accept an invitation to some neighbouring family. She was even surprised by Clara, on more than one occasion, in tears, as she walked slowly among the trees in the beautiful grounds; but when she tried to draw from her the cause, she was unable to do so, so successfully did Jane evade her tender inquiries.

Mrs. Clarence, too, with all her selfishness, could not help noticing the sad change which had taken place in her daughter; and, her maternal fears once thoroughly aroused, she became seriously alarmed, and remarked to Mr. Carlton that Jane was certainly failing in health.

His attention thus called to her, he, too, became aware that there was evidently something wrong. Jane had lost the glow of health, and her step its elastic lightness; and though her mild eyes still beamed upon him with the same gentle affection as of yore, he felt that he was blameable in his conduct towards her. He should have insisted upon her taking more exercise, instead of permitting her to confine herself to the school-room. He should have kept more company, and conformed his house more to the ways she had been accustomed to in England. He should have gone out with her more. In fact, he should have done everything he had not done; and yet when, with the affectionate interest of a parent, he besought Jane to impart to him the cause of her evident uneasiness, all his efforts to make her acknowledge she was unhappy were unavailing. She was profuse in her acknowledgments of his kindness, and delighted to call him her friend and protector; but she persisted that nothing ailed her—she was well, quite well in health, and perfectly happy.

One evening, shortly after Mr. Carlton first sought an explanation of Jane, he entered the room where Mrs. Clarence and her daughter usually sat. Jane was standing at a window, seemingly lost in thought. She did not immediately perceive his entrance, and he stood for a few minutes regarding her sad and anxious countenance.

"Perhaps," he thought, "though she has refused to tell me the cause of her uneasiness as yet, I may at last succeed in gaining her confidence; and then, what a pleasure it would be to me to secure her happiness!"

As he thus mused, he approached the window. Jane turned round, and he saw instantly that she had been weeping; and a deep blush suffused her face when she saw him.

"My dear young lady," he said, taking her not unwilling hand within his own, "something afflicts you. Why will you deny me the gratification of trying at least to remove the cause? Am I not your friend and guardian, in the place even of a father to you?—did I not promise your dear little nephew on his death-bed that I would consider you as my own child—bestowing upon you at once the love and anxiety of a parent? If then I have neglected anything that might have contributed in the slightest degree to your happiness, tell me, that I may remedy it. Give me only the lightest intimation of your wishes, and I will prove it my greatest pleasure to fulfil them."

"Oh, no, sir," returned Jane, quickly; "you have neglected nothing—you have been all kindness since the first moment of our acquaintance, and I can never express to you half the gratitude I feel for your care and goodness."

"You are very good to say so," returned Mr. Carlton. "But remember that in afflicting yourself, you afflict me also. If in truth you wish me to think you regard me as a friend and protector, tell me how I may serve you. May I venture upon a somewhat delicate subject?" he continued.

Jane blushed and cast down her eyes; but as he did not read disapproval on her countenance, he again went on—

"Mr. Fergusson, a friend of yours, called some time since; but for various reasons, I considered it right to deny you. I acted in this respect as if I were in truth your parent—not that I attribute other than generous and honourable motives to the young man—but your relative positions are such, that I judged it both wise and prudent to discourage, as far as possible, any intimacy between you. If this is in any remote manner even the cause of your present disquietude, I entreat you to repose full and free confidence in me."

Jane coloured yet more deeply than before, and sighed as she answered, that so far from such a circumstance having caused her the slightest uneasiness, she felt obliged and grateful to him for the kind interest he had taken in her welfare.

"Well, then," he inquired, "would you like to live part of the year in town? It is certainly very dull for one of your age to pass so much time in the country; and I shall be most happy to live part of the year at any place you like better."

"Do not distress me, dear sir, by talking thus," replied Jane, overcome by the kindness of Mr. Carlton. "Indeed, I wish for no society but yours." She blushed as she gave utterance to the words, and added quickly—"and my mother's."

Mr. Carlton looked at her for a minute in silence, as if at a loss what next to mention; and after considering awhile, he said—

"Perhaps you are acquainted with some person whose absence you regret?"

"No, sir," she replied, not without an effort; "I regret the absence of no person."

He saw that she looked distressed as she gave utterance to these words, and could not endure the thought of having given her pain; so, placing his arm kindly round her waist, he said—

"Forgive me, my dear young lady—I shall hate myself if I wound you; but it is natural to suppose a girl of your age should have some favourite. You have lately made the acquaintance of several amiable and deserving men."

"Oh, pray do not mention this," said Jane; "I do not think of any of them —indeed, they are alike indifferent to me; and, I am sure, I should be the most ungrateful girl in the world if I did not prefer your society—your good opinion —above, far above, all others."

As she spoke, Jane bowed her head on his shoulder, hiding her face against his bosom. A sudden thought struck Mr. Carlton, an idea that made him almost start. He drew the trembling girl towards him, and pressing his lips to her fair brow, left her and walked hastily to his own apartment. He threw himself on a chair, and for some time the tumult of his thoughts was so great that he could scarcely recollect himself.

"And is it possible," he thought, "that she loves me? Can it indeed be possible that sweet gentle girl, of whose love the noblest might well be proud, and I well nigh old enough to bear towards her in truth the character of a parent, which I have assumed, as being the most suitable as regards us both? No! I must be mistaken, and yet what can I infer from her manners and behaviour? And I have been so unkind, so negligent, so cold, so unworthy of her." And he felt his indignation rise against himself, as he reflected on the youth and noble qualities of her whom he now fondly believed had long honoured him with her regard, a regard which he considered as so far above his merits. And yet he felt it must be so—he now recollected a thousand little instances of kindness and attention from Jane that had before passed unnoticed. Her fondness for his society, the attention with which she always listened to him, all contributed to confirm his opinion, and he wondered how it had never occurred to him before. In a moment all his previously established notions of perpetual widowhood vanished, his solitary rambles, his lonely retirements, and monotonous seclusion, all appeared desolate, unsocial, miserable, and the idea of being the chosen of the amiable and gentle Jane, alone occupied his mind. That evening was devoted to cool and calm reflection. He thought of his motherless children, and the loved and loving wife he had lost; but the image of Jane, her noble, yet unobtrusive worth rose before his mind's eye, in all its youthful purity, and he felt she was indeed both fit and worthy to fill the vacant corner of his heart, and replace to his children the parent they had lost. Visions too of bright and happy days flitted before him, blest with the love of that fair being in whom he had not long felt so deep an interest; and above all the blest thought, that in securing his own happiness, he would also be consummating hers, filled his heart with rapture and exultation. The following morning when they met at breakfast, Jane was if possible more than usually silent and melancholy, and Mr. Carlton, though his whole thoughts and attention were taken up by her alone, scarcely spoke, so Mrs. Clarence had the entire conversation to herself. After breakfast, Jane went into the garden which surrounded the house, and was fragrant with its rich perfumes of orange and pomegranate. She had not been gone more than a few minutes before Mr. Carlton took up his hat, and followed her. There was a walk at the bottom of the garden, which from being shaded by a row of large lime-trees, was usually called the lime walk; and after a short time, Mrs. Clarence getting tired of being alone, went to the window to see what was become of them, and caught a glimpse of Jane's white dress through an opening in the lime-trees, and at the next turn saw her and Mr. Carlton walking arm-in-arm up and down, apparently in earnest conversation.

"I am glad," she said to herself, "that poor Jane has taken a fancy to walk with some one, and not be always wandering alone, and though Mr. Carlton is so grave, yet he is also so kind-hearted and generous, that she cannot have a better companion."

So saying, she sat down quietly to her work, but dinner-time drew nigh and she was still alone.

"They have suddenly taken a great liking to that walk," said she, "if they are still there." And she went again to the window, and saw that they were still walking, and still, as it seemed, in earnest conversation; and then she thought she saw the hand of Jane pressed to the bosom of Mr. Carlton.

"Poor girl," she said, "she has at length opened her heart to him, and he is kindly advising her about something. I am sure he loves her as if she were his own daughter."

Some time after this they both entered, and any more observant person than Mrs. Clarence could not have failed to perceive that a look of deep settled joy and contentment had taken the place of the careworn look that Jane had lately worn, and that Mr. Carlton's countenance was lighted up with happiness.

"Dear Mamma," said Jane, as soon as they were alone, "I have much to tell you."

Mrs. Clarence, whom her late anxiety for her daughter's health had wonderfully improved, answered kindly, and even tenderly.

Thus encouraged, Jane poured out the deep confession of her heart without being once interrupted by her mother. At length, all being told, Mrs. Clarence replied—

"Well, Jane, you have certainly surprised me greatly, but have also given me a great deal of pleasure. I am sure I never could have thought of it; but if you do not mind the difference of age, I am sure you could not have a better or more amiable husband."

"I only hope," returned Jane, modestly, "that I may be worthy of such a one. I have loved before, and wept over the falsehood of one who had deceived my brightest hopes, and whose cruelty forced from my eyes many rebellious tears, little thinking of the sweet and peaceful destiny which was in store for me, or I should have rejoiced instead of mourned. There is now," she continued, with increasing animation. "not one hope of my heart which is not fulfilled; and I am sure I have every reason for gratitude and thankfulness, and I shall see no more sad looks, or have reason to fear again that your health is declining."

"Yes," said Mrs. Clarence, smiling.

Jane blushed, as she replied—

"Oh, no, mamma; forgive me if I have been selfishly forgetful of your comfort of late, but——"

"Not a word," returned her mother, as she affectionately kissed her cheek; "you have ever been to me the most kind and dutiful child parent ever was blest with. I have too often tried you, I am sure, by my peevishness and impatience, but you have never shown that you felt it in the slightest manner."

"Dear, dear mamma," said Jane, affected to tears by the unwonted confession of her mother, "you will be happy here; though far from our own loved England, this has become a dearer home to me; say, can I make it so to you?"

"You can, dear Jane," returned her mother; "my health is greatly improved, and I hope to live many years to witness and participate in your happiness."

"Thank God for those words, dear mamma," replied Jane, "the sweetest that have ever met my ears, not even excepting those I have so lately listened to, and which has confirmed the dearest hopes of my heart; the children, too—his children, whom I loved from the very first, how proud I shall be to hear them call me mother You must assist me, dear mamma, in the exercise of the many pleasant duties which will soon be mine."

Mrs. Clarence listened to her daughter, and gazed with maternal pride and fondness on her glowing cheek, her mild blue eyes reflecting the purity and happiness of her mind; and as she thus gazed and listened, conscience, that divine monitor which had been so long silent, made its still soft voice heard once again, and tears—blessed tears fell from her eyes and bedewed the upturned face of Jane, as she said—

"My child—my own dear child, God has, indeed, rewarded your filial affection, and blessed you with the love of one every way deserving your warmest affection; your early life has been strongly marked with sorrow and suffering; you have indeed been sorely tried, and have borne unrepiningly every ill, but all this is past, never I hope to return again—there are bright and happy days in store for us both."

"Indeed, indeed, there are," returned Jane, as she flung herself on the bosom of her mother, while tears of heart-felt joy forced themselves in torrents from her eyes. Now every wish and desire of her pure and honest heart was realised, every dark cloud had cleared away, and she walked in the bright noon-tide of existence. With what an easy tread did she shortly afterwards walk to the home of her cherished friend, to make her a participator in her new-found happiness. What a bright smile irradiated her animated countenance, and with what enthusiastic feelings did she open her whole heart to Clara, who listened with a throbbing breast to all she had to tell.

"And you love him?" said Clara, when her recital was ended.

"Love him?" replied Jane. "Oh, yes, I cannot tell you how dearly. I do not know," she continued with increasing animation, "when this love first took possession of my breast; but of this I am convinced, that I shall never, never cease to regard him with the fondest, the most devoted affection. But dear Clara, you are unwell, and I have been selfishly dwelling on my own happiness, instead of endeavouring to——"

"Stop," dear Jane interrupted her friend, "speak only of yourself, I love to listen to you. Oh, may you indeed be happy. I commend your choice; so noble, so generous and high-minded, you may well be proud of having won his heart; you have nothing to fear for the future."

"But one fear," returned Jane, "that I may not prove unworthy of him."

"You are too diffident of your own merits," said Clara; "none but yourself could possibly entertain so groundless an apprehension."

"Mr. Eardley is from home?" resumed Jane in a tone of inquiry, after both had been silent a short time; "is that the cause of your present uneasiness? for it is vain to attempt to conceal from me who have known you so long, that there is something amiss."

"I did not wish to distress you," returned Clara, "when you came to me so bright and happy, so like your former self, that all the sorrow which has passed over your head, seems as though it had never been; but I am indeed unhappy, more unhappy than I thought it possible I could be again."

"You seriously alarm me," returned Jane; "what can have occurred to disturb you thus? I entreat you, tell me all."

"The strange woman," faltered Clara, "of whom I told you, is here!" and as she spoke, she sank her voice to a whisper, and glanced round with a shudder.

"Here!" replied Jane, starting up with a movement of evident surprise.

"Do not alarm yourself," replied Clara, laying her hand kindly on her shoulder; "I do no mean in this room, but close by—so close that her shadow seems constantly hovering over me, like some warning spirit which foretells sorrow and desolation. I cannot seem even to breathe free, now that I know she is near—that she is incessantly watching my motions—ready at any momemt to force her hateful presence upon me—not for one instant can I feel safe from her intrusion; and there is something, too, so strange and fearful in her actions, and the manner in which she comes and goes; now gliding into the house, none know how, and with her wild dark eyes fixed upon my face, recalling the fatal curse which rests upon our family, and predicting its speedy fulfilment; and then, before I have time even to recover from the surprise and terror her presence occasions, she is gone, none daring to follow in her footsteps, so majestic and overawing are her manners."

"Dear Clara," replied Jane, tenderly, "do not distress yourself, I entreat of you."

"This is not all, Jane," returned Clara, while the tears coursed each other down her cheeks; "this is not all, or I could bear it patiently; but Richard is altered—oh, so sadly altered!" And here the emotion she could no longer restrain burst forth in smothered sobs and sighs.

Jane threw her arms affectionately round her friend, and soothed her sorrow with tender words and gentle caresses. At length, when the violence of her feelings were somewhat abated, Jane said, gently—

"Tell me, love, Richard is not less kind and affectionate?"

"Oh, no, no!" returned Clara, "he is all, nay, more than he has ever been; but a shadow has fallen on his once sunny brow—he seldom smiles, and his voice has lost the gladsome tones which once breathed such sweet music to my ears. That stranger woman seems to have cast a spell about him, and darkened every bright and joyous feeling of his breast; yet he never speaks of her save when troubled sleep forces from him words, terrible and tormenting for me to hear, and from which I gather that he has in some manner injured or oppressed her, and for which she now seeks retribution."

"Why, then," said Jane, after a few moments of thoughtful silence, and she tried to speak firmly, though her voice faltered as she gave utterance to the words; "why not leave here and remove to some distant spot where it may be a more arduous task to discover your retreat?"

"I have proposed this," returned Clara, "nay strenuously urged it, painful as a second parting would be to us both. I have yet repeatedly pressed Richard to consent, to fly once more from home and friends, and seek out some secluded spot where we may live in peace and happiness, but I cannot wring from him a consent to profit by my suggestion; he persists it would be useless, and were we to fly to the farthest ends of the earth, she would track us out and blight our every joy by her baneful presence. Alas!" she continued, "what can we do—what will become of us."

"She cannot be permitted ever to haunt you thus," replied Jane, indignantly. "Permit me, my dear Clara, to mention this strange circumstance to Mr. Carlton, who I am assured will aid you with counsel in this matter; he is better acquainted with the laws of the country than ourselves, and must therefore be more conversant with the best mode of ridding yourselves of her intolerable presence."

"Oh, no, no," returned Clara, eagerly, "not for the world. If aught could make Richard more wretched, it would surely be the idea of having this painful circumstance more generally known. He appears to regard the misery to which he is doomed, as a just penance for some early sin; and I must therefore strive to bear it patiently. But though I suffer deeply, it is not on my own account; I feel not for myself, but him."

Thus, with the warmest desire to promote the happiness and tranquillity of her friend, Jane was forced to abandon all hope even of doing so; she could only trust to the vague wish, that some fortunate occurrence might avail to restore her lost peace, and by kind attention and unremitting anxiety, do her utmost to reassure the trembling mind of Clara, and prevent her being, as she herself assured her, so very—very wretched.

CHAPTER LVIII.

"Yet never seemed her blooming brow
Younger or fairer than 'tis now;
Nay, rather, as the west winds sigh
Freshens the flower it passes by,
Time's wing but seemed in passing o'er
To leave her lovelier than before.
Yet on her smile a sadness hung;
And when as oft she spoke or sung
Of other worlds, there came a light,
From her dark eyes, so strangely bright,
   Like broken clouds, or like the stream
That, smiling, left the mountain's brow,
   As though its waters ne'er could sever;
Yet, ere it reached the plain below,
   Breaks into floods that part for ever."

THE scene of our story must now shift itself to the banks of the Guadalquiver, to Andalusia's capital, the princely Seville. In one of the most magnificent hotels, and in a room where the massive splendour, and luxurant decorations told plainly that it had once belonged to one of the wealthiest and noblest families of Spain, is seated Walter Eardley, busied in looking over some papers, and dictating occasionally to a secretary seated at some little distance from him.

The occupation, however, with which he was employed seemed irksome to him, and rising from his seat he said somewhat petulantly—

"That will do. We will finish this some other time."

The secretary immediately rose also, and bowing obedience, quitted the room. here was a look at once fraught with tenderness and pity, which the young

man cast upon Walter, as he lingered momentarily at the door, which could not fail to have attracted the remark even of the most casual observer; but Walter saw it not; his mind was evidently disturbed, and ill at ease. His thoughts, too, were wandering far away; and when the door closed behind his secretary, he gave vent to his agitated feelings aloud.

"She is, indeed, beautiful," he murmured; "but the remembrance of my lost Lucy still haunts me with regret, and poisons every joy. The curse, too, which rests upon our family, is a source of uneasiness which preys deeply on my mind. How can I link the destiny of one so young and lovely, so pure and free from guilt, with any own sorrow-stricken lot? No; it must not be. I have yet the power to retract, and will do so ere it be too late."

And yet, though he thus resolved, he was still perplexed with doubt and uncertainly. A thousand times had he thus resolved before, and as often broken faith with himself; for the facination of beauty still lured him on, and left him without the power to retrace his steps. While Walter was thus musing, the young man to whom we have already alluded as filling the situation of secretary in his household, had retired to the apartment specially appropriated to his use ; and throwing himself upon a chair, covered his face with both hands ; and by the convulsive heaving of his bosom, it was clearly perceptible that he was weeping bitterly. Some secret source of sorrow which he would impart to none evidently preyed upon his health and spirits ; for a deep melancholy was fixed upon his countenance, and he was rarely, if ever, seen to smile, and scarce a thing had power to draw him form the solitude of his chamber. He was a very young man, of rather slight make, and somewhat under the middle height. His looks told plainly that he was a foreigner. Indeed, the deep blue eyes, and aquiline vose, bespoke him of English birth. The circumstance of his first entering the service of Walter were so strange and romantic as to deserve a relation, which we think cannot be altogether unpleasing or distateful to the reader.

Immediately after his separation from Ada, Walter (who possessed a morbid sensibility, which prevented him resuming his parliamentary duties) thinking that the finger of scorn was ever ready to point him out as the deceived and betrayed husband of a gay and volatile wife, gladly accepted a ministerial appointment to a vacant office, which removed him far from the scenes of his wedded life ; and with a handsome retinue, took up his residence in the princely abode at Seville, which we have already described. Here he was surrounded by the bright and beautiful ; and, being forced upon from the high office he occupied to mingle again in society, lost for a time the deep sense of his injuries, which had so deeply affected him. Among others, he was introduced to the Senora Inez, who attracted his attention, not so much from her extreme loveliness as the versatile powers of her mind, which was of no common order. By times grave, and gay, brilliant in conversation, the light jest and witty repartee rivalling at times the depth of knowledge which her conversational powers betrayed, it is no wonder that Walter should become fascinated, and as it were spellbound by her presence. He knew his own danger, and felt that she was becoming too dear, too dangerous for his peace ; and yet, as we have seen, could not resolve to tear her image from his heart, the more especially as it was evident he was favoured beyond all her suitors. There was something, too, about her quiet grace and unostentatious manners, which forcibly reminded him of his lost Lucy ; and though, in most respects, they were essentially different, he pleased himself with the idea that they greatly resembled each other. In her society he lost much of his latent moodiness, and became once more the gay and fascinating being he had been in his early life. And his fond imagination loved to recur to past scenes, and please itself with the bright hope that he might yet regain his long lost happiness. Previously to quitting England he had instructed his lawyers to institute the necessary proceedings in order to procure a divorce from Ada, whose supposed unfaithfulness he conceived warranted such a line of conduct on his part ; he would therefore speedily be at liberty to offer his hand to the Senora Inez ; and the better he became acquainted with her temper and disposition, the more disposed he felt to adopt such a course ; still he held back, and had not even breathed a thought of love to any save his own heart ; they were friends, and as yet nothing more. He had now been in Spain six mouths, when one evening, returning home from her father's villa after a late party, where play had run high, and he had been a considerable winner, little heeding the lateness of the hour, and thinking of the charms of the peerless Inez, he was suddenly startled from his reverie by hearing some one exclaim in his own language—

"For God's sake draw, and protect yourself."

He turned at the moment, and was just in time to parry a thrust which would doubtless have proved fatal; his antagonists, two in number, though foiled, were not so easily beaten off; and Walter, though a good swordsman, had nearly his equal. His countryman, who had uttered the friendly warning, endeavoured to assist him, but being a stripling, and unarmed, ho was but of little use in the combat, which continued for some seconds, when a lucky thrust from Walter brought one of the assailants to the ground, and the noise of approaching footsteps induced the other to consult his own safety, by immediate flight. When, on stooping down to discover the extent of the injury he had inflicted, Walter, to his utter astonishment, recognised the wounded man as a member of one of the first families in Seville, and from whom he had won a considerable sum in the course of the evening. His late assailant shrank abashed from the indignant scorn which flashed from the eyes of Walter as he made this discovery, but who contented himself with merely remarking that he had thought the noble cavaliers of Spain were used to forewarn a man before they drew upon him, and not like an hired assassin strike in the dark. And then turning to his countryman whose pallid countenance denoted that he required immediate attention, he supported him in his arms till assistance was procured, and which was readily granted by the passengers whose fortunate approach had acted so favourably to Walter, with whose aid he had the youth immediately conveyed to his own princely abode, and would have sent for a surgeon had not the young man opposed most strenuously this measure; in all other things he was willing to be guided entirely by Walter; but though the pallor of his countenance, together with some spots of blood on his clothing, seemed to indicate that he was wounded, and he persisted in asserting that such was not the case, and assured him that nothing ailed him, beyond a slight faintness from which he would shortly recover, and the only desire he had was a few days quiet, when his health, which had been for some time declining, would, he hoped, be fully restored—the deep gratitude which Walter felt towards the youth for having been so instrumental in saving his life, induced him to yield implicit obedience to his wishes; and having assigned to him the most comfortable apartments of the mansion, and desired the servants to see that he wanted for nothing, Walter left him to undisturbed repose. Yet notwithstanding he still pertinaciously denied the circumstance, it was Walter's firm conviction that he had been wounded, though why he should persist in refusing to admit it or receive the advice and assistance of a surgeon, of course he could not conjecture; still his own opinion remained unaltered; nay, was further confirmed by weeks of evident, though as far as possible, concealed suffering on the part of his preserver. During all this time Walter contented himself by ministering as far as possible to the comfort and happiness of the youth, whom, however, he was sorry to observe, preserved a distant though respectful manner towards him, which all his efforts could not do away; indeed his presence seemed at all times so painful and embarrassing to the invalid, that he repeatedly did violence to his own feelings, and banished himself from the sick chamber.

At length returning health induced him once more to intrude upon the privacy of the stranger, and endeavour to learn something of his history. The youth as usual received him with a mixture of pleasure and uneasiness, scarcely once during the interview venturing to raise his eyes to his face. His story was short and simple, and consequenty soon told.

He was an orphan, he said, almost without friends or kindred, and had been induced to quit England by a promise of the situation of corresponding clerk to a house in Seville; but on his arrival found that the firm had failed, and at the time of his meeting with Walter, was remaining in Spain until he could return to his own country, or circumstances should throw something in his way.

On hearing this, Walter offered the situation of secretary to himself, with a handsome salary, which the youth gladly accepted. Herbert Brooks, such did the young man style himself, still remaind in such very delicate, that he had commenced his duties but a few weeks when we first introduced him to the reader, so that he had not yet been much employed by Walter ; he was conversant, however, with several circumstances respecting him, of which the servents made no secret, and among others, than he was deeply enamoured of a Spanish lady, whom they all thought it most probable he would marry, as she was high-born, beautiful, and wealthy. He sighed deeply, as he listened to the eulogy so often lavished upon this lady, and with a show of greater interest than he had ever been known to manifest before, inquired her name, and on being told she was called the Senora Inez, remarked that he should not forget it, and again inquired her style of beauty.

"Is she proud as well as fair?" he asked.

"She is beautiful," replied the person to whom he addressed himself, "but not fair, for she is dark complexioned, with eyes black as night, and hair which might well be said to rival the raven's glossy wing ; but for all that, she is gentle, kind, and amiable in the extreme, with no more pride about her than a peasant girl."

Again the youth sighed deeply, and from this moment melancholy seemed to mark him for its own. He performed the few duties required of, as it were, mechanically, and without the slightest show of interest. When Walter's eye was upon him, he never on any occasion encountered his glance ; but when he was himself busied, the youth would frequently drop his own pen, and remain for some minutes steadfastly gazing upon him ; but the slightest movement on the part of Walter, sufficed to recall the wandering mind of his secretary, and in an instant his attention would to all appearance be absorbed in his duties. Thus weeks and months rolled on, and Walter became conscious of a feeling of deep interest springing up in his mind for the friendless boy, to whom he was in all probability indebted for his existence ; his quiet inoffensive life rendered him likewise a great favourite with the entire household, to whom his deep and settled melancholy lent an additional charm. Yet it was all in vain they strove to draw from him the secret source of his sorrows ; on this subject he was invariably silent ; but it was currently reported among the servants that he had been crossed in love. This coming to Walter's ears, he ventured to question him on the subject.

"My poor boy," he said, one morning when the brow of the secretary wore a deeper gloom even than usual, "you are unhappy, and though I would wish to prove myself your best and truest friend, you hesitate to entrust me with the cause of your grief ; tell me how is this. Do you doubt the truth of my feelings or think it possible I am actuated by unworthy motives, in seeking to read the secret of your breast ?"

The youth hesitated, cast down his eyes, and sighed deeply. Walter crossed over to his side, and taking his hand, which trembled in his own, said kindly and frankly—

"Herbert, I do not wish to probe your feelings, but in your downcast eyes, and glowing cheeks, methinks I read your secret."

"Alas ! no," replied the secretary trembling yet more, "it is impossible," and as he spoke he raised his eyes momentarily to Walter's face. Walter started as he did so, for in that one little glance, there seemed shadowed forth the lineaments of some well-remembered countenance. And yet when he asked himself when and where he had seen it before he was puzzled, and could not by any possible effort of the imagination recall it to his memory. Convinced, therefore, that it was only one of those strange reminiscences which sometimes attract our observation, and lead us almost to believe that the scenes now passing before our eyes have already been enacted, though at so distant a period that it has faded from our memory, he again resumed the conversation by saying—

"It is possible I may be mistaken in my conjecture, and yet I can only attribute your deep-seated melancholy to one cause. Tell me, have you not been disappointed in love?"

The youth sighed heavily, and without again venturing to raise his eyes from the papers with which he affected to be busied, replied—

"I once loved fondly, how fondly none but myself ever knew."

"And the object of your affection," pursued Walter, "was she true or false?"

The secretary answered not.

"She was false then?" continued Walter, "and that sufficiently accounts for your dejection—yet take heart, and do not suffer yourself to be rendered miserable for life, by the heartless cruelty of one, who may have belied the truth and purity of her sex. Believe me, though one be false, there are many others with whom you may find solace and happiness."

"You have been in love yourself then," replied the secretary, "that you speak so feelingly?"

"I have, Herbert," replied Walter kindly, "but she was torn from me in early youth, and long, long have I mourned my irreparable loss."

"Yet you cannot enter into my feelings," returned the youth, "for the one upon whom I fixed my fondest affections still lives, lives to bless another with that love, to secure which to myself I would willingly lay down my life."

"But since she has proved false, you should look upon her as utterly unworthy of your regard, and cease to mourn her broken faith."

"I say not," returned the secretary, "either that she was false or true. I only say I loved, and fancied I was loved again. The miner knows not the value of the ore until he tries the vein; it may be deep and rich, or it may lay lightly on the surface."

"Herbert," said Walter, after a pause, "you shall take this letter to the Senora Inez; you will there see one of the loveliest of women, a paragon of beauty."

The secretary took the letter in silence.

"What think you," resumed Walter, "of the Spanish ladies? Are they not beautiful enough to eclipse the light of one, who has proved faithless and unkind?"

"To me," replied the youth modestly, "my own countrywomen are fairer than all others."

"Yes, yes," returned Walter hesitating, as the image of Lucy presented itself forcibly to his mind, "they are, as you say, fair and lovely, but they have no warmth, no feeling."

"Indeed," said the secretary with more boldness than he had before spoken. "Indeed you wrong them as an Englishman should not. They are true to their faith, gentle, tender, and full of love; but the wrongs they too often suffer from men make them seem cold and heartless. A woman whose heart is broken by an ill-requited affection may suffer in silence, but she feels as much, ay, more than those who are loudest in the expression of their passion. You do not know a woman's heart: it is not what you conceive it. But men unfortunately are easier led by words than actions."

"I think," said Walter after a moment's pause, "that you have been disappointed; but you speak in glowing terms of woman."

"I speak as I feel," replied the secretary. "I may have erred and wrecked my happiness in life, for that I feel is gone for ever; but why should I throw on others the fault which was entirely my own? You cannot understand my feelings, and I will not therefore obtrude them upon you. You appear to know but little of your own countrywomen, or you would not judge them so erroneously."

"Herbert," replied Walter, "I feel a deep and strange interest in all you say. Would that I could induce you to place full confidence in me. You will not, I am sure, find it misplaced."

"Some other time, perhaps no very distant one, you shall know all," returned the young man; "at present any disclosure would be premature and painful alike to us both."

"It shall be as you please," replied Walter; "but tell me, the object of your choice—was she handsome?"

"A lover," said the secretary, "always fancies the object of his affection beautiful beyond all others; it is possible, indeed, that you have overrated the charms of the Senora Inez."

"You will acquit me upon that point after you have seen her, I am sure," replied Walter, smiling; "but put aside those papers—the air is so fresh and beautiful, it will invigorate your health and spirits; and you too seldom go abroad, and, confined to one dull chamber, no wonder your ideas are tinged with misanthrophy."

The secretary rose to leave the room, and when he reached the door, turned to ask if there were any letters for England, as the post was just leaving?

"None," answered Walter.

The secretary still lingered, as though hoping for another answer; but none came; and as he left the room, an air of deep sorrow and dejection was plainly visible on his countenance.

CHAPTER LIX.

"How wonderful is Death!
Death, and his brother, Sleep.
One, pale as yonder waning moon,
With lips of lucid blue;
The other, rosy as the morn
When throned on ocean's wave,
It blushes o'er the world;
Yet both so passing wonderful."

GLORIOUSLY and beautiful, amid the rich volumes of the varied tinted clouds of an eastern sky, the sun sinks to rest. It is twilight; but not the dull lingering twilight of our English clime, which like the foreseen consequences of a distant evil, seems only to render the cold dews and sombre aspect of approaching darkness more sad and desolate.

One by one the stars, lovely in their soft refulgent glory, peep forth, till the vast and azure canopy of the horizon is one blaze of light, while the broad moon sheds a pure silvery light upon the earth. Sad that human suffering should pollute so pure a scene—sad that human anguish should exist amid so bright a landscape and such matchless beauty!

Alone in a small villa, far from her native land—far from her kindred—despised, forsaken, and rejected—the proud heart of Laura Eardley will soon cease to beat. Her raven hair is flung back from her pale and polished brow; her eyes, naturally large and wild, are fixed in a strange unearthly stare, and her hand is occasionally drawn restlessly across her damp and feverish forehead. She struggles for utterance, and with almost preternatural energy arrests for a time the hand of death, and gives vent to her feelings in disjointed sentences—

"Alas! it is but too true. I know it—I feel it: in vain do I struggle with the fierce disease which is consuming me. I must die, too, in the flower of my youth—stricken down by remorseless fever, which spares neither the young nor the strong. Not that I fear death, or would shrink from its approach, had I accomplished the one great object of my life, revenge—soul-satisfying revenge. But it fails me. Yes; what my heart has thirsted for during a life of benighted darkness, during a pilgrimage uncheered by one ray of sunshine: what I have prayed for, existed for, that for which I have alone supported the weight of this dreary world, the sneer of the cowardly, and the scorn of the righteous, the pity of the weak—fails me now, at the very moment, too, when retribution is at hand. Oh! that I could live but a few more months to accomplish the work of vengeance, then would I gladly lay me down and die without a murmur. But not now, oh, God! not now can I appear before thy throne with my thirst for revenge unsatisfied."

"Ha, art thou there?" she exclaimed, after a moment's silence.

"No, it must be a vision of this disturbed brain!" and again she passed her hand across her fevered brow. "No wonder that the ravings of delirium should present before my eyes the form of my bitterest enemy; one more unpitying, more wily than the serpent who fascinates his prey, and by blandishments draws on the unwary to their own destruction."

"Laura," said the voice of Richard Eardley, as he approached the bed-side of the sufferer, "I am come to close your eyes. The grave will soon hide for ever those waning and conflicting emotions. Struggle not, I entreat of you, against the decrees of Providence. Let us part in peace. Give me your hand, and pronounce my forgiveness."

The eyes of the injured Laura were fixed upon her betrayer with a glassy and unearthly wildness, and thrice she gasped for breath without being able to articulate even a word.

"You will forgive me," continued Richard, "and not carry animosity with you to the grave? I know I have acted unkind and dishonourable towards you, but mine was a youthful error, and has since been deeply repented of. Do not, then, withhold from me your pardon, or so near the confines of eternity yield your thoughts and feelings to revenge. Let your better angel triumph over all human weakness; and though, living, you have thirsted to revenge your injuries, dying, let them be forgiven and buried in oblivion. For this purpose I have come, and will remain by your side, watching the expiring flame of life, and offering you the affection of a fond devoted brother. I have brought with me one, too, of your own sex, gentle, loving, amiable, and kind, who will whisper to you words of hope and peace, to whom I have imparted all, and who, so far from upbraiding me with my past conduct, has taken me anew to her bosom, and voluntarily promised to love and cherish me with the tenderest love; who besought me, when she learnt your illness, to allow her to come to your bed-side, to watch by your sick couch, to minister to your wants, to cool your fevered brow, and hold your wasted hand, to talk to you peace and forgiveness, to join with me in seeking pardon at your hands; and yet so great is the delicacy of her of whom I speak, that she would not venture into your presence, unless assured that you were willing to receive her, to regard her as a dear and affectionate sister. Oh! Laura, can you refuse this? Though deeply I have sinned against you, let us part in peace. Do not carry enmity to the grave. Although you have hitherto rejected my aid, and for years despised and hated me, yet I pray—I entreat you to forgive me now."

"Leave me—begone!" she replied, at length, in a hoarse, sepulchral voice. "Canst thou not let me die in peace? Must I behold thee, the bane of my existence, here even at my death-bed, triumphing over me even to the last? Forgive," she continued, in a voice of suppressed, yet violent emotion, "thou, who through life hast ever been my evil genius—thou, who hast made my proud heart submit to indignity, to shame, that has almost burst the chords of existence —thou, who hast turned into poison the holiest sympathies of nature, making faith a mockery, and love the bitterest of all human ills—who hast blighted all the better feelings of my nature, and turned me adrift and benighted on a world of sorrow and trouble! Go," she added. "Go; I cannot die in peace. The breath refuses to leave this wretched frame whilst thou art here. Forgive thee, forsooth! God may forgive thee, but I never will. The curse of thy family, the bitter curse which has already begun to work, rest ever and heavily upon thee and thine! This is my last wish, my dying prayer."

As she spoke, she gradually sank upon the pillow, from which in the excitement of her feelings she had partially arisen. Her breath came thick and short for a few seconds, and then all was hushed in everlasting stillness—the stillness of death! Thus erished the proud and high minded Laura. Richard turned from the chamber of death, sad and sick at heart; and though he was received with open arms by the tender and affectionate Clara, who sought by every means in her power to sooth his anguish and cheer his drooping spirit, he refused to be comforted. The dying words of the injured Laura wrung mournfully in his ears, and forbade him to find rest or peace. In vain Clara, by every gentle effort, endeavoured to beguile his anguish. So deep and bitter were his emotions, that she entertained fears even for his reason. Nor was this without foundation; for the second evening from the death of Laura beheld him stricken down by the same fierce disease which had proved so fatal to her. Now, indeed, was the hour of bitter trial and suffering to Clara—poor Clara!—who had borne up so bravely under every misfortune, but was now cast down into the very abyss of sorrow. Still she watched by the sick bed of her husband, and despite her anguish, suffered none to tend or wait upon him but herself. From her hand he received the cooling draught, and she it was who wiped the damp dew from his forehead. And if love—fond, true, pure, devoted love—could have ava led to stay the hand of death, or turn his shaft aside, Richard had yet been spared to cheer and bless her. But human aid was useless; and after tossing for a few weary weeks backward and forward on his restless couch, death closed his mortal career, and Clara was left alone. Alas! what words can depict her utter desolation when he—the sole partner and sole part of all her joys—lay before her dead! The warm heart which had once beat so fondly against her own was still! The lips which had so fondly pressed her cheek were now cold and motionless! The eyes which had poured volumes of deep and everlasting love into her own were closed for ever! We part from those we love—we, to whom partings and meetings are common, and who, in our hearts bitterest grief, know that there are those from whom—if we ask for it—we can gain sympathy; we yet feel parting great anguish, and that "farewell for ever," is scarcely less poignant than death itself. How wasting, then, must have been the agony of Clara, when she beheld her first and idolized love dead before her, with none but her friend, Jane Clarence, to share her grief! No bosom upon which she could lay her head and find relief. Days and months rolled by, and the bright and beautiful world was filled with gay and lightsome hearts, wandering delightedly among its groves and glades by waterfalls, and trickling rills—wondering, while surrounded by the sunshine of their own hearts' happiness, and the matchless beauty of nature, how care and sorrow should ever have come into a world so fair. But Clara, patient, noble, and self-denying to the last, still hid herself in solitude, to weep alone and unheeded over the loss of all her earthly hopes.

CHAPTER LX.

Oh, ever thus from childhood's hour,
    I've seen my fondest hopes decay;
I never loved a tree or flower,
    But 'twas the first to fade away:
I never nursed a dear gazelle,
    To cheer with its soft blue eye,
But when it came to know me well,
    And love me, it was sure to die.

THE sad news of Richard's death speedily reached England, and though Lady Eardley shed some natural tears for the loss of her eldest son, her grief was greatly mitigated by the demise of Laura, which would in all probability secure the estates to Walter, and hide her shame for ever from the world. Felicitating herself, therefore, on her own forethought in having taken possession of Eardley Hall, she instantly wrote to acquaint Walter with the altered state of affairs, and entreat him to return home without delay. Pending his arrival, she endeavoured to discover the retreat of Ada, being anxious, if possible, to promote a reconciliation between her and Walter, in the hope that the line might be continued, and thus prevent the estates eventually passing to some distant branch of the family for lack of heirs; but all her efforts proved vain.

Ada had some time since left the abode where she had in the first instance retired, immediately after her separation from Walter, and gone none knew where. Consoling herself for this disappointment, in the belief than others (in the event of his succeeding in procuring a divorce) would undoubtedly marry again, Lady Eardley made some alterations in the household, which she thought could not fail to be pleasing to Walter, and prepared the servants for the speedy reception of their new master. In the meantime, Walter, utterly unconscious of all this, was still perplexed with doubts and fears, now resolving to tear himself for ever from the fascinating influence of the Senora Inez, and now on the very point of making her an offer of his hand and heart. In the midst of these conflicting feelings, the letter of Lady Eardley arrived. Strange, indeed, and startling was the news it contained: his brother dead, and himself summoned home to take possession of the estates. The letter dropped from his hands, and his face assumed an ashy paleness. The secretary was seated opposite to him, busied with some papers, but who, on remarking the violent emotion of Walter, started up exclaiming—

"You are ill. Alas! what can I do for you?"

"No Herbert, not ill," returned Walter recovering his self-composure at the sound of the other's voice, "but this letter has conveyed to me strange and unlooked-for intelligence. Sit down," he continued; "I owe you much; but for your friendly warning our race had been now extinct." The secretary changed colour, and dropping into a chair remained perfectly silent. "You have been a kind and true friend to me," resumed Walter, after a short silence, "and I feel a deep and powerful interest stirring in my breast for you, which induces me to open my heart, and take council and advice from one who, though young, is, I am sure, well calculated to give it."

"You refer to the Senora Inez?" replied the youth in faltering accents.

"You but anticipate my words," said Walter. "You have seen the lady; give me your impartial opinion of her."

"She is very beautiful, and seems both kind and amiable," replied the secretary with some hesitation.

"And you would think her worthy of wealth and title, of becoming, in short, the wife of an English baronet, of accompanying him to England, and shedding lustre on his house, ancient and honourable in its lineage?"

A bright ray of sunshine beamed for a moment on the countenance of the secretary, as he answered quickly—

"You do not then think of the Lady Inez in connection with yourself?"

"Yes, Herbert, it is of myself I speak. My brother's untimely death hasput me in possession of his title and estates."

The sunshine instantly disappeared from the face of the youth, as he stammered forth—

"Indeed, I wish you joy and happiness."

"Which you must share with me, or it would be incomplete," returned Walter hastily. "You say you have no friends or kindred; let me stand to you in the place of all. Together we will return to England, and you shall dwell with me in the home of my ancestors, an ancient venerable building, which I know will please you," he continued in a warmer strain, as he thought with pardonable pride on the noble building, which had for so many years appertained to the family of the Eardleys.

"Sir Walter Eardley," stammered forth the young man, "you have asked my opinion of the Senora Inez—will you think me too bold if I venture to implore you not to give her your hand unless your heart goes with it? That is the most priceless gem you can bestow, and of which I trust she may prove worthy. She may love you; but do not rest entirely upon that for happiness: neglect has too often withered the best and sweetest feelings. Therefore, if you would be happy, I beseech you to cultivate her affection, and never on any account permit her to depend on others for those attentions which should come alone from you."

The words of the secretary powerfully affected Walter; it brought vividly to his recollection the brief days of his wedded life, which had resulted in so much unhappiness, both to himself and the volatile being to whom he had entrusted his happiness; and as he listened, his brow grew dark, and, glancing angrily towards the youth, he answered harshly—

"Leave me—I wish to be alone."

The secretary, rising from his seat, replied meekly—

"If I have offended you with my boldness, I entreat your pardon."

"No, no," returned Walter; "your words, it is true, have opened wounds which time had but partially healed, yet I know your intention was good. Forgive my petulance, but I am ill at ease; leave me now, Herbert, I shall be calmer presently."

In the evening of this day, Walter paid a visit to the Senora Inez; but it was not altogether a pleasant one; the events of the morning, together with the warning words of the secretary, so singularly appropriate to himself, tended to excite feelings of a sorrowful and painful description. It was in this gloomy disposition that he returned late to his princely hotel. As he entered, he was informed that his secretary was dangerously ill, and wished most anxiously to see him. Walter hurried instantly to his chamber.

The night was far advanced, and the moon shed its soft pure light through the Gothic casement with unusual brightness, falling on the invalid's bed almost like a mid-day sun.

"My poor boy," said Walter, as he seated himself beside him, "you seem very ill—what has happened to you?"

The secretary motioned that those who were present should quit the room, leaving him alone with Walter. As soon as his desire was attended to, he said—

"You expressed a wish some short time since to learn my history. I refused you then, because I knew it would soon come to this. My heart was breaking day by day. And yet that which has happened to me has often happened before, and will again—I have loved and been deceived. It is an oft-told tale; and yet until we feel the bitter desolation of heart-broken despair, we know not how much we can suffer."

"You are unhappy," replied Walter; "but be not dispirited — better times may come, and the bright and sunny side of life may turn to your view; the gloomy shadows you are raising are but the offspring of your sudden illness."

"For me," returned the secretary, "there is no bright and sunny side. My hour is fast approaching—the subtle poison, Despair, has long been working in my veins, though I have concealed its effects from the observation of all; but now I have not long to live—nor would I wish to do so—for my own heart alone knows what it is to live as I have done."

As he gave utterance to the last words, the youth, with much difficulty raised himself in bed, and throwing aside the dark hair that Walter had always hitherto seen, allowed him to observe that it was false, while his real hair was a light rich auburn.

"Do you not recognise me?" he inquired, as Walter gazed upon him with astonishment; "or am I so changed that none can know me?"

"What do I see?" exclaimed Walter. "Can it be possible!—or do my eyes deceive me?—Ada here! What does it mean? Here is some fearful mystery I cannot explain."

"The meaning is soon told; but I fear I have not strength to do it. My brain is on fire, and my veins seem as though they would burst with each convulsive throb!"

"Nay, I will fly for assistance; some remedy may be found; it cannot be too late."

"Walter," replied Ada, for it was indeed her, "I command you to stay. I have but little now to tell, yet it is necessary for the happiness, the peace of others, that you should hear me. You must remember the evening when you abruptly entered my apartment and accused me of unfaithfulness, which you learnt from some reports that were circulated to my disadvantage. Walter," she added, solemnly, "listen to me while I own, by all my sufferings in this world, by all my hopes of happiness and peace in the next, here on my death-bed, from which I shall never rise again, hear me swear that those reports were false ! My heart—my love has never swerved from you. I have loved you, as Heaven knows, in purity and truth. My only sin was to secure your love—your consideration, at any and every hazard ; to do which I was vain and foolish enough to attempt to arouse your jealous feelings. In that bitter hour when you denounced me for ever, I longed, God only knows how ardently, to tell you all—to entreat your forgiveness of the weak part I had acted, and take me anew to your heart ; but pride chained my tongue, and we parted, I believed for ever. When you quitted England, which I learnt from the public papers, I determined to follow you. I knew I could not live long, and I was impressed with an earnest desire to see you again, and convince you, if possible, of my innocence. The disguise I assumed to accomplish all this you know ; but you do not know how hour by hour, and day by day, I followed your footsteps ; you do not know what I endured to be near you. But I will not repeat it ; suffice it, that I found myself forgotten, and another holding that place I alone had hope for. As regards Percy, he is innocent of all feeling towards me, incompatible with the deep regard he nourishes for my cousin." She paused a moment, and then resumed—"You may remember that you gave me this cross, bidding me when I loved you no longer, to return it to you. I have worn it ever since, because I have never ceased to love you ; but I can wear it no longer ; it should belong to another. Take it—take it from my sight. It was an ill-omened gift ; I have been unhappy from the moment that I first wore it," saying which she thrust it into his hands. "I feel happier now."

"Oh ! Ada," exclaimed Walter, overcome with the intensity of his feelings, "forgive me ; forget the past—I will be yours and yours only. I have erred—I know and feel it now. Look upon me and say that you forgive me. Will you not forgive me ?'

She spoke feebly, for her strength was fast leaving her, as she replied—

"Walter, there is my hand : I do forgive you ; but had I years to live in lieu of the few brief moments which remain to me, I would not be yours. I would not be again your wife in name, but not in your affections. No—no, I would not be your wife."

"On this cross, and before Heaven," exclaimed Walter, "I swear never to call another by the name of wife."

The vow had come too late, for she heard it not ; a deep sleep seemed to have fallen suddenly upon her—a sleep not like death's semblance, but death itself ! Her features were calm and placid, for no struggle marked the transition from sleep to death ; and it was some time ere Walter became convinced that she was indeed no more. He gazed for some time on the still beauteous form before him in silent contemplation, and then as he turned away he murmured—

"And this is my work. Oh, God ! the curse of my race is upon me, that all I have ever loved are torn from me, all who ever loved me turn to—No, no, she did not hate me. I have been in a dream—a hideous dream ; but the sad reality is before me, and now that it is too late, I feel I might have been happy, had I cultivated the growth of that passion which I have been the means of turning into gall and wormwood. Oh ! Ada, what you felt do I now feel. But it is too late to atone for past unkindness. You cannot hear me now ; but here I swear that none shall ever fill thy place. I will live and die a solitary man, and never more court affection ; my love shall rest in thy remembrance, and though living I have wronged you, such atonement as man can make will I make, by steeling my heart for ever from woman's love or friendship."

CHAPTER LXI.

"Thus did I dream—wild, wandering dreams, I own;
But such as haunt me ever, if alone,
Or in that pause 'twixt joy and joy I be,
Like a ship hushed between two waves at sea.
Then do these spirits, whispering like the sound
Of the dark future, come appalling round,
While those, if ev'n but half I tell,
Thou wilt but half believe—Farewell!"

READER! our tale is ended, and our task well-nigh done. We desire to take but a cursory glance more at the different characters we have brought under your notice, and will then detain you no longer. Shortly after the events recorded in our last chapter, Walter, banishing the image of the Lady Inez for ever from his heart, returned to England a sad and melancholy man, estranging himself from the world and its amusements, being constantly at the seat of his ancestors in the strictest seclusion. True to his vow, he died unmarried. The title and estates passing to a distant branch of the family, the curse is said to have ended with him, since to love or wed an Eardley is no longer considered the forerunner of some dire calamity. Lady Eardley for some time resided with her son at the family mansion, from whom she learnt the sad circumstances attending the death of Ada, and convinced of the utter inutility of urging her son to form a fresh alliance, speedily forbore to press him on so painful a subjet. After a few years of seclusion, an accidental circumstance again brought her in contact with Evereard Tracy, both were much altered. Sorrow and vicissitude had worked great changes in their minds; and when after a short interval, Evereard proposed that they should renew the vows so early broken, Lady Eardley offered no opposition, stipulating only that their previous union should be kept a secret from Walter. To this Evereard readily assented, and they were remarried. Thus, after the storms and buffets of their youth and meridian, the evening of life was passed in calm tranquillity. Mutually forgiving and forgiven, their destinies so long and cruelly separated were at length united together. They mourned the loss of those near relatives so early called away, and though they were destined to see their race become extinct, and were left childless and friendless save for their mutual attachment, they learnt to look forward to a brighter state of existence where they might eventually regain the friends they had lost in this. Percy, true to his better feelings, abandoned for ever his gay associates, and devoted himself entirely to the happiness of his gentle and affectionate partner; and though he worked hard for several years, his exertions were at length rewarded by regaining his lost footing in society, and had the pleasure of seeing both his sisters united to men capable of appreciating their good qualities, and making them contented and happy wives. Mr. Herbert continued to reside with them, and in the course of years was surrounded by a whole troop of merry grandchildren, who were at once the delight and solace of his old age. Mary continued to perform well the duties which appertained to her station; and while she was ever ready to extend a helping hand to all who were in distress, she more particularly turned her attention to those of her own sex, who were forced to procure a precarious livelihood by their needle. To these she was most kind and indulgent; and while she endeavoured, as far as her means permitted, to afford them employment, she made it a rule to purchase no ready-made article, save at a price that must ensure the poor needlewomen a fair remuneration for her labour. As early as circumstances permitted, Jane gave her hand to Mr. Carlton, and with it a pure, generous, honest heart, which he fully appreciated, and was proud to win. Mrs. Clarence lived long enough to witness her daughter's happiness, and proudly exult in the choice she had made. Poor Clara, too, was induced to make one of the family; and when the term of her widowhood had expired, received many eligible offers, all of which she unhesitatingly refused. Blest with the society of her dearest friend, respected by Mr. Carlton, loved and idolized by the children, Clara passed the remainder of her days in peaceful serenity; and though there were times when the tears would linger on her cheek, yet faith triumphed over human suffering, and she was enabled to bow submissively to the will of God.

Henry Fergusson and his wealthy bride, after their long sojourn in Italy, returned to England, and were rapturously received by Mrs. Belmont, who could not sufficiently admire the little stranger whom they presented to her as their son, and whom she declared to Henry was the very image of himself. She continued to occupy her usual apartments in Belgrave Square, and maintained her partiality to paintings, unimpaired by age or infirmity. Henry and Fanny, when alone, frequently laughed good-naturedly at her failing; but as it injured none, and was an evident source of gratification and amusement to herself, they never disputed her being a first-rate judge of the art.

It would be useless to conceal from the reader that the image of Jane would frequently present itself to the mind of Henry, or that he mourned in secret his broken vows. Notwithstanding, he was a most exemplary and devoted husband, and Fanny never had cause to repent the generosity of her conduct towards him.

Dear reader, will you forgive us for detaining you a moment longer, while we say a word for ourselves? We have so often met you, and each time with an increase of satisfaction arising from the kindness with which you have ever greeted our presence, that it behoves us to express our grateful sense of the same. We have endeavoured to extract for your amusement from the simple every-day occurrences of life—without having recourse to adventures wild and utterly improbable, with which some tales abound—not forgetting to depict virtue in its true and beautiful colours; while we have shown you the utter deformity and wretchedness of vice, which, though it may triumph for a season, must eventually bring sorrow and destruction on its votaries.

We have for so many weeks looked forward to meeting you with such lively satisfaction, that we linger on this our last page with a sad and regretful feeling; still, we anticipate, with renewed pleasure, at no distant period again entering the lists as caterers for your amusement and instruction. In the meantime, if we have succeeded in wiling away a tedious hour, or enlivening a dull one, our aim is so far accomplished; and for the present must bid you adieu—

> " Farewell! whatever may befall,
> Or bright, or dark, thou'lt know it all."

ELLEN T——.